JONAH'S GOURD VINE

MULES AND MEN

THEIR EYES
WERE WATCHING GOD

Zora Neale Hurston collecting folklore in the late 1930s.

JONAH'S GOURD VINE

Foreword by Rita Dove

MULES AND MEN

Preface by Franz Boas
Foreword by Arnold Rampersad
Illustrations by Miguel Covarrubias

THEIR EYES
WERE WATCHING GOD

Foreword by Mary Helen Washington

ZORA NEALE HURSTON

Series Editor: Henry Louis Gates, Jr.

Quality Paperback Books   New York

JONAH'S GOURD VINE

A NOVEL

ZORA NEALE HURSTON

WITH A NEW FOREWORD BY RITA DOVE

To
Bob Wunsch
Who is one of the long-wingded angels
Right round the throne
Go gator and muddy the water

FOREWORD

"You laks dat ole train Ah see," the Negro said to John, watching him as he all but fell down into the railroad cut, trying to keep sight of the tail of the train.

"Yeah, man Ah lakted dat. It say something but Ah ain't heered it 'nough tuh tell whut it say yit. You know whut it say?"

"It don't say nothin'. It jes' make uh powerful racket, dass all."

"Naw, it say some words too. Ahm comin' heah pleny mo' times and den Ah tell yuh whut it say."

When the publishing house of J. B. Lippincott inquired if the author of the short story "The Gilded Six Bits" was working on a novel, Zora Neale Hurston took paper and pencil and headed for home. She rented a room in Sanford, Florida, next door to the all-black town where she had grown up, and began to write *Jonah's Gourd Vine.* In October 1933, a scant four months later, the manuscript was accepted for publication.

Jonah's Gourd Vine takes the classic form of the *Bildungsroman:* John, an unlettered but determined young man, ventures forth to make his fortune. What he learns of the world and his own nature form the trajectory of his life and the novel.

Like those of many black Americans, John's origins are

murky. His mother Amy bears him while working on Alf Pearson's farm; she marries Ned Crittenden and moves to the other side of Big Creek. Ned, who was raised a slave, despises John for what he represents—for there is every indication that John is the illegitimate son of the white judge.

Even as a young man, John is aware of the power of utterance. His fear of the first locomotive he sees is quickly replaced by the desire to understand it. And though he never learns to speak to his own soul, he is fascinated by the infinite variety of nature's music:

> . . . John sat on the foot-log and made some words to go with the drums of the Creek. Things walked in the birch woods, creep, creep, creep. The hound dog's lyric crescendo lifted over and above the tree tops. He was on the foot-log, half way across the Big Creek where maybe people laughed and maybe people had lots of daughters. The moon came up. The hunted coon panted down to the Creek . . . [t]he tenor-singing hound dog went home. Night passed. No more Ned, no hurry. No telling how many girls might be living on the new and shiny side of the Big Creek. John almost trumpeted exultantly at the new sun. He breathed lustily. He stripped and carried his clothes across, then recrossed and plunged into the swift water and breasted strongly over.

This passage contains all the elements of John's spirit—his exuberant masculine energy, his gift for language, and his intense relationship between his interior self and the natural world, both his headstrong lustiness and his ability for provident forethought. (He carries his clothes across the river, then recrosses before swimming over.)

This scene, however, occurs right after his mother's repeated warning not to swim the Songahatchee and John's parting promise to her to stop "runnin' and uh rippin' and clambin' trees and rocks and jumpin'." The seeds of his inner conflict are evident.

In an ironic twist recalling the incestuous relationships in the South, John leaves home to find work under Alf Pearson, who remarks, "Your face looks sort of familiar but I can't place you" before giving him the cast-off clothes of his legitimate son. But when the judge's wife objects to John driving their coach, he is put to work in the barns.

John, who adopts Pearson as his surname, is an immediate success among the black workers, especially the women: they seduce him right and left. He focuses his attention on the fiery little Lucy Potts, the smartest black girl in the area. Her excellence inspires John to "eat up dat school," and he joins the church when he is told that Lucy sings in the choir. After a determined courtship, Lucy and John become man and wife.

Although John left home at the suggestion of his mother, he soon learns the temptation of flight. Whenever things get sticky, he runs away. And, just as he is able to break a promise to his mother minutes afterward without a second thought, John sees no discrepancy in enjoying a stream of women while swearing to love Lucy body and soul. Even before marriage, John must leave the Pearson place and find work at a logging camp to escape a jealous husband; and though he swears to Lucy that "Ah loves you and you alone," after marriage he still cannot stay away from other women. There is Mehaley and Big 'Oman and then Delphine, who comforts John while Lucy lies in labor with their fourth child. When Lucy's brother takes their marriage bed in partial payment of a debt, John beats him up and is consequently summoned to court. Alf Pearson gives him money along with some "fatherly" advice: "John, distance is the only cure for certain diseases."

John moves to the all-black settlement of Eatonville, Florida (Hurston's home town) and sends for Lucy. He grows in confidence and takes his place in the community as a man, while Lucy's energy is taken up by children; all her fierce intelligence is channeled into advising her husband. Together they forge John's reputation as minister of Zion Hope Church and eventually mayor in the neighboring town of Sanford.

Actually, John's "disease" is that he is too smooth a talker. He is carried away by his own words, just as he is carried away by his body. His stirring prayers convince him and everyone else at Zion Hope that he has been called to preach, although his wife warns him against confusing talent with commitment:

> "Lucy, look lak Ah jus' found out whut Ah kin do. De words dat sets de church on fire comes tuh me jus' so. Ah reckon de angels must tell 'em tuh me."
> "God don't call no man, John, and turn 'im loose uh fool."

Perhaps his most despicable flight occurs when his younger daughter Isis lies desperately ill; terrified that she will die, he runs into the arms of another woman until she recovers. (Ironically, later it is the nine-year-old Isis who stands by her dying mother.) John returns, shamefaced, with gifts for Lucy—a new dress and a pineapple—that seem as blasphemous as they are ludicrous.

The procession of women continues until John meets Hattie Tyson, who enjoins the aid of a conjure woman to keep him at her side. Lucy's sound advice grows wearisome to him, and her cautious inquiries into his infidelities finally enrage him. Remembering John's poor track record with promises, it is with foreboding that we hear him swear to Lucy: "Li'l Bit, Ah ain't never laid de weight uh mah hand on you in malice." When Lucy falls ill, John continues to see other women, and Lucy makes a decisive pronouncement on John's sin-now-atone-later attitude: "You can't clean yo'self wid yo' tongue lak uh cat." Stung by the truth, John slaps her. She turns her face to the wall, withdrawing her support from him, and dies.

This act of malice, which hastens Lucy's death, is the worm that cuts down the great vine:

> And the Lord God appointed a plant, and made it come up over Jonah, that it might be a shade over his head, to save him from this discomfort. So Jonah was exceedingly glad because of the plant. But when dawn came up the next day,

God appointed a worm which attacked the plant, so that it withered.

Jonah 4: 6–7

Indeed, John Pearson is a rapidly growing vine, and everything he touches blossoms under his hand: he is a favorite with the women, he is popular with the men, he is a good worker and a gifted storyteller, and finally, as minister and mayor, he becomes both a spiritual and a community leader. His philandering ways do not seem to slow him down until he commits the ghastly sin of striking his wife on her deathbed.

The worm, however, could also be Hattie, who is willing to use magic more compelling than feminine wiles to topple the preacher. John marries Hattie, and beats her after discovering that he's been "conjured." When Hattie slyly pleads her case before Deacon Harris (who is jealous of John's successes with women), Harris assures her, "Ah'd cut down dat Jonah's gourd vine in a uh minute, if Ah had all de say-so." When she files for divorce, John does not confute her testimony.

The worm of malice burrows through the church community. Long uneasy about the preacher's philanderings, the congregation of Zion Hope plans to dethrone him. On the day of reckoning, John preaches the sermon of his life.

John's final sermon is taken nearly verbatim from Hurston's field notes on a country preacher. It is a meditation on martyrdom and heroism, reflecting John's position before the church; after a brief rhapsodic digression on the creation of earth, he zeroes in on Jesus, come on his "train of mercy" to save mankind. In John's depiction of the Resurrection, the train of mercy turns into the "damnation train," which in a bizarre but effective conclusion is derailed when the cowcatcher rams into Jesus's side. Final Judgment is pictured as a convention where "de two trains of Time shall meet on de trestle."

Surrounded by enemies who had once been friends, bitten through at the root, John steps down from the pulpit and walks out of the church. He decides to earn a living as a carpenter, but his honest efforts fail in the face of the community's delight in persecuting a fallen idol.

Are we to sympathize with John as a victim of malicious ill-wishers, or condemn him for his despicable conduct toward his wife? Since Hattie has a spell put on him, is he to blame for his actions at all?

If we look at the Biblical story of Jonah and the vine, John's "case" becomes clearer: the prophet has predicted the fall of the great city of Nineveh, upon which its inhabitants repent by fasting and covering themselves in sackcloth and ashes. Moved to pity, the Lord revokes his sentence, and Jonah takes to the hills to sulk. After God has caused the vine to wither, he orders the sun to beat down until Jonah bemoans the loss of shade and exclaims that he is "angry enough to die." The Lord replies:

"You pity the plant, for which you did not labor, nor did you make it grown, which came into being in a night, and perished in a night. And should not I pity Nineveh, that great city, in which there are more than a hundred and twenty thousand persons who do not know their right hand from their left, and also much cattle?"

Jonah 4:10–11

Sudden growth—fame achieved without thought or labor—must maintain a precarious balance. Perhaps John's fatal flaw is his inability to listen to himself and consequently his reluctance to put any effort into changing his ways. Unable to accept responsibility for his actions, he either runs away or "licks himself clean" with fast talking. Even the heaped-on tribulations that follow Lucy's death fail to lead him to an understanding of his selfishness: all he can see is the hypocrisy of others. And when Lucy finally returns to him in a dream, he is oblivious to the warning:

He killed the snake and carried Lucy across in his arms to where Alf Pearson stood at the cross roads and pointed down a white shell road with his walking cane and said, "Distance is the only cure for certain diseases," and he and Lucy went racing down the dusty white road together. Somehow Lucy got lost from him, but there he was on the road—happy because the dead snake was behind him, but crying in his loneliness for Lucy.

Instead of seeing the dream as a condemning portrait of the pattern of his life, John believes he is meant to leave town—to run away again, and to seek his fortune elsewhere. The proper and rich widow Sally Lovelace takes him in, and John's luck begin to turn: they marry, his carpentry business picks up, and Zion Hope asks him back. His triumphant homecoming, resplendent in the new car Sally has bought him, brings with it the admiration of his former enemies as well as the irresistible blandishments of a sweet young thing named Ora. In no time at all, John succumbs to lust again; appalled at his weakness, he flees Sanford and heads back to his wife. So sunk in self-recrimination is he that he fails to see an oncoming train. He is killed instantly. A man who does not learn from his mistakes is doomed to repeat them. In many ways, John has cut himself down.

They called for the instrument that they had brought to America in their skins—the drum—and they played upon it. . . . The drum with the man skin that is dressed with human blood, that is beaten with a human shin-bone and speaks to gods as a man and to men as a God.

Does *Jonah's Gourd Vine* hold up today, apart from its unquestionable value as a portrait of Southern black life in the first decades of the twentieth century—or does a sympathetic portrait of a philandering preacher seem antiquated as a work of literature, politically retrograde? As his first name attests, John is Everyman, and Pearson is a surname with multitudinous echoes. In a bitter reference to the lost ancestry of black slaves, he is someone's (but whose?) son; like that archetypal Son of God, he is "pierced" by those he has trusted; conversely, he is a man, pierced by Adam's rib, and his human frailty eventually causes his downfall.

Lucy, on the other hand, is almost a parody of the faithful, betrayed wife: she subordinates her dreams to his ambitions, she is rebuked and dies, the husband remarries, the children get farmed out. And yet no one can take Lucy's place. She haunts the novel, and her absence is at least as compelling as John's suffering.

For its time, Zora Neale Hurston's first novel, produced in four months when the author was forty-two, is a remarkable achievement. Written in the vicinity of her birthplace, *Jonah's Gourd Vine*, unsurprisingly, does not stray far from the autobiographical—John and Lucy are based on Hurston's father and mother, and Lucy's deathbed scene can be found in its original (with Zora as the nine-year-old daughter) in Hurston's autobiography, *Dust Tracks on a Road.* What is striking, however, is that this young woman did not make one of the major mistakes of first novelists—sticking too faithfully to the "true story"—but knew how to fashion of her parents' lives a tale of compelling pathos and majesty.

As a work of fiction, *Jonah's Gourd Vine* certainly has its flaws: transitions that jog, a little too much "local color." And though Hurston can hardly be blamed for wanting to infuse the text with the fieldwork she had done as an anthropologist, all too often her eloquent commentary stands full-blown and self-contained, interrupting the narrative flow. John's final sermon is a case in point, for even its masterful train imagery seems too heavy-handed a foreshadowing when the locomotive comes barreling out of the blue, a modern-day *deus ex machina,* to seal John's fate.

But Hurston's language is superb, rich with wordplay and proverbs—not only compelling when it comes to rendering the dialect of the Southern rural black but also as an omniscient narrator who neither indulges nor condemns the actions of her characters but offers the complexity of life in a story that leaves judgment up to the reader. John Pearson is presented as a human being in all his individual paradoxes—troubled and gifted, dignified and lascivious, pure and selfish—and as the exemplification of the country preacher, he is both poet and philosopher. If language is the chief visible sign of human beings' pre-eminence over beasts, then poetry is the purest expression of man's spiritual quest. *Jonah's Gourd Vine* is a glorious paean to the power of the word, an attestation to the promise made in Langston Hughes's famous 1926 essay, "The Negro Artist and the Racial Mountain":

We younger Negro artists who create now intend to express our individual dark-skinned selves without fear or shame. If white people are pleased we are glad. If they are not, it doesn't matter. We know we are beautiful. And ugly too. The tom-tom cries and the tom-tom laughs. If colored people are pleased we are glad. If they are not, their displeasure doesn't matter either. We build our temples for tomorrow, strong as we know how, and we stand on top of the mountain, free within ourselves.

RITA DOVE

CHAPTER 1

God was grumbling his thunder and playing the zig-zag lightning thru his fingers.

Amy Crittenden came to the door of her cabin to spit out a wad of snuff. She looked up at the clouds.

"Ole Massa gwinter scrub floors tuhday," she observed to her husband who sat just outside the door, reared back in a chair. "Better call dem chaps in outa de cotton patch."

" 'Tain't gwine rain," he snorted, "you always talkin' more'n yuh know."

Just then a few heavy drops spattered the hard clay yard. He arose slowly. He was an older middle-age than his years gave him a right to be.

"And eben if hit do rain," Ned Crittenden concluded grudgingly, "ef dey ain't got sense 'nough tuh come in let 'em git wet."

"Yeah, but when us lef' de field, you told 'em not to come till you call 'em. Go 'head and call 'em 'fo' de rain ketch 'em."

Ned ignored Amy and shuffled thru the door with the chair, and somehow trod on Amy's bare foot. " 'Oman, why don't you git outa de doorway? Jes contrary tuh dat. You needs uh good head stompin', dass whut. You sho is one aggervatin' 'oman."

Amy flashed an angry look, then turned her face again to

the sea of wind-whipped cotton, turned hurriedly and took the cow-horn that hung on the wall and placed it to her lips.

"You John Buddy! You Zeke! You Zachariah! Come in!"

From way down in the cotton patch, "Yassum! Us comin'!"

Ned shuffled from one end of the cabin to the other, slamming to the wooden shutter of the window, growling between his gums and his throat the while.

The children came leaping in, racing and tumbling in tense, laughing competition—the three smaller ones getting under the feet of the three larger ones. The oldest boy led the rest, but once inside he stopped short and looked over the heads of the others, back over the way they had come.

"Shet dat door, John!" Ned bellowed, "you ain't got the sense you wuz borned wid."

Amy looked where her big son was looking. "Who dat comin' heah, John?" she asked.

"Some white folks passin' by, mama. Ahm jes' lookin' tuh see whar dey gwine."

"Come out dat do'way and shet it tight, fool! Stand dere gazin' dem white folks right in de face!" Ned gritted at him. "Yo' brazen ways wid dese white folks is gwinter git you lynched one uh dese days."

"Aw 'tain't," Amy differed impatiently, "who can't look at ole Beasley? He ain't no quality no-how."

"Shet dat door, John!" screamed Ned.

"Ah wuzn't de last one inside," John said sullenly.

"Don't you gimme no word for word," Ned screamed at him. "You jes' do lak Ah say do and keep yo' mouf shet or Ah'll take uh trace chain tuh yuh. Yo' mammy mought think youse uh lump uh gold 'cause you got uh li'l' white folks color in yo' face, but Ah'll stomp yo' guts out and dat quick! Shet dat door!"

He seized a lidard knot from beside the fireplace and limped threateningly towards John.

Amy rose from beside the cook pots like a black lioness.

"Ned Crittenden, you raise dat wood at mah boy, and you gointer make uh bad nigger outa me."

2

"Dat's right," Ned sneered, "Ah feeds 'im and clothes 'im but Ah ain't tuh do nothin' tuh dat li'l' yaller god cep'n wash 'im up."

"Dat's uh big ole resurrection lie, Ned. Uh slew-foot, drag-leg lie at dat, and Ah dare yuh tuh hit me too. You know Ahm uh fightin' dawg and mah hide is worth money. Hit me if you dare! Ah'll wash *yo'* tub uh 'gator guts and dat quick."

"See dat? Ah ain't fuh no fuss, but you tryin' tuh start uh great big ole ruction 'cause Ah tried tuh chesstize dat young-un."

"Naw, you ain't tried tuh chesstize 'im nothin' uh de kind. Youse tryin' tuh fight 'im on de sly. He is jes' ez obedient tuh you and jes' ez humble under yuh, ez he kin be. Yet and still you always washin' his face wid his color and tellin' 'im he's uh bastard. He works harder'n anybody on dis place. You ain't givin' 'im nothin'. He more'n makes whut he gits. Ah don't mind when he needs chesstizin' and you give it tuh 'im, but anytime you tries tuh knock any dese chillun 'bout dey head wid sticks and rocks, Ah'll be right dere tuh back dey fallin'. Ahm dey mama."

"And Ahm de pappy uh all but dat one."

"You knowed Ah had 'm 'fo' yuh married me, and if you didn't want 'im round, whut yuh marry me fuh? Dat ain't whut you said. You washed 'im up jes' lak he wuz gold den. You jes took tuh buckin' 'im since you been hangin' round sich ez Beasley and Mimms."

Ned sat down by the crude fireplace where the skillets and spiders (long-legged bread pans with iron cover) sprawled in the ashes.

"Strack uh light, dere, some uh y'all chaps. Hit's dark in heah."

John obediently thrust a piece of lightwood into the embers and the fire blazed up. He retreated as quickly as possible to the farther end of the cabin.

Ned smoked his strong home-grown tobacco twist for a few minutes. Then he thrust out his feet.

"Pour me some water in dat wash-basin, you chaps, and

3

some uh y'all git de washrag."

There was a scurry and bustle to do his bidding, but the drinking-gourd dropped hollowly in the water bucket. Ned heard it.

" 'Tain't no water in dat air water-bucket, Ah'll bound yuh!" He accused the room and glowered all about him, "House full uh younguns fuh me to feed and close, and heah 'tis dust dark and rainin' and not uh drop uh water in de house! Amy, whut kinda 'oman is you nohow?"

Amy said nothing. She sat on the other side of the fireplace and heaped fresh, red coals upon the lid of the spider in which the bread was cooking.

"John!" Ned thundered, "git yo' yaller behind up offa dat floor and go git me some water tuh wash mah foots."

"You been tuh de house longer'n he is," Amy said quietly. "You coulda done been got dat water."

"You think Ah'm gwine take uh 'nother man's youngun and feed 'im and close 'im fuh twelve years and den he too good tuh fetch me uh bucket uh water?" Ned bellowed.

"Iss rainin' out dere, an' rainin' hard," Amy said in the same level tones.

"Dass right," Ned sneered, "John is de house-nigger. Ole Marsa always kep' de yaller niggers in de house and give 'em uh job totin' silver dishes and goblets tuh de table. Us black niggers is de ones s'posed tuh ketch de wind and de weather."

"Ah don't want *none* uh mah chilluns pullin' tuh no spring in uh hard rain. Yo' foots kin wait. Come hawg-killin' time Ah been married tuh you twelve years and Ah done seen yuh let 'em wait uh powerful long spell some time. Ah don't want mah chilluns all stove-up wid uh bad cold from proagin' 'round in de rain."

"Ole Marse didn't ast *me* of hit wuz rainin' uh snowin' uh hot uh col'. When he spoke Ah had tuh move and move quick too, uh git a hick'ry tuh mah back. Dese younguns ain't uh bit better'n me. Let 'em come lak Ah did."

"Naw, Ned, Ah don't want mine tuh come lak yuh come nor neither lak me, and Ahm uh whole heap younger'n you.

4

You growed up in slavery time. When Old Massa wuz drivin' you in de rain and in de col'—he wasn't don' it tuh he'p you 'long. He wuz lookin' out for hisself. Course Ah wuz twelve years old when Lee made de big surrender, and dey didn't work me hard, but—but dese heah chillun is diffunt from us."

"How come dey's diffunt? Wese all niggers tuhgether, ain't us? White man don't keer no mo' 'bout one dan he do de other."

"Course dey don't, but we ain't got tuh let de white folks love our chillun fuh us, is us? Dass jest de pint. We black folks don't love our chillun. We couldn't do it when we wuz in slavery. We borned 'em but dat didn't make 'em ourn. Dey b'longed tuh old Massa. 'Twan't no use in treasurin' other folkses property. It wuz liable tuh be took uhway any day. But we's free folks now. De big bell done rung! Us chillun is ourn. Ah doan know, mebbe hit'll take some of us generations, but us got tuh 'gin tuh practise on treasurin' our younguns. Ah loves dese heah already uh whole heap. Ah don't want 'em knocked and 'buked."

Ned raked his stubbly fingers thru his grisly beard in silent hostility. He spat in the fire and tamped his pipe.

"Dey say spare de rod and spile de child, and Gawd knows Ah ain't gwine tuh spile nair one uh dese. Niggers wuz made tuh work and all of 'em gwine work right long wid me. Is dat air supper ready yit?"

"Naw hit ain't. How you speck me tuh work in de field right long side uh you and den have supper ready jes' ez soon ez Ah git tuh de house? Ah helt uh big-eye hoe in mah hand jes' ez long ez you did, Ned."

"Don't you change so many words wid me, 'oman! Ah'll knock yuh dead ez Hector. Shet yo' mouf!"

"Ah change jes' ez many words ez Ah durn please! Ahm three times seben and uh button. Ah knows whut's de matter wid *you*. Youse mad cause Beaseley done took dem two bales uh cotton us made las' yeah."

"Youse uh lie!"

"Youse uh nother one, Ned Crittenden! Don't you lak it,

5

don't you take it, heah mah collar come and you shake it! Us wouldn't be in dis fix ef you had uh lissened tuh me. Ah tole you when dey hauled de cotton tuh de gin dat soon ez everything wuz counted up and Beasley give us share for yuh tuh take and haul it straight tuh dis barn. But naw, yuh couldn't lissen tuh me. Beasley told yuh tuh leave hit in *his* barn and being he's uh white man you done whut he told yuh. Now he say he ain't got no cotton uh ourn. Me and you and all de chillun done worked uh whole year. Us done made sixteen bales uh cotton and ain't even got uh cotton seed to show."

"Us et hit up, Major Beasley say. Come to think of it 'tis uh heap uh moufs in one meal barrel."

"No sich uh thing, Ned Crittenden. Fust place us ain't had nothing but meal and sow-belly tuh eat. You mealy-moufin' round cause you skeered tuh talk back tuh Rush Beasley. What us needs tuh do is git offa dis place. Us been heah too long. Ah b'longs on de other side de Big Creek anyhow. Never did lak it over heah. When us gather de crops dis yeah less move."

"Aw, Ah reckon we kin make it heah all right, when us don't have so many moufs in de meal barrel we kin come out ahead. 'Tain't goin' be dat many dis time when Ah goes to de gin house."

"How come?"

"Cause Ah done bound John over tuh Cap'n Mimms. Dat's uh great big ole boy, Amy, sixteen years old and look lak he twenty. He eats uh heap and den you won't let me git de worth uh mah rations out of 'im in work. He could be de finest plowhand in Alabama, but you won't lemme do nothin' wid 'im."

"He don't do nothin'? He's uh better hand wid uh wide sweep plow right now dan you is, and he kin chop mo' cotton dan you, and pick mo' dan Ah kin and you knows Ah kin beat you anytime." Then, as if she had just fully heard Ned, "Whut dat you say 'bout boundin' John Buddy over tuh Cap'n Mimms? You ain't uh gonna do no sich uh thing."

"Ah done done it."

In the frenzied silence, Amy noticed that the rain had

6

ceased; that the iron kettle was boiling; that a coon dog struck a trail way down the Creek, and was coming nearer, singing his threat and challenge.

"Ned Crittenden, you know jes' ez good ez Ah do dat Cap'n Mimms ain't nothin' but po' white trash, and he useter be de overseer on de plantation dat everybody knowed wuz de wust one in southern Alabama. He done whipped niggers nigh tuh death."

"You call him po' when he got uh thousand acres under de plow and more'n dat in wood lot? Fifty mules."

"Don't keer if he is. How did he git it? When Massa Pinckney got kilt in de war and ole Miss Pinckney didn't had nobody tuh look atter de place she took and married 'im. He wan't nothin' but uh overseer, lived offa clay and black m'lasses. His folks is so po' right now dey can't sit in dey house. Every time you pass dere dey settin' in de yard jes' ez barefooted ez uh yard dawg. You ain't gwine put no chile uh mine under no Mimms."

"Ah done done it, and you can't he'p yo'seff. He gwine come git 'im tuhmorrer. He's gwine sleep 'im and feed 'im and effen John Buddy's any account, he say he'll give uh suit uh close come Christmas time."

"Dis heah bindin' over ain't nothin' but uh 'nother way uh puttin' us folks back intuh slavery."

"Amy, you better quit talkin' 'bout de buckra. Some of 'em be outside and hear you and turn over you tuh de patter roller, and dey'll take you outa heah and put uh hun'ed lashes uh raw hide on yo' back. Ah done tole yuh but you won't hear."

The clash and frenzy in the air was almost visible. Something had to happen. Ned stood up and shuffled towards the door.

"Reckon Ahm gwine swill dat sow and feed de mules. Mah vittles better be ready when Ah git back."

He limped on out of the door and left it open.

"John Buddy," Amy said, "you and Zeke go fetch uh bucket full uh water and hurry back tuh yo' supper. De rest uh y'all git yo' plates and come git some uh dese cow-peas and

7

pone bread. Lawd, Lawd, Lawd. Je-sus!"

There was a lively clatter of tin plates and spoons. The largest two boys went after water, Zeke clinging in the darkness to his giant of a brother. Way down in the cotton Zeke gave way to his tears.

"John Buddy, Ah don't want you way from me. John Buddy,—" he grew incoherent. So John Buddy carried him under his arm like a shock of corn and made him laugh. Finally John said, "Sometime Ah jes' ez soon be under Mimms ez pappy. One 'bout ez bad as tother. 'Nother thing. Dis ain't slavery time and Ah got two good footses hung onto me." He began to sing lightly.

They returned with the water and were eating supper when Ned got back from the barn. His face was sullen and he carried the raw hide whip in his hand.

Amy stooped over the pot, giving second-helpings to the smaller children. Ned looked about and seeing no plate fixed for him uncoiled the whip and standing tiptoe to give himself more force, brought the whip down across Amy's back.

The pain and anger killed the cry within her. She wheeled to fight. The raw hide again. This time across her head. She charged in with a stick of wood and the fight was on. This had happened many times before. Amy's strength was almost as great as Ned's and she had youth and agility with her. Forced back to the wall by her tigress onslaught, Ned saw that victory for him was possible only by choking Amy. He thrust his knee into her abdomen and exerted a merciless pressure on her throat.

The children screamed in terror and sympathy.

"Help mama, John Buddy," Zeke screamed. John's fist shot out and Ned slid slowly down the wall as if both his legs and his insides were crumbling away.

Ned looked scarcely human on the floor. Almost like an alligator in jeans. His drooling blue lips and snaggled teeth were yellowed by tobacco.

"Lawd, Ah speck you done kilt yo' pappy, John. You didn't mean tuh, and he didn't had no business hittin' me wid dat raw

hide and neither chokin' me neither. Jesus, Jesus, Jesus, Jee-
sus!"

"He ain't dead, mama. Ah see 'im breathin'." Zachariah
said, "John Buddy sho is strong! Ah bet he kin whip ev'ry
body in Notasulga."

Ned got up limpingly. He looked around and sat upon the
bed.

"Amy, Ahm tellin' yuh, git dat punkin-colored bastard outa
dis house. He don't b'long heah wid us nohow."

"He ain't de onliest yaller chile in de world. Wese uh
mingled people."

Ned limped to the fireplace and Amy piled his plate with
corn bread and peas.

"Git dat half-white youngun uh yourn outa heah, Amy.
Heah Ah done took 'im since he wus three years old and done
for 'im when he couldn't do for hisseff, and he done raised his
hand tuh me. Dis house can't hol' bofe uh us. Yaller niggers
ain't no good nohow."

"Oh yes dey is," Amy defended hotly, "yes dey is—jes' ez
good ez anybody else. You jes' started tuh talk dat foolishness
since you been hangin' 'round old Mimms. Monkey see, monkey do."

"Well, iss de truth. Dese white folks orta know and dey say
dese half-white niggers got de worst part uh bofe de white and
de black folks."

"Dey ain't got no call tuh say dat. Is mo' yaller folks on de
chain-gang dan black? Naw! Is dey harder tuh learn? Naw! Do
dey work and have things lak other folks? Yas. Naw dese po'
white folks says dat 'cause dey's jealous uh de yaller ones.
How come? Ole Marse got de yaller nigger totin' his silver
cup and eatin' Berksher hawg ham outa his kitchin when po'
white trash scrabblin' 'round in de piney woods huntin' up uh
razor back. Yaller nigger settin' up drivin' de carriage and de
po' white folks got tuh step out de road and leave 'im pass by.
And den agin de po' white man got daughters dat don't never
eben smell de kitchin at the big house and all dem yaller
chillun got mammas, and no black gal ain't never been up

9

tuh de big house and dragged Marse Nobody out. Humph! Talkin' after po' white trash! If Ah wuz ez least ez dey is, Ah speck Ah'd fret mahself tuh death.''

"Aw naw,'' Ned sneered, "de brother in black don't fret tuh death. White man fret and worry and kill hisself. Colored folks fret uh li'l' while and gwan tuh sleep. 'Nother thing, Amy, Hagar's chillun don't faint neither when dey fall out, dey jes have uh hard old fit.''

"Dass awright, Ned. You always runnin' yo' race down. We ain't had de same chance dat white folks had. Look lak Ah can't sense you intuh dat.''

"Amy, niggers can't faint. Jes' ain't in 'em.''

"Dass awright. Niggers gwine faint too. May not come in yo' time and it may not come in mine, but way after while, us people is gwine faint jes' lak white folks. You watch and see.''

"Table dat talk. Dat John is gwine offa dis place effen Ah stay heah. He goes tuh Mimms uh he goes apin' on down de road way from heah. Ah done spoke.''

"Naw Ned,'' Amy began, but John cut her off.

"It's all right, mama, lemme go. Ah don't keer. One place is good ez 'nother one. Leave him do all de plowin' after dis!''

With his mouth full of peas and corn bread, Ned gloated, "De crops is laid by.''

"Yeah, but nex' year's crops ain't planted yit,'' John countered.

So John put on his brass-toed shoes and his clean shirt and was ready to leave. Amy dug out a crumpled and mouldy dollar and gave it to him.

"Where you goin', son?''

"Over de Big Creek, mama. Ah ever wanted tuh cross over.''

"Ah'll go piece de way wid yuh tuh de Creek, John. Gimme uh li'dud knot, dere, Zeke, so's Ah kin see de way back.''

"Good bye, pap,'' John called from the door. Ned grunted over a full mouth. The children bawled dolefully when John called to them.

Amy threw a rag over her bruised head and closed the door

after her. The night was black and starry.

"John, you wuz borned over de Creek."

"You wuz tellin' me dat one day, Ah 'member."

"Dey knows me well, over dere. Maybe Ah kin pint yuh whar some work is at."

"Yassum. Ah wants tuh make money, so's Ah kin come back and git yuh."

"Don't yuh take me tuh heart. Ah kin strain wid Ned. Ah jes' been worried 'bout you and him. Youse uh big boy now and you am gwine take and take offa 'im and swaller all his filth lak you been doin' here of late. Ah kin see dat in yo' face. Youse slow, but wid him keerin' on lak he do now, hit takes uh Gawd tuh tell whut gwine happen in dat house. He didn't useter 'buke yuh lak dat. But his old mammy and dat old cock-eyed sister uh his'n put 'im up tuh dat. He useter be crazy 'bout yuh. 'Member dat big gol' watch chain he bought fuh you tuh wear tuh big meetin'? Dey make lak he love you better'n he do de rest on 'count youse got color in your face. So he tryin' side wid dem and show 'em he don't. Ahm kinda glad fuh yuh tuh be 'way from 'round 'im. Massa Alf Pearson, he got uh big plantation and he's quality white folks. He know me too. Go in Notasulga and ast fuh 'im. Tell 'im whose boy you is and maybe he mought put yuh tuh work. And if he do, son, you scuffle hard so's he'll work yuh reg'lar. Ah hates tuh see yuh knucklin' under 'round heah all de time. G'wan, son, and be keerful uh dat foot-log 'cross de creek. De Songahatchee is strong water, and look out under foot so's yuh don't git snake bit."

"Ah done swum dat ole creek, mama—'thout yuh knowin'. Ah knowed you'd tell me not tuh swim it."

"Dat's how come Ah worries 'bout yuh. Youse always uh runnin' and uh rippin' and clambin' trees and rocks and jumpin', flingin' rocks in creeks and sich like. John, promise me yuh goin' quit dat."

"Yassum."

"Come tuh see me when yuh kin. G'bye."

Amy was gone back up the rocky path thru the blooming

11

cotton, across the barren hard clay yard. For a minute she had felt free and flighty down there as she stood in the open with her tall, bulky son. Now the welts on her face and body hurt her and the world was heavy.

John plunged on down to the Creek, singing a new song and stomping the beats. The Big Creek thundered among its rocks and whirled on down. So John sat on the foot-log and made some words to go with the drums of the Creek. Things walked in the birch woods, creep, creep, creep. The hound dog's lyric crescendo lifted over and above the tree tops. He was on the foot-log, half way across the Big Creek where maybe people laughed and maybe people had lots of daughters. The moon came up. The hunted coon panted down to the Creek, swam across and proceeded leisurely up the other side. The tenor-singing hound dog went home. Night passed. No more Ned, no hurry. No telling how many girls might be living on the new and shiny side of the Big Creek. John almost trumpeted exultantly at the new sun. He breathed lustily. He stripped and carried his clothes across, then recrossed and plunged into the swift water and breasted strongly over.

CHAPTER 2

There was a strange noise that John had never heard. He was sauntering along a road with his shoes in his hand. He could see houses here and there among the fields—not miles apart like where he had come from. Suddenly thirty or forty children erupted from a log building near the roadside, shouting and laughing. He had been to big meeting but this was no preaching. Not all them li'l' chaps. A chunky stern-faced man stood in the door momentarily with a bunch of hickories in his hand. So! This must be the school house that he had heard about. Negro children going to learn how to read and write like white folks. See! All this going on over there and the younguns over the creek chopping cotton! It must be very nice, but maybe it wasn't for over-the-creek-niggers. These girls all had on starchy little aprons over Sunday-go-to-meeting dresses. He stopped and leaned upon the fence and stared.

One little girl with bright black eyes came and stood before him, arms akimbo. She must have been a leader, for several more came and stood back of her. She looked him over boldly from his tousled brown head to his bare white feet. Then she said, "Well, folks! Where you reckon dis big yaller bee-stung nigger come from?"

Everybody laughed. He felt ashamed of his bare feet for the

13

first time in his life. How was he to know that there were colored folks that went around with their feet cramped up like white folks. He looked down at the feet of the black-eyed girl. Tiny little black shoes. One girl behind her had breasts, must be around fourteen. He looked at her again. Some others were growing up too. In fact all were looking a little bit like women—all but the little black-eyed one. When he looked back into her face he felt ashamed. Seemed as if she had caught him doing something nasty. He shifted his feet in embarrassment.

"Ah think he musta come from over de Big Creek. 'Tain't nothin' lak dat on dis side," the little tormenter went on. Then she looked right into his eyes and laughed. All the others laughed. John laughed too.

"Dat's whar Ah come from sho 'nuff," he admitted.

"Whut you doin' over heah, then?"

"Come tuh see iffen Ah could git uh job uh work. Kin yuh tell me whar Marse Alf Pearson live at?"

The little girl snorted, "Marse Alf! Don't y'all folkses over de creek know slavery time is over? 'Tain't no mo' Marse Alf, no Marse Charlie, nor Marse Tom neither. Folks whut wuz borned in slavery time go 'round callin' dese white folks Marse but we been born since freedom. We calls 'em Mister. Dey don't own nobody no mo'."

"Sho don't," the budding girl behind the little talker chimed in. She threw herself akimbo also and came walking out hippily from behind the other, challenging John to another appraisal of her person.

"Ah calls 'em anything Ah please," said another girl and pulled her apron a little tight across the body as she advanced towards the fence.

"Aw, naw, yuh don't, Clary," the little black-eyed girl disputed, "youse talkin' at de big gate now. You jus' want somebody tuh notice yuh."

"Well, effen you calls 'em Mista, Ah kin call 'em Mista too," John talked at the little spitfire. "Whar at is Mista Alf Pearson's place?"

"Way on down dis road, 'bout uh mile uh mo'. When yuh git long dere by de cotton-gin, ast somebody and dey'll tell yuh mo' exact."

John shifted from one foot to another a time or two, then started off with the long stride known as boaging.

"Thankee, thankee," he threw back over his shoulder and strode on.

The teacher poked his head out of the door and all the other girls ran around behind the school house lest he call them to account for talking to a boy. But the littlest girl stood motionless, not knowing that the others had fled. She stood still akimbo watching John stride away. Then suddenly her hands dropped to her sides and she raced along the inside of the fence and overtook John.

"Hello agin," John greeted her, glad at her friendliness.

"Hello yuhself, want uh piece uh cawn bread look on de shelf."

John laughed boisterously and the girl smiled and went on in another tone, "Whyn't *you* come tuh school too?"

" 'Cause dey never sont me. Dey tole me tuh go find work, but Ah wisht dey had uh tole me school. Whut Ah seen of it, Ah lakted it."

From behind her the irate voice of a man called, "Lucy! Lucy!! Come heah tuh me. Ah'll teach yuh 'bout talkin' wid boys!"

"See yuh later, and tell yuh straighter," John said and walked off.

John strode on into Notasulga, whistling; his tousled hair every which away over his head. He saw a group of people clustered near a small building and he timidly approached.

"Dis heah mus' be de cotton-gin wid all dem folks and hawses and buggies tied tuh de hitchin' postes."

Suddenly he was conscious of a great rumbling at hand and the train schickalacked up to the station and stopped.

John stared at the panting monster for a terrified moment, then prepared to bolt. But as he wheeled about he saw everybody's eyes upon him and there was laughter on every face.

He stopped and faced about. Tried to look unconcerned, but that great eye beneath the cloud-breathing smoke-stack glared and threatened. The engine's very sides seemed to expand and contract like a fiery-lunged monster. The engineer leaning out of his window saw the fright in John's face and blew a sharp blast on his whistle and John started violently in spite of himself. The crowd roared.

"Hey, dere, big-un," a Negro about the station called to John, "you ain't never seed nothin' dangerous lookin' lak dat befo', is yuh?"

"Naw suh and hit sho look frightenin'," John answered. His candor took the ridicule out of the faces of the crowd. "But hits uh pretty thing too. Whar it gwine?"

"Oh eve'y which and whar," the other Negro answered, with the intent to convey the impression to John that he knew so much about trains, their habits and destinations that it would be too tiresome to try to tell it all.

The train kicked up its heels and rattled on off. John watched after it until it had lost itself down its shiny road and the noise of its going was dead.

"You laks dat ole train Ah see," the Negro said to John, watching him as he all but fell down into the railroad cut, trying to keep sight of the tail of the train.

"Yeah, man, Ah lakted dat. It say something but Ah ain't heered it 'nough tuh tell whut it say yit. You know whut it say?"

"It don't say nothin'. It jes' make uh powerful racket, dass all."

"Naw, it say some words too. Ahm comin' heah plenty mo' times and den Ah tell yuh whut it say." He straightened up and suddenly remembered.

"Whar de cotton-gin at?"

"Hit's right over dere, but dey ain't hirin' nobody yit."

"Ain't lookin' tuh git hiahed. Lookin' fuh Mist' Alf Pearson."

"Dere he right over dere on de flat-form at de deepo', whut yuh want wid 'im?"

16

"Wants tuh git uh job."

"Reckon you kin git on. He done turned off his coachman fuh stovin' up one uh his good buggy hawses."

John stalked over to the freight platform.

"Is you Mist' Alf?" he asked the tall broad-built man, who was stooping over some goods.

"Why yes, what're you want?"

"Ah wants uh job uh work, please suh."

The white man continued to examine invoices without so much as a glance at the boy who stood on the ground looking up at him. Not seeing what he wanted, he straightened up and looked about him and saw John at last. Instead of answering the boy directly he stared at him fixedly for a moment, whistled and exclaimed, "What a fine stud! Why boy, you would have brought five thousand dollars on the block in slavery time! Your face looks sort of familiar but I can't place you. What's your name?"

"Mama, she name me Two-Eye-John from a preachin' she heered, but dey call me John Buddy for short."

"How old are you, John?"

"Sixteen, goin' on sebenteen."

"Dog damn! Boy you're almost as big as I am. Where'd you come from?"

"Over de Big Creek. Mama she sont me over here and told me tuh ast you tuh gimme uh job uh work. Ah kin do mos' anything."

"Humph, I should think you could. Boy, you could go bear-hunting with your fist. I believe I can make a lead plow-hand out of you."

"Yassuh, thankee, Mista Alf, Ah knows how."

"Er, who is your mama?"

"Amy Crittenden. She didn't useter be uh Crittenden. She wuz jes' Amy and b'longed tuh you 'fo surrender. She say Ah borned on yo' place."

"Oh yes. I remember her. G'wan get in my rig. The bay horses with the cream colored buggy. Fetch it on over here and drive me home."

John went over by the courthouse to get the rig. It was some distance. As soon as he was out of earshot, one of Alf Pearson's friends asked him, "Say, Judge, where'd you get the new house-nigger from?"

"Oh a boy born on my place since surrender. Mama married some stray darky and moved over the Big Creek. She sent him over here to hunt work and he ran into me and I'm hiring him. Did you ever see such a splendid specimen? He'll be a mighty fine plow hand. Too tall to be a good cotton-picker. Sixteen years old."

"Humph! Plow-hand! Dat's uh house-nigger. His kind don't make good field niggers. It's been tried. In his case it's a pity, because he'd be equal to two hands ordinary."

"Oh well, maybe I can do something with him. He seems willing enough. And anyway I know how to work 'em."

When John brought the horses to a satisfactory halt before the white pillars of the Pearson mansion, his new boss got down and said, "Now John, take those horses on to the stable and let Nunkie put 'em away. He'll show you where the quarters are. G'wan to 'em and tell old Pheemy I said fix you some place to sleep."

"Yassuh, thankee suh."

"And John, I might need you around the house sometimes, so keep clean."

"Yassuh."

"Where's the rest of your clothes?"

"Dese is dem."

"Well, you'll have to change sometime or other. I'll look around the house, and perhaps I can scare you up a change or two. My son Alfred is about your size, but he's several years older. And er, er, I'll fetch 'em down to the quarters in case I find anything. Go 'long."

Ole Pheemy gave John a bed in her own cabin, "Take dis bed heah if hit's good 'nough fuh yuh," she said pointing to a high feather bed in one corner.

"Yassum, thankee ma'am. Ah laks it jes' fine, and dis sho is uh pritty house."

18

He was looking at the newspapers plastered all over the walls.

Pheemy softened.

"Oh you ain't one uh dese uppity yaller niggers then?"

"Oh no ma'am. Ahm po' folks jes' lak you. On'y we ain't got no fine houses over de Creek lak dis heah one."

"Whus yo' name?"

"John, but Zeke and Zack and dem calls me John Buddy, yassum."

"Who yo' folks is over de Big Creek?"

"Mama she name Amy Crittenden—she—"

"Hush yo' mouf, you yaller rascal, you! Ah knowed, Ah seed reckerlection in yo' face." Pheemy rushed upon John, beating him affectionately and shoving him around. "Well, Lawd a'mussy boy! Ahm yo' granny! Yo' nable string is buried under dat air chanyberry tree. 'Member so well de very day you cried." (First cry at birth.) "Eat dis heah tater pone."

The field hands came in around dusk dark, eyeing John suspiciously, but his utter friendliness prevented the erection of barriers on his birth place. Amy's son was welcome. After supper the young folks played "Hide the Switch" and John overtook and whipped most of the girls soundly. They whipped him too. Perhaps his legs were longer, but anyway when he was "it" he managed to catch every girl in the quarters. The other boys were less successful, but girls were screaming under John's lash behind the cowpen and under the sweet-gum trees around the spring until the moon rose. John never forgot that night. Even the strong odor of their sweaty bodies was lovely to remember. He went in to bed when all of the girls had been called in by their folks. He could have romped till morning.

In bed he turned and twisted.

"Skeeters botherin' yuh, John Buddy?" Pheemy asked.

"No'm Ahm jes' wishin' Mist' Alf would lak mah work and lemme stay heah all de time." Then the black eyes of the little girl in the school yard burned at him from out of the darkness and he added, "Wisht Ah could go tuh school too."

19

"G'wan tuh sleep, chile. Heah 'tis way in de midnight and you ain't had no night rest. You gotta sleep effen you wanta do any work. Whut Marse Alf tell yuh tuh do?"

"He ain't tole me nothin' yit."

"Well, you stay heah tuh de house. Ontell he send fuh yuh. He ain't gwine overwork yuh. He don't break nobody down. Befo' surrender he didn't had no whippin' boss on *dis* place. Nawsuh. Come tuh 'membrance, 'tain't nothin' much tuh do now. De crops is laid by, de ground peas ain't ready, neither de cawn. But Ah don't speck he gointer put you in de fiel' nohow. Maybe you hand him his drinks uh drive de carridge fuh him and Ole Miss."

"Yassum," drifted back from John as he slid down and down into sleep and slumber.

That night he dreamed new dreams.

"John."

"Yassuh."

"I see the clothes fit you."

"Yassuh, Ahm powerful glad dey do, 'cause Ah laks 'em."

"John, I don't reckon I'll have you to drive us again. I thought to make a coachman out of you, but the mistress thinks you're too, er, er—large sitting up there in front. Can't see around you."

"Yassuh," John's face fell. He wasn't going to be hired after all.

"But I've got another job for you. You feed the chickens and gather the eggs every morning before breakfast. Have the fresh eggs in the pantry at the big house before seven o'clock so Emma can use some for our breakfast."

"Yassuh."

"And John, see to it that Ceasar and Bully and Nunkie keep the stables, pig pens and the chicken houses clean. Don't say anything to 'em, but when you find 'em dirty you let me know."

"Yassuh."

"And another thing, I want you to watch all of my brood

20

sows. As soon as a litter is born, you let me know. And you must keep up with every pig on the place. Count 'em every morning, and when you find one missing you look around and find out what's become of it. I'm missing entirely too many shoats. I'm good to my darkies but I can't let 'em eat up all my hogs. Now, I'm going to see if I can trust you."

"Yassuh."

"Can you read and write, John?"

"Nawsuh."

"Never been to school?"

"Nawsuh, yassuh, Ah passed by dat one d'other day."

"Well, John, there's nothing much to do on the place now, so you might as well go on down to the school and learn how to read and write. I don't reckon it will hurt you. Don't waste your time, now. Learn. I don't think the school runs but three months and it's got to close for cotton-picking. Don't fool around. You're almost grown. Three or four children on this place go so you go along with them. Go neat. I didn't have slouchy folks on my place in slavery time. Mister Alfred, my son, is studying abroad and he's left several suits around that will do for you. Be neat. Let's see your feet. I don't believe you can wear his shoes but I'll buy you a pair and take it out of your wages. You mind me and I'll make something out of you."

"Yassuh, Mister Alf. Thankee. Youse real good tuh me. Mama said you wuz good."

"She was a well-built-up girl and a splendid hoe hand. I never could see why she married that darky and let him drag her around share-cropping. Those backwoods white folks over the creek make their living by swindling the niggers."

John didn't go to school the next day. He had truly been delighted at the prospect of attending school. It had kept him glowing all day. But that night the young people got up a game of "Hide and Seek." It started a little late, about the time that the old heads were going to bed.

Bow-legged, pigeon-toed Minnie Turl was counting, "Ten, ten, double ten, forty-five, fifteen. All hid? All hid?"

From different directions, as the "hiders" sought cover, "No!"

> "Three li'l' hawses in duh stable,
> One jumped out and skint his nable.
> All hid? All hid?"

"No!" from farther away.

John ran down hill towards the spring where the bushes were thick. He paused at a clump. It looked like a good place. There was a stealthy small sound behind it and he ran on. Some one ran down the path behind him. A girl's hand caught his. It was Phrony, the womanish fourteen-year-old who lived in the third cabin from Pheemy's.

"Ah'll show yuh uh good place tuh hide," she whispered, "nobody can't find yuh."

She dragged him off the path to the right and round and about to a clump of sumac overrun with wild grape vines.

"Right under heah," she panted from running, "nobody can't find yuh."

"Whar you goin' hide yuhself?" John asked as he crept into the arboreal cave.

"Iss plenty room," Phrony whispered. "Us bofe kin hide in heah."

She crept in also and leaned heavily upon John, giggling and giggling as the counting went on.

> "Ah got up 'bout half-past fo'
> Forty fo' robbers wuz 'round mah do'
> Ah got up and let 'em in
> Hit 'em ovah de head wid uh rollin' pin.
> All hid? All hid?"

"Yeah."

"All dem ten feet round mah base is caught. Ahm comin'!"

There were screams and shouts of laughter. "Dere's Gold-Dollar behind dat chanyberry tree. Ah got yuh."

22

"Whoo-ee! Ahm free, Minnie, Ah beat yuh in home."

"Less we run in whilst she gone de other way," John whispered.

"Naw, less we lay low 'til she git tired uh huntin' us and give us free base."

"Aw right, Phrony, but Ah loves tuh outrun 'em and beat 'em tuh de base. 'Tain't many folks kin run good ez me."

"Ah kin run good, too."

"Aw, 'tain't no girl chile kin run good ez me."

"Ah betcha 'tis. Lucy Potts kin outrun uh yearlin' and rope 'im."

"Humph! Where she at?"

"She live over in Pottstown. Her folks done bought de ole Cox place. She go to school. Dey's big niggers."

"She uh li'l' bitty gal wid black eyes and long hair plats?"

"Yeah, dat's her. She leben years ole, but she don't look it. Ahm fourteen. Ahm big. Maybe Ah'll git married nex' year."

"Ahm gwine race huh jes' soon ez Ah gits tuh school. Mista Alf gwine lemme go too."

"Dat's good. Ah done been dere las' yeah. Ah got good learnin'. Reckon Ah'll git uh husban' nex'."

Cry from up the hill, "John and Phrony, come on in. You get free base!"

They scrambled out. John first, then Phrony more slowly, and trudged up the hill. A boy was kneeling at the woods chopping-block base when they came into the crowd. The crowd began to disperse again. John started off in another direction. He looked back and saw Phrony coming behind him, but Mehaley cut in from behind a bush and reached him first.

"Come on wid me, John, lemme show yuh uh good place." He started to say that he didn't want to hide out and talk as he had done with Phrony. He wanted to pit his strength and speed against the boy who was counting. He wanted to practise running, but he felt a flavor come out from Mehaley. He could almost sense it in his mouth and nostrils. He was cross with Phrony for following them. He let Mehaley take his hand

and they fled away up the hill and hid in the hay.

"De hair on yo' head so soft lak," Mehaley breathed against his cheek. "Lemme smoothen it down."

When John and Mehaley came in, Minnie Turl was counting. Everybody was hid except Phrony who sat bunched up on the door step.

"Y'all better go hide agin," she said.

"Somebody else count and lemme hide," Minnie wailed. "Ah been countin' most all de time." She came and stood near John.

"G'wan hide, Minnie, Ah'll count some," John said.

"Heh! Heh!" Phrony laughed maliciously at Minnie. Minnie looked all about her and went inside the house and to bed.

"Haley, where mah hair comb you borried from me las' Sunday? Ah wuz nice enough tuh len' it tuh yuh, but you ain't got manners 'nough tuh fetch it back." Phrony advanced upon Mehaley and John.

"You kin git yo' ole stink hair comb any time. Ah'll be glad tuh git it outa mah house. Mama tole me not tuh comb wid it 'cause she skeered Ah'd git boogers in mah haid."

"Youse uh lie! Ah ain't got no boogers in mah haid, and if you' mamy say so she's uh liar right long wid you! She ain't so bad ez she make out. Ah'll stand on yo' toes and tell yuh so."

"Git back outa mah face, Phrony. Ah don't play de dozens!" Mehaley shoved. Phrony struck, and John and all the hiders, who came running in at the sound of battle, had trouble stopping the rough and tumble.

"Did y'all had words befo' yuh fell out?" Charlie asked.

"We ain't had no words," said Mehaley.

"Whut y'all fightin' 'bout, if yuh ain't mad?"

"Aw, ole fish-mouf Phrony mad 'cause John wouldn't hide wid her and he took and hid wid me."

"Youse uh liar, madam! He did so hide wid me."

"He wouldn't stay, and Ah'll betcha Alabama wid uh fence 'round it he won't never hide wid yuh no mo'."

24

Mehaley preened herself akimbo and rotated her hips insolently.

"Sh-sh—" Charlie cautioned, "de old heads liable tuh wake up, and dey'll haul off and take and frail everybody. Less all tip in tuh bed. Iss way after midnight anyhow."

So John overslept next morning and by the time that he had gathered the eggs and counted the hogs it was too late for school. He didn't want to see Lucy anyway. Not the way he felt that day, but late in the afternoon as he wandered over the place, he found a tiny clearing hidden by trees.

"Dis is uh prayin' ground," he said to himself.

"O Lawd, heah 'tis once mo' and again yo' weak and humble servant is knee-bent and body bowed—Mah heart beneath mah knees and mah knees in some lonesome valley cryin' fuh mercy whilst mercy kinst be found. O Lawd! you know mah heart, and all de ranges uh mah deceitful mind—and if you find any sin lurkin' in and about mah heart please pluck it out and cast it intuh de sea uh fuhgitfulness whar it'll never rise tuh condemn me in de judgment."

That night John, deaf to Mehaley's blandishments, sat in the doorway and told tales. And Brer Rabbit and Brer Fox and Raw-Head-and-Bloody-Bones walked the earth like natural men.

Next morning, bright and soon he stood at the school-house door. The teacher was a stodgy middle-aged man who prided himself on his frowns. Every few moments he lifted his head and glared about the room. He yearned to hold his switches in his hand. He had little ambition to impart knowledge. He reigned. Later John found out he was Lucy's uncle.

"Come heah, you," he pointed his ruler at John. "Don't you know no better'n to come in my school and sit yo'self down without sayin' a word to me?"

"Yassuh," he approached the deal table that went by the name of desk.

"If you know better, why did you do it? I ought to put forty lashes on yo' bare back. You come to school?"

"Yassuh."

"Don't say 'yassuh' to me. Say 'Yes suh.' "

The room tittered.

"What's yo' name?"

"John."

"John whut? You got some other name besides John."

"Mama, she name me Two-Eye John—"

They burst into loud laughter. John colored and he stole a glance at Lucy. She wasn't laughing. Her hands and lips were tense. She must be put out with him for being a fool. She wasn't laughing like the rest.

"But mama and all of 'em at home calls me John Buddy."

"Buddy is a nickname. What's yo' papa' name?"

John scratched his head and thought a minute.

" 'Deed Ah don't know, suh."

There was another short silence.

"Where do you live?"

"On Mista Alf Pearson's place."

"Was you born there?"

"Yes suh."

"Well, Ah'll jus' put you down as John Pearson and you answer by that, you hear?"

"Yes suh."

"Ever been to school before?"

"Naw suh."

"Well, you get over there in de A B C class and don't let me ketch you talkin' in school."

John was amazed at the number of things to be learned. He liked to watch Lucy's class recite. They put so many figures on the board and called it long division. He would certainly be well learnt when he could do that. They parsed sentences. They spelt long words.

He studied hard because he caught Lucy watching him every time he recited. He wrote on the ground in the quarters and in a week he knew his alphabet and could count to a hundred.

"Whut you learnin' in school, John—A, B, Ab's?" Charlie asked him.

26

"Ah already know dat, Charlie. Ah kin spell 'baker' too."

"Don't b'lieve it. Not dis quick, yuh can't."

"B-a-k-bak-e-r-er baker."

"Boy, you sho is eatin' up dat school!"

"Ain't ez smart ez some. Take Lucy Potts for instink. She's almost uh 'fessor now. Nobody can't spell her down. Dey say she kin spell eve'y word in Lippincott's Blue-back Speller."

"Shucks! You ain't tryin' tuh buck up tuh her in book learnin', is yuh? Dey tell me she kin spell 'compresstibility,' and when yuh git dat fur 'tain't much mo' fuhther fur yuh tuh go."

"She sho kin spell it, 'cause Ah heered 'er do it. Some say she kin spell 'Constan-ti-nople' too."

"Ah b'lieve it. All dem Potts is smart. Her brother leads de choir at Macedony Baptis' Church, and she trebles right 'long wid dem grown women and kin sing all de notes—de square ones, de round ones, de triangles."

"Ah'll be dere tuh heah her do it nex' big meetin'. Charlie, Ah loves tuh heah singin'."

"Whyn't yuh join de choir? You oughter be able tuh sing lak git out wid all dat ches' you got."

"B'lieve Ah will, Charlie. Ah laks big meetin'."

It was three weeks from the time that John started to school 'til cotton-picking time. Prodded on all sides, he had learned to read a little and write a few words crudely.

He was sorry when school closed for the cotton-picking but he kept on studying. When the school re-opened for its final month he wanted to get promoted again. He found himself spelling out words on barns and wagons, almanacs, horse-medicine-bottles, wrapping-paper.

He had been to church; he hadn't enough courage to join the choir, but every meeting he was there. Lucy tossed her head and sang her treble and never missed a note.

When the cotton-picking began on his place, Alf Pearson said to John, "You better go across the Creek and let your mama know how you're getting along. If you see any good cotton pickers—anybody that can pick more than two hundred

27

a day—tell 'em I need some hands, and you be back by tomor-row night. I bought a brood sow over round Chehaw and I want you to go get her."

There was great rejoicing in Amy's house when John climbed the hill from the Creek.

They didn't know him in his new clothes. They made great " 'miration" over everything. Amy cried.

"Jes' tuh think, mah boy gittin' book-learnt! Ned, de rest uh dese chillun got tuh go tuh school nex' yeah. Sho is."

"Whut fur? So dey kin lay in de peni'ten'ry? Dat's all dese book-learnt niggers do—fill up de jails and chain-gangs. Dese boys is comin' 'long all right. All dey need tuh learn is how tuh swing uh hoe and turn a furrer. Ah ain't rubbed de hair offa mah haid 'gin no college walls and Ah got good sense. Day ain't goin' tuh no school effen Ah got anythin' tuh say 'bout it. Jes' be turnin' 'em fools!"

Stormy weather. John cut in.

"Mama, Mista Alf say if Ah could find some good cotton pickers tuh tell 'em he need hands. You know any? He payin' fifty cent uh hund'ed."

"Dat's more'n dey payin' over heah," Ned cut in eagerly, "Amy, whyn't you take Zeke and Zack and y'all g'wan make dat li'l' change? Ah'll take keer de li'l' chillun and pick up whut li'l' Ah kin git over heah. Cotton open dat side de Creek fust anyhow. By time y'all finish over dere hit'll jis' be gittin' in full swing over heah."

"Reckon us could make li'l' money. Tell 'im, 'Yeah,' John Buddy, we's comin'."

"Zack!" Ned called, "Take dis heah jug and run over tuh de Turk place and tell Ike tuh send me uh gallon. Pay 'im nex' week some time."

When the cotton was all picked and the last load hauled to the gin, Alf Pearson gave the hands two hogs to barbecue.

That was a night. Hogs roasting over the open pit of oak coals. Negroes from three other plantations. Some brought "likker." Some crocus sacks of yellow yam potatoes, and bush-els of peanuts to roast, and the biggest syrup-kettle at Pearson's canemill was full of chicken perleau. Twenty hens and six water-buckets full of rice. Old Purlee Kimball was stirring it with a shovel.

Plenty of music and plenty of people to enjoy it. Three sets had been danced when Bully took the center of the hard-packed clay court upon which they were dancing. He had the whole rib of a two-hundred-pound hog in his hands and gnawed it as he talked.

"Hey, everybody! Stop de music. Don't vip another vop 'til Ah says so. Hog head, hog bosom, hog hips and every kind of hog there ever wuz is ready! Come git yourn. De chickens is cacklin' in de rice and dey say 'Come git it whilst iss fitten 'cause t'morrer it may be frost-bitten!' De yaller yams is spilin' in de ashes. It's uh shame! Eat it all up, and den we's gointer dance, 'cause we'll have somethin' tuh dance offa."

The hogs, the chickens, the yams disappeared. The old folks played "Ole Horse" with the parched peanuts. The musicians drank and tuned up. Bully was calling figures.

"Hey you, dere, us ain't no white folks! Put down dat fiddle! Us don't want no fiddles, neither no guitars, neither no banjoes. Less clap!"

So they danced. They called for the instrument that they had brought to America in their skins—the drum—and they played upon it. With their hands they played upon the little dance drums of Africa. The drums of kid-skin. With their feet they stomped it, and the voice of Kata-Kumba, the great drum, lifted itself within them and they heard it. The great drum that is made by priests and sits in majesty in the juju house. The drum with the man skin that is dressed with human blood, that is beaten with a human shin-bone and speaks to gods as a man and to men as a God. Then they beat upon the drum and danced. It was said, "He will serve us better if we bring him from Africa naked and thing-less." So the buckra reasoned. They tore away his clothes that Cuffy might bring nothing away, but Cuffy seized his drum and hid it in his skin under the skull bones. The shin-bones he bore openly, for he thought, "Who shall rob me of shin-bones when they see no drum?" So he laughed with cunning and said, "I, who am borne away to become an orphan, carry my parents with me. For Rhythm is she not my mother and Drama is her man?" So he groaned aloud in the ships and hid his drum and laughed.

"Dis is jes' lak when Ah wuz uh girl," Amy told Pheemy and offered her body to the voice.

Furious music of the little drum whose body was still in Africa, but whose soul sung around a fire in Alabama. Flourish. Break.

> Ole cow died in Tennessee
> Send her jawbone back to me
> Jawbone walk, Jawbone talk
> Jawbone eat wid uh knife and fork.
> Ain't Ah right?
>
> CHORUS: Yeah!
> Ain't I right? Yeah!

Hollow-hand clapping for the bass notes. Heel and toe stomping for the little one. Ibo tune corrupted with Nango. Congo gods talking in Alabama.

> If you want to see me jabber
> Set me down to uh bowl uh clabber
> Ain't Ah right? Yeah!
> Now, ain't Ah right? Yeah!
>
> Ole Ant Dinah behind de pine
> One eye out and de other one blind
> Ain't Ah right? Yeah! Yeah!
> Now, ain't Ah right? Yeah!

"Looka dat boy uh yourn, Amy!" Zeke Turk urged. "Didn't thought he knowed how tuh dance. He's rushin' de frog tuh de frolic! And looka 'Big 'Oman,' dat gal dancin' wid 'im. Lawd, she shakin' yonder skirt."

Wisht Ah had uh needle
Fine ez Ah could sew
Ah'd sew mah baby to my side
And down de road Ah'd go.

Double clapping—

Down de road baby
Down de road baby
It's killing mama
Oh, it's killing mama.

Too hot for words. Fiery drum clapping.

"Less burn dat old moon down to a nub! Is dat you, Pheemy?"

"Yeah Lawd. Mah head is tilted to de grave, but Ah'll show y'all Ah ain't fuhgit how. Come on out heah, Dink, and help ole Pheemy do de Parse me lah."

"Heel and toe. Don't call no figgers."

"Aw yeah, less call figgers. Go 'head Bully, but don't call it lak you call for white folks and dey go praipsin 'cross the floor lake dey steppin on eggs. Us kin dance. Call 'em, Bully."

"Awright, choose yo' partners."

"Couples tuh yo' places lak hawse tuh de traces."

"Sixteen hands up!"

"Circle four."

"Y'all ain't clappin' right. Git dat time.

Raccoon up de 'simmon tree
Possum on de ground
Raccoon shake dem 'simmons down
Possum pass 'em round."

The fire died. The moon died. The shores of Africa receded. They went to sleep and woke up next day and looked out on dead and dying cotton stalks and ripening possum persimmons.

As the final day of school closing drew near, John found life tremendously exciting. The drama of Pearson's plantation yielded to the tenseness around the school house. He had learned to spell his way thru several pages in his reader. He could add, subtract and divide and multiply. He proved his new power to communicate his thoughts by scratching Lucy's name in the clay wherever he found a convenient spot: with a sharp stick he had even scratched it on the back of Pheemy's chimney.

He saw Lucy at school every day. He saw her in church, and she was always in his consciousness, but he had never talked with her alone. When the opportunity presented itself he couldn't find words. Handling Big 'Oman, Lacey, Semmie, Bootsie and Mehaley merely called for action, but with Lucy he needed words and words that he did not have. One day during the practice for school closing he crowded near her and said, "Wisht Ah could speak pieces lak you do."

"You kin speak 'em better'n me," Lucy said evenly, "you got uh good voice for speakin'."

"But Ah can't learn no long ones lak you speaks. When do you learn 'em?"

"In de night time round home after Ah git thru wid mah lessons."

"You ain't got many mo' days tuh be studyin' of nights. Den whut you gwine do wid yo'self?"

"Mama always kin find plenty fuh folks tuh do."

"But Ah mean in de night time, Lucy. When youse thru wid yo' work. Don't you do nothin' but warm uh chair bottom?"

Lucy drew away quickly, "Oooh, John Buddy! You talkin' nasty."

John in turn was in confusion. "Whuss nasty?"

"You didn't hafta say 'bottom.'"

John shriveled up inside. He had intended to recite the rhymes to Lucy that the girls on the plantation thought so witty, but he realized that—

32

Some love collards, some love kale
But I loves uh gal wid uh short skirt tail

would drive Lucy from him in disgust. He could never tell her that. He felt hopeless about her. Soon she was recalled to the platform to recite and John's chance was gone. He kept on thinking, however, and he kept on making imaginary speeches to her. Speeches full of big words that would make her gasp and do him "reverence." He was glad when he was selected as the soldier to sing opposite Lucy in the duet, "Oh Soldier, Will You Marry Me?" It meant something more than singing with gestures beside a girl. Maybe she would realize that he could learn things too, even if she could read the better. He meant to change all that as quickly as possible. One day he shyly overtook her on her way home.

"Dey tell me you kin run fast," he began awkwardly.

"Dey told you right," Lucy answered saucily, "whoever tole you. Ah kin outrun most anybody 'round heah."

"Less we race tuh dat sweet-gum tree and see who kin beat," John challenged.

They were off. Lucy's thin little legs pumping up and down. The starchy strings of her blue sunbonnet fluttering under her chin, and her bonnet lying back of her neck.

"Ah beat yuh!" John gloated over the foot or two that he had gained with difficulty.

"Yeah, you beat me, but look how much mo' legs you got to run wid," Lucy retorted. "Bet if Ah had dem legs nobody couldn't never outrun me."

"Ah didn't mean tuh beat yuh. Gee, us done come uh good ways! How much further you live from heah, Lucy?"

"Oh uh little ways cross de branch."

"B'lieve Ah'll go see how yo' ole branch look. Maybe it got uh heap uh fish in it."

" 'Tain't got no fish in it worth talkin' 'bout. 'Tain't hardly knee deep, John, but iss uh great big ole snake down dere."

"Whut kinda snake?"

"Uh great big ole cotton-mouf moccasin. He skeers me,

John. Everytime Ah go 'cross dat foot-log Ah think maybe Ah might fall in and den he'll bite me, or he might reah hisself up and bite me anyhow."

"How come y'all don't take and kill 'im?"

"Who you reckon goin' down in de water tuh strain wid uh moccasin? He got uh hole back under the bank where you kin see 'im, but you can't git 'im 'thout you wuz down in de branch. He lay all 'round dere on de ground and even on de foot-log, but when he see somebody comin' he go in his hole, all ready for yuh and lay dere and dare yuh tuh bother 'im."

"You jes' show 'im tuh me. Ah can't stand tuh be aggravated by no ole snake and then agin Ah don't want 'im slurrin' *you*."

"Sh-sh, watch out, John! He 'round heah somewhere. Can't you smell 'im? Dere he is goin' in his hole!"

John took a good look at the snake, then looked all about him for a weapon. Finding none he sat down and began to remove his shoes.

"You ain't goin' in dat branch!" Lucy gasped.

"Turn me go, Lucy. If you didn't want yo' ole snake kilt yuh oughta not showed 'im tuh me." He exulted, but pretended not to see her concern was for him.

He looked carefully to see that no other snakes were about, then stepped cautiously down into the water. The snake went on guard, slowly, insolently. Lucy was terrified. Suddenly, he snatched the foot-log from its place and, leaning far back to give it purchase, he rammed it home upon the big snake and held it there. The snake bit at the log again and again in its agony, but finally the biting and the thrashing ceased. John fished the snake out and stretched it upon the grass.

"Ooh, John, Ahm so glad you kilt dat ole devil. He been right dere skeerin' folks since befo' Ah wuz borned."

"He won't skeer nobody else, lessen dey skeered uh dead snakes," John answered in the tone that boys use to girls on such occasions.

"Reckon his mate ain't gonna follow us and try tuh bite us for killin' dis one?"

"Lucy, he can't foller bofe us, lessen us go de same way."

"Thass right, John. Ah done forgot, you live over on de Alf Pearson place."

"Yeah, dat's right."

"Where M'haley and Big 'Oman live."

"Unh hunh, Ah speck dey do live dere. Ah seen uh lot uh pullet-size girl chillun 'bout de place. Nearly uh hund'ed head uh folks on dat plantation."

A heavy silence fell. Lucy looked across the shallow stream and said,

"You ain't put de foot-log back, John."

"Dat's right. Sho nuff Ah done fuhgot. Lemme tote you cross den. Ah kin place it back for de other folks."

"Doncha lemme fall, John. Maybe 'nother ole snake down dere."

"How Ahm gonna let uh li'l' bit lak you fall? Ah kin tote uh sack uh feed-meal and dat's twice big ez you. Lemme tote yuh. Ah 'clare Ah won't drop yuh."

John bore Lucy across the tiny stream and set her down slowly.

"Oh you done left yo' book-sack, Lucy. Got tuh take yuh back tuh git it."

"Naw, you hand it tuh me, John."

"Aw, naw, you come git it."

He carried Lucy back and she recrossed the stream the third time. As he set her down on her home side he said, "Little ez *you* is nobody wouldn't keer how fur he hafta tote you. You ain't even uh handful."

Lucy put herself akimbo, "Ahm uh li'l' piece uh leather, but well put t'gether, Ah thankee, Mist' John."

"Mah comperments, Miss Lucy."

Lucy was gone up the hill in a blue whirlwind. John replaced the foot-log and cut across lots for home.

"She is full uh pepper," John laughed to himself, "but ah laks dat. Anything 'thout no seasonin' in it ain't no good."

At home, Lucy rushed out back of the corn crib and tiptoed

35

to see if her head yet touched the mark she had made three weeks before.

"Ah shucks!" She raged, "Ah ain't growed none hardly. Ah ain't never gointer get grown. Ole M'haley way head uh me!"

She hid and cried until Emmeline, her mama, called her to set the table for supper.

The night of school closing came. John in tight new shoes and with a standing collar was on hand early. Saw Lucy enter followed by the Potts clan. Frowning mama, placid papa, strapping big sister, and the six grown brothers. Boys with "rear-back" hair held down by a thick coating of soap. Boys hobbling in new shoes and tight breeches. Girls whose hair smelled of fresh hog-lard and sweet william, and white dresses with lace, with pink or blue sashes, with ruffles, with mothers searching their bosoms for pins to yank up hanging petticoats. Tearful girls who had forgotten their speeches. Little girls with be-ribboned frizzed-out hair who got spanked for wetting their starchy panties. Proud parents. Sulky parents and offspring. Whispered envy.

"Dere's Lucy Potts over dere in uh fluted dress. Dey allus gives her de longest piece tuh speak."

"Dat's 'cause she kin learn more'n anybody else."

"Naw 'tain't, dey muches her up. Mah Semmie could learn jes' ez long uh piece ez anybody if de give it tuh her—in time. Ahm gwine take mah chillun outa school after dis and put 'em tuh work. Dey ain't learnin' 'em nothin' nohow. Dey makes cake outa some uh de chillun and cawn bread outa de rest."

Opening prayer. Song. Speech by white superintendent. Speeches rattled off like beans poured into a tin can.

"A speech by Miss Lucy Potts."

The shining big eyes in the tiny face. Lacy whiteness. Fierce hand-clapping. Lucy calm and self-assured.

"A chieftain to the highland bound, cried 'Boatman do not tarry' "—to the final "My daughter, oh my daughter." More applause. The idol had not failed her public.

"She kin speak de longest pieces and never miss uh word

36

and say 'em faster dan anybody Ah ever seed." It was agreed Lucy was perfect. Time and speeches flew fast.

> Little fishes in de brook
> Willie ketch 'em wid uh hook
> Mama fry 'em in de pan
> Papa eat 'em lak uh man.

"Duet—Miss Lucy Potts, bassed by Mr. John Pearson." They sang and their hearers applauded wildly. Nobody cared whether the treble was treble or the bass was bass. It was the gestures that counted and everybody agreed that John was perfect as the philandering soldier of the piece and that Lucy was just right as the over-eager maid. They had to sing it over twice. John began to have a place of his own in the minds of folks, more than he realized.

CHAPTER 3

One morning in the early spring John found Amy sitting before the fire in Pheemy's house.

"Howdy, mam."

"Howdy, son."

She rubbed her teeth and gums with the tiny snuff-brush. She had something to say and John knew it.

"How's everybody makin' it over de Big Creek, maw?"

"Right middlin', John. Us could do better but yo' pappy always piddlin' from piller tuh post and dat keep de rest uh us in hot water."

"Yessum. What's de trouble now?"

"Yuh know Beasley took and beat us out uh our cotton and we ain't hardly had nothin' tuh eat, so day 'fo' yistiddy Ned took and kilt one uh Beasley's yearlings way down dere in de hammock and fetched it home dere and us cooked and et some of it and put some of it down in salt. We thinkin' nobody'd ever know de diffunce, but Beasley heard de cows bellerin' when dey smelt de blood where it wuz kilt and went down dere and found de hide. So us had tuh pack up our things in meal sacks and when it wuz black dark us went on over tuh de Shelby place, and us goin' work dere dis year."

"Dat's uh whole heap better'n Beasley's place, but 'tain't

39

nigh good ez heah. Wisht y'all would come work fuh Mist' Alf.''

"Ned, he too hard-headed tuh do dat. Ah done tried and tried but his back don't bend. De only difference 'tween him and uh mule is, de mule got four good foots, and he ain't got nairn. De minute anybody mention crossin' dat creek, he's good tuh make disturbiment and tear up peace. He been over dat creek all his life jes' ez barefooted ez uh yard dawg and know he ain't even got uh rooster tuh crow fuh day, yet and still you can't git 'im 'way from dere.''

"How come you don't quit 'im? Come on, and fetch de chillun wid you!''

"You can't know intuh dat yit, John. In times and seasons, us gwine talk dat, but Ah come tuh take you back wid me, John.''

"Me, mama?'' John asked in agonized surprise, "you know Ah don't want no parts of over dat Creek.''

"Mama know, son, but Mist' Shelby asted where wuz you de fust thing and say he don't want us 'thout you.''

"Mama, Ah don't wanta go 'way back over dere in dem woods. All you kin hear 'bout over dere is work, push-hard and pone-bread, ole cawn bread wid nothin' in it but salt and water! Ah laks it over here where dey talks about biscuit-bread some time.''

"Yeah, John Buddy, mama know jes' how yuh feels and her heart is beatin' right wid yourn. Mama love flour bread too. But, you know, lots uh white folks ain't gwine be bothered wid Ned, and us got tuh find some place tuh lay our heads. Mist' Shelby ain't uh mean man, but he don't b'lieve us kin make de crop 'thout you. Reckon you better git yo' things and come 'long.''

Amy got up wearily, the ruffles of her faded calico skirt sweeping the floor as she moved.

"Ahm goin' and see Marse Alf 'bout takin' yuh. Be ready 'ginst Ah git back, John Buddy.''

John watched her out of the door, then slowly he went out himself and wandered about; but finally he was standing back

40

of Pheemy's cabin and gazing at the rude scratching on the adobe chimney. "Lucy," "Lucy Ann," "Lucy Potts," "Lucy and John," "Lucy is John's girl," "No 'nife can cut our love into," "Lucy Pearson."

"Oh," John sobbed, "she ain't gonna want no over-de-creek-nigger."

He stood there a long time before he went inside and began to collect his things. Then he came upon the song book that Lucy's terrifying brother had given him when he joined the choir. There was a crude drawing of a railroad train on it. No, he couldn't leave Notasulga where the train came puffing into the depot twice a day. No, no! He dropped everything and tore out across the fields and came out at last at the railroad cut just below the station. He sat down upon the embankment and waited. Soon in the distance he heard the whistle, "Wah-ooom! Wahup, wahup!" And around the bend came first the smoke stack, belching smoke and flames of fire. The drivers turning over chanting "Opelika-black-and-dirty! Opelika-black-and-dirty." Then as she pulled into the station, the powerful whisper of steam. Starting off again, "Wolf coming! Wolf coming! Wolf coming! Opelika-black-and-dirty, Opelika-black-and-dirty! Auh—wah-hoooon"—into the great away that gave John's feet such a yearning for distance.

The train had been gone a long time when Alf Pearson's buggy pulled up beside John.

"What are you doing down here, John, with Amy looking all over Macon County for you?"

"Jes' come down tuh hear whut de train say one mo' time, Mist' Alf."

"Get in and drive me down to get the mail, John. How's the hogs getting on?"

"Jes' fine, Mist' Alf. S'pectin' two mo' litters dis week. Dat make five litters since New Year's. Ain't lost one since Chris'-mas, neither."

"Splendid, John, splendid."

"Mist' Alf, Ah don't treasure 'cross dat creek. Lemme stay heah wid you, please suh."

"John, I'm not sending you over there. Your mother is taking you. If you're ever in need of a job, come on back here and behave yourself and I'll look after you. No matter where you are, don't steal and don't get too biggety and you'll get along. Touch the horses up a little. I'm in a hurry."

CHAPTER 4

There was work a plenty on the Shelby place. John and Ned were plowing the rocky hillsides. As they turned the furrows John always strode several feet in advance of Ned. The older man limped behind his plow, stumbling now and then, slashing the mule and swearing incessantly.

"Gawd uhmighty! Git up heah, you hard-tailed bastard! Confound yuh, gee! John Buddy, whar you gwine?"

"Ahm goin' tuh git me uh sweat-rag tuh wipe mah face wid. Ahm tired uh sweat runnin' intuh mah eyes."

"You jes' tries tuh keep from workin', John. Out nearly all night proagin' over de Creek and now yuh don't wanta do nothin'."

"Ah done plowed uh acre and uh half tuh yo' one, and nowhere you put yo' foot down but whut 'tain't uh rock dere. Nobody can't make nothin' on dis place—look lak God jus' stood up and throwed uh handful uh rocks. If dis ain't work, 'tain' uh hound dawg in Georgy."

"Jes' you stay from over dat Creek, runnin' after all dem gals and git yo' night rest, dem rocks wouldn't be so worrysome."

"Ah do mo' of it than you right now. Dis ain't no slavery time," John flung back over his shoulder as he started towards the house.

"Yuh done got powerful biggity since yuh been on dat Pearson place," Ned muttered to himself, "Can't say uh word, 'thout he got tuh gimme two fuh one."

Amy stood trembling between her son and her husband. The other children were growing up and imitating everything that John did, as closely as possible. Zack and Zeke were already trying on John's hats and ties. Their whole talk was "over de Creek," and "man when us git on dat ole train." Amy had managed to keep things on an even keel by soothing John's feelings and reminding Ned that if John went over to Notasulga to choir practice and meeting, that he was now seventeen and ought to have a little freedom. So it had gone, and now the cotton was knee-high. The crops more than half made. She breathed a little easier. She was at the house putting on a pot of collard greens when John came in for the sweat-rag.

"Mama, better tell Ned tuh leave me be. Tell 'im tuh stop his bulldozia. Ah done heered 'im lyin' tuh Mist' Shelby makin' out Ah don't do nothin'—hard ez Ah works."

"He be's drunk when he keer on lak dat and his likker tell 'im tuh talk. Don't pay 'im no mind."

"But, mama, ev'ry time Ah go cross de Creek he look lak he go crazy and git tuh blasphemin' 'bout no 'count gals. Ah don't keer if he do be peepin' through his likkers he got tuh quit dat. Sho ez gun's iron, he got tuh quit dat. He don't know nothin' 'bout—'bout no gal Ah keeps comp'ny wid."

"Heah de rag yuh wanted, John. Go 'long back tuh work and Ah'll give Ned uh straightenin'. Dat is if he kin stand uh straightenin'."

Ned was sullen when John returned but he said nothing. He took part of his humor out on the mule and held the other inside him. He said to himself as he stumbled along behind his plow, "Damn biggity rascal! Wisht Ah had 'im tied down so he couldn't move! I'd put uh hund'ed lashes on his bare back. He know he got de advantage uh me. He don't even know his pappy and he ought tuh be proud Ah took and married his ma and made somethin' out of 'im. He ought to be humble,

44

but he ain't, and plenty folks right now on account uh his yaller skin will put 'im above me. Wisht Ah knowed somethin' that would crumple his feathers! But he sho' is makin' dis crop, though. Ah oughter clear more'n uh hund'ed dollars. Effen Ah do, Ahm gwine buy me uh hawse and buggy, and ain't gwine 'low nobody tuh hitch it up but me."

That evening the things unsaid laid a steamy blanket over talk. John made the long journey over the creek and Ned fumed.

"Whyn't you tell John whut yuh got tuh say, Ned?" Amy slapped back, "You *been* tellin' 'im."

" 'Cause Ah don't want tuh hafta kill 'im, dat's how come. He must smell hisself—done got so mannish. Some fast 'omanish gal is grinnin' in his face and he tries tuh git sides hisself."

Amy smoked her pipe and went on to bed. The children too. Zeke and Zack were in the woods trying out a new coon dog and came in after moon-up. John came home later.

When Amy brought dinner to the field next day John took his bucket and went off alone to eat. With a huge hickory tree between him and the others, he pulled out the three cornered note and read again and again.

Sweet Notasulga, Chocklit Alabama Date of kisses, month of love Dere John, you is my honey. I won't never love nobody else but you. I love choir practise now. Sugar is sweet, and lard is greasy, you love me, don't be uneasy.

Your darling,
LUCY ANN POTTS

Ned called several times before John heard him.

"John Buddy! You John! Come heah and take holt uh dese plow lines."

"Yes suh," John said at last.

"Don't set dere and answer me. When Ah speak, you move!"

"Ah, Ahm comin', but Ah ain't goin' tuh run fuh nobody."

45

"Looka heah, John, Ahm sick uh yo' sass. Ah got it in me tuh tell yuh and if Ah don't tell yuh, Ah'll purge when Ah die. Youse uh good fuh nothin' trashy yaller rascal—ain't fit tuh tote guts tuh uh bear." A sudden frenzy took Ned, "Anyhow, Ah done made up mah mind tuh beat you nelly tuh death. You jes' spilin' fuh uh good killin'! Drop dem britches below yo' hocks, and git down on yo' knees. Ah means tuh straighten you out dis day."

As he said this, Ned snatched off the trace-chain from the plow and turned upon John who was still twenty feet or more from his step-father. When Ned whirled about with the doubled trace-chain in his right fist he found not a cowering bulk of a boy but a defiant man, feet spread wide, a large rock drawn back to hurl.

"Don't you vary! Dog damn yuh!" John challenged. "Come uhnother step and Ah'll bust yuh wide open, wid dis rock. You kin cuff and kick Zeke and them around but Ah done promised Gawd and uh couple uh other men tuh stomp yo' guts out nex' time you raise yo' hand tuh me."

For a throbbing space the two stood face to face. Ned turned and hobbled off.

"Stand dere! Jes' you stand dere till Ah go git mah double-barrel britch-loader and Ahm gointer blow yo' brains out!"

Ned limped off towards the house. John held his pose until the older man dipped below the first rise. Then he let fall his arm, and walked back towards the hickory tree.

"Ahm gointer git behind dis tree and if dat ugly-rump nigger come back here wid dat gun, Ahm gointer bust 'im wide open wid uh rock 'fore he know whut hit 'im. Humph! Ah don't b'lieve he gone at no britch-loader nohow. He gone 'cause he got skeered Ah wuz goin' take dat trace-chain 'way from 'im and lay it 'cross his own back."

John waited a long time. Ned could have gone twice the distance and returned with a gun. If he could have looked over the hill he would have seen Ned "proaging" off to the Turk place to get a gallon of red-eye-for-courage. Finally John came out from behind the hickory tree and loosed the mules from the plows and looped up the plow lines on the hames.

"Shucks! Ahm goin' 'way from heah." It came to John like a revelation. Distance was escape. He stopped before the burnt-off trunk of a tree that stood eight or ten feet high and threw the character of Ned Crittenden upon it.

"And you, you ole battle-hammed, slew-foot, box-ankled nubbin, you! You ain't nothin' and ain't got nothin' but whut God give uh billy-goat, and then round tryin' tuh hell-hack folks! Tryin' tuh kill somebody wid talk, but if you wants tuh fight,—dat's de very corn Ah wants tuh grind. You come grab me now and Ah bet yuh Ah'll stop *you* from suckin' eggs. Hit me now! G'wan hit me! Bet Ah'll break uh egg in yuh! Youse all parts of uh pig! You done got me jus' ez hot ez July jam, and Ah ain't got no mo' use fuh yuh than Ah is for mah baby shirt. Youse mah race but you sho ain't mah taste. Jus' you break uh breath wid me, and Ahm goin' tuh be jus' too chastisin'.

"Ahm jus' lak uh old shoe—soft when yuh rain on me and cool me off, and hard when yuh shine on me and git me hot. Tuh keep from killin' uh sorry somethin' like yuh, Ahm goin' way from heah. Ahm goin' tuh Zar, and dat's on de other side of far, and when you see me agin Ahm gointer be somebody. Mah li'l' finger will be bigger than yo' waist. Don't you part yo' lips tuh me no mo' jes' ez long ez heben is happy—do Ah'll put somethin' on yuh dat lye soap won't take off. You ain't nothin' but uh big ole pan of fell bread. Now dat's de word wid de bark on it."

John stepped back a few paces, balanced his rock, hurled it against the stump with all his might and started across the field to the creek.

The involuntary beauty of sunset found him once again upon the plantation of his birth exulting among the herd, and finding Pheemy's cabin good to be in.

47

CHAPTER 5

"Hello, John."

"Hello, Bully."

"Whut you doin' back over here?"

"Come tuh git me uh job uh work again. Whuss de news?"

"Oh de white folks is still in de lead. Seen Mist' Alf yit?"

"Naw, goin' up tuh de big house now."

"Soon's yuh git back tuh de quarters Ah got uh bug tuh put in yo' ear."

"Awright, be back tuhreckly."

There were more used suits in Alf Pearson's clothes closet and John received them.

"My son, Mister Alfred's, clothes don't fit you now as well as they did last year, John. Too tight. Reckon I'll have to give you mine from now on. By the way, John, I've lost two hogs since you've been gone. Get back on your same job. Can you read and write fairly well now, John?"

"Yes suh."

"That's fine. I want you to take this note book and keep up with the groceries and fertilizer and feed that the folks in the quarters draw. It's hard for me to do it with running the bank and watching slick politicians. I had thought my son would have been home by now to help me, but it seems to take quite a long time to finish studying in Paris."

"Yes suh."

"You just take everybody's name on a separate page and put down everything they get the moment you hand it to 'em."

"Yes suh."

"And John, if you've been fooling around Duke's wife, leave her alone. He's been up here to me about it. Don't start no fight about it. There's plenty single girls around here."

"Ah ain't studyin' 'bout his Exie, Mist' Alf. He better talk tuh *her*. She de one come pullin' on me."

Alf Pearson laughed heartily and gave John a playful shove.

"Get along you rascal you! You're a walking orgasm. A living exultation."

"Whut's dat, Mist' Alf?"

"Oh never mind about that. Keep up with the pigs."

That night M'haley and Big 'Oman and Bootsie got up a game of "Hide and Seek" but John counted and let the other boys hide. The game ended fairly early. John had been around behind the house to look at his writing and the chimney and found it all defaced, so he didn't want to play. When the game was over he called Bully aside.

"Bully, Ah wrote some writin' on de back uh An' Pheemy's chimbley."

"Yeah, Ah know you did. Fack is, ev'rybody know yuh did, and dat's de very crow Ah wants tuh pick wid yuh."

"Is you heard who took and scratched it, and put smut out de chimbley all over it and mommucked it all up?"

"You ain't mad, is yuh?"

"Yeah, Ahm mad. Ahm jes' ez hot ez Tucker when de mule kicked his mammy, and any man dat tell me tuh mah face dat he done it he got tuh smell mah fist. You know who done it, Bully?"

"Don't yuh say Ah tole yuh and when you go tuh git atter her, don't you call my name, but M'haley took and done dat when she heered you wuz singin' in de choir. Some of 'em say you jes' done it so you could git a chance tuh see Lucy Potts."

"Whut M'haley got tuh do wid dat? Ah feel lak Ah could take and lam her wid lightnin'."

50

"Why doncher do it, John? If 'twas me felt bad lak you do, Ah'd beat her jes' ez long ez she last. Anyhow she takin' de under currents on you."

"Naw, Ah don't choose beatin' lady people. Uh man is crazy tuh do dat—when he know he got tuh submit hisself tuh 'em. Ahm gittin' sleepy. B'lieve Ah'll turn in."

Bully went away whistling, and John made to go inside to bed.

"John!" in a soft whisper from around the corner of the house. "Come heah, John."

John stepped to the corner, "Who dat callin' me?"

"Aw, you come see," the voice retreated into the shoulder-high cotton. John followed.

"Whut you want wid me, M'haley?"

"Look lak you ain't glad youse back."

"Yes Ah is, M'haley, but 'tain't lak de fust night Ah come. Ah reckon all de new done wore off de plantation."

" 'Tain't de plantation. Dat's jes' de same. Ah reckon you jes' ain't got time tuh strain wid us quarters niggers now. You sings on de choir at Macedony."

"Whut's singin' notes got tuh do wid it? It jus' 'tain't new no mo'."

"Naw, you jes' stuck on dat li'l' ole Lucy Ann, and she ain't nothin' but uh baby. She ain't but leben years ole."

"She twelve now, goin' on thirteen. She had her birth night de day befo' mines. Her'n on December 31, and mine's January 1. Ain't dat funny?"

"Ahm fifteen, so goody, goody, goody."

John said nothing. After a while M'haley said, "John, Ah thought once me and you wuz gointer make uh wed." He stood stolid and silent.

In the silence she threw her arms about John's passive neck and swung herself off the ground, then lay still against him.

"John."

"Hunh."

"Feel mah heart. Put yo' hand right heah. Ain't it beatin' hard? Dat's 'cause Ahm so glad youse back. Feel it again. My

51

heart is rearin' and pitchin' fur you lak uh mule in uh tin stable. John, Ah loves you, Ah swear Ah does. You so pretty and you ain't color-struck lak uh whole heap uh bright-skin people. John?"

"Hunh."

"John, hug me till mah dress fit tight."

The next day John whitewashed Pheemy's chimney, and wrote Lucy's name in huge letters across it, and on Sunday he was at church far ahead of anybody else, with a three-cornered note in his hymn-book.

"Hope ole big-mouf M'haley don't come pukin' her guts 'round heah," he thought aloud. This was another day and another place. Pearson's quarters and M'haley had no business here. His eye wandered out of the window and down the dusty road. A bunch of girls approached in starchy elegance. "Lawd, dat look lak M'haley now—comin' heah tuh bull-doze and dominize."

John fell to his knees and prayed for cleansing. He prayed aloud and the empty house threw back his resonant tones like a guitar box.

"Dat sho sound good," John exulted. "If mah voice sound *dat* good de first time Ah ever prayed in de church house, it sho won't be de las'." He arose from his knees and before the drove of girls had reached the steps John had forgotten all about his sins and fears, but he retreated to the choir-stand out of M'haley's reach.

As soon as Lucy took her seat before him he leaned forward and thrust his hymn-book into her hand. She coyly dropped hers, and he picked it up and pretended to search for a song. Lucy slyly did the same and read:

Dere Lucy:
>Whin you pass a mule tied to a tree,
>Ring his tail and think of me.

>>>Your sugger-lump,
>>>JOHN

John read:

> Long as the vine grow 'round the stump
> You are my dolling sugar lump.
> Mama whipped me last night, because Bud told her we
> was talking to each other.

Your sweet heart,
LUCY ANN

John was so sweetly distracted by this note that he was blind and deaf to his surroundings. Bud Potts had rapped loudly and importantly and had gestured with his hands as if he were pushing a wash-basket of clothes up on a high shelf for the choir to rise. Everyone was standing but John. He never noticed this until Oral Johnson nudged him.

"Get yo' pitch!" Bud ordered as if he were giving the order to fire on Fort Sumter.

"Basses—duh-h-h-h. Y'all got it? Altos—fah-h-h—Trebles—me-e-e-e—. Pay 'tension dere, Lucy!"

Satisfied in the matter of the pitch, Bud took a full breath and broke out thru his nose—"Duh, duh, duh, duh! Dole la fee so lah so fee." The altos were right behind the basses and fighting in haughty jerks for sound supremacy—"fah! fah! me! sol! fah-so-la-so-lah-so-fah!" The trebles pitched out in full, Ory behind the pack and keened furiously to make up for lost time, "—me, me, ray, do! Me-fah-lah-so-lah-so-fah! Oh me, me, me,—"

It was a hard race and hotly contended at the top of the lungs all the way. The trebles won because while altos, basses and even other trebles forgot their notes in confusion and fell by the wayside, Lucy never missed a note. Bud growled away in the bass but Lucy treed him and held him growling in discomfiture out upon a limb until the end of the piece cut him down.

John beat the bass notes by a vigorous side-to-side motion of his head and everybody in the audience thought they heard him singing them.

The preacher arose.

"Ah takes mah tex' and Ah takes mah time." He pursed up his wrinkled black face and glared all over the church. No one accepting the challenge he went on—"Ah takes mah tex' 'tween de lids uh de Bible," and slammed it shut. Another challenging glare about the room. Same results. "Don't you take and meddle wid *whar* Ah takes mah tex'. Long ez Ah gives yuh de word uh Gawd, 'tain't none uh yo' business whar Ah gits it from."

For two hours his voice beat about the ears of the people and the "Amen's" rocked and rolled back to the pulpit.

John heard little of it. He studied the back of Lucy's head and shoulders and the way the white rice buttons ran down her back and found plenty to entertain him the whole while.

When the cotton had been picked and ginned, Alf had John to pick out the hogs for the barbecue. The same elaborate preparations as usual. Same high laughter, but John sat passively in a doorway with Zeke who was getting tall and emitting ram odors.

"Less we dance, John Buddy. Ah wants tuh swing one dem gals."

John laughed scornfully, "Whut you know 'bout swingin' gals? You don't eben know how tuh dance."

"Dat's much ez *you* know. Ah done been tuh four, five frolics 'cross de Creek since you been gone."

Phrony came dashing up, hair wrapped with blue rag strings and reeking of lemon extract used as a perfume.

"John how come you ain't dancin'?"

"Ah got uh bone in mah leg," John bantered.

"Aw come on, John."

"Go head on, Phrony. You got plenty boys 'sides me. Ah tell yuh Ah got uh bone in mah leg."

"Sho 'nuff, John? When did you git it in dere? You wuz walkin' all righ' jes' fo' dark."

"He jes' funnin' wid yuh," Zeke cut in, " 'Course he got uh bone in his leg. How he goin' tuh walk if he ain't? Come on and lemme switch yo' coat."

54

Zeke grabbed Phrony by the point of her elbow and they plunged into the cauldron of sound.

John sat on, thinking of the words on the chimney back, but soon Exie found him.

"John, how come you ain't in de play party? M'haley dancin' wid Bully."

"She's uh much-right gal. Much right for Bully ez it is for me."

Exie laughed happily, "Big 'Oman huntin' you too and plenty mo'."

"Whut for?"

"Dey say de dance don't go so good 'thout you. Dey say de boys neither de gals don't do 'round when you ain't dere lak dey do when yo' is."

"Dey done 'thout me 'fo' dey seen me. Ah jes' don't feel lak no dancin' and whoopin' and hollerin' t'night."

"Me neither. Less we all jes' set and talk, John."

"Naw, Gawd! Ah don't want Duke pickin' no fight wid me over you. You his'n."

"Us ain't got no courthouse papers. Dat's commissary license us got. Ah kin quit anytime, and then agin effen Ah had courthouse license Ah got divorce in mah heels." She picked up John's hand and pulled it into her lap. Just then M'haley walked up to them.

"Oh 'scuse me," she turned away scornfully, "Ah didn't reckon you wuz so busy, John," she whirled and ran back to the dance.

"You better g'wan back tuh de play party, Exie. M'haley's goin' tuh tell Duke on you."

"Let her tell 'im, tell 'im, turn 'im up and smell 'im."

John rose. "Ah got tuh step off a li'l' piece. Ah'll be right back." He walked off and Exie started on back to the fire. Half way she met Duke, and John could hear the struggle of battle. He turned about and hurried to them.

"Whut you beatin' Exie 'bout? She ain't done nothin'."

"If she wan't doin' nothin', whut y'all doin' up heah in de

55

dark?" He struck her violently in the face again. John stepped between them.

"Don't lam dis 'oman no mo', Duke. She ain't did a thing wrong. You wanta beat on somebody, hop me. Mah shoulders is broad."

Besides the ones who had heard M'haley say out loud that John and Exie were up the hill in the dark too busy to dance, there were others who had heard what Duke said when he left the fire-lit circle. So the crowd had surrounded the three. Exie, bruised but exultant, John and Duke standing face to face.

"Fight, fight, you no kin. Kill on 'nother 'twon't be no sin," Nunkie shouted.

Old Pheemy stepped between and scattered the crowd.

"Neb mind," Duke threatened as he was led away, "Ah ain't through wid you, John Pearson. Ahm goin' git yuh! Ahm goin' tuh git yuh if Ah have tuh steal yuh! Youse bigger'n me, but mah Barlow knife'll even us up."

The dance went on. John danced a little with Big 'Oman and Bootsie but he wasn't flamboyant.

In the bed with Zeke later he said, "Zeke, Ahm goin' 'way from here."

"You ain't skeered uh Duke, is yuh?"

"Naw, Duke cuts and shoots too, but all de shootin' he do is shoot fuh home if somebody git behind 'im, and cut fuh de nearest way. He don't fight no men-folks. He's uh woman-jessie. Beat up women and run from mens. Ah ain't got him tuh study 'bout, but Ah feel lak Ah weighs uh thousand pounds and it's mah heart make me feel that away."

"How come?"

"Y'know dat li'l' gal dat trebles in de choir at Macedony—de one whut don't wrop her hair, de onliest one up dere dat don't wrop her hair no time wid all dat cord-string lake de rest? Well, Ah loves her, and she say she love me too, and Ah betcha old moufy M'haley uh some uh dese other niggers goin' make out Ahm goin' wid Exie, and dat's whut me and Duke lak tuh fought over, and then agin Mist' Alf done tole me not tuh fool wid Exie and Duke goin' up tuh de big house and tell uh lie on me."

"If yuh go off somewhere, John Buddy, lemme go wid yuh, heah, Please?"

"You too little. Ain't but fourteen, and if Ah go 'way from heah atall, Ahm goin' tuh de tie-camp and cut cross ties. Man asted me tuh go yistiddy in Notasulga. Yuh makes good money too."

"John Buddy, please. Heah?"

"Naw, you stay 'round heah and watch out for Lucy. Git word tuh me iffen any ole mullet-head tries tuh cut me out. Ahm gointer write tuh you and you way-lay her and git her tuh read it fuh yuh."

"Aw, Ah kin read too. Ah kin read some."

"Whut kin you read?"

"In de fust reader it say, 'This is Ned. He has a dog,' Ah kin read dat lak anything. Dat's uh heap, ain't it?"

"Dat'll do, but Ah ain't goin tuh write 'bout no Ned in de fust reader, and neither no dawg. You do lak Ah tell yuh, and if she say she don't pay dese niggers' talk no mind, you git de word tuh me quick ez yuh kin, heah, Zeke?"

"Unhunh."

"Yuh see, she got de advantage uh me 'cause she knows Ah love her, but Ah don't know whether she love me or not. Lots uh folks makes 'miration at her. You stay 'round heah and back mah fallin', and then nex' time Ah'll take you 'long."

"Aw right, John Buddy."

The next morning John was gone—walked to Opelika and on to the tie-woods on the Alabama River.

CHAPTER 6

I t was dusk-dark when John walked into the tie-camp. At some distance away he could see a group of men bunched on the ground beside a small fire. Gaming. They were so intent that John was right on them before they knew. When somebody saw him, there was a breathy cry, "De buckra!" Somebody grabbed up the dice and everyone made to run. John laughed and stepped up among them.

"Ha, ha! Y'all thought Ah wuz white, didn't yuh?"

Everyone laughed except Coon Tyler. He was every bit as large as John and several years older. He looked up at John out of red, angry eyes and growled, "You oughter quit goin' 'round skeering folks. You better hail fo' you tuh walk up on *me* agin."

John kept on laughing. "Lawd, y'all sho wuz snatchin' and grabbin'. Ah ought not tuh uh said nothin' and some uh y'all would uh been to Selma in five minutes."

Coon would not be amused, "You scoundrel-beast, you git from over de game!"

John stepped back a little, not in fear but in surprise.

"You ain't mad, is yuh?" he asked.

One of the men said, "Don't pay Coon no mind, he jes' funnin' wid yuh."

Seeing the passive attitude in John, Coon blazed, "Funnin'?

59

Y'all know Ah don't joke and Ah don't stand no jokin'. 'Tain't nothin' in de drug store'll kill yuh quick ez me.''

"Mah name is Ezeriah Hill, but de lady people calls me Uncle Dump,'' the oldest man in the group said to John, "Whuss yo' name, boy?''

"John. Where de boss at?''

"He gone intuh town. Be back tuhreckly. He goin' hiah yuh 'cause us needs help. Come on lemme show yuh uh place tuh sleep.''

John followed him into the bunk house. "Heah whar you sleep at. Eve'ybody scorch up dey own grub. Be ready tuh hit de grit by daylight.''

"Yes suh.''

"Chaw tuhbacker uh smoke?''

"Naw suh.''

"Wall you gwine learn 'cause you can't keep dis camp grub on yo' stomach lessen yuh do. Got tuh learn how tuh cuss too. Ah kin see you ain't nothin' but uh lad of uh boy. Mens on dese camps is full uh bulldocia 'til dey smell uh good size fist. Den dey dwindles down tuh nelly nothin'.''

All next day John wielded a broad axe, a maul and pestle with the rest. He found that he liked the rhythmic swing, the chant "Cuttin' timber!'' with the up stroke of the axe. Then the swift, sure descent, "Hanh!'' Up again, "Cuttin' ties! Hanh.'' All day long, "Cuttin' timber! Hanh! Cuttin' ties, hanh!''

A boy called Do-dirty because of his supposed popularity with and his double-crossing of women, took John to town with him Saturday night. John was eager to go so he could buy writing paper and a pencil. He got it and then Do-dirty proudly showed him the town, and the town's women. It was late Sunday evening when they returned to camp and from one thing to another it was two weeks before John wrote to Ezekiel.

And when a month passed and he got no answer he began to feel that there would never be a word from Lucy. He went to town often. On the nights that he stayed in camp he was the center of camp life. He could chin the bar more times than anyone there. He soon was the best shot, the fastest runner and in wrestling no man could put his shoulders to the ground. The boss began to invite his friends out to watch the fun. John won his first match by pinning Nelse Watson from another camp to the ground, but his greatest stunt was picking up an axe by the very tip end of the helve and keeping the head on a level with his shoulders in his out-stretched arm. Coon could muscle out one axe, but John could balance two. He could stand like a cross, immobile for several seconds with an axe muscled out in each hand. Next to showing muscle-power, John loved to tell stories. Sometimes the men sat about the fire and talked and John loved that. One night Do-dirty began, "Y'all wanta heah some lies?"

"Yeah," said Too-Sweet, "Ah evermore loves lies but you can't tell none. Leave John tell 'em 'cause he kin act 'em out. He take de part uh Brer Rabbit and Brer B'ar and Brer Fox jes' ez natche'l."

"Aw, 'tain't nothin' tuh 'im," Coon grumbled, "y'all make me sick."

Saturday afternoon Do-dirty looked off towards the West and cried, "Looka yonder! Who dat comin' runnin'?"

Everybody looked but John. He was inside getting ready to go to town.

"Do John Buddy work at dis heah camp?" he heard and recognized Zeke's voice.

"Come inside, Zeke!" he called out quickly.

Zeke came in and sat down on the bunk beside John. No words. Happiness radiated from one to the other.

"You seen Lucy?"

"Yeah, two times."

"Whut she say?"

Zeke tugged at a letter inside his clothes.

"She writ dis tuh yuh and tole me tuh mail it, but Ah run off and bring it tuh yuh. Yuh see Ah ain't got yo' letter till day befo' yestiddy. 'Cause pappy wouldn't leave me go tuh town tuh de Post Office. John Buddy, you goin' tuh leave me stay wid yuh? Hunh?"

John spelled slowly thru his letter and smiled, "Yeah, you kin stay whut li'l' time Ahm goin' tuh be heah. Two mo' pay days and Ahm gone. Got tuh take uh birthday gif' tuh Lucy. Wisht Ah could give her Georgy under fence."

"John Buddy, Ahm hongry. Feel lak Ah ain't dirtied uh plate dis week."

"Wait uh minute. Ah'll stir yuh up uh Ash-cake and you kin sop it in some syrup. Maybe Ah ain't goin' tuh town nohow now."

John went outside and fixed the fire and put the bread in the hot ashes and covered it up.

"Reckon Ah better git uh bucket uh water, Zeke. You watch de bread. It's uh good li'l' piece tuh de spring."

Zeke watched the bread and took it out of the ashes when it was thoroughly brown. John had not returned. Most of the men lounged about outside. Finally Coon said to Zeke, "You better run down de hill dere and see whut's de matter wid yo' big buddy. Pant'er got 'im, maybe."

All alarm, Ezekiel leaped up and flew down the path he had seen John take. In a few minutes he saw John coming.

"Where you goin', Zeke?"

"Huntin' yuh. Skeered uh brute-beast had done kotched yuh."

When they got back to the bunk house, John gave Zeke his tin plate and set the gallon jug of syrup before him.

"He'p yo'self, Zeke, and grow hair on yo' chest."

Zeke poured a plate full of syrup and looked for the Ash-cake. "Whar at de bread is?" he asked John.

"You seen it since me," John answered. He looked about and seeing the suppressed laughter on the men's faces he asked, "Where de bread Ah took and cooked fuh mah li'l' bubber?"

General laughter. John got angry. "Ah say, who took and done 'way wid mah bread? Whoever done it mus' be skeered tuh own it."

Coon first, laughing instantly, "Ah et yo' damn bread. Don't you lak it, don't yuh take it, heah mah collar, come and shake it."

"Yeah and Ahm gointer shake it too dis day and year of our Lawd, and if Ah don't, Gawd knows, Ahm gointer give it uh common trial. My gal don't 'speck me tuh run."

They flew at each other and the others scrambled out of the way. Coon was too wise to clinch. He stayed his distance and slugged, but his wariness wore him out. Trying to hit and duck at the same time, he struck out ten or twelve times and landed one high on the enemy's head. John ran in and landed one smack in his enemy's mouth, and while Coon was spitting out his teeth, he ripped a mule-kicking right to the pit of Coon's stomach and the fight was over and done.

John felt good. His first real fight. Something burned inside him. He tasted blood in his mouth, but there was none actually. He wished somebody else would hit him. He wanted to feel himself taking and giving blows.

"You be keerful how you hit folks, Jawn," Uncle Dump cautioned, "you don't know yo' own strength. Dat man (indicating Coon) is hurt bad."

"He been pickin' on me ever since Ah been heah, and Ah been takin' and takin' 'til mah guts is full."

An hour before Lucy's letter had arrived Coon might have eaten John's Ash-cake and offered other insults safely. Now John was different. There was something about Lucy that stuck another and stiffer bone down his back.

He walked over and looked upon the fallen Coon. His surly black face was relaxed in a vacuous manner—blowing bloody foam out thru his swollen lips at every breath.

"Nex' time he fool wid me, Ah bet Ah'll try mah bes' tuh salivate 'im. He try tuh be uh tush hawg—puttin' out his brags everywhere."

He cooked Zeke more bread and soon the camp had settled down to normal. Somebody put Coon in his bunk, and he never spoke a word until after John had taken Zeke to town.

"Know whut," he lisped to the others, "dat boy slipped up

63

on me, but Ahm gwine git even wid him. 'Tain't too late. Seben years ain't too long fuh uh coudar tuh wear uh ruffled bosom shirt. Ahm gwine gently chain-gang fuh dat same nigger."

"Aw," Dump disparaged, "you got uh belly full uh John. You ain't wantin' no mo' uh him."

"Yeah Ah wants tuh fight 'im, but not wid no fist. Ah flies hot quick but Ahm very easy cooled when de man Ahm mad wid is bigger'n me."

CHAPTER 7

John and Zeke got back to Notasulga in time for the Christmas tree at Macedony, and John put a huge China doll on the tree for Lucy. She didn't know he had returned until he walked in during the singing and sat across the aisle from her.

At home, Emmeline Potts pounced upon the large package. "Dis is uh stray bundle dat didn't come from de Sunday School and it didn't come from dis house." She opened it. "Lucy Ann, read dis piece uh paper and tell me who give you dis great big play-pritty."

Lucy faltered. She turned the paper around two or three times.

"John Pearson."

"Dat big yaller boy from cross de Creek?"

"Yes ma'am."

"Whut he doin' givin' *you* uh present?"

"Ah don't know'm."

"Yes you do, madam. Dere's uh bug under dat chip. Mind yuh now, mah young lady; Ah ketch you foolin' wid boys, 'specially uh yaller bastard, Ahm uh goin' tuh put hick'ries tuh yo' back tuh set, Miss Potts. Ah done tole Artie Mimms he kin have yuh when yuh git sixteen."

CHAPTER 8

Alf Pearson welcomed John back with a bluff cursing out.

"I told you to leave Duke's woman alone. I didn't tell you to leave the place. Don't gimme excuses nor back talk. G'wan to work. I'll be glad when some good girl grabs you and makes something out of you. Stop running away. Face things out."

That Sunday Mehaley got two of her friends to go to Macedony with her, though they all belonged to Shiloh.

"Less go slur dat li'l' narrer-contracted Potts gal," she urged. "Somebody say John put uh great big doll-baby on de tree fuh her and den agin he bought her gold hoop ear-rings fuh her birthday. Course Ah don't believe he done no sich uh hot-do, but she fool wid me tuhday Ah means tuh beat her 'til she rope lak okra, and den agin Ah'll stomp her 'til she slack lak lime."

They crowded near Lucy after preaching, but old Emmeline was ever at Lucy's elbow. John had written Lucy to meet him at the spring, but Lucy was not permitted the liberty.

"Naw, you ain't goin' lolly-gaggin' down tuh no spring wid all dese loose gals. You goin' git in dis road 'head uh me and g'wan home."

Emmeline was most emphatic, but while she said her good

byes to her friends, John came up and tipped his hat.

"How yuh do, Mis' Potts."

"Howdy John," she glared like noon.

"Mis' Potts, kin Ah scorch Mis' Lucy home?"

"Lucy ain't takin' no comp'ny yit. She ain't but fourteen and Ah don't turn mah gals loose tuh take comp'ny 'til dey sixteen, and when Ah does Ah picks de comp'ny mahself. Ah ain't raisin' no gals tuh throw 'way on trash."

Richard Potts spoke up. "Whut make you got tuh plow so deep, Emmeline? Ack lak 'tain't nobody got feelings but you. All right, son, Ah reckon it won't hurt nothin' if yuh walk 'long wid Lucy jes' ahead uh us. But she too young tuh court."

The world turned to red and gold for Lucy. She had read the jealousy and malice in Mehaley's face, and John had asked for her company right in front of Mehaley and her crowd! He had faced her hard-to-face mama! She stretched up another inch. There was little to say on the way home, but she had made those big girls stand back. There was one moment when they reached the bend in the road a moment before Richard and Emmeline and John had squeezed her arm. The whole world took on life. Lucy gave no sign that she noticed the touch but in one flash she discovered for herself old truths.

John noted the prosperous look of the Potts place. It was different from every other Negro's place that he had ever seen. Flowers in the yard among whitewashed rocks. Tobacco hanging up to dry. Peanuts drying on white cloth in the sun. A smoke-house, a spring-house, a swing under a china-berry tree, bucket flowers on the porch.

"Stay and have dinner wid us," Richard Potts invited.

John stayed but ate little, and in his presence Lucy cut peas in two and split grains of rice, for which she was coarsely teased by her brothers until John left her, shamefaced.

Another look from his gray eyes that Lucy knew was her look and nobody else's, and John loped on off to Pearson's.

The next morning Lucy found a hair upon her body and exulted.

"Ahm uh woman now."

The following Saturday when she stripped to bathe in the wooden wash tub, she noted that tiny horizontal ridges had lifted her bust a step away from childhood.

She wrote John a long letter and granted him her special company.

CHAPTER 9

You Lucy!" Emmeline scolded as she struggled along behind John and Lucy on the way from church, "Ain't Ah done tole yuh and tole yuh not tuh let no boys be puttin' dey hand all over yuh? You John! You stay arm-length from dat gal and talk it out. You got uh tongue."

Lucy and John sniggered together slyly and walked an inch or two farther apart.

"Good Gawd, dey could drive uh double team between us now," John complained.

"Talk loud, Ah don't 'low no whisperin' tuh no gal uh mine."

They talked about the preaching and the new hymn-books and the proposed church organ. Some were for the innovation but the majority of the congregation thought that kind of music in a church would be sinful to the extreme. Emmeline stayed close enough to hear every word.

At home Lucy's married sister, Dink, sympathetically inveigled Emmeline into the kitchen where she was dishing up dinner. Lucy and John sat in the parlor with the crayon enlargements on easels and the gilded moustache-cups and saucers on wire props and the religious mottoes on the wall.

John cleared his throat to speak, but Emmeline popped in at that moment and took her seat beside the center table. John

71

was on one side of the room behind her and Lucy was on the other side facing her.

"Ah been keepin' comp'ny wid you uh long time, ain't Ah, Lucy?"

"Yeah, mighty nigh uh year now."

"And you ain't never had manners 'nough tuh ast *me* fuh her comp'ny reg'lar," Emmeline snapped.

Conversation died. On the lower shelf of the center table John spied Lucy's double slate with the slate-pencil suspended from it by a string.

"Dis de same slate you use in school, ain't it, Lucy?"

"Unhunh."

John opened the slate and wrote a few words in it as softly as possible. Emmeline seemed neither to see nor hear the scratching of the pencil, but when John leaned forward and tried to hand the slate past Emmeline to Lucy, Emmeline's hand flew out like a cat's paw and grabbed the slate. She looked on both sides and saw no writing, then she opened it and looked hard at the message, "I got something to tell you. Less go for a walk." Emmeline couldn't read a word and she was afraid that no one would read it correctly for her, but one thing she was sure of, she could erase as well as the world's greatest professor. She spoiled out the words with a corner of her apron, and put the slate back under the table. Not a word was passed.

"Mama!" from the kitchen.

"Whut you want, Dink?"

"Come turn dis sweet bread out on uh plate. Ahm skeered Ah'll make it fall uh tear it, tryin' tuh git it out de pan."

Emmeline went grumbling to the rear.

"Less set on de piazza," John suggested, "Maybe us kin git uh word in edgeways 'fo' she git back."

"Aw right."

They went out on the porch and sat slyly side by side—Lucy in the old red rocker, and John on a cow-hided straight chair.

"Lucy, Ah loves yuh."

Emmeline burst out of the parlor.

"Lucy! Whut you doin' settin' on top uh dat boy?"

"Ah ain't settin' on top of 'im. Uh milk cow could git between us."

"Don't you back talk *me*. When Ah speak you *move*. You hear me Lucy?"

"Yessum."

"How come you ain't movin'? Mah orders is five feet apart. Dink know befo' she married Ah never 'lowed her tuh set closer dan five feet and you know it and when Ah don't 'low tuh one, Ah ain't gwine 'low tuh de other. Heifer! Move dat chear 'way from dat boy!"

Silence.

"Lucy!"

"Yessum."

"Is you deef?"

"No'm."

Richard came in from the barn at that moment and called his wife.

"Aw, Emmeline, don't plow so deep. You puts de shamery on folks. Come on inside and hep Dink fix de dinner. Ahm hongry."

"Naw, Ah see she done got hard-headed, and Ahm gwine pray fuh her. Hard-headed chillun never come tuh no good end. Mind whut Ah say! Ahm gwine tell God about *you*, madam."

She pulled back the curtain in the parlor so that she could see every move on the porch and prayed.

"O Lawd and our Gawd, You know Ah tries tuh raise mah chillun right and lead 'em in de way dat dey should go, and Lawd You know it 'tain't right fuh boys and gals tuh be settin' on top one 'nother; and Lawd You know You said You'd strike disobedient chillun dead in dey tracks, and Lawd make mine humble and obedient, and tuh serve Thee and walk in Thy ways and please tuh make 'em set five feet apart, and when Ah done sung mah last song, done prayed mah last prayer, please suh, Jesus, make up mah dyin' bed and keep mah chillun's feet p'inted tuh de starry pole in glory and make

73

'em set five feet 'part. Dese and all other blessin's Ah ast in Jesus name, Amen, and thang Gawd.''

"Aw Emmeline, dat prayer uh yourn ain't got out de house," Richard commented, "it's bumblin' 'round 'mong de rafters right now and dat's fur as it'll ever git."

Out on the porch John said softly, "Meet me tuhmorrer 'cross de branch by dat swee' gum tree 'bout fo' o'clock."

"Aw right. Aincha goin' tuh stay and have some dinner wid us?"

"Naw, Ah don't choose none. Dey got baked chicken at de big house and Ah eats from dere whenever Ah wants tuh. You gointer be sho' tuh be at our tree?"

"Unhunh."

"Sho now?"

"Unhunh."

"S'pos'n yo' mah uh some of de rest of 'em ketch yuh?"

Lucy threw herself akimbo. "Humph, dey can't do nothin' but beat me, and if dey beat me, it sho won't kill me, and if dey kill me dey sho can't eat me. Ah'll be dere jus' as sho as gun's iron."

" 'Bye den, Lucy. Sho wisht Ah could smack yo' lips."

"Whut's dat you say, John?"

"Oh nothin'. 'Bye. Do'an let de booger man ketch yuh."

"Don't let ole Raw-Head-and-Bloody-Bones waylay yuh neither."

John was at the tree long before Lucy. He was sitting on the knurly-roots tying his handkerchief into a frogknot when he saw her coming diffidently down the hill on the Potts side of the branch. Presently she was standing before him.

" 'Lo, Lucy."

"Hello, John. Ah see you fixin' tuh make soap."

"Whut make you say dat, Lucy?"

"Ah see yuh got yo' bones piled up."

She pointed to his crossed legs and they both laughed immoderately.

"Miss Lucy, uh Lucy, whyn't yuh have some set down?"

"Unrack yo' bones den and make room."

Lucy sat down. John untied his handkerchief and Lucy plaited rope-grass. John attempted another knot but fumbled it nervously. Lucy caught hold of the handkerchief also.

"Lemme he'p yuh wid dat, John. Ah know how tuh tie dat. Heah, you take dem two corners and roll 'em whilst Ah git dese fixed."

They both held the handkerchief taut between them. But before the knot could be tied John pulled hard and made Lucy lean towards him.

"Lucy, something been goin' on inside uh me fuh uh long time."

Diffidently, "Whut, John?"

"Ah don't know, Lucy, but it boils up lak syrup in de summer time."

"Maybe you needs some sassafras root tuh thin yo' blood out."

"Naw, Lucy, Ah don't need no sassafras tea. You know whuss de matter wid me—but ack lak you dumb tuh de fack."

Lucy suddenly lost her fluency of speech. She worked furiously at the love-knot.

"Lucy, you pay much 'tention tuh birds?"

"Unhunh. De jay bird say 'Laz'ness will kill you,' and he go to hell ev'ry Friday and totes uh grain uh sand in his mouf tuh put out de fire, and den de doves say, 'Where you *been* so long?'"

John cut her short. "Ah don't mean dat way, Lucy. Whut Ah wants tuh know is, which would you ruther be, if you had yo' ruthers—uh lark uh flyin', uh uh dove uh settin'?"

"Ah don't know whut you talkin' 'bout, John. It mus' be uh new riddle."

"Naw 'tain't, Lucy. Po' me, Lucy. Ahm uh one wingded bird. Don't leave me lak dat, Lucy."

Suddenly Lucy shouted, "Look, John, de knot is tied right, ain't it pretty?"

"Yeah, Lucy iss sho pretty. We done took and tied dis knot, Miss Lucy, less tie uh 'nother one."

"You got mo' han'kerchiefs in yo' pocket?"

"Naw. Ah ain't studyin' 'bout no hankechers neither. De knot Ah wants tuh tie wid you is de kind dat won't come uh loose 'til us rises in judgment. You knows mah feelings."

"How Ah know whut you got inside yo' mind?"

"Yeah yuh do too. Y'all lady people sho do make it hard fuh us men folks. Look me in de eye Lucy. Kiss me and loose me so Ah kin talk."

There was an awkward bumping of mouths. Lucy had had her first kiss.

"Lucy, Ah looked up intuh Heben and Ah seen you among de angels right 'round de throne, and when Ah seen *you,* mah heart swole up and put wings on mah shoulders, and Ah 'gin tuh fly 'round too, but Ah never would uh knowed yo' name if ole Gab'ull hadn't uh whispered it tuh me."

He extended his hands appealingly.

"Miss Lucy, how 'bout changin' frum Potts tuh Pearson?"

"Yeah, John."

"When?"

"Whenever you ready fuh me. You know mo' 'bout dat dan Ah do."

"How 'bout on yo' birthday, Lucy? Us kin make merry fuh uh heap uh things den at de same time."

"Aw right, John."

It was coldish on the December night, as Lucy made ready to meet John at the church. She had only finished her wedding-dress the day before, and only her father had seemed to care whether she had one or not. Now the puffed and laced little dress of light gray cashmere lay across the bed with her new shoes and six starchy petticoats loaded down with lace of her own making.

"Lucy Ann!" Emmeline bawled from the kitchen.

"Whut, mama?"

"Don't you answer *me* no 'whut'! Ah'll come in dere and stomp yo' guts out. Whut you got all dis fiah goin' fuh?"

"Mama, you know Ah got tuh bath mah self 'fo' Ah put on dese clothes."

"Ah keers nothin' 'bout no bathin'. 'Nother thing, you

76

done kilt up fo' uh mah fryin'-size chickens, madam, and got 'em all cooked."

"No'm, Ah ain't kilt none uh yo' chickens. Dem wuz mah own Ah kilt fuh mah weddin'."

"How come dey yourn? You stinkin' li'l' heifer you!"

" 'Cause dem is some uh Lay-over's biddies dat Ah raised. Papa gimme dat hen las' year, and tole me tuh start raisin' mahself some chickens, so's Ah have uh good start when Ah git married, and you know Ah got twenty odd from her now."

"Youse uh lie, madam. Eve'y chicken on dis place is mines. Ah woulda give yuh uh few fuh seed if you wuz marryin' anybody. Here Artie Mimms is wid sixty acres under plow and two mules and done ast me fuh yuh ever since yuh wuz ten years old and Ah done tole 'im he could have yuh and here you is jumpin' up, goin' over mah head, and marryin' uh nigger dat ain't hardly got changin' clothes."

"He is got changin' clothes."

"Hush up! Maybe he got clothes, but he ain't got uh chamber pot tuh his name nor uh bed tuh push it under. Still he kin take you outa uh good home and drag yuh off tuh Pearson's quarters."

"Mama, yuh been hell-hackin' me eve' since us tole yuh us wuz gointer git married. Whut Ah keer 'bout ole Artie Mimms?"

"He ain't ole!"

"He is so ole, too. Ah looked at 'im good last big meetin'. His knees is sprung and his head is blossomin' fuh de grave. Ah don't want no ole springy-leg husband."

"You better want one dat kin feed yuh! Artie got dat farm and dem mules is paid fuh. He showed me and yo' paw de papers las' week."

"Whut Ah keer how many mules he got paid fuh? Ah ain't speckin' tuh live wid no mules. You tryin' tuh kill me wid talk. Don't keer whut yuh say, Ahm gointer marry John dis night, God bein' mah helper."

Lucy had been fixing her bath all during the talk. She now closed the room door, flung off her clothes with a savage

77

gesture and stepped into the tub.

Instantly Emmeline's angry hand pushed against the latched door. "Whose face you slammin' uh door in, madam? Ah means tuh bring you down offa yo' high horse! Whar dem peach hick'ries? Somebody done done 'way wid mah switches. Aaron! You go cut me five uh six good peach switches and don't bring me nothin' dat ain't long ez mah arm. Dis gal done provoked me. Ah been tryin' tuh keep offa her back 'til dat trashy yaller bastard git her outa dis house, but she won't lemme do it. Go git dem hick'ries so Ah kin roast 'em in dis fiah. Ah birthed her, she didn't birth me, and Ah'll show her she can't run de hawg over me."

"Yessum, mama, Ahm gwine."

"Make haste, Aaron. Go in uh speedy hurry!"

Lucy spoke from the wash-tub, "Mama, 'tain't no use in you sendin' Aaron out tuh be cuttin' and ruinin' papa's peach trees, 'cause Ahm tellin' anybody, ole uh young, grizzly or gray, Ah ain't takin' no whippin' tuhnight. All mah switches done growed tuh trees."

"Whuss dat you say in dere, madam?"

Richard drove 'round to the front and hitched the horse and buggy at that moment.

"Whut's all dis racket gwine on in heah?" he demanded.

"Dat youngest gal uh your'n done sassed me out, and dared me tuh hit uh. Ah birthed uh but now she's older'n me. She kin marry dat yaller wretch, but Ah means fuh her tuh tote uh sore back when he gits uh."

"Aw dry up, Emmeline, dry up! She done done her pickin', now leave her be. If she make her bed hard, she de one got tuh lay on it. 'Tain't you. Git yo' clothes on fuh de weddin'. Us Potts can't leave our baby gal go off tuh git married by herself."

"Me! Ah ain't gointer put mah foot in de place. Ahm gointer let folks see whar Ah stand. Ah sho ain't gwine squench mah feelin's fuh Lucy and dat John and you and nobody else—do Ah'll purge when Ah die."

Richard tucked Lucy into the buckboard and drove the

78

silent little bundle to the church huddled against him. His arm about her gave his blessing but he knew that she would have gone anyway. He but made the way easier for her little feet.

To Lucy, Macedony, so used to sound and fervor, seemed cold and vacant. Her family, her world that had been like a shell about her all her life was torn away and she felt cold and naked. The aisle seemed long, long! But it was like climbing up the stairs to glory. Her trembling fear she left on the climb. When she rode off beside John at last she said, "John Buddy, look lak de moon is givin' sunshine."

He toted her inside the house and held her in his arms infant-wise for a long time. "Lucy, don't you worry 'bout yo' folks, hear? Ahm gointer be uh father and uh mother tuh you. You jes' look tuh me, girl chile. Jes' you put yo' 'pendence in me. Ah means tuh prop you up on eve'y leanin' side."

CHAPTER 10

A month after he was married John had moved up into the house-servants' quarters just back of the big house. John had achieved a raise in his wages. Alf Pearson had given them among other things a walnut bed with twisted posts, as a wedding present, and Lucy loved it above all else. She made it a spread and bolster of homemade lace.

After a few months Mehaley began to waylay John at the pig pens and in devious ways to offer herself. John gradually relaxed and began to laugh with her. She grew bolder. The morning after Lucy's first son was born, when he found her at the chicken house before him, he said, "Mehaley, Ah ain't gonna say Ah ain't laked you 'cause youse soft and nice, but Ah got Lucy, and Ah don't keer how she feel uh nothin', Ah'll want her right on. Ah tastes her wid mah soul, but if Ah didn't take holt uh you Ah'd might soon fuhgit all 'bout yuh. Pomp love you—you go marry Pomp. He'll do fuh yuh lak uh man. You better take and marry 'im."

"Ah don't want no Pomp! John Buddy, you know'd me 'fo' yuh knowed Lucy. If y'all wuz ever tuh quit would yuh marry me, John Buddy?"

"Us ain't never gonna do no quittin' 'til one uh us is six feet in de ground, and if you git de notion tuh run tell her a whole mess tuh back her feelin's and tear up peace, you better take wings and fly 'fo' Ah find it out. You hear me? Nothin' ain't gointer part us."

So when Pomp Lamar, the new hoe hand, fell beneath Mehaley's mango call—exotic, but fibrous and well-bodied—she answered "Yes" quickly with a persuasive kiss.

"But Ahm got tuh be married real, Pomp."

"And dat's whut Ah means tuh do, M'haley, come nex' pay-day."

"And less we g'wan off dis farm, Pomp. You know is too much back-bendin' and mule-smellin' on cotton plantations. Less go on some public works, lak uh sawmill uh sumpin'. Ah kin git 'long wid anybody any whar so long ez you half-way treat me right."

"M'haley, you might not know it, but youse gittin' uh do-right man. Whenever you needs somebody tuh do uh man's part Ah'll be 'round dere walkin' heavy over de floor."

Next pay-day the quarters was gathered at Mehaley's mother's cabin. Quantities of sweet biscuits had been cooked up along with the chickens. The wedding was set for eight o'clock and the crowd was there—all except Pomp. People began to ask questions that had no answers. Mehaley didn't get dressed. She was asked why she was still in her working clothes.

"Humph! Y'all think Ahm gwine put mah trunk on mah back and de tray on mah head, and dat man don't never come? Naw indeed! Ah ain't gwine tuh dress tuh marry no man 'til unless he be's in de house."

"You reckon he done run off?" Nunkie asked.

"Aw naw," Duke dissented. "He tole me he wuz crazy tuh marry Haley. He jus' keepin' colored folks time. When white folks say eight o'clock dey mean eight o'clock. When uh colored person say eight o'clock, dat jes' mean uh hour ago. He'll be heah in plenty time."

It was after nine when the bridegroom arrived. "Where you been at all dis time?" Mehaley's mother wanted to know.

"Ah couldn't stand on de flo' wid M'haley in dem ole

sweaty britches. Ah been off tuh borry me some clothes tuh git married in."

Mehaley began to dress with the interference of ten or more ladies. Finally she was ready, but a quarrel arose as to who was to perform the ceremony. Mehaley's father wanted to do it, but her mother had invited the pastor.

"Ah don't keer if you *is* her pappy," the mother stated, "you ain't nothin' but uh stump-knocker and Ah wants dis done real. Youse standin' in uh sho 'nuff preacher's light. G'wan set down and leave Elder Wheeler hitch 'em right. You can't read, no-how."

"Yes, Ah kin too."

"Naw, you can't neither. G'wan sit down. If us wuz down in de swamp whar us couldn't git tuh no preacher, you'd do, but here de pastor is. You ain't nothin' but uh jack-leg. Go set in de chimbley corner and be quiet."

"You always tryin' tuh make light uh mah preachin'," the husband defended, "but Gawd don't. Dis de fust one uh mah chillun tuh jump over de broomstick and Ah means tuh tie de knot mah own self."

Around eleven o'clock, the pastor, worn out by the stubbornness of the father, retired from the field, and the couple stood upon the floor.

"Whar yo' shoes, Pomp?" Mehaley asked. "You ain't gwine marry me barefooted, is yuh?"

"Dey over dere under de bed. Yo' paw and the preacher argued so long and dem new shoes hurted mah foots so bad, Ah took 'em off. Now Ah can't git 'em back on. Dat don't make uh bit uh diff'rence. You goin' tuh see mah bare foots uh whole heap after dis."

So Mehaley Grant stood up to marry Pomp Lamar and her father Woody Grant, who had committed the marriage ceremony to memory anyway, grabbed an almanac off the wall and held it open pompously before him as he recited the questions to give the lie to the several contentions that he could not read.

"Ah now puhnounce you man and wife."

"Bus' her, Pomp, bus' her rat in de mouf. She's yourn now, g'wan Pomp. Les see yuh kiss her!"

After many boisterous kisses, the women took Mehaley by the arm and led her off.

"Us goin' and bath M'haley fuh huh weddin'-night. Some uh y'all men folks grab Pomp, and give him uh washin' off."

Mehaley got out of bed that night after the guests had all gone home.

"Whar yuh gwine, Haley?"

"Huntin' fuh mah box uh snuff."

"Yo' box uh snuff? Gal, don't you know you jes' got done married tuh uh husband? Put out dat light and come git back under dese kivvers."

"Naw, Pomp, not 'til Ah gits uh dip uh snuff. Ah wants it real bad."

She hunted about until she found it. "Lawd," she cried, "you see some dem women done messed 'round and spilt soap suds in mah snuff!"

She sat down before the fireplace and wept, hard racking sobs. Pomp's assurance that she would have a dozen boxes from the Commissary first thing in the morning did not comfort her, and it was only when her stormy tears had exhausted her that she let her new husband lead her back to bed. In his arms, she said, "Pomp, don't fuhgit you said you wuz gwine take me 'way fuhm heah."

"Cose Ah is, Haley. Nex' pay-day, sho." He kept his word.

At sundown on the evening of their leaving, Lucy was on her knees at the praying ground, telling God all her feelings.

"And oh, Ah know youse uh prayer-hearin' God. Ah know you kin hit uh straight lick wid uh crooked stick. You heard me when Ah laid at hell's dark door and cried three long days and nights. You moved de stumblin' stone out my way, and now, Lawd, you know Ahm uh po' child, and uh long ways from home. You promised tuh be uh rock in uh weary land—uh shelter in de time uh storm. Amen."

Lucy and John raced around their house in the later afternoons playing "Hail Over" and "Hide the Switch," and Lucy grew taller. The time came when she could no longer stand under John's outstretched arm. By the time her third son was born she weighed ninety-five pounds.

John had added weight to his inches and weighed two hundred and fifteen pounds, stripped. There was no doubt about it now. John was foreman at Pearson's. His reading and writing had improved to the degree where Alf could trust him with all the handling of supplies.

"John," Alf said to him one day, "you damn rascal! that girl you married is as smart as a whip and as pretty as a speckled pup. She's making a man of you. Don't let her git away."

"Oh good Lawd, naw! Mist' Alf, she even nice. Don't talk 'bout her never partin' from me. Dat sho would put de affliction on me."

"Well, John, you'd better keep Big 'Oman out of that Commissary after dark. Aha! You didn't think I knew, did you? Well, I know a lot of things that would surprise folks. You better clean yourself up."

The hand of John's heart reached out and clutched on fear. Alf Pearson shoved him on out of his office and returned to work, chuckling. Two days later Big 'Oman was gone. It got said that she was shacked up with somebody in a tie-camp on the Alabama River.

A month later John said, "Lucy, somebody done wrote Mist' Alf 'bout uh drove uh cows dey wants tuh sell 'im. He say fuh me tuh go look over 'em and see whut dey worth. Be back Sad'day."

"Iss been rainin' uh lot fuh you tuh be goin' uh long way, John."

"Goin' on horse-back, Lucy. De water ain't goin' bother me."

Lucy said no more. John didn't notice her silence in the haste of his departure, but a few miles on down the road he said, "Humph! Lucy ain't frailed me none wid uh tongue. Wonder how come dat?"

On Thursday John was cheerfully riding away from Lucy,

but at daybreak on Saturday he was dressed and ready to ride back.

"John, you ain't gwine leave me, is yuh?" Big 'Oman sobbed, "thought you come to stay. De big boss say you kin git uh job right heah."

"Ah got uh job, Big 'Oman. Done been off too long now."

The weeping girl clung to his stirrup. "When you comin' back tuh me, John?"

"In times and seasons, Big 'Oman. Lemme go now. All at rain yistiddy and las' night makes bad travelin'. Bad 'nough when Ah wuz comin'. De later it gits, de higher de river."

He dashed off quickly and rode hard, counting the miles as he went.

"Eighteen miles from home. 'Leben mo' miles. Heah 'tis de river—eight mo' miles."

The river was full of water and red as judgment with chewed-up clay land. The horse snorted and went mincing down to the bridge. Red water toting logs and talking about trouble, wresting with timber, pig-pens, and chicken coops as the wind hauls feathers, gouging out banks with timber and beating up bridges with logs.

"Git up, Roxy! Us got tuh cross dis river, don't keer if she run high ez uh bell-tower, us got tuh cross. Come on up dere. Let de damn bridge shake, bofe us kin swim."

Midway over, a huge log struck the far end of the bridge and tore it loose from the shore and it headed down stream. The whole structure loosened, rolled over and shot away.

John freed himself and struck out for shore. Fifty feet or more down stream Roxy landed, snorting her loss of faith in the judgment of man. John felt himself being carried with the stream in spite of his powerful stroke, but inch by inch he was surely gaining land. The neighing of Roxy had attracted the attention of a white squatter on the farther shore and John saw people looking on his fight with the Alabama.

There was a cry from the shore, a thud at the back of his head and he sank.

John strode across infinity where God sat upon his throne and looked off towards immensity and burning worlds dropped from his teeth. The sky beneath John's tread crackled and flashed eternal lightning and thunder rolled without ceasing in his wake.

Way off he heard crying, weeping, weeping and wailing— wailing like the last cry of Hope when she fled the earth. Where was the voice? He strained his eye to see. None walked across the rim bones of nothingness with him, but the wailing wailed on. Slowly John saw Lucy's face. Lucy wept at a far, far distance, but the breath of her weeping sent a cold wind across the world. Then her voice came close and her face hung miserably above his, weeping. She brought the world with her face and John could see without moving his head the familiar walls of their house.

Gradually things came closer. The gourd dipper, the water-bucket, the skillets and spiders, and his wife so close above him, forearm across her face, retching in tears.

"Whuss de matter, Lucy? You thought Ah wuzn't never comin' back? Don't you know nothin' couldn't keep me 'way from you?"

"John! Ah thought you wuz dead."

"Naw, Ah ain't dead. Whatever give you de idea Ah wuz dead, Lucy?"

"Dey brought yuh home fuh dead dis mawnin' and iss nelly sundown now and you ain't moved, and you ain't spoke 'til jus' now."

"Who brung me home?"

"De Bickerstaffs. Say de bridge washed uhway wid yuh and de hawse on it, and you got hit by de timber. Yo' lip is cut deep and yo' head is hurted in de back and uh bad place right dere side yo' nose."

"Umph, umph, umph! Lawd have mussy. Ah thought Ah been sleep. So dat's how come Ahm all wet up and mah face hurt me so, eh?"

"Yeah, and John, Ahm so glad you ain't dead 'way from me and mah li'l' chillun, and then agin Ah hated tuh think 'bout you herded tuh judgment in yo' sins."

A silent wait.

"You can't lay on dis floor all night. Ah got tuh git yuh in de bed some way uh 'nother. Lemme go call somebody tuh he'p me muscle yuh. Ah sent fuh mah folks but 'tain't been nobody from dat side yet."

The next day John called Lucy to him.

"Lucy."

"Yeah, John."

"Dey done tole you 'bout Big 'Oman and me?"

"Yeah, John, and some uh yo' moves Ah seen mahself, and if you loves her de bes', John, you gimme our chillun and you go on where yo' love lie."

"Lucy, don't tell me nothin' 'bout leavin' you, 'cause if you do dat, you'll make two winters come in one year."

There was a feeling silence.

"Lucy, Ah loves you and you alone. Ah swear Ah do. If Ah don't love you, God's gone tuh Dothan."

"Whut make yuh fool wid scrubs lak Big 'Oman and de rest of 'em?"

"Dat's de brute-beast in me, but Ah sho aim tuh live clean from dis on if you 'low me one mo' chance. Don't tongue-lash me—jes' try me and see. Here you done had three younguns fuh me and fixin' have uh 'nother. Try me Lucy."

The next big meeting John prayed in church, and when he came to his final:

You are de same God, Ah
Dat heard de sinner man cry.
Same God dat sent de zigzag lightning tuh
Join de mutterin' thunder.
Same God dat holds de elements
In uh unbroken chain of controllment.
Same God dat hung on Cavalry and died,
Dat we might have a right tuh de tree of life—

We thank Thee that our sleeping couch
Was not our cooling board,
Our cover was not our winding sheet . . .
Please tuh give us uh restin' place
Where we can praise Thy name forever,

                                                        Amen.

"Uh prayer went up tuhday," Deacon Moss exulted to Deacon Turl. "Dat boy got plenty fire in 'im and he got uh good
strainin' voice. Les' make 'im pray uh lot."

Deacon Turl agreed and went on home to his chicken
dumplings.

John never made a balk at a prayer. Some new figure, some
new praise-giving name for God, every time he knelt in
church. He rolled his African drum up to the altar, and called
his Congo Gods by Christian names. One night at the altar-call
he cried out his barbaric poetry to his "Wonder-workin" God
so effectively that three converts came thru religion under the
sound of his voice.

"He done more'n de pastor," Moss observed. "Dat boy is
called tuh preach and don't know it. Ahm gwine tell him so."

But Moss never did. Lucy's time was drawing nigh and a
woman named Delphine drifted into town from Opelika. John
was away from both home and church almost continually in
the next month.

Alf went to see Lucy.

"Lucy Ann, where's that husband of yours?"

"He's out 'round de barn somewheres, ain't he, Mist' Alf?"
Lucy asked. She knew he was not there. She knew that Alf
Pearson knew he was not there and that Alf Pearson knew that
she knew he was not there, but he respected her reticence.

"Lucy, you oughta take a green club and flail John good. No
matter what I put in his way to help him along, he flings it away
on some slut. You take a plow-line and half kill him."

When Alf was gone Lucy looked drearily up the path for her
husband and saw her oldest brother coming with his double
team.

89

"Lawd a mussy!" she groaned and dropped into a chair. A heavy knocking at the door.

"Who dat?"

"Iss me, Bud. Lemme come in right now. Ahm in uh big hurry."

Lucy opened the door feebly and Bud's stumpy figure thrust itself inside aggressively as if it said in gestures, "Who you tryin' tuh keep out?"

"Lucy, Ah come tuh git dat three dollars you borried offa me."

"Well, Bud, tuh tell yuh de truth, Ah ain't got it right dis minute. Mah husband ain't here, but he'll be here pretty soon, then he'll pay yuh sho, Bud."

"Who don't know he ain't here? How he gointer be here, and layin' all 'round de jook behind de cotton gin wid Delphine?"

"You better come back, Bud, when he's here and tell 'im all dat tuh his face."

"And whut it takes tuh tell 'im, Ah got it! He ain't nothin' but uh stinkin' coward or he wouldn't always be dodgin' back uh yuh. Ah'll tell 'im all right. 'Tain't no fight in him."

"G'wan home, Bud. If papa wuzn't dead you wouldn't come heah lak dis—and me in mah condition."

"Ah know you done wished many's de time you had married Artie Mimms."

"Naw. Not nary time."

"Gimme mah money and lemme go 'fo' Ah git mad agin."

"Ah tole you Ah ain't got no money and won't have none till John come."

"You ain't gonna git none den—dat is if he ever come. Some folks say he done quit you fuh dat Delphine. She strowin' it herself all over Macon County and laffin' at yuh. You jes' dumb tuh de fact."

"You can't pay no 'tention tuh talk. Dey's talkin' everywhere. De folks is talkin' in Georgy and dey's talkin' in Italy. Ah don't pay dese talkers no mind."

"Gimme de money, Lucy, and lemme go."

90

"Done tole yuh Ah ain't got no money. Come back heah when John is home."

"Naw, Ah ain't gonna do nothin' lak dat. Ah come heah wid de determination tuh git mah money uh satisfaction, one."

"But, don't you see Ah ain't in no fix tuh be fretted all up this uh way? G'wan leave me uh lone."

Bud looked around him contemptuously. "Humph! Here mah sister is cooped up wid three li'l' chillun in uh place ain't big uhnough tuh cuss uh cat in 'thout gittin yo' mouf full uh hair."

"G'wan way from me, Bud. Ahm too sick tuh be worried."

"Naw, Ah means tuh have something fuh mah money. Gimme dat bed."

"Dat big one wid de knobs on it?"

"Yep. Who you reckon want de tother one dat dem chillun done wet in? Move! Don't you git in mah way. Move! If you wuz married tuh anybody you wouldn't be in no sich uh fix."

The bed was down in a twinkling, the feather mattress and bolster heaped upon the floor, while Bud dragged out the head and foot pieces. Lucy sank down upon the mattress and fought the lump in her throat. When her brother returned for the rails and slats, Lucy was crumpled in a little dark ball in the center of the deep mound of feathers.

"Bud, you ought'n tuh take dat bed. Mist' Alf give it tuh us. Dat's our weddin' bed."

"He oughta give 'im mo'. Git up offa dat air mattress!"

"Ah ain't, and if you don't git offa dis place Ah'll call Mist' Alf. Ah bet you'll leave here then."

"Aw Ah ain't skeered uh no white man. Ah been free ever since Grant took Richmond."

But in a few moments Bud was gone and Lucy was shivering and weeping upon the feather mattress.

"Hezekiah," she called to her oldest boy, "run down tuh de quarters lak uh li'l' man and tell An' Pheemy tuh come quick. Run on, son. Youse five years ole now, youse uh great big boy. Hurry up."

"Mama, Ahm hungry."

91

"Mama know it too. Run on now. Run fast, Hezekiah! Show mama how fas' you kin run. Oh Gawd have mussy on me! Have mussy in uh mos' puhticular manner. Have mussy on mah ever-dyin' soul!"

Before midnight Lucy in awful agony upon her pallet on the floor had given birth to her first daughter.

The odor of airless childbirth hung over the stuffy room. Pheemy with the help of Old Edy and Della performed the ancient rites.

Edy and Della sweetened the mother and put a clean meal-sack sheet beneath Lucy, but only Pheemy could handle the after-birth in the proper way, so that no harm could come to Lucy. That is she buried it shoulder deep to the east of the house beneath a tree, then she returned and attended to the navel string of the baby and adjusted the belly-band.

"Della, you and Edy kin go 'long now. Ah kin see after Lucy."

They went reluctantly. As soon as the sound of their feet died away Pheemy asked, "How you feelin' inside, honey?"

"Lawd, An' Pheemy, Ah got somethin' in mah heart ain't got no name. Ah layin' here right now tryin' tuh find some words for feelin's. Look lak mah right heart ain't beatin' no mo'."

"Neb mine, Lucy, 'bout de words. You needs sleep and rest and some chicken gruel. Ah gwine bring yuh some. Ahm gwine find some sheep pills so de baby kin have some sheep shadney."

That night Pheemy fell asleep in a chair before the fire. The children full of corn pone and buttermilk had been asleep since early night. Lucy alone saw John when he crept in towards morning. She shut her eyes and pretended sleep. John stood looking down upon her for a long time. Lucy, later, thru the crack of her eye saw him examining the new-born baby, and felt him timidly tucking the covers under her feet, and heard him stretching himself on the floor beside the mattress; heard the deep breathing of his sleep. She raised herself upon her elbows and looked at him hard. She looked at the flickering fire, the rude dingy walls and everything in the room and knew that she'd never lose the picture as long as she lived. She stretched out her hand nearest her husband and rested the fingers on his tousled head. With her other arm she cuddled her baby close, and fell into a deep, healthful sleep.

When Lucy woke up, old Hannah was riding high. The light was strong in her face. She looked about and asked Pheemy, "Where John?"

"He at de barn—done chopped up uh tree for wood. Oughter be 'bout through wid his work by now. You better suckle dat chile."

John crept in and stood before Lucy while her fat daughter searched hungrily for the nipple.

"Lucy, whut you doin' sleepin' on de floor?"

"Dat's all Ah got tuh sleep on, John Buddy."

"Where de weddin' bed at?"

"Bud come took it fuh dat li'l' change us owe 'im fuhm las' year."

"When he come got it?"

"Yistiddy."

He hung his head a moment.

"Lucy, kin Ah see de baby?"

"She nussin' now, John. Soon's she git through."

"Dat ain't no trouble." He stooped and picked up mother and child and sat with them in his lap. "Lucy, Ahm sho proud uh dis li'l' girl chile you done had. Dat's jus' whut Ah wanted—uh girl so us could have it fuh uh doll-baby. An' Pheemy, don't Lucy have de biggest babies? Dis chile it almost big as her. She so little Ah hafta shake de sheets tuh find her in de bed."

She slapped him feebly.

"Ain't you got no better sense dan tuh set in uh man's lap and box his jaws? He's liable tuh let yuh fall thru his legs." He stopped laughing abruptly. "An' Pheemy you fed mah wife and slopped mah three li'l' pigs?"

"Look in de meal-barrel and see."

John didn't look. Pheemy's words told him. He laid Lucy

93

again upon the pallet and left. As he stepped thru the wire fence gap at Bud's place he saw Bud riding up the path behind him on his mule, his huge bull whip coiled upon his saddle-horn.

"Gid up dere, Sooky!" Bud Potts held his eyes stubbornly before him. John Pearson's hand flung out, grasped the mule's bridle close to the bit, and shoved the animal back upon its haunches.

"Gid down, Bud. You might kin beat me, but if you do, eve'ybody goin tuh know you been in uh fight. So good uh man, so good uh man."

"Whut you mean, John, comin' here pickin' uh fuss lak dat?"

"Ah ain't come tuh pick no fuss, Ahm come tuh fight. God bein' mah helper Ah means tuh teach yuh how tuh go proagin' 'round takin' folkses weddin' beds when dey ain't home and flinging dey wives on de floor. Gid down!"

"If you wuz any kind uh man, all dis wouldn't come tuh pass. De white folks and eve'ybody is sick and tiahed uh de way you keerin' on. Nohow you can't beat *me*. Ahm uh *man*."

"Maybe Ah can't, but Ahm so goin' tuh give it uh common trial. Hit de ground! If Ah don't beat yuh, you kin go and tell de word Ah give it uh po' man's trial."

Bud tried to ride off, but he was snatched scuffling to the ground and hammered to his knees time and time again. When he swore no more, when he begged for mercy no more, John picked him up and heaved him across the rump of the mule and recrossed the branch.

Almost home he remembered the empty meal-barrel and swerved off into the Weens' wood lot where droves of piney wood rooters nosed for ground nuts. John laid a shoat by the heels and stuck it expertly before it had squealed more than three or four times. Looking all about to see if he was seen, he swung the hog over his shoulder and took the back way home.

By that time the sun was washing herself in the bloody sea and splashing her bedclothes in red and purple. John built a

94

fire under the washpot, and dressed his meat before he came inside the house. When Lucy opened her eyes from a nap, crude slabs of pork steak were sizzling in the skillets.

"Where you git all dat fresh meat from, John?"

"Neb' mind where Ah got de meat from. You jes' eat 'til you git plenty. Ah'll get out and throw uh natural fuh you any time. You got uh *man* tuh fend fuh yuh."

"Lawd knows Ah do needs one. Me and mah po' li'l chillun been singin' mighty low 'round here."

"Now, Lucy, don't start dat talk 'bout breakin' up and quittin' 'cause Ah ain't goin' tuh hear dat. Youse mah wife and all Ah want you tuh do is gimme uh chance tuh show mah spunk."

"Good Lawd, John, dat's all justice been beggin' righteous tuh do—be uh *man.* Cover de ground you stand on. Jump at de sun and eben if yuh miss it, yuh can't help grabbin' holt uh de moon."

"Li'l' Bit, please don't tongue lash me," there was a short pause, " 'cause Ah done beat Bud nelly tuh death, and dat's plenty tuh think uhbout—by rights Ah oughta kilt 'im." He rubbed his swollen knuckles.

"Oh mah Gawd! When?"

"Dis evenin'—jus' 'fo' Ah come home, Lucy. Ah wouldn't be no man atall tuh let yo' brother uh nobody else snatch uh bed out from under you, mo' special in yo' condition."

"John dat's goin' tuh cause trouble and double, Bud hate you and now you done hit 'im he ain't goin' tuh let his shirt-tail touch 'im till he tell it tuh de white folks. Lawd, me and mah po' chilluns. If dey ever git yuh on dat chain-gang Ah never speck tuh see you live no mo'."

"Ah ain't goin' tuh no chain-gang. If dey ever git in behind me, Ah'll tip on 'cross de good Lawd's green. Ah'll give mah case tuh Miss Bush and let Mother Green stand mah bond."

"Dey liable tuh grab yuh, 'fo' yuh know it."

"Aw les' squat dat rabbit and jump uh 'nother one. You ack lak you done cut loose."

"Naw, Ah ain't cut loose but look lak wese tied tuhgether

95

by uh long cord string and youse at one end and Ahm at de other. Way off."

"You kin take in some de slack."

"Don't look lak it."

"Aw, lemme see de caboose uh dat. Less eat dis hog meat and hoe-cake. Jes' 'cause women folks ain't got no big muscled arm and fistes lak jugs, folks claims they's weak vessels, but dass uh lie. Dat piece uh red flannel she got hung 'tween her jaws is equal tuh all de fistes God ever made and man ever seen. Jes' take and ruin a man wid dey tongue, and den dey kin hold it still and bruise 'im up jes' ez bad."

"Say whut yuh will or may, you tryin' tuh loud talk me, but, John, you gives mah folks too much tuh go on. Ah wants mah husband tuh be uh great big man and look over 'em all so's Ah kin make 'em eat up dey talk. Ah wants tuh uphold yuh in eve'ything, but yuh know John, nobody can't fight war wid uh brick."

CHAPTER 11

Duke came panting up to Lucy's late the next afternoon. Lucy was propped up in a rocker and Pheemy was washing baby rags.

"Hates tuh tell yuh, Lucy, but dey done got 'im."

"Do, Jesus."

"Yassum, de high sheriff put his hand on his shoulder down dere by de deepo' 'bout uh hour uh go. Bud Potts swo' out de warrant, and den Weens say he goin' have 'im bound over tuh de big cote. Sho is bad, and you in yo' condition."

"Where dey got 'im, Duke?"

"In de big jail. Cy Perkins, Jestice uh de Peace, goin' tuh bind 'im over. Den Judge Pearson'll set on de case nex' cote day."

Lucy rose abruptly, "Ahm goin', Pheemy. You take keer mah chillun."

"Lucy, yo' body ain't healed up yit. You can't go."

"Ah specks tuh be back 'fo' dark, An' Pheemy."

"Gal, you ain't but three days out uh labor. De elements is pizen tuh yuh, and effen yuh git lated 'til after sundown, de pizen night air sho will be de last uh you."

Lucy flung the plaid shawl about her head and shoulders. "And, An' Pheemy, if de baby cries tuh nuss 'fo' Ah git back, jus' give her uh sugar-tit tuh suck on and keep her pacified."

Lucy stepped out of the cabin door and was gone. In due time she stood in Cy Perkins' office where he was holding court. She saw her brother's bruised and beaten face. She saw her husband handcuffed and humble, his eyes turned away from the world.

The court had not set. She still had time if she worked fast. She held her shawl under the chin with the frail fingers of one hand as she went and stood before her brother.

"Don't come puttin' up no po' mouf tuh me, Lucy. Git out mah face," Bud shouted before she could speak. "Dis case ain't uh goin' tuh be nol prossed uh nothin' else. Ah wouldn't squash it fuh mah mammy. You made yo' bed now lay in it."

She turned away. Cy Perkins called her.

"Howdy, Lucy."

"Well, Ah thankee, Mist' Perkins. Ah come tuh see 'bout mah husband."

"Got any bail money, Lucy? That's what you need."

"Naw suh. Ah come wid jus' whut Ah stand in, 'cause Ah ain't got nothin' else, but Ah come."

Cy Perkins looked hard at the forlorn little figure. Lucy stood before him with her large bright eyes staring and not knowing she stared. Suddenly she sat down because she couldn't stand any more.

"Look like you're sick, Lucy."

"Mah troubles is inward. Mist' Perkins."

"Her new baby ain't but three days old," Duke volunteered.

Perkins fumbled with his papers, never looking at Lucy the while. John remained with head hung down and face averted except for one begging glance at Lucy. Finally the Justice of the Peace arose and beckoned Lucy into his back office.

"Don't try to stand up, Lucy. Set down before you fall down. It's too bad that you are out at a time like this. Listen, Lucy, this is serious. Your family is well thought of 'round here and lots of folks think John needs a good whipping before he goes to the gang. If he's got any friends he better call on 'em now. Tell you the truth, Lucy, if it wasn't for you, and me knowing your papa so well, I wouldn't have parted my lips, but your husband is in a mess of trouble."

"Thankee, Mist' Perkins. Ah got fo' li'l' chillun 'round mah feet; if dey send John off Ah don't know whut'll 'come uh us all."

"Have you been to Judge Alf yet?"

"Naw suh. Ah hates tuh go 'cause he done cautioned John good tuh behave hisself, but Ah reckon Ah better."

"Hurry across there to his office. I won't set court until you get back."

Lucy didn't come back. She all but collapsed on the steps of Pearson's office, and he sent her home in his buggy. Alf Pearson strode across to Perkins' office and asked that the prisoner be released in his charge and it was done. Weens was paid for his hog, but John was bound over to the big court for the assault upon his brother-in-law. There was a great deal of loud whispering about night-riders and the dark of midnight, but nobody touched John as he drove Judge Pearson home.

"John, I'm not going to ask you why you've done these things, partly because I already know, and partly because I don't believe you do."

"If Ah had uh knowed 'twuz gointer raise all dis rukus."

Alf laughed sardonically, "Of course you did not know. Because God has given to all men the gift of blindness. That is to say that He has cursed but few with vision. Ever hear tell of a happy prophet? This old world wouldn't roll on the way He started it if men could see. Ha! In fact I think God Himself was looking off when you went and got yourself born."

"Yes suh, Ah speck so."

They turned into the cedar-lined drive that led up to the big, columned veranda.

"John, distance is the only cure for certain diseases. Here's fifty dollars. There are lots of other towns in the world besides Notasulga, and there's several hours before midnight. I know a man who could put lots of distance between him and this place before time, even wearing his two best suits—one over the other. He wouldn't fool with baggage because it would hold him back. He would get to a railroad twenty-five or thirty miles off."

John assisted Alf Pearson to alight.

"Good bye, John. I know how to read and write and I believe Lucy does too."

He strode up the steps of his veranda very straight and stiff, as if he had an extra backbone in his back.

In the early black dark John was gone. Lucy feverishly peeped thru first one crack then another, watching up the big road after him.

"Lucy, whyn't you stay in dat bed?" Pheemy grumbled. "You look lak youse jes' determined tuh be down sick and Ah already got mah hands full wid dese chilluns."

"An' Pheemy, Ahm standin' on de watch wall. Reckon de patter rollers'll ketch 'im?"

"Lawd naw. He pitched out towards Chehaw and dem folks is in Notasulga waitin' fuh midnight."

The hours went past on their rusty ankles and midnight stood looking both ways for day.

"Hush!" said Lucy, "dey's comin'!"

Pheemy listened hard but couldn't hear a thing.

"Dat's all right, An' Pheemy, Ah don't zakly hear nothin' neither, but uh far uhway whisper look lak it's puttin' on flesh."

They stood peering for a quarter of an hour or more at the narrow slit of the big road visible from the cabin. Then sure enough as silently as horsemen can, rode twenty or thirty men in the cloud-muddied moonlight. Slowly, watchfully, as they passed the big gate that led to the quarters and on past the stately cedar drive.

"How come dey ain't turned in?" Lucy asked, a tremble.

"Dey ain't gwine set foot on Judge Alf Pearson's place, if dey run on 'im outside dey'd grab 'im. Dey might go in some folks' quarters, but 'tain't never no patter roller set foot on dis place. Dey know big wood from brush."

Pheemy told the truth, but she was only embolden to speak

100

after the last rider had passed the big gate, and faded into the distance.

"Maybe dey already got 'im."

"Aw naw, gal, g'wan tuh rest. Dey jes' bluffin' tuh skeer us black folks."

The next day Chuck Portlock met Alf Pearson and tried to say casually, "Say, Judge dey tell me dat nigger run off. You got any notion which way he went?"

"Afraid not, Chuck. I've treed many a coon in my time, but I don't believe I've got a drop of bloodhound in me."

CHAPTER 12

John's destination was purely accidental. When he came out upon the big road to Chehaw, he overtook another Negro. They hailed each other gladly in the early dawn.

"Where you bound fuh?" John asked.

"Tuh ketch me uh high henry."

"Whuss dat?"

"Uh railroad train, man, where you been all yo' days you don't know de name of uh train?"

"Oh, 'bout in spots and places. Where you bound fuh when you git on de train?"

"Tuh Florida, man. Dat's de new country openin' up. Now git me straight, Ah don't mean West Florida, Ah means de real place. Good times, good money, and no mules and cotton."

"B'lieve Ah'll go 'long wid yuh."

"Man, dat calls fuh more'n talk. Dat calls fuh money."

"How much?"

"Twenty odd dollars. 'Cordin' tuh where at you goin'."

"Where you goin'?"

"Tuh uh town called Sanford. Got uh sister dere. She keepin' uh boardin' house," he looked John over, "she's uh fine lookin', portly 'oman; you better come 'long."

"Um already married, thankee jes' de same. Man, Ah got uh putty 'oman. Li'l' bitsa thing. Ahm sho tuh send fuh her soon ez Ah git settled some place."

"Aw shucks man, you ain't lak me. Ah don't take no women no place. Ah lets every town furnish its own."

They bought their tickets and John sat in a railway coach for the first time in his life, though he hid this fact from his traveling mate. To him nothing in the world ever quite equalled that first ride on a train. The rhythmic stroke of the engine, the shiny-buttoned porter bawling out the stations, the even more begilded conductor, who looked more imposing even than Judge Pearson, and then the red plush splendor, the gaudy ceiling hung with glinting lamps, the long mournful howl of the whistle. John forgot the misery of his parting from Lucy in the aura of it all. That is, he only remembered his misery in short snatches, while the glory lay all over him for hours at the time. He marvelled that just anybody could come along and be allowed to get on such a glorified thing. It ought to be extra special. He got off the train at every stop so that he could stand off a piece and feast his eyes on the engine. The greatest accumulation of power that he had ever seen.

CHAPTER 13

As John and his mate stepped off the train at Sanford, they were met by a burly, red-faced white man who looked them over sharply—which gave them both the fidgets. Finally he asked, "Where y'all come from?"

"Up de road uh piece in Wes' Florduh," John's partner answered, much to his relief.

"Want work?"

"Ah kinda got uh job promised tuh me already," John's mate answered again.

"How 'bout you, Big Yaller?"

"Nawsuh, Ah ain't got no job. Ah would love tuh hear tell uh one."

"Come along then. Ever done any work on uh railroad?"

"Nawsuh, but Ah wants tuh try."

"Git yo duds then. We going over to Wildwood. Dollar a day. Seaboard puttin' thru uh spur."

That night John slept in the railroad camp and at sun-up he was swinging a nine-pound hammer and grunting over a lining bar.

The next day he wrote Lucy and sent her all of his ready money.

All day long it was strain, sweat and rhythm. When they were lining track the water-boy would call out, "Mr. Dugan!"

The straining men would bear down on the lining bars and grunt, "Hanh!"

"Hanh!"

"Got de number ten!"

"Hanh!"

"Got de pay-car!"

"Hanh!"

"On de rear end."

"Hanh!"

"Whyncher pick 'em up!"

"Hanh!"

"Set it over."

"Hanh!"

And the rail was in place. Sometimes they'd sing it in place, but with the same rhythm.

> When Ah get in Illinois
> Ahm gointer spread de news about de Floriduh boys
> Sho-ove it over
> Hey, hey, can't you live it?

Then a rhythmic shaking of the nine-hundred-pound rail by bearing down on the bars thrust under it in concert.

"Ahshack - uh - lack - uh - lack - uh - lack - uh - lack - uh - lack - uh - hanh!"

Rail in place.

"Hey, hey, can't you try?"

He liked spiking. He liked to swing the big snub-nosed hammer above his head and drive the spike home at a blow. And then the men had a song that called his wife's name and he liked that.

"Oh Lulu!"

"Hanh!" A spike gone home under John's sledge.

"Oh, oh, gal!"

"Hanh!"

"Want to see you!"

"Hanh!"

"So bad."

"Hanh!"

And then again it was fun in the big camp. More than a hundred hammer-muscling men, singers, dancers, liars, fighters, bluffers and lovers. Plenty of fat meat and beans, women flocking to camp on pay-day.

On Sunday John and his breaster went into town to church. The preacher snatched figure after figure from the land of images, and the church loved it all. Back in camp that night, John preached the sermon himself for the entertainment of the men who had stayed in camp and he aped the gestures of the preacher so accurately that the crowd hung half-way between laughter and awe.

"You kin mark folks," said Blue. "Dass jes' lak dat preacher fuh de world. Pity you ain't preachin' yo'self."

"Look, John," said his breaster, "dey's uh colored town out 'cross de woods uh piece—maybe fifteen tuh twenty miles, and dey's uh preacher—"

"You mean uh whole town uh nothin' but colored folks? Who bosses it, den?"

"Dey bosses it deyself."

"You mean dey runnin' de town 'thout de white folks?"

"Sho is. Eben got uh mayor and corporation."

"Ah sho wants tuh see dat sight."

"Dat's jes' whar Ah wants tuh take yuh nex' Sunday. Dey got uh Meth'dis' preacher over dere Ah wants yuh tuh mark. He talk thru his nose and he preaches all his sermons de same way. Sho would love tuh hear you mark 'im."

"Ah'll sho do it. Whut's de name uh dat town?"

"Eatonville, Orange County."

The Negro mayor filled John with almost as much awe as the train had. When he was leaving town that Sunday night he told his friend, "Ahm comin' back tuh dis place. Uh man kin be sumpin' heah 'thout folks tramplin' all over yuh. Ah wants mah wife and chillun heah."

There were many weeks between John and the little Negro village. He would resolve to move there on next pay-day, but trips to town, and visitors to camp defeated his plans.

But a letter from Lucy nerved him and he found work pruning orange trees in Maitland, the adjacent white town, and went to live in Eatonville.

He had meant to send for Lucy within the month, but one thing and another delayed him. One day, however, in a fit of remorse he went and drew down a month's wages in advance and sent the money to Judge Pearson for his wife because he was ashamed to write to her.

He was working for Sam Mosely, the second most prosperous man in Eatonville, and borrowed his team to meet Lucy at the train.

He wouldn't let her walk down the coach steps, but held wide his arms and made her jump into his bosom. He drove the one mile from the depot in Maitland to the heart of Eatonville with a wagon full of laughter and shouts of questions.

"Glad tuh see me, Lucy?" John asked as soon as he had loaded the battered tin trunk and the feather bed on the wagon and sprung into the driver's seat.

" 'Course, John."

"Is you only mouf glad or yuh sho nuff glad?"

"Sho nuff, but one time Ah thought you sho took uh long time tuh write tuh me and send fuh us."

"You looks lak new money 'round heah, honey. Ah'd send fuh you, if Ah didn't had bread tuh eat. Look how our li'l' gal done growed."

"Yeah she walkin' and talkin'. You been 'way from us might nigh uh yeah."

The children exclaimed at the fruit clustered golden among the dark glistening foilage.

"Ah got y'all plenty oranges at de house, y'all chaps. Yo' papa lookin' out fuh yuh."

"You got us uh house, John?" Lucy asked happily.

"Ah mean where Ah been stayin' at. Ah reckon us all kin git in dere."

" 'Tain't no mo' houses in town?"

"Yeah, two, three vacant, but us ain't got much money.

Sendin' fuh y'all and all, and den us ain't got nothin' tuh go in uh house but ourselves."

"Dat ain't nothin'. You go git us house of our own. 'Tain't nothin' lak being yo' own boss. Us kin sleep on de floor 'til we kin do better."

Lucy sniffed sweet air laden with night-blooming jasmine and wished that she had been born in this climate. She seemed to herself to be coming home. This was where she was meant to be. The warmth, the foliage, the fruits all seemed right and as God meant her to be surrounded. The smell of ripe guavas was new and alluring but somehow did not seem strange.

So that night John and his family were housekeeping again. John went to the woods at the edge of town and filled three crocus sacks with moss and each of the larger children had a sack apiece for a mattress. John and Lucy took the baby girl upon the feather mattress with them.

Next morning Lucy awoke at daylight and said to John in bed, "John, dis is uh fine place tuh bring up our chillun. Dey won't be seein' no other kind uh folks actin' top-superior over 'em and dat'll give'em spunk tuh be bell cows theyselves, and you git somethin' tuh do 'sides takin' orders offa other folks. Ah 'bominates dat."

"Whut's it goin' tuh be, Lucy?"

"You knows how tuh carpenter. Go ast who want uh house built, and den you take and do it. You kin prop up shacks jus' as good as some uh dem dat's doin' it."

And to John's surprise people wanted houses built all over Orange County. Central Florida was in the making.

"And now less don't pay Joe Clarke no mo' rent. Less buy dis place, John."

"Dat's uh bigger job than Ah wants tuh tackle, Lucy. You so big-eyed. Wese colored folks. Don't be so much-knowin'."

But the five acre plot was bought nevertheless, and John often sat on Joe Clarke's store porch and bragged about his determination to be a property owner.

"Aw, 'tain't you, Pearson," Walter Thomas corrected, "iss dat li'l' handful uh woman you got on de place."

109

"Yeah," Sam Mosely said earnestly, "Anybody could put hisself on de ladder wid her in de house. Dat's de very 'oman Ah been lookin' fuh all mah days."

"Yeah, but Ah seen uh first, Sam, so you might jus' ez well quit lookin'," John said and laughed.

"Oh Ah knows dat, John. 'Twon't do me no good tuh look, but yet and still it won't hurt me neither. You might up and die uh she might quit yuh and git uh sho nuff husband, and den she could switch uh mean Miss Johnson in dat big house on Mars Hill."

"Hold on dere uh minute, Sam," John retorted half in earnest amid the general laughter, "less squat dat rabbit and jump uhnother one. Anyhow mah house liable tuh be big ez your'n some uh dese days."

"Aw, he jes' jokin' yuh, Pearson," Joe Clarke, the mayor intervened, "I god, you takin' it serious."

When John got home that night Lucy was getting into bed. John stopped in the hallway and took his Winchester rifle down from the rack and made sure that it was loaded before he went into the bedroom, and sat on the side of the bed.

"Lucy, is you sorry you married me instid uh some big nigger wid uh whole heap uh money and titles hung on tuh him?"

"Whut make you ast me dat? If you tired uh me, jus' leave me. Another man over de fence waitin fuh yo' job."

John stood up, "Li'l' Bit, Ah ain't never laid de weight uh mah hand on you in malice. Ain't never raised mah hand tuh yuh eben when you gits mad and slaps mah jaws, but lemme tell you somethin' right now, and it ain't two, don't you never tell me no mo' whut you jus' tole me, 'cause if you do, Ahm goin' tuh kill yuh jes' ez sho ez gun is iron. Ahm de first wid you, and Ah means tuh be de last. Ain't never no man tuh breathe in yo' face but me. You hear me? Whut made you say dat nohow?"

"Aw, John, you know dat's jus' uh by-word. Ah hears all de women say dat."

"Yeah, Ah knows dat too, but *you* ain't tuh say it. Lemme

110

tell you somethin'. Don't keer whut come uh go, if you ever start out de door tuh leave me, you'll never make it tuh de gate. Ah means tuh blow yo' heart out and hang fuh it."

"You done—"

"Don't tell me 'bout dem trashy women Ah lusts after once in uh while. Dey's less dan leaves uh grass. Lucy do you still love me lak yuh useter?"

"Yeah John, and mo'. Ah got mo' tuh love yuh fuh now."

John said, "Neb mine mah crazy talk. Jus' you hug mah neck tight, Ah'd sweat in hell fuh yuh. Ah'd take uh job cleaning out de Atlantic Ocean jus' fuh yuh. Look lak Ah can't git useter de thought dat you married me, Lucy, and you got chillun by *me!*"

And he held Lucy tightly and thought pityingly of other men.

The very next Sunday he arose in Covenant Meeting and raised the song, "He's a Battle-Axe in de Time Uh Trouble," and when it was done he said, "Brothers and Sisters, Ah rise befo' yuh tuhday tuh tell yuh, God done called me tuh preach."

"Halleluyah! Praise de Lawd!"

"He called me long uhgo, but Ah wouldn't heed tuh de voice, but brothers and sisters, God done whipped me tuh it, and like Peter and Paul Ah means tuh preach Christ and Him crucified. He tole me tuh go, and He'd go with me, so Ah ast yo' prayers, Church, dat Ah may hold up de blood-stained banner of Christ and prove strong dat Ah may hold out tuh de end."

The church boiled over with approval, "Ah knowed it! Tole 'im long time uhgo dat's whut he wuz cut out fuh. Thang God. He's goin' tuh be uh battle-axe sho 'nuff—Hewin' down sinners tuh repentance."

His trial sermon had to be preached in a larger church—so many people wanted to hear him. He had a church to pastor before the hands had been laid on his head. The man who preached his ordination sermon was thrown in deep shadow by the man who was to be ordained.

The church he pastored at Ocoee did all they could to hold him, but the membership was less than a hundred. Zion Hope, of Sanford, membership three hundred, took him to her bosom, and her membership mounted every month.

John dumped a heavy pocketbook into Lucy's lap one Monday morning before he took off his hat.

Lucy praised him. "We goin' tuh finish payin' fuh dis place wid dis money. De nex' time, us buy de chillun some changin' clothes. You makin' good money now, John. Ah always knowed you wuz goin' tuh do good."

He wore the cloak of a cloud about his shoulders. He was above the earth. He preached and prayed. He sang and sinned, but men saw his cloak and felt it.

"Lucy, look lak Ah jus' found out whut Ah kin do. De words dat sets de church on fire comes tuh me jus' so. Ah reckon de angels must tell 'em tuh me."

"God don't call no man, John, and turn 'im loose uh fool. Jus' you handle yo' members right and youse goin' tuh be uh sho 'nuff big nigger."

"Ain't Ah treatin' 'em good, Lucy? Ah ain't had no complaints."

"Naw, you wouldn't hear no complaints 'cause you treatin' 'em too good. Don't pomp up dem deacons so much. Dey'll swell up and be de ruination of yuh. Much up de young folks and you got somebody tuh strain wid dem ole rams when dey git dey habits on. You lissen tuh me. Ah hauled de mud tuh make ole Cuffy. Ah know whuts in 'im.

"Don't syndicate wid none of 'em, do dey'll put yo' business in de street." Lucy went on, "Friend wid few. Everybody grin in yo' face don't love yuh. Anybody kin look and see and tell uh snake trail when dey come cross it but nobody kin tell which way he wuz goin' lessen he seen de snake. You keep outa sight, and in dat way, you won't give nobody uh stick tuh crack yo' head wid."

As he swaggered up to Joe Clarke's store porch in his new clothes, putting and taking with his yellow cane, Sam Mosely teased, "Well, John done got tuh be uh preacher."

"Yeah Ah is, and Ah ain't no stump-knocker neither. Ah kin go hard."

"Maybe so, John, but anybody kin preach. Hard work and hot sun done called uh many one. Anybody kin preach."

"Naw dey can't neither. Take you for instance."

"Don't want tuh. Ahm de mayor."

"You ain't goin' tuh be it after de 18th day of August. Watch and see."

"Who gointer be it; Joe Clarke? He said he wuzn't runnin'."

"Naw, Ahm gointer be de mayor."

"You runnin' fuh mayor?"

"Not now but Ahm goin' tuh run when de time come, and if you want tuh be mayor agin you better *run.* Don't fool wid it—run! Go hard uh go home. You and Clarke ain't had nobody tuh run against, but dis time big Moose done come down from de mountain. Ahm goin' tuh run you so hard 'til they can't tell yo' run-down shoe from yo' wore out sock."

General laughter.

"I God," Joe Clarke declared, "Ah never seen two sworn buddies dat tries tuh out do on 'nother lak y'all do. You so thick 'til one can't turn 'thout de other one, yet and still you always buckin' 'ginst each other."

" 'Tain't me," Sam Mosely defended, "Iss him, but he can't never ekal up tuh me 'cause Ah come heah from Wes' Flordah uh porpoise, but look whut Ah got now. Ahm uh self-made man."

"Ah come heah right out de tie woods in uh boot and uh shoe, but Ah got proppity too. Whut you goin' tuh call *me?*" He thrust out his chest.

"Uh wife-made man," Mosely retorted amid boisterous laughter, "if me and him wuz tuh swap wives Ah'd go past 'im so fast you'd think it wuz de A.C.L. passin' uh gopher."

"Better say joe, 'cause you don't know. Anyhow when you run for mayor next time git ready tuh take yo' whippin'. De time done come when big britches goin' tuh fit li'l' Willie."

And Rev. Pearson did win. He was swept into office by the

113

overwhelming majority of seventeen to three.

"Tell yuh how yuh beat me, John," Mosely said on the store porch that night, "course 'twan't fair, but it wuz de way you and Lucy led de gran' march night 'fo' las' at de hall, but by rights uh preacher ain't got no business dancin'."

"Grand marchin' ain't dancin'. Ah never cut uh step."

"Dat's right too, y'all," Joe Lindsay put in, "you ain't dancin' 'til yuh cross yo' feet, but Rev. John, no sinner man couldn't uh led dat march no better'n you and Lucy. Dat li'l' 'oman steps it lightly, slightly and politely."

"Tuh make short talk outa long," added Walter Thomas, "Sam, youse uh good man. Ah don't know no better conditioned man in dese parts. Yo' morals is clean ez uh fish—and he been in bathin' all his life, but youse too dry fuh de mayor business. Jes' lak it 'twuz wid Saul and David."

Lucy was going to have another baby and in her condition she missed John a lot. Now that he was called here and there over the state to conduct revivals, she knew that he must go. She was glad to see him in new suits that his congregation proudly bestowed upon him without his asking. She loved to see him the center of admiring groups. She loved to hear him spoken of as "The Battle-Axe." She even loved his primitive poetry and his magnificent pulpit gestures, but, even so, a little cold feeling impinged upon her antennae. There was another woman.

Time and time over the dish-pan, she'd find herself talking aloud.

"Lawd lemme quit feedin' on heart meat lak Ah do. Dis baby goin' tuh be too fractious tuh live." And then again, "Lawd, if Ah meet dat woman in heben, you got tuh gimme time tuh fight uh while. Jus' ruin dis baby's temper 'fo' it git tuh dis world. 'Tain't mah fault, Lawd, Ahm jus' ez clean ez yo' robes."

This was her second baby since coming to Florida, and she remembered how happy he had been at the coming of the fourth boy. A new baby might change things, perhaps, and she was right. When the new little girl was a month old, he took the lacy, frilly little bundle out of Lucy's arms and carried it out to the waiting horse and buggy.

"You ain't got time tuh fool wid dat youngun, John. You goin' up tuh Sanford tuh preach, ain't yuh?"

"Yeah, and de church got tuh see dis baby. Dis is sho mah work. De very spit uh me. 'Cep'n—"

" 'Cep'n what? Dem sho yo' gray eyes."

"Dey ain't whut Ah wuz fixin' tuh say. Dat's mah eye color alright but her eyes look at yuh lak she know sumpin. Anybody'd think she's grown. Wonder whut she thinkin' 'bout?"

"Take uh God tuh tell. Ah toted de rest uh de chillun in mah belly, but dat one wuz bred in mah heart. She bound tuh be diffunt."

"Git yo' things on, Lucy, and come on tuh Sanford wid me. De church ain't seen mah wife in six months. Put on dat li'l' red dress and come switchin' up de aisle and set on de front seat so you kin be seen. Ahm goin' tuh tote de baby, lessen you want me tuh tote bofe of yuh."

"Go 'way, Ah don't hafta wear dat ole red dress 'cause Ah got uh brand new princess, laced down de back wid uh silk cord wid tassels on it."

With her bangs above her shining eyes and the door-knob knot of hair at the back, Lucy sat on that front seat in church and felt a look strike her in the back and slide off helplessly. Her husband's glance fell on her like dew. Her look and nobody else's was in his gray eyes, and the coldness melted from the pit of her stomach, and at the end of the sermon John came down from the pulpit and took the baby from her arms and standing just before the pulpit proudly and devotedly called, "Come heah eve'ybody, one at de time and pass by and look on yo' pastor's baby girl chile. Ah could shout tuhday." And they came.

There came other times of cold feelings and times of triumphs. Only the coldnesses grew numerous.

Once she had sent him off to Alabama when she felt such a coldness that it laid her in a sick-bed. She knew that the glory of his broadcloth and Stetson would humble Bud, chagrin old

115

Ned and make Amy happy, and in his present glory the "leaf of grass" would wither. Lucy prayed often now, but sometimes God was tired and slept a little and didn't hear her. Maybe He had other Johns somewhere that needed His ear, but Lucy didn't get too tired. She didn't worry God too much. She had her husband and seven children now and her hands were kept busy. John had to be pushed and shoved and there was no one to do it but Lucy.

There came the day, with Lucy's maneuvering, when John stood up in the State Association and was called Moderator. "Wisht ole Ned and Bud could see me now," John gloated, "always makin' out Ah wuzn't goin' tuh be nothin'. Ah uh big nigger now. Ain't Ah Lucy?"

"You sho is. All you got tuh do now is tuh *ack* lak one."

"Don't you reckon Ah know how tuh ack, Lucy? You ain't out dere wid Brown and Battle and Ford and all dem big mens, lak Ah is. You always tryin' tuh tell me whut tuh do. Ah wouldn't be where Ah is, if Ah didn't know no more'n you think Ah do. You ain't mah guardzeen nohow."

John strode off in his dark blue broadcloth, his hand-made alligator shoes, and his black Stetson, and left Lucy sitting on their porch. The blue sky looked all wrinkled to Lucy thru the tears.

And soon Lucy knew who the woman was, and once or twice the thought troubled her that John knew she knew, but didn't care.

One night as she sang the sleep song to the younger children she noticed a sallow listlessness in Isis, her younger girl. The next day she knew it was typhoid. For a week she fought it alone. John was down the East Coast running a revival and didn't come at once. When he did come, the doctor said, "Well, Reverend, I'm glad you're here. If she can last 'til midnight she's got a chance to get over it, but—but I doubt if she will live 'til dark."

The restrained Lucy stood at the far side of the bed looking at her child, looking at John. The agony of the moment sweated great drops from his forehead. He would have fallen on the bed but Lucy led him outside.

"Ah can't stand 'round and see mah baby girl die. Lucy! Lucy! God don't love me. Ah got tuh go 'way 'til it's all over. Ah jus' can't stay."

So John fled to Tampa away from God, and Lucy stayed by the bedside alone. He was gutted with grief, but when Hattie Tyson found out his whereabouts and joined him, he suffered it, and for some of his hours he forgot about the dying Isis, but when he returned a week later and found his daughter feebly recovering, he was glad. He brought Lucy a new dress and a pineapple.

CHAPTER 14

People in Sanford began to call Lucy aside. There was much under-voice mention of Hattie Tyson, Oviedo and shame, Gussie, Tillie, Della, church court, making changes in the pulpit and monthly conference.

"John," Lucy began abruptly one day, "you kin keep from fallin' in love wid *anybody,* if you start in time."

"Now whut you drivin' at?"

"You either got tuh stop lovin' Hattie Tyson uh you got tuh stop preachin'. Dat's whut de people say."

"Ah don't love no Hattie Tyson. De niggers lyin' on me."

"Maybe so, but if you don't you oughta stay from 'round her. Ah done seen de green tree ketch on fire, so you know uh dry one will burn."

"Lawd how some folks kin lie! Dey don't wait tuh find out a thing. Some of 'em so expert on mindin' folks' business dat dey kin look at de smoke comin' out yo' chimbley and tell yuh whut yuh cookin'."

"Yo' church officers is talkin' it too, John."

"Sho 'nuff, Lucy?"

"Dey talkin' 'bout settin' you down."

"Lawd have mussy! You ain't 'ginst me too, is yuh Lucy?"

"Naw, Ah'll never be 'ginst yuh, John, but Ah did thought you done strayed off and don't love me no mo'."

"You musta thought it, Lucy, 'cause nobody sho didn't tell yuh. If you don't know, ast somebody."

"John, now don't you go 'round dat church mealy-moufin 'round dem deacons and nobody else. Don't you break uh breath on de subjick. Face 'em out, and if dey wants tuh handle yuh in conference, go dere totin' uh high head and Ah'll be right dere 'long side of yuh."

Conference night came and the church was full. It was evident that the entire congregation was keyed up. The routine business was gotten out of the way quickly. Beulah Tansill flung her low look at the pastor and then at Deacon Tracy Patton. Deacon Patton cleared his throat and did a great deal of head scratching. The look on the pastor's face didn't seem to belong there. It was bold and unusual. It sort of dared him and the words he had brought there with him wouldn't slide off his tongue. He scratched his head some more. He had stirred up the side front the first time, he tried the opposite side back.

"Uh, ruh, uh ruh, any onfinished business?" prompted Deacon Harris.

Deacon Patton almost rose that time. Another look at Pearson and Lucy and he laid down his hat and scratched with both hands. Gave his entire head a thorough scratching and held his mouth open in sympathy.

"Shet yo' mouf, Tracy Patton!" Sister Berry cautioned. "De flies will blow yo' liver tuhreckly."

"Shet your'n. You tries tuh be so much-knowin'. You got tuh learn how tuh speak when you spokin to, come when youse called."

"Ah ain't got tuh do but two things—stay black and die," Sister Berry snapped.

"Less stand adjourned," Deacon Harris hurried, "us don't want no fight."

That was as far as the conference went. The Chairman realized that the Chief spokesman was not going to speak, hastily adjourned, hoping that Beulah and Tracy wouldn't implicate him if they talked it. He made it his business to walk home with the pastor and drop a defensive suggestion in his ear in advance.

"Rev. Ahm diggin' mah sweet pitaters tuhmorrer. Goin' tuh bring you some too."

"Thanks, Aleck. Mah wife and chillun all loves dem good ole yeller yams, good ez Ah do."

"Dey sho gointer git some. Look heah, Elder Pearson Ah reckon you done heard dat some dese niggers is throwin' lies 'bout you and some woman over 'bout Oviedo. Ah ain't tole yuh nothin', and you be keerful uh dese folks dat totes yuh news. Uh dog dat'll bring uh bone will keep one. You know dat's de truth. Good night."

John had read the hostility in the meeting and his relief at his temporary deliverance was great. He said nothing to his wife, but he bought a dozen mangoes and thrust the bag into her hand.

As they undressed for bed Lucy asked in a matter of fact tone, "Whut tex' you goin' tuh preach on Sunday comin'?"

"Iss Communion so Ah reckon Ah'll preach de Passover Supper in de upper room."

"Don't you preach it. Dis thing ain't thru wid yit. 'Tain't never goin' tuh be finished 'til you tackle dey feelings and empty out dey hearts—do, it'll lay dere and fester and after while it would take God hisself tuh clean up de mess."

"Whut mo' kin Ah do? Ah wuz dere fuh dem tuh handle me and dey didn't do it."

"Dat wuz 'cause de folks didn't have no leader. They wuz plenty fight in dere. All dey needed wuz uh lead hound. You git yo'self out dey mouf and stay out of it, hear me?"

"Whut mus' Ah do?"

"You preach uh sermon on yo'self, and you call tuh they remembrance some uh de good things you done, so they kin put it long side de other and when you lookin' at two things at de same time neither one of 'em don't look so big, but don't tell uh lie, John. If youse guilty you don't need tuh git up dere and put yo' own name on de sign post uh scorn, but don't say you didn't do it neither. Whut you say, let it be de truth. Dat what comes from de heart will sho reach de heart agin."

"Mah chillun, Papa Pearson don't feel lak preachin' y'all tuh-day," he began on Sunday after he had sung a song, "y'all been looking at me fuh eight years now, but look lak some uh y'all been lookin' on me wid unseein' eye. When Ah speak tuh yuh from dis pulpit, dat ain't me talkin', dat's de voice uh God speakin' thru me. When de voice is thew, Ah jus' uhnother one uh God's crumblin' clods. Dere's seben younguns at mah house and Ah could line 'em all up in de courthouse and swear tuh eve'yone of 'em, Ahm uh natchel man but look lak some uh y'all is dumb tuh de fack.

"Course, mah children in Christ, Ah been here wid y'all fuh eight years and mo'. Ah done set by yo' bedside and buried de dead and joined tuhgether de hands uh de livin', but Ah ain't got no remembrance. Don't keer if Ah laugh, don't keer if Ah cry, when de sun, wid his blood red eye, go intuh his house at night, he takes all mah remembrance wid 'im, but some yuh y'all dat got remembrance wid such long tangues dat it kin talk tuh yuh at a distance, when y'all is settin' down and passin' nations thew yo' mouf, look close and see if in all mah doin's if dere wuz anything good mingled up uhmoungst de harm Ah done yuh. Ah ain't got no mind. Y'all is de one dat is so much-knowin' dat you kin set in judgment.

"Maybe y'all got yo' right hand uh fellership hid behind yuh. De Lawd's supper is heah befo' us on de table. Maybe mah hands ain't tuh break de bread fuh yuh, maybe mah hands ain't tuh tetch de cup no mo'. So Ahm comin' down from de pulpit and Ah ain't never goin' back lessen Ah go wid yo' hearts keepin' comp'ny wid mine and yo' fire piled on mah fire, heapin' up."

He closed the great Bible slowly, passed his handkerchief across his face and turned from the pulpit, but when he made to step down, strong hands were there to thrust him back. The church surged up, a weeping wave about him. Deacons Hambo and Harris were the first to lay hands upon him. His

122

weight seemed nothing in many hands while he was roughly, lovingly forced back into his throne-like seat.

After a few minutes of concerted weeping, he moved down to the Communion table and in a feeling whisper went thru the sacrifice of a God.

CHAPTER 15

An' Dangie Dewoe's hut squatted low and peered at the road from behind a mass of Palma Christi and elderberry. The little rag-stuffed windows hindered the light and the walls were blackened with ancient smoke.

She had thrown several stalks of dried rabbit tobacco on the fire for power and sat with her wrinkled old face pursed up like a black fist, watching the flames.

Three quick sharp raps on the door.

"Who come?"

"One."

"Come on in, Hattie." As the woman entered An' Dangie threw some salt into the flame without so much as a look at her visitor. "Knowed you'd be back. Set down."

Hattie sat a moment impatiently, then she looked anxiously at An' Dangie and said, "He ain't been."

"He will. Sich things ez dat takes time. Did yuh feed 'im lak Ah tole yuh?"

"Ain't laid eyes on 'im in seben weeks. How Ahm goin' do it?"

"Hm-m-m." She struggled her fatness up from the chair and limped over to an old tin safe in the corner. She fumbled with the screw top of a fruit jar and returned with a light handful of wish-beans. "Stan' over de gate whar he sleeps and eat dese

125

beans and drop de hulls 'round yo' feet. Ah'll do de rest."

"Lawd, An' Dangie, dere' uh yard full uh houn' dawgs and chillun. Eben if none uh dem chillun see me, de dawgs gwine bark. Ah wuz past dere one day 'thout stoppin'."

"G'wan do lak Ah tell yuh. Ahm gwine hold de bitter bone in mah mouf so's you kin walk out de sight uh men. You bound tuh come out more'n conquer. Jes' you pay me whut Ah ast and 'tain't nothin' built up dat Ah can't tear down."

"Ah know you got de power."

"Humph! Ah reckon Ah is. Y' ever hear 'bout me boilin' uh wash-pot on uh sail needle?"

"Yas ma'am and mo' besides."

"Well don't come heah doubtin' lak you done jes' now. Aw right, pay me and g'wan do lak Ah tell yuh."

Hattie took the knotted handkerchief out of her stocking and paid. As she reached the door, the old woman called after her, " 'Member now, you done started dis and it's got tuh be kep' up do hit'll turn back on yuh."

"Yas'm."

The door slammed and An' Dangie crept to her altar in the back room and began to dress candles with war water. When the altar had been set, she dressed the coffin in red, lit the inverted candles on the altar, saying as she did so, "Now fight! Fight and fuss 'til you part." When all was done at the altar she rubbed her hands and forehead with war powder, put the catbone in her mouth, and laid herself down in the red coffin facing the altar and went into the spirit.

CHAPTER 16

Lucy was lying sick. The terrible enemy had so gnawed away her lungs that her frame was hardly distinguishable from the bed things.

"Isie?"

"Yes ma'am."

"Come give mama uh dose uh medicine."

"Yes'm."

The skinny-legged child of nine came bringing a cheap glass pitcher of water. "Ah pumped it off so it would be cool and nice fuh yuh."

"Thankee, Isie. Youse mah chile 'bove all de rest. Yo' pa come yet?"

"Yes'm, he out 'round de barn somewhere."

"Tell 'im Ah say tuh step heah uh minute."

John Pearson crossed the back porch slowly and heavily and entered the bedroom with downcast eyes.

"Whut you want wid me, Lucy?"

"Here 'tis Wednesday and you jus' gittin' home from Sanford, and know Ahm at uh mah back too. You know dat Hezekiah and John is uhway in school up tuh Jacksonville, and dese other chillun got tuh make out de bes' dey kin. You ought tuh uh come on home Monday and seen after things."

He looked sullenly at the floor and said nothing. Lucy used her spit cup and went on.

"Know too Ahm sick and you been home fuh de las' longest and ain't been near me tuh offer me uh cup uh cool water uh ast me how Ah feel."

"Oh you sick, sick, sick! Ah hates tuh be 'round folks always complainin', and then again you always doggin' me 'bout sumpin'. Ah gits sick and tired uh hearing it!"

"Well, John, you puts de words in mah mouf. If you'd stay home and look after yo' wife and chillun, Ah wouldn't have nothin' tuh talk uhbout."

"Aw, yes you would! Always jawin' and complainin'."

Lucy said, "If you keep ole Hattie Tyson's letters out dis house where mah chillun kin git holt of 'em and you kin stop folkses mouf by comin' on home instid uh layin' 'round wid her in Oviedo."

"Shet up! Ahm sick an' tired uh you' yowin' and jawin'. 'Tain't nothin' Ah hate lak gittin' sin throwed in mah face dat done got cold. Ah do ez Ah please. You jus' uh hold-back tuh me nohow. Always sick and complainin'. Uh man can't utilize hisself."

He came to the bed and stood glaring down upon her. She seemed not to notice and said calmly after a short pause, "Ahm glad tuh know dat, John. After all dese years and all dat done went on dat Ah ain't been nothin' but uh stumblin'-stone tuh yuh. Go 'head on, Mister, but remember—youse born but you ain't dead. 'Tain't nobody so slick but whut they kin stand uh 'nother greasin'. Ah done told yuh time and time uhgin dat ignorance is de hawse dat wisdom rides. Don't git miss-put on yo' road. God don't eat okra."

"Oh you always got uh mouf full uh opinions, but Ah don't need you no mo' nor nothing you got tuh say, Ahm uh man grown. Don't need no guardzeen atall. So shet yo' mouf wid me."

"Ah ain't going' tuh hush nothin' uh de kind. Youse livin' dirty and Ahm goin' tuh tell you 'bout it. Me and mah chillun got some rights. Big talk ain't changin' whut you doin'. You can't clean yo'self wid yo' tongue lak uh cat."

There was a resounding smack. Lucy covered her face with her hand, and John drew back in a sort of horror, and instantly strove to remove the brand from his soul by words, "Ah tole yuh tuh hush." He found himself shaking as he backed towards the door.

"De hidden wedge will come tuh light some day, John. Mark mah words. Youse in de majority now, but God sho don't love ugly."

John shambled out across the back porch, and stood for an unknowing time among the palmetto bushes in a sweating daze feeling like Nebuchadnezer in his exile.

Lucy turned her face to the wall and refused her supper that her older daughter Emmeline cooked and that Isis brought to her.

"But mama, you said special you wanted some batter-cakes."

"You eat 'em, Isie. Mama don't want uh thing. Come on in when you thru wid yo' supper lak you always do and read mama something out yo' reader."

But Isis didn't read. Lucy lay so still that she was frightened. She turned down the lamp by the head of the bed and started to leave, but Lucy stopped her.

"Thought you was sleep, mama."

"Naw, Isie, been watchin' dat great big ole spider."

"Where?"

"Up dere on de wall next tuh de ceilin'. Look lak he done took up uh stand."

"Want me tuh kill 'im wid de broom?"

"Naw, Isie, let 'im be. You didn't put 'im dere. De one dat put 'im dere will move 'im in his own time."

Isis could hear the other children playing in the back room.

"Reckon you wanta go play wid de rest, Isie, but mama wants tuh tell yuh somethin'."

"Whut is it, mama?"

"Isie, Ah ain't goin' tuh be wid yuh much longer, and when Ahm dead Ah wants you tuh have dis bed. Iss mine. Ah sewed

129

fuh uh white woman over in Maitland and she gimme dis bedstead fuh mah work. Ah wants you tuh have it. Dis mah feather tick on here too."

"Yes'm mama, Ah—"

"Stop cryin', Isie, you can't hear whut Ahm sayin', 'member tuh git all de education you kin. Dat's de onliest way you kin keep out from under people's feet. You always strain tuh be de bell cow, never be de tail uh nothin'. Do de best you kin, honey, 'cause neither yo' paw nor dese older chillun is goin' tuh be bothered too much wid yuh, but you goin' tuh git 'long. Mark mah words. You got de spunk, but mah po' li'l' sandy-haired chile goin' suffer uh lot 'fo' she git tuh de place she kin 'fend fuh herself. And Isie, honey, stop cryin' and lissen tuh me. Don't you love nobody better'n you do yo'self. Do, you'll be dying befo' yo' time is out. And, Isie, uh person kin be killed 'thout being stuck un blow. Some uh dese things Ahm tellin' yuh, you wont understand 'em fuh years tuh come, but de time will come when you'll know. And Isie, when Ahm dyin' don't you let 'em take de pillow from under mah head, and be covering up de clock and de lookin' glass and all sich ez dat. Ah don't want it done, heah? Ahm tellin' you in prefer-ence tuh de rest 'cause Ah know you'll see tuh it. Go wash yuh face and turn tuh de Twenty-Sixth Chapter of de Acts fuh me. Den you go git yo' night rest. If Ah want yuh, Ah'll call yuh."

Way in the night Lucy heard John stealthily enter the room and stand with the lamp in his hand peering down into her face. When she opened her eyes she saw him start.

"Oh," he exclaimed sharply with rising inflection. Lucy searched his face with her eyes but said nothing.

"Er, er, Ah jus' thought Ah'd come see if you wanted anything," John said nervously, "if you want anything, Lucy, all you got tuh do is tuh ast me. De favor is in me."

Lucy looked at her husband in a way that stepped across the ordinary boundaries of life and said, "Jus' have patience, John, uh few mo' days," and pulled down her lids over her eyes, and John was glad of that.

John rushed from Lucy's bedside to the road and strode up

and down in the white moonlight. Finally he took his stand beneath the umbrella tree before the house and watched the dim light in Lucy's room. Nothing came to him there and he awoke Emmeline at daybreak, "Go in yo' ma's room Daught' and come back and tell me how she makin' it."

"She say she ain't no better," Daught' told him.

The spider was lower on the wall and Lucy entertained herself by watching to see if she could detect it move.

She sent Isis to bed early that Thursday night but she herself lay awake regarding the spider. She thought that she had not slept a moment, but when in the morning Isis brought the wash basin and tooth brush, Lucy noted that the spider was lower and she had not seen it move.

That afternoon Mrs. Mattie Clarke sat with her and sent Isis out to play.

"Lucy, how is it 'tween you and God?"

"You know Ah ain't never been one to whoop and holler in church, Sister Clarke, but Ah done put on de whole armor uh faith. Ah ain't afraid tuh die."

"Ahm sho glad tuh hear dat, Sister Pearson. Yuh know uh person kin live uh clean life and den dey kin be so fretted on dey dyin' bed 'til dey lose holt of de kingdom."

"Don't worry 'bout me, Sister Clarke. Ah done been in sorrow's kitchen and Ah done licked out all de pots. Ah done died in grief and been buried in de bitter waters, and Ah done rose agin from de dead lak Lazarus. Nothin' kin touch mah soul no mo'. It wuz hard tuh loose de string-holt on mah li'l' chillun." Her voice sank to a whisper, "But Ah reckon Ah done dat too."

"Put whip tuh yo' hawses, honey. Whip 'em up."

Despite Lucy's all-night vigil she never saw the spider when he moved, but at first light she noted that he was at least a foot from the ceiling but as motionless as a painted spider in a picture.

The evening train brought her second son, John, from Jacksonville. Lucy brightened.

"Where's Hezekiah?" she asked eagerly.

131

"He's comin'. His girl is gointer sing uh solo at de church on Sunday and he wants to hear her. Then he's coming right on. He told me to wire him how you were."

"Don't do it, John. Let 'im enjoy de singin'."

John told her a great deal about the school and the city and she listened brightly but said little.

After that look in the late watches of the night John was afraid to be alone with Lucy. His fear of her kept him from his bed at night. He was afraid lest she should die while he was asleep and he should awake to find her spirit standing over him. He was equally afraid of her reproaches should she live, and he was troubled. More troubled than he had ever been in all his life. In all his struggles of sleep, the large bright eyes looked thru and beyond him and saw too much. He wished those eyes would close and was afraid again because of his wish.

Lucy watched the spider each day as it stood lower. And late Sunday night she cried out, "O Evening Sun, when you git on de other side, tell mah Lawd Ahm here waitin'."

And God awoke at last and nodded His head.

In the morning she told Emmeline to fry chicken for dinner. She sent Isis out to play. "You been denyin' yo' pleasure fuh me. G'wan out and play wid de rest. Ah'll call yuh if Ah want yuh. Tell everybody tuh leave me alone. Ah don't want no bother. Shet de door tight."

She never did call Isis. Late in the afternoon she saw people going and coming, coming and going. She was playing ball before the house, but she became alarmed and went in.

The afternoon was bright and a clear light streamed into the room from the bare windows. They had turned Lucy's bed so that her face was to the East. The way from which the sun comes walking in red and white. Great drops of sweat stood out on her forehead and trickled upon the quilt and Isis saw a pool of sweat standing in a hollow at the elbow. She was breathing hard, and Isis saw her set eyes fasten on her as she came into the room. She thought that she tried to say something to her as she stood over her mother's head, weeping with her heart.

"Get her head offa dat pillow!" Mattie Mosely ordered. "Let her head down so she kin die easy."

Hoyt Thomas moved to do it, but Isis objected. "No, no, don't touch her pillow! Mama don't want de pillow from under her head!"

"Hush Isie!" Emmeline chided, "and let mama die easy. You makin' her suffer."

"Naw, naw! she said *not* tuh!" As her father pulled her away from her place above Lucy's head, Isis thought her mother's eyes followed her and she strained her ears to catch her words. But none came.

John stood where he could see his wife's face, but where Lucy's fixed eyes might not rest upon him. They drew the pillow from beneath Lucy's head and she gulped hard once, and was dead. "6:40" someone said looking at a watch.

"Po' thing," John wept. "She don't have tuh hear no mo' hurtin' things." He hurried out to the wood pile and sat there between two feelings until Sam Mosely led him away.

"She's gone!" rang out thru the crowded room and they heard it on the porch and Mattie Mosely ran shouting down the street, "She's gone, she's gone at last!"

And the work of the shrouding began. Little Lucy, somewhat smaller in death than she had been even in life, lay washed and dressed in white beneath a sheet upon the cooling board when her oldest son arrived that evening to break his heart in grief.

That night a wind arose about the house and blew from the kitchen wall to the clump of oleanders that screened the chicken house, from the oleanders to the fence palings and back again to the house wall, and the pack of dogs followed it, rearing against the wall, leaping and pawing the fence, howling, barking and whining until the break of day, and John huddled beneath his bed-covers shaking and afraid.

CHAPTER 17

They put Lucy in a little coffin next day, the shiny coffin that held the beginning and the ending of so much. And the September woods were ravished by the village to provide tight little bouquets for the funeral. Sam Mosely, tall, black and silent, hitched his bays to his light wagon and he bore Lucy from her house and children and husband and worries to the church, while John, surrounded by his weeping family, walked after the wagon, shaking and crying. The village came behind and filled the little church with weeping and wild-flowers. People were stirred. The vital Lucy was gone. The wife of Moderator Pearson was dead.

"There is rest for the weary" rose and fell like an organ. Harmony soaked in tears.

"She don't need me no mo' nohow," John thought defensively.

"On the other side of Jordan, in the sweet fields of Eden—where the tree of life is blooming—"

And the hot blood in John's veins made him deny kinship with any rider of the pale white horse of death.

"Man born of woman has but a few days."

Clods of damp clay falling hollowly on the box. Out of sight of the world, and dead men heard her secrets.

That night they sat in the little parlor about the organ and the older children sang songs while the smaller ones cried and whimpered on. John sat a little apart and thought. He was free. He was sad, but underneath his sorrow was an exultation like a live coal under gray ashes. There was no longer guilt. But a few days before he had shuddered at the dread of discovery and of Lucy's accusing eye. There was no more sin. Just a free man having his will of women. He was glad in his sadness.

The next day John Pearson and Sam Mosely met on Clarke's porch. Sam remarked, "Funny thing, ain't it John—Lucy come tuh town twelve years uhgo in mah wagon and mah wagon took her uhway."

"Yeah, but she b'longed tuh me, though, all de time," John said and exulted over his friend.

CHAPTER 18

Deacons Hambo, Watson, Hoffman and Harris waited
on Rev. Pearson in his study at the parsonage.

"No mealy-moufin', Harris. No whippin' de Devil
'round de stump. He got tuh be told." Hambo urged.

"Ahm goin' tuh tell 'im how we feel. You too hot tuh talk.
You ain't in yo' right mind."

"Oh yes, Ah is too, Ahm hot, though. Ahm hot ez July jam.
Jee-esus Christ!"

John entered the room radiating cheer.

"Hello, boys. How yuh do?"

"Don't do all dey say, but Ah do mah share," said Hambo
quickly, "and damned if you don't do yourn."

Pearson didn't know whether it was one of the bluff
Hambo's jokes or not. He started to laugh, then looked at the
men's faces and quit.

"Oh."

"Now lemme handle dis, Hambo, lak we said," begged
Harris.

"Naw, lemme open mah mouf 'fo' Ah bust mah gall. John,
is you married tuh dat Hattie Tyson?"

"Yeah."

"DeG—D—hell you is, man! Yo' wife ain't been dead but

three months, and you done jumped up and married befo' she got col' in her grave!"

"Ah got dese li'l' chillun and somebody got tuh see after 'em."

"Well de somebody you got sho ain't seein' after 'em. They's 'round de streets heah jes' ez raggedy ez jay-birds in whistlin' time. Dey sho ain't gittin' uh damn bit uh 'tention."

"Course Ah didn't marry her jus' tuh wait on de chillun. She got tuh have some pleasure."

"Course she is! Dat strumpet ain't never done nothin' but run up and down de road from one sawmill camp tuh de other and from de looks of her, times was hard. She ain't never had nothin'—not eben doodly-squat, and when she gits uh chance tuh git holt uh sumpin de ole buzzard is gone on uh rampage. She ain't got dis parsonage and dem po' li'l' motherless chillun tuh study 'bout."

"Hold on dere, Hambo, y'all. Dat's mah wife."

"Sh-h-ucks! Who don't know dat Hattie Tyson! Ah ain't gonna bite mah tongue uh damn bit and if you don't lak it, you kin jus' try me wid yo' fist. Ahm three times seben and uh button! And whut makes me mad 'nough tuh fight uh circle-saw is, you don't want uh yo'self. You done got trapped and you ain't got de guts tuh take uh rascal-beater and run her 'way from here. She done moved you 'way from Eatonville 'cause 'tain't 'nough mens and likker dere tuh suit her."

"Wait uh minute, Hambo."

"Ain't gonna wait nothin' uh de kind. Wait broke de wagon down. Ah jes' feel lak takin' uh green club and waitin' on dat wench's head until she acknowledge Ahm God and besides me there's no other! Gimme lief, John, and Ah'll make haste and do it. Ah feels lak stayin' wid yo' head uh week. Dey tell me you eben drawed uh knife on yo' son John, 'cause he tried tuh keep dah strumpet out his mama's feather bed dat she give tuh li'l' Isis on her death-bed, and nobody but uh lowdown woman would want you scornin' yo' name all up lak dat."

Pearson hung his head.

"If y'all come heah tuh 'buke me, g'wan do it."

Hoffman spoke up.

"We ain't come to 'buke you, Reverend, but de church sho is talkin' and gittin' onrestless 'bout yo' marriage."

"Yeah, dat's jus' whut Ah come fuh—tuh 'buke yuh. Ah ain't come tuh make yuh no play-party. Stoopin' down from where you stand, fuh whut?" Hambo broke out again, "Jus 'cause you never seen no talcum powder and silk kimonos back dere in Alabama."

Harris and Hoffman took him by the arms and led him forth, and John went back upstairs and wept.

Hattie had heard it all, but she stayed out of sight until the rough tongued Hambo was gone. She went to John, but first she combed her hair and under-braided the piece of John-de-conquer root in her stiff back hair. "Dey can't move me—not wid de help Ah got," she gloated and went in to John where he lay weeping.

"Thought you tole me dat Hambo wuz yo' bosom friend?"

"He is, Hattie. Ah don't pay his rough talk no mind."

"Ah don't call dat no friend—comin' right in yo' house and talkin' 'bout yo' wife lak she wuz uh dog. If you wuz any kind of uh man you wouldn't 'low it."

"Uh preacher can't be fightin' and keerin' on. Mo' special uh Moderator. Hambo don't mean no harm. He jus' 'fraid de talk might hurt me."

"Him and them sho treats me lak uh show man treats uh ape. Come right in mah house and run de hawg over me and tryin' tuh put you 'ginst me. Youse over dem and you ought not tuh 'low 'em tuh cheap, but 'stid uh dat they comes right to yo' face and calls yo' wife uh barrel uh dem things. Lawd knows Ah ain't got no puhtection uh tall! If Miss Lucy had tuh swaller all Ah does, Ah know she glad she dead."

"Lucy ain't never had nobody to call her out her name. Dey better not. Whut make *you* call her name? Hambo is de backbone uh mah church. Ah don't aim to tear de place tuh pieces fuh nobody. Put dat in yo' pipe and smoke it."

Hattie heard and trembled. The moment that John left town to conduct a revival meeting, she gathered what money she could and hurried to the hut of An' Dangie Dewoe.

CHAPTER 19

The Lord of the wheel that turns on itself slept, but the world kept spinning, and the troubled years sped on. Tales of weakness, tales of vice hung about John Pearson's graying head. Tales of wifely incontinence which Zion Hope swallowed hard. The old ones especially. Sitting coolly in the shade of after-life, they looked with an utter lack of tolerance upon the brawls of Hattie and John. They heard her complaints often and believed her and only refused action because they knew the complainant to be equally guilty, but less popular than the man against whom she cried. Besides, the younger generation winked at what their elders cried over. Lucy had counselled well, but there were those who exulted in John's ignominious fall from the Moderatorship after nine years tenure, and milled about him like a wolf pack about a tired old bull—looking for a throat-hold, but he had still enough of the former John to be formidable as an animal and enough of his Pagan poesy to thrill. The pack waited. John knew it and was tired unto death of fighting off the struggle which must surely come. The devouring force of the future leered at him at unexpected moments. Then too his daily self seemed to be wearing thin, and the past seeped thru and mastered him for increasingly longer periods. He whose present had always been so bubbling that it crowded out past and future now found himself with a memory.

He began to remember friends who had lain back on the shelf of his mind for years. Now and then he surprised them by casual visits, but the pitying look would send him away and it would be a long time before he made such a call again.

He began to see a good deal of Zeke who had moved with his family to Florida, a year or two before Lucy died. He loved seeing Zeke because he was just as great a hero in his brother's eyes as he had been when he was the biggest Negro Baptist in the State and when Zion Hope had nine hundred members instead of the six hundred now on its roll. Zeke talked but always spared him.

Yes, John Pearson found himself possessed of a memory at a time when he least needed one.

"Funny thing," he said sitting in Zeke's kitchen with his wife, "things dat happened long time uhgo used to seem way off, but now it all seems lak it wuz yistiddy. You think it's dead but de past ain't stopped breathin' yet."

"Eat supper wid us, John Buddy, and stay de night."

"Thankee, Zeke. B'lieve Ah will fuh uh change." He went to bed at Zeke's after supper. Slept a long time. He awoke with a peculiar feeling and crept out of the house and went home.

"Hattie, whut am Ah doin' married tuh you?" John was standing in his wife's bedroom beside her bed and looking down on her, a few minutes later.

Hattie sat up abruptly, pulling up the shoulder straps of her nightgown.

"Is dat any way fuh you tuh do? Proagin' 'round half de night lak uh damn tom cat and den come heah, wakin' me up tuh ast uh damn fool question?"

"Well, you answer me den. Whut is us doin' married?"

"If you been married tuh uh person seben years and den come ast sich uh question, you mus' be crazy uh drunk one. You *is* drunk! You oughta know whut us doin' married jus' ez well ez Ah do."

"But Ah don't. God knows Ah sho don't. Look lak Ah been sleep. Ah ain't never meant tuh marry you. Ain't got no recollection uh even tryin' tuh marry yuh, but here us is married, Hattie, how come dat?"

"Is you crazy sho 'nuff?"

"Naw, Ah ain't crazy. Look lak de first time Ah been clothed in mah right mind fuh uh long time. Look lak uh whole heap uh things been goin' on in mah sleep. You got tuh tell me how come me and you is married."

"Us married 'cause you said you wanted me. Dat's how come."

"Ah don't have no 'membrance uh sayin' no sich uh thing. Don't b'lieve Ah said it neither."

"Well you sho said so—more'n once too. Ah married yuh jes' tuh git rid of yuh."

"Aw naw. Ah ain't begged you tuh marry me, nothin' uh de kind. Ah ain't said nothing' 'bout lovin' yuh tuh my knowin', but even if Ah did, youse uh experienced woman—had plenty experience 'fo' Ah ever seen yuh. You know better'n tuh b'lieve anything uh man tell yuh after ten o'clock at night. You know so well Ah ain't wanted tuh marry you. Dat's how come Ah know it's uh bug under dis chip."

"Well—if you didn't want me you made lak yuh did," Hattie said doggedly.

"Dat sho is funny, 'cause Ah know Ah wanted Miss Lucy and Ah kin call tuh memory eve'y li'l' thing 'bout our courtin' and 'bout us gittin' married. Couldn't fuhgit it if Ah wuz tuh try. Mo' special and particular, Ah remember jus' how Ah felt when she looked at me and when Ah looked at her and when we touched each other. Ah recollect how de moon looked de night us married, and her li'l' bare feets over de floor, but Ah don't remember nothin' 'bout *you*. Ah don't know how de moon looked and even if it rained uh no. Ah don't 'call to mind making no 'rangements tuh marry yuh. So you mus' know mo' 'bout it than Ah do."

Hattie pulled her long top lip down over the two large chalky-white false teeth in front and thought a while. She sank

143

back upon her pillow with an air of dismissal. "Youse drunk and anybody'd be uh fool tuh talk after yuh. You know durned well how come you married me."

"Naw, Ah don't neither. Heap uh things done went on Ah ain't meant tuh be. Lucy lef' seben chillun in mah keer. Dey ain't here now. Where is mah chillun, Hattie? Whut mah church doin' all tore up? Look at de whiskey bottles settin' 'round dis house. Dat didn't useter be."

"Yeah, and you sho drinks it too."

"But Ah didn't useter. Not in Lucy's time. She never drunk none herself lak you do, and she never brought none in de house tuh tempt me."

"Aw g'wan out heah! Don't keer if Ah do take uh swaller uh two. You de pastor uh Zion Hope, not me. You don't hav' to do lak me. Youse older'n me. Hoe yo' own row. De niggers fixin' tuh put yuh out dat pulpit 'bout yo' women and yo' likker and you tryin' tuh blame it all on me."

"Naw it's jus' uh hidden mystery tuh me—what you doin' in Miss Lucy's shoes."

And like a man arisen, but with sleep still in his eyes, he went out of the door and to his own bedroom.

Hattie lay tossing, wondering how she could get to An' Dangie Dewoe without arousing suspicion.

"Wonder is Ah done let things go too long, or is de roots jus' done wore out and done turn'd back on me?"

There was no sleep in either bedroom that night.

Hattie crept into John's bed at dawn and tried her blandishments but he thrust her rudely away.

"Don't you want me tuh love yuh no mo'?"

"Naw."

"How come?"

"It don't seem lak iss clean uh sumpin."

"Is you mad cause Ah learnt tuh love yuh so hard way back dere 'fo' Miss Lucy died?"

"Ah didn't mind you lovin' me, but Ah sho is mad wid yuh fuh marryin' me. Youse jus' lak uh blowfly. Spoil eve'y thing yuh touch. You sho ain't no Lucy Ann."

"Naw, Ah ain't no Miss Lucy, 'cause Ah ain't goin' tuh cloak yo' dirt fuh yuh. Ah ain't goin' tuh take offa yuh whut she took so you kin set up and be uh big nigger over mah bones."

" 'Tain't no danger uh me bein' no big nigger wid *you* uhround. Ah sure ain't de State Moderator no mo'."

"And dat ain't all. You fool wid me and Ah'll jerk de cover offa you and dat Berry woman. Ah'll throw uh brick in yo' coffin and don't keer how sad de funeral will be, and Ah dare yuh tuh hit me too. Ah ain't gonna be no ole man's fool."

"You know Ah don't beat no women folks. Ah married Lucy when she wuzn't but fifteen and us lived tuhgether twenty-two years and Ah ain't never lifted mah hand—"

Suddenly a seven-year-old picture came before him. Lucy's bright eyes in the sunken face. Helpless and defensive. The look. Above all, the look! John stared at it in fascinated horror for a moment. The sea of the soul, heaving after a calm, giving up its dead. He drove Hattie from his bed with vile imprecations.

"You, you!" he sobbed into the crook of his arm when he was alone, "you made me do it. And Ah ain't never goin' tuh git over it long ez Ah live."

During breakfast they quarreled over the weak coffee and Hattie swore at him.

"No woman ain't never cussed me yet and you ain't gonna do it neither—not and tote uh whole back," he gritted out between his teeth and beat her severely, and felt better. Felt almost as if he had not known her when Lucy was sick. He panged a little less. So after that he beat her whenever she vexed him. More interest paid on the debt of Lucy's slap. He pulled the crayon enlargement of Hattie's out of its frame and belligerently thrust it under the wash-pot while she was washing and his smoking eyes warned her not to protest.

"Rev'und," she began at breakfast one morning, "Ah needs uh pair uh shoes."

"Whyn't yuh go git 'em den?"

"Where Ahm goin' tuh git 'em from?"

145

"Speer got plenty and J. C. Penney swear he sells 'em."

"Dat ain't doin' me no good lessen Ah got de money tuh buy 'em wid."

"Ain't yuh got no money?"

"You ain't gimme none, is yuh? Not in de last longest."

"Oh you got shoes uh plenty. Ah see yuh have five uh six pairs 'round out under de dresser. Miss Lucy never had nothin' lak dat."

"Miss Lucy agin! Miss Lucy dis, Miss Lucy dat!"

"Yeah Miss Lucy, and Ahm gointer put uh headstone at her grave befo' anybody git shoes 'round heah—eben me."

"Mah shoes is nelly wore out, man. Dat headstone kin wait."

"Naw, Hattie, 'tain't gonna wait. Don't keer if youse so nelly barefooted 'til yo' toes make prints on de ground. She's gointer git her remembrance-stone first. You done wore out too many uh her shoes already. Here, take dis two bits and do anything you wanta wid it."

She threw it back viciously. "Don't come lounchin' me out no two bits when Ah ast you fuh shoes."

Hattie reported this to certain church officers and displayed her general shabbiness. Harris sympathized.

"Iss uh shame, Sister. Ah'd cut down dat Jonah's gourd vine in uh minute, if Ah had all de say-so. You know Ah would, but de majority of 'em don't keer whut he do, some uh dese people stands in wid it. De man mus' is got roots uh got piece uh dey tails buried by his door-step. Know whut some of 'em tole me? Says he ain't uh bit worse dan de rest uh y'all 'round de altar dere. Y'all gits all de women yuh kin. He jus' de bes' lookin' and kin git mo' of 'em dan de rest. Us pays him tuh preach and he kin sho do dat. De best in de State, and whut make it so cool, he's de bes' lookin'. Eben dem gray hairs becomes 'im. Nobody don't haft do lak he *do,* jus' do lak he *say* do. Yes ma'am, Sister Pearson 'twon't do fuh us tuh try tuh handle 'im. He'd beat de case. De mo' he beat you de better some of 'em laks it. Dey chunkin stones at yo' character and sayin' you ain't fit. Pot calling de kittle black. Dey points de finger uh scorn at yuh and say yo' eye is black. All us kin do is tuh lay low and wait on de Lawd."

"Sho wisht Ah could he'p mahself," Hattie whimpered.

"They *is* help if you knows how tuh git it. Some folks kin hit uh straight lick wid uh crooked stick. They's sich uh thing ez two-headed men."

"You b'lieve in all dat ole stuff 'bout hoodoo and sich lak, Brer Harris?" Hattie watched Harris's face closely.

"Yeah, Ah do, Mrs. Rev'und. Ah done seen things done. Why hit's in de Bible, Sister! Look at Moses. He's de greatest hoodoo man dat God ever made. He went 'way from Pharaoh's palace and stayed in de desert nigh on to forty years and learnt how tuh call God by all his secret names and dat's how he got all dat power. He knowed he couldn't bring off all dem people lessen he had power unekal tuh man! How you reckon he brought on all dem plagues if he didn't had nothin' but human power? And then agin his wife wuz Ethiopian. Ah bet she learnt 'im whut he knowed. Ya, indeed, Sister Pearson. De Bible is de best conjure book in de world."

"Where Ahm goin' ter fin' uh two-headed doctor? Ah don't know nothin' 'bout things lak dat, but if it kin he'p mah condition—"

"An' Dangie Dewoe wuz full uh power, but she dead now, but up t'wards Palatka is uh 'nother one dat's good. He calls hisself War Pete."

The old black woman of the sky chased the red-eyed sun across the sky every evening and smothered him in her cloak at last. This had happened many times. Night usually found John at his brother's house until late or at the bluff Deacon Hambo's who kept filthy epithets upon his tongue for his pastor, but held down the church with an iron hand.

A fresh rumor spread over the nation. It said war. It talked of blood and glory—of travel, of North, of Oceans and transports, of white men and black.

And black men's feet learned roads. Some said good bye cheerfully . . . others fearfully, with terrors of unknown dangers in their mouths . . . others in their eagerness for distance

147

said nothing. The daybreak found them gone. The wind said North. Trains said North. The tides and tongues said North, and men moved like the great herds before the glaciers.

Conscription, uniforms, bands, strutting drum-majors, and the mudsills of the earth arose and skipped like the mountains of Jerusalem on The Day. Lowly minds who knew not their State Capitals were talking glibly of France. Over there. No man's land.

"Gen'l Pushin', Gen'l Punishin', Gen'l Perchin', Gen'l Pershin'. War risk, war bread, insurance, Camp dis-and-dat. Is you heard any news? Dead? Lawd a mussy! Sho hope mah boy come thew aw-right. De black man ain't got no voice but soon ez war come who de first man dey shove in front? De nigger! Ain't it de truth? Bet if Ole Teddy wuz in de chear he'd straighten out eve'ything. Wilson! Stop dat ole lie. Wilson ain't de man Teddy Roosevelt wuz. De fightin'est man and the rulin'est man dat God ever made. Ain't never been two sho 'nuff smart mens in dese United States—Teddy Roosevelt and Booger T. Washington. Nigger so smart he et at de White House. Built uh great big ole school wuth uh thousand dollars, maybe mo'. Teddy wuz allus sendin' fuh 'im tuh git 'im tuh he'p 'im run de Guv'ment. Yeah man, dat's de way it 'tis—niggers think up eve'ything good and de white folks steal it from us. Dass right. Nigger invented de train. White man seen it and run right off and made him one jes' lak it and told eve'ybody he thought it up. Same way wid 'lectwicity. Nigger thought dat up too. DuBois? Who is dat? 'Nother smart nigger? Man, he can't be smart ez Booger T.! Whut did dis DuBois ever do? He writes up books and papers, hunh? Shucks! dat ain't nothin', anybody kin put down words on uh piece of paper. Gimme da paper sack and lemme see dat pencil uh minute. Shucks! Writing! Man Ah thought you wuz talkin' 'bout uh man whut had done sumpin. Ah thought maybe he wuz de man dat could make sidemeat taste lak ham."

Armistice. Demobilized. Home in khaki. "Yeah man, parlez vous, man, don't come bookooin' 'round heah, yuh liable tuh git hurt. Ah could uh married one uh dem French

women but shucks, gimme uh brown skin eve'y time. Blacker
de berry sweeter de juice. Come tuh mah pick, gimme uh
good black gal. De wine wuz sour, and Ah says parlez vous,
hell! You gimme mah right change! Comme telly vous. Nar,
Ah ain't goin' back tuh no farm no mo'. Ah don't mean tuh
say, 'Git up' tuh nary 'nother mule lessen he's setting down
in mah lap. God made de world but he never made no hog
outa me tuh go 'round rootin' it up. Done done too much
bookoo plowing already! Woman quick gimme mah sumpin
t' eat. Toot sweet.''

World gone money mad. The pinch of war gone, people
must spend. Buy and forget. Spend and solace. Silks for sor-
rows. Jewels to bring back joy. The factories roared and cried,
"Hands!" and in the haste and press white hands became
scarce. Scarce and dear. Hands? Who cares about the color of
hands? We need hands and muscle. The South—land of muscled hands.

"George, haven't you got some relatives and friends down
South who'd like a job?"

"Yes, suh."

"Write 'em to come."

Some had railroad fare and quickly answered the call of the
North and sent back for others, but this was too slow. The
wheels and marts were hungry. So the great industries sent out
recruiting agents throughout the South to provide transportation to the willing but poor.

"Lawd, Sanford gettin' dis Nawth bound fever lak eve'y-
where else,'' Hambo complained one Sunday in church.
"Elder, you know we done lost two hund'ed members in three
months?''

"Co'se Ah knows it, Hambo. Mah pocketbook kin tell it, if
nothing else. Iss rainin' in mah meal barrel right uh long.''

"Dat's awright. De celery farms is making good. All dese
folks gone Nawth makes high wages 'round heah. Less raise
de church dues,'' and it was done.

But a week later Hambo was back. "Looka heah, John, dis
thing is gittin' serious sho 'nuff. De white folks is gittin' wor-

ried too. Houses empty eve'ywhere. Not half 'nough people tuh work de farms—crops rotting in de ground. Folks plantin' and ain't eben takin' time tuh reap. Mules lef' standin' in de furrers. Some de folks gone 'thout lettin' de families know, and dey say iss de same way, only wurser, all over de South. Dey talkin' 'bout passin' laws tuh keep black folks from buying railroad tickets. Dey tell me dey stopped uh train in Georgy and made all de colored folks git off. Up dere iss awful, de pullman porters tell me. Ride half uh day and see nothin' but farms wid nobody on 'em.''

"Yeah," Pearson answered, "had uh letter from mah son in Tennessee. Same way. In some parts de white folks jails all them recruitin' agents so dey hafta git de word uhround in secret. Folks hafta slip off. Drive off in cars and ketch trains further up de line.''

"Tell yuh whut Ah seen down tuh Orlando. De man wuz skeered tuh git offa de train, but he seen uh colored man standin' 'round de deepo', so he took and called 'im and he says, 'Ahm uh labor agent, wanta work?' He tole him, 'Yes suh.' 'Well git some mo' men and have 'em down heah tuh meet de Nawth bound train at 2:40 o'clock. Ah'll stick mah hand out de winder and show wid mah fingers how many Ah got transportation for. Y'all watch good and count mah fingers right,' and he done it. Wanted sixteen. He beckoned one of 'em onto de train and fixed up wid him fuh de rest and dey all went wid 'im. Dat's all yuh kin heah. On de streets—in de pool-room—pickin' beans on de farm—in de cook kitchen— over de wash board—before dey go in church and soon ez dey come out, tellin' who done already went and who fixin' tuh go.''

"Yeah," agreed Rev. Pearson, "we preachers is in uh tight fix. Us don't know whether tuh g'wan Nawth wid de biggest part of our churches or stay home wid de rest.''

"Some of 'em done went. Know one man from Palatka done opened up uh church in Philadelphy and most of 'em is his ole congregation. Zion Hope sho done lost uh many one. Most of 'em young folks too.''

"Well maybe they won't stay Nawth. Most of 'em ain't useter col' weather fuh one thing."

"Yeah, but dey'll git used tuh it. Dey up dere now makin' big money and livin' in brick houses. Iss powerful hard tuh git uh countryman outa town. He's jus' ez crazy 'bout it ez uh hog is 'bout town swill. Dey won't be back soon."

Do what they would, the State, County and City all over the South could do little to halt the stampede. The cry of "Goin' Nawth" hung over the land like the wail over Egypt at the death of the first-born. The railroad stations might be watched, but there could be no effective censorship over the mails. No one could keep track of the movements of cars and wagons and mules and men walking. Railroads, hardroads, dirt roads, side roads, roads were in the minds of the black South and all roads led North.

Whereas in Egypt the coming of the locust made desolation, in the farming South the departure of the Negro laid waste the agricultural industry—crops rotted, houses careened crazily in their utter desertion, and grass grew up in streets. On to the North! The land of promise.

CHAPTER 20

Hattie was rubbing in the first water and dropping the white things into the wash-pot when Deacon Harris hurried up to her back gate.

"Mawnin', Sister Pearson," opening the gate.

"Howdy do, Deacon?"

"Ain't got no right tuh grumble. How you?"

"Not so many, dis mawnin'. You look lak you in uh kinda slow hurry."

"Nope, jes' anxious tuh tell yuh uh thing uh two."

"If is sumpin tuh better mah condition, hurry up and tell it. God knows Ah sho needs somebody tuh give aid and assistance. Reverend and his gang sho is gripin' me. Ah feels lak uh cat in hell wid no claws."

"First thing, Ah got uh man Ah b'lieve, if de crowd ever git tuh hear 'im, dey'd lak 'im better'n de Rev'und."

"Where he come from?"

"Wes' Floriduh. Man he kin cold preach! Preached over in Goldsborough las' night and strowed fire all over de place. Younger man dan Pearson too."

"Can't you fix it fuh 'im tuh speak at Zion Hope?"

"Sho. Done 'bout got it fixed fuh de fourth Sunday night. Dat ain't Pastoral Sunday, but its de nex' bes'. De crowd'll be almos' ez big."

"Dat's fine! Some uh dem niggers don't b'lieve nobody kin preach but John Pearson. Let 'em see. Den maybe dey'll set 'im down. Ah don't keer whut dey do wid 'im. Ah do know one thing, Ah sho got mah belly full. Whus de other things you wuz goin' tuh tell me 'bout?"

"Well, in looking over de books, I saw where mos' of the folks whut would stand up for Rev'und so hard, is gone. If we wuz tuh bring de thing tuh uh vote Ah b'lieve we kin dig up de hidden wedge. Ah been sorta feelin' 'round 'mong some de members and b'lieve de time done come when we kin chop down dis Jonah's gourd vine."

"Dat sho would be all de heben Ah ever want to see. How kin we bring it uhbout? You got tuh have plenty tuh show do some uh dat crowd won't hear it."

"You git uh divorce from 'im. You kin git plenty witnesses tuh bear yuh out in dat. Ah'll be one mahself."

"Chile, he wouldn't keer nothin' 'bout dat. He'd be glad, Ah speck, so he kin run loose wid dat Gertie Burden. Dat's de one he sho 'nuff crazy 'bout."

"Who you tellin'? Ever since she wuz knee high. Us knowed it all de time, but thought yuh didn't."

"He don't try tuh keep it out mah sight. He washes mah face wid her night and day."

"You jokin'!"

"Know whut he told me las' time Ah got 'im 'bout her? Says, 'Don't be callin' dat girl all out her name, Miss Lucy didn't call *you* nothin'.' Deacon Harris, Ah wuz so mad Ah could uh lammed 'im wid lightnin', but how de divorce goin' set 'im down?"

"Yuh see de church punishes fuh things de law don't chastize fuh, and if iss so bad 'til de law'll handle it, de church is bound tuh. Don't need no mo' trial."

"But Ah can't eben start uh divorce trial jus' dry long so."

"You kin pick uh fight outa Sister Beery uh Gertie Burden, can't yuh? Dat'll th'ow de fat in de fiah, and bring eve'ything out in de day light, and when iss all over wid, he'll be uh lost ball in de high grass. Ah sick and tiahed uh all dese so-called

154

no-harm sins. Dis ain't no harm, and dat ain't no harm, and all dese li'l' no-harm sins is whut leads folks straight to hell."

"De one Ah wants tuh beat de worse is dat ole Beery Buzzard. Right on de church ground she ast me one Sunday, if Miss Lucy's bed wudden still hot when Ah got in it."

"Jump on her, den."

"She's rawbony, but she look real strong tuh me. Ole long, tall, black huzzy! Wisht Ah could hurt 'er."

"She don't eat iron biscuits and she don't sop cement gravy. She kin be hurt, and den agin, you kin git help—not open, yuh know, but on de sly. Somebody tuh hand yuh sumpin jes' when you need it bad."

"When mus' Ah tackle de slut?"

"De very nex' time Rev'und goes off somewhere tuh preach. If he's dere he'd git it stopped too quick. Befo' it make uhnough disturbment."

Two incidents nerved Hattie's hand. The first, that same evening Rev. Pearson came in from some carpentry work he had been doing out around Geneva, obviously crestfallen, but nothing she did succeeded in making him tell her the reason.

If she could have seen her husband at noon time of that very same day she would have seen him seated beside the luscious Gertie on a cypress log with her left hand in his and his right arm about her waist.

"John, Ah b'lieve Ahm goin' ter marry."

"Please, Gertie, don't say dat."

"You married, ain'tcha? Ahm twenty-two. Papa and mama spectin' me tuh marry some time uh other and dey think Ah oughter take dis chance. You know he got uh big orange grove wid uh house on it and seben hund'ed dollars in de bank."

"Dat's right, Gertie. Take yo' chance when it comes. Don't think—don't look at me. Ahm all spoilt now. Kiss me one mo' time. Den Ah got tuh go back tuh work. Lawd, Ah hope you be happy. Iss wonderful tuh marry somebody when you wants tuh. You don't keer whut you do tuh please 'em. Some women you wouldn't mind tearin' up de pavements uh hell tuh built

155

'em uh house, but some you don't give 'em nothin'. You jes' consolate 'em by word uh mouf and fill 'em full uh melody.''

Therefore the next morning at breakfast when John grumbled about the scorched grits and Hattie threatened to dash hot coffee in John's face, he beat her soundly. The muscular exercise burnt up a portion of his grief, but it urged Hattie on. A few days later, when she learned of Gertie's engagement, she was exultant. "Now maybe, it'll hurt 'im, if Ah quit 'im. Gittin' loose from me might gripe 'im now—anyhow it sho ain't gwine he'p 'im none wid Gertie.''

Hattie knew, as do other mortals, that half the joy of quitting any place is the loneliness we leave behind.

CHAPTER 21

The fourth Sunday came shining with the dangerous beauty of flame. Between Sunday School and the 11:00 o'clock service, Andrew Berry called Rev. Pearson aside.

"Is de deacon board tole yuh?"

" 'Bout whut?"

"De new preacher dey got here tuh try out tuhnight?"

"Naw, but Hambo did tell me tuh strow fire dis mawnin'. Reckon he wuz throwin' me uh hint right den."

"Ahm sho he wuz. De Black Herald got it dat dey got *you* on de let-loose and de onliest thing dat keeps some of 'em hangin' on is dey don't b'lieve nobody kin preach lak you, but if dis man dey got here tuhday kin surpass yuh, den dere'll be some changes made. Harris and de Black Dispatch say he kin drive all over yuh."

"Maybe he kin, Andrew. Ain't dat him over dere, talkin' tuh Sister Williams?"

"Yeah. He'll be tuh de service tuh hear *you* so he kin know how tuh do tuhnight when he gits up tuh preach."

John Pearson shook hands politely when he was introduced to Rev. Felton Cozy when he entered the church. Rev. Cozy was cordially invited to sit in the pulpit, which he did very pompously. All during the prayer service that led up to the sermon he was putting on his Oxford glasses, glaring about the church and taking them off again.

Rev. Pearson preached his far-famed, "Dry Bones" sermon, and in the midst of it the congregation forgot all else. The church was alive from the pulpit to the door. When the horse in the valley of Jehoshaphat cried out, "Ha, ha! There never was a horse like me!" He brought his hearers to such a frenzy that it never subsided until two Deacons seized the preacher by the arms and reverently set him down. Others rushed up into the pulpit to fan him and wipe his face with their own kerchiefs.

"Dat's uh preachin' piece uh plunder, you hear me?" Sister Hall gloated. "Dat other man got tuh go some if he specks tuh top dat."

"Can't do it," Brother Jeff avowed, "can't be done."

"Aw, you don't know," contended Sister Scale. "Wait 'til you hear de tother one."

"Elder Pearson ain't preached lak dat in uh long time. Reckon he know?"

"Aw naw. Dey kep' it from 'im. When he know anything, de church'll be done done whut dey going tuh do."

When Rev. Cozy arose that night the congregation slid forward to the edge of its seat.

"Well, y'all done heard one sermon tuhday, and now Ah stand before you, handlin' de Alphabets." He looked all about him to get the effect of his statement. "Furthermo', Ah got uhnother serus job on mah hands. Ahm a race man! Ah solves the race problem. One great problem befo' us tuhday is whut is de blacks gointer do wid de whites?"

After five minutes or more Sister Boger whispered to Sister Pindar, "Ah ain't heard whut de tex' wuz."

"Me neither."

Cozy had put on and removed his glasses with the wide black ribbon eight times.

"And Ah say unto you, de Negro has got plenty tuh feel proud over. Ez fur back ez man kin go in his-to-ree, de black man wuz always in de lead. When Caesar stood on de Roman

158

forum, uccordin' tuh de best authority, uh black man stood beside him. Y'all say 'Amen.' Don't let uh man preach hisself tuh death and y'll set dere lak uh bump on uh log and won't he'p 'im out. Say 'Amen'!!

"And fiftly, Je-sus, Christ, wuz uh colored man hisself and Ah kin prove it! When he lived it wuz hot lak summer time, all de time, wid de sun beamin' down and scorchin' hot—how could he be uh white man in all dat hot sun? Say 'Amen'! Say it lak you mean it, and if yuh do mean it, tell me so! Don't set dere and say nothin'!

"Furthermo' Adam musta been uh colored man 'cause de Bible says God made 'im out de dust uh de earth, and where is anybody ever seen any white dust? Amen! Come on, church, say 'Amen'!

"And twelfth and lastly, all de smartest folks in de world got colored blood in 'em. Wese de smartest people God ever made and de prettiest. Take our race—wese uh mingled people. Jes' lak uh great bouquet uh flowers. Eve'y color and eve'y kind. Nobody don't need tuh go hankerin' after no white womens. We got womens in our own race jes' ez white ez anybody. We got 'em so black 'til lightnin' bugs would follow 'em at twelve o'clock in de day—thinkin' iss midnight and us got 'em in between.

"And nothin' can't go on nowhere but whut dere's uh nigger in it! Say 'Amen'!"

"Amen! He sho is tellin' de truth now!"

At the close of the service, many came forward and shook Cozy's hand and Harris glowed with triumph. He was dry and thirsty for praise in connection with his find so he tackled Sisters Watson and Boger on the way home.

"How y'all lak de sermon tuhnight?"

"Sermon?" Sister Boger made an indecent sound with her lips, "dat wan't no sermon. Dat wuz uh lecture."

"Dat's all whut it wuz," Sister Watson agreed and switched on off.

Harris knew that he must find some other weapon to move the man who had taken his best side-girl from him.

CHAPTER 22

Harris, Hattie and one-eyed Fred Tate went on with their plans for the complete overthrow of Rev. Pearson thru the public chastisement of Sister Berry, but things began to happen in other directions.

While she held a caucus one afternoon with supporters, Hambo sat at Zeke's house and sent one of Zeke's children to find John.

"John, youse in boilin' water and tuh you—look lak 'tain't no help fuh it. Dat damn 'oman you got b'lieves in all kinds uh roots and conjure. She been feedin' you outa her body fuh years. Go home now whilst she's off syndicatin' wid her gang—and rip open de mattress on yo' bed, de pillow ticks, de bolsters, dig 'round de door-steps in front de gate and look and see 'ain't some uh yo' draws and shirt-tails got pieces cut offa 'em. Hurry now, and come back and let us know whut you find out. G'wan! Don't stop tuh race yo' lip wid mine, and don't try tuh tell me whut you think. Jes' you g'wan do lak Ah tell yuh."

John Pearson went and returned with a miscellany of weird objects in bottles, in red flannel, and in toadskin.

"Lawd, Hambo, here's uh piece uh de tail uh—uh shirt Ah had 'fo' Lucy died. Umph! Umph! Umph!"

"Ha! Ah wuz spectin' dat!"

"Whut kin Ah do 'bout it, Hambo?"

"Give it here. Less take it tuh uh hoodoo doctor and turn it back on her, but whut you got tuh do is tuh beat de blood outa her. When you draw her wine dat breaks de spell—don't keer whut it is."

"Don't you fret 'bout dat. Ah 'bominates sich doings. She gointer git her wine drawed dis day, de Lawd bein' may helper. Ahm goin' on home and be settin' dere when she come."

Hattie saw the hole at the gate and the larger one at the front steps before she entered the yard. Inside, the upturned rugs, the ripped-up beds, all had fearful messages for her. Who had done this thing? Had her husband hired a two-headed doctor to checkmate her? How long had he been suspecting her? Where was he now?

"Hattie," John called from the dining-room. She would have bolted, but she saw he made ready to stop her. She stood trembling in the hallway like a bird before a reptile.

"Whut you jumpin' on me fuh?" she cried out as he flung himself upon her.

"You too smart uh woman tuh ast dat, and when Ah git th'ew wid you, you better turn on de fan, and make me some tracks Ah ain't seen befo' do Ahm gointer kill yuh. Hoodooin' me! Stand up dere, 'oman, Ah ain't hit you yet."

And when the neighbors pulled him from her weakening body he dropped into a chair and wept hard. Wept as he had not wept since his daughter's serious illness, emptying out his feelings.

Hattie fled the house, not even waiting to bathe her wounds nor change her clothes. When John's racking sobs had ceased, the stillness after the tumult soothed him. He bathed and slept fourteen hours. In the morning he wrote to each of his children a shy letter. On the third day Hattie struck. He was sued for divorce.

"Ahm sho glad," he told Zeke and Hambo, "she made me

jes' ez happy by quittin' ez Lucy did when she married me."

"Yeah, but if she prove adultery on you in de cotehouse, you sho goin' tuh lose yo' church," Hambo warned. "You got tuh fight it."

CHAPTER 23

Time is long by the courthouse clock.

John Pearson sat restlessly in his seat. Sitting alone except for Zeke's oldest son. Zeke had to work that day and his sister-in-law excused herself on the grounds that she "never had been to any courthouse and she didn't want no bother with it. Courthouses were back luck to colored people—best not to be 'round there." Many of the people John had approached for witnesses had said the same thing. "Sho, sho," they wanted him to win, but "you know dese white folks—de laws and de cotehouses and de jail houses all b'longed tuh white folks and po' colored folks—course, Ah never done nothin' tuh be 'rested 'bout, but— Ah'll be prayin' fuh yuh, Elder. You bound tuh come out more'n conquer."

So John sat heavily in his seat and thought about that other time nearly thirty years before when he had sat handcuffed in Cy Perkins' office in Alabama. No fiery little Lucy here, thrusting her frailty between him and trouble. No sun of love to rise upon a gray world of hate and indifference. Look how they huddled and joked on the other side of the room. Hattie, the destroyer, was surrounded by cheer. Sullen looks his way. Oh yes, she had witnesses!

Mule-faced, slew-foot Emma Hales was there—rolling her cock-eye triumphantly at him. Why should she smite out at his head? He remembered the potato pones, the baked chicken with corn-bread dressing, the marble cake, the potato pies that he had eaten in her house many times. He had eaten but never tarried. Never said a word out of the way to her in all his life. He wondered, but Emma knew. She remembered too well how often he had eaten her dinners and hurried away to the arms of the gray-eyed Ethel.

Deacon Harris now outwardly friendly, but he had been told weeks before of Harris's activity against him. Harris should not be hostile, he had taken no woman who loved Harris, for none had wanted him. His incompetence was one of the behind-hand jokes of the congregation. He was blind to human motives but Harris hated him with all the fury of the incompetent for the full-blooded loins.

The toadies were there. Armed with hammers. Ever eager to break the feet of fallen idols. Contemptuous that even the feet of idols should fall among them. No fury so hot as that of a sycophant as he stands above a god that has toppled from a shrine. Faces of gods must not be seen of him. He has worshipped beneath the feet so long that if a god but lowers his face among them, they obscene it with spit. "Ha!" they cried, "what kind of a divinity is this that levels his face with mine? Gods show feet—not faces. Feet that crush—feet that crumble—feet that have no eyes for men's suffering nor ears for agony, lest indeed it be a sweet offering at God's feet. If gods have no power for cruelty, why then worship them? Gods tolerate sunshine, but bestir themselves that men may have storms. From the desolation of our fireplaces, let us declare the glory. If he rides upon the silver-harnessed donkey, let us cry 'hosanna'. If he weeps in compassion, let us lynch him. The sky-rasping mountain-peak fills us with awe, but if it tumbles into the valley it is but boulders. It should be burst asunder. Too long it has tricked us into worship and filled our souls with envy. Crush! Crush! Crush! Lord, thou hast granted thy servant the boon of pounding upon a peak."

So the toadies were there. Vindictively setting the jaw-muscles. Taking folks for fools! But, yes they would testify.

Their injury was great. Let his silk-lined broadcloth look to itself. They meant to rip it from his back today. Think of it, folks! We rip up broadcloth and step on Stetsons. Costly walking-sticks can be made into wood for the cook stove.

Hattie was a goddess for the moment. She sat between the Cherubim on the altar of destruction. She chewed her gum and gloated. Those who held themselves above me, shall be abased. Him who pastored over a thousand shall rule over none. Even as I. His name shall be a hissing, and Hattie's shall be the hand that struck the harp. Selah. Let the world hiss with Hattie. If he but looked with longing! But no, only hurt and scorn was in his eyes. Hurt that so many of his old cronies surrounded her and scorn of herself. Let him ache! If she could but ache him more!

Court was set. The waves of pang that palpitated in the room did not reach up to the judge's bench. No. His honor took his seat as a walrus would among a bed of clams. He sat like a brooding thought with his eyes outside the room. It was just another day with the clerk and the stenographer.

"Hattie Pearson, pwop wah blah!"

John saw the smirking anticipation on the faces of the lawyers, the Court attendants, the white spectators, and felt as if he had fallen down a foul latrine.

"Now, how was it, Hattie?" The look around the room at the other whites, as if to say, "Now listen close. You're going to hear something rich. These niggers!"

"So you wanta quit yo' husband, do you, Hattie? How come? Wasn't he all right? Is *that* him? Why he looks like he oughta be okeh. Had too many women, eh? Didn't see you enough, is that it? Ha! ha! couldn't you get yo'self another man on the side? What you worrying about a divorce for? Why didn't you g'wan leave him and get yourself somebody else? You got divorce in yo' heels, ain't you? You must have the next one already picked out. Ha! ha! Bet he ain't worth the sixty dollars."

So it went on with each of the witnesses in turn. John laughed grimly to himself at the squirming of prospective

167

witnesses who would have fled but found it too late. One by one he saw four of his erstwhile intimates take the stand against him.

Finally the Clerk cast about for defense witnesses, "Say, Reverend, where's *yo'* witnesses?"

"Ain't got none."

"Why? Couldn't you find anybody to witness for you?"

"Yes suh, but who kin tell de truth and swear dat he know uh man ain't done nothin' lak dat?"

The Court laughed, but sobered with a certain respect.

"You want to enter a plea of denial?"

"Naw suh. Ahm goin' tuh say Ah did it all."

"You don't care, then, if Hattie has her freedom?"

"Naw suh, Ah sho don't. Matters uh difference tuh me whut she do, uh where she go."

The fun was over in the Court. Whisperings. Formalities. Papers. It was all over. He saw former friends slinking off to avoid his eye. Hattie was outside, flourishing her papers with over-relish. Loud talking and waving them as if they were a certificate of her virtue.

Hambo's short sturdy legs overtook John as he went down the marble steps, and Hambo's big hand smacked his shoulders.

"Well, you, ole mullet-headed tumble-bug, you!"

John eyed him wearily, "How come didn't but four uh y'all testify aginst me? Ah thought Ah had five friends."

"You ———!" Hambo went into a fit of most obscene swearing, "why didn't you call me fuh uh witness? Didn't Ah tell yuh to?"

"Yeah, but—"

"Take yo' but out my face. Ah wanted tuh git up dere and talk some chat so bad 'til de seat wuz burning me. Ah wanted tuh tell 'bout de mens Ah've knowed Hattie tuh have. She could make up uh 'scursion train all by herself. Ah wanted tuh tell de judge 'bout all dat conjure and all dem roots she been workin' on you. Feedin' you outa her body—."

"And dat's how come Ah didn't have 'em tuh call yuh. Ah

168

didn't want de white folks tuh hear 'bout nothin' lak dat. Dey knows too much 'bout us as it is, but dey some things dey ain't tuh know. Dey's some strings on our harp fuh us tuh play on and sing all tuh ourselves. Dey thinks wese all ignorant as it is, and dey thinks wese all alike, and dat dey knows us inside and out, but you know better. Dey wouldn't make no great 'miration if you had uh tole 'em Hattie had all dem mens. Dey spectin' dat. Dey wouldn't zarn 'tween uh woman lak Hattie and one lak Lucy, uh yo' wife befo' she died. Dey thinks all colored folks is de same dat way. De only difference dey makes is 'tween uh nigger dat works hard and don't sass 'em, and one dat don't. De hard worker is uh good nigger. De loafer is bad. Otherwise wese all de same. Dass how come Ah got up and said, 'Yeah, Ah done it,' 'cause dey b'lieved it anyhow, but dey b'lieved de same thing 'bout all de rest.''

It was late afternoon when John stumbled out of the court-house with his freedom that had been granted to Hattie.

"You tellin' de truth, John," Hambo agreed at last, "but don't you come puttin' me in wid dem other crabs. Don't you come talkin' tuh *me* lak dat! Ah knock yuh so dead dat yuh can't eben fall. Dey'll have tuh push yuh over. Pick up dem damn big foots uh your'n and come on up tuh mah house. Ah got barbecued spare-ribs and death puddin' ready cooked.''

On the way over there was a great deal of surface chatter out of Hambo. John kept silent except when he had to answer. At Hambo's gate he paused. "Ain't it funny, Hambo, you know all uhbout me. Us been friends fuh twenty years. Don't it look funny, dat all mah ole pleasures done got tuh be new sins? Maybe iss 'cause Ahm gittin' ole. Havin' women didn't useter be no sin. Jus' got sinful since Ah got ole.''

" 'Tain't de sin so much, John. You know our people is jus' lak uh passle uh crabs in uh basket. De minute dey see one climbin' up too high, de rest of 'em reach up and grab 'em and pull 'im back. Dey ain't gonna let nobody git nowhere if dey kin he'p it.''

CHAPTER 24

Second Sunday in the month came rolling around. Pastoral day. Covenant meeting. Communion service. But before all this must come Conference meeting on the Saturday night before, and John knew and everybody knew what the important business of the meeting would be. Zion Hope, after seventeen years, was going to vote on a pastor. Was John Pearson to be given a vote of confidence? Not if Hattie's faction prevailed. Would Felton Cozy receive the call? Not if Hambo and the John Pearson faction was still alive.

Everybody was there. John opened the meeting as usual, then stepped down and turned the chair over to Deacon Hoffman. "I know we all come here tuhnight tuh discuss some things. Ah'd ruther not tuh preside. Deacon Hoffman."

Hoffman took the chair. "Y'all know whut we come here for. Less get thru wid de most urgent business and den we kin take up new business."

He fumbled with the pile of hymnals on the table and waited. There was an uneasy shuffling of feet all over the room, but nobody arose to put a motion. Finally Hattie got up about the middle of the center aisle.

"Brother Cherman."

"Sister Pearson."

"Ah wants tuh lay charges 'ginst mah husband."

Hambo was on his feet.

"Brother Cherman! Brother Cherman!"

"Sister Pearson got de flo', Brer Hambo."

"She ain't got no business wid it. She's entirely out uh order."

"She ain't. She says she got charges tuh make uhginst her husband. Dat's whut uh Conference meetin' is for in uh Baptis' Church—tuh hear charges and tuh rectify, ain't it?"

"Yeah," Hambo answered, "but dis woman ain't got no husband in dis church, Brother Cherman. We ain't got no right listenin' tuh nothin' she got tuh say. G'wan back where you come from, Hattie, and try to improve up from uh turpentine still."

"Dat's right, too," shouted Sister Watson, "been divorced two weeks tuh mah knowin'."

"Better set down, Sister Pearson, 'til we kin git dis straight," Hoffman said, reluctantly.

"Iss straight already," Andrew Berry shouted, "when uh woman done gone tuh de cotehouse and divorcted uh man she done got her satisfaction. She ain't got no mo' tuh say. Let de mess drop. Ah ain't goin' tuh hear it."

"And another thing," Hambo put in. "Elder Pearson, you oughta git up and tell whut you found in yo' bed. Course he beat uh, and 'tain't uh man under de sound uh mah voice but whut wouldn't uh done de same. G'wan tell it, Rev'und."

"Naw, no use tuh sturry up de stink. Let it rest. Y'all g'wan do whut yuh want tuh."

There was a long, uncomfortable silence.

"G'wan talk, Harris, you and de rest dat's so anxious tuh ground-mole de pastor, but be sho and tell where *you* wuz yo'self when you seen him do all of dis y'all talkin' 'bout. Be sho and tell dat too. Humph! Youse jes' ez deep in de mud ez he is in de mire."

Another long silence. Finally Hoffman said, "De hour is growin' late. Less table dis discussion and open up de house fuh new business."

Soon the meeting was over. John, Hambo and Berry walked home together.

"If Harris and dem had uh called dat meetin' de nex' day after cote, it would a been uh smuttie rub, nelly eve'ybody would have been uhginst yuh, but two weeks is too long fuh colored tuh hold onto dey feeling. Most of 'em don't keer one way uh 'nother by now."

"Still plenty of 'em is 'ginst me," John spoke at last. "It made mah flesh crawl—Ah felt it so when Ah wuz in dere."

"But dey ain't got no guts. Dey wants tuh do dey work under cover. Dey got tuh fight war if dey wants tuh win dis battle, and dey needs cannon-guns. You can't fight war wid uh brick."

John said nothing. His words had been very few since his divorce. He was going about learning old truths for himself as all men must, and the knowledge he got burnt his insides like acid. All his years as pastor at Zion Hope he had felt borne up on a silken coverlet of friendship, but the trial had shown him that he reclined upon a board, thinly disguised. Hambo had tried vainly to bring him around. A few others had done their share. A few he recognized among the congregation as foes, avowedly; a few friends in the same degree. The rest he saw would fall in line and toady if he triumphed, and execrate him if he failed. He felt inside as if he had been taking calomel. The world had suddenly turned cold. It was not new and shiny and full of laughter. Mouldy, maggoty, full of suck-holes—one had to watch out for one's feet. Lucy must have had good eyes. She had seen so much and told him so much it had wearied him, but she hadn't seen all this. Maybe she had, and spared him. She would. Always spreading carpets for his feet and breaking off the points of thorns. But and oh, her likes were no more on this earth! People whom he had never injured snatched at his shoddy bits of carpet and sharpened the thorns for his flesh.

Nobody pushed him uphill, but everybody was willing to lend a hand to the downward shove. Oh for the wings, for the

173

wings of a dove! That he might see no more what men's faces held!

Sunday afternoon, the sunlight filtered thru the colored glass on the packed and hushed church. Women all in white. Three huge bouquets of red hibiscus below him and behind the covered Communion table. As he stood looking down into the open Bible and upon the snow-white table, his feelings ran riot over his body. "He that soppeth in the dish with me." He knew he could not preach that Last Supper. Not today. Not for many days to come. He turned the pages while he swallowed the lump in his throat and raised:

> Beloved, Beloved, now are we the sons of God
> And it doth not yet appear what we shall be
> But we know, but we know
> When He shall appear, when He shall appear
> We shall be like Him
> We shall see Him as He is.

The audience sang with him. They always sang with him well because group singers follow the leader.

Then he began in a clear, calm voice.

"Brothers and Sisters: De song we jus' sung, and seein' so many uh y'all out here tuh day, it reaches me in uh most particular manner. It wakes up uh whole family uh thoughts, and Ahm gointer speak tuh yuh outa de fullness uh mah heart. Ah want yuh tuh pray wid me whilst Ah break de bread uh life fuh de nourishment uh yo' souls.

"Our theme this morning is the wounds of Jesus. When the father shall ast, 'What are these wounds in thine hand?' He shall answer, 'Those are they with which I was wounded in the house of my friends.' Zach. 13:6.

"We read in the 53rd Chapter of Isaiah where He was wounded for our transgressions and bruised for our iniquities, and the apostle Peter affirms that His blood was spilt from before the foundation of the world.

"I have seen gamblers wounded. I have seen desperadoes

174

wounded; thieves and robbers and every other kind of characters, law-breakers and each one had a reason for his wounds.
Some of them was unthoughtful, and some for being overbearing, and some by the doctor's knife, but all wounds dis-
figure a person.

"Jesus was not unthoughtful. He was not overbearing. He
was never a bully. He was never sick. He was never a criminal
before the law and yet He was wounded. Now, a man usually
gets wounded in the midst of his enemies, but this man was
wounded, says the text, in the house of His friends. It is not
your enemies that harm you all the time. Watch that close
friend. Every believer in Christ is considered His friend, and
every sin we commit is a wound to Jesus. The blues we play
in our homes is a club to beat up Jesus, and these social card
parties.
Jesus have always loved us from the foundation of the world
When God
Stood out on the apex of His power
Before the hammers of creation
Fell upon the anvils of Time and hammered out the ribs of the
      earth
Before He made any ropes
By the breath of fire
And set the boundaries of the ocean by the gravity of His
      power
When God said, ha!
Let us make man
And the elders upon the altar cried, ha!
If you make man, ha!
He will sin
God my master, ha!
Father!! Ha-aa!
I am the teeth of time
That comprehended de dust of de earth
And weighed de hills in scales
That painted de rainbow dat marks de end of de parting storm
Measured de seas in de holler of my hand

175

That held de elements in a unbroken chain of controllment.
Make man, ha!
If he sin I will redeem him
I'll break de chasm of hell
Where de fire's never quenched
I'll go into de grave
Where de worm never dies, Ah!
So God A'mighty, Ha!
Got His stuff together
He dipped some water out of de mighty deep
He got Him a handful of dirt
From de foundation sills of de earth
He seized a thimble full of breath
From de drums of de wind, ha!
God, my master!
Now I'm ready to make man
Aa-aah!
Who shall I make him after? Ha!
Worlds within worlds begin to wheel and roll
De Sun, Ah!
Gethered up de fiery skirts of her garments
And wheeled around de throne, Ah!
Saying, Ah, make man after me, ha!
God gazed upon the sun
And sent her back to her blood-red socket
And shook His head, ha!
De Moon, ha!
Grabbed up de reins of de tides.
And dragged a thousand seas behind her
As she walked around de throne
Ah-h, please make man after me
But God said "NO!"
De stars bust out from their diamond sockets
And circled de glitterin' throne cryin'
A-aah! Make man after me
God said, "NO!"
I'll make man in my own image, ha!

I'll put him in de garden
And Jesus said, ha!
And if he sin,
I'll go his bond before yo' mighty throne
Ah, He was yo' friend
He made us all, ha!
Delegates to de judgment convention
Ah!
Faith hasn't got no eyes, but she' long-legged
But take de spy-glass of Faith
And look into dat upper room
When you are alone to yourself
When yo' heart is burnt with fire, ha!
When de blood is lopin' thru yo' veins
Like de iron monasters (monsters) on de rail
Look into dat upper chamber, ha!
We notice at de supper table
As He gazed upon His friends, ha!
His eyes flowin' wid tears, ha! He said
"My soul is exceedingly sorrowful unto death, ha!
For this night, ha!
One of you shall betray me, ha!
It were not a Roman officer, ha!
It were not a centurion
But one of you
Who I have chosen my bosom friend
That sops in the dish with me shall betray me."
I want to draw a parable.
I see Jesus
Leaving heben with all of His grandeur
Dis-robin' Hisself of His matchless honor
Yielding up de scepter of revolvin' worlds
Clothing Hisself in de garment of humanity
Coming into de world to rescue His friends.
Two thousand years have went by on their rusty ankles
But with the eye of faith, I can see Him
Look down from His high towers of elevation

I can hear Him when He walks about the golden streets
I can hear 'em ring under His footsteps
Sol me-e-e, Sol do
Sol me-e-e, Sol do
I can see Him step out upon the rim bones of nothing
Crying I am de way
De truth and de light
Ah!
God A'mighty!
I see Him grab de throttle
Of de well ordered train of mercy
I see kingdoms crush and crumble
Whilst de archangels held de winds in de corner chambers
I see Him arrive on dis earth
And walk de streets thirty and three years
Oh-h-hhh!
I see Him walking beside de sea of Galilee wid His disciples
This declaration gendered on His lips
"Let us go on to the other side"
God A'mighty!
Dey entered de boat
Wid their oarus (oars) stuck in de back
Sails unfurled to de evenin' breeze
And de ship was now sailin'
As she reached de center of de lake
Jesus was sleep on a pillow in de rear of de boat
And de dynamic powers of nature became disturbed
And de mad winds broke de heads of de Western drums
And fell down on de lake of Galilee
And buried themselves behind de gallopin' waves
And de white-caps marbilized themselves like an army
And walked out like soldiers goin' to battle
And de zig-zag lightning
Licked out her fiery tongue
And de flying clouds
Threw their wings in the channels of the deep
And bedded de waters like a road-plow

And faced de current of de chargin' billows
And de terrific bolts of thunder—they bust in de clouds
And de ship begin to reel and rock
God A'mighty!
And one of de disciples called Jesus
"Master!! Carest Thou not that we perish?"
And He arose
And de storm was in its pitch
And de lightnin' played on His raiments as He stood on the
    prow of the boat
And placed His foot upon the neck of the storm
And spoke to the howlin' winds
And de sea fell at His feet like a marble floor
And de thunders went back in their vault
Then He set down on de rim of de ship
And took de hooks of His power
And lifted de billows in His lap
And rocked de winds to sleep on His arm
And said, "Peace, be still."
And de Bible says there was a calm.
I can see Him wid de eye of faith.
When He went from Pilate's house
Wid the crown of seventy-two wounds upon His head
I can see Him as He mounted Calvary and hung upon de cross
    for our sins.
I can see-eee-ee
De mountains fall to their rocky knees when He cried
"My God, my God! Why hast Thou forsaken me?"
The mountains fell to their rocky knees and trembled like a
    beast
From the stroke of the master's axe
One angel took the flinches of God's eternal power
And bled the veins of the earth
One angel that stood at the gate with a flaming sword
Was so well pleased with his power
Until he pierced the moon with his sword
And she ran down in blood

And de sun
Batted her fiery eyes and put on her judgment robe
And laid down in de cradle of eternity
And rocked herself into sleep and slumber
He died until the great belt in the wheel of time
And de geological strata fell aloose
And a thousand angels rushed to de canopy of heben
With flamin' swords in their hands
And placed their feet upon blue ether's bosom, and looked
  back at de dazzlin' throne
And de arc angels had veiled their faces
And de throne was draped in mournin'
And de orchestra had struck silence for the space of half an
  hour
Angels had lifted their harps to de weepin' willows
And God had looked off to-wards immensity
And blazin' worlds fell off His teeth
And about that time Jesus groaned on de cross, and
Dropped His head in the locks of His shoulder and said, "It
  is finished, it is finished."
And then de chambers of hell exploded
And de damnable spirits
Come up from de Sodomistic world and rushed into de smoky
  camps of eternal night,
And cried, "Woe! Woe! Woe!"
And then de Centurion cried out,
"Surely this is the Son of God."
And about dat time
De angel of Justice unsheathed his flamin' sword and ripped
  de veil of de temple
And de High Priest vacated his office
And then de sacrificial energy penetrated de mighty strata
And quickened de bones of de prophets
And they arose from their graves and walked about in de
  streets of Jerusalem
I heard de whistle of de damnation train

Dat pulled out from Garden of Eden loaded wid cargo goin'
　　to hell
Ran at break-neck speed all de way thru de law
All de way thru de prophetic age
All de way thru de reign of kings and judges—
Plowed her way thru de Jurdan
And on her way to Calvary, when she blew for de switch
Jesus stood out on her track like a rough-backed mountain
And she threw her cow-catcher in His side and His blood
　　ditched de train
He died for our sins.
Wounded in the house of His friends.
That's where I got off de damnation train
And dat's where you must get off, ha!
For in dat mor-ornin', ha!
When we shall all be delegates, ha!
To dat Judgment Convention
When de two trains of Time shall meet on de trestle
And wreck de burning axles of de unformed ether
And de mountains shall skip like lambs
When Jesus shall place one foot on de neck of de sea, ha!
One foot on dry land, ah
When His chariot wheels shall be running hub-deep in fire
He shall take His friends thru the open bosom of an un-
　　clouded sky
And place in their hands de "hosanna" fan
And they shall stand 'round and 'round his beatific throne
And praise His name forever, Amen.

There had been a mighty response to the sermon all thru its
length. The "bearing up" had been almost continuous, but as
Pearson's voice sank dramatically to the final Amen, Anderson
lifted a chant that kept the church on fire for several seconds
more. During this frenzy John Pearson descended from the
pulpit. Two deacons sprang to assist him at the Communion
table, but he never stopped there. With bowed head he
walked down the center aisle and out of the door—leaving
stupefaction in his wake. Hoffman and Nelse Watson posted

after him and stopped him as he left the grounds, but he brushed off their hands.

"No, chillun, Ah—Ah can't break—can't break de bread wid y'all no mo'," and he passed on.

"Man, ain't you goin' on back tuh yo' pulpit lak you got some sense?" Hambo asked that night. "If you don't some of 'em is sho tuh strow it uhround dat you wuz put out."

"Naw, Hambo. Ah don't want y'all fightin' and scratchin' over me. Let 'em talk all dey wanta."

"Ain't yuh never tuh preach and pastor no mo?"

"Ah won't say never 'cause— Never is uh long time. Ah don't b'lieve Ahm fitted tuh preach de gospel—unless de world is wrong. Yuh see dey's ready fuh uh preacher tuh be uh man uhmongst men, but dey ain't ready yet fuh 'im tuh be uh man uhmongst women. Reckon Ah better stay out de pulpit and carpenter fuh mah livin'. Reckon Ah kin do dat 'thout uh whole heap uh rigmarole."

But after a while John was not so certain. Several people who formerly had felt that they would rather wait for him several weeks to do a job now discovered that they didn't even have time to get him word. Some who already had work done shot angry, resentful looks after him and resolved not to pay him. It would be lacking in virtue to pay carpenter-preachers who got into trouble with congregations. Two men who had been glad of a chance to work under him on large jobs kept some of his tools that he had loaned them and muttered that it was no more than their due. He had worked them nearly to death in the damp and cold and hadn't paid them. One man grew so indignant that he pawned a spirit-level and two fine saws.

John was accused of killing one man by exposure and over-work. It was well known that he died of tuberculosis several months after he had worked a day or two for John, but nobody was going to be behind hand in accusations. Every bawdy in town wept over her gin and laid her downfall at John's door. He was the father of dozens of children by women he had never seen. Felton Cozy had stepped into his shoes at Zion

Hope and made it a point to adjust his glasses carefully each time he saw John lest too much sin hit him in his virtuous eye. John came to recognize all this eventually and quit telling people his troubles or his plans. He found that they rejoiced at the former and hurried away to do what they could to balk the latter.

As one man said, "Well, since he's down, less keep 'im down."

He saw himself growing shabby. It was hard to find food in variety.

One evening he came home most dejected.

"Whuss de matter, big foots?" Hambo asked. "You look all down in de mouf."

"Look lak lightnin' done struck de po' house. Dey got me in de go-long Ah reckon. All de lies dese folks strowing 'round 'bout me done got some folks in de notion Ah can't drive uh clean nail in they lumber. Look lak dey spectin' uh house Ah build tuh git tuh fornication befo' dey could get de paint on it. Lawd Jesus!"

"Come in and eat some dese snap peas and okra Ah got cooked. It'll give you mo' guts than uh goat."

"Naw thankee, Hambo. Ahm goin' lie down."

He went into his room and shut the door. "Oh Lucy! Lucy! Come git me. You knowed all dis—whut yuh leave me back heah tuh drink dis cup? Please, Lucy, take dis curse offa me. Ah done paid and paid. Ah done wept and Ah done prayed. If you see God where you is over dere ast Him tuh have mercy! Oh Jesus, Oh Jesus, Oh-wonder-workin' God. Take dis burden offa mah sobbin' heart or else take me 'way from dis sin-sick world!"

He sought Lucy thru all struggles of sleep, mewing and crying like a lost child, but she was not there. He was really searching for a lost self and crying like the old witch with her shed skin shrunken by red pepper and salt, "Ole skin, doncher know me?" But the skin was never to fit her again. Sometimes in the dark watches of the night he reproached Lucy bitterly

183

for leaving him. "You meant to do it," he would sob. "Ah saw yo' eyes."

By day he gave no sign of his night-thoughts. His search and his tears were hidden under bed quilts.

When Hambo woke him for breakfast next morning he didn't get up.

"Don't b'lieve Ahm goin' out tuhday, 'cause if Ah meet Cozy wid dat sham-polish smile uh his'n de way Ah feel tuhday, dey'll be tryin' me fuh murder nex' time."

His courage was broken. He lay there in bed and looked back over days that had had their trial and failure. They had all been glorious tomorrows once gilded with promise, but when they had arrived, they turned out to be just days with no more fulfillment—no more glad realities than those that had preceded—more betrayal, so why look forward? Why get up?

His divorce trial stayed with him. He saw that though it was over at the courthouse the judge and jury had moved to the street corners, the church, the houses. He was on trial everywhere, and unlike the courthouse he didn't have a chance to speak in his own behalf.

Sisters White and Carey came over around sundown with a gingerbread and melon-rind preserves.

"Always remembered you had uh sweet tooth," Sister Carey said.

They wanted to know if he was thinking of pastoring again. Certain people had crowded Cozy in, but the real folks had "chunked him out again. His shirttail may be long but we kin still spy his hips."

"He never could preach, nohow," Sister White complained, "and he been strainin' hisself tryin' tuh be stronger wid de women folks than you wuz. Settin' 'round de houses drinkin' and sayin' toastes 'bout, 'Luck tuh de duck dat swims de pond—' Bet if some dese men folks ketch 'im dey'll luck his duck fuh 'im. Since you won't consider, us callin' uh man from Savannah."

"Oh, he's more'n welcome to all de women folks," John rejoined.

"Where you keepin' yo'self dese days, anyhow, and whut you doin'?"

"Oh well, Sister White, since yuh ast me, Ah do any kind of uh job Ah kin git tuh make uh dollar, and Ah keeps mahself at home. Sometimes Ah reads de Bible and sometimes Ah don't feel tuh. Den Ah jus' knock uhround from pillar tuh post and sort of dream. Seem lak de dreams is true sho 'nuff sometime—iss so plain befo' me, but after while dey fades. But even while they be fadin', Ah have others. So it goes from day tuh day."

One night John had a dream. Lucy sat beside a stream and cried because she was afraid of a snake. He killed the snake and carried Lucy across in his arms to where Alf Pearson stood at the cross roads and pointed down a white shell road with his walking cane and said, "Distance is the only cure for certain diseases," and he and Lucy went racing down the dusty white road together. Somehow Lucy got lost from him, but there he was on the road—happy because the dead snake was behind him, but crying in his loneliness for Lucy. His sobbing awoke him and he said, "Maybe it's meant for me tuh leave Sanford. Whut Ahm hangin' 'round heah for, anyhow?"

At breakfast he said to Hambo, "Well, Hambo, Ah been thinkin' and thinkin' and Ah done decided dat Ahm goin' tuh give you dis town. You kin have it."

"You better say Joe, 'cause you don't know. Us been here batchin' tuhgether and gittin 'long fine. Ahm liable not tuh let yuh go. Me, Ahm in de 'B' class, be here when you leave and be here when you git back."

"Oh yeah, Ahm goin'. Gointer spread mah jenk in unother town."

"Where you figgerin' on goin'?"

"Don't know yet. When Ah colleck dem few pennies Ah got owing tuh me, iss good bye Katy, bar de door. Some uh dese mawnin's, and it won't be long, you goin' tuh wake up callin' me and Ah'll be gone."

And that is the way he went. It was equally haphazard that he landed in Plant City and went about looking for work.

Several times he passed the big white building that Baptist pride had erected and that he had been invited as Moderator to dedicate, but he passed it now with shuttered eyes. He avoided the people who might remember him.

A week and no work. Walking the streets with his tool kit. Hopeful, smiling ingratiatingly into faces like a dog in a meat house. Desperation nettling his rest.

"How yuh do, suh? Ain't you Rev'und Pearson?"

He looked sidewise quickly into the face of a tall black woman who smiled at him over a gate. Yard chock full of roses in no set pattern.

"Yes ma'am. Well, Ah thank yuh."

"Thought Ah knowed yuh. Heard yuh preach one time at our church."

"Pilgrim Rest Baptis' Church?"

"Dat's right. Dat wuz uh sermon! Come in."

John was tired. He sat heavily upon the step.

"Don't set on de do' step. Elder, heah's uh chear."

"Iss all right, Sister, jus' so Ahm settin' down."

"Naw, it 'tain't. If you set on de steps you'll git all de pains in de house. Ha, ha! Ah reckon you say niggers got all de signs and white folks got all de money."

He sat in the comfortable chair she placed for him and surrendered his hat.

"You got tuh eat supper wid me, lessen you got somewhere puhticklar tuh go. Mah dead husband said you wuz de best preacher ever borned since befo' dey built de Rocky Mountains."

Rev. Pearson laughed a space-filling laugh and waited on her lead.

"You goin' tuh be in our midst uh while?"

"Don't know, Sister—er—"

"Sister Lovelace. Knowed you wouldn't know me. Maybe you would eben disremember mah husband, but Ah sho is glad tuh have yuh in our midst. 'Scuse me uh minute whilst

186

Ah go skeer yuh up suppin' tuh eat."

She bustled inside but popped out a moment later with a palm-leaf fan.

"Cool yo'self off, Rev'und."

She was back in a few minutes with a pitcher clinking with ice.

"Have uh cool drink uh water, Elder—mighty hot. Ain't aimin' tuh fill yuh up on water, ha! ha! jes' keepin' yuh cool 'til it git done."

From the deep porch, smothered in bucket flowers the street looked so different. The world and all seemed so different—it seemed changed in a dream way. "Maybe nothin' ain't real sho 'nuff. Maybe 'tain't no world. No elements, no nothin'. Maybe wese jus' somewhere in God's mind," but when he wiggled his tired toes the world thudded and throbbed before him.

"Walk right intuh de dinin'-room and take uh chear, Rev'und. Right in dis big chear at de head uh de table. Maybe you kin make uh meal outa dis po' dinner Ah set befo' yuh, but yuh know Ahm uh widder woman and doin' de bes' ah kin."

"Dis po' dinner," consisted of fried chicken, hot biscuits, rice, mashed sweet potatoes, warmed over greens, rice pudding and iced tea.

"You goin' tuh set down and eat wid me, ain't yuh Sister Lovelace?"

"Naw, you go right uhead and eat. Ahm goin' tuh fan de flies. Dey right bad dese days. Ah been laying off tuh have de place screened, but jes' ain't got 'round tuh it. De wire is easy tuh git but dese carpenters 'round heah does sich shabby work 'til Ah ruther not be bothered."

"Ahm uh carpenter."

"You ain't got time tuh fool wid nothin' lak dat. Youse too big uh man."

"Oh, Ah got plenty time."

John felt warm heart-beats that night in his room. He de-

187

cided to drop a line or two to Sanford. He sent a cheerful line to Hambo first of all.

He wrote to Mamie Lester for news and comfort. She never answered. She felt injured that he should ask such a thing of her. Her indignation burst out of her. She asked many people, "Who do John Pearson think Ah am to be totin' news for him? He ain't nothin'." She said "nothin'" as if she had spat a stinking morsel out of her mouth.

After a long time, when he didn't get an answer, John Pearson understood, and laughed in his bed. The virtuous indignation of Mamie Lester! He could see her again as he had first seen her twenty years ago, as she had tramped into Sanford as barefooted as a yard dog with her skimpy, dirty calico dress and uncombed head; and her guitar hanging around her neck by a dirty red ribbon. How she had tried to pick him up and instead had gotten an invitation to his church. Respectability and marriage to a deacon. She, who had had no consciousness of degradation on the chain-gang and in the brothel, had now discovered she had no time for talk with fallen preachers.

Now that he had work to do, he wrote to George Gibson, asking him to return his tools that George had borrowed. George ignored the letter. He was really angry, "The son of a bum! Won't pay nobody and then come astin' me 'bout dem tools. Ah wish he would come to my face and ast me for 'em."

"Do Pearson owe you too?" another impostor asked.

"Do he? Humph!" he left the feeling that if he only had the money that John Pearson owed him, he need never worry any more.

George was indignant at being asked favors by the weak. His blood boiled.

It became the fashion that whoever was in hard luck, whoever was in debt—John Pearson had betrayed him. Gibson habitually wore a sorrowful look of infinite betrayal. In the meanwhile he used John's tools and came finally to feel that he deserved them.

The next day after the chance meeting John began his task of screening the house of Sally Lovelace, and when he was thru he hesitated over taking the money agreed upon.

"You done fed me more'n de worth uh de job," he said.

"Aw shucks, man, uh woman dat's useter havin' uh man tuh do fuh got tuh wait on somebody. Take de money. You goin' tuh be tuh church dis Sunday?"

"Er—er—Ah don't jus' exactly know, tuh tell yuh truth, Sister Lovelace."

"You jokin', Ah know. Whut you goin' tuh do, if you don't go?"

"Not tuh turn yuh no short answer, Ah don't know."

"Oh come uhlong wid me. Deacon Turner and dem wuz overglad tuh know youse in town. Dey wants yuh tuh run our revival meetin' and dey did say suppin' 'bout yuh preachin' Communion Service."

John flinched, and Mrs. Lovelace saw it. He had to stay to supper then, and at eleven o'clock that night she knew everything. He had not spared himself, and lay with his head in her lap sobbing like a boy of four.

"Well, youse gointer pastor right here at Pilgrim Rest and none of 'em bet' not come 'round here tryin' tuh destroy yo' influence!" Sally blazed. "Ain't doodley squat dey self and goin' 'round tromplin' on folks dat's 'way uhbove 'em." She ran her fingers soothingly thru John's curly hair, and he fell asleep at her knee.

John escorted Sally to church on Sunday and preached.

"Man, you preached!" Sally said warmly during dinner— "only thing Ah heahed so many folks wuz shoutin' Ah couldn't half hear whut you wuz sayin'. You got tuh preach dat at home some time. Special fuh me."

"Preach it anytime you say, but sho 'nuff Ah felt lak ole times tuhday. Felt lak Samson when his hair begin tuh grow out agin."

"Dat's de way fuh yuh tuh feel, John. Oh yeah, 'fo' Ah fuhgit it, dere's uh lady got twenty-seben houses. She wants you tuh look over and patch up wherever dey needs fixin'. Ain't been nothin' done on 'em in two years. 'Bout two weeks steady work and den de Meth'dis' parsonage got tuh have new

189

shingles all over and me and de pastor's wife stands in. Oh you goin' tuh git 'long good in this town."

John had finished the work on the houses before he found out that they belonged to Sally. The Methodist preacher had paid him. He found himself displeased when he heard of Sally's ownership. What would she with all that property, want with him?

"John, dey's fixin' tuh loose de pastor uh Pilgrim Rest and Ahm quite sho dey's 'bout tuh call you. So go git yo' things tuhgether and less git married tuhday so nobody can't start no talk."

"Thank yuh, Sally."

"You wuz aimin' tuh ast me anyhow, wuzn't yuh?"

"Sho wuz, jus' ez soon ez Ah could git tuh de place where Ah could make support fuh yuh."

"Well, den eve'ything is all right between us. We ain't no chillun no mo', and we don't need tuh go thru uh whole lot uh form and fashion—uh kee-kee-in' and eatin' up pocket handkerchers. You done got de church and dat calls fuh over uh hund'ed dollars uh month and besides whut you got comin' in from carpenterin', and Ah got three hund'ed dollars eve'y month from de rent uh dem houses. Ahm gointer marry you, 'cause Ah love yuh and Ah b'liève you love me, and 'cause you needs marryin'.''

"Ah sho do, Sally. Less go git married and den got set on de fish pond and ketch us uh mess uh speckled perches fuh supper. Iss uh heap mo' fun than buyin' 'em."

"Less do. Ah always wanted tuh go sich places, but Oscar never would take me. He wuz uh good puhvider tho'."

Sally went to bed as a matter of course that night, but John was as shy as a girl—as Lucy had been. His bride wondered at that. He stayed a long time on his knees and Sally never knew how fervently he prayed that Sally might never look at him out of the eyes of Lucy. How abjectly he begged his God to keep his path out of the way of snares and to bear him up lest he bruise his feet against a stumbling-stone, and he vowed vows, if God would only keep his way clean. "Let Lucy see it too, Lawd, so she kin rest. And be so pleased as to cast certain memories in de sea of fuhgitfulness where dey will never rise tuh condemn me in de judgment. Amen and thang God."

CHAPTER 25

Sally, you never ought tuh bought me no car. Dat's too much money tuh take out de bank."

"Who else Ahm goin' tuh spend it on? Ah ain't got uh chick nor uh chile 'ceptin' you. If us ever goin' tuh enjoy ourselves, dis is de world tuh do it in."

"But uh Chevrolet would uh done me. You didn't hafta go buy no Cadillac."

"Wanted yuh tuh set up in uh Cadillac. Dat's yo' weddin' present and our first anniversary present all two together."

"Don't look lak us been married no year, Sally."

"But us is. Dat's 'cause we happy. Tuh think Ah lived tuh git forty-eight 'fo' Ah ever knowed whut love is."

"Ah love you de same way, Sally."

"Look here, John, you ain't been back tuh Sanford since yuh lef' dere."

"Don't keer if Ah never see it no mo' 'twill be too soon."

"Yeah, but honey, yo' buddy Hambo done been down here and paid you uh visit. You oughter go up and spend uh few days wid him, and let dem niggers see how well you gittin' uhlong."

"Awright; when you wanta go?"

"Me? Ah ain't goin'. Ah got mah guava jelly tuh put up. Ah don't trust ridin' so fur in dese cars, nohow. You go and tell me all uhbout it. You been right up under me ever since us been married. Do yuh good tuh git off uh spell."

"Naw, Sally, Ah don't want tuh go 'thout you."

"Fool, how you goin' tuh git uh rest from me and take me wid yuh? You jes' lak uh li'l' boy and dass whut make Ah love yuh so, but you g'wan."

"Naw, Ah promised mahself never tuh sleep uh night 'way from you. Ah don't wanta break mah vow."

Sally exulted in her power and sipped honey from his lips, but she made him go, seeing the pain in John's face at the separation. It was worth her own suffering ten times over to see him that way for her.

The next morning he turned the long nose of his car northwards and pulled up at Hambo's gate. He was affectionately called every vile name in the language and fed on cow peas, but it seemed good to be there.

Three girls in their late teens stood about his gleaming chariot when he emerged towards sundown to visit the new pastor of Zion Hope church. They admired it loudly and crudely hinted for rides, but John coolly drove off without taking any hints. He was used to admiration of his car now and he had his vows.

Sanford was warm. From what he heard now as he sat under the wheel of his car, Sanford had had not a moment of happiness since he left. Zion Hope was desolate. The choir in heaven had struck silence for the space of half an hour. Wouldn't he consider a recall?

"Naw, it would be de same ole soup-bone—jus' warmed over—dat's all. Ah got uh church bigger'n dis one."

"You could give dem two Sundays and us two, couldn't yuh?" Trustee John Hall pled.

"Ah couldn't see de way tuh be 'way from home dat much. We got too much proppity down dere fuh me tuh look after."

"You got proppity?"

"Yep. Thirty houses tuh rent. Three of 'em brand new. Ah jus' finished 'em off las' week and dey was rented 'fo' de roof got on." He pulled out the huge roll of bills in his pocket,

194

"And Ah jus' got th'ew collectin' de month's rent 'fo' Ah come off."

"God uhmighty man, youse rich! You got bucks above suspicion! Oh shucks, Ah lak tuh fuhgit. Here's dat fo' dollars Ah owe you fuh buildin' dat shed-room 'fo' you went way from here. Ah could uh been done paid yuh, but Ah let talk keep me from it."

John pocketed the money without thanking him. He was grinning sardonically inside, thinking of the heat of the pavements and empty belly, the cold cruelty of want, how much men hit and beat at need when it pleads its gauntness.

But Hall was looking upon plenty and heard no miserable inside gnawings. He heard not John's cold lack of courtesy.

"But you got tuh preach for us dis comin' Sunday. Dat's Communion service. Nobody in de world kin preach dat lak you. Lemme go put it out right now, so's de whole church will know."

"You reckon Ah'd fine uh welcome, Hall?"

"Lawd yes, Rev. Pearson. You left a welcome at Zion Hope when you left here, and you kerried a welcome wid yuh where you went and you brought a welcome back wid you. Come preach for us one mo' time. God a'mighty man, Zion Hope couldn't hold all de folks dat would be dere. We'd lift a collection lak on big rally day."

But John was fingering the four dollars in his mind. He would buy a chicken for supper. Hambo would like that. He would still have enough left over to service the car and take him home.

"Nope, Brother Hall. Thankee for de invitation, but Ah feels to get on back home tuh mah wife. Can't be off too long."

He went on thinking how to show Sally how he could guard their money. Sure three dollars and a quarter would take him home. Maybe less. He wrote Sally about it, wrote her some kind of a letter every day.

While he and Hambo ate supper he heard voices on the porch—gay giggling. He motioned to see who it was.

"Aw, don't go," Hambo continued, " 'Tain't nobody but

195

dem three li'l' chippies from up de street. Dey gone crazy 'bout dat car. Dat kinda plump one is Ora Patton—jes' ez fresh ez dishwater. Always grinnin' up in some man's face. She's after yo' money right now. I seen her pass here eve'y few minutes—switchin' it and lookin' back at it. Set down and finish yo' supper man. Ah wouldn't pay her no rabbit-foot. She ain't wuth it."

"Oh, Ah ain't studyin' 'bout dem gals. Jus' don't want nobody tuh mess wid dat car. Dat radiator cap cost twenty-six dollars. Soon ez Ah git th'ew supper Ahm goin' tuh put de car up."

"You better, dey steal gas 'round here too, but dat Ora is hot after yuh. Her egg-bag ain't gonna rest easy 'til she git nex' tuh yuh. Money crazy. Don't give 'er uh damn cent. Be lak me. Ah wouldn't give uh bitch uh bone if she treed uh terrapin."

"She won't git nothin' outa me. Ahm lak de cemetery. Ahm takin' in, but never no put out. 'Ceptin' tuh Sally. She come tuh me in hell and Ah love her for it."

When John stepped to the door of his car he found Ora on the running-board.

"Hello, daddy."

"Oh, er, hello, daughter."

"Don't call me no daughter. Take me fuh uh short ride."

"Ahm jus' goin' tuh de garage. Two—three blocks, you kin ride dat fur if you wanta."

"Okay, stingy papa. You eben wear uh stingy-rim hat." As the car moved off silently, "Lawd! Ah wonder how it feels tuh be drivin' uh great big ole 'Kitty.'"

"Kin you drive?"

"Yeah. Lemme take de wheel jes' uh minute. Every body in town is talkin' 'bout dis blue and silver 'Kitty.' You mus' got money's mammy, and grandpa change."

"Nope, broke ez uh he-ha'nt in torment. All dis b'longs tuh mah wife. Here's de garage. Youse goin' on past it."

"Aw, gimme uh li'l' bit uh ride, daddy. Don't be so mean and hateful."

196

"Nope, Ahm goin' home tuhmorrer and Ah got tuh be in bed so Ah wont go tuh sleep drivin'. Move over."

He reached for the wheel and Ora shot down on the gas. They had nosed out on the road to Osteen before John dared to struggle for possession of the wheel. He hated to think of even a scratch on his paint. Then Ora pulled to the side of the road and parked and threw her arms about his neck and began to cry.

"Ora so bad and now, big, good-looking daddy is mad wid her! Po' Ora can't he'p who she like. Please don't be mad, you pretty, curly headed man."

John unwrapped her arms from 'round his neck gently.

"Well, Ah'll give you uh li'l' short ride, if thass all yuh want. Can't burn up too much gas."

Ora kissed him fleshily, "Dat's right sweet daddy. Let de wheels roll, Ah loves cars. Ride me 'til Ah sweat."

In twenty minutes John was back at the garage and Ora got out pouting. "You mus' figger Ah sweats mighty easy, papa. Ah ast yuh fuh uh ride, but you ain't gimme none hardly."

Friday came and John was glad. He was going home and Ora had failed of her purpose. He was convincing himself that God and Sally could trust him.

Friday night Ora waited for him outside the garage. Standing in the dark of a clump of hibiscus.

"Thought you wuz goin' home Tuesday?" she accused. "Here 'tis Friday night and you ain't gone yet. Ah know you jes' wants tuh git rid uh me."

"Naw, 'tain't dat. First place Ah got uh wife and second place Ahm goin' home sho 'nuff tuhmorrer and therefo' Ah ain't got no time tuh talk. Needs mah sleep. Ahm gittin' ole."

"Aw, naw, you ain't. Come on less take uh good bye ride. Less don't make it stingy lak de las' time. Less ride out tuh Oviedo and back."

She climbed in beside him and put her hands on top of his wheel and eye-balled him sweetly.

"Don't go in dis ole garage. Drive on."

CHAPTER 26

Two hours later when John found himself dressing in a
dingy back room in Oviedo he was mad—mad at his
weakness—mad at Ora, though she did not know it as
yet. She was putting on her shoes on the other side of the bed.

"Daddy, you got twenty dollars you kin gimme? Ah needs
so many things and you got plenty."

"Naw, Ah tole you befo' Ah didn't have nothin'. Anything
you see on me b'longs tuh Sally." He laced his shoes and put
on his vest, then he remembered the remainder of the four
dollars he had collected. He pulled it out of his pocket and
threw it at her, "Here! Take dat. Iss all Ah got, and Ah hope
you rot in hell! Ah hope you never rise in judgment!" He
seized his coat and put it on as he hurried out to the car. Ora
grabbed up her dress and dashed after him, but he was under
the wheel before she left the room, and the motor was humming when she reached the running-board. John viciously
thrust her away from the car door without uttering a word. He
shoved her so hard that she stumbled into the irrigation ditch,
as the car picked up speed and in a moment was a red eye in
the distance.

"Well, de ole gray-head bastard! Wonder whut got intuh
him? Dis li'l' ole three dollars and some odd change is gonna
do me uh lot uh good. Ah been strainin' up tuh git tuh Oviedo

fuh de last longest and here Ah is, but Ah wisht Ah knowed whut he flew hot over. Sho do. He done lef' me right where Ah wants tuh be, wid pay-day at de packin' house tuhmorrer. Jes' lak de rabbit in de briar patch.

"Bright and soon tuhmorrer Ah means tuh git me uh bottle uh perfume and some new garters—one red one tuh draw love and one yeller one tuh draw money. Hey, hey, Ah can't lose—not wid de help Ah got."

When Hambo awoke John was gone. Ten dollars was on the dresser beside the clock, and a couple of brand new nightshirts were on a chair.

"Well de hen-fired son-of-a-gun done slipped off and never tole me good bye again! Bet de wop-sided, holler-headed—— thought Ah wuz gointer cry, but he's uh slew-footed liar!" Whereupon Hambo cried over the stove as he fried his sowbosom and made a flour hoe-cake. Then he found he couldn't eat. Frog in his throat or something so that even his coffee choked him.

The ground-mist lifted on a Florida sunrise as John fled homeward. The car droned, "ho-o-ome" and tortured the man. False pretender! Outside show to the world! Soon he would be in the shelter of Sally's presence. Faith and no questions asked. He had prayed for Lucy's return and God had answered with Sally. He drove on but half-seeing the railroad from looking inward.

The engine struck the car squarely and hurled it about like a toy. John was thrown out and lay perfectly still. Only his foot twitched a little.

"Damned, if I kin see how it happened," the engineer declared. "He musta been sleep or drunk. God knows I blowed for him when I saw him entering on the track. He wasn't drunk. Couldn't smell no likker on him, so he musta been asleep. Hell, now I'm on the carpet for carelessness, but I got witnesses I blowed."

Sally wept hard. "Naw, Ah don't want de seben thousand

dollars from de railroad. Ahm goin' tuh give it tuh his chillun. Naw, Ah don't want none of it. Ah loved 'im too much tuh rob his chillun. Jes' lemme be buried right side uh him when Ah die. Us two off by ourselves. Dass how come Ah bought uh new burial lot. Ah can't git over it, people. Jes' ez he wuz gittin ready tuh live, he got tuh git taken uhway, but Ah got one consolation, he sho wuz true tuh me. Jes' tuh think Ah had tuh live fifty years tuh git one sweet one and it throwed de light over all de other ones. Ah'll never regret uh thing. He wuz true tuh me." She said it over and over. It was a song for her heart and she kept singing it.

She sat shining darkly among the multitudes from all over the State who had come to do John Pearson homage. She sat among his children and made them love her, and when he was laid to rest she was invited to attend memorial services in twenty or more cities.

Sanford was draped in mourning on the second Sunday when Zion Hope held her memorial for John Pearson. The high-backed, throne-like chair was decorated. Tight little sweaty bouquets from the woods and yards were crowded beside ornate floral pieces. Hattie in deep mourning came back to town for the service.

She would have seated herself on the front seat before the flower-banked chair that represented the body of Rev. Pearson, but someone stopped her. "His wife is in de seat," they whispered and showed her to a place among the crowd.

Hambo rolled his eyes at the black-veiled Hattie and gritted his teeth, and whispered to Watson:

"Uhhunh, Ad done heered she wuz comin' back tuh ast us all tuh he'p her git his lodge insurances. Wisht Ah wuz God. Ah'd take and turn her intuh uh damn hawg and den Ah'd concrete de whole world over, so she couldn't find uh durned place tuh root."

And the preacher preached a barbaric requiem poem. On the pale white horse of Death. On the cold icy hands of Death. On the golden streets of glory. Of Amen Avenue. Of Halleluyah Street. On the delight of God when such as John

201

appeared among the singers about His throne. On the weeping sun and moon. On Death who gives a cloak to the man who walked naked in the world. And the hearers wailed with a feeling of terrible loss. They beat upon the O-go-doe, the ancient drum. O-go-doe, O-go-doe, O-go-doe! Their hearts turned to fire and their shinbones leaped unknowing to the drum. Not Kata-Kumba, the drum of triumph, that speaks of great ancestors and glorious wars. Not the little drum of kidskin, for that is to dance with joy and to call to mind birth and creation, but O-go-doe, the voice of Death—that promises nothing, that speaks with tears only, and of the past.

So at last the preacher wiped his mouth in the final way and said, "He wuz uh man, and nobody knowed 'im but God," and it was ended in rhythm. With the drumming of the feet, and the mournful dance of the heads, in rhythm, it was ended.

GLOSSARY

Lidard knot, fat pine wood, generally used for kindling.   p. 2

Chaps, children. Old English use.   p. 13

Buckra, white people.   p. 7

Patter roller, "Patrollers," an organization of the late slavery days that continued through the Reconstruction period. Its main objective was the intimidation of Negroes. Similar to the KKK.   p. 7

Hagar's chillun, Negroes, as against Sarah's children, the whites.
     p. 10

Apin' down de road, running away.   p. 10

Talkin' at de big gate, boasting. Making pretence of bravery behind the back of a powerful person. The allusion comes from the old slavery-time story of the Negro who boasted to another that he had given Ole Massa a good cussin' out. The other one believed him and actually cussed Ole Massa out the next time that he was provoked, and was consequently given a terrible beating. When he was able to be at work again he asked the first Negro how it was that he was not whipped for cussing Ole Massa. The first Negro asked the other if he had cussed Ole Massa to his face. "Sho Ah did. Ain't dat whut you tole me you done?" "Aw naw, fool. Ah ain't tole yuh nothin' uh de kind. As said Ah give Ole Massa uh good cussin' out and Ah did. But when Ah did dat, he wuz settin' up on de verandah and Ah wuz down at de big gate. You sho is uh big fool. It's uh wonder Ole Massa didn't kill you dead." p. 14

Shickalacked, a sound-word to express noise of a locomotive. p. 15

Nable string, umbilical cord. p. 19

Boogers, head lice. p. 24

Make 'miration, pay flattering compliments. p. 28

Parched peanuts, roasted peanuts. p. 29

Cuffy, West African word meaning Negro. p. 29

Branch, colloquial for small stream. p. 34

Smell hisself, reaching puberty (girl or boy becoming conscious of). p. 45

Lies, stories, tales. p. 61

Tush hawg, wild boar, very vicious, hence a tough character. The tusks of the wild boar curve out and are dangerous weapons. p. 63

Seben years ain't too long fuh uh coudar tuh wear uh ruffled bosom shirt, it's never too late for me to get even with you. p. 64

Coudar, a striped, hard-shell fresh-water turtle. p. 64

Bucket flower, potted plant. Old buckets and tubs being used for flower pots. A delicate, well-cared-for person. p. 68

Lay-over, hen with a full drooping comb. Domestic animals and fowls often named for some striking characteristic. p. 77

Jook, the pleasure houses near industrial work. A combination of bawdy, gaming, and dance hall. Incidentally the cradle of the "blues." p. 90

Strowin', spreading abroad. p. 90

Sheep shadney, tea made from sheep droppings. It is sweetened and fed to very young babies. p. 92

Old Hannah, the sun. p. 93

Piney wood rooters, razor-back hogs. Wild hogs. They never get really fat. Inclined to toughness.   p. 94

Justice been beggin' righteous tuh do, this is your duty so clearly that it is not debatable.   p. 95

He ain't goin' tuh let his shirt-tail touch 'im, he won't sit down.   p. 95

Ah'll give mah case tuh Miss Bush and let Mother Green stand mah bond, I'll hide in the woods. I won't need a lawyer because I'll be hidden and no one will have to stand my bond for I have put my person in care of the bushes.   p. 95

Squat dat rabbit, let the matter drop, cease.   p. 95

De caboose uh dat, the end; i.e., the caboose is the tail end of a freight train.   p. 96

Loud talk me, making your side appear right by making more noise than the others.   p. 96

Big Moose done come down from de mountain, "When the half-gods go, the gods arrive." He will make all that has gone before seem trivial beside his works.   p. 113

Porpoise, pauper.   p. 113

Gopher, land tortoise, native of Florida which is locally known as a gopher.   p. 113

Better say Joe, that is doubtful.   p. 113

Big britches goin' tuh fit li'l' Willie, he who was small is now grown. The underdog is now in position to fight for topdog place.
                                    p. 113

Bitter bone, the all-power black-cat bone. Some hoodoo doctors select it by boiling the cat alive with appropriate ceremonies (see "Hoodoo in America," *Journal of American Folk-Lore,* Vol. 44, No. 174, p. 387) and passing the bones thru the mouth until one arrives at the bitter bone.   p. 126

Catbone, same as above, though some doctors do not seek a bone by taste (see "Hoodoo in America," *Journal of American Folk-Lore,* Vol. 44, No. 174, p. 396).   p. 126

God don't eat okra, okra when cooked is slick and slimy, i.e., God does not like slickness, crooked ways. p. 128

When Ahm dying don't you let 'em take de pillow from under mah head. The pillow is removed from beneath the head of the dying because it is said to prolong the death struggle if left in place. All mirrors, and often all glass surfaces, are covered because it is believed the departing spirit will pause to look in them and if it does they will be forever clouded afterwards. p. 130

Doodly-squat, nothing more valuable than dung. Hence the person is in extreme poverty. p. 138

Cold preach, cold used as a superlative to mean unsurpassed. Very common usage. p. 153

Black Herald, Black Dispatch, Negro gossip. p. 157

In his cooler passages the colored preacher attempts to achieve what to him is grammatical correctness, but as he warms up he goes natural. The "ha" in the sermon marks a breath. The congregation likes to hear the preacher breathing or "straining." p. 157

Sow-bosom, salt pork, a very important item in the diet of both Negroes and poor whites in the South. p. 200

MULES
AND MEN

ZORA NEALE HURSTON

PREFACE BY FRANZ BOAS
WITH A NEW FOREWORD BY ARNOLD RAMPERSAD
ILLUSTRATIONS BY MIGUEL COVARRUBIAS

To
my dear friend
Mrs. Annie Nathan Meyer
who hauled the mud to make me
but loves me just the same

CONTENTS

vii

PREFACE

Ever since the time of Uncle Remus, Negro folklore has exerted a strong attraction upon the imagination of the American public. Negro tales, songs and sayings without end, as well as descriptions of Negro magic and voodoo, have appeared; but in all of them the intimate setting in the social life of the Negro has been given very inadequately.

It is the great merit of Miss Hurston's work that she entered into the homely life of the southern Negro as one of them and was fully accepted as such by the companions of her childhood. Thus she has been able to penetrate through that affected demeanor by which the Negro excludes the White observer effectively from participating in his true inner life. Miss Hurston has been equally successful in gaining the confidence of the voodoo doctors and she gives us much that throws a new light upon the much discussed voodoo beliefs and practices. Added to all this is the charm of a loveable personality and of a revealing style which makes Miss Hurston's work an unusual contribution to our knowledge of the true inner life of the Negro.

To the student of cultural history the material presented is valuable not only by giving the Negro's reaction to everyday events, to his emotional life, his humor and passions, but it throws into relief also the peculiar amalgamation of African and European tradition which is so important for understanding historically the character of American Negro life, with its strong African background in the West Indies, the importance of which diminishes with increasing distance from the south.

FRANZ BOAS

FOREWORD

On December 14, 1927, according to her biographer Robert Hemenway, Zora Neale Hurston boarded a midafternoon train at Pennsylvania Station in New York City, bound for Mobile, Alabama. From Mobile she would travel on to Florida and then to Louisiana, in a major effort to gather material on African-American folklore and other folk practices, including voodoo.

Hurston did not begin her project with the utmost confidence. After all, her first significant venture as a collector of folklore in the South had ended earlier that year with a frank admission on her part of failure. That professional setback was particularly galling for two reasons. First, Hurston was no stranger to the South, having been born and reared in Eatonville, Florida; as she later boasted in her autobiography *Dust Tracks on a Road* (1942), she had "the map of Dixie on my tongue." Secondly, she had carried out this first project collecting folklore in the South with the solid backing and encouragement of Franz Boas, unquestionably the dominant figure in American anthropology and Hurston's most influential professor at Barnard College, which she had entered as a student in 1925.

Still, Hurston had been unable to make the most of these advantages and had returned to New York with raw material in her notebooks rather than with a mature, complex grasp of the implications of that material that would have enabled her to move from being simply a transcriber to becoming a profound interpreter of Southern folklore's place in the culture of black America. She had returned to Boas with little to show for her efforts. However, her second expedition into the South as a gatherer of folklore would end differently, even though several years passed before its success was crowned with the publication in 1935 of *Mules and Men*. Filtered through a matured consciousness, and organized according to effective journalistic and literary strategies, the material she gathered mainly between 1927 and 1928 (with additional work up to 1931 and 1932) resulted in one of the outstanding books of its kind ever published in the United States. In 1960, the year Hurston died, the celebrated American collector Alan Lomax appraised *Mules and Men* as "the most engaging, genuine, and skillfully written book in the field of folklore."

Although Hurston is far better known for the publication of her feminist novel *Their Eyes Were Watching God* (1937), no understanding of her mind and her art, or of her contribution to African-American culture or to the study of folklore, can ignore the achievement of *Mules and Men*. Almost certainly, there would have been no *Their Eyes Were Watching God* without the process of growth and maturation that resulted first from *Mules and Men*. In this book, Hurston first effected a genuine reconciliation between herself and her past, which is to say between herself as a growing individual with literary ambitions on the one hand and the evolving African-American culture and history on the other. Here, in an extended literary act—her most ambitious to date—she found at last the proper form for depicting herself in relationship to the broad range of forces within the African-American culture that had produced her, as well as for portraying the people of which she was but one member. Here she came to terms at last with the full range of black folk traditions, practices, expressions, and types of behavior, and began to trust her understanding of their multiple meanings as an index to the African-American world. "From the earliest rocking of my cradle," she wrote in *Mules and Men*, "I had known about the capers Brer Rabbit is apt to cut and what the Squinch Owl says from the house top. But it was fitting me like a tight chemise. I couldn't see it for wearing it. It was only when I was off in college, away from my native surroundings, that I could see myself like somebody else and stand off and look at my garment. Then I had to have the spy-glass of Anthropology to look through at that."

In the case of Zora Neale Hurston, one speaks of this "coming to terms" with black folk culture carefully or not at all. Struggling to find a lofty place for herself in the world, she nevertheless arrived in New York in 1925 displaying from the start little ambivalence about traditional black culture. She was one of W.E.B. Du Bois's talented tenth—the gifted and educated leadership of the race on whom Du Bois based his hopes for African-American ascendance—without seeing herself, as members of the tenth often saw themselves, as victim caught tragically between two worlds, black and white. Instead, she draped black folk culture about herself like a fabulous robe, creating an inimitable and unforgettable personality, according to virtually everyone who recalled her, based on her mastery of jokes and stories, insights and attitudes, that derived almost directly from the black folk experience. As a fledgling writer, too, her earliest stories depended proudly—and shrewdly—on the black voices she had heard as a child growing up in Florida, the people who had taught her how to speak. She moved ambitiously among whites, often with guile and not infrequently in a servile manner; but consistently she offered herself as a child of the black South who had little desire ever to forget, much less repudiate, her folk and country roots.

This degree of identification set her apart from virtually all other writers, black and white. In his landmark study *The Souls of Black Folk* (1903), Du Bois had delved into folk culture to illustrate his thesis of black dignity and historicity. However, he had concentrated almost exclusively, in the area of psychology and philosophy, on approaches by blacks to Christianity;

in the area of art, he clung almost entirely to the noble and transcendent music of the spirituals. Other black writers, such as William Wells Brown and Charles Chesnutt, had drawn on black folkways, including both in music and in religion, in certain areas of their work, but none approached Hurston's knowledge of and commitment to folk culture. By far the best-known explorer of the black folk tradition among writers was Joel Chandler Harris, whose Uncle Remus stories, in tying animal tales to the plantation tradition, severely limited their applicability to black culture as a whole. Within what passed in those days for folklore science (as Hemenway points out, not one American university then boasted a department of folklore), efforts by white collectors to gather black material were often stymied by preconceptions about black character and by the reticence of blacks to lower their guard before such strangers. Notable among such work available in Hurston's days as a student were Guy Johnson and Howard Odum's *The Negro and His Sons* (1925) and *Negro Workaday Songs* (1926), as well as the white Mississippi folklorist Newbell Niles Puckett's *Folk Beliefs of the Southern Negro* (1927), in which Puckett had masqueraded as a voodoo priest himself in order to gain information.

As her letters to her academic mentor Franz Boas attest, Hurston had little regard for the work of these writers, especially Odum and Johnson, whom she saw as presumptuous in their confidence that they understood fully the black folk material. "Folklore is not as easy to collect as it sounds," she warned. "The best source is where there are the least outside influences and these people, being usually under-privileged, are the shyest." She was fortunate in that Boas, although a white man himself, was perhaps the outstanding champion of the notion of cultural relativism. He urged that cultures be seen on their own terms and not according to a scale that held European civilization to be the supreme standard. For all her advantages, however, Hurston still found it difficult to effect a breakthrough. In part, this was owing to the complexity of the task of understanding the material; in part, it derived from

Hurston's personal life experience, and especially from the fact that she was living at least one major lie as a student at Barnard. The two elements—the scholarly or intellectual, on the one hand, and the "purely" personal, on the other—were perhaps finally inseparable.

Hurston was born in the black town of Eatonville, Florida, on January 7, 1891—but so willfully misrepresented herself later that even her diligent biographer believed that her year of birth was 1901. This lost decade is perhaps only the major mystery of her life. What happened to Hurston between 1891 and 1917, when she started high school at Morgan Academy (later Morgan State University) in Baltimore, Maryland, is barely illuminated either by independent research or by her autobiography *Dust Tracks on a Road* (1942). Both, however, tell of a loving mother who urged her to "jump at de sun" and a dominating father, an Eatonville preacher and carpenter, whose remarriage following his wife's death began a long season of sorrow for Hurston. Apparently unable to find common ground with her new stepmother, Zora was passed around among relatives before she struck out on her own. She worked variously as a maid and a waitress, and may even have been married for a while, before she entered Morgan Academy in 1917. After being graduated from Morgan, she briefly attended Howard University in Washington, D.C., before going to New York in 1925 to study at Barnard College. *Mules and Men* is dedicated to Annie Nathan Meyer ("who hauled the mud to make me but loves me just the same"), the founder and a trustee of the college and the person directly responsible for Hurston's presence there.

As Hurston wrote, "the spy-glass of Anthropology" offered at Barnard and Columbia, especially in the persons of Boas and his associates Melville Herskovits and Ruth Benedict, enabled her to begin to see her Southern black culture accurately and comprehensively. And yet her deliberate obscuring of a decade of her life suggests that she could have approached her past, which is to say the wellspring of her folkloric knowledge, only with a certain amount of caution, perhaps even distaste. In dropping a decade from her life, she was almost certainly denying the existence of experiences and involvements that, however unpalatable to her later on as she strove for success, had been a major part of her knowledge of her world. However, one other person was at least as important as these academics in pushing Hurston not only back into the arms of her past, as exemplified by her literal reentry into Eatonville to gather the material for the first part of *Mules and Men,* but also toward the radical belief in parapsychology and occultism, in voodoo and other forms of African religion, that generated the second, even more extraordinary part of the volume. That person was her patron Mrs. R. Osgood Mason, as Hurston reveals in *Mules and Men,* who "backed my falling in a hearty way, in a spiritual way, and in addition, financed the whole expedition in the manner of the Great Soul that she is. The world's most gallant woman."

This tribute appears at the end of Hurston's introduction, which places her in a motorcar (paid for by Mrs. Mason) precisely on the border of Eatonville—home. The wealthy septuagenarian widow of a doctor who had been himself an expert in parapsychology, Mrs. Mason was already "Godmother" to various Harlem Renaissance figures, including Alain Locke and Langston Hughes, when she took up Zora Neale Hurston and bankrolled her second folklore expedition into the South. As with Langston Hughes, whose novel *Not Without Laughter* (1930) Mrs. Mason virtually commissioned and edited, she did much more than provide Hurston with money. Volatile in personality, contemptuous of European rationalism and radically devoted to the idea of extrasensory communication, and a champion of the notion of the artistic and spiritual superiority of the darker races, Mrs. Mason, more than any of Hurston's academic advisers, paved the way for Hurston's plunging not simply into the Eatonville community of her childhood but, far more radically, into voodoo and black magic in Louisiana.

Although the voodoo section (a slightly edited version of her 1931 article "Hoodoo in America" in the *Journal of Ameri-*

can Folklore) was added at the last minute to the book in 1934 to please its publisher, Lippincott, the two sections are intimately related. The world of Eatonville and Florida in general—the world of tales spun by black men and women—is linked directly in this book to the world of New Orleans and Louisiana, where "two-headed doctors" preside over a community that believes devoutly in spells and conjures, hexes and divinations. Linking Eatonville and New Orleans is the communality and adaptability, the indomitable resilience of the imagination of Africans terrorized in the New World by objective reality in the form of slavery, segregation, and poverty. And both elements, I believe, were linked integrally to Hurston's interior world, to the fantastic personality and the altered personal history she had created for herself. "I thought about the tales I had heard as a child," Hurston recalled fancifully but pointedly during her approach by car to Eatonville. "How even the Bible was made over to suit our vivid imagination. How the devil always outsmarted God and how that over-noble hero Jack or John—not *John Henry,* who occupies the same place in Negro folklore that Casey Jones does in white lore and if anything is more recent—outsmarted the devil."

She who had been living to some extent by her wits, by her imagination, by the "lies" she created for her empowerment and salvation, as well as by her more structured, conventionally disciplined intelligence as a college student, now had begun to see her personal predicament and her imaginative response to it in a broader historical and cultural sense. To her black sources, their marvelous tales were—"lies." (" 'Zora,' George Thomas informed me, 'you come to de right place if lies is what you want. Ah'm gointer lie up a nation.' ") In one sense, it is possible to say that Hurston had become more of an African-American cultural nationalist, seeing more of the world and herself in terms of race and her own blackness. This would be true only to a limited degree, as Hurston's later involvement with reactionary political forces and personalities suggests. The power she gained from seeing her life in coherence with the storytelling imagination of country blacks and with the world of conjure and black magic represented by voodoo was placed largely in a different service—self-empoweringly, to facilitate her emergence as a writer of fiction. Even before *Mules and Men* appeared in 1935, she published her first novel, *Jonah's Gourd Vine* (1934), which drew on her parents' history for inspiration. Two years after *Mules and Men* came *Their Eyes Were Watching God,* in which she effected her most harmonious blending of the themes of folklore and individualism, in a story now recognized as one of the main foundations of African-American literature.

In both main sections of *Mules and Men*— the seventy stories that make up "Folk Tales" and her encounters with five doctors in "Hoodoo"—the most fertile single device is the portrait of the narrator, Hurston herself. In both cases, she is both familiar with the culture into which she is moving and also an initiate. She is known in Eatonville, but everywhere else she must ingratiate herself into the confidence of the people, her great source. ("I stood there awkwardly, knowing that the too-ready laughter and aimless talk was a window-dressing for my benefit. The brother in black puts a laugh in every vacant place in his mind. His laugh has a hundred meanings.") So, too, with the world of hoodoo, which she approaches not as a scientific scholar, taking notes, or fraudulently, as Newbell Niles Puckett had done for his own book in representing himself as a conjure man. "None may wear the crown of power," she writes of her initiation, "without preparation. *It must be earned.*" Instead, she would be a true believer. "Belief in magic is older than writing," she declared tellingly. In the end, her teacher Luke Turner (called elsewhere Samuel Thompson by Hurston), who offered himself as the grand-nephew of Marie Leveau, the most fabled figure in New Orleans hoodoo lore, invites Hurston to devote her life to the field. "He wanted me to stay with him to the end," she soberly reveals. "It has been a great sorrow to me that I could not say yes."

Much has been made about Hurston's scholarly shortcomings in compiling *Mules and Men.* It seems certain that not all the stories and anecdotes in the book originated in the course of her research. Some of them, picked up elsewhere, may have been substantially ornamented by Hurston, and perhaps she invented a few. Rival versions of certain passages, published elsewhere by her, raise questions about her scholarly integrity. For the sake of symmetry, she appears to have telescoped certain periods of time into more convenient arrangements. "I had spent a year in gathering and culling over folk-tales," she wrote, when in fact she had spent a much longer period. Above all, some readers find Hurston insufficiently analytical and too much a part of her text, without that text revealing her definitively. Her shifts from the third person to the first are sometimes disconcerting. Scientific purists may find her language at times too colloquial and even racy, her sense of humor often reckless, her poetic license too frequently invoked. Her approach, some would say, was journalistic rather than scientific, self-indulgent rather than profound.

I would respond that the key to *Mules and Men* is precisely Hurston's finding of herself in the black folk world she described, and finding that black folk world, approached first by her as a student of anthropology, finally to be an unmistakable, ineradicable part of herself, her intimate psychology and history, and her desires, especially her desire to be an artist.

ARNOLD RAMPERSAD

INTRODUCTION

I was glad when somebody told me, "You may go and collect Negro folklore."

In a way it would not be a new experience for me. When I pitched headforemost into the world I landed in the crib of negroism. From the earliest rocking of my cradle, I had known about the capers Brer Rabbit is apt to cut and what the Squinch Owl says from the house top. But it was fitting me like a tight chemise. I couldn't see it for wearing it. It was only when I was off in college, away from my native surroundings, that I could see myself like somebody else and stand off and look at my garment. Then I had to have the spy-glass of Anthropology to look through at that.

Dr. Boas asked me where I wanted to work and I said, "Florida," and gave, as my big reason, that "Florida is a place that draws people—white people from all over the world, and Negroes from every Southern state surely and some from the North and West." So I knew that it was possible for me to get a cross section of the Negro South in the one state. And then I realized that I was new myself, so it looked sensible for me to choose familiar ground.

First place I aimed to stop to collect material was Eatonville, Florida.

And now, I'm going to tell you why I decided to go to my

native village first. I didn't go back there so that the home folks could make admiration over me because I had been up North to college and come back with a diploma and a Chevrolet. I knew they were not going to pay either one of these items too much mind. I was just Lucy Hurston's daughter, Zora, and even if I had—to use one of our down-home expressions—had a Kaiser baby,[1] and that's something that hasn't been done in this Country yet, I'd still be just Zora to the neighbors. If I had exalted myself to impress the town, somebody would have sent me word in a match-box that I had been up North there and had rubbed the hair off of my head against some college wall, and then come back there with a lot of form and fashion and outside show to the world. But they'd stand flat-footed and tell me that they didn't have me, neither my sham-polish, to study 'bout. And that would have been that.

I hurried back to Eatonville because I knew that the town was full of material and that I could get it without hurt, harm or danger. As early as I could remember it was the habit of the men folks particularly to gather on the store porch of evenings and swap stories. Even the women folks would stop and break a breath with them at times. As a child when I was sent down to Joe Clarke's store, I'd drag out my leaving as long as possible in order to hear more.

Folklore is not as easy to collect as it sounds. The best source is where there are the least outside influences and these people, being usually under-privileged, are the shyest. They are most reluctant at times to reveal that which the soul lives by. And the Negro, in spite of his open-faced laughter, his seeming acquiescence, is particularly evasive. You see we are a polite people and we do not say to our questioner, "Get out of here!" We smile and tell him or her something that satisfies the white person because, knowing so little about us, he doesn't know what he is missing. The Indian resists curiosity by a stony silence. The Negro offers a feather-bed resistance. That is, we let the probe enter, but it never comes out. It gets

[1] Have a child by the Kaiser.

2

smothered under a lot of laughter and pleasantries.

The theory behind our tactics: "The white man is always trying to know into somebody else's business. All right, I'll set something outside the door of my mind for him to play with and handle. He can read my writing but he sho' can't read my mind. I'll put this play toy in his hand, and he will seize it and go away. Then I'll say my say and sing my song."

I knew that even *I* was going to have some hindrance among strangers. But here in Eatonville I knew everybody was going to help me. So below Palatka I began to feel eager to be there and I kicked the little Chevrolet right along.

I thought about the tales I had heard as a child. How even the Bible was made over to suit our vivid imagination. How the devil always outsmarted God and how that over-noble hero Jack or John—not *John Henry*, who occupies the same place in Negro folk-lore that Casey Jones does in white lore and if anything is more recent—outsmarted the devil. Brer Fox, Brer Deer, Brer 'Gator, Brer Dawg, Brer Rabbit, Ole Massa and his wife were walking the earth like natural men way back in the days when God himself was on the ground and men could talk with him. Way back there before God weighed up the dirt to make the mountains. When I was rounding Lily Lake I was remembering how God had made the world and the elements and people. He made souls for people, but he didn't give them out because he said:

"Folks ain't ready for souls yet. De clay ain't dry. It's de
strongest thing Ah ever made. Don't aim to waste none
thru loose cracks. And then men got to grow strong
enough to stand it. De way things is now, if Ah give it out
it would tear them shackly bodies to pieces. Bimeby, Ah
give it out."

So folks went round thousands of years without no souls.
All de time de soul-piece, it was setting 'round covered up
wid God's loose raiment. Every now and then de wind
would blow and hist up de cover and then de elements
would be full of lightning and de winds would talk. So

3

people told one 'nother that God was talking in de mountains.

De white man passed by it way off and he looked but he wouldn't go close enough to touch. De Indian and de Negro, they tipped by cautious too, and all of 'em seen de light of diamonds when de winds shook de cover, and de wind dat passed over it sung songs. De Jew come past and heard de song from de soul-piece then he kept on passin' and all of a sudden he grabbed up de soul-piece and hid it under his clothes, and run off down de road. It burnt him and tore him and throwed him down and lifted him up and toted him across de mountain and he tried to break loose but he couldn't do it. He kept on hollerin' for help but de rest of 'em run hid 'way from him. Way after while they come out of holes and corners and picked up little chips and pieces that fell back on de ground. So God mixed it up wid feelings and give it out to 'em. 'Way after while when He ketch dat Jew, He's goin' to 'vide things up more ekal'.

So I rounded Park Lake and came speeding down the straight stretch into Eatonville, the city of five lakes, three croquet courts, three hundred brown skins, three hundred good swimmers, plenty guavas, two schools, and no jail-house.

Before I enter the township, I wish to make acknowledgments to Mrs. R. Osgood Mason of New York City. She backed my falling in a hearty way, in a spiritual way, and in addition, financed the whole expedition in the manner of the Great Soul that she is. The world's most gallant woman.

4

PART I

❖

FOLK TALES

ONE

As I crossed the Maitland-Eatonville township line I could see a group on the store porch. I was delighted. The town had not changed. Same love of talk and song. So I drove on down there before I stopped. Yes, there was George Thomas, Calvin Daniels, Jack and Charlie Jones, Gene Brazzle, B. Moseley and "Seaboard." Deep in a game of Florida-flip. All of those who were not actually playing were giving advice—"bet straightening" they call it.

"Hello, boys," I hailed them as I went into neutral.

They looked up from the game and for a moment it looked as if they had forgotten me. Then B. Moseley said, "Well, if it ain't Zora Hurston!" Then everybody crowded around the car to help greet me.

"You gointer stay awhile, Zora?"

"Yep. Several months."

"Where you gointer stay, Zora?"

"With Mett and Ellis, I reckon."

"Mett" was Mrs. Armetta Jones, an intimate friend of mine since childhood and Ellis was her husband. Their house stands under the huge camphor tree on the front street.

"Hello, heart-string," Mayor Hiram Lester yelled as he hurried up the street. "We heard all about you up North. You back home for good, I hope."

"Nope, Ah come to collect some old stories and tales and Ah know y'all know a plenty of 'em and that's why Ah headed straight for home."

"What you mean, Zora, them big old lies we tell when we're jus' sittin' around here on the store porch doin' nothin'?" asked B. Moseley.

"Yeah, those same ones about Ole Massa, and colored folks in heaven, and—oh, y'all know the kind I mean."

"Aw shucks," exclaimed George Thomas doubtfully. "Zora, don't you come here and tell de biggest lie first thing. Who you reckon want to read all them old-time tales about Brer Rabbit and Brer Bear?"

"Plenty of people, George. They are a lot more valuable than you might think. We want to set them down before it's too late."

"Too late for what?"

"Before everybody forgets all of 'em."

"No danger of that. That's all some people is good for—set 'round and lie and murder groceries."

"Ah know one right now," Calvin Daniels announced cheerfully. "It's a tale 'bout John and de frog."

"Wait till she get out her car, Calvin. Let her get settled at 'Met's' and cook a pan of ginger bread then we'll all go down and tell lies and eat ginger bread. Dat's de way to do. She's tired now from all dat drivin'."

"All right, boys," I agreed. "But Ah'll be rested by night. Be lookin' for everybody."

So I unloaded the car and crowded it into Ellis' garage and got settled. Armetta made me lie down and rest while she cooked a big pan of ginger bread for the company we expected.

Calvin Daniels and James Moseley were the first to show up.

"Calvin, Ah sure am glad that you got here. Ah'm crazy to hear about John and dat frog," I said.

"That's why Ah come so early so Ah could tell it to you and go. Ah got to go over to Wood Bridge a little later on."

"Ah'm glad you remembered me first, Calvin."

8

"Ah always like to be good as my word, and Ah just heard about a toe-party over to Wood Bridge tonight and Ah decided to make it."

"A toe-party! What on earth is that?"

"Come go with me and James and you'll see!"

"But, everybody will be here lookin' for me. They'll think Ah'm crazy—tellin' them to come and then gettin' out and goin' to Wood Bridge myself. But Ah certainly would like to go to that toe-party."

"Aw, come on. They kin come back another night. You gointer like this party."

"Well, you tell me the story first, and by that time, Ah'll know what to do."

"Ah, come on, Zora," James urged. "Git de car out. Calvin kin tell you dat one while we're on de way. Come on, let's go to de toe-party."

"No, let 'im tell me this one first, then, if Ah go he can tell me some more on de way over."

James motioned to his friend. "Hurry up and tell it, Calvin, so we kin go before somebody else come."

"Aw, most of 'em ain't comin' nohow. They all 'bout goin' to Wood Bridge, too. Lemme tell you 'bout John and dis frog:

It was night and Ole Massa sent John,[1] his favorite slave, down to the spring to get him a cool drink of water. He called John to him.

"John!"

"What you want, Massa?"

"John, I'm thirsty. Ah wants a cool drink of water, and Ah wants you to go down to de spring and dip me up a nice cool pitcher of water."

John didn't like to be sent nowhere at night, but he always tried to do everything Ole Massa told him to do, so he said, "Yessuh, Massa, Ah'll go git you some!"

Ole Massa said: "Hurry up, John. Ah'm mighty thirsty."

John took de pitcher and went on down to de spring.

[1]Negro story-hero name. See glossary.

There was a great big ole bull frog settin' right on de edge of de spring, and when John dipped up de water de noise skeered de frog and he hollered and jumped over in de spring.

John dropped de water pitcher and tore out for de big house, hollerin' "Massa! Massa! A big ole booger[2] done got after me!"

Ole Massa told him, "Why, John, there's no such thing as a booger."

"Oh, yes it is, Massa. He down at dat Spring."

"Don't tell me, John. Youse just excited. Furthermore, you go git me dat water Ah sent you after."

"No, indeed, Massa, you and nobody else can't send me back there so dat booger kin git me."

Ole Massa begin to figger dat John musta seen somethin' sho nuff because John never had disobeyed him before, so he ast: "John, you say you seen a booger. What did it look like?"

John tole him, "Massa, he had two great big eyes lak balls of fire, and when he was standin' up he was sittin' down and when he moved, he moved by jerks, and he had most no tail."

Long before Calvin had ended his story James had lost his air of impatience.

"Now, Ah'll tell one," he said. "That is, if you so desire."

"Sure, Ah want to hear you tell 'em till daybreak if you will," I said eagerly.

"But where's the ginger bread?" James stopped to ask.

"It's out in the kitchen," I said. "Ah'm waiting for de others to come."

"Aw, naw, give us ours now. Them others may not get here before forty o'clock and Ah'll be done et mine and be in Wood Bridge. Anyhow Ah want a corner piece and some of them others will beat me to it."

So I served them with ginger bread and buttermilk.

[2]A bogey man.

10

"You sure going to Wood Bridge with us after Ah git thru tellin' this one?" James asked.

"Yeah, if the others don't show up by then," I conceded.

So James told the story about the man who went to Heaven from Johnstown.

You know, when it lightnings, de angels is peepin' in de lookin' glass; when it thunders, they's rollin' out de rain-barrels; and when it rains, somebody done dropped a barrel or two and bust it.

One time, you know, there was going to be big doin's in Glory and all de angels had brand new clothes to wear and so they was all peepin' in the lookin' glasses, and therefore it got to lightning all over de sky. God tole some of de angels to roll in all de full rain barrels and they was in such a hurry that it was thunderin' from the east to the west and the zig-zag lightning went to join the mutterin' thunder and, next thing you know, some of them angels got careless and dropped a whole heap of them rain barrels, and didn't it rain!

In one place they call Johnstown they had a great flood. And so many folks got drownded that it looked jus' like Judgment day.

So some of de folks that got drownded in that flood went one place and some went another. You know, everything that happen, they got to be a nigger in it—and so one of de brothers in black went up to Heben from de flood.

When he got to the gate, Ole Peter let 'im in and made 'im welcome. De colored man was named John, so John ast Peter, says, "Is it dry in dere?"

Ole Peter tole 'im, "Why, yes it's dry in here. How come you ast that?"

"Well, you know Ah jus' come out of one flood, and Ah don't want to run into no mo'. Ooh, man! You ain't *seen* no water. You just oughter seen dat flood we had at Johnstown."

Peter says, "Yeah, we know all about it. Jus' go wid Gabriel and let him give you some new clothes."

So John went on off wid Gabriel and come back all dressed up in brand new clothes and all de time he was changin' his clothes he was tellin' Ole Gabriel all about dat flood, jus' like he didn't know already.

So when he come back from changin' his clothes, they give him a brand new gold harp and handed him to a gold bench and made him welcome. They was so tired of hearing about dat flood they was glad to see him wid his harp 'cause they figgered he'd get to playin' and forget all about it. So Peter tole him, "Now you jus' make yo'self at home and play all de music you please."

John went and took a seat on de bench and commenced to tune up his harp. By dat time, two angels come walkin' by where John was settin' so he throwed down his harp and tackled 'em.

"Say," he hollered, "Y'all want to hear 'bout de big flood Ah was in down on earth? Lawd, Lawd! It sho rained, and talkin' 'bout water!"

Dem two angels hurried on off from 'im jus' as quick as they could. He started to tellin' another one and he took to flyin'. Gab'ull went over to 'im and tried to get 'im to take it easy, but John kept right on stoppin' every angel dat he could find to tell 'im about dat flood of water.

Way after while he went over to Ole Peter and said: "Thought you said everybody would be nice and polite?"

Peter said, "Yeah, Ah said it. Ain't everybody treatin' you right?"

John said, "Naw. Ah jus' walked up to a man as nice and friendly as Ah could be and started to tell 'im 'bout all dat water Ah left back there in Johnstown and instead of him turnin' me a friendly answer he said, 'Shucks! You ain't seen no water!' and walked off and left me standin' by myself."

"Was he a *ole* man wid a crooked walkin' stick?" Peter ast John.

"Yeah."

"Did he have whiskers down to here?" Peter measured down to his waist.

12

"He sho did," John tol' 'im.

"Aw shucks," Peter tol' 'im. "Dat was Ole Nora.[3] You can't tell *him* nothin' 'bout no flood."

There was a lot of horn-honking outside and I went to the door. The crowd drew up under the mothering camphor tree in four old cars. Everybody in boisterous spirits.

"Come on, Zora! Le's go to Wood Bridge. Great toe-party goin' on. All kinds of 'freshments. We kin tell you some lies most any ole time. We never run outer lies and lovin'. Tell 'em tomorrow night. Come on if you comin'—le's go if you gwine."

So I loaded up my car with neighbors and we all went to Wood Bridge. It is a Negro community joining Maitland on the north as Eatonville does on the west, but no enterprising souls have ever organized it. They have no schoolhouse, no post office, no mayor. It is lacking in Eatonville's feeling of unity. In fact, a white woman lives there.

While we rolled along Florida No. 3, I asked Armetta where was the shindig going to be in Wood Bridge. "At Edna Pitts' house," she told me. "But she ain't givin' it by herself; it's for the lodge."

"Think it's gointer be lively?"

"Oh, yeah. Ah heard that a lot of folks from Altamonte and Longwood is comin'. Maybe from Winter Park too."

We were the tail end of the line and as we turned off the highway we could hear the boys in the first car doing what Ellis Jones called bookooing[4] before they even hit the ground. Charlie Jones was woofing[5] louder than anybody else. "Don't y'all sell off all dem pretty li'l pink toes befo' Ah git dere."

Peter Stagg: "Save me de best one!"

Soddy Sewell: "Hey, you mullet heads! Get out de way

<hr>

[3] Noah.

[4] Loud talking, bullying, woofing. From French *beaucoup*.

[5] Aimless talking. See glossary.

there and let a real man smoke them toes over."

Gene Brazzle: "Come to my pick, gimme a vaseline brown!"

Big Willie Sewell: "Gimme any kind so long as you gimme more'n one."

Babe Brown, riding a running-board, guitar in hand, said, "Ah want a toe, but if it ain't got a good looking face on to it, don't bring de mess up."

When we got there the party was young. The house was swept and garnished, the refreshments on display, several people sitting around; but the spot needed some social juices to mix the ingredients. In other words, they had the carcass of a party lying around up until the minute Eatonville burst in on it. Then it woke up.

"Y'all done sold off any toes yet?" George Brown wanted to know.

Willie Mae Clarke gave him a certain look and asked him, "What's dat got to do with you, George Brown?" And he shut up. Everybody knows that Willie Mae's got the business with George Brown.

"Nope. We ain't had enough crowd, but I reckon we kin start now," Edna said. Edna and a sort of committee went inside and hung up a sheet across one end of the room. Then she came outside and called all of the young women inside. She had to coax and drag some of the girls.

"Oh, Ah'm shame-face-ted!" some of them said.

"Nobody don't want to buy *mah* ole rusty toe." Others fished around for denials from the male side.

I went on in with the rest and was herded behind the curtain.

"Say, what *is* this toe-party business?" I asked one of the girls.

"Good gracious, Zora! Ain't you never been to a toe-party before?"

"Nope. They don't have 'em up North where Ah been and Ah just got back today."

"Well, they hides all de girls behind a curtain and you stick out yo' toe. Some places you take off yo' shoes and some places you keep 'em on, but most all de time you keep 'em on. When all de toes is in a line, sticking out from behind de sheet they let de men folks in and they looks over all de toes and buys de ones they want for a dime. Then they got to treat de lady dat owns dat toe to everything she want. Sometime they play it so's you keep de same partner for de whole thing and sometime they fix it so they put de girls back every hour or so and sell de toes agin."

Well, my toe went on the line with the rest and it was sold five times during the party. Everytime a toe was sold there was a great flurry before the curtain. Each man eager to see what he had got, and whether the other men would envy him or ridicule him. One or two fellows ungallantly ran out of the door rather than treat the girls whose toe they had bought sight unseen.

Babe Brown got off on his guitar and the dancing was hilarious. There was plenty of chicken perleau and baked chicken and fried chicken and rabbit. Pig feet and chitterlings[6] and hot peanuts and drinkables. Everybody was treating wildly.

"Come on, Zora, and have a treat on me!" Charlie Jones insisted. "You done et chicken-ham and chicken-bosom wid every shag-leg in Orange County *but* me. Come on and spend some of *my* money."

"Thanks, Charlie, but Ah got five helpin's of chicken inside already. Ah either got to get another stomach or quit eatin'."

"Quit eatin' then and go to thinking. Quit thinkin' and start to drinkin'. What you want?"

"Coca-Cola right off de ice, Charlie, and put some salt in it. Ah got a slight headache."

"Aw naw, my money don't buy no sweet slop. Choose some coon dick."

"What is coon dick?"

"Aw, Zora, jus' somethin' to make de drunk come. Made

6Hog intestines.

out uh grape fruit juice, corn meal mash, beef bones and a few mo' things. Come on le's git some together. It might make our love come down."

As soon as we started over into the next yard where coon dick was to be had, Charlie yelled to the barkeep, "Hey, Seymore! fix up another quart of dat low wine—here come de boom!"

It was handed to us in a quart fruit jar and we went outside to try it.

The raw likker known locally as coon dick was too much. The minute it touched my lips, the top of my head flew off. I spat it out and "choosed" some peanuts. Big Willie Sewell said, "Come on, heart-string, and have some gospel-bird[7] on me. My money spends too." His Honor, Hiram Lester, the Mayor, heard him and said, "There's no mo' chicken left, Willie. Why don't you offer her something she can get?"

"Well there *was* some chicken there when Ah passed the table a little while ago."

"Oh, so you offerin' her some chicken *was*. She can't eat that. What she want is some chicken *is*."

"Aw shut up, Hiram. Come on, Zora, le's go inside and make out we dancin'." We went on inside but it wasn't a party any more. Just some people herded together. The high spirits were simmering down and nobody had a dime left to cry so the toe-business suffered a slump. The heaped-up tables of refreshments had become shambles of chicken bones and empty platters anyway so that there was no longer any point in getting your toe sold, so when Columbus Montgomery said, "Le's go to Eatonville," Soddy Sewell jumped up and grabbed his hat and said, "I heard you, buddy."

Eatonville began to move back home right then. Nearly everybody was packed in one of the five cars when the delegation from Altamonte arrived. Johnny Barton and Georgia Burke. Everybody piled out again.

"Got yo' guitar wid you, Johnnie?"

[7]Chicken. Preachers are supposed to be fond of them.

16

"Man, you know Ah don't go nowhere unless Ah take my box wid me," said Johnnie in his starched blue shirt, collar pin with heart bangles hanging on each end and his cream pants with the black stripe. "And what make it so cool, Ah don't go nowhere unless I play it."

"And when you git to strowin' yo' mess and Georgy gits to singin' her alto, man it's hot as seven hells. Man, play dat 'Palm Beach.'"

Babe Brown took the guitar and Johnnie Barton grabbed the piano stool. He sung. Georgia Burke and George Thomas singing about Polk County where the water taste like wine.

My heart struck sorrow, tears come running down.

At about the thirty-seventh verse, something about:

Ah'd ruther be in Tampa with the Whip-poor-will,
Ruther be in Tampa with the Whip-poor-will
Than to be 'round here—
Honey with a hundred dollar bill,

I staggered sleepily forth to the little Chevrolet for Eatonville. The car was overflowing with passengers but I was so dull from lack of sleep that I didn't know who they were. All I knew is they belonged in Eatonville.

Somebody was woofing in my car about love and I asked him about his buddy—I don't know why now. He said, "Ah ain't got no buddy. They kilt my buddy so they could raise me. Jus' so Ah be yo' man Ah don't want no damn buddy. Ah hope they kill every man dat ever cried, 'titty-mamma' but me. Lemme be yo' kid."

Some voice from somewhere else in the car commented, "You sho' Lawd is gointer have a lot of hindrance."

Then somehow I got home and to bed and Armetta had Georgia syrup and waffles for breakfast.

TWO

The very next afternoon, as usual, the gregarious part of the town's population gathered on the store porch. All the Florida-flip players, all the eleven-card layers.[1] But they yelled over to me they'd be over that night in full. And they were.

"Zora," George Thomas informed me, "you come to de right place if lies is what you want. Ah'm gointer lie up a nation."

Charlie Jones said, "Yeah, man. Me and my sworn buddy Gene Brazzle is here. Big Moose done come down from de mountain."[2]

"Now, you gointer hear lies above suspicion," Gene added.

It was a hilarious night with a pinch of everything social mixed with the story-telling. Everybody ate ginger bread; some drank the buttermilk provided and some provided coon dick for themselves. Nobody guzzled it—just took it in social sips.

But they told stories enough for a volume by itself. Some of the stories were the familiar drummer-type of tale about two Irishmen, Pat and Mike, or two Jews as the case might be.

[1]Coon-can players. A two-handed card game popular among Southern Negroes.

[2]Important things are about to happen.

19

Some were the European folk-tales undiluted, like Jack and the Beanstalk. Others had slight local variations, but Negro imagination is so facile that there was little need for outside help. A'nt Hagar's son, like Joseph, put on his many-colored coat an paraded before his brethren and every man there was a Joseph.

Steve Nixon was holding class meeting across the way at St. Lawrence Church and we could hear the testimony and the songs.[3] So we began to talk about church and preachers.

"Aw, Ah don't pay all dese ole preachers no rabbit-foot,"[4] said Ellis Jones. "Some of 'em is all right but everybody dats up in de pulpit whoopin' and hollerin' ain't called to preach."

"They ain't no different from nobody else," added B. Moseley. "They mouth is cut cross ways, ain't it? Well, long as you don't see no man wid they mouth cut up and down, you know they'll all lie jus' like de rest of us."

"Yeah; and hard work in de hot sun done called a many a man to preach," said a woman called Gold, for no evident reason. "Ah heard about one man out clearin' off some new ground. De sun was so hot till a grindstone melted and run off in de shade to cool off. De man was so tired till he went and sit down on a log. 'Work, work, work! Everywhere Ah go de boss say hurry, de cap' say run. Ah got a durn good notion not to do nary one. Wisht Ah was one of dese preachers wid a whole lot of folks makin' my support for me.' He looked back over his shoulder and seen a narrer li'l strip of shade along side of de log, so he got over dere and laid down right close up to de log in de shade and said, 'Now, Lawd, if you don't pick me up and chunk me on de other side of dis log, Ah know you done called me to preach.'

"You know God never picked 'im up, so he went off and tol' everybody dat he was called to preach."

"There's many a one been called just lak dat," Ellis corroborated. "Ah knowed a man dat was called by a mule."

[3] See glossary.

[4] I ignore these preachers.

20

"A mule, Ellis? All dem b'lieve dat, stand on they head," said Little Ida.

"Yeah, a mule did call a man to preach. Ah'll show you how it was done, if you'll stand a straightenin'."

"Now, Ellis, don't mislay de truth. Sense us into dis mule-callin' business."

Ellis: These was two brothers and one of 'em was a big preacher and had good collections every Sunday. He didn't pastor nothin' but big charges. De other brother decided he wanted to preach so he went way down in de swamp behind a big plantation to de place they call de prayin' ground, and got down on his knees.

"O Lawd, Ah wants to preach. Ah feel lak Ah got a message. If you done called me to preach, gimme a sign."

Just 'bout dat time he heard a voice, "Wanh, uh wanh! Go preach, go preach, go preach!"

He went and tol' everybody, but look lak he never could git no big charge. All he ever got called was on some saw-mill, half-pint church or some turpentine still. He knocked around lak dat for ten years and then he seen his brother. De big preacher says, "Brother, you don't look like you gittin' holt of much."

"You tellin' dat right, brother. Groceries is scarce. Ah ain't dirtied a plate today."

"Whut's de matter? Don't you git no support from your church?"

"Yeah, Ah gits it such as it is, but Ah ain't never pastored no big church. Ah don't git called to nothin' but saw-mill camps and turpentine stills."

De big preacher reared back and thought a while, then he ast de other one, "Is you sure you was called to preach? Maybe you ain't cut out for no preacher."

"Oh, yeah," he told him. "Ah *know* Ah been called to de ministry. A voice spoke and tol' me so."

"Well, seem lak if God called you He is mighty slow in puttin' yo' foot on de ladder. If Ah was you Ah'd go back and ast 'im agin."

21

So de po' man went on back to de prayin' ground agin and got down on his knees. But there wasn't no big woods like it used to be. It has been all cleared off. He prayed and said, "Oh, Lawd, right here on dis spot ten years ago Ah ast you if Ah was called to preach and a voice tole me to go preach. Since dat time Ah been strugglin' in Yo' moral vineyard, but Ah ain't gathered no grapes. Now, if you really called me to preach Christ and Him crucified, please gimme another sign."

Sho nuff, jus' as soon as he said dat, de voice said "Wanh-uh! Go preach! Go preach! Go preach!"

De man jumped up and says, "Ah knowed Ah been called. Dat's de same voice. Dis time Ah'm goin ter ast Him where *must* Ah go preach."

By dat time de voice come agin and he looked 'way off and seen a mule in de plantation lot wid his head all stuck out to bray agin, and he said, "Unh hunh, youse de very son of a gun dat called me to preach befo'."

So he went on off and got a job plowin'. Dat's whut he was called to do in de first place.

Armetta said, "A many one been called to de plough and they run off and got up in de pulpit. Ah wish dese mules knowed how to take a pair of plow-lines and go to de church and ketch some of 'em like they go to de lot with a bridle and ketch mules."

Ellis: Ah knowed one preacher dat was called to preach at one of dese split-off churches. De members had done split off from a big church because they was all mean and couldn't git along wid nobody.

Dis preacher was a good man, but de congregation was so tough he couldn't make a convert in a whole year. So he sent and invited another preacher to come and conduct a revival meeting for him. De man he ast to come was a powerful hard preacher wid a good strainin' voice. He was known to get converts.

Well, he come and preached at dis split-off for two whole weeks. De people would all turn out to church and jus' set dere and look at de man up dere strainin' his lungs out and nobody would give de man no encouragement by sayin' "Amen," and not a soul bowed down.

It was a narrer church wid one winder and dat was in de pulpit and de door was in de front end. Dey had a mean ole sexton wid a wooden leg. So de last night of de protracted meetin' de preacher come to church wid his gripsack in his hand and went on up in de pulpit. When he got up to preach he says, "Brother Sexton, dis bein' de last night of de meetin' Ah wants you to lock de do' and bring me de key. Ah want everybody to stay and hear whut Ah got to say."

De sexton brought him de key and he took his tex and went to preachin'. He preached and he reared and pitched, but nobody said "Amen" and nobody bowed down. So 'way after while he stooped down and opened his suitsatchel and out wid his .44 Special. "Now," he said, "you rounders and brick-bats—yeah, you women, Ah'm talkin' to you. If you ain't a whole brick, den you must be a bat— and gamblers and 'leven-card layers. Ah done preached to you for two whole weeks and not one of you has said 'Amen,' and nobody has bowed down."

He thowed de gun on 'em. "And now Ah say bow down!" And they beginned to bow all over dat church.

De sexton looked at his wooden leg and figgered he couldn't bow because his leg was cut off above de knee. So he ast, "Me too, Elder?"

"Yeah, you too, you peg-leg son of a gun. You bow down too."

Therefo' dat sexton bent dat wooden leg and bowed down. De preacher fired a couple of shots over they heads and stepped out de window and went on 'bout his business. But he skeered dem people so bad till they all rushed to one side of de church tryin' to git out and carried dat church buildin' twenty-eight miles befo' they thought to turn it loose.

"Now Ellis," chided Gold when she was thru her laughter, "You know dat's a lie. Folks over there in St. Lawrence holdin' class meetin' and you over here lyin' like de crossties from Jacksonville to Key West."

"Naw, dat ain't no lie!" Ellis contended, still laughing himself.

"Aw, yes it 'tis," Gold said. "Dat's all you men is good for—settin' 'round and lyin'. Some of you done quit lyin' and gone to flyin'."

Gene Brazzle said, "Get off of us mens now. We *is* some good. Plenty good too if you git de right one. De trouble is you women ain't good for nothin' exceptin' readin' Sears and Roebuck's bible and hollerin' 'bout, 'gimme dis and gimme dat' as soon as we draw our pay."

Shug[5] said, "Well, we don't git it by astin' you mens for it. If we work for it we kin git it. You mens don't draw no pay. You don't do nothin' but stand around and draw lightnin'."

"Ah don't say Ah'm detrimental," Gene said dryly, "but if Gold and Shug don't stop crackin' us, Ah'm gointer get 'em to go."

Gold: "Man, if you want me any, some or none, do whut you gointer do and stop cryin'."

Gene: "You ain't seen me cryin'. See me cryin', it's sign of a funeral. If Ah even look cross somebody gointer bleed."

Gold: "Aw, shut up, Gene, you ain't no big hen's biddy if you do lay gobbler eggs. You tryin' to talk like big wood when you ain't nothin' but brush."

Armetta sensed a hard anger creepin' into the teasing so she laughed to make Gene and Gold laugh and asked, "Did y'all have any words before you fell out?"

"We ain't mad wid one 'nother," Gene defended. "We jus' jokin'."

"Well, stop blowin' it and let de lyin' go on," said Charlie Jones. "Zora's gittin' restless. She think she ain't gointer hear no more."

"Oh, no Ah ain't," I lied. After a short spell of quiet, good

---

[5]Short for sugar.

humor was restored to the porch. In the pause we could hear Pa Henry over in the church house sending up a prayer:

. . . You have been with me from the earliest rocking of my
  cradle up until this present moment.
You know our hearts, our Father,
And all de range of our deceitful minds,
And if you find anything like sin lurking
In and around our hearts,
Ah ast you, My Father, and my Wonder-workin' God
To pluck it out
And cast it into de sea of Fuhgitfulness
Where it will never rise to harm us in dis world
Nor condemn us in de judgment.
You heard me when Ah laid at hell's dark door
With no weapon in my hand
And no God in my heart,
And cried for three long days and nights.
You heard me, Lawd,
And stooped so low
And snatched me from the hell
Of eternal death and damnation.
You cut loose my stammerin' tongue;

25

You established my feet on de rock of Salvation
And yo' voice was heard in rumblin' judgment.
I thank Thee that my last night's sleepin' couch
Was not my coolin' board
And my cover
Was not my windin' sheet.
Speak to de sinner-man and bless 'im.
Touch all those
Who have been down to de doors of degradation.
Ketch de man dat's layin' in danger of consumin' fire;
And Lawd,
When Ah kin pray no mo';
When Ah done drunk down de last cup of sorrow
Look on me, yo' weak servant who feels de least of all;
'Point my soul a restin' place
Where Ah kin set down and praise yo' name forever
Is my prayer for Jesus sake
Amen and thank God.

As the prayer ended the bell of Macedonia, the Baptist church, began to ring.

"Prayer meetin' night at Macedony," George Thomas said.

"It's too bad that it must be two churches in Eatonville," I commented. "De town's too little. Everybody ought to go to one."

"Dey wouldn't do dat, Zora, and you know better. Fack is, de Christian churches nowhere don't stick together," this from Charlie.

Everybody agreed that this was true. So Charlie went on. "Look at all de kind of denominations we got. But de people can't help dat 'cause de church wasn't built on no solid foundation to start wid."

"Oh yes, it 'twas!" Johnnie Mae disputed him. "It was built on solid rock. Didn't Jesus say 'On dis rock Ah build my church?' "

"Yeah," chimed in Antie Hoyt. "And de songs says, 'On Christ de solid rock I stand' and 'Rock of Ages.' "

Charlie was calm and patient. "Yeah, he built it on a rock,

26

but it wasn't solid. It was a pieced-up rock and that's how come de church split up now. Here's de very way it was:

Christ was walkin' long one day wid all his disciples and he said, "We're goin' for a walk today. Everybody pick up a rock and come along." So everybody got their selves a nice big rock 'ceptin' Peter. He was lazy so he picked up a li'l bit of a pebble and dropped it in his side pocket and come along.

Well, they walked all day long and de other 'leven disciples changed them rocks from one arm to de other but they kept on totin' 'em. Long towards sundown they come 'long by de Sea of Galilee and Jesus tole 'em, "Well, le's fish awhile. Cast in yo' nets right here." They done like he tole 'em and caught a great big mess of fish. Then they cooked 'em and Christ said, "Now, all y'all bring up yo' rocks." So they all brought they rocks and Christ turned 'em into bread and they all had a plenty to eat wid they fish exceptin' Peter. He couldn't hardly make a moufful offa de li'l bread he had and he didn't like dat a bit.

Two or three days after dat Christ went out doors and looked up at de sky and says, "Well, we're goin' for another walk today. Everybody git yo'self a rock and come along."

They all picked up a rock apiece and was ready to go. All but Peter. He went and tore down half a mountain. It was so big he couldn't move it wid his hands. He had to take a pinch-bar to move it. All day long Christ walked and talked to his disciples and Peter sweated and strained wid dat rock of his'n.

Way long in de evenin' Christ went up under a great big ole tree and set down and called all of his disciples around 'im and said, "Now everybody bring up yo' rocks."

So everybody brought theirs but Peter. Peter was about a mile down de road punchin' dat half a mountain he was bringin'. So Christ waited till he got dere. He looked at de rocks dat de other 'leven disciples had, den he seen dis great big mountain dat Peter had and so he got up and walked over to it and put one foot up on it and said, "Why

27

Peter, dis is a fine rock you got here! It's a noble rock! And Peter, on dis rock Ah'm gointer build my church."

Peter says, "Naw you ain't neither. You won't build no church house on *dis* rock. You gointer turn dis rock into bread."

Christ knowed dat Peter meant dat thing so he turnt de hillside into bread and dat mountain is de bread he fed de 5,000 wid. Den he took dem 'leven other rocks and glued 'em together and built his church on it.

And that's how come de Christian churches is split up into so many different kinds—cause it's built on pieced-up rock.

There was a storm of laughter following Charlie's tale. "Zora, you come talkin' bout puttin' de two churches together and not havin' but one in dis town," Armetta said chidingly. "You know better'n dat. Baptis' and Methdis' always got a pick out at one 'nother. One time two preachers—one Methdis' an de other one Baptis' wuz on uh train and de engine blowed up and bein' in de colored coach right back of de engine they got blowed up too. When they saw theyself startin' up in de air de Baptis' preacher hollered, 'Ah bet Ah go higher than you!' "

Then Gold spoke up and said, "Now, lemme tell one. Ah know one about a man as black as Gene."

"Whut you always crackin' me for?" Gene wanted to know. "Ah ain't a bit blacker than you."

"Oh, yes you is, Gene. Youse a whole heap blacker than Ah is."

"Aw, go head on, Gold. Youse blacker than me. You jus' look my color cause youse fat. If you wasn't no fatter than me you'd be so black till lightnin' bugs would follow you at twelve o'clock in de day, thinkin' it's midnight."

"Dat's a lie, youse blacker than Ah ever dared to be. Youse lam' black. Youse so black till they have to throw a sheet over yo' head so de sun kin rise every mornin'. Ah know yo' ma cried when she seen *you.*"

28

"Well, anyhow, Gold, youse blacker than me. If Ah was as fat as you Ah'd be a yaller man."

"Youse a liar. Youse as yaller as you ever gointer git. When a person is poor he look bright and de fatter you git de darker you look."

"Is dat yo' excuse for being so black, Gold?"

Armetta soothed Gold's feelings and stopped the war. When the air cleared Gold asked, "Do y'all know how come we are black?"

"Yeah," said Ellis. "It's because two black niggers got together."

"Aw, naw," Gold disputed petulantly. "Well, since you so smart, tell me where dem two black niggers come from in de first beginnin'."

"They musta come from Zar, and dat's on de other side of far."

"Uh, hunh!" Gold gloated. "Ah knowed you didn't know whut you was talkin' about. Now Ah'm goin' ter tell you how come we so black:

Long before they got thru makin' de Atlantic Ocean and haulin' de rocks for de mountains, God was makin' up de people.[6] But He didn't finish 'em all at one time. Ah'm compelled to say dat some folks is walkin' 'round dis town right now ain't finished yet and never will be.

Well, He give out eyes one day. All de nations come up and got they eyes. Then He give out teeth and so on. Then He set a day to give out color. So seven o'clock dat mornin' everybody was due to git they color except de niggers. So God give everybody they color and they went on off. Then He set there for three hours and one-half and no niggers. It was gettin' hot and God wanted to git His work done and go set in de cool. So He sent de angels. Rayfield and Gab'ull[7] to go git 'em so He could 'tend some mo' business.

[6]See glossary.
[7]The angels Raphael and Gabriel.

29

They hunted all over Heben till dey found de colored folks. All stretched out sleep on de grass under de tree of life. So Rayfield woke 'em up and tole 'em God wanted 'em.

They all jumped up and run on up to de th'one and they was so skeered they might miss sumpin' they begin to push and shove one 'nother, bumpin' against all de angels and turnin' over foot-stools. They even had de th'one all pushed one-sided.

So God hollered "Git back! Git back!" And they misunderstood Him and thought He said, "Git black," and they been black ever since.

Gene rolled his eyeballs into one corner of his head.

"Now Gold call herself gettin' even wid me—tellin' dat lie. 'Tain't no such a story nowhere. She jus' made dat one up herself."

"Naw, she didn't," Armetta defended. "Ah *been* knowin' dat ole tale."

"Me too," said Shoo-pie.

"Don't you know you can't git de best of no woman in de talkin' game? Her tongue is all de weapon a woman got," George Thomas chided Gene. "She could have had mo' sense, but she told God no, she'd ruther take it out in hips. So God give her her ruthers. She got plenty hips, plenty mouf and no brains."

"Oh, yes, womens is got sense too," Mathilda Moseley jumped in. "But they got too much sense to go 'round braggin' about it like y'all do. De lady people always got de advantage of mens because God fixed it dat way."

"Whut ole black advantage is y'all got?" B. Moseley asked indignantly. "We got all de strength and all de law and all de money and you can't git a thing but whut we jes' take pity on you and give you."

"And dat's jus' de point," said Mathilda triumphantly. "You *do* give it to us, but how come you do it?" And without

30

waiting for an answer Mathilda began to tell why women always take advantage of men.

You see in de very first days, God made a man and a woman and put 'em in a house together to live. 'Way back in them days de woman was just as strong as de man and both of 'em did de same things. They useter get to fussin' 'bout who gointer do this and that and sometime they'd fight, but they was even balanced and neither one could whip de other one.

One day de man said to hisself, "B'lieve Ah'm gointer go see God and ast Him for a li'l mo' strength so Ah kin whip dis 'oman and make her mind. Ah'm tired of de way things is." So he went on up to God.

"Good mawnin', Ole Father."

"Howdy man. Whut you doin' 'round my throne so soon dis mawnin'?"

"Ah'm troubled in mind, and nobody can't ease mah spirit 'ceptin' you."

God said: "Put yo' plea in de right form and Ah'll hear and answer."

"Ole Maker, wid de mawnin' stars glitterin' in yo' shinin' crown, wid de dust from yo' footsteps makin' worlds upon worlds, wid de blazin' bird we call de sun flyin' out of yo' right hand in de mawnin' and consumin' all day de flesh and blood of stump-black darkness, and comes flyin' home every evenin' to rest on yo' left hand, and never once in all yo' eternal years, mistood de left hand for de right, Ah ast you *please* to give me mo' strength than dat woman you give me, so Ah kin make her mind. Ah know you don't want to be always comin' down way past de moon and stars to be straightenin' her out and its got to be done. So give me a li'l mo' strength, Ole Maker and Ah'll do it."

"All right, Man, you got mo' strength than woman."

So de man run all de way down de stairs from Heben till he got home. He was so anxious to try his strength on de woman dat he couldn't take his time. Soon's he got in de house he hollered "Woman! Here's yo' boss. God done

31

tole me to handle you in which ever way Ah please. Ah'm yo' boss."

De woman flew to fightin' 'im right off. She fought 'im frightenin' but he beat her. She got her wind and tried 'im agin but he whipped her agin. She got herself together and made de third try on him vigorous but he beat her every time. He was so proud he could whip 'er at last, dat he just crowed over her and made her do a lot of things she didn't like. He told her, "Long as you obey me, Ah'll be good to yuh, but every time yuh rear up Ah'm gointer put plenty wood on yo' back and plenty water in yo' eyes."

De woman was so mad she went straight up to Heben and stood befo' de Lawd. She didn't waste no words. She said, "Lawd, Ah come befo' you mighty mad t'day. Ah want back my strength and power Ah useter have."

"Woman, you got de same power you had since de beginnin'."

"Why is it then, dat de man kin beat me now and he useter couldn't do it?"

"He got mo' strength than he useter have. He come and ast me for it and Ah give it to 'im. Ah gives to them that ast, and you ain't never ast me for no mo' power."

"Please suh, God, Ah'm astin' you for it now. Jus' gimme de same as you give him."

God shook his head. "It's too late now, woman. Whut Ah give, Ah never take back. Ah give him mo' strength than you and no matter how much Ah give you, he'll have mo'."

De woman was so mad she wheeled around and went on off. She went straight to de devil and told him what had happened.

He said, "Don't be dis-incouraged, woman. You listen to me and you'll come out mo' than conqueror. Take dem frowns out yo' face and turn round and go right on back to Heben and ast God to give you dat bunch of keys hangin' by de mantel-piece. Then you bring 'em to me and Ah'll show you what to do wid 'em."

So de woman climbed back up to Heben agin. She was mighty tired but she was more out-done that she was tired so she climbed all night long and got back up to Heben agin. When she got befo' de throne, butter wouldn't melt in her mouf.

"O Lawd and Master of de rainbow, Ah know yo' power. You never make two mountains without you put a valley in between. Ah know you kin hit a straight lick wid a crooked stick."

"Ast for whut you want, woman."

"God, gimme dat bunch of keys hangin' by yo' mantelpiece."

"Take 'em."

So de woman took de keys and hurried on back to de devil wid 'em. There was three keys on de bunch. Devil say, "See dese three keys? They got mo' power in 'em than all de strength de man kin ever git if you handle 'em right. Now dis first big key is to de do' of de kitchen, and you know a man always favors his stomach. Dis second one is de key to de bedroom and he don't like to be shut out from dat neither and dis last key is de key to de cradle and he don't want to be cut off from his generations at all. So now you take dese keys and go lock up everything and wait till he come to you. Then don't you unlock nothin' until he use his strength for yo' benefit and yo' desires."

De woman thanked 'im and tole 'im, "If it wasn't for you, Lawd knows whut us po' women folks would do."

She started off but de devil halted her. "Jus' one mo' thing: don't go home braggin' 'bout yo' keys. Jus' lock up everything and say nothin' until you git asked. And then don't talk too much."

De woman went on home and did like de devil tole her. When de man come home from work she was settin' on de porch singin' some song 'bout "Peck on de wood make de bed go good."

When de man found de three doors fastened what useter stand wide open he swelled up like pine lumber after a rain. First thing he tried to break in cause he figgered his strength would overcome all obstacles. When he saw he couldn't do it, he ast de woman, "Who locked dis do'?"

She tole 'im, "Me."

"Where did you git de key from?"

"God give it to me."

33

He run up to God and said, "God, woman got me locked 'way from my vittles, my bed and my generations, and she say you give her the keys."

God said, "I did, Man, Ah give her de keys, but de devil showed her how to use 'em!"

"Well, Ole Maker, please gimme some keys jus' lak 'em so she can't git de full control."

"No, Man, what Ah give Ah give. Woman got de key."

"How kin Ah know 'bout my generations?"

"Ast de woman."

So de man come on back and submitted hisself to de woman and she opened de doors.

He wasn't satisfied but he had to give in. 'Way after while he said to de woman, "Le's us divide up. Ah'll give you half of my strength if you lemme hold de keys in my hands."

De woman thought dat over so de devil popped and tol her, "Tell 'im, naw. Let 'im keep his strength and you keep yo' keys."

So de woman wouldn't trade wid 'im and de man had to mortgage his strength to her to live. And dat's why de man makes and de woman takes. You men is still braggin' 'bout yo' strength and de women is sittin' on de keys and lettin' you blow off till she git ready to put de bridle on you.

B. Moseley looked over at Mathilda and said, "You just like a hen in de barnyard. You cackle so much you give de rooster de blues."

Mathilda looked over at him archly and quoted:

> Stepped on a pin, de pin bent
> And dat's de way de story went.

"Y'all lady people ain't smarter *than* all men folks. You got plow lines on some of us, but some of us is too smart for you. We go past you jus' like lightnin' thru de trees," Willie Sewell boasted. "And what make it so cool, we close enough to you to have a scronchous time, but never no halter on our necks.

34

Ah know they won't git none on dis last neck of mine."

"Oh, you kin be had," Gold retorted. "Ah mean dat abstifically."

"Yeah? But not wid de trace chains. Never no shack up. Ah want dis tip-in love and tip yo' hat and walk out. Ah don't want nobody to have dis dyin' love for me."

Richard Jones said: "Yeah, man. Love is a funny thing; love is a blossom. If you want yo' finger bit poke it at a possum."

Jack Oscar Jones, who had been quiet for some time, slumped way down in his chair, straightened up and said, "Ah know a speech about love."

Ruth Marshall laughed doubtfully. "Now, Jack, you can't make me b'lieve you know de first thing about no love."

"Yeah he do, too," Clara, Jack's wife defended.

"Whut do he know, then?" Ruth persisted.

"Aw, Lawd," Clara wagged her head knowingly. "You ain't got no business knowing dat. Dat's *us* business. But he know jus' as much about love as de nex' man."

"You don't say!" Johnnie Mae twitted her sister-in-law. "Blow it out, then, Jack, and tell a blind man somethin'."

"Ah'm gointer say it, then me and Zora's goin' out to Montgomery and git up a cool watermelon, ain't we, Zora?"

"If you got de price," I came back. "Ah got de car so all we need is a strong determination and we'll have melon."

"No, Zora ain't goin' nowhere wid my husband," Clara announced. "If he got anything to tell her—it's gointer be right here in front of me."

Jack laughed at Clara's feigned jealousy and recited:

SONG POEM

When the clock struck one I had just begun. Begun with Sue, begun with Sal, begun with that pretty Johnson gal.

When the clock struck two, I was through, I was through with Sue, through with Sal, through with that pretty Johnson gal.

When the clock struck three I was free, free with Sue, free with Sal, free with that pretty Johnson gal.

When the clock struck four I was at the door, at the door with Sue, at the door with Sal, at the door with that pretty Johnson gal.

When the clock struck five I was alive, alive with Sue, alive with Sal, alive with that pretty Johnson gal.

When the clock struck six I was fixed, fixed with Sue, fixed with Sal, fixed with that pretty Johnson gal.

When the clock struck seven I was even, even with Sue, even with Sal, even with that pretty Johnson gal.

When the clock struck eight I was at your gate, gate with Sue, gate with Sal, gate with that pretty Johnson gal.

When the clock struck nine I was behind, behind with Sue, behind with Sal, behind with that pretty Johnson gal.

When the clock struck ten I was in the bin, in the bin with Sue, in the bin with Sal, in the bin with that pretty Johnson gal.

When the clock struck eleven, I was in heaven, in heaven with Sue, in heaven with Sal, in heaven with that pretty Johnson gal.

When the clock struck twelve I was in hell, in hell with Sue, in hell with Sal, in hell with that pretty Johnson gal.

"Who was all dis Sue and dis Sal and dat pretty Johnson gal?" Clara demanded of Jack.

"Dat ain't for you to know. My name is West, and Ah'm so different from de rest."

"You sound like one man courtin' three gals, but Ah know a story 'bout three mens courtin' one gal," Shug commented.

"Dat's bogish,"[8] cried Bennie Lee thickly.

"Whut's bogish?" Shug demanded. She and Bennie were step-brother and sister and they had had a lawsuit over the property of his late father and her late mother, so a very little of Bennie's sugar would sweeten Shug's tea and vice versa.

"Ah don't want to lissen to no ole talk 'bout three mens

[8]Bogus.

36

after no one 'oman. It's always more'n three womens after every man."

"Well, de way Ah know de story, there was three mens after de same girl," Shug insisted. "You drunk, Bennie Lee. You done drunk so much of dis ole coon dick till you full of monkies."

"Whut you gointer do?" Bennie demanded. "Whut you gointer do?" No answer was expected to this question. It was just Bennie Lee's favorite retort. "De monkies got me, now whut you gointer do?"

"Ah ain't got you to study about, Bennie Lee. If God ain't payin' you no mo' mind than Ah is, youse in hell right now. Ah ain't talkin' to you nohow. Zora, you wanter hear dis story?"

"Sure, Shug. That's what Ah'm here for."

"Somebody's gointer bleed," Bennie Lee threatened. Nobody paid him any mind.

"God knows Ah don't wanter hear Shug tell nothin'," Bennie Lee complained.

"Ah wish yo' monkies would tell you to go hide in de hammock and forgit to tell you de way home." Shug was getting peeved.

"You better shut up befo' Ah whip yo' head to de red. Ah wish Ah was God. Ah'd turn you into a blamed hawg, and then Ah'd concrete de whole world over so you wouldn't have not one nary place to root."

"Dat's dat two-bits in change you got in yo' pocket now dat's talkin' for you. But befo' de summer's over *you'll* be rootin' lak a hawg. You already lookin' over-plus lak one now. Don't you worry 'bout me."

Bennie Lee tried to ask his well-known question but the coon dick was too strong. He mumbled down into his shirt bosom and went to sleep.

THREE

Youse in de majority, now Shug," B. Moseley said,
seeing Bennie asleep. "Le's hear 'bout dat man wid
three women."

Shug said:

Naw, it was three mens went to court a girl, Ah told
you. Dis was a real pretty girl wid shiny black hair and coal
black eyes. And all dese men wanted to marry her, so they
all went and ast her pa if they could have her. He looked
'em all over, but he couldn't decide which one of 'em
would make de best husband and de girl, she couldn't
make up her mind, so one Sunday night when he walked
into de parlor where they was all sittin' and said to 'em,
"Well, all y'all want to marry my daughter and youse all
good men and Ah can't decide which one will make her de
best husband. So y'all be here tomorrow mornin' at daybreak and we'll have a contest and de one dat can do de
quickest trick kin have de girl."

Nex' mornin' de first one got up seen it wasn't no water
in de bucket to cook breakfas' wid. So he tole de girl's
mama to give him de water bucket and he would go to the
spring and git her some.

He took de bucket in his hand and then he found out
dat de spring was ten miles off. But he said he didn't mind

39

dat. He went on and dipped up de water and hurried on back wid it. When he got to de five-mile post he looked down into de bucket and seen dat de bottom had done dropped out. Then he recollected dat he heard somethin' fall when he dipped up de water so he turned round and run back to de spring and clapped in dat bottom before de water had time to spill.

De ole man thought dat was a pretty quick trick, but de second man says, "Wait a minute. Ah want a grubbin' hoe and a axe and a plow and a harrow." So he got everything he ast for. There was ten acres of wood lot right nex' to de house. He went out dere and chopped down all de trees, grubbed up de roots, ploughed de field, harrowed it, planted it in cow-peas, and had green peas for dinner.

De ole man says "Dat's de quickest trick. Can't nobody beat dat. No use in tryin'. He done won de girl."

De last man said, "You ain't even givin' me a chance to win de girl."

So he took his high-powered rifle and went out into de woods about seben or eight miles until he spied a deer. He took aim and fired. Then he run home, run round behind de house and set his gun down and then run back out in de woods and caught de deer and held 'im till de bullet hit 'im.

So he won de girl.

Robert Williams said:
Ah know another man wid a daughter.

The man sent his daughter off to school for seben years, den she come home all finished up. So he said to her, "Daughter, git yo' things and write me a letter to my brother!" So she did.

He says, "Head it up," and she done so.

"Now tell 'im, 'Dear Brother, our chile is done come home from school and all finished up and we is very proud of her.'"

Then he ast de girl "Is you got dat?"

She tole 'im "yeah."

40

"Now tell him some mo'. 'Our mule is dead but Ah got another mule and when Ah say (clucking sound of tongue and teeth) he moved from de word.'"

"Is you got dat?" he ast de girl.

"Naw suh," she tole 'im.

He waited a while and he ast her again, "You got dat down yet?"

"Naw suh, Ah ain't got it yet."

"How come you ain't got it?"

"Cause Ah can't spell (clucking sound)."

"You mean to tell me you been off to school seben years and can't spell (clucking sound)? Why Ah could spell dat myself and Ah ain't been to school a day in mah life. Well jes' say (clucking sound) he'll know what yo' mean and go on wid de letter."

Henry "Nigger" Byrd said:
I know one about a letter too.

My father owned a fas' horse—I mean a *fast* horse. We was livin' in Ocala then. Mah mother took sick and mah father come and said, "Skeet,"—he uster call me Skeet—"You oughter wire yo' sister in St. Petersburg."

"I jus' wired her," I tole him.

"Whut did you put in it?"

I tole 'im.

He says, "Dat ain't right. I'm goin' ketch it." He went out in de pasture and caught de horse and shod 'im and curried 'im and brushed 'im off good, put de saddle on 'im and got on 'im, and caught dat telegram and read it and took it on to mah sister.

Soon as he left de house, mama said, "You chillun make a fire in de stove and fix somethin' for de ole man to eat."

Befo' she could git de word out her mouf, him and mah sister rode up to de do' and said "Whoa!"

By dat time a flea ast me for a shoe-shine so I left.

Armetta said: "Nigger, I didn't know you could lie like that."

41

"I ain't lyin', Armetta. We had dat horse. We had a cow too and she was so sway-backed that she could use de bushy part of her tail for a umbrella over her head."

"Shet up, Nig!" "Seaboard" Hamilton pretended to be outraged. "Ah knowed you could sing barytone but Ah wouldn't a b'lieved de lyin' was in you if Ah didn't hear you myself. Whut makes you bore wid such a great big augur?"

Little Julius Henry, who should have been home in bed spoke up. "Mah brother John had a horse 'way back dere in slavery time."

"Let de dollars hush whilst de nickel speak," Charlies Jones derided Julius' youth. "Julius, whut make you wanta jump in a hogshead when a kag[1] will hold yuh? You hear dese hard ole coons lyin' up a nation and you stick in yo' bill."

"If his mouf is cut cross ways and he's two years ole, he kin lie good as anybody else," John French defended. "Blow it, Julius."

Julius spat out into the yard, trying to give the impression that he was skeeting tobacco juice like a man.[2]

De rooster chew t'backer, de hen dip snuff.
De biddy can't do it, but he struts his stuff.
Ole John, he was workin' for Massa and Massa had two hawses and he lakted John, so he give John one of his hawses.

When John git to workin' 'em he'd haul off and beat Massa's hawse, but he never would hit his'n. So then some white folks tole ole Massa 'bout John beatin' his hawse and never beatin' his own. So Massa tole John if he ever heard tell of him layin' a whip on his hawse agin he was gointer take and kill John's hawse dead as a nit.

John tole 'im, "Massa, if you kill my hawse, Ah'll beatcher makin' money."

One day John hit ole Massa's hawse agin. Dey went and tole Massa' bout it. He come down dere where John was

<hr/>

[1]Keg.

[2]This story is of European origin, but has been colored by the negro mouth.

haulin' trash, wid a great big ole knife and cut John's hawse's th'oat and he fell dead.

John jumped down off de wagon and skint his hawse, and tied de hide up on a stick and throwed it cross his shoulder, and went on down town.

Ole John was a fortune teller hisself but nobody 'round dere didn't know it. He met a man and de man ast John, "Whut's dat you got over yo' shoulder dere, John?"

"It's a fortune teller, boss."

"Make it talk some, John, and I'll give you a sack of money and a hawse and saddle, and five head of cattle."

John put de hide on de ground and pulled out de stick and hit 'cross de hawse hide and hold his head down dere to lissen.

"Dere's a man in yo' bed-room behind de bed talkin' to yo' wife."

De man went inside his house to see. When he come back out he said, "Yeah, John, you sho tellin' de truth. Make him talk some mo'."

John went to puttin' de stick back in de hide. "Naw, Massa, he's tired now."

De white man says, "Ah'll give you six head of sheeps and fo' hawses and fo' sacks of money."

John pulled out de stick and hit down on de hide and hold down his head to lissen.

"It's a man in yo' kitchen openin' yo' stove." De man went back into his house and come out agin and tole John, "Yo, fortune-teller sho is right. Here's de things Ah promised you."

John rode on past Ole Massa's house wid all his sacks of money and drivin' his sheeps and cattle, whoopin' and crackin' his whip. "Yee, whoo-pee, yee!" Crack!

Massa said, "John, where did you git all dat?"

John said, "Ah tole you if you kilt mah hawse Ah'd beatcher makin' money."

Massa said to 'im, "Reckon if Ah kilt mah hawse Ah'd make dat much money?"

"Yeah, Massa, Ah reckon so."

So ole Massa went out and kilt his hawse and went to town hollerin', "Hawse hide for sale! Hawse hide for sale!"

43

One man said, "Hold on dere. Ah'll give you two-bits for it to bottom some chears."

Ole Massa tole 'im, "Youse crazy!" and went on hollerin' "Hawse hide for sale!"

"Ah'll gi' you twenty cents for it to cover some chears," another man said.

"You must be stone crazy! Why, dis hide is worth five thousand dollars."

De people all laughed at 'im so he took his hawse hide and throwed it away and went and bought hisself another hawse.

Ole John, he already rich, he didn't have to work but he jus' love to fool 'round hawses so he went to drivin' hawse and buggy for Massa. And when nobody wasn't wid him, John would let his grandma ride in Massa's buggy. Dey tole ole Massa 'bout it and he said, "John, Ah hear you been had yo' grandma ridin' in mah buggy. De first time Ah ketch her in it, Ah'm gointer kill 'er."

John tole 'im, "If you kill my grandma, Ah'll beatcher makin' money."

Pretty soon some white folks tole Massa dat John was takin' his gran'ma to town in his buggy and was hittin' his hawse and showin' off. So ole Massa come out dere and cut John's gran'ma's th'oat.

So John buried his gran'ma in secret and went and got his same ole hawse hide and keered it up town agin and went 'round talkin' 'bout, "Fortune-teller, fortune-teller!"

One man tole 'im, "Why, John, make it talk some for me. Ah'll give you six head of goats, six sheeps, and a hawse and a saddle to ride 'im wid."

So John made it talk and de man was pleased so he give John more'n he promised 'im, and John went on back past Massa's house wid his stuff so ole Massa could see 'im.

Ole Massa run out and ast, "Oh, John, where did you git all dat?"

John said, "Ah tole you if you kill mah gran'ma Ah'd beatcher makin' money."

Massa said, "You reckon if Ah kill mine, Ah'll make all dat?"

"Yeah, Ah reckon so."

So Massa runned and cut his gran'ma's th'oat and went up town hollerin' "gran'ma for sale! gran'ma for sale!"

Wouldn't nobody break a breath wid him. Dey thought he was crazy. He went on back home and grabbed John and tole 'im, "You made me kill my gran'ma and my good hawse and Ah'm gointer throw you in de river."

John tole 'im, "If you throw me in de river, Ah'll beatcher makin' money."

"Naw you won't neither," Massa tole 'im. "You done made yo' last money and done yo' las' do."

He got ole John in de sack and keered 'im down to de river, but he done forgot his weights, so he went back home to git some.

While he was gone after de weights a toad frog come by dere and John seen 'im. So he hollered and said, "Mr. Hoptoad, if you open dis sack and let me out Ah'll give you a dollar."

Toad frog let 'im out, so he got a soft-shell turtle and put it in de sack wid two big ole bricks. Then ole Massa got his weights and come tied 'em on de sack and throwed it in de river.

Whilst Massa was down to de water foolin' wid dat sack, John had done got out his hawse hide and went on up town agin hollerin', "Fortune-teller! fortune-teller!"

One rich man said "Make it talk for me, John."

John pulled out de stick and hit on de hide, and put his ear down. "Uh man is in yo' smoke-house stealin' meat and another one is in yo' money-safe."

De man went inside to see and when he come back he said, "You sho kin tell de truth."

So John went by Massa's house on a new hawse, wid a sack of money tied on each side of de saddle. Ole Massa seen 'im and ast, "Oh, John, where'd you git all dat?"

"Ah tole you if you throw me in de river Ah'd beatcher makin' money."

Massa ast, "Reckon if Ah let you throw me in de river, Ah'd make all dat?"

"Yeah, Massa, Ah *know* so."

John got ole Massa in de sack and keered 'im down to de river. John didn't forgit *his* weights. He put de weights on ole Massa and jus' befo' he throwed 'im out he said, "Goodbye, Massa, Ah hope you find all you lookin' for."

And dat wuz de las' of ole Massa.

"Dat wuz a long tale for a li'l boy lak you," George Thomas praised Julius.

"Ah knows a heap uh tales," Julius retorted.

Whut is de workinest pill you ever seen? Lemme tell you whut kind of a pill it was and how much it worked.

It wuz a ole man one time and he had de rheumatism so bad he didn't know what to do. Ah tole 'im to go to town and git some of dem conthartic pills.[3]

He went and got de pills lak Ah tole 'im, but on his way back he opened de box and went to lookin' at de pills. He wuz comin' cross some new ground where dey hadn't even started to clear up de land. He drop one of de pills but he didn't bother to pick it up—skeered he might hurt his back stoopin' over.

He got to de house and say, "Ole lady, look down yonder whut a big smoke! Whut is dat, nohow?"

She say, "Ah don't know."

"Well," he say. "Guess Ah better walk down dere and see whut dat big smoke *is* down dere."

He come back. "Guess whut it is, ole lady? One of dem conthartic pills done worked all dem roots out de ground and got 'em burning!"

"Julius, you little but you loud. Dat's a over average lie you tole," Shug laughed. "Lak de wind Ah seen on de East Coast. It blowed a crooked road straight and blowed a well up out de ground and blowed and blowed until it scattered de days of de week so bad till Sunday didn't come till late Tuesday evenin'."

"Shug, Whuss yuh gonna do?" Bennie Lee tried to rise to the surface but failed and slumped back into slumber.

"A good boy, but a po' boy," somebody commented as

[3]Compound cathartic.

46

John French made his mind up.

"Zora, Ah'm gointer tell one, but you be sho and tell de folks Ah tole it. Don't say Seymore said it because he took you on de all-day fishin' trip to Titusville. Don't say Seaboard Hamilton tole it 'cause he always give you a big hunk of barbecue when you go for a sandwich. Give ole John French whut's comin' to 'im."

"You gointer tell it or you gointer spend de night tellin' us you gointer tell it?" I asked.

Ah got to say a piece of litery (literary) fust to git mah wind on.
Well Ah went up on dat meat-skin
And Ah come down on dat bone
And Ah grabbed dat piece of corn-bread
And Ah made dat biscuit moan.
Once a man had two sons. One was name Jim and de other one dey call him Jack for short. Dey papa was a most rich man, so he called de boys to 'im one night and tole 'em, "Ah don't want y'all settin' 'round waitin' for me tuh die tuh git whut Ah'm gointer give yuh. Here's five hundred dollars apiece. Dat's yo' sheer of de proppity. Go put yo'selves on de ladder. Take and make men out of yourselves."

Jim took his and bought a big farm and a pair of mules and settled down.

Jack took his money and went on down de road skinnin' and winnin'. He won from so many mens till he had threbbled his money. Den he met a man says, "Come on, le's skin some." De man says "Money on de wood" and he laid down a hundred dollars.

Jack looked at de hund'ud dollars and put down five hund'ud and says, "Man, Ah ain't for no spuddin'.[4] You playin' wid yo' stuff out de winder.[5] You fat 'round de heart.[6] Bet some money."

---

[4]Playing for small change.

[5]Risking nothing, i.e. hat, coat and shoes out the window so that the owner can run if he loses.

[6]Scared.

De man covered Jack's money and dey went to skinnin'.
Jack was dealin' and he thought he seen de other man on
de turn so he said, "Five hund'ud mo' my ten spot is de
bes'."

De other man covered 'im and Jack slapped down another five hund'ud and said, "Five hund'ud mo' you fall dis
time."

De other man never said a word. He put down five
hund'ud mo'.

Jack got to singin':

"When yo' card git-uh lucky, oh pardner
You oughter be in a rollin' game."

He flipped de card and bless God it wuz de ten spot!
Jack had done fell hisself instead of de other man. He was
all put out.

Says, "Well, Ah done los' all mah money so de game is
through."

De other man say, "We kin still play on. Ah'll bet you
all de money on de table against yo' life."

Jack agreed to play 'cause he figgered he could out-shoot
and out-cut any man on de road and if de man tried to kill
him he'd git kilt hisself. So dey shuffled agin and Jack
pulled a card and it fell third in hand.

Den de man got up and he was twelve foot tall and Jack
was so skeered he didn't know whut to do. De man looked
down on 'im and tole 'im says, "De Devil[7] is mah name
and Ah live across de deep blue sea. Ah could kill you
right now, but Ah'll give yuh another chance. If you git to
my house befo' de sun sets and rise agin Ah won't kill yuh,
but if you don't Ah'll be compelled to take yo' life."

Den he vanished.

Jack went on down de road jus' a cryin' till he met uh
ole man.

Says, "Whuss de matter, Jack?"

"Ah played skin wid de Devil for mah life and he
winned and tole me if Ah ain't to his house by de time de
sun sets and rise agin he's gointer take mah life, and he live
way across de ocean."

[7]See glossary.

De ole man says, "You sho is in a bad fix, Jack. Dere ain't but one thing dat kin cross de ocean in dat time."

"Whut is dat?"

"It's uh bald eagle. She come down to de edge of de ocean every mornin' and dip herself in de sea and pick off all de dead feathers. When she dip herself de third time and pick herself she rocks herself and spread her wings and mount de sky and go straight across de deep blue sea. And every time she holler, you give her piece uh dat yearlin' or she'll eat you.

"Now if you could be dere wid a yearlin' bull and when she git thru dippin' and pick herself and rock to mount de sky and jump straddle of her back wid dat bull yearlin' you could make it."

Jack wuz dere wid de yearlin' waitin' for dat eagle to come. He wuz watchin' her from behind de bushes and seen her when she come out de water and picked off de dead feather and rocked to go on high.

He jumped on de eagle's back wid his yearlin' and de eagle was out flyin' de sun. After while she turned her head from side to side and her blazin' eyes lit up first de north den de south and she hollered, "Ah-h-h, Ah, ah! One quarter cross de ocean! Don't see nothin' but blue water, uh!"

Jack was so skeered dat instead of him givin' de eagle uh quarter of de meat, he give her de whole bull. After while she say, "Ah-h-h, ah, ah! One half way cross de ocean! Don't see nothin' but blue water!"

Jack didn't have no mo' meat so he tore off one leg and give it to her. She swallowed dat and flew on. She hollered agin, "Ah-h-h. Ah, ha! Mighty nigh cross de ocean! Don't see nothin' but blue water! Uh!"

Jack tore off one arm and give it to her and she et dat and pretty soon she lit on land and Jack jumped off and de eagle flew on off to her nest.

Jack didn't know which way de Devil lived so he ast. "Dat first big white house 'round de bend in de road," dey tole 'im.

Jack walked to de Devil's house and knocked on de do'.

"Who's dat?"

49

"One of de Devil's friends. One widout uh arm and widout uh leg."

Devil tole his wife, says: "Look behind de do' and hand dat man uh arm and leg." She give Jack de arm and leg and Jack put 'em on.

Devil says, "See you got here in time for breakfas'. But Ah got uh job for yuh befo' you eat. Ah got uh hund'ud acres uh new ground ain't never had uh brush cut on it. Ah want you to go out dere and cut down all de trees and brushes, grub up all de roots and pile 'em and burn 'em befo' dinner time. If you don't, Ah'll hafta take yo' life."

Jus' 'bout dat time de Devil's chillen come out to look at Jack and he seen he had one real pretty daughter, but Jack wuz too worried to think 'bout no girls. So he took de tools and went on out to de wood lot and went to work.

By de time he chopped down one tree he wuz tired and he knowed it would take 'im ten years to clear dat ground right, so Jack set down and went to cryin'. 'Bout dat time de Devil's pretty daughter come wid his breakfas'. "Whuss de matter, Jack?"

"Yo papa done gimme uh job he know Ah can't git through wid, and he's gonna take mah life and Ah don't wanna die."

"Eat yo' breakfas' Jack, and put yo' head in mah lap and go to sleep."

Jack done lak she tole 'im and went to sleep and when he woke up every tree was down, every bush—and de roots grubbed up and burnt. Look lak never had been a blade uh grass dere.

De Devil come out to see how Jack wuz makin' out and seen dat hundred acres cleaned off so nice and said, "Uh, huh, Ah see youse uh wise man, 'most wise as me. Now Ah got another job for yuh. Ah got uh well, uh hundred feet deep and Ah want yuh to dip it dry. Ah mean dry, Ah want it so dry till Ah kin see dust from it and den Ah want you to bring me whut you find at de bottom."

Jack took de bucket and went to de well and went to work but he seen dat de water wuz comin' in faster dan he could draw it out. So he sat down and begin to cry.

De Devil's daughter come praipsin long wid Jack's dinner and seen Jack settin' down cryin'. "Whuss de matter, Jack? Don't cry lak dat lessen you wanta make me cry too."

"Yo' pa done put me to doin' somethin' he know Ah can't never finish and if Ah don't git thru he is gonna take mah life."

"Eat yo' dinner, Jack and put yo' head in mah lap and go to sleep."

Jack done lak she tole 'im and when he woke up de well wuz so dry till red dust wuz boilin' out of it lak smoke. De girl handed 'im a ring and tole 'im "Give papa dis ring. Dat's whut he wanted. It's mama's ring and she lost it in de well de other day."

When de Devil come to see whut Jack wuz doin', Jack give 'im de ring and de Devil looked and seen all dat dust pourin' out de well. He say, "Ah see youse uh very smart man. Almos' as wise as me. All right, Ah got just one mo' job for you and if you do dat Ah'll spare yo' life and let you marry mah daughter to boot. You take dese two geeses and go up dat cocoanut palm tree and pick 'em, and bring me de geeses when you git 'em picked and bring me every feather dat come off 'em. If you lose one Ah'll have to take yo' life."

Jack took de two geeses and clammed up de cocoanut palm tree and tried to pick dem geeses. But he was more'n uh hundred feet off de ground and every time he'd pull uh feather often one of dem birds, de wind would blow it away. So Jack began to cry agin. By dat time Beatrice Devil come up wid his supper. "Whuss de matter, Jack?"

"Yo' papa is bound tuh kill me. He know Ah can't pick no geeses up no palm tree, and save de feathers."

"Eat yo' supper Jack and lay down in mah lap."

When Jack woke up all both de geeses wuz picked and de girl had all de feathers even; she had done caught dem out de air dat got away from Jack. De Devil said, "Well, now you done everything Ah tole you, you kin have mah daughter. Y'all take dat ole house down de road apiece. Dat's where me and her ma got our start."

So Jack and de Devil's daughter got married and went to keepin' house.

Way in de night, Beatrice woke up and shook Jack.

51

"Jack! Jack! Wake up! Papa's comin' here to kill you. Git up and go to de barn. He got two horses dat kin jump a thousand miles at every jump. One is named Hallowed-be-thy-name and de other, Thy-kingdom-come. Go hitch 'em to dat buck board and head 'em dis way and le's go."

Jack run to de barn and harnessed de hawses and headed towards de house where his wife wuz at. When he got to de do' she jumped in and hollered, "Le's go, Jack. Papa's comin' after us!"

When de Devil got to de house to kill Jack and found out Jack wuz gone, he run to de barn to hitch up his fas' hawses. When he seen dat dey wuz gone, he hitched up his jumpin' bull dat could jump five hundred miles at every jump, and down de road, baby!

De Devil wuz drivin' dat bull! Wid every jump he'd holler, "Oh! Hallowed-be-thy-name! Thy-kingdom-come!" And every time de hawses would hear 'im call 'em they'd fall to they knees and de bull would gain on 'em.

De girl say, "Jack, he's 'bout to ketch us! Git out and drag yo' feet backwards nine steps, throw some sand over yo' shoulders and le's go!"

Jack done dat and de hawses got up and off they went, but every time they hear they master's voice they'd stop till de girl told Jack to drag his foot three times nine times and he did it and they gained so fast on de Devil dat de hawses couldn't hear 'im no mo', and dey got away.

De Devil passed uh man and he say, "Is you seen uh man in uh buck board wid uh pretty girl wid coal black hair and red eyes behind two fas' hawses?"

De man said, "No, Ah speck dey done made it to de mountain and if dey gone to de mountain you can't over-take 'em."

"Jack and his wife wuz right dere den listenin' to de Devil. When de daughter saw her pa comin' she turned herself and de hawses into goats and they wuz croppin' grass. Jack wuz so tough she couldn't turn him into nothin' so she saw a holler log and she tole 'im to go hide in it, which he did. De Devil looked all around and he seen dat log and his mind jus' tole 'im to go look in it and he went and picked de log up and said, "Ah, ha! Ah gotcher!"

Jack wuz so skeered inside dat log he begin to call on de Lawd and he said, "O Lawd, have mercy."

You know de Devil don't lak tuh hear de name uh de Lawd so he throwed down dat log and said, "Damn it! If Ah had of knowed dat God wuz in dat log Ah never would a picked it up."

So he got back in and picked up de reins and hollered to de bull, "Turn, bull, turn! Turn clean roh-hound. Turn bull tu-urn, turn clee-ean round!"

De jumpin' bull turnt so fast till he fell and broke his own neck and throwed de Devil out on his head and kilt 'im. So dat's why dey say Jack beat de Devil.

"Boy, how kin you hold all dat in yo' head?" Jack Jones asked John. "Bet if dat lie was somethin' to do yuh some good yuh couldn't remember it."

Johnnie Mae yawned wide open and Ernest seeing her called out, "Hey, there, Johnnie Mae, throw mah trunk out befo' you shet up dat place!"

This reflection upon the size of her mouth peeved Johnnie Mae no end and she and Ernest left in a red hot family argument. Then everybody else found out that they were sleepy. So in the local term everybody went to the "pad."

Lee Robinson over in the church was leading an ole spiritual, "When I come to Die," to which I listened with one ear, while I heard the parting quips of the story-tellers with the other.

Though it was after ten the street lights were still on. B. Moseley had not put out the lights because the service in the church was not over yet, so I sat on the porch for a while looking towards the heaven-rasping oaks on the back street, towards the glassy silver of Lake Sabelia. Over in the church I could hear Mrs. Laura Henderson finishing her testimony . . . "to make Heben mah home when Ah come to die. Oh, Ah'll never forget dat day when de mornin' star bust in mah heart! Ah'll never turn back! O evenin' sun, when you git on de other side, tell mah Lawd Ah'm here prayin'."

The next afternoon I sat on the porch again. The young'uns had the grassy lane that ran past the left side of the house playing the same games that I had played in the same lane years before. With the camphor tree as a base, they played "Going 'Round de Mountain." Little Hubert Alexander was in the ring. The others danced rhythmically 'round him and sang:

> Going around de mountain two by two
> Going around de mountain two by two
> Tell me who love sugar and candy.
>
> Now, show me your motion, two by two
> Show me your motion two by two
> Tell me who love sugar and candy.

I tried to write a letter but the games were too exciting. "Little Sally Walker," "Draw a bucket of water," "Sissy in de barn," and at last that most raucous, popular and most African of games, "Chirck, mah Chick, mah Craney crow." Little Harriet Staggers, the smallest girl in the game, was contending for the place of the mama hen. She fought hard, but the larger girls promptly overruled her and she had to take her place in line behind the other little biddies, two-year-old Donnie Brown, being a year younger than Harriet, was the hindmost chick.

During the hilarious uproar of the game, Charlie Jones and Bubber Mimms came up and sat on the porch with me.

"Good Lawd, Zora! How kin you stand all dat racket? Why don't you run dem chaps 'way from here?" Seeing his nieces, Laura and Melinda and his nephew, Judson, he started to chase them off home but I made him see that it was a happy accident that they had chosen the lane as a playground. That I was enjoying it more than the chaps.

That settled, Charlie asked, "Well, Zora, did we lie enough for you las' night?"

"You lied good but not enough," I answered.

"Course, Zora, you ain't at de right place to git de bes' lies. Why don't you go down 'round Bartow and Lakeland and 'round in dere—Polk County? Dat's where they really lies up a mess and dats where dey makes up all de songs and things lak dat. Ain't you never hea'd dat in Polk County de water drink lak cherry wine?"

"Seems like when Ah was a child 'round here Ah heard de folks pickin' de guitar and singin' songs to dat effect."

"Dat's right. If Ah was you, Ah'd drop down dere and see. It's liable to do you a lot uh good."

"If Ah wuz in power[8] Ah'd go 'long wid you, Zora," Bubber added wistfully. "Ah learnt all Ah know 'bout pickin' de box[9] in Polk County. But Ah ain't even got money essence. 'Tain't no mo' hawgs 'round here. Ah cain't buy no chickens. Guess Ah have tuh eat gopher."[10]

"Where you gointer git yo' gophers, Bubber?" Charlie asked. "Doc Biddy and his pa done 'bout cleaned out dis part of de State."

"Oh, Ah got a new improvement dat's gointer be a lot of help to me and Doc Biddy and all of us po' folks."

"What is it, Bubber?"

"Ah'm gointer prune a gang of soft-shells (turtles) and grow me some gophers."

The sun slid lower and lower and at last lost its grip on the western slant of the sky and dipped three times into the bloody sea—sending up crimson spray with each plunge. At last it sunk and night roosted on the tree-tops and houses.

Bubber picked the box and Charlie sang me songs of the railroad camps. Among others, he taught me verses of JOHN HENRY, the king of railroad track-laying songs which runs as follows:[11]

[8]Funds.

[9]Playing the guitar.

[10]Dry land tortoise.

[11]See glossary.

John Henry driving on the right hand side,
Steam drill driving on the left,
Says, 'fore I'll let your steam drill beat me down
I'll hammer my fool self to death,
Hammer my fool self to death.

John Henry told his Captain,
When you go to town
Please bring me back a nine pound hammer
And I'll drive your steel on down,
And I'll drive your steel on down.

John Henry told his Captain,
Man ain't nothing but a man,
And 'fore I'll let that steam drill beat me down
I'll die with this hammer in my hand,
Die with this hammer in my hand.

Captain ast John Henry,
What is that storm I hear?
He says Cap'n that ain't no storm,
'Tain't nothing but my hammer in the air,
Nothing but my hammer in the air.

John Henry told his Captain,
Bury me under the sills of the floor,
So when they get to playing good old Georgy skin,
Bet 'em fifty to a dollar more,
Fifty to a dollar more.

John Henry had a little woman,
The dress she wore was red,
Says I'm going down the track,
And she never looked back.
I'm going where John Henry fell dead,
Going where John Henry fell dead.

Who's going to shoe your pretty lil feet?
And who's going to glove your hand?
Who's going to kiss your dimpled cheek?
And who's going to be your man?
Who's going to be your man?

My father's going to shoe my pretty lil feet;
My brother's going to glove my hand;
My sister's going to kiss my dimpled cheek;
John Henry's going to be my man,
John Henry's going to be my man.

Where did you get your pretty lil dress?
The shoes you wear so fine?
I got my shoes from a railroad man,
My dress from a man in the mine,
My dress from a man in the mine.

They talked and told strong stories of Ella, Wall, East Coast Mary, Planchita and lesser jook[12] lights around whom the glory of Polk County surged. Saw-mill and turpentine bosses and prison camp "cap'ns" set to music passed over the guitar strings and Charlie's mouth and I knew I had to visit Polk County right now.

A hasty good-bye to Eatonville's oaks and oleanders and the wheels of the Chevvie split Orlando wide open—headed south-west for corn (likker) and song.

[12]A fun house. Where they sing, dance, gamble, love, and compose "blues" songs incidentally.

FOUR

Twelve miles below Kissimmee I passed under an arch that marked the Polk County line. I was in the famed Polk County.

> How often had I heard "Polk County Blues."
> "You don't know Polk County lak Ah do.
> Anybody been dere, tell you de same thing too."

The asphalt curved deeply and when it straightened out we saw a huge smoke-stack blowing smut against the sky. A big sign said, "Everglades Cypress Lumber Company, Loughman, Florida."

We had meant to keep on to Bartow or Lakeland and we debated the subject between us until we reached the opening, then I won. We went in. The little Chevrolet was all against it. The thirty odd miles that we had come, it argued, was nothing but an appetizer. Lakeland was still thirty miles away and no telling what the road held. But it sauntered on down the bark-covered road and into the quarters just as if it had really wanted to come.

We halted beside two women walking to the commissary and asked where we could get a place to stay, despite the signs all over that this was private property and that no one could enter without the consent of the company.

One of the women was named "Babe" Hill and she sent me to her mother's house to get a room. I learned later that Mrs. Allen ran the boarding-house under patronage of the company. So we put up at Mrs. Allen's.

That night the place was full of men—come to look over the new addition to the quarters. Very little was said directly to me and when I tried to be friendly there was a noticeable disposition to *fend* me off. This worried me because I saw at once that this group of several hundred Negroes from all over the South was a rich field for folk-lore, but here was I figuratively starving to death in the midst of plenty.

Babe had a son who lived at the house with his grandmother and we soon made friends. Later the sullen Babe and I got on cordial terms. I found out afterwards that during the Christmas holidays of 1926 she had shot her husband to death, had fled to Tampa where she had bobbed her hair and eluded capture for several months but had been traced thru letters to her mother and had been arrested and lodged in Bartow jail. After a few months she had been allowed to come home and the case was forgotten. Negro women *are* punished in these parts for killing men, but only if they exceed the quota. I don't remember what the quota is. Perhaps I did hear but I forgot. One woman had killed five when I left that turpentine still where she lived. The sheriff was thinking of calling on her and scolding her severely.

James Presley used to come every night and play his guitar. Mrs. Allen's temporary brother-in-law could play a good second but he didn't have a box so I used to lend him mine. They would play. The men would crowd in and buy soft drinks and woof at me, the stranger, but I knew I wasn't getting on. The ole feather-bed tactics.

Then one day after Cliffert Ulmer, Babe's son, and I had driven down to Lakeland together he felt close enough to tell me what was the trouble. They all thought I must be a revenue officer or a detective of some kind. They were accustomed to strange women dropping into the quarters, but not in shiny gray Chevrolets. They usually came plodding down the big road or counting railroad ties. The car made me look too prosperous. So they set me aside as different. And since most of them were fugitives from justice or had done plenty time, a detective was just the last thing they felt they needed on that "job."

I took occasion that night to impress the job with the fact that I was also a fugitive from justice, "bootlegging." They were hot behind me in Jacksonville and they wanted me in Miami. So I was hiding out. That sounded reasonable. Bootleggers always have cars. I was taken in.

The following Saturday was pay-day. They paid off twice a month and pay night is big doings. At least one dance at the section of the quarters known as the Pine Mill and two or three in the big Cypress Side. The company works with two kinds of lumber.

You can tell where the dances are to be held by the fires. Huge bonfires of faulty logs and slabs are lit outside the house in which the dances are held. The refreshments are parched[1] peanuts, fried rabbit, fish, chicken and chitterlings.

The only music is guitar music and the only dance is the ole square dance. James Presley is especially invited to every party to play. His pay is plenty of coon dick, and he *plays.*

Joe Willard is in great demand to call figures. He rebels occasionally because he likes to dance too.

But all of the fun isn't inside the house. A group can always be found outside about the fire, standing around and woofing and occasionally telling stories.

The biggest dance on this particular pay-night was over to the Pine Mill. James Presley and Slim assured me that they would be over there, so Cliffert Ulmer took me there. Being the reigning curiosity of the "job" lots of folks came to see what I'd do. So it was a great dance.

The guitars cried out "Polk County," "Red River" and just instrumental hits with no name, that still are played by all good

[1]Roasted.

box pickers. The dancing was hilarious to put it mildly. Babe, Lucy, Big Sweet, East Coast Mary and many other of the well-known women were there. The men swung them lustily, but nobody asked me to dance. I was just crazy to get into the dance, too. I had heard my mother speak of it and praise square dancing to the skies, but it looked as if I was doomed to be a wallflower and that was a new role for me. Even Cliffert didn't ask me to dance. It was so jolly, too. At the end of every set Joe Willard would trick the men. Instead of calling the next figure as expected he'd bawl out, "Grab yo' partners and march up to de table and treat." Some of the men did, but some would bolt for the door and stand about the fire and woof until the next set was called.

I went outside to join the woofers, since I seemed to have no standing among the dancers. Not exactly a hush fell about the fire, but a lull came. I stood there awkwardly, knowing that the too-ready laughter and aimless talk was a window-dressing for my benefit. The brother in black puts a laugh in every vacant place in his mind. His laugh has a hundred meanings. It may mean amusement, anger, grief, bewilderment, chagrin, curiosity, simple pleasure or any other of the known or undefined emotions. Clardia Thornton of Magazine Point, Alabama, was telling me about another woman taking her husband away from her. When the show-down came and he told Clardia in the presence of the other woman that he didn't want her—could never use her again, she tole me "Den, Zora, Ah wuz so outdone, Ah just opened mah mouf and laffed."

The folks around the fire laughed and boisterously shoved each other about, but I knew they were not tickled. But I soon had the answer. A pencil-shaped fellow with a big Adam's apple gave me the key.

"Ma'am, whut might be yo' entrimmins?" he asked with what was supposed to be a killing bow.

"My whut?"

"Yo entrimmins? Yo entitlum?"

The "entitlum" gave me the cue, "Oh, my name is Zora Hurston. And whut may be yours?"

More people came closer quickly.

"Mah name is Pitts and Ah'm sho glad to meet yuh. Ah asted Cliffert tuh knock me down tuh yuh but he wouldn't make me 'quainted. So Ah'm makin' mahseff 'quainted."

"Ah'm glad you did, Mr. Pitts."

"Sho nuff?" archly.

"Yeah. Ah wouldn't be sayin' it if Ah didn't mean it."

He looked me over shrewdly. "Ah see dat las' crap you shot, Miss, and Ah fade yuh." ·

I laughed heartily. The whole fire laughed at his quick comeback and more people came out to listen.

"Miss, you know uh heap uh dese hard heads wants to woof at you but dey skeered."

"How come, Mr. Pitts? Do I look like a bear or panther?"

"Naw, but dey say youse rich and dey ain't got de nerve to open dey mouf."

I mentally cursed the $12.74 dress from Macy's that I had on among all the $1.98 mail-order dresses. I looked about and noted the number of bungalow aprons and even the rolled down paper bags on the heads of several women. I did look different and resolved to fix all that no later than the next morning.

"Oh, Ah ain't got doodley squat,"[2] I countered. "Mah man brought me dis dress de las' time he went to Jacksonville. We wuz sellin' plenty stuff den and makin' good money. Wisht Ah had dat money now."

Then Pitts began woofing at me and the others stood around to see how I took it.

"Say, Miss, you know nearly all dese niggers is after you. Dat's all dey talk about out in de swamp."

"You don't say. Tell 'em to make me know it."

"Ah ain't tellin' nobody nothin'. Ah ain't puttin' out nothin' to no ole hard head but ole folks eyes and Ah ain't doin' dat till they dead. Ah talks for Number One. Second stanza: Some of 'em talkin' 'bout marryin' you and dey wouldn't know whut to do wid you if they had you. Now, dat's a fack."

"You reckon?"

"Ah know dey wouldn't. Dey'd 'spect you tuh git out de bed and fix dem some breakfus' and a bucket. Dat's 'cause dey don't know no better. Dey's thin-brainded. Now me, Ah wouldn't let you fix me no breakfus'. Ah git up and fix mah own and den, whut make it so cool, Ah'd fix *you* some and set it on de back of de cook-stove so you could git it when you wake up. Dese mens don't even know how to talk to nobody lak you. If you wuz tuh ast dese niggers somethin' dey'd answer you 'yeah' and 'naw.' Now, if you wuz some ole gator-back 'oman dey'd be tellin' you jus' right. But dat ain't de way tuh talk tuh nobody lak *you.* Now you ast *me* somethin' and see how Ah'll answer yuh."

"Mr. Pitts, are you havin' a good time?"

(In a prim falsetto) "Yes, Ma'am. See, dat's de way tuh talk tuh *you.* "

I laughed and the crowd laughed and Pitts laughed. Very successful woofing. Pitts treated me and we got on. Soon a boy came to me from Cliffert Ulmer asking me to dance. I found out that that was the social custom. The fellow that wants to broach a young woman doesn't come himself to ask. He sends

[2]Nothing.

64

his friend. Somebody came to me for Joe Willard and soon I was swamped with bids to dance. They were afraid of me before. My laughing acceptance of Pitts' woofing had put everybody at his ease.

James Presley and Slim spied noble at the orchestra. I had the chance to learn more about "John Henry" maybe. So I strolled over to James Presley and asked him if he knew how to play it.

"Ah'll play it if you sing it," he countered. So he played and I started to sing the verses I knew. They put me on the table and everybody urged me to spread my jenk,[3] so I did the best I could. Joe Willard knew two verses and sang them. Eugene Oliver knew one; Big Sweet knew one. And how James Presley can make his box cry out the accompaniment!

By the time that the song was over, before Joe Willard lifted me down from the table I knew that I was in the inner circle. I had first to convince the "job" that I was not an enemy in the person of the law; and, second, I had to prove that I was their kind. "John Henry" got me over my second hurdle.

After that my car was everybody's car. James Presley, Slim and I teamed up and we had to do "John Henry" wherever we appeared. We soon had a reputation that way. We went to Mulberry, Pierce and Lakeland.

After that I got confidential and told them all what I wanted. At first they couldn't conceive of anybody wanting to put down "lies." But when I got the idea over we held a lying contest and posted the notices at the Post Office and the commissary. I gave four prizes and some tall lying was done. The men and women enjoyed themselves and the contest broke up in a square dance with Joe Willard calling figures.

The contest was a huge success in every way. I not only collected a great deal of material but it started individuals coming to me privately to tell me stories they had no chance to tell during the contest.

Cliffert Ulmer told me that I'd get a great deal more by

[3]Have a good time.

going out with the swamp-gang. He said they lied a plenty while they worked. I spoke to the quarters boss and the swamp boss and both agreed that it was all right, so I strowed it all over the quarters that I was going out to the swamp with the boys next day. My own particular crowd, Cliffert, James, Joe Willard, Jim Allen and Eugene Oliver were to look out for me and see to it that I didn't get snake-bit nor 'gator-swallowed. The watchman, who sleeps out in the swamps and gets up steam in the skitter every morning before the men get to the cypress swamp, had been killed by a panther two weeks before, but they assured me that nothing like that could happen to me; not with the help I had.

Having watched some members of that swamp crew handle axes, I didn't doubt for a moment that they could do all that they said. Not only do they chop rhythmically, but they do a beautiful double twirl above their heads with the ascending axe before it begins that accurate and bird-like descent. They can hurl their axes great distances and behead moccasins or sink the blade into an alligator's skull. In fact, they seem to be able to do everything with their instrument that a blade can do. It is a magnificent sight to watch the marvelous co-ordination between the handsome black torsos and the twirling axes.

So next morning we were to be off to the woods.

It wasn't midnight dark and it wasn't day yet. When I awoke the saw-mill camp was a dawn gray. You could see the big saw-mill but you couldn't see the smoke from the chimney. You could see the congregation of shacks and the dim outlines of the scrub oaks among the houses, but you couldn't see the grey quilts of Spanish Moss that hung from the trees.

Dick Willie was the only man abroad. It was his business to be the first one out. He was the shack-rouser. Men are not supposed to over-sleep and Dick Willie gets paid to see to it that they don't. Listen to him singing as he goes down the line.

Wake up, bullies, and git on de rock. 'Tain't quite daylight but it's four o'clock.

66

Coming up the next line, he's got another song.

Wake up, Jacob, day's a breakin'. Git yo' hoe-cake a bakin' and yo' shirt tail shakin'.

What does he say when he gets to the jook and the long-house?[4] I'm fixing to tell you right now what he says. He raps on the floor of the porch with a stick and says:

"Ah ha! What make de rooster crow every morning at sun-up?

"Dat's to let de pimps and rounders know de workin' man is on his way."

About that time you see a light in every shack. Every kitchen is scorching up fat-back and hoe-cake. Nearly every skillet is full of corn-bread. But some like biscuit-bread better. Break your hoe-cake half in two. Half on the plate, half in the dinner-bucket. Throw in your black-eyed peas and fat meat left from supper and your bucket is fixed. Pour meat grease in your plate with plenty of cane syrup. Mix it and sop it with your bread. A big bowl of coffee, a drink of water from the tin dipper in the pail. Grab your dinner-bucket and hit the grit. Don't keep the straw-boss[5] waiting.

This morning when we got to the meeting place, the foreman wasn't there. So the men squatted along the railroad track and waited.

Joe Willard was sitting with me on the end of a cross-tie when he saw Jim Presley coming in a run with his bucket and jumper-jacket.

"Hey, Jim, where the swamp boss? He ain't got here yet."

"He's ill—sick in the bed Ah hope, but Ah bet he'll git here yet."

"Aw, he ain't sick. Ah bet you a fat man he ain't," Joe said.

"How come?" somebody asked him and Joe answered:

[4]See glossary.

[5]The low-paid poor white section boss on a railroad; similar to swamp boss who works the gang that gets the timber to the sawmill.

"Man, he's too ugly. If a spell of sickness ever tried to slip up on him, he'd skeer it into a three weeks' spasm."

Blue Baby[6] stuck in his oar and said: "He ain't so ugly. Ye all jus' ain't seen no real ugly man. Ah seen a man so ugly till he could get behind a jimpson weed and hatch monkies."

Everybody laughed and moved closer together. Then Officer Richardson said: "Ah seen a man so ugly till they had to spread a sheet over his head at night so sleep could slip up on him."

They laughed some more, then Cliffert Ulmer said:

"Ah'm goin' to talk with my mouth wide open. Those men y'all been talkin' 'bout wasn't ugly at all. Those was pretty men. Ah knowed one so ugly till you could throw him in the Mississippi river and skim ugly for six months."

"Give Cliff de little dog," Jim Allen said. "He done tole the biggest lie."

"He ain't lyin'," Joe Martin tole them. "Ah knowed dat same man. He didn't die—he jus' uglied away."

They laughed a great big old kah kah laugh and got closer together.

"Looka here, folkses," Jim Presley exclaimed. "Wese a half hour behind schedule and no swamp boss and no log train here yet. What yo' all reckon is the matter sho' 'nough?"

"Must be something terrible when white folks get slow about putting us to work."

"Yeah," says Good Black. "You know back in slavery Ole Massa was out in de field sort of lookin' things over, when a shower of rain come up. The field hands was glad it rained so they could knock off for a while. So one slave named John says:

"More rain, more rest."

"Ole Massa says, 'What's dat you say?'

"John says, 'More rain, more grass.' "

"There goes de big whistle. We ought to be out in the woods almost."

[6]See glossary.

68

The big whistle at the saw-mill boomed and shrilled and pretty soon the log-train came racking along. No flats for logs behind the little engine. The foreman dropped off the tender as the train stopped.

"No loggin' today, boys. Got to send the train to the Everglades to fetch up the track gang and their tools."

"Lawd, Lawd, we got a day off," Joe Willard said, trying to make it sound like he was all put out about it. "Let's go back, boys. Sorry you won't git to de swamp, Zora."

"Aw, naw," the Foreman said. "Y'all had better g'wan over to the mill and see if they need you over there."

And he walked on off, chewing his tobacco and spitting his juice.

The men began to shoulder jumper-jackets and grab hold of buckets.

Allen asked: "Ain't dat a mean man? No work in the swamp and still he won't let us knock off."

"He's mean all right, but Ah done seen meaner men than him," said Handy Pitts.

"Where?"

"Oh, up in Middle Georgy. They had a straw boss and he was so mean dat when the boiler burst and blowed some of the men up in the air, he docked 'em for de time they was off de job."

Tush Hawg up and said: "Over on de East Coast Ah used to have a road boss and he was so mean and times was so hard till he laid off de hands of his watch."

Wiley said: "He's almost as bad as Joe Brown. Ah used to work in his mine and he was so mean till he wouldn't give God an honest prayer without snatching back 'Amen.' "

Ulmer says: "Joe Wiley, youse as big a liar as you is a man! Whoo-wee. Boy, you molds 'em. But lemme tell y'all a sho nuff tale 'bout Ole Massa."

"Go 'head and tell it, Cliff," shouted Eugene Oliver. "Ah love to hear tales about Ole Massa and John. John sho was one smart nigger."

So Cliff Ulmer went on.

You know befo' surrender Ole Massa had a nigger name John and John always prayed every night befo' he went to bed and his prayer was for God to come git him and take him to Heaven right away. He didn't even want to take time to die. He wanted de Lawd to come git him just like he was—boot, sock and all. He'd git down on his knees and say: "O Lawd, it's once more and again yo' humble servant is knee-bent and body-bowed—my heart beneath my knees and my knees in some lonesome valley, crying for mercy while mercy kin be found. O Lawd, Ah'm astin' you in de humblest way I know how to be *so* pleased as to come in yo' fiery chariot and take me to yo' Heben and its immortal glory. Come Lawd, you know Ah have such a hard time. Old Massa works me *so* hard, and don't gimme no time to rest. So come, Lawd, wid peace in one hand and pardon in de other and take me away from this sin-sorrowing world. Ah'm tired and Ah want to go home."

So one night Ole Massa passed by John's shack and heard him beggin' de Lawd to come git him in his fiery chariot and take him away; so he made up his mind to find out if John meant dat thing. So he goes on up to de big house and got hisself a bed sheet and come on back. He throwed de sheet over his head and knocked on de door.

John quit prayin' and ast: "Who dat?"

Ole Massa say: "It's me, John, de Lawd, done come wid my fiery chariot to take you away from this sin-sick world."

Right under de bed John had business. He told his wife: "Tell Him Ah ain't here, Liza."

At first Liza didn't say nothin' at all, but de Lawd kept right on callin' John: "Come on, John, and go to Heben wid me where you won't have to plough no mo' furrows and hoe no mo' corn. Come on, John."

Liza says: "John ain't here, Lawd, you hafta come back another time."

Lawd says: "Well, then Liza, you'll do."

Liza whispers and says: "John, come out from underneath dat bed and g'wan wid de Lawd. You been beggin' him to come git you. Now g'wan wid him."

John back under de bed not saying a mumblin' word. De Lawd out on de door step kept on callin'.

Liza says: "John, Ah thought you was so anxious to get to Heben. Come out and go on wid God."

John says: "Don't you hear him say 'You'll do'? Why don't you go wid him?"

"Ah ain't a goin' nowhere. Youse de one been whoopin' and hollerin' for him to come git you and if you don't come out from under dat bed Ah'm gointer tell God youse here."

Ole Massa makin' out he's God, says: "Come on, Liza, you'll do."

Liza says: "O, Lawd, John is right here underneath de bed."

"Come on John, and go to Heben wid me and its immortal glory."

John crept out from under de bed and went to de door and cracked it and when he seen all dat white standin' on de doorsteps he jumped back. He says: "O, Lawd, Ah can't go to Heben wid you in yo' fiery chariot in dese ole dirty britches; gimme time to put on my Sunday pants."

"All right, John, put on yo' Sunday pants."

John fooled around just as long as he could, changing them pants, but when he went back to de door, de big white glory was still standin' there. So he says agin: "O, Lawd, de Good Book says in Heben no filth is found and I got on his dirty sweaty shirt. Ah can't go wid you in dis old nasty shirt. Gimme time to put on my Sunday shirt!"

"All right, John, go put on yo' Sunday shirt."

John took and fumbled around a long time changing his shirt, and den he went back to de door, but Ole Massa was still on de door step. John didn't had nothin' else to change so he opened de door a little piece and says:

"O, Lawd, Ah'm ready to go to Heben wid you in yo' fiery chariot, but de radiance of yo' countenance is *so* bright, Ah can't come out by you. Stand back jus' a li'l way please."

Ole Massa stepped back a li'l bit.

John looked out agin and says: "O, Lawd, you know dat po' humble me is less than de dust beneath yo' shoe soles. And de radiance of yo' countenance is so bright Ah can't come out by you. Please, please, Lawd, in yo' tender mercy, stand back a li'l bit further."

Ole Massa stepped back a li'l bit mo'.

John looked out agin and he says: "O, Lawd, Heben is
so high and wese so low; youse so great and Ah'm so weak
and yo' strength is too much for us poor sufferin' sinners.
So once mo' and agin yo' humber servant is knee-bent and
body-bowed askin' you one mo' favor befo' Ah step into
yo' fiery chariot to go to Heben wid you and wash in yo'
glory—be so pleased in yo' tender mercy as to stand back
jus' a li'l bit further."

Ole Massa stepped back a step or two mo' and out dat
door John come like a streak of lightning. All across de
punkin patch, thru de cotton over de pasture—John wid
Ole Massa right behind him. By de time dey hit de corn-
field John was way ahead of Ole Massa.

Back in de shack one of de children was cryin' and she
ast Liza: "Mama, you reckon God's gointer ketch papa and
carry him to Heben wid him?"

"Shet yo' mouf, talkin' foolishness!" Liza clashed at de
chile. "You know de Lawd can't outrun yo' pappy—
specially when he's barefooted at dat."

Kah, Kah, Kah! Everybody laughing with their mouths
wide open. If the foreman had come along right then he
would have been good and mad because he could tell their
minds were not on work.

Joe Willard says: "Wait a minute, fellows, wese walkin' too
fast. At dis rate we'll be there befo' we have time to talk some
mo' about Ole Massa and John. Tell another one, Cliffert."

"Aw, naw," Eugene Oliver hollered out.

Let *me* talk some chat. Dis is de real truth 'bout Ole
Massa 'cause my grandma told it to my mama and she told
it to me.

During slavery time, you know, Ole Massa had a nigger
named John and he was a faithful nigger and Ole Massa
lakted John a lot too.

One day Ole Massa sent for John and tole him, says:

"John, somebody is stealin' my corn out de field. Every mornin' when I go out I see where they done carried off some mo' of my roastin' ears. I want you to set in de corn patch tonight and ketch whoever it is."

So John said all right and he went and hid in de field.

Pretty soon he heard somethin' breakin' corn. So John sneaked up behind him wid a short stick in his hand and hollered: "Now, break another ear of Ole Massa's corn and see what *Ah'll* do to you."

John thought it was a man all dis time, but it was a bear wid his arms full of roastin' ears. He throwed down de corn and grabbed John. And him and dat bear!

John, after while got loose and got de bear by the tail wid de bear tryin' to git to him all de time. So they run around in a circle all night long. John was so tired. But he couldn't let go of de bear's tail, do de bear would grab him in de back.

After a stretch they quit runnin' and walked. John swingin' on to de bear's tail and de bear's nose 'bout to touch him in de back.

Daybreak, Ole Massa come out to see 'bout John and he seen John and de bear walkin' 'round in de ring. So he run up and says: "Lemme take holt of 'im, John, whilst you run git help!"

John says: "All right, Massa. Now you run in quick and grab 'im just so."

Ole Massa run and grabbed holt of de bear's tail and said: "Now, John you make haste to git somebody to help us."

John staggered off and set down on de grass and went to fanning hisself wid his hat.

Ole Massa was havin' plenty trouble wid dat bear and he looked over and seen John settin' on de grass and he hollered:

"John, you better g'wan git help or else I'm gwinter turn dis bear aloose!"

John says: "Turn 'im loose, then. Dat's whut Ah tried to do all night long but Ah couldn't."

Jim Allen laughed just as loud as anybody else and then he said: "We better hurry on to work befo' de buckra⁷ get in behind us."

"Don't never worry about work," says Jim Presley. "There's more work in de world than there is anything else. God made de world and de white folks made work."

"Yeah, dey made work but they didn't make us do it," Joe Willard put in. "We brought dat on ourselves."

"Oh, yes, de white folks did put us to work too," said Jim Allen.

Know how it happened? After God got thru makin' de world and de varmints and de folks, he made up a great big bundle and let it down in de middle of de road. It laid dere for thousands of years, then Ole Missus said to Ole Massa: "Go pick up dat box, Ah want to see whut's in it." Ole Massa look at de box and it look so heavy dat he says to de nigger, "Go fetch me dat big ole box out dere in de road." De nigger been stumblin' over de box a long time so he tell his wife:

"'Oman, go git dat box." So de nigger 'oman she runned to git de box. She says:

"Ah always lak to open up a big box 'cause there's nearly always something good in great big boxes." So she run and grabbed a-hold of de box and opened it up and it was full of hard work.

Dat's de reason de sister in black works harder than anybody else in de world. De white man tells de nigger to work and he takes and tells his wife.

"Aw, now, dat ain't de reason niggers is working so hard," Jim Presley objected.

Dis is de way *dat* was.
God let down two bundles 'bout five miles down de road. So de white man and de nigger raced to see who

⁷West African word meaning white people.

would git there first. Well, de nigger out-run de white man
and grabbed de biggest bundle. He was so skeered de
white man would git it away from him he fell on top of de
bundle and hollered back: "Oh, Ah got here first and dis
biggest bundle is mine." De white man says: "All right,
Ah'll take yo' leavings," and picked up de li'l tee-ninchy
bundle layin' in de road. When de nigger opened up his
bundle he found a pick and shovel and a hoe and a plow
and chop-axe and then de white man opened up his bundle
and found a writin'-pen and ink. So ever since then de nigger been out in de hot sun, usin' his tools and de white
man been sittin' up figgerin', ought's a ought, figger's a
figger; all for de white man, none for de nigger.

"Oh lemme spread my mess. Dis is Will Richardson doin'
dis lyin'."

You know Ole Massa took a nigger deer huntin' and
posted him in his place and told him, says: "Now you wait
right here and keep yo' gun reformed and ready. Ah'm
goin' 'round de hill and skeer up de deer and head him dis
way. When he come past, you shoot."
De nigger says: "Yessuh, Ah sho' will, Massa."
He set there and waited wid de gun all cocked and after
a while de deer come tearin' past him. He didn't make a
move to shoot de deer so he went on 'bout his business.
After while de white man come on 'round de hill and ast
de nigger: "Did you kill de deer?"
De nigger says: "Ah ain't seen no deer pass here yet."
Massa says: "Yes, you did. You couldn't help but see
him. He come right dis way."
Nigger says: "Well Ah sho' ain't seen none. All Ah seen
was a white man come along here wid a pack of chairs on
his head and Ah tipped my hat to him and waited for de
deer."

"Some colored folks ain't got no sense, and when Ah see
'em like dat," Ah say, "My race but not my taste."

FIVE

Y'all ever hear dat lie 'bout big talk?" cut in Joe Wiley. "Yeah we done heard it, Joe, but Ah kin hear it some 'gin. Tell it, Joe," pleaded Gene Oliver.

During slavery time two ole niggers wuz talkin' an' one said tuh de other one, "Ole Massa made me so mad yistiddy till Ah give 'im uh good cussin' out. Man, Ah called 'im everything wid uh handle on it."

De other one says, "You didn't cuss *Ole Massa,* didja? Good God! Whut did he do tuh you?"

"He didn't do *nothin',* an' man, Ah laid one cussin' on 'im! Ah'm uh man lak dis, Ah won't stan' no hunchin'. Ah betcha he won't bother *me* no mo'."

"Well, if you cussed 'im an' he didn't do nothin' tuh you, de nex' time he make me mad Ah'm goin' tuh lay uh hearin' on him."

Nex' day de nigger did somethin'. Ole Massa got in behind 'im and he turnt 'round an' give Ole Massa one good cussin' an Ole Massa had 'im took down and whipped nearly tuh death. Nex' time he saw dat other nigger he says tuh 'im. "Thought you tole me, you cussed Ole Massa out and he never opened his mouf."

"Ah did."

"Well, how come he never did nothin' tuh yuh? Ah did

77

it an' he come nigh uh killin' *me.*"

"Man, you didn't go cuss 'im tuh his face, didja?"

"Sho Ah did. Ain't dat whut you tole me you done?"

"Naw, Ah didn't say Ah cussed 'im tuh his face. You sho is crazy. Ah thought you had mo' sense than dat. When Ah cussed Ole Massa he wuz settin' on de front porch an' Ah wuz down at de big gate."

De other nigger wuz mad but he didn't let on. Way after while he 'proached de nigger dat got 'im de beatin' an' tole 'im, "Know whut Ah done tuhday?"

"Naw, whut you done? Give Ole Massa 'nother cussin'?"

"Naw, Ah ain't never goin' do dat no mo'. Ah peeped up under Ole Miss's drawers."

"Man, hush yo' mouf! You knows you ain't looked up under ole Miss's clothes!"

"Yes, Ah did too. Ah looked right up her very drawers."

"You better hush dat talk! Somebody goin' hear you and Ole Massa'll have you kilt."

"Well, Ah sho done it an' she never done nothin' neither."

"Well, whut did she say?"

"Not uh mumblin' word, an' Ah stopped and looked jus' as long as Ah wanted tuh an' went on 'bout mah business."

"Well, de nex' time Ah see her settin' out on de porch Ah'm goin' tuh look too."

"Help yo'self."

Dat very day Ole Miss wuz settin' out on de porch in de cool uh de evenin' all dressed up in her starchy white clothes. She had her legs all crossed up and de nigger walked up tuh de edge uh de porch and peeped up under Ole Miss's clothes. She took and hollored an' Ole Massa come out an' had dat nigger almost kilt alive.

When he wuz able tuh be 'bout agin he said tuh de other nigger, "Thought you tole me you peeped up under Ole Miss's drawers?"

"Ah sho did."

"Well, how come she never done nothin' tuh *you?* She got me nearly kilt."

"Man, when Ah looked under Ole Miss's drawers they

wuz hangin' out on de clothes line. You didn't go look up in 'em while she had 'em on, didja? You sho is uh fool! Ah thought you had mo' sense than dat, Ah claire Ah did. It's uh wonder he didn't kill yuh dead. Umph, umph, umph. You sho ain't got no sense atall."

"Yeah," said Black Baby, "But dat wasn't John de white folks was foolin' wid. John was too smart for Ole Massa. He never got no beatin'!"

De first colored man what was brought to dis country was name John. He didn't know nothin' mo' than you told him and he never forgot nothin' you told him either. So he was sold to a white man.

Things he didn't know he would ask about. They went to a house and John never seen a house so he asked what it was. Ole Massa tole him it was his kingdom. So dey goes on into de house and dere was the fireplace. He asked what was that. Ole Massa told him it was his flame 'vaperator.

The cat was settin' dere. He asked what it was. Ole Massa told him it was his round head.

So dey went upstairs. When he got on de stair steps he asked what dey was. Ole Massa told him it was his jacob ladder. So when they got up stairs he had a roller foot bed. John asked what was dat. Ole Massa told him it was his flowery-bed-of-ease. So dey came down and went out to de lot. He had a barn. John asked what was dat. Ole Massa told him, dat was his mound. So he had a Jack in the stable, too. John asked, "What in de world is dat?" Ole Massa said: "Dat's July, de God dam."

So de next day Ole Massa was up stairs sleep and John was smokin'. It flamed de 'vaperator and de cat was settin' dere and it got set afire. The cat goes to de barn where Ole Massa had lots of hay and fodder in de barn. So de cat set it on fire. John watched de Jack kicking up hay and fodder. He would see de hay and fodder go up and come down but he thought de Jack was eatin' de hay and fodder. So he goes upstairs and called Ole Massa and told him to get up off'n his flowery-bed-of-ease and come down on his jacob ladder. He said: "I done flamed the 'vaperator and it caught de round head and set him on fire. He's gone to de mound and set it on fire, and July the God dam is eatin' up everything he kin git his mouf on."

Massa turned over in de bed and ast, "Whut dat you say, John?"

John tole 'im agin. Massa was still sleepy so he ast John agin whut he say. John was gittin' tired so he say, "Aw, you better git up out dat bed and come on down stairs. Ah done set dat ole cat afire and he run out to de barn and set it afire and dat ole Jackass is eatin' up everything he git his mouf on."

Gene Oliver said: "Y'all hush and lemme tell this one befo' we git to de mill. This ain't no slavery time talk."

Once they tried a colored man in Mobile for stealing a goat. He was so poorly dressed, and dirty—that de judge told him, "Six months on de country road, you stink so."

A white man was standing dere and he said, "Judge, he don't stink, Ah got a nigger who smells worser than a billy goat." De judge told de man to bring him on over so he could smell him. De next day de man took de billy goat and de nigger and went to de court and sent de judge word dat de nigger and de billy goat wuz out dere and which one did he want fust.

The judge told him to bring in de goat. When he carried de goat he smelled so bad dat de judge fainted. Dey got ice water and throwed it in de Judge's face 'til he come to. He told 'em to bring in de nigger and when dey brung in de nigger de goat fainted.

Joe Wiley said: "Ah jus' got to tell this one, do Ah can't rest."

In slavery time dere was a colored man what was named John. He went along wid Ole Massa everywhere he went. He used to make out he could tell fortunes. One day him

80

and his Old Massa was goin' along and John said, "Ole Massa, Ah kin tell fortunes." Ole Massa made out he didn't pay him no attention. But when they got to de next man's plantation Old Massa told de landlord, "I have a nigger dat kin tell fortunes." So de other man said, "Dat nigger can't tell no fortunes. I bet my plantation and all my niggers against yours dat he can't tell no fortunes."

Ole Massa says: "I'll take yo' bet. I bet everything in de world I got on John 'cause he don't lie. If he say he can tell fortunes, he can tell 'em. Bet you my plantation and all my niggers against yours and throw in de wood lot extry."

So they called Notary Public and signed up de bet. Ole Massa straddled his horse and John got on his mule and they went on home.

John was in de misery all that night for he knowed he was gointer be de cause of Ole Massa losin' all he had.

Every mornin' John useter be up and have Old Massa's saddle horse curried and saddled at de door when Ole Massa woke up. But *this* mornin' Old Massa had to git John out of de bed.

John useter always ride side by side with Massa, but on de way over to de plantation where de bet was on, he rode way behind.

So de man on de plantation had went out and caught a coon and had a big old iron wash-pot turned down over it.

There was many person there to hear John tell what was under de wash-pot.

Ole Massa brought John out and tole him, say: "John, if you tell what's under dat wash pot Ah'll make you independent, rich. If you don't, Ah'm goin' to kill you because you'll make me lose my plantation and everything I got."

John walked 'round and 'round dat pot but he couldn't git de least inklin' of what was underneath it. Drops of sweat as big as yo' fist was rollin' off of John. At last he give up and said: "Well, you got de ole coon at last."

When John said that, Ole Massa jumped in de air and cracked his heels twice befo' he hit de ground. De man that was bettin' against Ole Massa fell to his knees wid de cold sweat pourin' off him. Ole Massa said: "John, you done won another plantation fo' me. That's a coon under that pot sho 'nuff."

So he give John a new suit of clothes and a saddle horse. And John quit tellin' fortunes after that.

Going back home Ole Massa said: "Well, John, you done made me vast rich so I goin' to Philly-Me-York and won't be back in three weeks. I leave everything in yo' charge."

So Ole Massa and his wife got on de train and John went to de depot with 'em and seen 'em off on de train bid 'em goodbye. Then he hurried on back to de plantation. Ole Massa and Ole Miss got off at de first station and made it on back to see whut John was doin'.

John went back and told de niggers, "Massa's gone to Philly-Me-York and left everything in my charge. Ah want one of you niggers to git on a mule and ride three miles north, and another one three miles west and another one three miles south and another one three miles east. Tell everybody to come here—there's gointer be a ball here tonight. The rest of you go into the lot and kill hogs until you can walk on 'em."

So they did. John goes in and dressed up in Ole Massa's swaller-tail clothes, put on his collar and tie; got a box of cigars and put under his arm, and one cigar in his mouth.

When the crowd come John said: "Y'all kin dance and Ah'm goin' to call figgers."

So he got Massa's biggest rockin' chair and put it up in Massa's bed and then he got up in the bed in the chair and begin to call figgers:

"Hands up!" "Four circle right." "Half back." "Two ladies change." He was puffing his cigar all de time.

'Bout this time John seen a white couple come in but they looked so trashy he figgered they was piney woods crackers, so he told 'em to g'wan out in de kitchen and git some barbecue and likker and to stay out there where they belong. So he went to callin' figgers agin. De git Fiddles[1] was raisin' cain over in de corner and John was callin' for de new set:

[1] Guitars.

"Choose yo' partners." "Couples to yo' places like horses to de traces." "Sashay all." "Sixteen hands up." "Swing Miss Sally 'round and 'round and bring her back to me!"

Just as he went to say "Four hands up," he seen Ole Massa comin' out the kitchen wipin' the dirt off his face.

Ole Massa said: "John, just look whut you done done! I'm gointer take you to that persimmon tree and break yo' neck for this—killing up all my hogs and havin' all these niggers in my house."

John ast, "Ole Massa, Ah know you gointer kill me, but can Ah have a word with my friend Jack before you kill me?"

"Yes, John, but have it quick."

So John called Jack and told him; says: "Ole Massa is gointer hang me under that persimmon tree. Now you get three matches and get in the top of the tree. Ah'm gointer pray and when you hear me ast God to let it lightning Ah want you to strike matches."

Jack went on out to the tree. Ole Massa brought John on out with the rope around his neck and put it over a limb.

"Now, John," said Massa, "have you got any last words to say?"

"Yes sir, Ah want to pray."

"Pray and pray damn quick. I'm clean out of patience with you, John."

So John knelt down. "O Lord, here Ah am at de foot of de persimmon tree. If you're gointer destroy Old Massa tonight, with his wife and chillun and everything he got, lemme see it lightnin'."

Jack up the tree, struck a match. Ole Massa caught hold of John and said: "John, don't pray no more."

John said: "Oh yes, turn me loose so Ah can pray. O Lord, here Ah am tonight callin' on Thee and Thee alone. If you are gointer destroy Ole Massa tonight, his wife and chillun and all he got, Ah want to see it lightnin' again."

Jack struck another match and Ole Massa started to run. He give John his freedom and a heap of land and stock. He run so fast that it took a express train running at the rate of ninety miles an hour and six months to bring him back, and that's how come niggers got they freedom today.

83

Well, we were at the mill at last, as slow as we had walked. Old Hannah[2] was climbing the road of the sky, heating up sand beds and sweating peoples. No wonder nobody wanted to work. Three fried men are not equal to one good cool one. The men stood around the door for a minute or two, then dropped down on the shady side of the building. Work was too discouraging to think about. Phew! Sun and sawdust, sweat and sand. Nobody called a meeting and voted to sit in the shade. It just happened naturally.

Jim Allen said, "Reckon we better go inside and see if they want us?"

"Oh hell, naw!" shouted Lennie Barnes. "We ain't no mill-hands nohow. Let's stay right where we is till they find us. We got plenty to do—lyin' on Ole Massa and slavery days. Lemme handle a li'l language long here wid de rest. Y'all ever hear 'bout dat nigger dat found a gold watch?"

"Yeah, Ah done heard it," said Cliff, "but go on and tell it, Lonnie, so yo' egg bag kin rest easy."[3]

"Well, once upon a time was a good ole time.
Monkey chew tobacco and spit white lime."
A colored man was walking down de road one day and he found a gold watch and chain. He didn't know what it was, so the first thing he met was a white man, so he showed the white man de watch and ast him what it was. White man said, "Lemme see it in my hand."

De colored man give it to him and de white man said, "Why this is a gold watch, and de next time you find anything kickin' in de road put in yo' pocket and sell it."

With that he put the watch in his pocket and left de colored man standing there.

So de colored man walked on down de road a piece further and walked up on a little turtle. He tied a string to it

[2] The Sun.

[3] So you can be at ease. A hen is supposed to suffer when she has a fully developed egg in her.

and put de turtle in his pocket and let de string hang out.

So he met another colored fellow and the fellow ast him says: "Cap, what time you got?"

He pulled out de turtle and told de man, "It's a quarter past leben and kickin' lak hell for twelve."

Larkins White says: "Y'all been wearin' Ole Massa's southern can[4] out dis mornin'. Pass him over here to me and lemme handle some grammar wid him."

"You got him, Ah just hope dat straw boss don't come sidlin' 'round here," somebody said.

"Ah got to tell you 'bout Old Massa down in de piney woods."

During slavery uh nigger name Jack run off from his marster and took and hid hisself down in de piney woods.

Ole Massa hunted and hunted but he never could ketch dat nigger.

But Jack had uh good friend on de plantation dat useter slip 'im somethin' t' eat and fetch de banjo down and play 'im somethin' every day so's he could dance some. Jack wuz tryin' to make it on off de mountain where Old Massa couldn't fetch 'im back. So Ole Massa got on to dis other nigger slippin' out to Jack but he couldn't ketch 'im so he tole 'im if he lead 'im to where Jack wuz he'd give 'im a new suit uh clothes. So he said, "All right."

So he tole Old Massa to follow him and do whutever he sing. So Ole Massa said, "All right."

So dat day de nigger took Jack some dinner and de Banjo. So Jack et. Den he tole him, say: "Jack I got uh new song fuh yuh today."

"Play it and lemme dance some."

"It's about Ole Massa."

Jack said, "I don't give uh damn 'bout Ole Massa. Ah don't b'long tuh him no mo'. Play it and lemme dance."

So he started to playin'.

[4]His hips.

85

"From pine to pine, Mister Pinkney.
From pine to pine, Mister Pinkney."

Jack was justa dancin' fallin' off de log and cuttin' de pigeon wing—(diddle dip, diddle dip—diddle dip) "from pine to pine Mr. Pinkney."

> White man coming closer all de time.
> "Now take yo' time Mister Pinkney.
> Now take yo' time Mister Pinkney."
> (Diddle dip, diddle dip, diddle dip, diddle dip)
> "Now grab 'im now Mister Pinkney
> Now grab 'im now Mister Pinkney."
> (Diddle dip, diddle dip, diddle dip, diddle dip)
> "Now grab 'im now Mister Pinkney."

So they caught Jack and put uh hundred lashes on his back and put him back to work.

"Now Ah tole dat one for myself, now Ah got to tell one for my wife."

"Aw, g'wan tell de lie, Larkins, if you want to. You know you ain't tellin' no lie for yo' wife. No mo' than de rest of us. You lyin' cause you like it." James Presley put in. "Hurry up so somebody else kin plough up some literary and lay-by some alphabets."

Two mens dat didn't know how tuh count good had been haulin' up cawn and they stopped at de cemetery wid de last load 'cause it wuz gittin' kinda dark. They thought they'd git thru instead uh goin' 'way tuh one of 'em's barn. When they wuz goin' in de gate two ear uh cawn dropped off de waggin, but they didn't stop tuh bother wid 'em, just then. They wuz in uh big hurry tuh git home. They wuz justa vidin' it up. "You take dis'n an Ah'll take dat'un, you take dat'un and Ah'll take dis'un."

An ole nigger heard 'em while he wuz passin' de cemetery an' run home tuh tell ole Massa 'bout it.

"Massa, de Lawd and de devil is down in de cemetery 'vidin' up souls. Ah heard 'em. One say, 'you take that 'un an' Ah'll take dis'un'."

Ole Massa wuz sick in de easy chear, he couldn't git about by hisself, but he said, "Jack, Ah don't know whut dis foolishness is, but Ah know you lyin'."

"Naw Ah ain't neither, Ah swear it's so."

"Can't be, Jack, youse crazy."

"Naw, Ah ain't neither; if you don' believe me, come see for yo'self."

"Guess Ah better go see whut you talkin' 'bout; if you fool me, Ah'm gointer have a hundred lashes put on yo' back in de mawnin' suh."

They went on down tuh de cemetery wid Jack pushin' Massa in his rollin' chear, an' it wuz sho dark down dere too. So they couldn't see de two ears uh cawn layin' in de gate.

Sho nuff Ole Massa heard 'em sayin' "Ah'll take dis'un," and de other say, "An' Ah'll take dis'un." Ole Massa got skeered hisself but he wuzn't lettin' on, an' Jack whispered tuh 'im, "Unh hunh, didn't Ah tell you de Lawd an' de devil wuz down here 'vidin' up souls?"

They waited awhile there in de gate listenin' den they heard 'em say, "Now, we'll go git dem two at de gate."

Jack says, "Ah knows de Lawd gwine take you, and Ah ain't gwine let de devil get me—Ah'm gwine home." An' he did an' lef' Ole Massa settin' dere at de cemetery gate in his rollin' chear, but when he got home, Ole Massa had done beat 'im home and wuz settin' by de fire smokin' uh seegar."

Jim Allen began to fidget. "Don't y'all reckon we better g'wan inside? They might need us."

Lonnie Barnes shouted, "Aw naw—you sho is worrysome. You bad as white folks. You know they say a white man git in some kind of trouble, he'll fret and fret until he kill hisself. A nigger git into trouble, he'll fret a while, then g'wan to sleep."

"Yeah, dat's right, too," Eugene Oliver agreed. "Didja ever hear de white man's prayer?"

"Who in Polk County ain't heard dat?" cut in Officer Richardson.

"Well, if you know it so good, lemme hear *you* say it," Eugene snapped back.

"Oh, Ah don't know it well enough to say it. Ah jus' know it well enough to know it."

"Well, all right then, when Ah'm changing my dollars, you keep yo' pennies out."

"Ah don't know it, Eugene, say it for me," begged Peter Noble. "Don't pay Office no mind."

Well, it come a famine and all de crops was dried up and Brother John was ast to pray. He had prayed for rain last year and it had rained, so all de white folks 'sembled at they church and called on Brother John to pray agin, so he got down and prayed:

"Lord, first thing, I want you to understand that this ain't no nigger talking to you. This is a white man and I want you to hear me. Pay some attention to me. I don't worry and bother you all the time like these niggers—asking you for a whole heap of things that they don't know what to do with after they git 'em—so when I do ask a favor, I want it granted. Now, Lord, we want some rain. Our crops is all burning up and we'd like a little rain. But I don't mean for you to come in a hell of a storm like you did last year— kicking up racket like niggers at a barbecue. I want you to come calm and easy. Now, another thing, Lord, I want to speak about. Don't let these niggers be as sassy as they have been in the past. Keep 'em in their places, Lord, Amen."

Larkins White burst out:

And dat put me in de mind of a nigger dat useter do a lot of prayin' up under 'simmon tree, durin' slavery time. He'd go up dere and pray to God and beg Him to kill all de white folks. Ole Massa heard about it and so de next day he got hisself a armload of sizeable rocks and went up de 'simmon tree, before de nigger got dere, and when he begin to pray and beg de Lawd to kill all de white folks, Ole Massa let one of dese rocks fall on Ole Nigger's head. It was a heavy rock and knocked de nigger over. So when he got up he looked up and said: "Lawd, I ast you to kill all de white folks, can't you tell a white man from a nigger?"

Joe Wiley says: "Y'all might as well make up yo' mind to bear wid me, 'cause Ah feel Ah got to tell a lie on Ole Massa for my mamma. Ah done lied on him enough for myself. So Ah'm gointer tell it if I bust my gall tryin'."

Ole John was a slave, you know. And there was Ole Massa and Ole Missy and de two li' children—a girl and a boy.

Well, John was workin' in de field and he seen de children out on de lake in a boat, just a hollerin'. They had done lost they oars and was 'bout to turn over. So then he went and tole Ole Massa and Ole Missy.

Well, Ole Missy, she hollered and said: "It's so sad to lose these 'cause Ah ain't never goin' to have no more children." Ole Massa made her hush and they went down to de water and follered de shore on 'round till they found 'em. John pulled off his shoes and hopped in and swum out and got in de boat wid de children and brought 'em to shore.

Well, Massa and John take 'em to de house. So they was all so glad 'cause de children got saved. So Massa told 'im to make a good crop dat year and fill up de barn, and den when he lay by de crops nex' year, he was going to set him free.

So John raised so much crop dat year he filled de barn and had to put some of it in de house.

So Friday come, and Massa said, "Well, de day done come that I said I'd set you free. I hate to do it, but I don't like to make myself out a lie. I hate to git rid of a good nigger lak you."

So he went in de house and give John one of his old suits of clothes to put on. So John put it on and come in to shake hands and tell 'em goodbye. De children they cry, and Ole Missy she cry. Didn't want to see John go. So John took his bundle and put it on his stick and hung it crost his shoulder.

Well, Ole John started on down de road. Well, Ole Massa said, "John, de children love yuh."

"Yassuh."

"John, I love yuh."

"Yassuh."

"And Missy *like* yuh!"

"Yassuh."

"But 'member, John, youse a nigger."

"Yassuh."

Fur as John could hear 'im down de road he wuz hollerin', "John, Oh John! De children loves you. And I love you. De Missy *like* you."

John would holler back, "Yassuh."

"But 'member youse a nigger, tho!"

Ole Massa kept callin' 'im and his voice was pitiful. But John kept right on steppin' to Canada. He answered Ole Massa every time he called 'im, but he consumed on wid his bag.

90

SIX

Tookie Allen passed by the mill all dressed up in a tight shake-baby.[1] She must have thought she looked good because she was walking that way. All the men stopped talking for a while. Joe Willard hollered at her.

"Hey, Tookie, how do you like your new dress?"

Tookie made out she didn't hear, but anybody could tell that she had. That was why she had put on her new dress, and come past the mill a wringing and twisting—so she could hear the men talking about her in the dress.

"Lawd, look at Tookie switchin' it and lookin' back at it! She's done gone crazy thru de hips." Joe Willard just couldn't take his eyes off of Tookie.

"Aw, man, you done seen Tookie and her walk too much to be makin' all dat miration over it. If you can't show me nothin' better than dat, don't bring de mess up," Cliff Ulmer hooted. "Less tell some more lies on Ole Massa and John."

"John sho was a smart nigger now. He useter git de best of Ole Massa all de time," gloated Sack Daddy.

"Yeah, but some white folks is smarter than you think," put in Eugene Oliver.

[1]A dress very tight across the hips but with a full short skirt; very popular on the "jobs."

91

For instance now, take a man I know up in West Florida. He hired a colored man to clear off some new ground, but dat skillet blonde[2] was too lazy to work. De white man would show him what to do then he's g'wan back to de house and keep his books. Soon as he turned his back de nigger would flop down and go to sleep. When he hear somebody comin' he'd hit de log a few licks with de flat of de ax and say, "Klunk, klunk, you think Ah'm workin' but Ah ain't."

De white man heard him but he didn't say a word. Sat'-day night come and Ole Cuffee went up to de white man to git his pay. De white man stacked up his great big ole silver dollars and shook 'em in his hand and says, "Clink, clink, you think I'm gointer pay you, but I ain't."

By that time somebody saw the straw boss coming so everybody made it on into the mill. The mill boss said, "What are y'all comin' in here for? Ah ain't got enough work for my own men. Git for home."

The swamp gang shuffled on out of the mill. "Umph, umph, umph," said Black Baby. "We coulda *done* been gone if we had a knowed dat."

"Ah told y'all to come an' go inside but you wouldn't take a listen. Y'all think Ah'm an ole Fogey. Young Coon for running but old coon for cunning."

We went on back to the quarters.

When Mrs. Bertha Allen saw us coming from the mill she began to hunt up the hoe and the rake. She looked under the porch and behind the house until she got them both and placed them handy. As soon as Jim Allen hit the steps she said:

"Ah'm mighty proud y'all got a day off. Maybe Ah kin git dis yard all clean today. Jus' look at de trash and dirt! And it's so many weeds in dis yard, Ah'm liable to git snake bit at my own door."

"Tain' no use in you gittin' yo' mouf all primped up for no hoein' and rakin' out of me, Bertha. Call yo' grandson and let

[2]Very black person.

92

him do it. Ah'm too old for dat," said Jim testily.

"Ah'm standin' in my tracks and steppin' back on my abstract[3]—Ah ain't gointer rake up no yard. Ah'm goin' fishin'," Cliffert Ulmer snapped back. "Grandma, you worries mo' 'bout dis place than de man dat owns it. You ain't de Everglades Cypress Lumber Comp'ny sho nuff. Youse just shacking in one of their shanties. Leave de weeds go. Somebody'll come chop 'em some day."

"Naw, Ah ain't gointer leave 'em go! You and Jim would wallow in dirt right up to yo' necks if it wasn't for me."

Jim threw down his jumper and his dinner bucket. "Now, *Ah'm* goin' fishin' too. When Bertha starts her jawin' Ah can't stay on de place. Her tongue is hung in de middle and works both ways. Come on Cliff, less git de poles!"

"Speck Ah'm gointer have to make a new line for my trout pole," Cliff said. "Dat great big ole fish Ah hooked las' time carried my other line off in his mouth, 'member?"

"Aw, dat wasn't no trout got yo' line; dat's whut you tell us, but dat was a log bit yo' hook dat time." Larkins White twitted.

"Yes dat was a trout, too now. Ah'm a real fisherman. Ah ain't like y'all. Ah kin ketch fish anywhere. All Ah want to know, is there any water. Man, Ah kin ketch fish out a water bucket. Don't b'lieve me, just come on down to de lake. Ah'll bet, Ah'll pull 'em all de fish out de lake befo' y'all git yo' bait dug."

"Dat's a go," shouted Larkins. "Less go! Come on de rest of y'all to see dis thing out. Dis boy 'bout to burst his britches since he been chawin' tobacco reg'lar and workin' in de swamp wid us mens."

Cliff picked up the hoe and went 'round behind the house to dig some bait. Old Jim went inside and got the spool of No. 8 cotton and a piece of beeswax and went to twisting a trout line. He baptized the hook in asafetida and put his hunting knife in his pocket, met Cliffert at the gate and they were off

[3] I am standing my ground.

93

to join the others down by the jook. Big Sweet and Lucy got out their poles and joined us. It was almost like a log-rolling[4] or a barbecue. The quarters were high. The men didn't get off from work every day like this.

We proaged on thru the woods that was full of magnolia, pine, cedar, oak, cypress, hickory and many kinds of trees whose names I do not know. It is hard to know all the trees in Florida. But everywhere they were twined with climbing vines and veiled in moss.

"What's de matter, Ah don't hear no birds?" complained Eugene Oliver. "It don't seem natural."

Everybody looked up at one time like cows in a pasture.

"Oh you know how come we don't hear no birds. It's Friday and de mocking bird ain't here," said Big Sweet after a period of observation.

"What's Friday got to do with the mockin' bird?" Eugene challenged.

"Dat's exactly what Ah want to know," said Joe Wiley.

"Well," said Big Sweet. "Nobody never sees no mockin' bird on Friday. They ain't on earth dat day."

"Well, if they ain't on earth, where is they?"

"They's all gone to hell on Friday with a grain of sand in they mouth to help out they friend." She continued:

Once there was a man and he was very wicked. He useter rob and steal and he was always in a fight and killin' up people. But he was awful good to birds and mockin' birds was his favorite. This was a long time ago before de man first started to buildin' de Rocky Mountains. Well, 'way after while somebody kilt him, and being he had done lived so bad, when he died he went straight to hell.

De birds all hated it mighty bad when they seen him in hell, so they tried to git him out. But the fire was too hot so they give up—all but de mockin' birds. They come to-gether and decided to tote sand until they squenched de

[4]When people used to get out logs to build a house they would get the neighbors to help. Plenty of food and drink served. Very gay time.

fire in hell. So they set a day and they all agreed on it. Every Friday they totes sand to hell. And that's how come nobody don't never see no mockin' bird[5] on Friday.

Joe Wiley chuckled. "If them mockin' birds ever speck to do dat man any good they better git some box-cars to haul dat sand. Dat one li'l grain they totin' in their bill ain't helpin' none. But anyhow it goes to show you dat animals got sense as well as peoples." Joe went on—

Now take cat-fish for instances. Ah knows a man dat useter go fishin' every Sunday. His wife begged him not to do it and his pastor strained wid him for years but it didn't do no good. He just would go ketch him a fish every Sabbath. One Sunday he went and just as soon as he got to de water he seen a great big ole cat-fish up under some water lilies pickin' his teeth with his fins. So de man baited his pole and dropped de hook right down in front of de big fish. Dat cat grabbed de hook and took out for deep water. De man held on and pretty soon dat fish pulled him in. He couldn't git out. Some folks on de way to church seen him and run down to de water but he was in too deep. So he went down de first time and when he come up he hollered—"Tell my wife." By dat time de fish pulled him under again. When he come up he hollered, "Tell my wife—" and went down again. When he come up de third time he said: "Tell my wife to fear God and cat-fish," and went down for de last time and he never come up no mo'.

"Aw, you b'lieve dat old lie?" Joe Willard growled. "Ah don't."

"Well, Ah do. Nobody ain't gointer git me to fishin' on Sunday," said Big Sweet fervently.

"How come nothin' don't happen to all dese white folks dat go fishin' on Sunday? Niggers got all de signs and white folks got all de money," retorted Joe Willard.

[5]Some say it is a jay bird.

95

"Yeah, but all cat-fish ain't so sensible." Joe Wiley cut in with a sly grin on his face. "One time when Ah was livin' in Plateau, Alabama—dat's right on de Alabama river you know—Ah put out some fish lines one night and went on home. Durin' de night de river fell and dat left de hooks up out de water and when Ah went there next morning a cat-fish had done jumped up after dat bait till he was washed down in sweat."

Jim Presley said, "I know you tellin' de truth, Joe, 'cause Ah saw a coach whip after a race runner one day. And de race runner was running so fast to git away from dat coach whip dat his tail got so hot it set de world on fire, and dat coach whip was running so hard to ketch him till he put de fire out wid his sweat."

Jim Allen said, "Y'all sho must not b'long to no church de way y'all tells lies. Y'all done quit tellin' 'em. Y'all done gone to moldin' 'em. But y'all want to know how come snakes got poison in they mouth and nothin' else ain't got it?"

"Yeah, tell it, Jim," urged Arthur Hopkins.

Old man Allen turned angrily upon Arthur.

"Don't you be callin' me by my first name. Ah'm old enough for yo' grand paw! You respect my gray hairs. Ah don't play wid chillun. Play wid a puppy and he'll lick yo' mouf."

"Ah didn't mean no harm."

"Dat's all right, Arthur. Ah ain't mad. Ah jus' don't play wid chillun. You go play wid Cliff and Sam and Eugene. They's yo' equal. Ah was a man when yo' daddy was born."

"Well, anyhow, Mr. Jim, please tell us how come de snakes got poison."

Well, when God made de snake he put him in de bushes to ornament de ground. But things didn't suit de snake so one day he got on de ladder and went up to see God.

"Good mawnin', God."

"How do you do, Snake?"

"Ah ain't so many, God, you put me down there on my

96

belly in de dust and everything trods upon me and kills off my generations. Ah ain't got no kind of protection at all."

God looked off towards immensity and thought about de subject for awhile, then he said, "Ah didn't mean for nothin' to be stompin' you snakes lak dat. You got to have some kind of a protection. Here, take dis poison and put it in yo' mouf and when they tromps on you, protect yo' self."

So de snake took de poison in his mouf and went on back.

So after awhile all de other varmints went up to God.

"Good evenin', God."

"How you makin' it, varmints?"

"God, please do somethin' 'bout dat snake. He' layin' in de bushes there wid poison in his mouf and he's strikin' everything dat shakes de bush. He's killin' up our generations. Wese skeered to walk de earth."

So God sent for de snake and tole him:

"Snake, when Ah give you dat poison, Ah didn't mean for you to be hittin' and killin' everything dat shake de bush. I give you dat poison and tole you to protect yo'self when they tromples on you. But you killin' everything dat moves. Ah didn't mean for you to do dat."

De snake say, "Lawd, you know Ah'm down here in de dust. Ah ain't got no claws to fight wid, and Ah ain't got no feets to git me out de way. All Ah kin see is feets comin' to tromple me. Ah can't tell who my enemy is and who is my friend. You gimme dis protection in my mouf and Ah uses it."

God thought it over for a while then he says:

"Well, snake, I don't want yo' generations all stomped out and I don't want you killin' everything else dat moves. Here take dis bell and tie it to yo' tail. When you hear feets comin' you ring yo' bell and if it's yo' friend, he'll be keerful. If it's yo' enemy, it's you and him."

So dat's how de snake got his poison and dat's how come he got rattles.

Biddy, biddy, bend my story is end.

Turn loose de rooster and hold de hen.

"Don't tell no mo' 'bout no snakes—specially when we walkin' in all dis tall grass," pleaded Presley. "Ah speck Ah'm gointer be seein' 'em in my sleep tonight. Lawd, Ah'm skeered of snakes."

"Who ain't?" cut in Cliff Ulmer. "It sho is gittin' hot. Ah'll be glad when we git to de lake so Ah kin find myself some shade."

"Man, youse two miles from dat lake yet, and otherwise it ain't hot today," said Joe Wiley. "He ain't seen it hot, is he Will House?"

"Naw, Joe, when me and you was hoboing down in Texas it was so hot till we saw old stumps and logs crawlin' off in de shade."

Eugene Oliver said, "Aw dat wasn't hot. Ah seen it so hot till two cakes of ice left the ice house and went down the street and fainted."

Arthur Hopkins put in: "Ah knowed two men who went to Tampa all dressed up in new blue serge suits, and it was so hot dat when de train pulled into Tampa two blue suits got off de train. De men had done melted out of 'em."

Will House said, "Dat wasn't hot. Dat was chilly weather. Me and Joe Wiley went fishin' and it was so hot dat before we got to de water, we met de fish, coming swimming up de road in dust."

"Dat's a fact, too," added Joe Wiley. "Ah remember dat day well. It was so hot dat Ah struck a match to light my pipe and set de lake afire. Burnt half of it, den took de water dat was left and put out de fire."

Joe Willard said "Hush! Don't Ah hear a noise?"

Eugene and Cliffert shouted together, "Yeah—went down to de river—

> Heard a mighty racket
> Nothing but de bull frog
> Pullin' off his jacket!"

"Dat ain't what Ah hea'd," said Joe.

"Well, whut did you hear?"

"Ah see a chigger[6] over in de fence corner wid a splinter in his foot and a seed tick is pickin' it out wid a fence rail and de chigger is hollerin', 'Lawd, have mercy.' "

"Dat brings me to de boll-weevil," said Larkins White. "A boll-weevil flew onto de steerin' wheel of a white man's car and says, 'Mister, lemme drive yo' car.'

"De white man says, 'You can't drive no car.'

"Boll-weevil says: 'Oh yeah, Ah kin. Ah drove in five thousand cars last year and Ah'm going to drive in ten thousand dis year.'

"A man told a tale on de boll-weevil agin. Says he heard a terrible racket and noise down in de field, went down to see whut it was and whut you reckon? It was Ole Man Boll-Weevil whippin' li' Willie Boll-Weevil 'cause he couldn't carry two rows at a time."

Will House said, "Ah know a lie on a black gnat. Me and my buddy Joe Wiley was ramshackin' Georgy over when we come to a loggin' camp. So bein' out of work we ast for a job. So de man puts us on and give us some oxes to drive. Ah had a six-yoke team and Joe was drivin' a twelve-yoke team. As we was comin' thru de woods we heard somethin' hummin' and we didn't know what it was. So we got hungry and went in a place to eat and when we come out a gnat had done et up de six-yoke team and de twelve-yoke team, and was sittin' up on de wagon pickin' his teeth wid a ox-horn and cryin' for somethin' to eat."

"Yeah," put in Joe Wiley, "we seen a man tie his cow and calf out to pasture and a mosquito come along and et up de cow and was ringin' de bell for de calf."

"Dat wasn't no full-grown mosquito at dat," said Eugene Oliver, "Ah was travellin' in Texas and laid down and went to sleep. De skeeters bit me so hard till Ah seen a ole iron

[6]A young flea.

99

wash-pot, so Ah crawled under it and turned it down over me good so de skeeters couldn't git to me. But you know dem skeeters bored right thru dat iron pot. So I up wid a hatchet and bradded their bills into de pot. So they flew on off 'cross Galveston bay wid de wash pot on their bills."

"Look," said Black Baby, "on de Indian River we went to bed and heard de mosquitoes singin' like bull alligators. So we got under four blankets. Shucks! dat wasn't nothin'. Dem mosquitoes just screwed off dem short bills, reached back in they hip-pocket and took out they long bills and screwed 'em on and come right on through dem blankets and got us."

"Is dat de biggest mosquito you all ever seen? Shucks! Dey was li'l baby mosquitoes! One day my ole man took some men and went out into de woods to cut some fence posts. And a big rain come up so they went up under a great big ole tree. It was so big it would take six men to meet around it. De other men set down on de roots but my ole man stood up and leaned against de tree. Well, sir, a big old skeeter come up on de other side of dat tree and bored right thru it and got blood out of my ole man's back. Dat made him so mad till he up wid his ax and bradded dat mosquito's bill into dat tree. By dat time de rain stopped and they all went home.

"Next day when they come out, dat mosquito had done cleaned up ten acres dying. And two or three weeks after dat my ole man got enough bones from dat skeeter to fence in dat ten acres."

Everybody liked to hear about the mosquito. They laughed all over themselves.

"Yeah," said Sack Daddy, "you sho is tellin' de truth 'bout dat big old mosquito 'cause my ole man bought dat same piece of land and raised a crop of pumpkins on it and lemme tell y'all right now—mosquito dust is de finest fertilizer in de world. Dat land was so rich and we raised pumpkins so big dat we et five miles up in one of 'em and five miles down and ten miles acrost one and we ain't never found out how far it went. But my ole man was buildin' a scaffold inside so we could cut de pumpkin meat without so much trouble, when he dropped his hammer. He tole me, he says, 'Son, Ah done dropped my hammer. Go git it for me.' Well, Ah went down in de pumpkin and begin to hunt dat hammer. Ah was foolin' 'round in there all day, when I met a man and he ast me what Ah was lookin' for. Ah tole him my ole man had done dropped his hammer and sent me to find it for him. De man tole me Ah might as well give it up for a lost cause, he had been lookin' for a double mule-team and a wagon that had got lost in there for three weeks and he hadn't found no trace of 'em yet. So Ah stepped on a pin, de pin bent and dat's de way de story went."

"Dat was rich land but my ole man had some rich land too," put in Will House. "My ole man planted cucumbers and he went along droppin' de seeds and befo' he could git out de way he'd have ripe cucumbers in his pockets. What is the richest land you ever seen?"

"Well," replied Joe Wiley, "my ole man had some land dat was so rich dat our mule died and we buried him down in our bottom-land and de next mornin' he had done sprouted li'l jackasses."

"Aw, dat land wasn't so rich," objected Ulmer. "My ole man had some land and it was so rich dat he drove a stob[7] in de ground at de end of a corn-row for a landmark and next morning there was ten ears of corn on de corn stalk and four ears growin' on de stob."

"Dat lan' y'all talkin' 'bout might do, if you give it plenty commercial-nal[8] but my ole man wouldn't farm no po' land like dat," said Joe Wiley. "Now, one year we was kinda late puttin' in our crops. Everybody else had corn a foot high when papa said, 'Well, chillun, Ah reckon we better plant some corn.' So Ah was droppin' and my brother was hillin' up behind me. We had done planted 'bout a dozen rows when Ah looked back and seen de corn comin' up. Ah didn't want it to grow too fast 'cause it would make all fodder and no

[7]Stake.

[8]Commercial fertilizer.

101

roastin' ears so Ah hollered to my brother to sit down on some of it to stunt de growth. So he did, and de next day he dropped me back a note—says: "passed thru Heben yesterday at twelve o'clock sellin' roastin' ears to de angels."

"Yeah," says Larkins White, "dat was some pretty rich ground, but whut is de poorest ground you ever seen?"

Arthur Hopkins spoke right up and said:

"Ah seen some land so poor dat it took nine partridges to holler 'Bob White.' "

"Dat was rich land, boy," declared Larkins. "Ah seen land so poor dat de people come together and 'cided dat it was too poor to raise anything on, so they give it to de church, so de congregation built de church and called a pastor and held de meetin'. But de land was so poor they had to wire up to Jacksonville for ten sacks of commercial-nal before dey could raise a tune on dat land."

The laughter was halted by the sound of a woodpecker against a cypress. Lonnie Barnes up with his gun to kill it, but Lucy stopped him.

"What you want to kill dat ole thing for? He ain't fitten to eat. Save dat shot and powder to kill me a rabbit. Ah sho would love a nice tender cotton-tail. Slim Ellis brought me a great big ole fat ham off a rabbit last night, and Ah lakted dat."

"Ah kin shoot you a rabbit just as good as Slim kin," Lonnie protested. "Ah wasn't gointer kill no ole tough peckerwood for you to eat, baby. Ah was goin' to shoot dat red-head for his meanness. You know de peckerwood come pretty nigh drownin' de whole world once."

"How was dat?"

Well, you know when de Flood was and dey had two of everything in de ark—well, Ole Nora[9] didn't take on no trees, so de woodpecker set 'round and set 'round for a week or so then he felt like he just had to peck himself some wood. So he begin to peck on de Ark. Ole Nora

[9]Noah.

come to him and tole him, "Don't peck on de Ark. If you peck a hole in it, we'll all drown."

Woodpecker says: "But Ah'm hungry for some wood to peck."

Ole Nora says, "Ah don't keer how hongry you gits don't you peck on dis ark no mo. You want to drown everybody and everything?"

So de woodpecker would sneak 'round behind Ole Nora's back and peck every chance he got. He'd hide hisself way down in de hold where he thought nobody could find him and peck and peck. So one day Ole Nora come caught him at it. He never opened his mouth to dat woodpecker. He just hauled off and give dat peckerwood a cold head-whipping wid a sledge hammer, and dat's why a peckerwood got a red head today—'cause Ole Nora bloodied it wid dat hammer. Dat's how come Ah feel like shootin' every one of 'em Ah see. Tryin' to drown *me* before Ah was born.

"A whole lot went on on dat ole Ark," Larkins White commented. "Dat's where de possum lost de hair off his tail."

"Now don't you tell me no possum ever had no hair on dat slick tail of his'n," said Black Baby, " 'cause Ah know better."

Yes, he did have hair on his tail one time. Yes, indeed. De possum had a bushy tail wid long silk hair on it. Why, it useter be one of de prettiest sights you ever seen. De possum struttin' 'round wid his great big ole plumey tail. Dat was 'way back in de olden times before de big flood.

But de possum was lazy—jus' like he is today. He sleep too much. You see Ole Nora had a son name Ham and he loved to be playin' music all de time. He had a banjo and a fiddle and maybe a guitar too. But de rain come up so sudden he didn't have time to put 'em on de ark. So when rain kept comin' down he fretted a lot 'cause he didn't have nothin' to play. So he found a ole cigar box and made hisself a banjo, but he didn't have no strings for it. So he seen de possum stretched out sleeping wid his tail all spread 'round. So Ham slipped up and shaved de possum's tail and made de strings for his banjo out de hairs. When dat possum woke up from his nap, Ham was playin' his tail hairs down to de bricks and dat's why de possum ain't got no hair on his tail today. Losin' his pretty tail sorta broke de possum's spirit too. He ain't never been de same since. Dat's how come he always actin' shame-faced. He know his tail ain't whut it useter be; and de possum feel mighty bad about it.

"A lot of things ain't whut they useter be," observed Jim Presley. "Now take de 'gator for instance. He been changed 'round powerful since he been made."

"Yeah," cut in Eugene Oliver, "He useter have a nice tongue so he could talk like a nat'chal man, but Brer Dog caused de 'gator to lose his tongue, and dat's how come he hate de dog today."

"Brer 'Gator didn't fall out wid Brer Dog 'bout no tongue," retorted Presley.

Brer Dog done de 'gator a dirty trick 'bout his mouth. You know God made de dog and the 'gator without no mouth. So they seen everybody else had a mouth so they made it up to git theirselves a mouth like de other var- mints. So they agreed to cut one 'nothers' mouth, and each one said dat when de other one tole 'em to stop cuttin' they would. So Brer Dog got his mouth first. Brer 'Gator took de razor and cut. Brer Dog tole him, "Stop," which he did. Den Brer Dog took de razor and begin to cut Brer 'Gator a mouth. When his mouth was big as he wanted it, Brer 'Gator says, "Stop, Brer Dog. Dat'll do, I thank you, please." But Brer Dog kept right on cuttin' till he ruint Brer 'Gator's face. Brer 'Gator was a very handsome gent'- man befo' Brer Dog done him that a way, and everytime he look in de lookin' glass he cry like a baby over de dis- figgerment of his face. And dat's how come de 'gator hate de dog.

"My people, my people," lamented Oliver. "They just will talk whut they don't know."

"Go on Oliver."

De 'gator didn't fall out wid de dog 'bout no mouth cuttin' scrape. You know all de animals was havin' a ball down in de pine woods, and so they all chipped in for refreshments and then they didn't have no music for de dance. So all de animals what could 'greed to furnish music. So de dog said he'd be de trumpet in de band, and de horse and de frog and de mockin' bird and all said they'd be there and help out all they could. But they didn't have no bass drum, till somebody said, "Whut's de matter wid Brer 'Gator, why he don't play de bass drum for us?" Dey called Brer 'Gator but he wasn't at de meetin' so de varmints depitized Brer Dog to go call on Brer 'Gator and see if he wouldn't furnish de drum music for de dance. Which he did.

"Good evenin', Brer 'Gator."

"My compliments, Brer Dog, how you makin' out? Ah'm always glad when folks visit me. Whut you want?"

"Well Brer 'Gator, de varmints is holdin' a big convention tonight in de piney woods and we want you to furnish us a little bit of yo' drum music."

"It's like this, Brer Dog, tell de other animals dat Ah'm mighty proud they wants me and de compliments run all over me, but my wife is po'ly and my chillun is down sick. But Ah'll lend you my drum if you know anybody kin play it, and know how to take keer of it too!"

"Oh, Ah'll do *dat,* Brer 'Gator. You just put it in my keer. You don't have to worry 'bout dat atall."

So de dog took Brer 'Gator's tongue to de ball dat night and they beat it for a drum. De varmints lakted de bass drum so well till they didn't play nothin' else hardly. So by daybreak it was wore clean out. Brer Dog didn't want to go tell Brer 'Gator they had done wore his tongue out so he hid from Brer 'Gator. Course de 'gator don't like it 'bout his tongue so he's de sworn enemy of de dog.

Big Sweet says, "Dat's de first time Ah ever heard 'bout de dawg wearin' out de 'gator's tongue, but Ah do know he useter be a pretty varmint. He was pure white all over wid red and yeller stripes around his neck. He was pretty like dat 'till he met up wid Brer Rabbit. Kah, kah, kah! Ah have to laugh everytime Ah think how sharp dat ole rabbit rascal is."

"Yeah," said Sam Hopkins. "At night time, at de right time; Ah've always understood it's de habit of de rabbit to dance in de wood."

"When Ah'm shellin' my corn; you keep out yo' nubbins, Sam," Big Sweet snapped as she spat her snuff.

Ah'm tellin' dis lie on de 'gator. Well, de 'gator was a pretty white varmint wid coal black eyes. He useter swim in de water, but he never did bog up in de mud lak he do now. When he come out de water he useter lay up on de clean grass so he wouldn't dirty hisself all up.

So one day he was layin' up on de grass in a marsh sunnin' hisself and sleepin' when Brer Rabbit come bustin' cross de marsh and run right over Brer 'Gator before he stopped. Brer 'Gator woke up and seen who it was trompin' all over him and trackin' up his pretty white hide. So he seen Brer Rabbit, so he ast him, "Brer Rabbit, what you mean by runnin' all cross me and messin' up my clothes lak dis?"

Brer Rabbit was up behind a clump of bushes peerin' out to see what was after him. So he tole de 'gator, says: "Ah

106

ain't got time to see what Ah'm runnin' over nor under. Ah got trouble behind me."

'Gator ast, "Whut is trouble? Ah ain't never heard tell of dat befo'."

Brer Rabbit says, "You ain't never heard tell of trouble?"

Brer 'Gator tole him, "No."

Rabbit says: "All right, you jus' stay right where you at and Ah'll show you whut trouble is."

He peered 'round to see if de coast was clear and loped off, and Brer 'Gator washed Brer Rabbit's foot tracks off his hide and went on back to sleep agin.

Brer Rabbit went on off and lit him a li'dard knot[10] and come on back. He sat dat marsh afire on every side. All around Brer 'Gator de fire was burnin' in flames of fire. De 'gator woke up and pitched out to run, but every which a way he run de fire met him.

He seen Brer Rabbit sittin' up on de high ground jus' killin' hisself laughin'. So he hollered and ast him:

"Brer Rabbit, whut's all dis goin' on?"

"Dat's trouble, Brer 'Gator, dat's trouble youse in."

De 'gator run from side to side, round and round. Way after while he broke thru and hit de water "ker ploogum!" He got all cooled off but he had done got smoked all up befo' he got to de water, and his eyes is all red from de smoke. And dat's how come a 'gator is black today—cause de rabbit took advantage of him lak dat.

---

[10]Lightwood, fat pine. So called because it is frequently used as a torch.

SEVEN

Joe Wiley said, " 'Tain't nothin' cute as a rabbit. When they come cuter than him, they got to have 'cute indigestion." He cleared his throat and continued:

Dat's de reason de dog is mad wid de rabbit[1] now—'cause he fooled de dog.

You know they useter call on de same girl. De rabbit useter g'wan up to de house and cross his legs on de porch and court de girl. Brer Dog, he'd come in de gate wid his banjo under his arm.

"Good evenin', Miss Saphronie."

"My compliments, Brer Dog, come have a chair on de pe-azza."

"No thank you ma'am, Miss Saphronie. B'lieve Ah'll set out here under de Chinaberry tree."

So he'd set out dere and pick de banjo and sing all 'bout:

If Miss Fronie was a gal of mine
She wouldn't do nothin' but starch and iron.

So de girl wouldn't pay no mind to Brer Rabbit at all. She'd be listenin' to Brer Dog sing. Every time he'd stop

[1]See glossary.

109

she'd holler out dere to him, "Wont you favor us wid another piece, Brer Dog? Ah sho do love singin' especially when they got a good voice and picks de banjo at de same time."

Brer Rabbit saw he wasn't makin' no time wid Miss Saphronie so he waylaid Brer Dog down in de piney woods one day and says:

"Brer Dog, you sho is got a mellow voice. You can sing. Wisht Ah could sing like dat, den maybe Miss Fronie would pay me some mind."

"Gawan, Brer Rabbit, you makin' great 'miration at nothin'. Ah can whoop a little, but Ah really do wish Ah could sing enough to suit Miss Fronie."

"Well, dat's de very point Ah'm comin' out on. Ah know a way to make yo' voice sweeter."

"How? Brer Rabbit, how?"

"Ah knows a way."

"Hurry up and tell me, Brer Rabbit. Don't keep me waitin' like dis. Make haste."

"Ah got to see inside yo' throat first. Lemme see dat and Ah can tell you exactly what to do so you can sing more better."

Brer Dog stretched his mouth wide open and the rabbit peered way down inside. Brer Dog had his mouth latched back to de last notch and his eyes shut. So Brer Rabbit pulled out his razor and split Brer Dog's tongue and tore out across de mountain wid de dog right in behind him. Him and him! Brer Rabbit had done ruint Brer Dog's voice, but he ain't had time to stop at Miss Fronie's nor nowhere else 'cause dat dog is so mad he won't give him time.

"Yeah," said Cliff.

De dog is sho hot after him. Run dem doggone rabbits so that they sent word to de dogs dat they want peace. So they had a convention. De rabbit took de floor and said they was tired of runnin', and dodgin' all de time, and they asted de dogs to please leave rabbits alone and run somethin' else. So de dogs put it to a vote and 'greed to leave off runnin' rabbits.

So after de big meetin' Brer Dog invites de rabbit over to his house to have dinner wid him.

He started on thru de woods wid Brer Dog but every now and then he'd stop and scratch his ear and listen. He stop right in his tracks. Dog say:

"Aw, come on Brer Rabbit, you too suscautious. Come on."

Kept dat up till they come to de branch just 'fore they got to Brer Dog's house. Just as Brer Rabbit started to step out on de foot-log, he heard some dogs barkin' way down de creek. He heard de old hound say, "How o-l-d is he?" and the young dogs answer him: "Twenty-one or two, twenty-one or two!" So Brer Rabbit say, "Excuse me, but Ah don't reckon Ah better go home wid you today, Brer Dog."

"Aw, come on, Brer Rabbit, you always gitten scared for nothin'. Come on."

"Ah hear dogs barkin', Brer Dog."

"Naw, you don't, Brer Rabbit."

"Yes, Ah do. Ah know, dat's dogs barkin'."

"S'posin' it is, it don't make no difference. Ain't we done held a convention and passed a law dogs run no mo' rabbits? Don't pay no 'tention to every li'l bit of barkin' you hear."

Rabbit scratch his ear and say,

"Yeah, but all de dogs ain't been to no convention, and anyhow some of dese fool dogs ain't got no better sense than to run all over dat law and break it up. De rabbits didn't go to school much and he didn't learn but three letter, and that's trust no mistake. Run every time de bush shake."

So he raced on home without breakin' another breath wid de dog.

"Dat's right," cut in Larkins White. "De Rabbits run from everything. They held a meetin' and decided. They say, 'Le's all go drown ourselves 'cause ain't nothin' skeered of us.' So it was agreed.

111

"They all started to de water in a body fast as time could wheel and roll. When they was crossin' de marsh jus' befo' they got to de sea, a frog hollered, 'Quit it, quit it!' So they say, 'Somethin' is 'fraid of us, so we won't drown ourselves.' So they all turnt 'round and went home."

"Dat's as bad as dat goat Ah seen back in South Carolina. We was on de tobacco truck goin' after plants when we passed a goat long side de road. He was jus' chewin' and he looked up and ast, 'Whose truck is dat?' Nobody answered him. When we come on back Ah said, 'Mr. Rush Pinkney's, why?' De goat says, 'Oh nothin',' and kept right on chewin'."

"Ow, Big Sweet! gimme dat lyin' goat! You know damn well dat goat ain't broke a breath wid you and nobody else," scolded Jim Allen.

"But a goat's got plenty sense, ugly as he is," said Arthur Hopkins.

Ah know my ole man had a goat and one Sunday mornin' he got mama to wash his shirt so't would be clean for him to wear to church. It was a pretty red silk shirt and my ole man was crazy about it.

So my ole lady washed it and hung it out to dry so she could iron it befo' church time. Our goat spied pa's shirt hangin' on de line and et it up tiddy umpty.

My ole man was so mad wid dat goat 'bout his shirt till he grabbed him and tied him on de railroad track so de train could run over him and kill him.

But dat old goat was smart. When he seen dat train bearin' down on him, he coughed up dat red shirt and waved de train down.

Dad Boykin said: "No ef and ands about it. A goat is a smart varmint, but my feets sho is tired."

"Dat *was* a long two miles," Jim Allen added. "Ah see de lake now, and Ah sho am glad."

"Doggone it!" said Lonnie Barnes, "here we is almost at de lake and Ah ain't got myself no game yet. But maybe Ah'll

112

have mo' luck on de way back."

"Yeah," Lucy remarked dryly, "dat gun you totin' ain't doin' you much good! Might just as well left it home."

"He act just like dat nigger did in slavery time wid Ole Massa's gun," laughed Willie Roberts.

"How as dat?"

Well, you know John was Ole Massa's pet nigger. He give John de best of everything and John thought Ole Massa was made outa gold. So one day Massa decided he wanted a piece of deer meat to eat so he called John and some more of his niggers together and told 'em:

"Now Ah want y'all to go git me a deer today. Ah'm goin' to give John my new gun and Ah want de rest of y'all go 'round and skeer up de deer and head him towards John, and he will shoot him wid de gun." When de others got there they said, "Did you git him, John?"

He said, "Naw, Ah didn't."

They said, "Well how come you didn't? He come right dead down de hill towards you."

"Y'all crazy! You think Ah'm gointer sprain Massa's brand new gun shootin' up hill wid it?"

"Dat's put me in de mind of a gun my ole man had," said Gene Oliver. "He shot a man wid it one time and de bullet worked him twice befo' it kilt him and three times after. If you hold it high, it would sweep de sky; if you hold it level, it'd kill de devil."

"Oh Gene, stop yo' lyin'! You don't stop lyin' and gone to flyin'."

"Dat ain't no lie, dat's a fact. One night I fired it myself," said Pitts.

"It's a wonder you didn't shoot it off dat time when de quarters boss was hot behind you."

"Let dat ride! Ah didn't want to kill dat ole cracker. But one night Ah heard somethin' stumblin' 'round our woodpile, so Ah grabbed de gun, stepped to de back door and fired it at de woodpile, and went on back to bed. All night long Ah

113

heard somethin' goin' 'round and 'round de house hummin' like a nest of hornets. When daybreak come Ah found out what it was. What you reckon? It was dat bullet. De night was so dark it was runnin' 'round de house waitin' for daylight so it could find out which was the way to go!"

"Dat was a mighty gun yo' pa had," agreed Larkins, "but Ah had a gun dat would lay dat one in the shade. It could shoot so far till Ah had to put salt down de barrel so de game Ah kilt wid it would keep till Ah got to it."

"Larkins—" Jim Allen started to protest.

"Mr. Allen, dat ain't no lie. Dat's a fack. Dat gun was so bad dat all Ah need to do was walk out in de woods wid it to skeer all de varmints. Ah went huntin' one day and saw three thousand ducks in a pond. Jus' as Ah levelled dis gun to fire, de weather turned cold and de water in de lake froze solid and them ducks flew off wid de lake froze to their feets."

"Larkins, s'posin' you was to die right now, where would you land?—jus' as straight to hell as a martin to his gourd. Whew! you sho kin lie. You'd pass slap thru hell proper. Jus' a bouncin' and a jumpin' and go clear to Ginny Gall, and dat's four miles south of West Hell; you better stop yo' lyin', man."

"Dat ain't no lie, man. You jus' ain't seen no real guns and no good shootin'."

"Ah don't want to see none. Less fish. Here we is at de lake. You can't talk and ketch fish too. You'll skeer all de fish away."

"Aw, nobody ain't even got a hook baited yet. Leave Larkins lie till we git set!" suggested Joe Wiley. "You gittin' old, Jim, when you can't stand good lyin'. It's jus' like sound doctrine. Everybody can't stand it."

"Who gittin' old? Not me! Ah laks de lies. All I said is yo' talkin' skeers off all de trouts and sheepheads. Ah can't eat no lies."

"Aw, gran'pa, don't be so astorperious! We all wants to hear Larkins' tale. I'm goin' ketch you some fish. We ain't off lak dis often. Tomorrow we'll be back in de swamp 'mong de cypress knees, de 'gators, and de moccasins, and strainin' wid de swamp boss," pleaded Cliff. "Go head on, and talk, Larkins, God ain't gonna bother you."

"Well," says Larkins:

A man had a wife and a whole passle of young 'uns, and they didn't have nothin' to eat.

He told his ole lady, "Well, Ah got a load of ammunition in my gun, so Ah'm gointer go out in de woods and see what Ah kin bring back for us to eat."

His wife said: "That's right, go see can't you kill us somethin'—if 'tain't nothin' but a squirrel."

He went on huntin' wid his gun. It was one of dese muzzle-loads. He knowed he didn't have but one load of ammunition so he was very careful not to stumble and let his gun go off by accident.

He had done walked more'n three miles from home and he ain't saw anything to shoot at. He got worried. Then all of a·sudden he spied some wild turkeys settin' up in a tree on a limb. He started to shoot at 'em, when he looked over in de pond and seen a passle of wild ducks; and down at de edge of de pond he saw a great big deer. He heard some noise behind him and he looked 'round and seen some partiges.

He wanted all of 'em and he didn't know how he could get 'em. So he stood and he thought and he thought. Then he decided what to do.

He took aim, but he didn't shoot at de turkeys. He shot de limb de turkeys was settin' on and de ball split dat limb and let all dem turkeys' feets dropped right down thru de crack and de split limb shet up on 'em and helt 'em right dere. De ball went on over and fell into de pond and kilt all dem ducks. De gun had too heavy a charge in her, so it bust and de barrel flew over and kilt dat deer. De stock kicked de man in de breast and he fell backwards and smothered all dem partiges.

Well, he drug his deer up under de tree and got his

ducks out de pond and piled them up wid de turkeys and so forth. He seen he couldn't tote all dat game so he went on home to git his mule and wagon.

Soon as he come in de gate his wife said:

"Where is de game you was gointer bring back? you musta lost yo' gun, you ain't got it."

He told his wife, "Ah wears de longest pants in dis house. You leave me tend to my business and you mind yours. Jus' you put on de pot and be ready. Plenty rations is comin'."

He took his team on back in de woods wid him and loaded up de wagon. He wouldn't git up on de wagon hisself because he figgered his mule had enough to pull without him.

Just as he got his game all loaded on de wagon, it commenced to rain but he walked on beside of the mule pattin' him and tellin' him to "come up," till they got home.

When he got home his wife says: "De pot is boilin'. Where is de game you tole me about?"

He looked back and seen his wagon wasn't behind de mule where it ought to have been. Far as he could see— nothin' but them leather traces, but no wagon.

Then he knowed de rain had done made dem traces stretch, and de wagon hadn't moved from where he loaded it.

So he told his wife, "De game will be here. Don't you worry."

So he just took de mule out and stabled him and wrapped dem traces 'round de gate post and went on in de house.

De next day it was dry and de sun was hot and it shrunk up dem traces, and about twelve o'clock they brought dat wagon home, "Cluck-cluck, cluck-cluck," right on up to de gate.

In spite of the laughter and talk, Cliff had landed two perch already, so Jim Allen laughed with the rest.

"Now," he said, beaming upon the fish his grandson had hooked, "I'm goin' to tell y'all about de hawk and de buzzard.

You know de hawk and de buzzard was settin' up in a pine tree one day, so de hawk says: "How you get yo' livin', Brer Buzzard?"

"Oh Ah'm makin' out pretty good, Brer Hawk. Ah waits on de salvation of de Lawd."

Hawk says, "Humph, Ah don't wait on de mercy of nobody. Ah takes mine."

"Ah bet, Ah'll live to pick yo' bones, Brer Hawk."

"Aw naw, you won't, Brer Buzzard. Watch me git my livin'."

He seen a sparrer sittin' on a dead limb of a tree and he sailed off and dived down at dat sparrer. De end of de limb was stickin' out and he run his breast right up on de sharp point and hung dere. De sparrer flew on off.

After while he got so weak he knowed he was gointer die. So de buzzard flew past just so—flyin' slow you know, and said, "Un hunh, Brer Hawk, Ah told you Ah was gointer live to pick yo' bones. Ah waits on de salvation of de Lawd." And dat's de way it is wid some of you young colts."

"Heh, heh, heh! Y'all talkin' 'bout me being old. Ah betcher Ah'll be here when a many of y'all is gone."

Joe Wiley said: "Less table discussion 'bout dyin' and open up de house for new business.

Y'all want to know how come they always use raw-hide on mule, so Ah'm gointer tell you. Whenever they make a whip they gointer have raw-hide on it, if it ain't nothin' but de tip.

A man had a mule you know and he had a ox too. So he used to work 'em together.

Both of 'em used to get real tired befo' knockin' off time but dat ole ox had mo' sense than de mule, so he played off sick.

Every day de mule would go out and work by hisself and de ox stayed in de stable. Every night when de mule come in, he'd ast, "Whut did Massa say 'bout me today?"

De mule would say, "Oh nothin'," or maybe he'd say,

117

"Ah heard him say how sorry he was you was sick and couldn't work."

De ox would laugh and go on to sleep.

One day de mule got tired, so he said, "Massa dat ox ain't sick. 'Tain't a thing de matter wid him. He's jus' playin' off sick. Ah'm tired of doin' all dis work by myself."

So dat night when he got in de stable, de ox ast him. "What did Ole Massa say 'bout me today?"

Mule told him, "Ah didn't hear him say a thing, but Ah saw him talkin' to de butcher man."

So de ox jumped up and said, "Ah'm well. Tell Ole Massa Ah'll be to work tomorrow."

But de next mornin' bright and soon de butcher come led him off.

So he said to de mule, "If you hadn't of told Massa on me, Ah wouldn't be goin' where Ah am. They're gointer kill me, but Ah'll always be war on yo' back."

And that's why they use raw-hide on mule's back—on account of dat mule and dat ox."

"Oh, well, if we gointer go way back there and tell how everything started," said Ulmer, "Ah might just as well tell how come we got gophers."

"Pay 'tention to yo' pole, Cliff," Jim Allen scolded. "You gittin' a bite. You got 'im! A trout too! If dat fool ain't lucky wid fish!"

Old Man Jim strung the trout expertly. "Now, Cliff, you kin do all de talkin' you want, just as long as you ketch me some fish Ah don't keer."

"Well," began Cliff:

God was sittin' down by de sea makin' sea fishes. He made de whale and throwed dat in and it swum off. He made a shark and throwed it in and then he made mullets and shad-fish and cats and trouts and they all swum on off.

De Devil was standin' behind him lookin' over his shoulder.

Way after while, God made a turtle and throwed it in de

118

water and it swum on off. Devil says, "Ah kin make one of those things."

God said, "No, you can't neither."

Devil told him, "Aw, Ah kin so make one of those things. 'Tain't nothin' to make nohow. Who couldn't do dat? Ah jus' can't blow de breath of life into it, but Ah sho kin make a turtle."

God said: "Devil, Ah know you can't make none, but if you think you kin make one go 'head and make it and Ah'll blow de breath of life into it for you."

You see, God was sittin' down by de sea, makin' de fish outa sea-mud. But de Devil went on up de hill so God couldn't watch him workin', and made his outa high land dirt. God waited nearly all day befo' de Devil come back wid his turtle.

As soon as God seen it, He said, "Devil, dat ain't no turtle you done made."

Devil flew hot right off. "Dat ain't no turtle? Who say dat ain't no turtle? Sho it's a turtle."

God shook his head, says, "Dat sho *ain't* no turtle, but Ah'll blow de breath of life into it like Ah promised."

Devil stood Him down dat dat was a turtle.

So God blowed de breath of life into what de Devil had done made, and throwed him into de water. He swum out. God throwed him in again. He come on out. Throwed him in de third time and he come out de third time.

God says: "See, Ah told you dat wasn't no turtle."

"Yes, suh, dat *is* a turtle."

"Devil, don't you know dat all turtles loves de water? Don't you see whut you done made won't stay in there?"

Devil said, "Ah don't keer, dat's a turtle, Ah keep a 'tellin' you."

God disputed him down dat it wasn't no turtle. Devil looked it over and scratched his head. Then he says, "Well, anyhow it will go for one." And that's why we have gophers!

"Dat gopher had good sense. He know he was a dry-land turtle so he didn't try to mix wid de rest. Take for instance de time they had de gopher up in court.

"De gopher come in and looked all around de place. De judge was a turtle, de lawyers was turtles, de witnesses was turtles and they had turtles for jurymen.

"So de gopher ast de judge to excuse his case and let him come back some other time. De judge ast him how come he wanted to put off his case and de gopher looked all around de room and said, 'Blood is thicker than water,' and escused hisself from de place.

"Yeah," said Floyd Thomas, "but even God ain't satisfied wid some of de things He makes and changes 'em Hisself."

Jim Presley wanted to know what God ever changed, to Floyd's knowledge.

Well, He made butterflies after de world wuz all finished and thru. You know de Lawd seen so much bare ground till He got sick and tired lookin' at it. So God tole 'em to fetch 'im his prunin' shears and trimmed up de trees and made grass and flowers and throwed 'em all over de clearin's and dey growed dere from memorial days.

Way after while de flowers said, "Wese put heah to keep de world comp'ny but wese lonesome ourselves." So God said, "A world is somethin' ain't never finished. Soon's you make one thing you got to make somethin' else to go wid it. Gimme dem li'l tee-ninchy shears."

So he went 'round clippin' li'l pieces offa everything—de sky, de trees, de flowers, de earth, de varmints and every one of dem li'l clippin's flew off. When folks seen all them li'l scraps fallin' from God's scissors and flutterin' they called 'em flutter-bys. But you know how it is wid de brother in black. He got a big mouf and a stambling tongue. So he got it all mixed up and said, "butter-fly" and folks been calling 'em dat ever since. Dat's how come we got butterflies of every color and kind and dat's why dey hangs 'round de flowers. Dey wuz made to keep de flowers company.

"Watch out, Cliffert!" yelled Jim Allen. "A 'gator must be on yo' hook! Look at it! It's dived like a duck."

"Aw, 'tain't nothin' but a gar fish on it. Ah kin tell by his bite!" said Cliff.

"You pull him up and see!" Jim commanded.

Cliff hauled away and landed a large gar on the grass.

"See, Ah told you, Gran'pa. Don't you worry. Ah'm gointer ketch you mo' fish than you kin eat. Plenty for Mama and Gran'ma too. Less take dis gar-fish home to de cat."

"Yeah," said Jim Presley. "Y' take de cat a fish, too. They love it better than God loves Gabriel—and dat's His best angel."

"He sho do and dat's how cats got into a mess of trouble—'bout eatin' fish," added Jim Presley.

"How was dat? I done forgot if Ah ever knowed."

"If, if, if," mocked Jim Allen. "Office Richardson, youse always iffin'! If a frog had wings he wouldn't bump his rump so much."

"Gran'pa is right in wid de cats," Cliff teased. "He's so skeered he ain't gointer git all de fish he kin eat, he's just like a watch-dog when de folks is at de table. He'll bite anybody then. Think they cheatin' 'im outa his vittles."

Jim Presley spat in the lake and began:

Once upon a time was a good ole time—monkey chew tobacco and spit white lime.

Well, this was a man dat had a wife and five chillun, and a dog and a cat.

Well, de hongry times caught 'em. Hard times everywhere. Nobody didn't have no mo' then jus' enough to keep 'em alive. First they had a long dry spell dat parched up de crops, then de river rose and drowned out everything. You could count anybody's ribs. De white folks all got faces look lak blue-John[2] and de niggers had de white mouf.[3]

So dis man laid in de bed one night and consulted wid his piller. Dat means he talked it over wid his wife. And he

[2]Skimmed milk.

[3]A very hungry person is supposed to look ashy-gray around the mouth.

told her, "Tomorrow less git our pole and go to de lake and see kin we ketch a mess of fish. Dat's our last chance. De fish done got so skeerce and educated they's hard to ketch, but we kin try."

They was at de lake bright and soon de next day. De man took de fishin' pole hisself 'cause he was skeered to trust his wife er de chillun wid it. It was they last chance to git some grub.

So de man fished all day long till he caught seven fishes. Not no great big trouts nor mud-cats but li'l perches and brims. So he tole 'em, "Now, Ah got a fish apiece for all of us, but Ah'm gointer keep on till Ah ketch one apiece for our dog and our cat."

So he fished on till sundown and caught a fish for the dog and de cat, and then they went on home and cooked de fish.

After de fish was all cooked and ready de woman said: "We got to have some drinkin' water. Less go down to de spring to git some. You better come help me tote it 'cause Ah feel too weak to bring it by myself."

So de husband got de water bucket off de shelf and went to de spring wid his wife. But 'fore he went, he told de chillun, "Now, y'all watch out and keep de cat off de fish. She'll steal it sho if she kin."

De chillun tole him, "Yessuh," but they got to foolin' 'round and playin' and forgot all about de cat, and she jumped up on de table and et all de fish but one. She was so full she jus' couldn't hold another mouthful without bustin' wide open.

When de old folks come back and seen what de cat had done they bust out cryin'. They knowed dat one li'l fish divided up wouldn't save they lives. They knowed they had to starve to death. De man looked at de cat and he knowed dat one mo' fish would kill her so he said, "Ah'm gointer make her greedy gut kill her." So he made de cat eat dat other fish and de man and his wife and chillun and de dog and cat all died.

De cat died first so's he was already in Heben when de rest of de family got there. So when God put de man's soul on de scales to weigh it, de cat come up and was lookin' at

122

de man, and de man was lookin' at de cat.

God seen how they eye-balled one 'nother so He ast de man, "Man, what is it between you and dis cat?"

So de man said, "God, dat cat's got all our nine lives in her belly." And he told God all about de fish.

God looked hard at dat cat for a hundred years, but it seem lak a minute.

Then he said: "Gabriel, Peter, Rayfield, John and Michael, all y'all ketch dat cat, and throw him outa Heben."

So they did and he was fallin' for nine days, and there ain't been no cats in Heben since. But he still got dem nine lives in his belly and you got to kill him nine times befo' he'll stay dead.

> Stepped on a pin, de pin bent
> And dat's de way de story went.

"Dat may be so, Presley," commented Jim Allen, "but if Ah ketch one messin' 'round *my* fish, Ah bet Ah kin knock dat man and woman and dem five chillun, de dog *and* de cat outa any cat Ah ever seen wid one lick."

"Dat's one something, Ah ain't never gointer kill," announced Willard forcefully. "It's dead bad luck."

"Me neither," assented Sack Daddy. "Everybody know it's nine years hard luck. Ah shot a man once up in West Florida, killed him dead for bull-dozin' me in a skin game, and got clean away. Ah got down in de phosphate mines around Mulberry and was doin' fine till Ah shacked up wid a woman dat had a great big ole black cat wid a white star in his bosom. He had a habit of jumpin' up on de bed all durin' de night time. One night Ah woke up and he was on my chest wid his nose right to mine, suckin' my breath.

"Ah got so mad Ah grabbed dat sucker by de tail and bust his brains out aginst a stanchion. My woman cried and carried on 'bout de cat and she tole me Ah was gointer have bad luck. Man, you know it wasn't two weeks befo' Sheriff Joe Brown laid his hand on my shoulder and tole me, 'Le's go.' Ah made five years for dat at Raiford. Killin' cats is bad luck."

"Talkin' 'bout dogs," put in Gene Oliver, "they got plenty sense. Nobody can't fool dogs much."

"And speakin' 'bout hams," cut in Big Sweet meaningly, "if Joe Willard don't stay out of dat bunk he was in last night, Ah'm gointer sprinkle some salt down his back and sugar-cure *his* hams."

Joe snatched his pole out of the water with a jerk and glared at Big Sweet, who stood sidewise looking at him most pointedly.

"Aw, woman, quit tryin' to signify."[4]

"Ah kin signify all Ah please, Mr. Nappy-chin, so long as Ah know what Ah'm talkin' about."

"See dat?" Joe appealed to the other men. "We git a day off and figger we kin ketch some fish and enjoy ourselves, but naw, some wimmins got to drag behind us, even to de lake."

"You didn't figger Ah was draggin' behind you when you was bringin' dat Sears and Roebuck catalogue over to my house and beggin' me to choose my ruthers.[5] Lemme tell *you* something, *any* time Ah shack up wid any man Ah gives myself de privilege to go wherever he might be, night or day. Ah got de law in my mouth."

"Lawd, ain't she specifyin'!" sniggered Wiley.

"Oh, Big Sweet does dat," agreed Richardson. "Ah knowed she had somethin' up her sleeve when she got Lucy and come along."

"Lawd," Willard said bitterly. "My people, my people," as de monkey said. "You fool wid Aunt Hagar's[6] chillun and they'll sho distriminate you and put yo' name in de streets."

Jim Allen commented: "Well, you know what they say—a man can cackerlate his life till he git mixed up wid a woman or git straddle of a cow."

Big Sweet turned viciously upon the old man. "Who you

[4]To show off.

[5]Make a choice.

[6]Negroes are in similie children of Hagar; white folks, of Sarah.

callin' a cow, fool? Ah know you ain't namin' *my* mama's daughter no cow."

"Now all y'all heard what Ah said. Ah ain't called nobody no cow," Jim defended himself. "Dat's just an old time by-word 'bout no man kin tell what's gointer happen when he gits mixed up wid a woman or set straddle of a cow."

"I done heard my gran'paw say dem very words many and many a time," chimed in Larkins. "There's a whole heap of them kinda by-words. Like for instance:

" 'Ole coon for cunnin', young coon for runnin',' and 'Ah can't dance, but Ah know good moves.' They all got a hidden meanin', jus' like de Bible. Everybody can't understand what they mean. Most people is thin-brained. They's born wid they feet under de moon. Some folks is born wid they feet on de sun and they kin seek out de inside meanin' of words."

"Fack is, it's a story 'bout a man sittin' straddle of a cow," Jim Allen went on.

A man and his wife had a boy and they thought so much of him that they sent him off to college. At de end of seven years, he schooled out and come home and de old man and his ma was real proud to have de only boy 'round there dat was book-learnt.

So de next mornin' after he come home, de ma was milkin' de cows and had one young cow dat had never been to de pail befo' and she used to kick every time anybody milked her.

She was actin' extry bad dat mornin' so de woman called her husband and ast him to come help her wid de cow. So he went out and tried to hold her, but she kept on rearin' and pitchin' and kickin' over de milk pail, so he said to his wife: "We don't need to strain wid dis cow. We got a son inside that's been to school for seben years and done learnt everything. He'll know jus' what to do wid a kickin' cow. Ah'll go call him."

So he called de boy and told him.

De boy come on out to de cow-lot and looked everything over. Den he said, "Mama, cow-kickin' is all a matter of scientific principle. You see before a cow can kick she has to hump herself up in the back. So all we need to do is to take the hump out the cow's back."

His paw said, "Son, Ah don't see how you gointer do dat. But 'course you been off to college and you know a heap mo' than me and yo' ma ever will know. Go 'head and take de hump outa de heifer. We'd be mighty much obliged."

De son put on his gold eye glasses and studied de cow from head to foot. Then he said, "All we need to keep this animal from humping is a weight on her back."

"What kinda weight do she need, son?"

"Oh, any kind of a weight, jus' so it's heavy enough, papa," de son told him. "It's all in mathematics."

"Where we gointer git any weight lak dat, son?"

"Why don't you get up there, papa? You're just about the weight we need."

"Son, you been off to school a long time, and maybe you done forgot how hard it is for anybody to sit on a cow, and Ah'm gittin' old, you know."

"But, papa, I can fix that part, too. I'll tie your feet together under her belly so she can't throw you. You just get on up there."

"All right, son, if you say so, Ah'll git straddle of dis cow. You know more'n Ah do, Ah reckon."

So they tied de cow up short to a tree and de ole man got on by de hardest,[7] and de boy passed a rope under her belly and tied his papa on. De old lady tried to milk de cow but she was buckin' and rearin' so till de ole man felt he couldn't stand it no mo'. So he hollered to de boy; "Cut de rope, son, cut de rope! Ah want to git down."

Instead of de boy cuttin' loose his papa's feet he cut de rope dat had de cow tied to de tree and she lit out 'cross de wood wid de ole man's feet tied under de cow. Wasn't no way for him to git off.

De cow went bustin' on down de back-road wid de ole man till they met a sister he knowed. She was surprised to

[7]With great difficulty.

126

see de man on de cow, so she ast: "My lawd, Brother So-and-so, where you goin'?"

He tole her, "Only God and dis cow knows."

"Wonder what de swamp boss is studyin' 'bout whilst we out here fishin'?" Oliver wondered.

"Nobody don't know and here's one dat don't keer," Cliff Ulmer volunteered. "Ah done caught me a nice mess of fish and Ah'm gointer bust dat jook wide open tonight.

"Ah was over there last night and maybe de boys didn't get off lyin'! Somebody tole one on de snail.

"You know de snail's wife took sick and sent him for de doctor.

"She was real low ill-sick and rolled from one side of de bed to de other. She was groanin', 'Lawd knows Ah got so much misery Ah hope de Doctor'll soon git here to me.'

"After seben years she heard a scufflin' at de door. She was real happy so she ast, 'Is dat you baby, done come back wid de doctor? Ah'm so glad!'

"He says, 'Don't try to rush me—Ah ain't gone yet.' He had been seben years gettin' to de door."

"Yeah, Ah was over there too," said Larkins White, "and somebody else tole a lie on de snail. A snail was crossin' de road for seben years. Just as he got across a tree fell and barely missed him 'bout a inch or two. If he had a been where he was six months before it would er kilt him. De snail looked back at de tree and tole de people, 'See, it pays to be fast.' "

"Look at de wind risin'!" Willard exclaimed.

"We ain't no hogs, Joe, we can't see no wind."

"You kin see it, if you squirt some sow milk in yo' eyes. Ah seen it one time," Jim Allen announced.

"How did it look, gran'pa? Dat's a sight Ah sho would love to see," cried Cliff.

"Naw, you wouldn't, son. De wind is blood red and when you see it comin' it look lak a bloody ocean rushin' down on you from every side. It ain't got no sides and no top. Youse jus' drownin' in blood and can't help yo'self. When Ah was

127

a li'l chap dey tole me if Ah put hawg milk in mah eyes Ah could see de wind, and—"

"Why they say 'hawg milk'? Can't you try some cow milk?" Cliffert asked.

"De hawg is de onliest thing God ever made whut kin see de wind. Ain't you never seen uh sow take a good look in one direction and go tuh makin' up a good warm nest? She see great winds a comin' a whole day off."

"Well, how didja quit seein' de wind, gran'pa?"

"De sow milk wore outa mah eyes gradual lak, but Ah seen dat wind fo' more'n a week. Dey had to blindfold me tuh keep me from runnin' wild."

Cliff Ulmer said:

De wind is a woman, and de water is a woman too. They useter talk together a whole heap. Mrs. Wind useter go set down by de ocean and talk and patch and crochet.

They was jus' like all lady people. They loved to talk about their chillun, and brag on 'em.

Mrs. Water useter say, "Look at *my* chillun! Ah got de biggest and de littlest in de world. All kinds of chillun. Every color in de world, and every shape!"

De wind lady bragged louder than de water woman: "Oh, but Ah got mo' different chilluns than anybody in de world. They flies, they walks, they swims, they sings, they talks, they cries. They got all de colors from de sun. Lawd, my chillun sho is a pleasure. 'Tain't nobody got no babies like mine."

Mrs. Water got tired of hearin' 'bout Mrs. Wind's chillun so she got so she hated 'em.

One day a whole passle of her chillun come to Mrs. Wind and says: "Mama, wese thirsty. Kin we go git us a cool drink of water?"

She says, "Yeah chillun. Run on over to Mrs. Water and hurry right back soon."

When them chillun went to squinch they thirst Mrs. Water grabbed 'em all and drowned 'em.

When her chillun didn't come home, de wind woman got

worried. So she went on down to de water and ast for her babies.

"Good evenin' Mis' Water, you see my chillun today?"

De water woman tole her, "No-oo-oo."

Mrs. Wind knew her chillun had come down to Mrs. Water's house, so she passed over de ocean callin' her chillun, and every time she call de white feathers would come up on top of de water. And dat's how come we got white caps on waves. It's de feathers comin' up when de wind woman calls her lost babies.

When you see a storm on de water, it's de wind and de water fightin' over dem chillun.

" 'Bout dat time a flea wanted to get a hair cut, so Ah left."

EIGHT

Y 'all been tellin' and lyin' 'bout all dese varmints but you ain't yet spoke about de high chief boss of all de world which is de lion," Sack Daddy commented.

"He's de King of de Beasts, but he ain't no King of de World, now Sack," Dad Boykin spoke up. "He *thought* he was de King till John give him a straightenin'."

"Don't put dat lie out!" Sack Daddy contended. "De lion won't stand no straightenin'."

"Course I 'gree wid you dat everybody can't show de lion no deep point, but John showed it to him. Oh, yeah, John not only straightened him out, he showed dat ole lion where in."

"When did he do all of dis, Dad? Ah ain't never heard tell of it." Dad spoke up:

Oh, dis was way befo' yo' time. Ah don't recolleck myself. De old folks told me about John and de lion. Well, John was ridin' long one day straddle of his horse when de grizzly bear come pranchin' out in de middle of de road and hollered: "Hold on a minute! They tell me you goin' 'round strowin' it dat youse de King of de World."

John stopped his horse: "Whoa! Yeah, Ah'm de King of

de World, don't you b'lieve it?" John told him.

"Naw, you ain't no King. Ah'm de King of de World. You can't be no King till you whip me. Git down and fight."

John hit de ground and de fight started. First, John grabbed him a rough-dried brick and started to work de fat offa de bear's head. De bear just fumbled 'round till he got a good holt, then he begin to squeeze and squeeze. John knowed he couldn't stand dat much longer, do he'd be jus' another man wid his breath done give out. So he reached into his pocket and got out his razor and slipped it between dat bear's ribs. De bear turnt loose and reeled on over in de bushes to lay down. He had enough of dat fight.

John got back on his horse and rode on off.

De lion smelt de bear's blood and come runnin' to where de grizzly was layin' and started to lappin' his blood.

De bear was skeered de lion was gointer eat him while he was all cut and bleedin' nearly to death, so he hollered and said: "*Please* don't touch me, Brer Lion. Ah done met de King of de World and he done cut me all up."

De lion got his bristles all up and clashed down at de bear: "Don't you lay there and tell me you done met de King of de World and not be talkin' 'bout me! Ah'll tear you to pieces!"

"Oh, don't tetch me, Brer Lion! Please lemme alone so Ah kin git well."

"Well, don't you call nobody no King of de World but me."

"But Brer Lion, Ah done *met* de King sho' nuff. Wait till you see him and you'll say Ah'm right."

"Naw, Ah won't, neither. Show him to me and Ah'll show you how much King he is."

"All right, Brer Lion, you jus' have a seat right behind dese bushes. He'll be by here befo' long."

Lion squatted down by de bear and waited. Fust person he saw goin' up de road was a old man. Lion jumped up and ast de bear, "Is dat him?"

Bear say, "Naw, dat's Uncle Yistiddy, he's a useter-be!"

After while a li'l boy passed down de road. De lion seen him and jumped up agin. "Is dat him?" he ast de bear.

Bear told him, "Naw, dat's li'l tomorrow, he's a gointer-be, you jus' lay quiet. Ah'll let you know when he gits here."

Sho nuff after while here come John on his horse but he had done got his gun. Lion jumped up agin and ast, "Is dat him?"

Bear say: "Yeah, dat's him! Dat's de King of de World."

Lion reared up and cracked his tail back and forwards like a bull-whip. He 'lowed, "You wait till Ah git thru wid him and you won't be callin' him no King no mo'."

He took and galloped out in de middle of de road right in front of John's horse and laid his years back. His tail was crackin' like torpedoes.

"Stop!" de lion hollered at John. "They tell me you goes for de King of de World!"

John looked him dead in de ball of his eye and told him, "Yeah, Ah'm de King. Don't you like it, don't you take it. Here's mah collar, come and shake it!"

De lion and John eye-balled one another for a minute or two, den de lion sprung on John.

Talk about fightin'! Man, you ain't seen no sich fightin' and wrasslin' since de mornin' stars sung together. De lion clawed and bit John and John bit him right back.

Way after while John got to his rifle and he up wid de muzzle right in ole lion's face and pulled de trigger. Long, slim black feller, snatch 'er back and hear 'er beller! Dog damn! Dat was too much for de lion. He turnt go of John and wheeled to run to de woods. John levelled down on him agin and let him have another load, right in his hind-quarters.

Dat ole lion give John de book; de bookity book.[1] He hauled de fast mail back into de woods where de bear was laid up.

"Move over," he told de bear. "Ah wanta lay down too."

[1]Sound word meaning running.

133

"How come?" de bear ast him.

"Ah done met de King of de World, and he done ruint me."

"Brer Lion, how you know you done met de King?"

" 'Cause he made lightnin' in my face and thunder in my hips. Ah know Ah done met de King, move over."

"Dad, dat lie of your'n done brought up a high wind," said Jim Allen, measuring the weather with his eye. "Look a li'l bit like rain."

"Tain't gonna rain, but de wind's too high for fish to bite. Le's go back," suggested Presley. "All them that caught fish got fish. All them that didn't got another chance."

Everybody began to gather up things. The bait cans were kicked over so that the worms could find homes. The strings of fish were tied to pole ends. When Joe Wiley went to pull up his string of fish, he found a water moccasin stealin' them and the men made a great ceremony of killin' it. Then they started away from the water. Cliff had a long string of fish.

"Look, Gran'pa" he said, "Ah reckon you satisfied, ain't you?"

"Sho Ah'm satisfied, Ah must *is* got cat blood in me 'cause Ah never gits tired of fish. Ah knows how to eat 'em too, and dat's somethin' everybody don't know."

"Oh, anybody can eat fish," said Joe Willard.

"Yeah," Jim conceded grudgingly, "they kin eat it, but they can't git de real refreshment out de meat like they oughter."

"If you kin git any mo' refreshment off a fish bone than me, you must be got two necks and a gang of bellies," said Larkins.

"You see," went on Jim, "y'all ain't got into de techincal apex of de business. When y'all see a great big platter of fried fish y'all jus' grab hold of a fish and bite him any which way, and dat's wrong."

"Dat's good enough for me!" declared Willard emphatically. "Anywhere and any place Ah ketch a fish Ah'm ready to bite him 'ceptin' he's raw."

"Me too."

"See dat?" Jim cried, exasperated. "You young folks is just like a passle of crows in a corn patch. Everybody talkin' at one time. Ain't nary one of you tried to learn how to eat a fish right."

"How you eat 'em, Mr. Allen?" Gene Oliver asked to pacify him.

"Well, after yo' hands is washed and de blessin' is said, you look at de fried fish, but you don't grab it. First thing you chooses a piece of corn-bread for yo' plate whilst youse lookin' de platter over for a nice fat perch or maybe it's trout. Nobody wid any manners or home-raisin' don't take de fork and turn over every fish in de dish in order to pick de best one. You does dat wid yo' eye whilst youse choosin' yo' pone bread. Now, then, take yo' fork and stick straight at de fish you done choosed, and if somebody ast you to take two, you say 'No ma'am, Ah thank you. This un will do for right now.'

"You see if you got too many fishes on yo' plate at once, folkses, you can't lay 'em out proper. So you take one fish at de time. Then you turn him over and take yo' fork and start at de tail, liff de meat all off de bone clear up to de head, 'thout misplacin' a bone. You eats dat wid some bread. Not a whole heap of bread—just enough to keep you from swallerin' de fish befo' you enjoy de consequences. When you thru on dat side of de fish turn him over and do de same on de other side. Don't eat de heads. Shove 'em to one side till you thru wid all de fish from de platter, den when there ain't no mo' fish wid sides to 'em, you reach back and pull dem heads befo' you and start at de back of de fish neck and eat right on thru to his jaw-bones.

"Now then, if it's summer time, go set on de porch and rest yo'self in de cool. If it's winter time, go git in front of de fireplace and warm yo'self—now Ah done tole you right. A whole heap of people talks about fish-eatin' but Ah done tole you real."

"He's tellin' you right," agreed Dad Boykin. "Ah'm older than he is, 'cause Ah was eighty-one las' November, and Ah was eatin' fish befo' Jim was born, but Ah never did get de gennywine schoolin' till Jim showed me. But Ah teached him somethin' too, didn't Ah, Jim?"

"Yeah, Dad, yo' showed me how to warm myself."

There was a great burst of laughter from the young men, but the two old men scowled upon them.

"You see," Dad said bitingly. "You young poots won't lissen to nothin'! Not a one of you knows how to warm hisself right and youse so hard-headed you don't want to be teached. Any fool kin lam hisself up in a chimbley corner and cook his shins, but when it comes right down to de en-trimmins, youse as ig'nant as a hog up under a acorn tree— he eats and grunts and never look up to see where de acorns is comin' from."

"Dad, *please* such, teach us how to warm ourselves," begged Cliff. "We all wants to know."

"Oh, y'all done wasted too much time, almost back in de quarters now, and de crowd will be scatterin'."

"Dat's all right, Dad," urged Joe Willard soothingly. "We ain't goin' nowhere till we been teached by you."

"Well, then, Ah'll tell y'all somethin'. De real way to git warm is first to git a good rockin' chear and draw it up to de fire. Don't flop yo'self down in it lak a cow in de pasture. Draw it right up in de center of de fireplace 'cause dat's de best. Some folks love to pile into de chimbley corner 'cause they's lazy and feared somebody gointer step on they foots. They don't want to have no trouble shiftin' 'em back and forth. But de center is de best place, so take dat. You even might have to push and shove a li'l bit to git dere, but dat's all right, go' head.

"When you git yo' chear all set where you wants it, then you walk up to de mantel piece and turn yo' back to de fire—dat's to knock de breezes offen yo' back. You know, all de time youse outside in de weather, li'l breezes and winds is jumpin' on yo' back and crawlin' down yo' neck, to hide. They'll stay right there if you don't do somethin' to git shet of 'em. They don't lak fires, so when you turn yo' back to de fire, de inflamed atmosphere goes up under yo' coat-tails and runs dem winds and breezes out from up dere. Sometimes, lessen you drive 'em off, they goes to bed wid you. Ain't y'all never been so you couldn't git warm don't keer how much kivver you put on?''

"Many's de time I been lak dat."

"Well," went on Dad, "Dat because some stray breezes had done rode you to bed. Now dat brings up to de second claw of de subjick. You done got rid of de back breezes, so you git in yo' chear and pull off yo' shoes and set in yo' sock feet. Now, don't set there all spraddle-legged and let de heat just hit you any which way, put yo' feet right close together so dat both yo' big toes is side by side. Then you shove 'em up close to de fire and let 'em git good and hot. Ah know it don't look lak it but dem toes'll warm you all over. You see when Ah was studyin' doctor Ah found out dat you got a leader dat runs from yo' big toe straight to yo' heart, and when you git dem toes hot youse hot all over."

"Yeah, Ah b'lieve youse right, Dad, 'bout dat warmin' business, but Ah wisht somebody'd tell us how to git cool right now."

The party was back in the camp. Everybody began to head for his own shack.

"See you tonight at de jook," Jim Presley called to Willard. "Don't you and Big Sweet put on no roll now. Ah hate to see men and wimmin folks fightin'."

"Me too," said Wiley emphatically. "If a man kin whip his woman and whip her good; all right, but when they don't do nothin' but fight, it makes my stomach turn."

"Well," said Big Sweet crisply. "If Joe Willard try to take dese few fishes he done caught where he shacked up last night,

Ah'm gointer take my Tampa switch-blade knife, and Ah'm goin' 'round de hambone lookin' for meat.''

"Aw, is *dat* so?'' Joe challenged her.

"Ah been baptized, papa, and Ah wouldn't mislead you,'' Big Sweet told him to his teeth.

"Hey, hey!'' Gene Oliver exclaimed. "Big Moose done come down from de mountain. Ah'm gointer be at dat jook tonight to see what Big Sweet and Ella Wall gointer talk about.''

"Me too. De time is done come where big britches gointer fit li'l Willie,''[2] Joe Wiley declared significantly.

"Oh, wese all gointer be there,'' Larkins said. "Say, Big Sweet, don't let de 'gator beat you to de pond,[3] do he'll give you mo' trouble than de day is long.''

So everybody got for home.

Back in the quarters the sun was setting. Plenty women over the cook-pot scorching up supper. Lots of them were already thru cooking, with the pots shoved to the back of the stove while they put on fresh things and went out in front of the house to see and be seen.

The fishermen began scraping fish and hot grease began to pop in happy houses. All but the Allen's. Mrs. Allen wouldn't have a thing to do with our fish because Mr. Allen and Cliffert had made her mad about the yard. So I fried the fish. She wouldn't touch a bite, but Mr. Allen, Cliffert and I pitched into it. Mr. Allen might have eaten by the rules but Cliffert and I went at it rough-and-tumble with no holds barred.

But we did sit down on the front porch to rest after the fish was eaten.

The men were still coming into the quarters from various parts of the "job." The children played "Shoo-round," and "Chick-mah-Chick" until Mrs. Williams called her four year

[2]Things have come to critical pass.

[3]Don't be out-done; or don't be too slow.

138

old Frankie and put her to sleep by rocking her and singing "Mister Frog."

It wasn't black dark, but night was peeping around the corner. The quarters were getting alive. Woofing, threats and brags up and down the line.

Three figures in the dusk-dark detached themselves from the railroad track and came walking into the quarters. A tall black grim-faced man with a rusty black reticule, followed by two women.

Everybody thought he was a bootlegger and yelled orders to him to that effect. He paid no attention, but set down his bag slowly, opened it still slower and took out a dog-eared Bible and opened it. The crowd quieted down. They knew he was a travelling preacher, a "stump-knocker" in the language of the "job."

Some fell silent to listen. Others sucked their teeth and either went back into their houses or went on to the jook.

When he had a reasonable amount of attention he nodded to the woman at his left and she raised "Death comes a Creepin' " and the crowd helped out. At the end the preacher began:[4]

You all done been over in Pentecost (got to feeling spiritual by singing) and now we going to talk about de woman that was taken from man. I take my text from Genesis two and twenty-one (Gen. 2:21)

Behold de Rib!
Now, my beloved,
Behold means to look and see.
Look at dis woman God done made,
But first thing, ah hah!
Ah wants you to gaze upon God's previous works.
Almighty and arisen God, hah!
Peace-giving and prayer-hearing God,

[4]See glossary.

139

High-riding and strong armded God
Walking acrost his globe creation, hah!

Wid de blue elements for a helmet
And a wall of fire round his feet
He wakes de sun every morning from his fiery bed
Wid de breath of his smile
And commands de moon wid his eyes.
And Oh—
Wid de eye of Faith
I can see him
Standing out on de eaves of ether
Breathing clouds from out his nostrils,
Blowing storms from 'tween his lips
I can see!
Him seize de mighty axe of his proving power
And smite the stubborn-standing space,
And laid it wide open in a mighty gash—
Making a place to hold de world
I can see him—
Molding de world out of thought and power
And whirling it out on its eternal track,

Ah hah, my strong armded God!
He set de blood red eye of de sun in de sky
And told it,
Wait, wait! Wait there till Shiloh come
I can see!
Him mold de mighty mountains
And melting de skies into seas.
Oh, Behold, and look and see! hah
We see in de beginning
He made de bestes every one after its kind,
De birds that fly de trackless air,
De fishes dat swim de mighty deep—
Male and fee-male, hah!
Then he took of de dust of de earth
And made man in his own image.
And man was alone,
Even de lion had a mate
So God shook his head
And a thousand million diamonds
Flew out from his glittering crown
And studded de evening sky and made de stars.
So God put Adam into a deep sleep
And took out a bone, ah hah!
And it is said that it was a rib.
Behold de rib!
A bone out of a man's side.
He put de man to sleep and made wo-man,
And men and women been sleeping together ever since.
Behold de rib!
Brothers, if God
Had taken dat bone out of man's head
He would have meant for woman to rule, hah
If he had taken a bone out of his foot,
He would have meant for us to dominize and rule.
He could have made her out of back-bone
And then she would have been behind us.
But, no, God Amighty, he took de bone out of his side
So dat places de woman beside us;
Hah! God knowed his own mind.
Behold de rib!

And now I leave dis thought wid you,
Let us all go marchin' up to de gates of Glory.
Tramp! tramp! tramp!
In step wid de host dat John saw.
Male and female like God made us
Side by side.
Oh, behold de rib!
And less all set down in Glory together
Right round his glorified throne
And praise his name forever.
              Amen.

At the end of the sermon the woman on the preacher's left
raised, "Been a Listenin' All de Night Long," and the
preacher descended from his fiery cloud and lifted the collection in his hat. The singers switched to, "You Can't Hide,
Sinners, You Can't Hide." The sparse contribution taken, the
trio drifted back into the darkness of the railroad, walking
towards Kissimmee.

NINE

The little drama of religion over, the "job" reverted to the business of amusing itself. Everybody making it to the jook hurriedly or slowly as the spirit moved.

Big Sweet came by and we went over together. I didn't go with Cliffert because it would mean that I'd be considered his property more or less and the other men would keep away from me, and being let alone is no way to collect folk-lore.

The jook was in full play when we walked in. The piano was throbbing like a stringed drum and the couples slow-dragging about the floor were urging the player on to new lows. "Jook, Johnnie, Ah know you kin spank dat ole pe-anner." "Jook it Johnnie!"[1] "Throw it in de alley!"[2]

The Florida-flip game was roaring away at the left. Four men playing skin game with small piles of loose change.[3]

"High, Jack, game," one side called.

"Low and not ashamed," from the other.

Another deal.

Dealer: (to play at left) "Whut yuh say?"

Player: "Beggin'."

[1] Play the piano in the manner of the jook or "blues."

[2] Get low down.

[3] See glossary.

Dealer: "Git up off yo' knees. Go 'head and tell 'em Ah sent you." (I give you one point.)

Dealer: "Pull off, partner."

A frenzied slapping of cards on the table. "Ha! we caught little britches!" (low) "Pull off again!"

"Can't. Ain't seen de deck but one time."

"Aw shucks. Ah got de wrong sign from you. Ah thought you had de king."

"Nope, Ah can't ketch a thing. Ah can't even ketch nobody lookin' at me."

The opponents grin knowingly and one of them sticks the Jack up on his forehead and gloats, "De Jack's a gentleman." It is now the highest card out.

A furious play to the end of the hand and the dealer cries: "Gone from three. Jus' like Jeff Crowder's eye" (out).

"Out!" cries the outraged opponents. "Out yo' head! Out wid whut!"

"We played high, low, game!"

"Take dat game right out yo' mouf. We got twenty by tens."

"Le's go to school." (Let's count game.)

One player slyly picks up the deck and tries to mix it with his cards.

"Aw naw, put down dat deck! You can't count it on me."

"Aw, you tryin' to bully de game, but if you ain't prepared to back yo' crap wid hot lead, don't bring de mess up."

Joe Wiley was on the floor in the crap game. He called me to come stand by him and give him luck. Big Sweet left me there and went on over to the skin game.

Somebody had squeezed the alcohol out of several cans of Sterno and added sugar, water and boiled-off spirits of nitre and called it wine. It was dealt out with the utmost secrecy. The quarters boss had a way of standing around in the dark and listening and he didn't allow a drop of likker on the job. Paynights used to mean two or three killings but this boss had ended the murders abruptly. And one caught with likker was sent down to Bartow to the jail and bound over to the Big

Court. So it had come to the place where "low" wine was about all the quarters could get and the drinker was taking two terrible risks at that—arrest and death,

But there was enough spirits about for things to keep lively. The crap game was frothy. Office had the dice when I walked up. He was shivering the dice and sliding them out expertly.

"Hah! good dice is findin' de money! Six is mah point."

"Whut's yo' come bet?" Blue asked.

"Two bits."

"Two bits you don't six."

Office picked up the dice stealthily, shook them, or rather failed to shake them craftily and slid them out. Blue stopped them. Office threw three times and three times Blue stopped them. Office took out his switch-blade knife and glared at Blue.

"Nigger, don't you stop mah dice befo' dey point."

"You chokin' dem dice. Shake and lemme hear de music."

I wanted to get into the game in a small way but Big Sweet was high balling[4] me to come over to the skin game. I went over to see what she wanted and was given her purse to hold. She wanted to play and she wanted a free hand. It was the liveliest and most intense game in the place. I got all worked up myself watching the falling cards.

A saddle-colored fellow called "Texas Red" was fighting the wine inside him by trying to tenor "Ol' Pal, Why Don't You Answer Me," while he hung over the game watching it. His nasal tones offended Big Sweet, who turned and asked him, "Did somebody hit yuh tuh start yuh? 'Cause if dey did Ah'm goin' ter hit yuh to stop yuh." Texas and Big Sweet did what is locally known as "eye-balling" each other. His eyes fell lower. Her knife was already open, so he strolled on off.

There had been a new deal. Everybody was getting a fresh card.

Dealer: "You want a card, Big Sweet?"

Big Sweet: "Yeah, Ah wanta scoop one in de rough."

4Waving ahead. A railroad term.

145

Dealer: "Aw right, yo' card is gointer cost you a dollar. Put yo' money on de wood and make de bet go good and then agin, put yo' money in sight and save a fight."

She drew a card from the deck and put it face up beside her, with a dollar bill.

Dealer: "Heah, Hardy, heah's a good card—a queen." He tossed the card to Hardy.

Hardy: "Aw naw, Ah don't play dem gals till way late in de night."

Dealer: "Well take de ace and go to wee-shoppy-tony and dat means East Hell. Ah'm gointer ketch you anyhow."

Hardy: "When you ketch me, you damn sho will ketch a man dat's caught a many one. Ah'm playin' up a nation."

Dealer: "Put down! You all owe de bet a dime. Damn sitters rob St. Peter, rob St. Paul."

Larkins: "Dat nigger is gointer top somebody. He's got a cub.[5] Ah ain't goin' in dat damn steel trap."

Dealer: "Aw naw, Ah ain't! You sap-sucker!" (To Hardy) "You owe de bet a dime if you never pay it."

The dealer starts down the deck, and the singing goes with it. Christopher Jenkins' deep baritone is something to remember.

> "Let de deal go down, boys.[6]
> Let de deal go down.
> When yo' card gits lucky, oh padner;
> You ought to be in a rollin' game."

Each line punctuated by "hah!" and a falling card.

Larkins: "Ah'm dead on de turn."

Dealer: "Ah heard you buddy."

"Ain't had no money, oh padner!"

(To Larkins) "You head-pecked shorty, drive up to de cryin'

[5]He has arranged the cards so he can deal winning cards to himself and losing cards to others.

[6]See appendix.

post and hitch up. You want another card?"

Larkins: "Shuffle and deal and ain't stop fallin' yet." (He means he stays in the game so he takes another hand.)

Dealer: "Put down dat chicken-change quarter you got in yo' hand."

The singing goes on—

"Ah'm goin' back to de Bama,
Won't be worried wid you."

(To Hardy) "De nine" (card dealer holds) "is de best. Is you got air nickel to cry?"

"Let de deal go down, boys;
Let de deal go down."

Big Sweet: "De four" (card she holds) "says a dollar mo'."

Dealer: "Oh hell and brothers! Ah'm strictly a two-bit man."

Big Sweet (arrogantly): "You full of dat ole ism blood. Fat covered yo' heart. Youse skeered to bet. Gamblin' wid yo' stuff out de window."[7]

Dealer: "Dollar mo'."

Hardy: "Hell broke loose in Georgy!"

Big Sweet: "Ah mean to carry y'all to Palatka and bring yuh back by de way of Winter Park."

Hardy: "Big Sweet, Ah don't b'lieve Ah'll see yo' raise."

Big Sweet: "Oh g'wan and bet. You got mo' sense than me. Look at dem damn kidneys all over yo' head."

"Ain't had no trouble, Lawd padner
Till Ah stop by here."

Dealer: "Take it and cry, children." (His card falls.) "Dey sent me out by de way of Sandusky. Lemme see kin Ah find me a clean card."

[7]Risking nothing. Ready to run.

Big Sweet: "Ah caught you guilty lyin'! Make a bet and tell a lie about it."

Hardy: "He done cocked a face card. Look out we don't ketch *you* guilty."

Big Sweet: "He got de cards in his hand."

> "Let de deal go down, boys,
> Let de deal go down."

Hardy: "Dat's me. Ah thought dat card was in Bee-luther-hatchee!"[8]

Dealer: "Tell de truth and stay in de church! Ah'm from down in Ginny-Gall where they eat cow-belly, skin and all. Big Sweet, everybody done fell but you. You must be setting on roots."

Big Sweet: "Nope, Ah got my Joe Moore in my hair."[9]

Dealer: "Well, Ah got de cards. I can cheat if I want to and beat you anyway."

Big Sweet: "You mess wid dem cards and see if Ah don't fill you full of looky-deres."

Hardy: "Whut a looky-dere?"

Big Sweet: "A knot on yo' head so big till when you go down de street everybody will point at it and say 'Looky-dere.'"

Dealer: (His card falls.) "Ah'm hot as seven hells."

Big Sweet: "Ah played de last card. Ah don't tell lies all de time. Now, you rich son of a bitch, pay off."

Larkins: "God! She must be sittin' on roots! Luck is a fortune."

Big Sweet raked in the money and passed it to me. She was about to place another bet when we heard a lot of noise outside. Everybody looked at the door at one time.

"Dat *must* be de Mulberry crowd. Nobody else wouldn't keep dat much noise. Ella Wall strowin' it."

---

[8] A mythical place, like "ginny gall."

[9] A piece of gamblers lucky hoodoo.

148

"She's plenty propaganda, all right."

Ella Wall flung a loud laugh back over her shoulder as she flourished in. Everybody looked at her, then they looked at Big Sweet. Big Sweet looked at Ella, but she seemed not to mind. The air was as tight as a fiddle string.

Ella wrung her hips to the Florida-flip game. Big Sweet stayed on at the skin game but didn't play. Joe Willard, knowing the imminence of forthright action, suddenly got deep into the crap game.

Lucy came in the door with a bright gloat in her eyes and went straight to Ella. So far as speaking was concerned she didn't see Big Sweet, but she did flirt past the skin game once, overcome with merriment.

"Dat li'l narrer contracted piece uh meatskin gointer make me stomp her right now!" Big Sweet exploded. "De two-faced heifer! Been hangin' 'round me so she kin tote news to Ella. If she don't look out she'll have on her last clean dress befo' de crack of day."

"Ah'm surprised at Lucy," I agreed. "Ah thought you all were de *best* of friends."

"She mad 'cause Ah dared her to jump *you*. She don't lak Slim always playing JOHN HENRY for you. She would have done cut you to death if Ah hadn't of took and told her."

"Ah can see she doesn't like it, but—"

"Neb' mind 'bout ole Lucy. She know Ah backs yo' fallin'. She know if she scratch yo' skin Ah'll kill her so dead till she can't fall. They'll have to push her over. Ella Wall look lak she tryin' to make me kill her too, flourishin' dat ole knife 'round. But she oughter know de man dat made one, made two. She better not vary, do Ah'll be all over her jus' lak gravy over rice."

Lucy and Ella were alternately shoo-shooing[10] to each other and guffawing. Then Ella would say something to the whole table and laugh.

Over at the Florida-flip game somebody began to sing that

[10]Whispering.

jook tribute to Ella Wall which has been sung in every jook and on every "job" in South Florida:

> Go to Ella Wall
> Oh, go to Ella Wall
> If you want good boody[11]
> Oh, go to Ella Wall
>
> Oh, she's long and tall
> Oh, she's long and tall
> And she rocks her rider
> From uh wall to wall
>
> Oh, go to Ella Wall
> Take yo' trunk and all—

"Tell 'em 'bout me!" Ella Wall snapped her fingers and revolved her hips with her hands.

"I'm raggedy, but right; patchey but tight; stringy, but I *will* hang on."

"Look at her puttin' out her brags." Big Sweet nudged me. "Loud-talkin' de place. But countin' from yo' little finger back to the thumb; if she start anything Ah got her some."

I knew that Big Sweet didn't mind fighting; didn't mind killing and didn't too much mind dying. I began to worry a bit. Ella kept on hurling slurs. So I said, "Come on, Big Sweet, we got to go to home."

"Nope, Ah ain't got to do nothin' but die and stay black. Ah stays right here till de jook close if anybody else stay. You look and see how much in dat pocket book."

I looked. "Forty-one dollars and sixty-three cents."

"Just you hold on to it. Ah don't want a thing in mah hands but dis knife."

Big Sweet turned to scoop a card in the rough. Just at that moment Ella chose to yell over, "Hey, bigger-than-me!" at Big Sweet. She whirled around angrily and asked me, "Didn't dat storm-buzzard throw a slam at me?"

[11]Sex.

"Naw, she was hollerin' at somebody else," I lied to keep the peace.

Nothing happening, Ella shouted, " 'Tain't nothin' to her. She ain't hit me yet."

Big Sweet heard that and threw in her cards and faced about. "If anything start, Little-Bit, you run out de door like a streak uh lightning and get in yo' car. They gointer try to hurt you too."

I thought of all I had to live for and turned cold at the thought of dying in a violent manner in a sordid saw-mill camp. But for my very life I knew I couldn't leave Big Sweet even if the fight came. She had been too faithful to me. So I assured her that I wasn't going unless she did. My only weapons were my teeth and toe-nails.

Ella crowded her luck. She yelled out, "Lucy, go tell Mr. Lots-of-Papa Joe Willard Ah say come here. Jus' tell 'im his weakness want 'im. He know who dat is."

Lucy started across. Ella stood up akimbo, but everybody knew she was prepared to back her brag with cold steel in some form, or she wouldn't have been there talking like she was.

A click beside me and I knew that the spring blade knife that Big Sweet carried was open.

"Stop right where you is, Lucy," Big Sweet ordered, "lessen you want to see yo' Jesus."

"Gwan Lucy," Ella Wall called out, " 'tain't nothin' stoppin' yuh. See nothin', say nothin'."

Big Sweet turned to Ella. "Maybe Ah ain't nothin'. But Ah say Lucy ain't gointer tell Joe Willard nothin'. What you sendin' *her* for? Why don't you go yo'self? Dere he is."

"Well, Ah kin go, now," Ella countered.

Big Sweet took a step forward that would put her right in Ella's path in case she tried to cross the room. "Ah can't hear what you say for yo' damn teeth rattlin'. Come on!"

Then the only thing that could have stopped the killing happened. The Quarters Boss stepped in the door with a .45

151

in his hand and another on his hip. Expect he had been eaves-dropping as usual.

"What's the matter here, y'all? Big Sweet, what you mean tuh do wid that knife?"

"Ahm jus' 'bout tuh send God two niggers. Come in here bull-dozin' me."

The Quarters Boss looked all around and pointed at Ella. "What tha hell *you* doin' in here wid weapons? You don't belong on this job nohow. Git the hell outa here and that quick. This place is for people that works on this job. Git! Somebody'll be in Barton jail in twenty minutes."

"You don't need tuh run her off, Cap'n," Big Sweet said. "Ah can git her tuh go. Jus' you stand back and gimme lief. She done stepped on mah starter and Ahm rearin' tuh go. If God'll send me uh pistol Ah'll send 'im uh man!"

"You ain't gonna kill nobody right under mah nose," the Quarters Boss snorted. "Gimme that knife you got dere, Big Sweet."

"Naw suh! Nobody gits *mah* knife. Ah bought it for dat storm-buzzard over dere and Ah means tuh use it on her, too. As long as uh mule go bareheaded she better not part her lips tuh me. Do Ah'll kill her, law or no law. Don't you touch me, white folks!"

"Aw she ain't so bad!" Ella sneered as she wrung her hips towards the door. "She didn't kill Jesse James."

"Git on 'way from here!" the Boss yelled behind her. "Lessen yuh wanna make time in Barton jail. Git off these premises and that quick! Gimme that knife!" He took the knife and gave Ella a shove. She moved sullenly behind her crowd away from the door, mumbling threats. He followed and stayed outside until the car pulled off. Then he stuck his head back inside and said, "Now you behave yo'self, Big Sweet. Ah don't wanna hafta jail yuh."

Soon as he was gone the mob got around Big Sweet. "You wuz noble!" Joe Willard told her, "You wuz uh whole woman and half uh man. You made dat cracker stand off a *you*."

"Who wouldn't?" said Presley. "She got loaded muscles.

152

You notice he don't tackle Big Sweet lak he do de rest round here. Dats cause she ain't got uh bit better sense then tuh make 'im kill her."

"Dats right," Big Sweet admitted, "and de nex' time Joe tell his Mulberry woman tuh come here bulldozin' *me*, Ahm gointer beat 'im to death grabbin' at 'im."

Joe Willard affected supreme innocence. "Will you lissen at dis 'oman? Ah ain't sent fuh nobody. Y'all see Ah didn't never go where she wuz, didn't yuh? Come on Big Sweet, less go home. How 'bout uh li'l keerless love? Ahm all ravalled out from de strain."

Joe and Big Sweet went home together and that was that.

When the quarters boss had gone, I saw Box-Car Daddy creeping back in the door. I didn't see him leave the place so I asked him where he had been.

"Had to step off a li'l piece," he told me with an effort at nonchalance.

"He always steps off whenever he see dat Quarters Boss, and he doing right, too," someone said.

"How come?" I asked. "Nobody else don't run."

Everybody laughed but nobody told me a thing. But after a while Box-Car began to sing a new song and I liked the swing of it.

"What's dat you singing, Box-Car?" I asked.

" 'Ah'm Gointer Loose dis Right-hand Shackle from 'Round my Leg.' Dat's a chain-gang song. Thought everybody knowed dat."

"Nope, never heard it. Ain't never been to de gang. How did you learn it?"

"Working on de gang."

"Whut you doin' on de gang, Box-Car? You look like a good boy, but a poor boy."

"Oh, dey put me under arrest one day for vacancy in Bartow. When de judge found out Ah had a job of work. He took and searched me and when he found out Ah had a deck of cards on me, he charged me wid totin' concealed cards, and attempt to gamble, and gimme three months. Then dey made out another charge 'ginst me. 'Cused me of highway shufflin', and attempt to gamble. You know dese white folks sho hates tuh turn a nigger loose, if every dey git dey hands on 'im. And dis very quarters boss was Cap'n on de gang where Ah wuz. Me and him ain't never gointer set hawses."[12] So he went on singing:

All day long, you heard me moan
Don't you tell my Cap'n which way I gone
Ah'm gointer lose dis right hand shackle from 'round my leg.

You work me late, you work me soon
Some time you work me by de light of de moon
Ah'm gointer lose dis right hand shackle from 'round my leg.

I learned several other songs. Thanks to James Presley and Slim; and Gene Oliver and his sister brought me many additional tales.

But the very next pay-night when I went to a dance at the Pine Mill, Lucy tried to steal me. That is the local term for an attack by stealth. Big Sweet saved me and urged me to stay on, assuring me that she could always defend me, but I shivered at the thought of dying with a knife in my back, or having my face mutilated. At any rate, I had made a very fine and full collection on the Saw-Mill Camp, so I felt no regrets at shoving off.

The last night at Loughman was very merry. We had a party at Mrs. Allen's. James Presley and Slim with their boxes; Joe Willard calling figures in his best mood. Because it was a special occasion and because I was urged, I actually took a sip of low-wine and found out how very low it was. The dancing stopped and I was hilariously toted off to bed and the party moved to my bedroom. We had had a rain flood early in the afternoon and a medium size rattlesnake had come in out of the wet. I had thrown away a pile of worn out stockings and he was asleep upon them there in the corner by the washstand.

[12]Never going to get along. As two horses pull together.

The boys wanted to kill it, but I begged them not to hurt my lowly brother. He rattled away for a while, but when everybody got around the bed on the far end of the room and got quiet, he moved in the manner of an hour-hand to a crack where the floor and wall had separated, and popped out of sight.

Cliffert told me the last Loughman story around midnight. "Zora, did yuh ever hear 'bout Jack and de Devil buckin' 'ginst one 'nother to see which one was de strongest?"

"Naw. Ah done heard a lot about de Devil and dat Jack, but not dat tale *you* know. Tell it."

Jack and de Devil wuz settin' down under a tree one day arguin' 'bout who was de strongest. De Devil got tired of talkin' and went and picked up a mule. Jack went and picked up de same mule. De Devil run to a great big old oak tree and pulled it up by de roots. Jack grabbed holt of one jus' as big and pulled it up. De Devil broke a anchor cable. Jack took it and broke it agin.

So de Devil says, "Shucks! Dis ain't no sho nuff trial. Dis is chillun foolishness. Meet me out in dat hund'ed acre clearin' tomorrow mornin' at nine o'clock and we'll see who kin throw mah hammer de furtherest. De one do dat is de strongest."

Jack says, "Dat suits me."

So nex' mawnin' de Devil wuz dere on time wid his hammer. It wuz bigger'n de white folks church house in Winter Park. A whole heap uh folks had done come out tuh see which one would win.

Jack wuz late. He come gallopin' up on hawseback and reined in de hawse so short till he reared up his hind legs.

Jack jumped off and says: "Wese all heah, le's go. Who goin' first?"

De Devil tole 'im, "Me. Everybody stand back and gimme room."

So he throwed de hammer and it went so high till it went clean outa sight. Devil tole 'em, "Iss Tuesday now. Y'all go home and come back Thursday mornin' at nine. It won't fall till then."

155

Sho 'nuff de hammer fell on Thursday mornin' at nine o'clock and knocked out a hole big as Polk County.

Dey lifted de hammer out de hole and levelled it and it wuz Jack's time to throw.

Jack took his time and walked 'round de hammer to de handle and took holt of it and throwed his head back and looked up at de sky.

"Look out, Rayfield! Move over, Gabriel! You better stand 'way back, Jesus! Ah'm fixin' to throw." He meant Heaven.

Devil run up to 'im, says, "Hold on dere a minute! Don't you throw mah damn hammer up dere! Ah left a whole lot uh mah tools up dere when dey put me out and Ah ain't got 'em back yet. Don't you *throw* mah hammer up dere!"

TEN

So I left most of my things at Loughman and ran down in the phosphate country around Mulberry. Around Mulberry, Pierce and Lakeland, I collected a mass of children's tales and games. The company operating the mines at Pierce maintains very excellent living conditions in their quarters. The cottages are on clean, tree-lined streets. There is a good hospital and a nine-months school. They will not employ a boy under seventeen so that the parents are not tempted to put minors to work. There is a cheerful community center with a large green-covered table for crap games under a shady oak.

We held a lying contest out under the trees in the night time, some sitting, some standing, everybody in a jolly mood. Mack C. Ford proved to be a mighty story teller before the Lord.

I found out about creation from him. The tail of the porpoise is on crosswise and he explains the mystery of that.

"Zora, did you ever see a porpoise?"

"Yep. Many times."

"Didja ever notice his tail?"

"Don't b'lieve Ah did. He moves so fast till Ah don't remember much except seeing him turning somersault and

157

shootin' up and down de Indian River like lightnin' thru de trees."

Well, it's on crossways. Every other fish got his tail on straight but de porpoise. His is on crossways and bent down lak dis. (He bent down the fingers of his left hand sharply from the knuckles.)

De reason for dat is, God made de world and de sky and de birds and animals and de fishes. He finished off de stars and de trees.

Den He made a gold track clear 'round de world and greased it, and called de sun to Him and says, "Now Sun, Ah done made everything but Time and Ah want you to make dat. Ah made dat gold track for you to run on and Ah want you to git on it and go 'round de world jus' as fas' as you kin stave it and de time it take you to go and come Ah'm gointer call it 'day' and 'night.' "

De porpoise was standin' 'round and heard God when He spoke to de sun. So he says, "B'lieve Ah'll take dat trip around de world myself."

So de sun lit out and de porpoise took out. Him and him! 'Round de world—lickety split!

So de porpoise beat de sun 'round de world by a hour and three minutes.

When God seen dat He shook His head and says, "Unh, unh! Dis ain't gointer do. Ah never meant for nothin' to be faster than de sun."

So He took out behind dat porpoise and run him for three days and nights befo' He overtook him. But when he *did* ketch dat ole porpoise He grabbed him by de tail and snatched it off and set it back on crossways to slow him up. He can't beat de sun no mo' but he's de next fastest thing in de world.

Everybody laughed one of those blow-out laughs, so Mack Ford said, "Mah lyin' done got good tuh me, so Ahm gointer tell yuh how come de dawg hates de cat."

De dog and de cat used to live next door to one 'nother and both of 'em loved ham. Every time they git a chance they'd buy a slice of ham.

One time both of 'em got holt of a li'l extry change so de dog said to de cat, "Sis Cat, we both got a li'l money, and it would be fine if bofe of us could buy a ham apiece. But neither one of us ain't got enough money to buy a whole ham by ourselves. Why don't we put our money together and buy us a ham together?"

"Aw right, Brer Dawg. T'morrer begin' Sat'day, le's we go to town and git ourselves a ham."

So de next day they went to town and bought de ham. They didn't have no convenience so they had to walk and tote it. De dawg toted it first and he said as he walked up de road wid de ham over his shoulder, "Ours! Ours! Ours! Our ham!"

After while it was de cat's time to tote de meat. She said, "My ham, my ham, my ham." Dawg heard her but he didn't say nothin'.

When de dawg took it agin he says, "Ours, ours, our ham!" Cat toted it and says, "My ham, my ham."

Dawg says, "Sis Cat, how come you keep on sayin' 'My ham' when you totes our meat. Ah always say, 'Our ham.' "

De Cat didn't turn him no answer, but every time she toted de ham she'd say "My ham" and every time de dawg toted it he'd say "Ours."

When they was almost home, de cat was carryin' de ham and all of a sudden she sprung up a tree and set up there eatin' up de ham. De dawg did all he could to stop her, but he couldn't clim' and so he couldn't do nothin' but bark. But he tole de cat, "You up dat tree eatin' all de ham, and Ah can't git to you. But when you come down ahm gointer make you take dis Indian River for uh dusty road."

"Didja ever pass off much time round de railroad camps, Zora?" asked Mr. Ford.

"Ah been round dere some."

"Ah wuz jus' fixin' tuh tell yuh if you ain't been there you missed some good singin', well ez some good lyin'. Ever hear dat song bout 'Gointer See my Long-haired Babe'?"[1]

"Naw, but ah sho wisht ah had. Can you sing it?"

"Sho can and then ahm gointer do it too, and that one bout 'Oh Lulu, oh Gal.'"

"Ah know you want to hear some more stories, don't you? Ah know ah feels lak tellin' some."

"Unh hunh," I agreed.

"Don't you know dat's one word de Devil made up?"

"Nope, Ah had never heard about it. It's a mighty useful word Ah know for lazy folks like me."

"Yes, everybody says 'unh hunh' and Ah'll tell you why."
He cleared his throat and continued:

Ole Devil looked around hell one day and seen his place was short of help so he thought he'd run up to Heben and kidnap some angels to keep things runnin' tell he got reinforcements from Miami.

Well, he slipped up on a great crowd of angels on de outskirts of Heben and stuffed a couple of thousand in his mouth, a few hundred under each arm and wrapped his tail 'round another thousand and darted off towards hell.

When he was flyin' low over de earth lookin' for a place to land, a man looked up and seen de Devil and ast 'im, "Ole Devil, Ah see you got a load of angels. Is you goin' back for mo'?"

Devil opened his mouth and tole 'im, "Yeah," and all de li'l angels flew out of his mouf and went on back to Heben. While he was tryin' to ketch 'em he lost all de others. So he went back after another load.

He was flyin' low agin and de same man seen him and says, "Ole Devil, Ah see you got another load uh angels."

[1] See appendix.

160

Devil nodded his head and said "unh hunh," and dat's
why we say it today.

"Dat's a fine story. Tell me some more."
"Ah'm gointer tell you all about Big Sixteen and High
Walker and Bloody Bones but first Ah want to ask you a
question."
"All right, go ahead and ask me."
"Zora, why do you think dese li'l slim women was put on
earth?"
"Couldn't tell you to save my life."
"Well, dese slim ones was put here to beautify de world."
"De big ones musta been put here for de same reason."
"Ah, naw, Zora. Ah don't agree wid you there."
"Well then, what *was* they put here for?"
"To show dese slim girls how far they kin stretch without
bustin'."
Everybody out under the trees laughed except Good Bread.
She took in a whole lot of breath and added to herself. Then
she rolled her eyes and said, "Mack Ford, Ah don't come in
yo' conversation atall. You jus' leave me out yo' mouf. And
furthermo' Ah don't crack."
"Nobody ain't called yo name, Good Bread, Ah wuz jus'
passin' uh joke."
"Oh yes you wuz hintin' at me."
"Aw, nobody ain't studyin' bout yuh. Jus' cause you done
set round and growed ruffles round yo' hips nobody can't
mention fat 'thout you makin' out they talkin' bout you. Ah
wuzn't personatin' yuh, but if de cap fit yuh, wear it."
"G'wan Mack, you knows dat a very little uh yo' sugar
sweetens mah tea. Don't git *me* started."
"G'wan start something if dats de way yuh feel. You kin be
stopped. Now you tryin' to make somebody believe you so
bad till you have tuh tote uh pistol tah bed tuh keep from
gettin' in uh fight wid yo' self! You got mo' poison in yuh than
dat snake dat wuz so poison tell he bit de railroad track and
killed de train, hunh?"

161

"Don't y'all break dis lyin' contest up in no fight," Christopher Jenkins said.

Mah Honey laughed scornfully. "Aw, tain't gointer be no fight. Good Bread jus' feel lak bull woofin' uh little t'night. Her likker told her tuh pick uh fight but let Mack make uh break at her now, and there'll hafta be some good runnin' done befo' dat fight come off. Tain't nothin' tuh her. She know she ugly. She look lak de devil ground up in pieces."

Good Bread jumped up with her pocket knife out. "Who y'all tryin tuh double teen? Trying tuh run de hawg over de wrong one now."

"Aw set down Good Bread, and put dat froe back in yo' pocket. Somebody's liable tuh take dat ole piece uh knife you got and wear it out round yo' own neck."

"Dats what Ah say," Christopher put in. "She always tryin' tuh loud talk somebody. Ah hates women wid men's overalls on anyhow."

"Let her holler all she wants tuh," Ford added off-hand. "Dis is uh holler day. She kin whoop lak de Seaboard and squall lak de A.C.L. Nobody don't keer, long as she don't put her hand on me. Sho as she do dat Ahm gointer light her shuck for her."

Good Bread got to her feet importantly as if she was going to do something. For a fraction of a second I held my breath in fear. Nobody else paid it the least bit of mind. Good Bread flounced on off.

"Ahm glad she gone," said Mah Honey. "She always pickin' fights and gittin beat. Dat 'oman hates peace and agreement." He looked after her a moment then yelled after her. "Hey, lady, you got all you' bust in de back!" Everybody laughed and Mah Honey went on. "She so mad now she'll stay way and let Mack tell Zora some lies. Gwan, Mack, you got de business."

"Aw, Ah feel lak singin'," Mack Ford said.

"Well nobody don't feel lak hearin' yuh, so g'wan tell dat lie on Big Sixteen. Ah never gits tired uh dat one."

"You ruther hear uh story, Zora?"

"Yeah, g'wan tell it. Dats jus' what Ah'm here for."
"Well alright then:

It was slavery time, Zora, when Big Sixteen was a man.
They called 'im Sixteen 'cause dat was de number of de
shoe he wore. He was big and strong and Ole Massa
looked to him to do everything.

One day Ole Massa said, "Big Sixteen, Ah b'lieve Ah
want you to move dem sills Ah had hewed out down in de
swamp."

"I yassuh, Massa."

Big Sixteen went down in de swamp and picked up dem
12×12's and brought 'em on up to de house and stack
'em. No one man ain't never toted a 12×12 befo' nor
since.

So Ole Massa said one day, "Go fetch in de mules. Ah
want to look 'em over."

Big Sixteen went on down to de pasture and caught dem
mules by de bridle but they was contrary and balky and he
tore de bridles to pieces pullin' on 'em, so he picked one
of 'em up under each arm and brought 'em up to Old
Massa.

He says, "Big Sixteen, if you kin tote a pair of balky
mules, you kin do anything. You kin ketch de Devil."

"Yassuh, Ah kin, if you git me a nine-pound hammer
and a pick and shovel!"

Ole Massa got Sixteen de things he ast for and tole 'im
to go ahead and bring him de Devil.

Big Sixteen went out in front of de house and went to
diggin'. He was diggin' nearly a month befo' he got where
he wanted. Then he took his hammer and went and
knocked on de Devil's door. Devil answered de door hisself.

"Who dat out dere?"

"It's Big Sixteen."

"What you want?"

"Wanta have a word wid you for a minute."

Soon as de Devil poked his head out de door, Sixteen
lammed him over de head wid dat hammer and picked 'im

163

up and carried 'im back to Old Massa.

Ole Massa looked at de dead Devil and hollered, "Take dat ugly thing 'way from here, quick! Ah didn't think you'd ketch de Devil sho 'nuff."

So Sixteen picked up de Devil and throwed 'im back down de hole.

Way after while, Big Sixteen died and went up to Heben. But Peter looked at him and tole 'im to g'wan 'way from dere. He was too powerful. He might git outa order and there wouldn't be nobody to handle 'im. But he had to go somewhere so he went on to hell.

Soon as he got to de gate de Devil's children was playin' in de yard and they seen 'im and run to de house, says, "Mama, mama! Dat man's out dere dat kilt papa!"

So she called 'im in de house and shet de door. When Sixteen got dere she handed 'im a li'l piece of fire and said, "You ain't comin' in here. Here, take dis hot coal and g'wan off and start you a hell uh yo' own."

So when you see a Jack O'Lantern in de woods at night you know it's Big Sixteen wid his piece of fire lookin' for a place to go.

"Give us somethin' to wet our goozles wid, and you kin git some lies, Zora," Jenkins prompted. I stood treats.

"Now g'wan, Mack, and lie some more," I said, and he remarked:

"De mosquitoes mighty bad right now, but down there on de East Coast they used to 'em. Know why we got so many skeeters heah and why we have so many storms?"

"Naw, but Ah'd love to know," I answered eagerly.

Well, one Christmas time, God was goin' to Palatka. De Devil was in de neighborhood too and seen God goin' long de big road, so he jumped behind a stump and hid. Not dat he was skeered uh God, but he wanted to git a Christmas present outa God but he didn't wanta give God nothin'.

So he squatted down behind dis stump till God come along and then he jumped up and said, "Christmas gift!"

164

God just looked back over his shoulder and said, "Take de East Coast," and kept on walkin'. And dat's why we got storms and skeeters—it's de Devil's property.

I should mention it is a custom in the deep South for the children to go out Christmas morning "catching" people by saying "Christmas gift." The one who says it first gets a present from the other. The adults usually prepare for this by providing plenty of hard candy, nuts, coconuts, fruits and the like. They never try to catch the neighbors' children but let themselves be caught.

"Ah know one mo' story on de devil. Reckon Ah'll tell it now.

"One day de Devil was walkin' along when he met Raw Head."

"Who is Raw Head?" I interrupted to ask. "Ah been hearin' his name called all my life, but never did find out who he was."

"Why, Zora! Ah thought everybody knowed who Raw Head was. Why he was a man dat was more'n a man. He was big and strong like Big Sixteen and he was two-headed. He knowed all de words dat Moses used to make. God give 'im de power to bring de ten plagues and part de Red Sea. He had done seen de Smokey Mountain and de Burnin' Bush. And his head didn't have no hair on it, and it sweated blood all de time. Dat's why he was named Raw Head."[2] Then Mr. Ford told the following story:

As Ah started to say, de Devil met Raw Head and they passed de time of day. Neither one wasn't skeered of de other, so they talked about de work they been doin'.

Raw Head said he had done turnt a man into a ground puppy. Devil said he been havin' a good time breakin' up couples. All over de world de Devil had husbands and wives fightin' and partin'.

[2]He was a conjure doctor. They are always referred to as "two-headed doctors," i.e. twice as much sense.

165

Tol 'im says, "Devil, youse my cousin and Ah know you got mo' power than me, but Ah know one couple you can't part. They lives cross de big creek in my district, and Ah done everything Ah could but nothin' can't come between 'em."

Devil says, "Dat's because de right one ain't tried yet. Ah kin part any two people. Jus' like Ah kin throw 'em together. You show 'em to me and Ah betcha half of hell Ah'll have 'em fightin' and partin' befo' Sunday."

So de Devil went to where dis couple lived and took up 'round de house.

He done everything he could but they wouldn't fight and they wouldn't part. Devil was real outdone. He had never had such a tussle since they throwed him outer Heben, and it was Friday. He seen he was 'bout to lose half of his kingdom and have to go back on his brag.

He was 'bout to give up and go somewhere else dat night when he met a woman as barefooted as a yard-dog. They spoke and she says, "You don't look so good. You been down sick?"

Devil told her, "Naw, but Ah been tryin' to break up dat lovin' couple up de road a piece there, but Ah can't do it."

De woman says, "Aw shucks, is dat all? Tell you whut: Ah ain't never had a pair of shoes in my life and if you promise to give me a pair of shoes tonight Ah'll part 'em for you."

"If you part 'em you get de shoes, and good ones at dat. But you got to do it first."

"Don't you worry 'bout dat, you jus' meet me at dat sweet-gum tree on de edge of de swamp tomorrer evenin' and bring de shoes."

Next mornin' she got up soon and went past de place to see where de man was workin' at. He was plowin' way off from de house. So she spoke to 'im nice and polite and went on up to de house where de wife was.

De wife asted her in and give her a chair. She took her seat and begin to praise everything on de place. It was de prettiest house she ever seen. It was de bes' lookin' yard in dat part of the state. Dat was de finest dawg she ever laid

166

eyes on. *Nobody* never had no cat as good as dat one was.

De wife thanked her for all her compliments and give her a pound of butter.

De woman told her, "Everything you got is pretty, but youse de prettiest of all."

De wife is crazy 'bout her husband and she can't stand to see him left out so she say, "My husband is prettier than Ah ever dared to be."

"Oh, yeah, he's pretty too. Almost as pretty as you. De only thing dat spoil his looks is dat long flesh-mole on his neck. Now if dat was off he'd be de prettiest man in de world."

De wife says, "Ah thinks he's already de prettiest man in de world, but if anything will make 'im *mo'* prettier still, Ah will too gladly do it."

"Well, then, you better cut dat big ole mole offa his neck."

"How kin Ah do dat? He skeered to cut it off. Say he might bleed to death."

"Aw naw, he won't neither. He won't lose more'n a drop of blood if you cut it off right quick wid a sharp razor and then wipe cob-web on de place. It's a pity he won't let you do it 'cause it sho do spoil his looks."

"If Ah knowed jus' how to do it, Ah sho would, 'cause Ah love him so and he is too pretty a man to be spoilt by a mole."

"Why don't you take de razor to bed wid you tonight. Then when he gets to sleep, you chop it off right quick and fix it lak Ah told you. He'll thank you for it next day."

De wife thanked de woman and give her a settin' of eggs and de woman told her good-bye and went on down to de field where de husband was plowin', and sidled up to him. "Good mornin' suh, you sho is a hard-workin' man."

"Yes ma'am, Ah works hard but Ah loves to work so Ah kin do for my wife. She's all Ah got."

"Yeah, and she sho got a man when she got you. 'Tain't many mens dat will hit from sun to sun for a woman."

The man said, "Sho ain't. But ain't no man got no wife as good as mine."

De woman spit on de ground and said, "It's good for a

person's mind to be satisfied. But lovin' a person don't make them love you. And youse a pitiful case."

"Why you say dat? Ain't I got de prettiest wife in de world. And what make it so cool, she's de sweetest wife God ever made."

"All Ah got to say is 'Watch out.'"

"Watch out for what? My wife don't need no watchin'. She's pretty, it's true, but Ah don't have to watch her."

"Somebody else done found out she pretty too and she's gointer gid rid of *you.* You better keep a close watch on her and when you go to bed tonight, make out you sleep and see if she don't try to cut yo' throat wid a razor!"

"Git off dis place—lyin' on my wife?"

De woman hid in de bushes outside de fence row and watched. Sho nuff, pretty soon he knocked off and went on towards de house. When he got dere he searched all over de place to see if anybody was there besides his wife. He didn't find nothin' but he watched everybody dat passed de gate, and he didn't say nothin' to his wife.

Dat night he got in bed right after supper and laid there wid his eyes shut. De wife went and got his razor and slipped it to bed wid her. When she thought he was good and sleep she got de cob-web in one hand and de razor in de other and leaned over him to cut his mole off. He had de cover up 'round his neck and soon as she started to ease it back he opened his eyes and grabbed her and took de razor.

"Unh, hunh! Ah was told you was goin' to cut my throat, but Ah didn't b'lieve it. From now on, we ain't no mo' husband and wife."

He dressed and left her cryin' in de bed.

De woman run on down to de sweet-gum tree to git her shoes. De Devil come brought 'em but he took and cut a long sapling and tied de shoe to de end of it and held 'em out to de woman and told her, "You parted 'em all right. Here's de shoes I promised you. But anybody dat kin create mo' disturbance than me is too dangerous. Ah don't want 'em round me. Here, take yo' shoes." And soon as she took 'em he vanished.

Horace Sharp said, "You lemme tell one now, Mack; you been talkin' all night. Tell yuh bout de farmer courtin' a girl.

Well, the startin' of it is, a farmer was courtin' a girl and after he decided to marry her, they married and started home. So when he passed a nice farm he said to the girl: "You see dat nice farm over yonder?" She said, "Yes." He said: "Well, all of these are mine." (Strokes his whiskers.)

Well, they traveled on further and they saw a herd of cattle and he said, "See dat nice herd of cattle?" She said. "Yes." "Well, all of these are mine." He smoothed his whiskers again.

So he traveled on a piece further and come to a big plantation with a big nice house on it, and he said: "All of these are mine."

So he traveled on further. He said, "See dat nice bunch of sheep?" She said, "Yes." "Well, all of these are mine."

Traveled on further. Come across a nice bunch of hogs and he said: "See dat nice bunch of hogs?" "Yes." "Well, all of these are mine."

So the last go 'round he got home and drove up to a dirty li'l shack and told her to get out and come in.

She says, "You got all those nice houses and want me to come in there? I couldn't afford to come in here. *Why you told me a story.* I'm going back home."

He says, "Why no, I didn't tell you a story. Everytime I showed you those things I said 'all of these were mine' and Ah wuz talkin' bout my whiskers." So the girl jumped out of the wagon and out for home she went.

Goat fell down and skint his chin
Great God A'mighty how de goat did grin.

"You do pretty good, Horace," Mah Honey drawled, "but how come you want to stick in yo' bill when Mack is talkin'? Dat story you told ain't doodly squat."

"Less see *you* tell one better'n dat one, then," Horace slashed back.

"Oh Ah can't tell none worth listenin' tuh and you can't neither. Only difference in us is Ah know Ah can't and you don't. Dat lie you told is po' ez owl harkey. Gwan tell some mo' Mack. Maybe somebody'll come long and help yuh out after while."

"Ah thought Horace's story wuz jus' alright," Lessie Lee Hudson said. "Can't eve'ybody talk de same."

"Course it wuz!" Horace yelled, "it wuz alright wid everybody 'ceptin Mah Honey. He's a nigger wid white folks' head—let *him* tell it. He make out he know every chink in China."

"What you gointer do?" Mah Honey asked. "Ah kin tell yuh fo' yuh part yo' lips. You ain't gointer do nothin' but mildew."

Somebody came along singing, "You Won't Do," and everybody looked round at one time like cows in a pasture. "Here come A.D. He kin lie good too. Hurry up, A.D. and help Mack out!"

"What Mack doin'?"

"Lyin' up a breeze."

"Awright, lemme git in dis shag-lag. Who lied last?"

"Mack. Youse next."

"Who all know what uh squinch owl[3] is?" Frazier lit out.

"Man, who you reckon it is, *don't* know what dat bad luck thing is?" Christopher Jenkins asked. "Sign uh death every time you hear one hollerin round yo' house. Ah shoots every one Ah kin find."

"You kin stop 'em without shootin' 'em. Jus' tie uh loose knot in uh string and every time he holler you pull de knot uh lil bit tighter. Dat chokes 'im. Keep on you choke 'im tuh death. Go out doors nex' mawnin and look ahround you'll find uh dead owl round dere somewhere." Said Mah Honey.

"All you need tuh do is turn somethin' wrong side outuds, pull off yo' coat and turn it or else you kin turn uh pocket," Carrie Jones added. "Me, Ah always pull off uh stockin' and turn it. Dat always drives 'im off."

"Throw some salt on de lamp or stick uh rusty fork in de

[3]Screech owl, sometimes known as a shivering owl.

170

floor will do de same thing. In fact its de best of all; Ah mean de salt in de lamp. Nothin' evil can't stand salt, let alone burnin' salt."

"Lemme tell y'all how come we got squinch owls and then y'all kin talk all yuh please bout how tuh kill 'em and drive 'em off de house top in de night time," said A.D.

Yuh know Ole Marster had uh ole maid sister that never been married. You know how stringy white folks necks gits when dey gits ole. Well hers had done got that-a-way and more special cause she never been married.

Her name wuz Miss Pheenie and Ole Marster had uh daughter so there wuz young mens round de parlor and de porch. All in de sittin' chairs and in de hammock under de trees. So Miss Pheenie useter stand round and peer at 'em and grin lak uh possum—wishin' she could git courted and married.

So one devilish young buck, he seen de feelin' in her so he 'gin tuh make manners wid her and last thing he done, he told her says, "If you go set up on de roof uh de house all night Ah'll marry yuh in de mawnin'."

It wuz uh bitter cold night. De wind searchin' lak de police. So she clambed up dere and set straddle of de highest part cause she couldn't stick nowhere's else. And she couldn't help but shake and shiver. And everytime de clock would strike de hour she'd say, "C-o-o-o-l-d on de housetop, but uh young man in de mawnin'." She kept dat up till de clock struck four, when she tumbled down, froze tuh death. But de very next night after they buried her, she took de shape of uh owl and wuz back dere shivverin' and cryin'. And dats how come us got squinch owls.

"Dat sho waz uh true lie, A.D.," Carrie said. "Ah sho is wished many de time dat Miss Pheenie had uh stayed off de top uh dat house."

"Ah knows one 'bout uh witch woman," A.D. went on. "Ah'll tell dat one too, whilst Ah got mah wind."

"Naw, Ah don't wanta hear bout no witches ridin' nobody," Baby-face Turl objected. "Ah been near rode tuh death in mah time. Can't bear tuh hear tell of it."

"Well then Ah kin tell yuh bout dat talkin' mule.

Ole feller one time had uh mule. His name wuz Bill. Every mornin' de man go tuh ketch 'im he say, "Come 'round, Bill!"

So one mornin' he slept late, so he decided while he wuz drinkin' some coffee he'd send his son tuh ketch Ole Bill.

Told 'im say, "Go down dere, boy, and bring me dat mule up here."

Boy, he sich a fast Aleck, he grabbed de bridle and went on down tuh de lot tuh ketch ole Bill.

He say, "Come round, Bill!"

De mule looked round at 'im. He told de mule, "Tain't no use you rollin' yo' eyes at *me.* Pa want yuh dis mawnin'. Come on round and stick yo' head in dis bridle."

Mule kept on lookin' at 'im and said, "Every mornin' it's 'Come round, Bill! Come round, Bill!' Don't hardly git no night rest befo' it's 'Come round, Bill!' "

De boy throwed down dat bridle and flew back tuh de house and told his Pa, "Dat mule is talkin'."

"Ah g'wan, boy, tellin' yo' lies! G'wan ketch dat mule."

"Naw suh, Pa, dat mule's done gone tuh talkin'. You hatta ketch dat mule yo' ownself. Ah ain't gwine."

Ole man looked at ole lady and say, "See whut uh lie dat boy is tellin'?"

So he gits out and goes on down after de mule his-self. When he got down dere he hollered, "Come round, Bill!"

Ole mule looked round and says, "Every mornin' it's come round, Bill!"

De old man had uh little fice dog useter foller 'im every-where he go, so he lit out wid de lil fice right behind 'im. So he told de ole lady, "De boy ain't told much of uh lie. Dat mule *is* talkin'. Ah never heered uh mule talk befo'."

Lil fice say, "Me neither."

De ole man got skeered agin. Right through de woods he went wid de fice right behind 'im. He nearly run hisself tuh death. He stopped and commenced blowin' and says, "Ahm so tired Ah don't know whut tuh do."

Lil dog run and set down in front of 'im and went to hasslin'[4] and says, "Me too."

Dat man is runnin' yet.

Everybody agreed that the old man did right by running, only some thought they could have bettered his record both for speed and distance.

"What make you love tuh tell dem skeery lies, A.D.?" Clarence Beale asked.

Lessie Lee snuggled up to Clarence with the eyes of Eve and said, "He skeers me too, Clarence. Less me and you hug up together." Clarence grabbed her and wrapped her up tight.

"Youse jus' all right, A.D. If you know another one skeerier than dat one, Ah'll give yuh five dollars tuh tell it. And then Ah'm gointer git de job uh keepin' de boogers offa Lessie Lee tuhnight. G'wan tell it."

"Yeah man!" Christopher Jenkins chimed in. "All dese frail eels gittin' skittish. Tell some mo' A.D. Skeer Carrie right up on me!"

So A.D. told another one.

This wuz uh man. His name was High Walker. He walked into a boneyard with skull-heads and other bones. So he would call them, "Rise up bloody bones and shake yo'self." And de bones would rise up and come together, and shake theirselves and part and lay back down. Then he would say to hisself, "High Walker," and de bones would say, "Be walkin'."

When he'd git off a little way he'd look back over his

---

[4]Panting.

shoulder and shake hisself and say, "High Walker and bloody bones," and de bones would shake theirselves. Therefore he knowed he had power.

So uh man sold hisself to de high chief devil. He give 'im his whole soul and body tuh do ez he pleased wid it. He went out in uh drift uh woods[5] and laid down flat on his back beyond all dese skull heads and bloody bones and said, "Go 'way Lawd, and come here Devil and do as you please wid me. Cause Ah want tuh do everything in de world dats wrong and never do nothing right."

And he dried up and died away on doin' wrong. His meat all left his bones and de bones all wuz separated.

And at dat time High Walker walked upon his skull head and kicked and kicked it on ahead of him a many and a many times and said tuh it, "Rise up and shake yo'self. High Walker is here."

Ole skull head wouldn't say nothin'. He looked back over his shoulder cause he heard some noises behind him and said, "Bloody bones you won't say nothin' yet. Rise tuh de power in de flesh."

Den de skull head said, "My mouf brought me here and if you don't mind, you'n will bring you here."

High Walker went on back to his white folks and told de white man dat a dry skull head wuz talkin' in de drift today. White man say he didn't believe it.

"Well, if you don't believe it, come go wid me and Ah'll prove it. And if it don't speak, you kin chop mah head off right where it at."

So de white man and High Walker went back in de drift tuh find dis ole skull head. So when he walked up tuh it, he begin tuh kick and kick de ole skull head, but it wouldn't say nothin'. High Walker looked at de white man and seen 'im whettin' his knife. Whettin' it hard and de sound of it said rick-de-rick, rick-de-rick, rick-de-rick! So High Walker kicked and kicked dat ole skull head and called it many and many uh time, but it never said nothin'. So de white man cut off High Walker's head.

[5]10,000 "faces" in the turpentine woods, i.e. tree trunks that have been cut on one side to make the sap run from which turpentine is made.

174

And de ole dry skull head said, "See dat now! Ah told you dat mouf brought me here and if you didn't mind out it'd bring you here."

So de bloody bones riz up and shook they selves seben times and de white man got skeered and said, "What you mean by dis?"

De bloody bones say, "We got High Walker and we all bloody bones now in de drift together."

The next day was Thursday and I got a letter from Big Sweet saying I must be back at Loughman by Saturday because that was pay night and Thelma and Cliffert were getting married and big doings would be going on.

Friday I arrived in Loughman. Thelma and Cliffert got married on Saturday and everybody that wasn't mad put out to give them a big time.

The biggest crowd was over at the Pine Mill where Jim Presley was playing so I wanted to go there. Big Sweet didn't want to go there much. At least that is what she told everybody, but she told me to go on. She might be over later. She gave me some advice about looking out for myself.

"Don't let nobody bring yuh nothin' tuh eat and drink, and don't let 'em send it neither. They liable tuh put uh spider in yo' dumplin'. Don't let nobody git yuh intuh no fuss, cause you can't do dis kind uh fightin'. You don't know no better'n tuh go face tuh face tuh fight. Lucy and dem ain't gointer fight nobody lak dat. They think it make 'em look big tuh cut yuh. Ah done went tuh her and put mah foot up on her door step and told her dat if she tetch yuh Ah'll gently chain-gang fuh her, but she don't aim tuh lemme ketch her. She mean tuh slip up on yuh sometime and hit yuh uh back hand lick wid her knife and turn her hand over right quick and hit yuh forward wid it and pull it down. Then she aims tuh run cross back yards and jump fences so fast till me and de law neither can't find her."

"Well, Big Sweet, if it's like dat, Ah speck Ah better not go out unless you be wid me," I told her.

"Oh yeah, you go on. You come here tuh see and lissen and Ah means fuh yuh tuh do it. Jus' watch out. Ah could give yuh uh knife tuh tote but dat wouldn't do you no good. You don't know how tuh handle it. Ah got two round here. One real good one Ah got down in Tampa, and one ole froe.[6] But you jus' gwan over dere and mind what Ah tell yuh. Ahm liable tuh be dere tuhreckly mahself. And don't git biggity wid nobody and let yuh head start more than yo' rump kin stand."

I promised sincerely and took Cliffert and Thelma in the car with me to the Pine Mill.

A new man had come from Groveland, where another big sawmill was located, and he was standing behind Jim Presley and Slim, singing new songs, and I was so glad that I had come. It didn't take me long to learn some new ones and I forgot all about Lucy.

Way after midnight Big Sweet came in. The place was hot by then. Everything was done got loud. The music, the dancing, the laughing, and nobody could say a thing even over the card games unless they made it sound something like singing. Heard one woman playing Coon Can sing out:

> Give mah man mah money, tuh play Coon Can
> He lost all mah money but he played his hand.

In a little while I heard her again:

> Befo' Ah'll lose mah rider's change
> Ah'll spread short deuces and tab de game.

Big Sweet nodded me over in a corner and said, "Ah done strowed it over on de other side dat Ahm gone home tuh bed. Jus' wanta see whut might come off."

"Lucy ain't been here atall," I told her. "Believe she skeered you might kill her sho 'nuff."

[6]A damaged pocket knife.

176

"She know Ah will lessen she kill me first. Ah hates uh two-facedted heifer lak her. And Ah ain't skeered tuh see Mah Jesus neither cause de Bible say God loves uh plain sinner and he's married tuh de backslider. Ah got jus' as good uh chance at Heben as anybody else. So have yo' correct amount uh fun. Ahm settin' right over dere in dat skin game."

Heard somebody at the Florida Flip game say, "Ahm gone—jus' lak uh turkey through de corn. Deal!"

Heard somebody else in the game say, "Beggin' " and the dealer told him, "Eat acorns."[7]

Heard Blue Baby ask Box-Car, "Who is dat new nigger over dere by de refreshments? God Amighty, ugly got de mug on him wid four wheel brakes."

"He's de new skitter man.[8] He sho' ain't nobody's pretty baby. Bet he have tuh slip up on de dipper tuh git uh drink uh water. B'lieve Ah'll holler at 'im. 'Hey Ugly, who made you? Don't start tuh lyin' on God now.' "

A general laugh followed this. Box-Car, a little proud of his crack, grabbed Blue Baby. "Come on less go over dere and marry Cliff and Thelma all over agin. Hey Cliff, you and Thelma git up on de floor and raise yo' right hand. Y'all ain't been hitched right till Box-Car git thew widja." The couple bashfully stood up.

"Join hands. Alright Cliff, Ahm de preacher—

Here's yo' woman, here's de ring,
Here's de banana, here's de skin
Now you married, go—

A huge burst of laughter drowned out Box Car's voice and when the laugh died out, I could hear Nunkie, "reading the deck" where the flip game used to be. Calling the names of the cards and laying them down rhythmically and dramatically as he read:

[7] I give you one point.
[8] A panther had killed the other one a week earlier.

Ace means the first time that Ah met you, Deuce means there was nobody there but us two, Trey means the third party, Charlie was his name, Four spot means the fourth time you tried dat same ole game, Five spot is five years you played me for a clown, Six spot, six feet of earth when de deal goes down, Now, Ahm holdin' de seben spot for each day in de week, Eight spot, eight hours you sheba-ed wid yo' sheik, Nine spot means nine hours Ah work hard every day, Ten spot de tenth of every month Ah brought you home mah pay, De Jack is Three Card Charlie who played me for a goat, De Queen, dat's you, pretty mama, also tryin' tuh cut mah throat, De King, dat hot papa Nunkie, and he's gointer wear de crown, So be keerful y'all ain't broke when de deal goes down.

Nunkie looked around belligerently on the last sentence and Joe Willard jumped up and pulled at Big Sweet.

"Play some music, Jim, y'all over dere, and less dance some mo'. Nunkie wants tuh pick uh fight wid Who Flung. Play us uh slow drag. Come on Big Sweet, less me and you have uh schronchuns dance."

"Dance wid Zora, honey, Ah don't choose tuh move from where Ahm at. Ah ain't mad wid nobody, baby, jus' wanta set and look on uh while yet."

Heard the new singing man climbing up on

> Tell me, tell me where de blood red river ru-u-un
> Oh tell me where de blood red river run
> From mah back door, straight to de risin' sun.

Heard Slim's bass strings under the singing throbbing like all Africa and Jim Presley's melody crying like repentance as four or five couples took the floor. Doing the slow drag, doing the schronch. Joe Willard doing a traveling buck and wing towards where I stood against the wall facing the open door.

Just about that time Lucy hopped up in the doorway with an open knife in her hands. She saw me first thing. Maybe she had been outside peeping a long time and there I was leaning against the wall right close to Slim. One door in the place and Lucy standing in it.

"Stop dat music," she yelled without moving. "Don't vip another vop till Ah say so! Ah means tuh turn dis place out right now. Ah got de law in mah mouf."

So she started walking hippily straight at me. She knew I couldn't get out easily because she had me barred and she knew not many people will risk running into a knife blade to stop a fight. So she didn't have to run. I didn't move but I was running in my skin. I could hear the blade already crying in my flesh. I was sick and weak. But a flash from the corner about ten feet off and Lucy had something else to think about besides me. Big Sweet was flying at her with an open blade and now it was Lucy's time to try to make it to the door. Big Sweet kicked her somewhere about the knees and she fell. A doubled back razor flew thru the air very close to Big Sweet's head. Crip, the new skitter man, had hurled it. It whizzed past Big Sweet and stuck in the wall; then Joe Willard went for Crip. Jim Presley punched me violently and said, "Run you chile! Run and ride! Dis is gointer be uh nasty ditch. Lucy been feedin' Crip under rations tuh git him tuh help her. Run clean off dis job! Some uh dese folks goin' tuh judgment and some goin' tuh jail. Come on, less run!"

Slim stuck out the guitar to keep two struggling men from blocking my way. Lucy was screaming. Crip had hold of Big Sweet's clothes in the back and Joe was slugging him loose. Curses, oaths, cries and the whole place was in motion. Blood was on the floor. I fell out of the door over a man lying on the steps, who either fell himself trying to run or got knocked down. I don't know. I was in the car in a second and in high just too quick. Jim and Slim helped me throw my bags into the car and I saw the sun rising as I approached Crescent City.

PART II

❖

HOODOO

ONE

Winter passed and caterpillars began to cross the road again. I had spent a year in gathering and culling over folk-tales. I loved it, but I had to bear in mind that there was a limit to the money to be spent on the project, and as yet, I had done nothing about hoodoo.

So I slept a night, and the next morning I headed my toe-nails toward Louisiana and New Orleans in particular.

New Orleans is now and has ever been the hoodoo capital of America. Great names in rites that vie with those of Hayti in deeds that keep alive the powers of Africa.

Hoodoo, or Voodoo, as pronounced by the whites, is burning with a flame in America, with all the intensity of a suppressed religion. It has its thousands of secret adherents. It adapts itself like Christianity to its locale, reclaiming some of its borrowed characteristics to itself, such as fire-worship as signified in the Christian church by the altar and the candles and the belief in the power of water to sanctify as in baptism.

Belief in magic is older than writing. So nobody knows how it started.

The way we tell it, hoodoo started way back there before everything. Six days of magic spells and mighty words and the world with its elements above and below was made. And now, God is leaning back taking a seventh day rest. When the

183

eighth day comes around, He'll start to making new again.

Man wasn't made until around half-past five on the sixth day, so he can't know how anything was done. Kingdoms crushed and crumbled whilst man went gazing up into the sky and down into the hollows of the earth trying to catch God working with His hands so he could find out His secrets and learn how to accomplish and do. But no man yet has seen God's hand, nor yet His finger-nails. All they could know was that God made everything to pass and perish except stones. God made stones for memory. He builds a mountain Himself when He wants things not forgot. Then His voice is heard in rumbling judgment.

Moses was the first man who ever learned God's power-compelling words and it took him forty years to learn ten words. So he made ten plagues and ten commandments. But God gave him His rod for a present, and showed him the back part of His glory. Then too, Moses could walk out of the sight of man. But Moses never would have stood before the Burning Bush, if he had not married Jethro's daughter. Jethro was a great hoodoo man. Jethro could tell Moses could carry power as soon as he saw him. In fact he felt him coming. Therefore, he took Moses and crowned him and taught him. So Moses passed on beyond Jethro with his rod. He lifted it up and tore a nation out of Pharaoh's side, and Pharaoh couldn't help himself. Moses talked with the snake that lives in a hole right under God's foot-rest. Moses had fire in his head and a cloud in his mouth. The snake had told him God's making words. The words of doing and the words of obedience. Many a man thinks he is making something when he's only changing things around. But God let Moses make. And then Moses had so much power he made the eight winged angels split open a mountain to bury him in, and shut up the hole behind them.

And ever since the days of Moses, kings have been toting rods for a sign of power. But it's mostly sham-polish because no king has ever had the power of even one of Moses' ten words. Because Moses made a nation and a book, a thousand million leaves of ordinary men's writing couldn't tell what Moses said.

Then when the moon had dragged a thousand tides behind her, Solomon was a man. So Sheba, from her country where she was, felt him carrying power and therefore she came to talk with Solomon and hear him.

The Queen of Sheba was an Ethiopian just like Jethro, with power unequal to man. She didn't have to deny herself to give gold to Solomon. She had gold-making words. But she was thirsty, and the country where she lived was dry to her mouth. So she listened to her talking ring and went to see Solomon, and the fountain in his garden quenched her thirst.

So she made Solomon wise and gave him her talking ring. And Solomon built a room with a secret door and everyday he shut himself inside and listened to his ring. So he wrote down the ring-talk in books.

That's what the old ones said in ancient times and we talk it again.

It was way back there—the old folks told it—that Raw-Head-And-Bloody-Bones had reached down and laid hold of the taproot that points to the center of the world. And they talked about High Walker too. But they talked in people's language and nobody knew them but the old folks.

Nobody knows for sure how many thousands in America are warmed by the fire of hoodoo, because the worship is bound in secrecy. It is not the accepted theology of the Nation and so believers conceal their faith. Brother from sister, husband from wife. Nobody can say where it begins or ends. Mouths don't empty themselves unless the ears are sympathetic and knowing.

That is why these voodoo ritualistic orgies of Broadway and popular fiction are so laughable. The profound silence of the initiated remains what it is. Hoodoo is not drum beating and dancing. There are no moon-worshippers among the Negroes in America.

I was once talking to Mrs. Rachel Silas of Sanford, Florida, so I asked her where I could find a good hoodoo doctor.

"Do you believe in dat ole fogeyism, chile? Ah don't see how nobody could do none of dat work, do you?" She laughed unnecessarily. "Ah been hearin' 'bout dat mess ever since Ah been big enough tuh know mahself, but shucks! Ah don't believe nobody kin do me no harm lessen they git somethin' in mah mouth."

"Don't fool yourself," I answered with assurance. "People can do things to you. I done seen things happen."

"Sho nuff? Well, well, well! Maybe things *kin* be done tuh harm yuh, cause Ah done heard *good* folks—folks dat ought to know—say dat it sho is a fact. Anyhow Ah figger it pays tuh be keerful."

"Oh yeah, Mrs. Rachel, Ah've seen a woman full of scorpions."

"Oh it kin be done, honey, no effs and ands 'bout de thing. There's things that kin be done. Ah seen uh' 'oman wid uh gopher in her belly. You could see 'm movin' 'round in her. And once every day he'd turn hisself clear over and then you could hear her hollerin' for more'n a mile. Dat hard shell would be cuttin' her insides. Way after 'while she took down ill sick from it and died. Ah knowed de man dat done dat trick. Dat wuz done in uh dish of hoppin-john."[1]

Mrs. Viney White, a neighbor, was sitting there so she spoke. "Ah knowed into dat mahself. It wuz done over her breaking de leg of one of his hens dat wuz scratchin' up her garden. When she took down sick Ah went to see her and Ah told her folks right then dat somebody had done throwed at her, but they didn't b'lieve in nothin'. Went and got a Medical doctor, and they can't do them kind of cases no good at all. Fact is it makes it worser." She stopped short and nodded her head apprehensively towards the window. Rachel nodded her head knowingly. "She out dere now, tryin' tuh eavesdrop."

"Who you talkin' 'bout?" I asked.

---

[1] Peas and rice cooked together.

"De one dat does all de underhand work 'round here. She even threwed at *me* once, but she can't do nothin'. Ah totes mah Big John de Conquerer[2] wid me. And Ah sprinkles mustard seed 'round my door every night before Ah goes tuh bed."

"Yeah, and another thing," Mrs. Rachel said, "Ah keeps her offa me too. She tries tuh come in dis yard so she kin put something down for me too, but air Lawd, Ah got something buried at dat gate dat she can't cross. She done been dere several times, but she can't cross."

"Ah'd git her tuh go if ah wuz you, Rachel," Mrs. Viney said.

"Wisht ah knowed how. Ah'd sho do it."

"You throw salt behind her, everytime she go out of her gate. Do dat nine times and Ah bet she'll move so fast she won't even know where she's going. Somebody salted a woman over in Georgetown and she done moved so much she done wore out her furniture on de movin' wagon. But looka here, Zora, whut you want wid a two-headed doctor? Is somebody done threwed a old shoe at *you?*"

"Not exactly neither one, Mrs. Viney. Just want to learn how to do things myself."

"Oh, honey, Ah wouldn't mess with it if Ah wuz you. Dat's a thing dat's got to be handled just so, do it'll kill you. Me and Rachel both knows somebody that could teach you if they will. Dis woman ain't lak some of these hoodoo doctors. She don't do nothin' but good. You couldn't pay her to be rottin' people's teeths out, and fillin' folks wid snakes and lizards and spiders and things like dat."

So I went to study with Eulalia, who specialized in Man-and-woman cases. Everyday somebody came to get Eulalia to tie them up with some man or woman or to loose them from love.

Eulalia was average sized with very dark skin and bushy eyebrows. Her house was squatting among the palmettoes and

---

[2] A root, extensively used in conjure.

the mossy scrub oaks. Nothing pretty in the house nor outside. No paint and no flowers. So one day a woman came to get tied to a man.

"Who is dis man?" Eulalia wanted to know.

"Jerry Moore," the woman told her. "He want me and Ah know it, but dat 'oman he got she got roots buried and he can't git shet of her—do we would of done been married."

Eulalia sat still and thought awhile. Then she said: "Course Ah'm uh Christian woman and don't believe in partin' no husband and wife but since she done worked roots on him, to hold him where he don't want to be, it tain't no sin for me to loose him. Where they live at?"

"Down Young's Quarters. De third house from dis end."

"Do she ever go off from home and stays a good while durin' de time he ain't there neither?"

"Yas Ma'am! She all de time way from dat house—off fanfootin' whilst he workin' lak a dog! It's a shame!"

"Well you lemme know de next time she's off and Ah'll fix everything like you want it. Put that money back in yo' purse, Ah don't want a thing till de work is done."

Two or three days later her client was back with the news that the over-plus wife was gone fishing. Eulalia sent her away and put on her shoes.

"Git dat salt-bowl and a lemon," she said to me. "Now write Jerry's name and his wife's nine times on a piece of paper and cut a little hole in the stem end of that lemon and pour some of that gun-powder in de hole and roll that paper tight and shove it inside the lemon. Wrap de lemon and de bowl of salt up and less go."

In Jerry Moore's yard, Eulalia looked all around and looked up at the sun a great deal, then pointed out a spot.

"Dig a little hole right here and bury dat lemon. It's got to be buried with the bloom-end down and it's got to be where de settin' sun will shine on it."

So I buried the lemon and Eulalia walked around to the kitchen door. By the time I had the lemon buried the door was open and we went inside. She looked all about and found some red pepper.

"Lift dat stove-lid for me," she ordered, and I did. She threw some of the pepper into the stove and we went on into the other room which was the bedroom and living-room all in one. Then Eulalia took the bowl and went from corner to corner "salting" the room. She'd toss a sprinkling into a corner and say, "Just fuss and fuss till you part and go away." Under the bed was sprinkled also. It was all over in a minute or two. Then we went out and shut the kitchen door and hurried away. And Saturday night Eulalia got her pay and the next day she set the ceremony to bring about the marriage.

TWO

N ow I was in New Orleans and I asked. They told me Algiers, the part of New Orleans that is across the river to the west. I went there and lived for four months and asked. I found women reading cards and doing mail order business in names and insinuations of well known factors in conjure. Nothing worth putting on paper. But they all claimed some knowledge and link with Marie Leveau. From so much of hearing the name I asked everywhere for this Leveau and everybody told me differently. But from what they said I was eager to know to the end of the talk. It carried me back across the river into the Vieux Carré. All agreed that she had lived and died in the French quarter of New Orleans. So I went there to ask.

I found an oil painting of the queen of conjure on the walls of the Cabildo, and mention of her in the guide books of New Orleans, but I did a lot of stumbling and asking before I heard of Luke Turner, himself a hoodoo doctor, who says that he is her nephew.

When I found out about Turner, I had already studied under five two-headed doctors and had gone thru an initiation ceremony with each. So I asked Turner to take me as a pupil. He was very cold. In fact he showed no eagerness even to talk with me. He feels sure of his powers and seeks no one. He refused to take me as a pupil and in addition to his habitual indifference I could see he had no faith in my sincerity. I could see him searching my face for whatever was behind what I said. The City of New Orleans has a law against fortune tellers, hoodoo doctors and the like, and Turner did not know me. He asked me to excuse him as he was waiting upon someone in the inner room. I let him go but I sat right there and waited. When he returned, he tried to shoo me away by being rude. I stayed on. Finally he named an impossible price for tuition. I stayed and dickered. He all but threw me out, but I stayed and urged him.

I made three more trips before he would talk to me in any way that I could feel encouraged. He talked about Marie Leveau because I asked. I wanted to know if she was really as great as they told me. So he enlightened my ignorance and taught me. We sat before the soft coal fire in his grate.

"Time went around pointing out what God had already made. Moses had seen the Burning Bush. Solomon by magic knowed all wisdom. And Marie Leveau was a woman in New Orleans.

"She was born February 2, 1827. Anybody don't believe I tell the truth can go look at the book in St. Louis Cathedral. Her mama and her papa, they wasn't married and his name was Christophe Glapion.

"She was very pretty, one of the Creole Quadroons and many people said she would never be a hoodoo doctor like her mama and her grandma before her. She liked to go to the balls very much where all the young men fell in love with her. But Alexander, the great two-headed doctor felt the power in her and so he tell her she must come to study with him. Marie, she rather dance and make love, but one day a rattlesnake come to her in her bedroom and spoke to her. So she went to Alexander and studied. But soon she could teach her teacher and the snake stayed with her always.

"She has her house on St. Anne Street and people come from the ends of America to get help from her. Even Queen

Victoria ask her help and send her a cashmere shawl with money also.

"Now, some white people say she hold hoodoo dance on Congo Square every week. But Marie Leveau never hold no hoodoo dance. That was a pleasure dance. They beat the drum with the shin bone of a donkey and everybody dance like they do in Hayti. Hoodoo is private. She give the dance the first Friday night in each month and they have crab gumbo and rice to eat and the people dance. The white people come look on, and think they see all, when they only see a dance.

"The police hear so much about Marie Leveau that they come to her house in St. Anne Street to put her in jail. First one come, she stretch out her left hand and he turn round and round and never stop until some one come lead him away. Then two come together—she put them to running and barking like dogs. Four come and she put them to beating each other with night sticks. The whole station force come. They knock at her door. She know who they are before she ever look. She did work at her altar and they all went to sleep on her steps.

"Out on Lake Pontchartrain at Bayou St. John she hold a great feast every year on the Eve of St. John's, June 24th. It is Midsummer Eve, and the Sun give special benefits then and need great honor. The special drum be played then. It is a cowhide stretched over a half-barrel. Beat with a jaw-bone. Some say a man but I think they do not know. I think the jawbone of an ass or a cow. She hold the feast of St. John's partly because she is a Catholic and partly because of hoodoo.

"The ones around her altar fix everything for the feast. Nobody see Marie Leveau for nine days before the feast. But when the great crowd of people at the feast call upon her, she would rise out of the waters of the lake with a great communion candle burning upon her head and another in each one of her hands. She walked upon the waters to the shore. As a little boy I saw her myself. When the feast was over, she went back into the lake, and nobody saw her for nine days again.

"On the feast that I saw her open the waters, she looked

hard at me and nodded her head so that her tignon shook. Then I knew I was called to take up her work. She was very old and I was a lad of seventeen. Soon I went to wait upon her Altar, both on St. Anne Street and her house on Bayou St. John's.

"The rattlesnake that had come to her a little one when she was also young was very huge. He piled great upon his altar and took nothing from the food set before him. One night he sang and Marie Leveau called me from my sleep to look at him and see. 'Look well, Turner,' she told me. 'No one shall hear and see such as this for many centuries.'

"She went to her Great Altar and made great ceremony. The snake finished his song and seemed to sleep. She drove me back to my bed and went again to her Altar.

"The next morning, the great snake was not at his altar. His hide was before the Great Altar stuffed with spices and things of power. Never did I know what become of his flesh. It is said that the snake went off to the woods alone after the death of Marie Leveau, but they don't know. This is his skin that I wear about my shoulders whenever I reach for power.

"Three days Marie, she set at the Altar with the great sun candle burning and shining in her face. She set the water upon the Altar and turned to the window, and looked upon the lake. The sky grew dark. The lightning raced to the seventeen quarters of the heavens and the lake heaved like a mighty herd of cattle rolling in a pasture. The house shook with the earth.

"She told me, 'You are afraid. That is right, you should fear. Go to your own house and build an altar. Power will come.' So I hurried to my mother's house and told them.

"Some who loved her hurried out to Bayou St. John and tried to enter the house but she try hard to send them off. They beat upon the door, but she will not open. The terrible strong wind at last tore the house away and set it in the lake. The thunder and lightning grow greater. Then the loving ones find a boat and went out to where her house floats on one side and break a window to bring her out, but she begs, 'NO! Please, no,' she tell them. 'I want to die here in the lake,' but they would not permit her. She did not wish their destruction, so she let herself be drawn away from her altar in the lake. And the wind, the thunder and lightning, and the water all ceased the moment she set foot on dry land.

"That night she also sing a song and is dead, yes. So I have the snake skin and do works with the power she leave me."

"How did Marie Leveau do her work?" I asked feeling that I had gotten a little closer to him.

"She go to her great Altar and seek until she become the same as the spirit, then she come out into the room where she listens to them that come to ask. When they finish she answer them as a god. If a lady have a bad enemy and come to her she go into her altar room and when she come out and take her seat, the lady will say to her:

" 'Oh, Good Mother. I come to you with my heart bowed down and my shoulders drooping, and my spirits broken; for an enemy has sorely tried me; has caused my loved ones to leave me; has taken from me my worldly goods and my gold; has spoken meanly of me and caused my friends to lose faith in me. On my knees I pray to you, Good Mother, that you will cause confusion to reign in the house of my enemy and that you will take their power from them and cause them to be unsuccessful.'

"Marie Leveau is not a woman when she answer the one who ask. No. She is a god, yes. Whatever she say, it will come so. She say:

" 'Oh, my daughter, I have heard your woes and your pains and tribulations, and in the depth of the wisdom of the gods I will help you find peace and happiness.

" 'It is written that you will take of the Vinagredes Four Volle[1] for him, and you will dip into it a sheet of pure parchment paper, and on this sheet you will write the names of your enemies and send it to the house of your enemies, tightly sealed with the wax of the porcupine plant.

" 'Then when the sun shall have risen and gone down three

_____
[1]Four Thieves Vinegar. For paraphernalia of conjure, see appendix.

195

times, you will take of the water of Mars, called War Water, and in front of the house of your enemy you will sprinkle it. This you will do as you pass by. If it be a woman, you will take the egg of a guinea fowl, and put it into the powder of the fruit of cayenne and the dust of Goofer,[2] and you will set it on the fire in your own house and in clear water from the skies you will boil it until it shall be hard. This you will do so that there shall be no fruit from her womb.

" 'And you shall take of the Damnation Powders, two drachmas, and of the water powders, two drachmas and make a package of it and send it to the home of the one who has spoken badly of you and has treated you mean, so that damnation and trouble shall be on the head of your enemy and not on you.

" 'You will do this so that you will undo your enemies and you will take the power to harm you away from your enemies.

" 'Oh daughter, go you in peace and do the works required of you, so that you will have rest and comfort from your enemies and that they will have not the power to harm you and lower you in the sight of your people and belittle you in the sight of your friends. So be it.' "

By the time that Turner had finished his recitation he wasn't too conscious of me. In fact he gave me the feeling that he was just speaking, but not for my benefit. He was away off somewhere. He made a final dramatic gesture with open hands and hushed for a minute. Then he sank deeper into himself and went on:

"But when she put the last curse on a person, it would be better if that man was dead, yes."

With an impatient gesture he signalled me not to interrupt him.

"She set the altar for the curse with black candles that have been dressed in vinegar. She would write the name of the person to be cursed on the candle with a needle. Then she place fifteen cents in the lap of Death upon the altar to pay the

[2]Dirt taken out of a grave.

spirit to obey her orders. Then she place her hands flat upon the table and say the curse-prayer.

" 'To The Man God: O great One, I have been sorely tried by my enemies and have been blasphemed and lied against. My good thoughts and my honest actions have been turned to bad actions and dishonest ideas. My home has been disrespected, my children have been cursed and ill-treated. My dear ones have been backbitten and their virtue questioned. O Man God, I beg that this that I ask for my enemies shall come to pass:

" 'That the South wind shall scorch their bodies and make them wither and shall not be tempered to them. That the North wind shall freeze their blood and numb their muscles and that it shall not be tempered to them. That the West wind shall blow away their life's breath and will not leave their hair grow, and that their finger nails shall fall off and their bones shall crumble. That the East wind shall make their minds grow dark, their sight shall fail and their seed dry up so that they shall not multiply.

" 'I ask that their fathers and mothers from their furtherest generation will not intercede for them before the great throne, and the wombs of their women shall not bear fruit except for strangers, and that they shall become extinct. I pray that the children who may come shall be weak of mind and paralyzed of limb and that they themselves shall curse them in their turn for ever turning the breath of life into their bodies. I pray that disease and death shall be forever with them and that their worldly goods shall not prosper, and that their crops shall not multiply and that their cows, their sheep, and their hogs and all their living beasts shall die of starvation and thirst. I pray that their house shall be unroofed and that the rain, the thunder and lightning shall find the innermost recesses of their home and that the foundation shall crumble and the floods tear it asunder. I pray that the sun shall not shed its rays on them in benevolence, but instead it shall beat down on them and burn them and destroy them. I pray that the moon shall not give them peace, but instead shall deride them and decry them and cause their minds to shrivel. I pray that their friends shall betray them and cause them loss of power, of gold and of silver, and that their enemies shall smite them until they beg for mercy which shall not be given them. I pray that their tongues shall forget how to speak in sweet words, and that it shall be paralyzed and that all about them will be desolation, pestilence and death. O Man God, I ask you for all these things because they have dragged me in the dust and destroyed my good name; broken my heart and caused me to curse the day that I was born. So be it.' "

Turner again made that gesture with his hands that meant the end. Then he sat in a dazed silence. My own spirits had been falling all during the terrible curse and he did not have to tell me to be quiet this time. After a long period of waiting I rose to go. "The Spirit say you come back tomorrow," he breathed as I passed his knees. I nodded that I had heard and went out. The next day he began to prepare me for my initiation ceremony, for rest assured that no one may approach the Altar without the crown, and none may wear the crown of power without preparation. *It must be earned.*

And what is this crown of power? Nothing definite in material. Turner crowned me with a consecrated snake skin. I have been crowned in other places with flowers, with ornamental paper, with cloth, with sycamore bark, with egg-shells. It is the meaning, not the material that counts. The crown without the preparation means no more than a college diploma without the four years' work.

This preparation period is akin to that of all mystics. Clean living, even to clean thoughts. A sort of going to the wilderness in the spirit. The details do not matter. My nine days being up, and possessed of the three snake skins and the new underwear required, I entered Turner's house as an inmate to finish the last three days of my novitiate. Turner had become so sure of my fitness as a hoodoo doctor that he would accept no money from me except what was necessary to defray the actual cost of the ceremony.

So I ate my final meal before six o'clock of the evening

before and went to bed for the last time with my right stocking on and my left leg bare.

I entered the old pink stucco house in the Vieux Carré at nine o'clock in the morning with the parcel of needed things. Turner placed the new underwear on the big Altar; prepared the couch with the snake-skin cover upon which I was to lie for three days. With the help of other members of the college of hoodoo doctors called together to initiate me, the snake skins I had brought were made into garments for me to wear. One was coiled into a high headpiece—the crown. One had loops attached to slip on my arms so that it could be worn as a shawl, and the other was made into a girdle for my loins. All places have significance. These garments were placed on the small altar in the corner. The throne of the snake. The Great One[3] was called upon to enter the garments and dwell there.

I was made ready and at three o'clock in the afternoon, naked as I came into the world, I was stretched, face downwards, my navel to the snake skin cover, and began my three day search for the spirit that he might accept me or reject me according to his will. Three days my body must lie silent and fasting while my spirit went wherever spirits must go that seek answers never given to men as men.

I could have no food, but a pitcher of water was placed on a small table at the head of the couch, that my spirit might not waste time in search of water which should be spent in search of the Power-Giver. The spirit must have water, and if none had been provided it would wander in search of it. And evil spirits might attack it as it wandered about dangerous places. If it should be seriously injured, it might never return to me.

For sixty-nine hours I lay there. I had five psychic experiences and awoke at last with no feeling of hunger, only one of exaltation.

I opened my eyes because Turner called me. He stood before the Great Altar dressed ceremoniously. Five others were with him.

[3]The Spirit.

"Seeker, come," Turner called.

I made to rise and go to him. Another laid his hand upon me lightly, restraining me from rising.

"How must I come?" he asked in my behalf.

"You must come to the spirit across running water," Turner answered in a sort of chant.

So a tub was placed beside the bed. I was assisted to my feet and led to the tub. Two men poured water into the tub while I stepped into it and out again on the other side.

"She has crossed the dangerous stream in search of the spirit," the one who spoke for me chanted.

"The spirit does not know her name. What is she called?"

"She has no name but what the spirit gives."

"I see her conquering and accomplishing with the lightning and making her road with thunder. She shall be called the Rain-Bringer."

I was stretched again upon the couch. Turner approached me with two brothers, one on either side of him. One held a small paint brush dipped in yellow, the other bore one dipped in red. With ceremony Turner painted the lightning symbol down my back from my right shoulder to my left hip. This was to be my sign forever. The Great One was to speak to me in storms.

I was now dressed in the new underwear and a white veil was placed over my head, covering my face, and I was seated in a chair.

After I was dressed, a pair of eyes was painted on my cheeks as a sign that I could see in more ways than one. The sun was painted on my forehead. Many came into the room and performed ceremonial acts, but none spoke to me. Nor could I speak to them while the veil covered my face. Turner cut the little finger of my right hand and caught the gushing blood in a wine cup. He added wine and mixed it with the blood. Then he and all the other five leaders let blood from themselves also and mixed it with wine in another glass. I was led to drink from the cup containing their mingled bloods, and each of them in turn beginning with Turner drank mine. At high noon

I was seated at the splendid altar. It was dressed in the center with a huge communion candle with my name upon it set in sand, five large iced cakes in different colors, a plate of honeyed St. Joseph's bread, a plate of serpent-shaped breads, spinach and egg cakes fried in olive oil, breaded Chinese okra fried in olive oil, roast veal and wine, two huge yellow bouquets, two red bouquets and two white bouquets and thirty-six yellow tapers and a bottle of holy water.

Turner seated me and stood behind me with his ceremonial hat upon his head, and the crown of power in his hand. "Spirit! I ask you to take her. Do you hear me, Spirit? Will you take her? Spirit, I want you to take her, she is worthy!" He held the crown poised above my head for a full minute. A profound silence held the room. Then he lifted the veil from my face and let it fall behind my head and crowned me with power. He lit my candle for me. But from then on I might be a candle-lighter myself. All the candles were reverently lit. We all sat down and ate the feast. First a glass of blessed oil was handed me by Turner. "Drink this without tasting it." I gulped it down and he took the glass from my hand, took a sip of the little that remained. Then he handed it to the brother at his right who did the same, until it went around the table.

"Eat first the spinach cakes," Turner exhorted, and we did. Then the meal began. It was full of joy and laughter, even though we knew that the final ceremony waited only for the good hour of twelve midnight.

About ten o'clock we all piled into an old Studebaker sedan—all but Turner who led us on a truck. Out Road No. 61 we rattled until a certain spot was reached. The truck was unloaded beside the road and sent back to town. It was a little after eleven. The swamp was dismal and damp, but after some stumbly walking we came to a little glade deep in the wood, near the lake. A candle was burning at each of the four corners of the clearing, representing the four corners of the world and the four winds. I could hear the occasional slap-slap of the water. With a whispered chant some twigs were gathered and tied into a broom. Some pine straw was collected. The sheets of typing paper I had been urged to bring were brought out and nine sheets were blessed and my petition written nine times on each sheet by the light from a shaded lantern. The crate containing the black sheep was opened and the sheep led forward into the center of the circle. He stood there dazedly while the chant of strange syllables rose. I asked Turner the words, but he replied that in good time I would know what to say. It was not to be taught. If nothing came, to be silent. The head and withers of the sheep were stroked as the chanting went on. Turner became more and more voluble. At last he seized the straw and stuffed some into the sheep's nostrils. The animal struggled. A knife flashed and the sheep dropped to its knees, then fell prone with its mouth open in a weak cry. My petition was thrust into its throat that he might cry it to the Great One. The broom was seized and dipped in the blood from the slit throat and the ground swept vigorously—back and forth, back and forth—the length of the dying sheep. It was swept from the four winds toward the center. The sweeping went on as long as the blood gushed. Earth, the mother of the Great One and us all, has been appeased. With a sharp stick Turner traced the outline of the sheep and the digging commenced. The sheep was never touched. The ground was dug from under him so that his body dropped down into the hole. He was covered with nine sheets of paper bearing the petition and the earth heaped upon him. A white candle was set upon the grave and we straggled back to the road and the Studebaker.

I studied under Turner five months and learned all of the Leveau routines; but in this book all of the works of any doctor cannot be given. However, we performed several of Turner's own routines.

Once a woman, an excited, angry woman wanted something done to keep her husband true. So she came and paid Turner gladly for his services.

Turner took a piece of string that had been "treated" at the altar and gave it to the woman.

"Measure the man where I tell you. But he must never know. Measure him in his sleep then fetch back the string to me."

The next day the woman came at ten o'clock instead of nine as Turner had told her, so he made her wait until twelve o'clock, that being a good hour. Twelve is one of the benign hours of the day while ten is a malignant hour. Then Turner took the string and tied nine knots in it and tied it to a larger piece of string which he tied about her waist. She was completely undressed for the ceremony and Turner cut some hair from under her left armpit and some from the right side of the groin and put it together. Then he cut some from the right arm-pit and a tuft from the left groin and it was all placed on the altar, and burned in a votive light with the wish for her husband to love her and forget all others. She went away quite happy. She was so satisfied with the work that she returned with a friend a few days later.

Turner, with his toothless mouth, his Berber-looking face, said to the new caller:

"I can see you got trouble." He shivered. "It is all in the room. I feel the pain of it; Anger, Malice. Tell me who is this man you so fight with?"

"My husband's brother. He hate me and make all the trouble he can," the woman said in a tone so even and dull that it was hard to believe she meant what she said. "He must leave this town or die. Yes, it is much better if he is dead." Then she burst out, "Yeah, he should be dead long time ago. Long before he spy upon me, before he tell lies, lies, lies. I should be very happy for his funeral."

"Oh I can feel the great hate around you," Turner said. "It follow you everywhere, but I kill nobody, I send him away if you want so he never come back. I put guards along the road in the spirit world, and these he cannot pass, no. When he go, never will he come back to New Orleans. You see him no more. He will be forgotten and all his works."

"Then I am satisfied, yes," the woman said. "When will you send him off?"

203

"I ask the spirit, you will know."

She paid him and he sent her off and Turner went to his snake altar and sat in silence for a long time. When he arose, he sent me out to buy nine black chickens, and some Four Thieves Vinegar.[4] He himself went out and got nine small sticks upon which he had me write the troublesome brother-in-law's name—one time on each stick. At ten that night we went out into the small interior court so prevalent in New Orleans and drove nine stakes into the ground. The left leg of a chicken was tied to each stake. Then a fire was built with the nine sticks on which the name had been written. The ground was sprinkled all over with the Four Thieves Vinegar and Turner began his dance. From the fire to the circle of fluttering chickens and back again to the fire. The feathers were picked from the heads of the chickens in the frenzy of the dance and scattered to the four winds. He called the victim's name each time as he whirled three times with the chicken's head-feathers in his hand, then he flung them far.

The terrified chickens flopped and fluttered frantically in the dim firelight. I had been told to keep up the chant of the victim's name in rhythm and to beat the ground with a stick. This I did with fervor and Turner danced on. One by one the chickens were seized and killed by having their heads pulled off. But Turner was in such a condition with his whirling and dancing that he seemed in a hypnotic state. When the last fowl was dead, Turner drank a great draught of wine and sank before the altar. When he arose, we gathered some ashes from the fire and sprinkled the bodies of the dead chickens and I was told to get out the car. We drove out one of the main highways for a mile and threw one of the chickens away. Then another mile and another chicken until the nine dead chickens had been disposed of. The spirits of the dead chickens had been instructed never to let the trouble-maker pass inward to New Orleans again after he had passed them going out.

[4]A conjure mixture. See Paraphernalia of Conjure.

204

*   *   *

One day Turner told me that he had taught me all that he could and he was quite satisfied with me. He wanted me to stay and work with him as a partner. He said that soon I would be in possession of the entire business, for the spirit had spoken to him and told him that I was the last doctor that he would make; that one year and seventy-nine days from then he would die. He wanted me to stay with him to the end. It has been a great sorrow to me that I could not say yes.

THREE

Anatol Pierre, of New Orleans, was a middle-aged octoroon. He is a Catholic and lays some feeble claim to kinship with Marie Leveau.

He had the most elaborate temple of any of the practitioners. His altar room was off by itself and absolutely sacrosanct.

He made little difficulty about taking me after I showed him that I had worked with others.

Pierre was very emotional and sometimes he would be sharp with his clients, indifferent as to whether they hired him or not. But he quickly adjusted himself to my being around him and at the end of the first week began to prepare me for the crown.

The ceremony was as follows:

On Saturday I was told to have the materials for my initiation bath ready for the following Tuesday at eleven o'clock. I must have a bottle of lavender toilet water, Jap honeysuckle perfume, and orange blossom water. I must get a full bunch of parsley and brew a pint of strong parsley water. I must have at hand sugar, salt and Vacher Balm. Two long pink candles must be provided, one to be burned at the initiation, one to be lit on the altar for me in Pierre's secret room.

He came to my house in Belville Court at a quarter to eleven to see if all was right. The tub was half-filled with warm water and Pierre put in all of the ingredients, along with a handful of salt and three tablespoons of sugar.

The candles had been dressed on Saturday and one was already burning on the secret altar for me. The other long pink candle was rolled around the tub three times, "In nomina patria, et filia, et spiritu sanctus, Amen." Then it was marked for a four day burning and lit. The spirit was called three times. "Kind spirit, whose name is Moccasin, answer me." This I was told to repeat three times, snapping my fingers.

Then I, already prepared, stepped into the tub and was bathed by the teacher. Particular attention was paid to my head and back and chest since there the "controls" lie. While in the tub, my left little finger was cut a little and his finger was cut and the blood bond made. "Now you are of my flesh and of the spirit, and neither one of us will ever deny you."

He dried me and I put on new underwear bought for the occasion and dressed with oil of geranium, and was told to stretch upon the couch and read the third chapter of Job night and morning for nine days. I was given a little Bible that had been "visited" by the spirit and told the names of the spirits to call for any kind of work I might want to perform. I am to call on Great Moccasin for all kinds of power and also to have him stir up the particular spirit I may need for a specific task. I must call on Kangaroo to stop worrying; call on Jenipee spirit for marriages; call on Death spirit for killing, and the seventeen "quarters"[1] of spirit to aid me if one spirit seems insufficient.

I was told to burn the marked candle every day for two hours—from eleven till one, in the northeast corner of the room. While it is burning I must go into the silence and talk to the spirit through the candle.

On the fifth day Pierre called again and I resumed my studies, but now as an advanced pupil. In the four months that followed these are some of the things I learned from him:

A man called Muttsy Ivins came running to Pierre soon after

[1]See appendix.

208

my initiation was over. Pierre looked him over with some instinctive antipathy. So he wouldn't help him out by asking questions. He just let Mr. Muttsy tell him the best way he could. So he began by saying, "A lot of hurting things have been done to me, Pierre, and now its done got to de place Ah'm skeered for mah life."

"That's a lie, yes," Pierre snapped.

"Naw it 'tain't!" Muttsy insisted. "Ah done found things 'round mah door step and in mah yard and Ah know who's doin' it too."

"Yes, you find things in your yard because you continue to sleep with the wife of another man and you are afraid because he has said that he will kill you if you don't leave her alone. You are crazy to think that you can lie to me. Tell me the truth and then tell me what you want me to do."

"Ah want him out de way—kilt, cause he swear he's gointer kill me. And since one of us got to die, Ah'd ruther it to be him than me."

"I knew you wanted a death the minute you got in here. I don't like to work for death."

"Please, Pierre, Ah'm skeered to walk de streets after dark, and me and de woman done gone too far to turn back. And he got de consumption nohow. But Ah don't wanter die before he do. Ah'm a well man."

"That's enough about that. How much money have you got?"

"Two hundred dollars."

"Two fifty is my terms, and I ain't a bit anxious for the job at that."

Pierre turned to me and began to give me a list of things to get for my own use and seemed to forget the man behind him.

"Maybe Ah kin git dat other fifty dollars and maybe not. These ain't no easy times. Money is tight."

"Well, goodbye, we're busy folks here. You don't have to do this thing anyway. You can leave town."

"And leave mah good trucking business? Dat'll never happen. Ah kin git yo' money. When yo' goin' ter do de work?"

"You pay the money and go home. It is not for you to know how and when the work is done. Go home with faith."

The next morning soon, Pierre sent me out to get a beef brain, a beef tongue, a beef heart and a live black chicken. When I returned he had prepared a jar of bad vinegar. He wrote Muttsy's enemy's name nine times on a slip of paper. He split open the heart, placed the paper in it, pinned up the opening with eighteen steel needles, and dropped it into the jar of vinegar, point downward.

The main altar was draped in black and the crudely carved figure of Death was placed upon it to shield us from the power of death.

Black candles were lit on the altar. A black crown was made and placed on the head of Death. The name of the man to die was written on paper nine times and placed on the altar one degree below Death, and the jar containing the heart was set on this paper. The candles burned for twelve hours.

Then Pierre made a coffin six inches long. I was sent out to buy a small doll. It was dressed in black to represent the man and placed in the coffin with his name under the doll. The coffin was left open upon the altar. Then we went far out to a lonely spot and dug a grave which was much longer and wider than the coffin. A black cat was placed in the grave and the whole covered with a cloth that we fastened down so that the cat could not get out. The black chicken was then taken from its confinement and fed a half glass of whiskey in which a paper had been soaked that bore the name of the man who was to die. The chicken was put in with the cat, and left there for a full month.

The night after the entombment of the cat and the chicken, we began to burn the black candles. Nine candles were set to burn in a barrel and every night at twelve o'clock we would go to the barrel and call upon the spirit of Death to follow the man. The candles were dressed by biting off the bottoms, as Pierre called for vengeance. Then the bottom was lighted instead of the top.

At the end of the month, the coffin containing the doll was carried out to the grave of the cat and chicken and buried upon their remains. A white bouquet was placed at the head and foot of the grave.

The beef brain was placed on a plate with nine hot peppers around it to cause insanity and brain hemorrhages, and placed on the altar. The tongue was slit, the name of the victim inserted, the slit was closed with a pack of pins and buried in the tomb.

"The black candles must burn for ninety days," Pierre told me. "He cannot live. No one can stand that."

Every night for ninety days Pierre slept in his holy place in a black draped coffin. And the man died.

Another conjure doctor solicited trade among Pierre's clients and his boasts of power, and his belittling comments of Pierre's power vexed him. So he said to me one day: "That fellow boasts too much, yes. Maybe if I send him a swelling he won't be out on the banquette bragging so much."

So Pierre took me with him to steal a new brick. We took the brick home and dressed nine black candles by writing the offensive doctor's name on each. His name was written nine times on a piece of paper and placed face down on the brick. It was tied there securely with twine. We put the black candles to burn, one each day for nine days, and then Pierre dug a well to the water table and slipped the brick slowly to the bottom. "Just like the brick soaks up the water, so that man will swell."

FOUR

I heard of Father Watson the "Frizzly Rooster" from afar, from people for whom he had "worked" and their friends, and from people who attended his meetings held twice a week in Myrtle Wreath Hall in New Orleans. His name is "Father" Watson, which in itself attests his Catholic leanings, though he is formally a Protestant.

On a given night I had a front seat in his hall. There were the usual camp-followers sitting upon the platform and bustling around performing chores. Two or three songs and a prayer were the preliminaries.

At last Father Watson appeared in a satin garment of royal purple, belted by a gold cord. He had the figure for wearing that sort of thing and he probably knew it. Between prayers and songs he talked, setting forth his powers. He could curse anybody he wished—and make the curse stick. He could remove curses, no matter who had laid them on whom. Hence his title The Frizzly Rooster. Many persons keep a frizzled chicken in the yard to locate and scratch up any hoodoo that may be buried for them. These chickens have, no doubt, earned this reputation by their ugly appearance—with all of their feathers set in backwards. He could "read" anybody at sight. He could "read" anyone who remained out of his sight if they but stuck two fingers inside the door. He could "read" anyone, no matter how far away, if he were given their height and color. He begged to be challenged.

He predicted the hour and the minute, nineteen years hence, when he should die—without even having been ill a moment in his whole life. God had told him.

He sold some small packets of love powders before whose powers all opposition must break down. He announced some new keys that were guaranteed to unlock every door and remove every obstacle in the way of success that the world knew. These keys had been sent to him by God through a small Jew boy. The old keys had been sent through a Jew man. They were powerful as long as they did not touch the floor—but if you ever dropped them, they lost their power. These new keys at five dollars each were not affected by being dropped, and were otherwise much more powerful.

I lingered after the meeting and made an appointment with him for the next day at his home.

Before my first interview with the Frizzly Rooster was fairly begun, I could understand his great following. He had the physique of Paul Robeson with the sex appeal and hypnotic what-ever-you-might-call-it of Rasputin. I could see that women would rise to flee from him but in mid-flight would whirl and end shivering at his feet. It was that way in fact.

His wife Mary knew how slight her hold was and continually planned to leave him.

"Only thing that's holding me here is this." She pointed to a large piece of brain-coral that was forever in a holy spot on the altar. "That's where his power is. If I could get me a piece, I could go start up a business all by myself. If I could only find a piece."

"It's very plentiful down in South Florida," I told her. "But if that piece is so precious, and you're his wife, I'd take it and let *him* get another piece."

"Oh my God! Naw! That would be my end. He's too powerful. I'm leaving him," she whispered this stealthily. "You get me a piece of that—you know."

The Frizzly Rooster entered and Mary was a different person at once. But every time that she was alone with me it was "That on the altar, you know. When you back in Florida, get me a piece. I'm leaving this man to his women." Then a quick hush and forced laughter at her husband's approach.

So I became the pupil of Reverend Father Joe Watson, "The Frizzly Rooster" and his wife, Mary, who assisted him in all things. She was "round the altar"; that is while he talked with the clients, and usually decided on whatever "work" was to be done, she "set" the things on the altar and in the jars. There was one jar in the kitchen filled with honey and sugar. All the "sweet" works were set in this jar. That is, the names and the thing desired were written on paper and thrust into this jar to stay. Already four or five hundred slips of paper had accumulated in the jar. There was another jar called the "break up" jar. It held vinegar with some unsweetened coffee added. Papers were left in this one also.

When finally it was agreed that I should come to study with them, I was put to running errands such as "dusting" houses, throwing pecans, rolling apples, as the case might be; but I was not told why the thing was being done. After two weeks of this I was taken off this phase and initiated. This was the first step towards the door of the mysteries.

My initiation consisted of the Pea Vine Candle Drill. I was told to remain five days without sexual intercourse. I must remain indoors all day the day before the initiation and fast. I might wet my throat when necessary, but I was not to swallow water.

When I arrived at the house the next morning a little before nine, as per instructions, six other persons were there,

215

so that there were nine of us—all in white except Father Watson who was in his purple robe. There was no talking. We went at once to the altar room. The altar was blazing. There were three candles around the vessel of holy water, three around the sacred sand pail, and one large cream candle burning in it. A picture of St. George and a large piece of brain coral were in the center. Father Watson dressed eight long blue candles and one black one, while the rest of us sat in the chairs around the wall. Then he lit the eight blue candles one by one from the altar and set them in the pattern of a moving serpent. Then I was called to the altar and both Father Watson and his wife laid hands on me. The black candle was placed in my hand; I was told to light it from all the other candles. I lit it at number one and pinched out the flame, and re-lit it at number two and so on till it had been lit by the eighth candle. Then I held the candle in my left hand, and by my right was conducted back to the altar by Father Watson. I was led through the maze of candles beginning at number eight. We circled numbers seven, five and three. When we reached the altar he lifted me upon the step. As I stood there, he called aloud, "Spirit! She's standing here without no home and no friends. She wants you to take her in." Then we began at number one and threaded back to number eight, circling three, five and seven. Then back to the altar again. Again he lifted me and placed me upon the step of the altar. Again the spirit was addressed as before. Then he lifted me down by placing his hands in my arm-pits. This time I did not walk at all. I was carried through the maze and I was to knock down each candle as I passed it with my foot. If I missed one, I was not to try again, but to knock it down on my way back to the altar. Arrived there the third time, I was lifted up and told to pinch out my black candle. "Now," Father told me, "you are made Boss of Candles. You have the power to light candles and put out candles, and to work with the spirits anywhere on earth."

Then all of the candles on the floor were collected and one of them handed to each of the persons present. Father took the black candle himself and we formed a ring. Everybody was given two matches each. The candles were held in our left hands, matches in the right; at a signal everybody stooped at the same moment, the matches scratched in perfect time and our candles lighted in concert. Then Father Watson walked rhythmically around the person at his right. Exchanged candles with her and went back to his place. Then that person did the same to the next so that the black candle went all around the circle and back to Father. I was then seated on a stool before the altar, sprinkled lightly with holy sand and water and confirmed as a Boss of Candles.

Then conversation broke out. We went into the next room and had a breakfast that was mostly fruit and smothered chicken. Afterwards the nine candles used in the ceremony were wrapped up and given to me to keep. They were to be used for lighting other candles only, not to be just burned in the ordinary sense.

In a few days I was allowed to hold consultations on my own. I felt insecure and said so to Father Watson.

"Of course you do now," he answered me, "but you have to learn and grow. I'm right here behind you. Talk to your people first, then come see me."

217

Within the hour a woman came to me. A man had shot and seriously wounded her husband and was in jail.

"But, honey," she all but wept, "they say ain't a thing going to be done with him. They say he got good white folks back of him and he's going to be let loose soon as the case is tried. I want him punished. Picking a fuss with my husband just to get chance to shoot him. We needs help. Somebody that can hit a straight lick with a crooked stick."

So I went in to the Frizzly Rooster to find out what I must do and he told me, "That a low fence." He meant a difficulty that was easily overcome.

"Go back and get five dollars from her and tell her to go home and rest easy. That man will be punished. When we get through with him, white folks or no white folks, he'll find a tough jury sitting on his case." The woman paid me and left in perfect confidence of Father Watson.

So he and I went into the workroom.

"Now," he said, "when you want a person punished who is already indicted, write his name on a slip of paper and put it in a sugar bowl or some other deep something like that. Now get your paper and pencil and write the name; alright now, you got it in the bowl. Now put in some red pepper, some black pepper—don't be skeered to put it in, it needs a lot. Put in one eightpenny nail, fifteen cents worth of ammonia and two door keys. You drop one key down in the bowl and you leave the other one against the side of the bowl. Now you got your bowl set. Go to your bowl every day at twelve o'clock and turn the key that is standing against the side of the bowl. That is to keep the man locked in jail. And every time you turn the key, add a little vinegar. Now I know this will do the job. All it needs is for you to do it in faith. I'm trusting this job to you entirely. Less see what you going to do. That can wait another minute. Come sit with me in the outside room and hear this woman out here that's waiting."

So we went outside and found a weakish woman in her early thirties that looked like somebody had dropped a sack of something soft on a chair.

The Frizzly Rooster put on his manner, looking like a brown, purple and gold throne-angel in a house.

"Good morning, sister er, er——"

"Murchison," she helped out.

"Tell us how you want to be helped, Sister Murchison."

She looked at me as if I was in the way and he read her eyes.

"She's alright, dear one. She's one of us. I brought her in with me to assist and help."

I thought still I was in her way but she told her business just the same.

"Too many women in my house. My husband's mother is there and she hates me and always puttin' my husband up to fight me. Look like I can't get her out of my house no ways I try. So I done come to you."

"We can fix that up in no time, dear one. Now go take a flat onion. If it was a man, I'd say a sharp pointed onion. Core the onion out, and write her name five times on paper and stuff it into the hole in the onion and close it back with the cut-out piece of onion. Now you watch when she leaves the house and then you roll the onion behind her before anybody else crosses the door-sill. And you make a wish at the same time for her to leave your house. She won't be there two weeks more." The woman paid and left.

That night we held a ceremony in the altar room on the case. We took a red candle and burnt it just enough to consume the tip. Then it was cut into three parts and the short lengths of candle were put into a glass of holy water. Then we took the glass and went at midnight to the door of the woman's house and the Frizzly Rooster held the glass in his hands and said, "In the name of the Father, in the name of the Son, in the name of the Holy Ghost." He shook the glass three times violently up and down, and the last time he threw the glass to the ground and broke it, and said, "Dismiss this woman from this place." We scarcely paused as this was said and done and we kept going and went home by another way because that was part of the ceremony.

Somebody came against a very popular preacher. "He's

getting too rich and big. I want something done to keep him down. They tell me he's 'bout to get to be a bishop. I sho' would hate for that to happen. I got forty dollars in my pocket right now for the work.''

So that night the altar blazed with the blue light. We wrote the preacher's name on a slip of paper with black ink. We took a small doll and ripped open its back and put in the paper with the name along with some bitter aloes and cayenne pepper and sewed the rip up again with the black thread. The hands of the doll were tied behind it and a black veil tied over the face and knotted behind it so that the man it represented would be blind and always do the things to keep himself from progressing. The doll was then placed in a kneeling position in a dark corner where it would not be disturbed. He would be frustrated as long as the doll was not disturbed.

When several of my jobs had turned out satisfactorily to Father Watson, he said to me, "You will do well, but you need the Black Cat Bone. Sometimes you have to be able to walk invisible. Some things must be done in deep secret, so you have to walk out of the sight of man."

First I had to get ready even to try this most terrible of experiences—getting the Black Cat Bone.

First we had to wait on the weather. When a big rain started, a new receptacle was set out in the yard. It could not be put out until the rain actually started for fear the sun might shine in it. The water must be brought inside before the weather faired off for the same reason. If lightning shone on it, it was ruined.

We finally got the water for the bath and I had to fast and "seek," shut in a room that had been purged by smoke. Twenty-four hours without food except a special wine that was fed to me every four hours. It did not make me drunk in the accepted sense of the word. I merely seemed to lose my body, my mind seemed very clear.

When dark came, we went out to catch a black cat. I must catch him with my own hands. Finding and catching black cats is hard work, unless one has been released for you to find.

Then we repaired to a prepared place in the woods and a circle drawn and "protected" with nine horseshoes. Then the fire and the pot were made ready. A roomy iron pot with a lid. When the water boiled I was to toss in the terrified, trembling cat.

When he screamed, I was told to curse him. He screamed three times, the last time weak and resigned. The lid was clamped down, the fire kept vigorously alive. At midnight the lid was lifted. Here was the moment! The bones of the cat must be passed through my mouth until one tasted bitter.

Suddenly, the Rooster and Mary rushed in close to the pot and he cried, "Look out! This is liable to kill you. Hold your nerve!" They both looked fearfully around the circle. They communicated some unearthly terror to me. Maybe I went off in a trance. Great beast-like creatures thundered up to the circle from all sides. Indescribable noises, sights, feelings. Death was at hand! Seemed unavoidable! I don't know. Many times I have thought and felt, but I always have to say the same thing. I don't know. I don't know.

Before day I was home, with a small white bone for me to carry.

FIVE

D r. Duke is a member of a disappearing school of folk magic. He spends days and nights out in the woods and swamps and is therefore known as a "swamper." A swamper is a root-and-conjure doctor who goes to the swamps and gathers his or her own herbs and roots. Most of the doctors buy their materials from regular supply houses.

He took me to the woods with him many times in order that I might learn the herbs by sight and scent. Not only is it important to be able to identify the plant, but the swamper must know when and how to gather it. For instance, the most widely used root known as John de Conqueror must be gathered before September 21st. Wonder of the World Root must be spoken to with ceremony before it is disturbed, or forces will be released that will harm whoever handles it. Snakes guard other herbs and roots and must not be killed.

He is a man past fifty but very active. He believes his power is unlimited and that nothing can stand against his medicine.

His specialty is law cases. People come to him from a great distance, and I know that he received a fee of one hundred and eighty five dollars from James Beasley, who was in the Parish prison accused of assault with attempt to murder.

For that particular case we went first to the cemetery. With his right hand he took dirt from the graves of nine children.

223

I was not permitted to do any of this because I was only a beginner with him and had not the power to approach spirits directly. They might kill me for my audacity.

The dirt was put in a new white bowl and carried back to the altar room and placed among the burning candles, facing the east. Then I was sent for sugar and sulphur. Three teaspoons each of sugar and sulphur were added to the graveyard dirt. Then he prayed over it, while I knelt opposite him. The spirits were asked to come with power more than equal to a man. Afterwards, I was sent out to buy a cheap suit of men's underclothes. This we turned wrong side out and dressed with the prepared graveyard dust. I had been told to buy a new pair .of tan socks also, and these were dressed in the same way.

As soon as Dr. Duke had been retained, I had been sent to the prison with a "dressed" Bible and Beasley was instructed to read the Thirty-fifth Psalm every day until his case should be called.

On the day he came up for trial, Dr. Duke took the new underclothes to the jail and put them on his client just before he started to march to the court room. The left sock was put on wrongside out.

Dr. Duke, like all of the conjure masters, has more than one way of doing every job. People are different and what will win with one person has no effect upon another. We had occasion to use all of the other ways of winning law suits in the course of practice.

In one hard case the prisoner had his shoes "dressed with the court." That was to keep the court under his control.

We wrote the judge's name three times, the prisoner's name three times, the district attorney's name three times, and folded the paper small, and the prisoner was told to wear it in his shoe.

Then we got some oil of rose geranium, lavender oil, verbena oil. Put three drops of oil of geranium in one-half ounce Jockey Club. Shook it and gave it to the client. He must use seven to nine drops on his person in court, but we had to dress his clothes, also. We went before court set to dress the court room and jury box and judge's stand, and have our client take perfume and rub it on his hand and rub from his face down his whole front.

To silence opposing witnesses, we took a beef tongue, nine pins, nine needles, and split the beef tongue. We wrote the names of those against our man and cut the names out and crossed them up in slit of tongue with red pepper and beef gall, and pinned the slit up with crossed needles and pins. We hung the tongue up in a chimney, tip up, and smoked the tongue for thirty-six hours. Then we took it down and put it in ice and lit on it from three to four black candles stuck in ice. Our client read the Twenty-second Psalm and Thirty-fifth also, because it was for murder. Then we asked the spirits for power more than equal to man.

So many people came to Dr. Duke to be uncrossed that he took great pains to teach me that routine. He never let me perform it, but allowed me to watch him do it many times.

Take seven lumps of incense. Take three matches to light the incense. Wave the incense before the candles on the altar. Make client bow over the incense three times. Then circle him with a glass of water three times, and repeat this three times. Fan him with the incense smoke three times—each time he bows his head. Then sprinkle him seven times with water, then lead him to and from the door and turn him around three times over incense that has been placed at the door. Then seat the client and sprinkle every corner of the room with water, three times, and also three times down the middle of the room, then go to another room and do the same. Smoke his underclothes and dress them. Don't turn the client's hand loose as he steps over the incense. Smoke him once at the door and three times at each corner. The room must be thoroughly smoked—even under the furniture—before the client leaves the room. After the evil has been driven out of him, it must also be driven from the room so it cannot return to him.

* * *

So much has been said and written about hoodoo doctors driving people away from a place that we cannot omit mentioning it. This was also one of Dr. Duke's specialties.

A woman was tired of a no-good husband; she told us about it.

"He won't work and make support for me, and he won't git on out the way and leave somebody else do it. He spend up all my money playing coon-can and kotch and then expect me to buy him a suit of clothes, and then he all the time fighting me about my wages."

"You sure you don't want him no more?" Dr. Duke asked her. "You know women get mad and say things they takes back over night."

"Lawd knows I means this. I don't want to meet him riding nor walking."

So. Dr. Duke told her what to do. She must take the right foot track of her hateful husband and parch it in an old tin frying pan. When she picks it up she must have a dark bottle with her to put the track in. Then she must get a dirt dauber nest, some cayenne pepper and parch that together and add it to the track. Put all of this into a dirty sock and tie it up. She must turn the bundle from her always as she ties it. She must carry it to the river at twelve noon. When she gets within forty feet of the river, she must run fast to the edge of the water, whirl suddenly and hurl the sock over her left shoulder into the water and never look back, and say, "Go, and go quick in the name of the Lord."

So she went off and I never saw her again.

Dr. Samuel Jenkins lives across the river in Marrero, Louisiana. He does some work, but his great specialty is reading the cards. I have seen him glance at people without being asked or without using his cards and making the most startling statements that all turned out to be true.

226

A young matron went out with me to Dr. Jenkins's one day just for the sake of the ride. He glanced at her and told her that she was deceiving her husband with a very worthless fellow. That she must stop at once or she would be found out. Her husband was most devoted, but once he mistrusted her he would accept no explanations. This was late in October, and her downfall came in December.

Dr. Charles S. Johnson, the well-known Negro sociologist, came to New Orleans on business while I was there and since I had to see Dr. Jenkins, he went with me. Without being asked, Dr. Jenkins told him that he would receive a sudden notice to go on a long trip. The next day, Dr. Johnson received a wire sending him to West Africa.

Once Dr. Jenkins put a light on a wish of mine that a certain influential white woman would help me, and assured me that she would never lose interest in me as long as she lived. The next morning at ten o'clock I received a wire from her stating that she would stand by me as long as she lived. He did this sort of thing day after day, and the faith in him is huge. Let me state here that most of his clients are white and upper-class people at that.

In appearance he is a handsome robust dark-skinned man around forty.

There are many superstitions concerning the dead.

All over the South and in the Bahamas the spirits of the dead have great power which is used chiefly to harm. It will be noted how frequently graveyard dust is required in the practice of hoodoo, goofer dust as it is often called.

It is to be noted that in nearly all of the killing ceremonies the cemetery is used.

The Ewe-speaking peoples[1] of the west coast of Africa all make offerings of food and drink—particularly libations of palm wine and banana beer upon the graves of the ancestor.

[1] A West African nation from which many slaves came to America.

227

It is to be noted in America that the spirit is always given a pint of good whiskey. He is frequently also paid for his labor in cash.

It is well known that church members are buried with their feet to the east so that they will arise on that last day facing the rising sun. Sinners are buried facing the opposite direction. The theory is that sunlight will do them harm rather than good, as they will no doubt wish to hide their faces from an angry God.

Ghosts cannot cross water—so that if a hoodoo doctor wishes to sic a dead spirit upon a man who lives across water, he must first hold the mirror ceremony to fetch the victim from across the water.

People who die from the sick bed may walk any night, but Friday night is the night of the people who died in the dark—who were executed. These people have never been in the light. They died with the black cap over the face. Thus, they are blind. On Friday nights they visit the folks who died from sick beds and they lead the blind ones wherever they wish to visit.

Ghosts feel hot and smell faintish. According to testimony all except those who died in the dark may visit their former homes every night at twelve o'clock. But they must be back in the cemetery at two o'clock sharp or they will be shut out by the watchman and must wander about for the rest of the night. That is why the living are frightened by seeing ghosts at times. Some spirit has lingered too long with the living person it still loves and has been shut out from home.

Pop Drummond of Fernandina, Fla., says they are not asleep at all. They "Sings and has church and has a happy time, but some are spiteful and show themselves to scare folks." Their voices are high and thin. Some ghosts grow very fat if they get plenty to eat. They are very fond of honey. Some who have been to the holy place wear seven-starred crowns and are very "suscautious" and sensible.

Dirt from sinners' graves is supposed to be very powerful, but some hoodoo doctors will use only that from the graves of infants. They say that the sinner's grave is powerful to kill, but his spirit is likely to get unruly and kill others for the pleasure of killing. It is too dangerous to commission.

The spirit newly released from the body is likely to be destructive. This is why a cloth is thrown over the face of a clock in the death chamber and the looking glass is covered over. The clock will never run again, nor will the mirror ever cast any more reflections if they are not covered so that the spirit cannot see them.

When it rains at a funeral it is said that God wishes to wash their tracks off the face of the earth, they were so displeasing to him.

If a murder victim is buried in a sitting position, the murderer will be speedily brought to justice. The victim sitting before the throne is able to demand that justice be done. If he is lying prone he cannot do this.

A fresh egg in the hand of a murder victim will prevent the murderer's going far from the scene. The egg represents life, and so the dead victim is holding the life of the murderer in his hand.

Sometimes the dead are offended by acts of the living and slap the face of the living. When this happens, the head is slapped one-sided and the victim can never straighten his neck. Speak gently to ghosts, and do not abuse the children of the dead.

It is not good to answer the first time that your name is called. It may be a spirit and if you answer it, you will die shortly. They never call more than once at a time, so by waiting you will miss probable death.[2]

[2]See Appendix for superstitions concerning sudden death.

SIX

✦

Before telling of my experiences with Kitty Brown I want to relate the following conjure stories which illustrate the attitude of Negroes of the Deep South toward this subject.

Old Lady Celestine went next door one day and asked her neighbor to lend her a quarter.

"I want it all in nickels, please, yes."

"Ah don't have five nickels, Tante Celestine, but Ah'll send a boy to get them for you," the obliging neighbor told her. So she did and Celestine took the money with a cold smile and went home.

Soon after another neighbor came in and the talk came around to Celestine.

"Celestine is not mad any more about the word we had last week. She was just in to pay me a visit."

"Humph!" snorted the neighbor, "maybe she come in to dust yo' door step. You shouldn't let people in that hate you. They come to do you harm."

"Oh no, she was very nice. She borrowed a quarter from me."

"Did she ask for small change?"

"Yes."

"Then she is still mad and means to harm you. They always

231

try to get small change from the ones they wish to harm. Celestine always trying to hurt somebody."

"You think so? You make me very skeered."

"Go send your son to see what she is doing. Ah'll bet she has a candle on yo' money now."

The boy was sent and came running back in terror. "Oh Mamma, come look at what Tante Celestine is doin'."

The two women crept to the crack in old Celestine's door. There in midsummer was the chimney ablaze with black candles. A cup in front of each candle, holding the money. The old woman was stretched out on her belly with her head in the fire-place twirling a huge sieve with a pair of shears stuck in the mesh, whirling and twirling the sieve and muttering the name of the woman who had loaned her the five nickels.

"She is cutting my heart with the shears!" the woman gasped; "the murderer should die." She burst into the house without ceremony and all the Treme[1] heard about the fight that followed.

Mrs. Grant lived down below Canal Street and was a faithful disciple of Dr. Strong, a popular hoodoo doctor who lived on Urquhart Street near St. Claude.

One hot summer night Mr. Grant couldn't sleep, so he sat on the upper balcony in his underwear chewing tobacco. Mrs. Grant was in bed.

A tall black woman lived two blocks down the street. She and Mrs. Grant had had some words a few days past and the black woman had been to a hoodoo doctor and bought a powder to throw at Mrs. Grant's door. She had waited till the hour of two in the morning to do it. Just as she was "dusting" the door, Mr. Grant on the balcony spit and some of the tobacco juice struck the woman.

She had no business at the Grant house at all, let alone at two o'clock in the morning throwing War Powder against the door. But even so, she stepped back and gave Mr. Grant a piece of her mind that was highly seasoned. It was a splendid

[1]The old French quarter of New Orleans.

bit of Creole invective art. He was very apologetic, but Mrs. Grant came to the door to see what was the trouble.

Her enemy had retreated, but as soon as she opened the door she saw the white powder against the door and on the steps. Moreover, there was an egg shell on each step.

Mrs. Grant shrieked in terror and slammed the door shut. She grabbed the chamber pot and ran out of the back door. Next door were three boys. She climbed into their back yard and woke up the family. She must have some urine from the boys. This she carried through the neighbor's front gate to her own door and dashed it over the door and steps. One of the boys was paid to take the egg shells away. She could not enter her front door until the conjure was removed. The neighborhood was aroused—she must have a can of lye. She must have some river water in which to dissolve the lye. All this was dashed against the door and steps.

Early next morning she was at the door of Dr. Strong. He congratulated her on the steps she had already taken, but told her that to be sure she had counteracted all the bad work, she must draw the enemy's "wine." That is, she must injure her enemy enough to draw blood.

So Mrs. Grant hurried home and half-filled three quart bottles with water. She put these in a basket, and the basket on her arm, and set out for the restaurant where the night-sprinkler-of-powders was a cook.

She asked to speak to her, and as soon as she appeared—bam! bam! bam! went the bottles over her head and the "wine" flowed. But she fought back and in the fracas she bit Mrs. Grant's thumb severely, drawing *her* "wine."

This complicated affairs again. Something must be done to neutralize this loss of blood. She hurried home and called one of the boys next door and said: "Son, here's five dollars. Go get me a black chicken—not a white feather on him—and keep the change for your trouble."

The chicken was brought. She seized her husband's razor and split the live bird down the breast and thrust her fist inside. As the hot blood and entrails enveloped her hand, she went into a sort of frenzy, shouting: "I got her, I got her, I got her now!"

A wealthy planter in Middle Georgia was very arrogant in his demeanor towards his Negro servants. He boasted of being "unreconstructed" and that he didn't allow no niggers to sass him.

A Negro family lived on his place and worked for him. The father, it seems, was the yard man, the mother, the cook. The boys worked in the field and a daughter worked in the house and waited on the table.

There was a huge rib-roast of beef one night for dinner. The white man spoke very sharply for some reason to the girl and she sassed right back. He jumped to his feet and seized the half-eaten roast by the naked ribs and struck her with the vertebrate end. The blow landed squarely on her temple and she dropped dead.

The cook was attracted to the dining-room door by the tumult. The white man resumed his seat and was replenishing his plate. He coolly told the mother of the dead girl to "Call Dave and you all take that sow up off the floor."

Dave came and the parents bore away the body of their daughter, the mother weeping.

Now Dave was known to dabble in hoodoo. The Negroes around both depended upon him and feared him.

He came back to clear away the blood of the murdered girl. He came with a pail and scrubbing brush. But first he sopped his handkerchief in the blood and put it into his pocket. Then he washed up the floor.

That night the Negro family moved away. They knew better than to expect any justice. They knew better than to make too much fuss about what had happened.

But less than two weeks later, the planter looked out of his window one night and thought he saw Dave running across the lawn away from the house. He put up the window and called to demand what he was doing on his place, but the figure disappeared in the trees. He shut the window and went to his wife's room to tell her about it and found her in laughing hysteria. She laughed for three days despite all that the doctors did to quiet her. On the fourth day she became maniacal and attacked her husband. Shortly it was realized that she was hopelessly insane and she had to be put in an institution. She made no attempt to hurt anyone except her husband. She was gentleness itself with her two children.

The plantation became intolerable to the planter, so he decided to move to more cheerful surroundings with his children. He had some friends in South Carolina, so he withdrew his large account at the bank and transferred it to South Carolina and set up a good home with the help of a housekeeper.

Two years passed and he became more cheerful. Then one night he heard steps outside his window and looked out. He saw a man—a Negro. He was sure it was Old Dave. The man ran away as before. He called and ran from the house in pursuit. He was determined to kill him if he caught him, for he began to fear ambush from the family of the girl he had murdered. He ran back to get his son, his gun and the dogs to trail the Negro.

As he burst into the front door he was knocked down by a blow on the head, but was not unconscious. His twenty year old son was raving and screaming above him with a poker in his hand. He struck blow after blow, his father dodging and covering himself as best he could. The housekeeper rushed up and caught the poker from behind and saved the man on the floor. The boy was led away weeping by the woman, but renewed his attack upon his father later in the night. This kept up for more than a month before the devoted parent would consent to his confinement in an institution for the criminally insane.

This was a crushing blow to the proud and wealthy ex-planter. He once more gathered up his goods and moved away. But a year later the visitation returned. He saw Dave. He was sure of it. This time he locked himself in his room and asked the housekeeper through the door about his daughter. She reported the girl missing. He decided at once that his black enemies had carried off his daughter Abbie. He made

235

ready to pursue. He unlocked his door and stepped into the hall to put on his overcoat. When he opened the closet his daughter pointed a gun in his face and pulled the trigger. The gun snapped. It happened to be unloaded. She had hidden in the closet to shoot him whenever he emerged from his room. Her disordered brain had overlooked the cartridges.

So he moved to Baltimore—out in a fashionable neighborhood. The nurse who came to look after his deranged daughter had become his mistress. He skulked about, fearful of every Negro man he saw. At no time must any Negro man come upon his premises. He kept guns loaded and handy, but hidden from his giggling, simpering daughter, Abbie, who now and then attacked him with her fists. His love for his children was tremendous. He even contrived to have his son released in his charge. But two weeks later, as he drove the family out, the young man sitting in the rear seat attacked him from behind and would have killed him but for the paramour and a traffic officer.

"When I was a boy[2] about ten years old there was a man named Levi Conway whom I knew well. He operated a ferry and had money and was highly respected by all. He was very careful about what he wore. He was tall and brown and wore a pompadour. He usually wore a broad-brimmed Stetson.

"He began to change. People thought he was going crazy. He owned lots of residential property but he quickly lost everything in some way that nobody seemed to understand. He grew careless in his dress and became positively untidy. He even got to the point where he'd buy ten cents worth of whiskey and drink it right out of the bottle.

"He began to pick up junk—old boilers, stones, wheels, pieces of harness, etc., and drag it around for miles every day. Then he'd bring it home and pile it in his backyard. This kept up for ten years or more.

"Finally he got sick in bed and couldn't get up.

[2]Told by Pierre Landeau of New Orleans.

"Tante Lida kept house for him. She was worried over his sickness, so she decided to get a woman from the Treme to find out what was wrong. The woman came. She was about fifty with a sore on her nose.

"She looked at Levi in the bed. Then she came out to Tante Lida. 'Sure, something has been done. I don't believe I can do anything to save him now, but I can tell you who did the work. You fix a place for me to stay here tonight and in the morning I will tell you.'

"Early next morning she sent for a heart of sheep or beef. She had them get her a package of needles and a new kettle. She lit a wood fire in the yard and filled the kettle one-third full of water and stood over the pot with the heart. She stuck the needles in one by one, muttering and murmuring as she stuck them in. When the water was boiling hard she dropped the heart in. It was about eleven o'clock in the morning.

" 'Now we shall know who has done this thing to Levi. In a few minutes the one who did it will come and ask for two things. Don't let him have either.'

"In a few minutes in came Pere Voltaire, a man whom all of us knew. He asked how Levi was. They told him pretty bad! He asked would they let him have two eggs and they said they had none. Then he asked would they lend him the wheelbarrow, and they said it wasn't there. The old woman winked and said, 'That is he.'

"He went on off. Then she told them to look into the pot, and they did. The heart was gone.

"A week later Levi died.

"This is the funny part. Some time after that my older brother, my cousin and I rowed over to the west bank of the river. Just knocking about as boys will, we found an old leaky boat turned upside down on the bank just out of reach of the water. I wondered who owned the piece of trash. My brother told me it belonged to Pere Voltaire. I said: 'Why doesn't he get a decent boat? This is too rotten to float.'

"I turned it over and found a great deal of junk under it—bundles tied up in rags, old bottles and cans and the like.

So I started to throwing the stuff into the water and my cousin helped me. We pushed the boat in, too. My brother tried to stop us.

"I forget now how it was that Pere Voltaire knew we did that. But two days later I began to shake as if I had an ague. Nothing the doctors could do stopped me. Two days later my cousin began to shake and two days after that my brother started to shake. It was three or four months before we could be stopped. But my brother stopped first. Then my cousin, then at last I stopped."

SEVEN

Kitty Brown is a well-known hoodoo doctor of New Orleans, and a Catholic. She liked to make marriages and put lovers together. She is squat, black and benign. Often when we had leisure, she told funny stories. Her herb garden was pretty full and we often supplied other doctors with plants. Very few raise things since the supply houses carry about everything that is needed. But sometimes a thing is wanted fresh from the ground. That's where Kitty's garden came in.

When the matter of my initiation came up she said, "In order for you to reach the spirit somebody has got to suffer. I'll suffer for you because I'm strong. It might be the death of you."

It was in October 1928, when I was a pupil of hers, that I shared in a hoodoo dance. This was not a pleasure dance, but ceremonial. In another generation African dances were held in Congo Square, now Beauregard Square. Those were held for social purposes and were of the same type as the fire dances and jumping dances of the present in the Bahamas. But the hoodoo dance is done for a specific purpose. It is always a case of death-to-the-enemy that calls forth a dance. They are very rare even in New Orleans now, even within the most inner circle, and no layman ever participates, nor has ever been allowed to witness such a ceremony.

This is how the dance came to be held. I sat with my teacher in her front room as the various cases were disposed of. It was my business to assist wherever possible, such as running errands for materials or verifying addresses, locating materials in the various drawers and cabinets, undressing and handling patients, writing out formulas as they were dictated, and finally making "hands."[1] At last, of course, I could do all of the work while she looked on and made corrections where necessary.

This particular day, a little before noon, came Rachael Roe. She was dry with anger, hate, outraged confidence and desire for revenge. John Doe had made violent love to her; had lain in her bed and bosom for the last three years; had received of Rachael everything material and emotional a woman can give. They had both worked and saved and had contributed to a joint savings account. Now, only the day before yesterday, he had married another. He had lured a young and pretty girl to his bed with Rachael's earnings; yes. Had set up housekeeping with Rachael's sweat and blood. She had gone to him and he had laughed at his former sweetheart, yes. The police could do nothing, no. The bank was sorry, but they could do nothing, no. So Rachael had come to Kitty.

Did she still love her John Doe? Perhaps; she didn't know. If he would return to her she should strive to forget, but she was certain he'd not return. How could he? But if he were dead she could smile again, yes—could go back to her work and save some more money, yes. Perhaps she might even meet a man who could restore her confidence in menfolk.

Kitty appraised her quickly. "A dance could be held for him that would carry him away right now, but they cost something."

"How much?"

"A whole lot. How much kin you bring me?"

"I got thirty-seven dollars."

"Dat ain't enough. Got to pay de dancers and set de table."

---

[1]Manufacturing certain luck charms.

240

One hundred dollars was agreed upon. It was paid by seven o'clock that same night. We were kept very busy, for the dance was set from ten to one the next day, those being bad hours. I ran to certain addresses to assemble a sort of college of bishops to be present and participate. The table was set with cake, wine, roast duck and barbecued goat.

By nine-thirty the next morning the other five participants were there and had dressed for the dance. A dispute arose about me. Some felt I had not gone far enough to dance. I could wait upon the altar, but not take the floor. Finally I was allowed to dance, as a delegate for my master who had a troublesome case of neuritis. The food was being finished off in the kitchen.

Promptly on the stroke of ten Death mounted his black draped throne and assumed his regal crown, Death being represented by a rudely carved wooden statue, bust length. A box was draped in black sateen and Kitty placed him upon it and set his red crown on. She hobbled back to her seat. I had the petition and the name of the man written on seven slips of paper—one for each participant. I was told to stick them in Death's grinning mouth. I did so, so that the end of each slip protruded. At the command I up-ended nine black tapers that had been dressed by a bath in whiskey and bad vinegar, and bit off the butt end to light, calling upon Death to take notice. As I had been instructed, I said: "Spirit of Death, take notice I am fixing your candles for you. I want you to hear me." I said this three times and the assembly gave three snaps with the thumb and middle finger.

The candles were set upside down and lighted on the altar, three to the left of Death, three to the right, and three before him.

I resumed my seat, and everyone was silent until Kitty was possessed. The exaltation caught like fire. Then B. arose drunkenly and danced a few steps. The clapping began lightly. He circled the room, then prostrated himself before the altar, and, getting to his hands and knees, with his teeth pulled one of the slips from the jaws of Death. He turned a violent somersault and began the dance, not intricate, but violent and muscle-twitching.

We were to dance three hours, and the time was divided equally, so that the more participants the less time each was called upon to dance. There were six of us, since Kitty could not actively participate, so that we each had forty minutes to dance. Plenty of liquor was provided so that when one appeared exhausted the bottle was pressed to his lips and he danced on. But the fury of the rhythm more than the stimulant kept the dancers going. The heel-patting was a perfect drum rhythm, and the hand clapping had various stimulating breaks. At any rate no one fell from exhaustion, though I know that even I, the youngest, could not have danced continuously on an ordinary dance floor unsupported by a partner for that length of time.

Nearly all ended on the moment in a twitchy collapse, and the next most inspired prostrated himself and began his dance with the characteristic somersault. Death was being continuously besought to follow the footsteps of John Doe. There was no regular formula. They all "talked to him" in their own way, the others calling out to the dancer to "talk to him." Some of the postures were obscene in the extreme. Some were grotesque, limping steps of old men and women. Some were mere agile leapings. But the faces! That is where the dedication lay.

When the fourth dancer had finished and lay upon the floor retching in every muscle, Kitty was taken. The call had come for her. I could not get upon the floor quickly enough for the others and was hurled before the altar. It got me there and I danced, I don't know how, but at any rate, when we sat about the table later, all agreed that Mother Kitty had done well to take me.

I have neglected to say that one or two of the dancers remained upon the floor "in the spirit" after their dance and had to be lifted up and revived at the end.

Death had some of all the food placed before him. An uncorked pint of good whiskey was right under his nose. He was paid fifteen cents and remained on his throne until one o'clock that night. Then all of the food before him was taken up with the tablecloth on which it rested and was thrown into the Mississippi River.

The person danced upon is not supposed to live more than nine days after the dance. I was very eager to see what would happen in this case. But five days after the dance John Doe deserted his bride for the comforting arms of Rachael and she hurried to Mother Kitty to have the spell removed. She said he complained of breast pains and she was fearfully afraid for him. So I was sent to get the beef heart out of the cemetery (which had been put there as of the routine), and John and Rachael made use of the new furniture bought for his bride. I think he feared that Rachael might have him fixed, so he probably fled to her as soon as the zest for a new wife had abated.

Kitty began by teaching me various ways of bringing back a man or woman who had left his or her mate. She had plenty to work on, too. In love cases the client is often told what to do at home. Minnie Foster was the best customer Kitty had. She wanted something for every little failing in her lover. Kitty said to her one day, "You must be skeered of yourself with that man of yours."

"No, Ma'am, I ain't. But I love him and I just want to make sure. Just you give me something to make his love more stronger."

"Alright, Minnie, I'll do it, but you ain't got no reason to be so unsettled with me behind you. Do like I say and you'll be alright.

"Use six red candles. Stick sixty pins in each candle—thirty on each side. Write the name of your sweetheart three times on a small square of paper and stick it underneath the candle. Burn one of these prepared candles each night for six nights. Make six slips of paper and write the name of the loved one once on each slip. Then put a pin in the paper on all four sides of the name. Each morning take up the sixty pins left from the burning of the candles, and save them. Then smoke the slip of paper with the four pins in it in incense smoke and bury it with the pins under your door step. The piece of paper with the name written on it three times, upon which each candle stands while burning, must be kept each day until the last candle is burned. Then bury it in the same hole with the rest. When you are sticking the pins in the candles, keep repeating: 'Tumba Walla, Bumba Walla, bring Gabe Staggers back to me.' "

Minnie paid her five dollars, thanked her loudly and hurried off to tighten the love-shackles on her Gabriel. But the following week she was back again.

"Ain't you got dat man to you wishes, yet, Minnie?" Kitty asked, half in fun and half in impatience.

"He love me, I b'lieve, but he gone off to Mobile with a construction gang and I got skeered he might not come back. Something might delay him on his trip."

"Oh, alright Minnie, go do like I say and he'll sure be back. Write the name of the absent party six times on paper. Put the paper in a water glass with two tablespoons full of quicksilver on it. Write his or her name three times each on six candles and burn one on a window sill in the daytime for six days."

Minnie paid and went home, but a week later she was back, washed down in tears. So Kitty gave her a stronger help.

"This is bound to bring him. Can't help it, Minnie. Now go home and stop fretting and do this:

"Write his name three times. Dig a hole in the ground. Get a left-foot soiled-sock from him secretly. His hatband may be used also. Put the paper with the name in the hole first. Then the sock or hatband. Then light a red candle on top of it all and burn it. Put a spray of Sweet Basil in a glass of water beside the candle. Light the candle at noon and burn until one. Light it again at six P.M. and burn till seven. (Always pinch out a candle—never blow it.) After the candle is lit, turn a barrel over the hole. When you get it in place, knock on it three times to call the spirit and say: 'Tumba Walla, Bumba Walla, bring Gabriel Staggers home to me.' "

We saw nothing of Minnie for six weeks, then she came in another storm of tears.

"Miss Kitty, Gabriel done got to de place I can't tell him his eye is black. What can I do to rule de man I love?"

"Do like I say, honey, and you can rule. Get his sock. Take one silver dime, some hair from his head or his hatband. Lay the sock out on a table, bottom up. Write his name three times and put it on the sock. Place the dime on the name and the hair or hatband on the dime. Put a piece of 'he' Lodestone[2] on top of the hair and sprinkle it with steel dust. As you do this, say, 'Feed the he, feed the she.' That is what you call feeding the Lodestone. Then fold the sock heel on the toe and roll it all up together, tight. Pin the bundle by crossing two needles. Then wet it with whiskey and set it up over a door. And don't 'low him to go off no more, do you going to lose all control.

"Now listen, honey, this is the way to change a man's mind about going away: Take the left shoe, set it up straight, then roll it one-half over first to the right, then to the left. Roll it to a coming-in door and point it straight in the door, and he can't leave. Hatband or sock can be made into a ball and rolled the same way: but it must be put under the sill or over the door."

Once Sis Cat got hongry and caught herself a rat and set herself down to eat 'im. Rat tried and tried to git loose but Sis Cat was too fast and strong. So jus' as de cat started to eat 'im he says, "Hol' on dere, Sis Cat! Ain't you got no manners atall? You going set up to de table and eat 'thout washing yo' face and hands?"

Sis Cat was mighty hongry but she hate for de rat to think she ain't got no manners, so she went to de water and washed her face and hands and when she got back de rat was gone.

So de cat caught herself a rat again and set down to eat. So de Rat said, "Where's yo' manners at, Sis Cat? You going to eat 'thout washing yo' face and hands?"

"Oh, Ah got plenty manners," de cat told 'im. "But Ah eats

[2]Magnetic iron ore.

mah dinner and washes mah face and uses mah manners afterwards." So she et right on 'im and washed her face and hands. And cat's been washin' after eatin' ever since.

I'm sitting here like Sis Cat, washing my face and usin' my manners.

GLOSSARY

Jack or John (not John Henry) is the great human culture hero in Negro folklore. He is like Daniel in Jewish folklore, the wish-fulfillment hero of the race. The one who, nevertheless, or in spite of laughter, usually defeats Ole Massa, God and the Devil. Even when Massa seems to have him in a hopeless dilemma he wins out by a trick. Brer Rabbit, Jack (or John) and the Devil are continuations of the same thing.   p. 9

Woofing is a sort of aimless talking. A man half seriously flirts with a girl, half seriously threatens to fight or brags of his prowess in love, battle or in financial matters. The term comes from the purposeless barking of dogs at night.   p. 13

Testimony. There is a meeting called a "love-feast" in the Methodist Church and an "experience meeting" with the Baptists. It is held once a month, either on a week-night or a Sunday morning preceding the Communion service. It is a Protestant confessional. No one is supposed to take communion unless he is on good terms with all of the other church members and is free from sin otherwise. The love-feast gives opportunity for public expression of good-will to the world. There are three set forms with variations. (1) The person who expects to testify raises a hymn. After a verse or two he or she speaks expressing (a) love for everybody, (b) joy at being present, (c) tells of the determination to stay in the field to the end. (2) Singing of a "hot" spiritual, giving the right hand of fellowship to the entire church, a shouting, tearful finish. (3) (a) Expresses joy at being present, (b) recites incident of conversion, telling in detail the visions seen and voices heard, (c) expresses determination to hold out to the end.   p. 20

It is singular that God never finds fault, never censures the Negro. He sees faults but expects nothing different. He is lacking in bitterness as is the Negro story-teller himself in circumstances that ordinarily would call for pity.   p. 29

The devil is not the terror that he is in European folk-lore. He is a powerful trickster who often competes successfully with God. There is a strong suspicion that the devil is an extension of the story-makers while God is the supposedly impregnable white masters, who are nevertheless defeated by the Negroes.   p. 48

John Henry. This is a song of the railroad camps and is suited to the spiking rhythm, though it is, like all the other work songs, sung in the jooks and other social places. It is not a very old song, being younger by far than Casey Jones and like that song being the celebration of an incidence of bravery. John Henry is not as widely distributed as "Mule on de Mount," "Uncle Bud" or several of the older songs, though it has a better air than most of the work songs. *John Henry has no place in Negro folk-lore except in this one circumstance.* The story told in the ballad is of John Henry, who is a great steel-driver, growing jealous when the company installs a steam drill. He boasts that he can beat the steam drill hammering home spikes, and asks his boss for a 9-pound hammer saying that if he has a good hammer he can beat the steam drill driving. The hammer is provided and he attempts to beat the drill. He does so for nearly an hour, then his heart fails him and he drops dead from exhaustion. It is told in direct dialogue for the greater part. The last three verses show internal evidence of being interpolated from English ballads. Judge the comparative newness of the song by the fact that he is competing with something as recent as a steam drill. For music for "John Henry" see Appendix.   p. 55

Long House. Another name for jook. Sometimes means a mere bawdy house. A long low building cut into rooms that all open on a common porch. A woman lives in each of the rooms.   p. 67

Blue Baby. Nicknames such as this one given from appearances or acts, i.e. "Blue Baby" was so black he looked blue. "Tush Hawg," a rough man; full of fight like a wild boar. p. 68

One notes that among the animals the rabbit is the trickster hero. Lacking in size, strength and natural weapons such as teeth and claws, he continues to overcome by cunning. There are other minor characters that are heroic, but Brer Rabbit is first. In Florida, Brer Gopher, the dry-land tortoise, is also a hero and perhaps nearly equal to the rabbit. p. 109

The colored preacher, in his cooler passages, strives for grammatical correctness, but goes natural when he warms up. The "hah" is a breathing device, done rhythmically to punctuate the lines. The congregation wants to hear the preacher breathing or "straining." p. 139

Georgia Skin Game. Any number of "Pikers" can play at a time, but there are two "principals" who do the dealing. Both of them are not dealing at the same time, however. But when the first one who deals "falls" the other principal takes the deal. If he in turn falls it goes back to the first dealer. The principals draw the first two cards. The pikers draw from the third card on. Unless a player or players want to "scoop one in the rough," he can choose his own card which can be any card in the deck except the card on top of the deck and that one goes to the dealer. The dealer charges anything he pleases for the privilege of "scooping," the money being put in sight. It is the player's bet. After the ones who wish to have scooped, then the dealer begins to "turn" the cards. That is, flipping them off the deck face upwards and the pikers choose a card each from among those turned off to bet on. Sometimes several pikers are on the same card. When all have selected their cards and have their bets down, they begin to chant "Turn 'em" to the dealer. He turns them until a player falls. That is, a card like the one he is holding falls. For instance one holds the 10 of hearts. When another 10 falls he loses. Then the players cry "hold 'em" until the player selects another clean card, one that has not fallen. The fresh side bets are down and the chant "turn 'em" and the singing "Let de deal go Down" until the deck is run out. p. 143

APPENDIX

I

NEGRO SONGS WITH MUSIC

JOHN HENRY

1 John Henry driving on the right hand side,
   Steam drill driving on the left,
   Says, 'fore I'll let your steam drill beat me down
   I'll hammer my fool self to death,
   Hammer my fool self to death.

2 John Henry told his Captain,
   When you go to town
   Please bring me back a nine pound hammer
   And I'll drive your steel on down.
   And I'll drive your steel on down.

3 John Henry told his Captain,
   Man ain't nothing but a man,
   And 'fore I'll let that steam drill beat me down
   I'll die with this hammer in my hand,
   Die with this hammer in my hand.

4 Captain ast John Henry,
   What is that storm I hear?
   He says Cap'n that ain't no storm,
   'Tain't nothing but my hammer in the air,
   Nothing but my hammer in the air.

5 John Henry told his Captain,
   Bury me under the sills of the floor,
   So when they get to playing good old Georgy skin,
   Bet 'em fifty to a dollar more,
   Fifty to a dollar more.

6 John Henry had a little woman,
   The dress she wore was red,
   Says I'm going down the track,
   And she never looked back.
   I'm going where John Henry fell dead,
   Going where John Henry fell dead.

7 Who's going to shoe your pretty li'l' feet?
   And who's going to glove your hand?
   Who's going to kiss your dimpled cheek?
   And who's going to be your man?
   Who's going to be your man?

8 My father's going to shoe my pretty li'l' feet;
   My brother's going to glove my hand;
   My sister's going to kiss my dimpled cheek;
   John Henry's going to be my man,
   John Henry's going to be my man.

9 Where did you get your pretty li'l' dress?
   The shoes you wear so fine?
   I got my shoes from a railroad man,
   My dress from a man in the mine,
   My dress from a man in the mine.

JOHN HENRY

(Work Song Series)

From the Zora Neale Hurston
Collection of Negro Folklore

Arranged by C. Spencer Tocus

Moderato

PIANO mf

VOICE

1. John Hen-ry driv-ing on the right hand side,

Steam drill driv-ing on the left, Says, 'fore I'll let your steam drill

beat me down   I'll ham-mer my fool self to

death,   Ham-mer my fool self to death.

REFRAIN   (spoken)

Hm ....   Hm .... hah!

EAST COAST BLUES

1 Don't you hear that East Coast when she blows,
   Oh, don't you hear that East Coast when she blows,
   Ah, don't you hear that East Coast when she blows.

2 I'm going down that long lonesome road,
   Oh, I'm going down that long lonesome road,
   Ah, I'm going down that long lonesome road.

3 I'm going where the chilly winds don't blow,
   Oh, I'm going where the chilly winds don't blow,
   Ah, I'm going where the chilly winds don't blow.

4 You treat me mean you sho going see it again,
   Oh, you treat me mean you sho going see it again,
   Ah, you treat me mean you sho going see it again.

5 I love you honey but your woman got me barred,
   Oh, I love you honey but your woman got me barred,
   Ah, I love you honey but your woman got me barred.

6 Love ain't nothing but the easy going heart disease,
   Oh, love ain't nothing but the easy going heart disease,
   Ah, love ain't nothing but the easy going heart disease.

EAST COAST BLUES

(Social Song Series)

From the Zora Neale Hurston Collection of Negro Folklore

PLEASE DON'T DRIVE ME

(Convict Song)

*From the Zora Neale Hurston
Collection of Negro Folklore*

Arranged by Porter Grainger

1 Please don't drive me because I'm blind,
   B'lieve I kin make it if I take my time.

2 Lift up de hammer and let it fall down,
   It's a hard rocky bottom and it must be found.

3 De cap'n say hurry, de boss say run,
   I got a damn good notion not to do nary one.

COLD RAINY DAY

Cold rain-y day. Some old cold rain-y day I'll be back some old cold rain-y day. Old Smok-ey Joe Lawd, he died on the road Say-ing I'll be back some day.

Cold rain-y day. Some old cold rain-y day I'll be back some old cold

rain-y day. All I want is my rail-road fare, Take me back

where I was born. Oh, the rocks may be my pil-low, Lawd, the sand may

be my bed. I'll be back some old cold rain-y day. Cold rain-y day,

Some old cold rain-y day, I'll be back some old cold rain-y day.

1   Cold rainy day, some old cold, rainy day,
    I'll be back some old cold, rainy day.

2   All I want is my railroad fare,
    Take me back where I was born.

3   Ole Smoky Joe, Lawd, he died on the road
    Saying I'll be back some day.

4   Oh, the rocks may be my pillow
    Lawd, the sand may be my bed,
    I'll be back some old cold, rainy day.

GOING TO SEE MY LONG-HAIRED BABE

SOLOIST:

Oh Lulu! Oh Gal!
Want to see you, so bad.

CHORUS:

Going to see my long-haired babe;
Going to see my long-haired babe,
Oh Lawd I'm going 'cross the water
See my long-haired babe.

SOLOIST:

What you reckon Mr. Treadwell
Said to Mr. Goff,
Lawd I b'lieve I'll go South,
Pay them poor boys off.

CHORUS:

SOLOIST:

Lawd I ast that woman
Lemme be her kid,
And she looked at me
And began to smile.

CHORUS:

SOLOIST:

Oh Lulu! Oh Gal!

ALL:

Want to see you, so bad.

GOING TO SEE MY LONG-HAIRED BABE

(Spiking Rhythm)

Oh, Lu-lu, Oh gal, want to see you, so bad. Going to see my long-haired babe, Going to see my long-haired babe. Oh Lawd, I'm going 'cross the

wa-ter see my long-haired babe. Lawd, I ast dat wom-an

lem-me be— her kid And she looked at me—and be-gan to smile.

After last verse

Oh, -Lu-lu, Oh gal, Want to see you so bad.

263

CAN'T YOU LINE IT?

NOTE: This song is common to the railroad camps. It is suited to the "lining" rhythm. That is, it fits the straining of the men at the lining bars as the rail is placed in position to be spiked down.

1 When I get in Illinois
   I'm going to spread the news about the Florida boys.
   Chorus: (All men straining at rail in concert.)
   Shove it over! Hey, hey, can't you line it?
   (Shaking rail.) Ah, shack-a-lack-a-lack-a-lack-a-lack-a-lack-a-lack.

   (Grunt as they move rail.) Can't you move it? Hey, hey, can't
      you try.

2 Tell what the hobo told the bum,
   If you get any corn-bread save me some.
CHORUS:

3 A nickle's worth of bacon, and a dime's worth of lard,
   I would buy more but the time's too hard.
CHORUS:

4 Wonder what's the matter with the walking boss,
   It's done five-thirty and he won't knock off.
CHORUS:

5 I ast my Cap'n what's the time of day,
   He got mad and throwed his watch away.
CHORUS:

6 Cap'n got a pistol and he try to play bad,
   But I'm going to take it if he make me mad.
CHORUS:

7 Cap'n got a burner* I'd like to have,
   A 32:20 with a shiny barrel.
CHORUS:

8 De Cap'n can't read, de Cap'n can't write,
   How do he know that the time is right?
CHORUS:

*Gun.

9 Me and my buddy and two three more,
   Going to ramshack Georgy everywhere we go.
CHORUS:

10 Here come a woman walking 'cross the field,
   Her mouth exhausting like an automobile.

CAN'T YOU LINE IT?

(Work Song Series)

From the Zora Neale Hurston
Collection of Negro Folklore

Arranged by Portia D. Dubart

THERE STANDS A BLUE BIRD (CHILDREN)

Another version: Going around de mountain, two by two (actions suit words).

1 There stands a blue-bird, tra, la, la, la.
There stands a blue-bird tra, la, la, la.
Gimme sugar, coffee and tea.

2 Now trip around the ocean, tra, la, la, la.
Now trip around the ocean, tra, la, la, la.
Gimme sugar, coffee and tea (one in ring dances around ring).

3 Show me your motion, tra, la, la, la (does solo dance).
Show me your motion, tra, la, la, la.
Gimme sugar, coffee and tea.

4 Show me a better one, tra, la, la, la (second solo step).
Show me a better one, tra, la, la, la.

5 Choose your partner, tra, la, la, la.
Choose your partner, tra, la, la, la.
Gimme sugar, coffee and tea.

(One in ring chooses partner and the new chosen partner takes his place in the ring and the other comes out.)

THERE STANDS A BLUE BIRD

(Children's Game)

From the Zora Neale Hurston   *Arranged by C. Spencer Tocus*
Collection of Negro Folklore

tra la la la, Gim-me su-gar cof-fee and tea. Now

skip a-round the o-cean, tra la la la—, Skip a-round the o-cean.

tra la la la—, Gim-me su-gar, cof-fee and tea.

MULE ON DE MOUNT

NOTE: The most widely distributed and best known of all Negro work songs. Since folk songs grow by incremental repetition the diversified subject matter that it accumulates as it ages is one of the evidences of its distribution and usage. This has everything in folk life in it. Several stories to say nothing of just lyric matter. It is something like the Odyssey, or the Iliad.

1 Cap'n got a mule, mule on the Mount called Jerry
Cap'n got a mule, mule on the Mount called Jerry
I can ride, Lawd, Lawd, I can ride.
(He won't come down, Lawd; Lawd, he won't come down, in another version.)

2 I don't want no cold corn bread and molasses,
I don't want no cold corn bread and molasses,
Gimme beans, Lawd, Lawd, gimme beans.

3 I don't want no coal-black woman for my regular,
I don't want no coal-black woman for my regular,
She's too low-down, Lawd, Lawd, she's too low-down.

4 I got a woman, she's got money 'cumulated,
I got a woman, she's got money 'cumulated,
In de bank, Lawd, Lawd, in de bank.

5 I got a woman she's pretty but she's too bulldozing,
I got a woman she's pretty but she's too bulldozing,
She won't live long, Lawd, Lawd, she won't live long.

6 Every pay day, pay day I gits a letter,
Every pay day, pay day I gits a letter,
Son come home, Lawd, Lawd, son come home.

7 If I can just make June, July and August,
If I can just make June, July and August,
I'm going home, Lawd, Lawd, I'm going home.

8 Don't you hear them, coo-coo birds keep a'hollering,
Don't you hear them, coo-coo birds keep a'hollering,
It's sign of rain, Lawd, Lawd, it's sign of rain.

9 I got a rain-bow wrapped and tied around my shoulder,
I got a rain-bow wrapped and tied around my shoulder,
It ain't goin' rain, Lawd, Lawd, it ain't goin' rain.

MULE ON DE MOUNT

(Work Song Series)

From the Zora Neale Hurston
Collection of Negro Folklore

Arranged by C. Spencer Tocus

LET THE DEAL GO DOWN

(Gaming song suited to the action of Georgia Skin Game.)

SOLOIST:

1   When your card gits lucky, oh partner,
     You ought to be in a rolling game.

CHORUS:

     Let the deal go down, boys,
     Let the deal go down.

SOLOIST:

2   I ain't had no money, Lawd, partner,
     I ain't had no change.

CHORUS:

SOLOIST:

3   I ain't had no trouble, Lawd, partner,
     Till I stop by here.

CHORUS:

SOLOIST:

4   I'm going back to de 'Bama, Lawd, partner,
     Won't be worried with you.

LET THE DEAL GO DOWN

You ought to be in a roll - ing game.

CHORUS

Let the deal go down, boys, Let the deal go down.

II

FORMULAE OF HOODOO DOCTORS[1]

CONCERNING SUDDEN DEATH

1. Put an egg in a murdered man's hand and the murderer can't get away. He will wander right around the scene.
2. If a murder victim falls on his face, the murderer can't escape punishment. He will usually be executed.
3. If the blood of the victim is put in a jug and buried at the north corner of his house, the murderer will be caught and convicted.
4. Bury the victim with his hat on and the murderer will never get away.
5. If you kill and step backwards over the body, they will never catch you.
6. If you are murdered or commit suicide, you are dead before your times comes. God is not ready for you, and so your soul must prowl about until your time comes.
7. If you suspect that a person has been killed by hoodoo, put a cassava stick in the hand and he will punish the murderer. If he is killed by violence, put the stick in one hand and a knife and fork in the other. The spirit of the murdered one will first drive the slayer insane, and then kill him with great violence.
8. If people die wishing to see someone, they will stay limp and warm for days. They are waiting.
9. If a person dies who has not had his fling in this world, he will turn on his face in the grave.
10. If a person dies without speaking his mind about matters, he will purge (foam at the mouth after death). Hence the expression: "I ain't goin' to purge when I die (I shall speak my mind)."

---

[1]The formulae, paraphernalia and prescriptions of conjure are reprinted through the courtesy of the *Journal of American Folklore*.

TO RENT A HOUSE

Tie up some rice and sycamore bark in a small piece of goods. Tie six fig leaves and a piece of John de Conquer root in another piece. Cheesecloth is good. Boil both bundles in a quart of water at the same time. Strain it out. Now sprinkle the rice and sycamore bark mixed together in front of the house. Put the fig leaves and John de Conquer root in a corner of the house and scrub the house with the water they were boiled in. Mix it with a pail of scrub water.

FOR BAD WORK—(DEATH)

Take a coconut that has three eyes. Take the name of the person you want to get rid of and write it on the paper like a coffin. (Put the name all over the coffin.) Put this down in the nut. (Pour out water.) Put beef gall and vinegar in the nut and the person's name all around the coconut. Stand nut up in sand and set one black candle on top of it. Number the days from one to fifteen days. Every day mark that coconut at twelve o'clock A.M. or P.M., and by the fifteenth day they will be gone. Never let the candle go out. You must light the new candle and set it on top of the old stub which has burnt down to a wafer.

COURT SCRAPES

a. Take the names of all the *good* witnesses (for your client), the judge and your client's lawyer. Put the names in a dish and pour sweet oil on them and burn a white candle each morning beside it for one hour, from nine to ten. The day of the trial when you put it upon the altar, don't take it down until the trial is over.

b. Take the names of the opponent of your client, his witnesses and his lawyer. Take all of their names on one piece of paper. Put it between two whole bricks. Put the top brick crossways. On the day of the trial set a bucket or dishpan on top of the bricks with ice in it. That's to freeze them out so they can't talk.

c. Take the names of your client's lawyer, witnesses and lawyer on paper. Buy a beef tongue and split it from the base towards the tip, thus separating top from bottom. Put the

274

paper with names in the split tongue along with eighteen pods of hot pepper and pin it through and through with pins and needles. Put it in a tin pail with plenty of vinegar and keep it on ice until the day of court. That day, pour kerosene in the bucket and burn it, and they will destroy themselves in court.

d. Put the names of the judge and all those *for* your client on paper. Take the names of the twelve apostles after Judas hung himself and write each apostle's name on a sage leaf. Take six candles and burn them standing in holy water. Have your client wear six of the sage leaves in each shoe and the jury will be made for him.

e. Write all the enemies' names on paper. Put them in a can. Then take soot and ashes from the chimney of your client and mix it with salt. Stick pins crosswise in the candles and burn them at a good hour. Put some ice in a bucket and set the can in it. Let your client recite the One Hundred Twentieth Psalm before Court and in Court.

f. To let John the conqueror win your case; take one-half pint whiskey, nine pieces of John the Conqueror Root one inch long. Let it soak thirty-eight hours till all the strength is out. (Gather all roots before September 21.) Shake up good and drain off roots in another bottle. Get one ounce of white rose or Jockey Club perfume and pour into the mixture. Dress your client with this before going to Court.

TO KILL AND HARM

Get bad vinegar, beef gall, filet gumbo with red pepper, and put names written across each other in bottles. Shake the bottle for nine mornings and talk and tell it what you want it to do. To kill the victim, turn it upside down and bury it breast deep, and he will die.

RUNNING FEET

To give anyone the running feet: Take sand out of one of his tracks and mix the sand with red pepper; throw some into a running stream of water and this will cause the person to run from place to place, until finally he runs himself to death.

TO MAKE A MAN COME HOME

Take nine deep red or pink candles. Write his name three times on each candle. Wash the candles with Van-Van. Put the name three times on paper and place under the candles, and call the name of the party three times as the candle is placed at the hours of seven, nine or eleven.

TO MAKE PEOPLE LOVE YOU

Take nine lumps of starch, nine of sugar, nine teaspoons of steel dust. Wet it all with Jockey Club cologne. Take nine pieces of ribbon, blue, red or yellow. Take a dessertspoonful and put it on a piece of ribbon and tie it in a bag. As each fold is gathered together call his name. As you wrap it with yellow thread call his name till you finish. Make nine bags and place them under a rug, behind an armoire, under a step or over a door. They will love you and give you everything they can get. Distance makes no difference. Your mind is talking to his mind and nothing beats that.

TO BREAK UP A LOVE AFFAIR

Take nine needles, break each needle in three pieces. Write each person's name three times on paper. Write one name backwards and one forwards and lay the broken needles on the paper. Take five black candles, four red and three green.

Tie a string across the door from it, suspend a large candle upside down. It will hang low on the door; burn one each day for one hour. If you burn your first in the daytime, keep on in the day; if at night, continue at night. A tin plate with paper and needles in it must be placed to catch wax in.

When the ninth day is finished, go out into the street and get some white or black dog dung. A dog only drops his dung in the street when he is running and barking, and whoever you curse will run and bark likewise. Put it in a bag with the paper and carry it to running water, and one of the parties will leave town.

III

PARAPHERNALIA OF CONJURE

It would be impossible for anyone to find out all the things that are being used in conjure in America. Anything may be conjure and nothing may be conjure, according to the doctor, the time and the use of the article.

What is set down here are the things most commonly used.

1. Fast Luck: Aqueous solution of oil of Citronella. It is put in scrub water to scrub the house. It brings luck in business by pulling customers into a store.
2. Red Fast Luck: Oil of Cinnamon and Oil of Vanilla, with wintergreen. Used as above to bring luck.
3. Essence of Van Van: Ten percent. Oil of Lemon Grass in alcohol. (Different doctors specify either grain, mentholated, or wood alcohol), used for luck and power of all kinds. It is the most popular conjure drug in Louisiana.
4. Fast Scrubbing Essence: A mixture of thirteen oils. It is burned with incense for fish-fry luck, i.e., business success. It includes:
   Essence Cinnamon
   Essence Wintergreen
   Essence Geranium
   Essence Bergamot
   Essence Orange Flowers, used also in initiation baths
   Essence Lavender, used also in initiation baths
   Essence Anice
   Essence St. Michael
   Essence Rosemary.
5. Water Notre Dame: Oil of White Rose and water. Sprinkle it about the home to make peace.
6. War Water: Oil of Tar in water (filtered). Break a glass of it on the steps wherever you wish to create strife. (It is sometimes made of creolin in water.)
7. Four Thieves Vinegar. It is used for breaking up homes,

277

for making a person run crazy, for driving off. It is sometimes put with a name in a bottle and the bottle thrown into moving water. It is used also to "dress" cocoanuts to kill and drive crazy.

8. Egyptian Paradise Seed (Amonium Melegreta). This is used in seeking success. Take a picture of St. Peter and put it at the front door and a picture of St. Michael at the back door. Put the Paradise seeds in little bags and put one behind each saint. It is known as "feeding the saint."

9. Guinea Paradise seed. Use as above.

10. Guinea pepper. This may also be used for feeding saints; also for breaking up homes or protecting one from conjure.

11. White Mustard seed. For protection against harm.

12. Black Mustard seed. For causing disturbance and strife.

13. Has-no-harra: Jasmine lotion. Brings luck to gamblers.

14. Carnation, a perfume. As above.

15. Three Jacks and a King. A perfume. As above.

16. Narcisse. As above but mild.

17. Nutmegs, bored and stuffed with quicksilver and sealed with wax, and rolled in Argentorium are very lucky for gamblers.

18. Lucky Dog is best of all for gamblers' use.

19. Essence of Bend-over. Used to rule and have your way.

20. Cleo-May, a perfume. To compel men to love you.

21. Jockey Club, a perfume. To make love and get work.

22. Jasmine Perfume. For luck in general.

23. White Rose. To make peace.

24. French Lilac. Best for vampires.

25. Taper Oil: perfumed olive oil. To burn candles in.

26. St. Joseph's Mixture:
    Buds from the Garden of Gilead
    Berries of the Fish
    Wishing Beans
    Juniper Berries
    Japanese scented Lucky Beans
    Large Star Anice

27. Steel dust is sprinkled over black load stone in certain

ceremonies. It is called "feeding the he, feeding the she."

28. Steel dust is attracted by a horse-shoe magnet to draw people to you. Used to get love, trade, etc.

29. Gold and silver magnetic sand. Powdered silver gilt used with a magnet to draw people to you.

30. *Saltpetre* is dissolved in water and sprinkled about to ward off conjure.

31. Scrub waters other than the Fast Lucks (see above, 1 and 2) are colored and perfumed and used as follows: red, for luck and protection; yellow, for money; blue (always colored with copperas), for protection and friends.

32. Roots and Herbs are used freely under widespread names:

Big John the Conqueror.

Little John the Conqueror. It is also put in Notre Dame Water or Waterloo in order to win.

World-wonder Root. It is used in treasure-hunts. Bury a piece in the four corners of the field; also hide it in the four corners of your house to keep things in your favor.

Ruler's Root. Used as above.

Rattlesnake Root.

Dragon's Blood (red root fibres). Crushed. Used for many purposes.

Valerian Root. Put a piece in your pillow to quiet nerves.

Adam and Eve Roots (paid). Sew together in bag and carry on person for protection.

Five-fingered grass. Used to uncross. Make tea, strain it and bathe in it nine times.

Waste Away Tea. Same as above.

33. Pictures of Saints, etc., are used also.

St. Michael, the Archangel. To Conquer.

St. Expedite. For quick work.

St. Mary. For cure in sickness.

St. Joseph with infant Jesus. To get job.

St. Peter without the key. For success.

St. Peter with the key. For great and speedy success.

St. Anthony de Padua. For luck.

St. Mary Magdalene. For luck in love (for women).

Sacred Heart of Jesus. For organic diseases.

34. Crosses. For luck.

35. Scapular. For protection.

36. Medals. For success.

37. Candles are used with set meanings for the different colors. They are often very large, one candle costing as much as six dollars.

White. For peace and to uncross and for weddings.

Red. For victory.

Pink. For love (some say for drawing success).

Green. To drive off (some say for success).

Blue. For success and protection (for causing death also).

Yellow. For money.

Brown. For drawing money and people.

Lavender. To cause harm (to induce triumph also).

Black. Always for evil or death.

Valive candles. For making Novenas.

38. The Bible. All hold that the Bible is the great conjure book in the world. Moses is honored as the greatest conjurer. "The names he knowed to call God by was what give him the power to conquer Pharaoh and divide the Red Sea."

IV

PRESCRIPTIONS OF ROOT DOCTORS

Folk medicine is practiced by a great number of persons. On the "jobs," that is, in the sawmill camps, the turpentine stills, mining camps and among the lowly generally, doctors are not generally called to prescribe for illnesses, certainly, nor for the social diseases. Nearly all of the conjure doctors practice "roots," but some of the root doctors are not hoodoo doctors. One of these latter at Bogaloosa, Louisiana, and one at Bartow, Florida, enjoy a huge patronage. They make medicine only, and white and colored swarm about them claiming cures.

The following are some prescriptions gathered here and there in Florida, Alabama and Louisiana:

GONORRHEA

a. Fifty cents of iodide potash in two quarts of water. Boil down to one quart. Add two teaspoons of Epsom salts. Take a big swallow three times a day.

b. Fifty cents iodide potash to one quart sarsaparilla. Take three teaspoons three times a day in water.

c. A good handful of May pop roots; one pint ribbon cane syrup; one-half plug of Brown's Mule tobacco cut up. Add fifty cents iodide potash. Take this three times a day as a tonic.

d. Parch egg shells and drink the tea.

e. For Running Range (Claps): Take blackberry root, sheep weed, boil together. Put a little blueing in (a pinch) and a pinch of laundry soap. Put all this in a quart of water. Take one-half glass three times a day and drink one-half glass of water behind it.

f. One quart water, one handful of blackberry root, one pinch of alum, one pinch of yellow soap. Boil together. Put in last nine drops of turpentine. Drink it for water until it goes through the bladder.

281

SYPHILIS

a. Ashes of one good cigar, fifteen cents worth of blue ointment. Mix and put on the sores.
b. Get the heart of a rotten log and powder it fine. Tie it up in a muslin cloth. Wash the sores with good castile soap and powder them with the wood dust.
c. When there are blue-balls (buboes), smear the swellings with mashed up granddaddies (daddy-long-legs) and it will bring them to a head.
d. Take a gum ball, cigar, soda and rice. Burn the gum ball and cigar and parch the rice. Powder it and sift and mix with vaseline. It is ready for use.
e. Boil red oak bark, palmetto root, fig root, two pinches of alum, nine drops of turpentine, two quarts of water together to one quart. Take one-half cup at a time. (Use no other water.)

FOR BLADDER TROUBLE

One pint of boiling water, two tablespoons of flaxseed, two tablespoons of cream of tartar. Drink one-half glass in the morning and one-half at night.

FISTULA

Sweet gum bark and mullen cooked down with lard. Make a salve.

RHEUMATISM

Take mullen leaves (five or six) and steep in one quart of water. Drink three to four wine glasses a day.

SWELLING

Oil of white rose (fifteen cents), oil of lavender (fifteen cents), Jockey Club (fifteen cents), Japanese honeysuckle (fifteen cents). Rub.

FOR BLINDNESS

a. Slate dust and pulverized sugar. Blow it in the eyes. (It must be finely pulverized to remove film.)
b. Get somebody to catch a catfish. Get the gall and put it in a bottle. Drop one drop in each eye. Cut the skin off. It gives the sight a free look.

LOCK-JAW

a. Draw out the nail. Beat the wound and squeeze out all the blood possible. Then take a piece of fat bacon, some tobacco and a penny and tie it on the wound.
b. Draw out the nail and drive it in a green tree on the sun-rise side, and the place will heal.

FLOODING[1]

One grated nutmeg, pinch of alum in a quart of water (cooked). Take one-half glass three times daily.

SICK AT STOMACH

Make a tea of parched rice and bay leaves (six). Give a cup at a time. Drink no other water.

LIVE THINGS IN STOMACH (FITS)

Take a silver quarter with a woman's head on it. Stand her on her head and file it in one-half cup of sweet milk. Add nine parts of garlic. Boil and give to drink after straining.

MEDICINE TO PURGE

Jack of War tea, one tablespoon to a cup of water with a pinch of soda after it is ready to drink.

---

[1]Menstruation.

LOSS OF MIND

Sheep weed leaves, bay leaf, sarsaparilla root. Take the bark and cut it all up fine. Make a tea. Take one tablespoon and put in two cups of water and strain and sweeten. You drink some and give some to patient.

Put a fig leaf and poison oak in shoe. (Get fig leaves off a tree that hasn't borne fruit. Stem them so that nobody will know.)

TO MAKE A TONIC

One quart of wine, three pinches of raw rice, three dusts of cinnamon (about one heaping teaspoon), five small pieces of the hull of pomegranate about the size of a fingernail, five tablespoons of sugar. Let it come to a boil, set one-half hour and strain. Dose: one tablespoon.

(When the pomegranate is in season, gather all the hulls you can for use at other times in the year.)

POISONS

There are few instances of actual poisoning. When a conjure doctor tells one of his patients, "Youse poisoned nearly to death," he does not necessarily mean that poison has been swallowed. He might mean that, but the instances are rare. He names that something has been put down for the patient. He may be: (1) "buried in the graveyard"; (2) "throwed in de river"; (3) "nailed up in a tree"; (4) put into a snake, rabbit, frog or chicken; (5) just buried in his own yard; (6) or hung up and punished. Juice of the nightshade, extract of polk root, and juice of the milkweed have been used as vegetable poisons, and poisonous spiders and powdered worms and insects are used as animal poisons. I have heard of one case of the poison sac of the rattlesnake being placed in the water pail of an enemy. But this sort of poisoning is rare.

It is firmly held in such cases that doctor's medicine can do the patient no good. What he needs is a "two-headed" doctor, that is, the conjure man. In some cases the hoodoo man does effect a cure where the physician fails because he has faith working with him. Often the patient is organically sound. He is afraid that he has been "fixed," and there is nothing that a medical doctor can do to remove that fear. Besides, some poisons of a low order, like decomposed reptiles and the like, are not listed in the American pharmacopoeia. The doctor would never suspect their presence and would not be prepared to treat the patient if he did.

THEIR EYES WERE
WATCHING GOD

A NOVEL

ZORA NEALE HURSTON

WITH A NEW FOREWORD BY MARY HELEN WASHINGTON

To
Henry Allen Moe

FOREWORD

I n 1987, the fiftieth anniversary of the first publication of *Their Eyes Were Watching God,* the University of Illinois Press inserted a banner in the lower right-hand corner of the cover of their anniversary reprint edition: "1987/50th Anniversary—STILL A BESTSELLER!" The back cover, using a quote from the *Saturday Review* by Doris Grumbach, proclaimed *Their Eyes,* "the finest black novel of its time" and "one of the finest of all time." Zora Neale Hurston would have been shocked and pleased, I believe, at this stunning reversal in the reception of her second novel, which for nearly thirty years after its first publication was out of print, largely unknown and unread, and dismissed by the male literary establishment in subtle and not so subtle ways. One white reviewer in 1937 praised the novel in the *Saturday Review* as a "rich and racy love story, if somewhat awkward," but had difficulty believing that such a town as Eatonville, "inhabited and governed entirely by Negroes," could be real.

Black male critics were much harsher in their assessments of the novel. From the beginning of her career, Hurston was severely criticized for not writing fiction in the protest tradition. Sterling Brown said in 1936 of her earlier book *Mules and Men* that it was not bitter enough, that it did not depict

vii

the harsher side of black life in the South, that Hurston made black southern life appear easygoing and carefree. Alain Locke, dean of black scholars and critics during the Harlem Renaissance, wrote in his yearly review of the literature for *Opportunity* magazine that Hurston's *Their Eyes* was simply out of step with the more serious trends of the times. When, he asks, will Hurston stop creating "these pseudo-primitives whom the reading public still loves to laugh with, weep over, and envy," and "come to grips with the motive fiction and social document fiction?" The most damaging critique of all came from the most well-known and influential black writer of the day, Richard Wright. Writing for the leftist magazine *New Masses*, Wright excoriated *Their Eyes* as a novel that did for literature what the minstrel shows did for theater, that is, make white folks laugh. The novel, he said, "carries no theme, no message, no thought," but exploited those "quaint" aspects of Negro life that satisfied the tastes of a white audience. By the end of the forties, a decade dominated by Wright and by the stormy fiction of social realism, the quieter voice of a woman searching for self-realization could not, or would not, be heard.

Like most of my friends and colleagues who were teaching in the newly formed Black Studies departments in the late sixties, I can still recall quite vividly my own discovery of *Their Eyes.* Somewhere around 1968, in one of the many thriving black bookstores in the country—this one, Vaughn's Book Store, was in Detroit—I came across the slender little paperback (bought for 75¢) with a stylized portrait of Janie Crawford and Jody Starks on the cover—she pumping water at the well, her long hair cascading down her back, her head turned just slightly in his direction with a look of longing and expectancy; he, standing at a distance in his fancy silk shirt and purple suspenders, his coat over one arm, his head cocked to one side, with the look that speaks to Janie of far horizons.

What I loved immediately about this novel besides its high poetry and its female hero was its investment in black folk traditions. Here, finally, was a woman on a quest for her own identity and, unlike so many other questing figures in black literature, her journey would take her, not away from, but deeper and deeper into blackness, the descent into the Everglades with its rich black soil, wild cane, and communal life representing immersion into black traditions. But for most black women readers discovering *Their Eyes* for the first time, what was most compelling was the figure of Janie Crawford—powerful, articulate, self-reliant, and radically different from any woman character they had ever before encountered in literature. Andrea Rushing, then an instructor in the Afro-American Studies Department at Harvard, remembers reading *Their Eyes* in a women's study group with Nellie McKay, Barbara Smith, and Gail Pemberton. "I loved the language of this book," Rushing says, "but mostly I loved it because it was about a woman who wasn't pathetic, wasn't a tragic mulatto, who defied everything that was expected of her, who went off with a man without bothering to divorce the one she left and wasn't broken, crushed, and run down."

The reaction of women all across the country who found themselves so powerfully represented in a literary text was often direct and personal. Janie and Tea Cake were talked about as though they were people the readers knew intimately. Sherley Anne Williams remembers going down to a conference in Los Angeles in 1969 where the main speaker, Toni Cade Bambara, asked the women in the audience, "Are the sisters here ready for Tea Cake?" And Williams, remembering that even Tea Cake had his flaws, responded, "Are the Tea Cakes of the world ready for us?" Williams taught *Their Eyes* for the first time at Cal State Fresno, in a migrant farming area where the students, like the characters in *Their Eyes,* were used to making their living from the land. "For the first time," Williams says, "they saw themselves in these characters and they saw their lives portrayed with joy." Rushing's comment on the female as hero and Williams's story about the joyful portrayal of a culture together epitomize what critics would later see as the novel's unique contribution to black literature: it affirms black cultural traditions while revising them to empower black women.

By 1971, *Their Eyes* was an underground phenomenon, surfacing here and there, wherever there was a growing interest in African-American studies—and a black woman literature teacher. Alice Walker was teaching the novel at Wellesley in the 1971–72 school year when she discovered that Hurston was only a footnote in the scholarship. Reading in an essay by a white folklorist that Hurston was buried in an unmarked grave, Walker decided that such a fate was an insult to Hurston and began her search for the grave to put a marker on it. In a personal essay, "Looking for Zora," written for *Ms.* magazine, Walker describes going to Florida and searching through waist-high weeds to find what she thought was Hurston's grave and laying on it a marker inscribed "Zora Neale Hurston/'A Genius of the South'/Novelist/Folklorist/Anthropologist/1901–1960." With that inscription and that essay, Walker ushered in a new era in the scholarship on *Their Eyes Were Watching God.*

By 1975, *Their Eyes,* again out of print, was in such demand that a petition was circulated at the December 1975 convention of the Modern Language Association (MLA) to get the novel back into print. In that same year at a conference on minority literature held at Yale and directed by Michael Cooke, the few copies of *Their Eyes* that were available were circulated for two hours at a time to conference participants, many of whom were reading the novel for the first time. In March of 1977, when the MLA Commission on Minority Groups and the Study of Language and Literature published its first list of out of print books most in demand at a national level, the program coordinator, Dexter Fisher, wrote: *"Their Eyes Were Watching God* is unanimously at the top of the list."

Between 1977 and 1979 the Zora Neale Hurston renaissance was in full bloom. Robert Hemenway's biography, *Zora Neale Hurston: A Literary Biography,* published in 1977, was a runaway bestseller at the December 1977 MLA convention. The new University of Illinois Press edition of *Their Eyes,* published a year after the Hemenway biography in March of 1978, made the novel available on a steady and dependable basis for the next ten years. *I Love Myself When I Am Laughing . . . And Then Again When I Am Looking Mean and Impressive: A Zora Neale Hurston Reader,* edited by Alice Walker, was published by the Feminist Press in 1979. Probably more than anything else, these three literary events made it possible for serious Hurston scholarship to emerge.

But the event that for me truly marked the beginning of the third wave of critical attention to *Their Eyes* took place in December 1979 at the MLA convention in San Francisco in a session aptly titled "Traditions and Their Transformations in Afro-American Letters," chaired by Robert Stepto of Yale with John Callahan of Lewis and Clark College and myself (then at the University of Detroit) as the two panelists. Despite the fact that the session was scheduled on Sunday morning, the last session of the entire convention, the room was packed and the audience unusually attentive. In his comments at the end of the session, Stepto raised the issue that has become one of the most highly controversial and hotly contested aspects of the novel: whether or not Janie is able to achieve her voice in *Their Eyes.* What concerned Stepto was the courtroom scene in which Janie is called on not only to preserve her own life and liberty but also to make the jury, as well as all of us who hear her tale, understand the meaning of her life with Tea Cake. Stepto found Janie curiously silent in this scene, with Hurston telling the story in omniscient third person so that we do not hear Janie speak—at least not in her own first-person voice. Stepto was quite convinced (and convincing) that the frame story in which Janie speaks to Pheoby creates only the illusion that Janie has found her voice, that Hurston's insistence on telling Janie's story in the third person undercuts her power as speaker. While the rest of us in the room struggled to find our voices, Alice Walker rose and claimed hers, insisting passionately that women did not have to speak when men thought they should, that they would choose when and where they wish to speak because while many women *had* found their own voices, they also knew when it was better not to use it. What was most remarkable about the energetic and at times heated discussion that followed Stepto's and Walker's remarks was the assumption of everyone in that room that *Their Eyes* was a shared text, that a novel that just ten years earlier was unknown and unavailable had entered into critical acceptance as perhaps the most widely known and the most privileged text in the African-American literary canon.

That MLA session was important for another reason. Walker's defense of Janie's choice (actually Hurston's choice) to be silent in the crucial places in the novel turned out to be the earliest feminist reading of voice in *Their Eyes,* a reading that was later supported by many other Hurston scholars. In a recent essay on *Their Eyes* and the question of voice, Michael Awkward argues that Janie's voice at the end of the novel is a communal one, that when she tells Pheoby to tell her story ("You can tell 'em what Ah say if you wants to. Dat's just de same as me 'cause mah tongue is in mah friend's mouf") she is choosing a collective rather than an individual voice, demonstrating her closeness to the collective spirit of the African-American oral tradition. Thad Davis agrees with this reading of voice, adding that while Janie is the teller of the tale, Pheoby is the bearer of the tale. Davis says that Janie's experimental life may not allow her to effect changes beyond what she causes in Pheoby's life; but Pheoby, standing within the traditional role of women, is the one most suited to take the message back to the community.

Although, like Stepto, I too am uncomfortable with the absence of Janie's voice in the courtroom scene, I think that silence reflects Hurston's discomfort with the model of the male hero who asserts himself through his powerful voice. When Hurston chose a female hero for the story she faced an interesting dilemma: the female presence was inherently a critique of the male-dominated folk culture and therefore could not be its heroic representative. When Janie says at the end of her story that "talkin' don't amount to much" if it's divorced from experience, she is testifying to the limitations of voice and critiquing the culture that celebrates orality to the exclusion of inner growth. Her final speech to Pheoby at the end of *Their Eyes* actually casts doubt on the relevance of oral speech and supports Alice Walker's claim that women's silence can be intentional and useful:

> 'Course, talkin' don't amount tuh uh hill uh beans when yuh can't do nothin' else . . . Pheoby, you got tuh *go* there tuh *know* there. Yo papa and yo mama and nobody else can't tell yuh and show yuh. Two things everybody's got tuh do fuh theyselves. They got tuh go tuh God, and they got tuh find out about livin' fuh theyselves.

The language of the men in *Their Eyes* is almost always divorced from any kind of interiority, and the men are rarely shown in the process of growth. Their talking is either a game or a method of exerting power. Janie's life is about the experience of relationships, and while Jody and Tea Cake and all the other talking men are essentially static characters, Janie and Pheoby pay closer attention to their own inner life—to experience—because it is the site for growth.

If there is anything the outpouring of scholarship on *Their Eyes* teaches us, it is that this is a rich and complicated text and that each generation of readers will bring something new to our understanding of it. If we were protective of this text and unwilling to subject it to literary analysis during the first years of its rebirth, that was because it was a beloved text for those of us who discovered in it something of our own experiences, our own language, our own history. In 1989, I find myself asking new questions about *Their Eyes*—questions about Hurston's ambivalence toward her female protagonist, about its uncritical depiction of violence toward women, about the ways in which Janie's voice is dominated by men even in passages that are about her own inner growth. In *Their Eyes*, Hurston has not given us an unambiguously heroic female character. She puts Janie on the track of autonomy, self-realization, and independence, but she also places Janie in the position of romantic heroine as the object of Tea Cake's quest, at times so subordinate to the magnificent presence of Tea Cake that even her interior life reveals more about him than about her. What *Their Eyes* shows us is a woman writer struggling with the problem of the questing hero as woman and the difficulties in 1937 of giving a woman character such power and such daring.

Because *Their Eyes* has been in print continuously since 1978, it has become available each year to thousands of new readers. It is taught in colleges all over the country, and its availability and popularity have generated two decades of the highest level of scholarship. But I want to remember the history that nurtured this text into rebirth, especially the collective spirit of the sixties and seventies that galvanized us into political action to retrieve the lost works of black women writers. There is a lovely symmetry between text and context in the case of *Their Eyes*: as *Their Eyes* affirms and celebrates black culture it reflects that same affirmation of black culture that rekindled interest in the text; Janie telling her story to a listening woman friend, Pheoby, suggests to me all those women readers who discovered their own tale in Janie's story and passed it on from one to another; and certainly, as the novel represents a woman redefining and revising a male-dominated canon, these readers have, like Janie, made their voices heard in the world of letters, revising the canon while asserting their proper place in it.

MARY HELEN WASHINGTON

CHAPTER 1

Ships at a distance have every man's wish on board. For some they come in with the tide. For others they sail forever on the horizon, never out of sight, never landing until the Watcher turns his eyes away in resignation, his dreams mocked to death by Time. That is the life of men.

Now, women forget all those things they don't want to remember, and remember everything they don't want to forget. The dream is the truth. Then they act and do things accordingly.

So the beginning of this was a woman and she had come back from burying the dead. Not the dead of sick and ailing with friends at the pillow and the feet. She had come back from the sodden and the bloated; the sudden dead, their eyes flung wide open in judgment.

The people all saw her come because it was sundown. The sun was gone, but he had left his footprints in the sky. It was the time for sitting on porches beside the road. It was the time to hear things and talk. These sitters had been tongueless, earless, eyeless conveniences all day long. Mules and other brutes had occupied their skins. But now, the sun and the bossman were gone, so the skins felt powerful and human. They became lords of sounds and lesser things. They passed

1

notions through their mouths. They sat in judgment.

Seeing the woman as she was made them remember the envy they had stored up from other times. So they chewed up the back parts of their minds and swallowed with relish. They made burning statements with questions, and killing tools out of laughs. It was mass cruelty. A mood come alive. Words walking without masters; walking altogether like harmony in a song.

"What she doin' coming back here in dem overhalls? Can't she find no dress to put on?—Where's dat blue satin dress she left here in?—Where all dat money her husband took and died and left her?—What dat ole forty year ole 'oman doin' wid her hair swingin' down her back lak some young gal?—Where she left dat young lad of a boy she went off here wid?— Thought she was going to marry?— Where he left *her?*— What he done wid all her money?— Betcha he off wid some gal so young she ain't even got no hairs—why she don't stay in her class?—"

When she got to where they were she turned her face on the bander log and spoke. They scrambled a noisy "good evenin' '' and left their mouths setting open and their ears full of hope. Her speech was pleasant enough, but she kept walking straight on to her gate. The porch couldn't talk for looking.

The men noticed her firm buttocks like she had grape fruits in her hip pockets; the great rope of black hair swinging to her waist and unraveling in the wind like a plume; then her pugnacious breasts trying to bore holes in her shirt. They, the men, were saving with the mind what they lost with the eye. The women took the faded shirt and muddy overalls and laid them away for remembrance. It was a weapon against her strength and if it turned out of no significance, still it was a hope that she might fall to their level some day.

But nobody moved, nobody spoke, nobody even thought to swallow spit until after her gate slammed behind her.

Pearl Stone opened her mouth and laughed real hard because she didn't know what else to do. She fell all over Mrs.

2

Sumpkins while she laughed. Mrs. Sumpkins snorted violently and sucked her teeth.

"Humph! Y'all let her worry yuh. You ain't like me. Ah ain't got her to study 'bout. If she ain't got manners enough to stop and let folks know how she been makin' out, let her g'wan!"

"She ain't even worth talkin' after," Lulu Moss drawled through her nose. "She sits high, but she looks low. Dat's what Ah say 'bout dese ole women runnin' after young boys."

Pheoby Watson hitched her rocking chair forward before she spoke. "Well, nobody don't know if it's anything to tell or not. Me, Ah'm her best friend, and *Ah* don't know."

"Maybe us don't know into things lak you do, but we all know how she went 'way from here and us sho seen her come back. 'Tain't no use in your tryin' to cloak no ole woman lak Janie Starks, Pheoby, friend or no friend."

"At dat she ain't so ole as some of y'all dat's talking."

"She's way past forty to my knowledge, Pheoby."

"No more'n forty at de outside."

"She's 'way too old for a boy like Tea Cake."

"Tea Cake ain't been no boy for some time. He's round thirty his ownself."

"Don't keer what it was, she could stop and say a few words with us. She act like we done done something to her," Pearl Stone complained. "She de one been doin' wrong."

"You mean, you mad 'cause she didn't stop and tell us all her business. Anyhow, what you ever know her to do so bad as y'all make out? The worst thing Ah ever knowed her to do was taking a few years offa her age and dat ain't never harmed nobody. Y'all makes me tired. De way you talkin' you'd think de folks in dis town didn't do nothin' in de bed 'cept praise de Lawd. You have to 'scuse me, 'cause Ah'm bound to go take her some supper." Pheoby stood up sharply.

"Don't mind us," Lulu smiled, "just go right ahead, us can mind yo' house for you till you git back. Mah supper is done.

You bettah go see how she feel. You kin let de rest of us know."

"Lawd," Pearl agreed, "Ah done scorched-up dat lil meat and bread too long to talk about. Ah kin stay 'way from home long as Ah please. Mah husband ain't fussy."

"Oh, er, Pheoby, if youse ready to go, Ah could walk over dere wid you," Mrs. Sumpkins volunteered. "It's sort of duskin' down dark. De booger man might ketch yuh."

"Naw, Ah thank yuh. Nothin' couldn't ketch me dese few steps Ah'm goin'. Anyhow mah husband tell me say no first class booger would have me. If she got anything to tell yuh, you'll hear it."

Pheoby hurried on off with a covered bowl in her hands. She left the porch pelting her back with unasked questions. They hoped the answers were cruel and strange. When she arrived at the place, Pheoby Watson didn't go in by the front gate and down the palm walk to the front door. She walked around the fence corner and went in the intimate gate with her heaping plate of mulatto rice. Janie must be round that side.

She found her sitting on the steps of the back porch with the lamps all filled and the chimneys cleaned.

"Hello, Janie, how you comin'?"

"Aw, pretty good, Ah'm tryin' to soak some uh de tiredness and de dirt outa mah feet." She laughed a little.

"Ah see you is. Gal, you sho looks *good.* You looks like youse yo' own daughter." They both laughed. "Even wid dem overhalls on, you shows yo' womanhood."

"G'wan! G'wan! You must think Ah brought yuh somethin'. When Ah ain't brought home a thing but mahself."

"Dat's a gracious plenty. Yo' friends wouldn't want nothin' better."

"Ah takes dat flattery offa you, Pheoby, 'cause Ah know it's from de heart." Janie extended her hand. "Good Lawd, Pheoby! ain't you never goin' tuh gimme dat lil rations you brought me? Ah ain't had a thing on mah stomach today

4

exceptin' mah hand." They both laughed easily. "Give it here and have a seat."

"Ah knowed you'd be hongry. No time to be huntin' stove wood after dark. Mah mulatto rice ain't so good dis time. Not enough bacon grease, but Ah reckon it'll kill hongry."

"Ah'll tell you in a minute," Janie said, lifting the cover. "Gal, it's *too* good! you switches a mean fanny round in a kitchen."

"Aw, dat ain't much to eat, Janie. But Ah'm liable to have something sho nuff good tomorrow, 'cause you done come."

Janie ate heartily and said nothing. The varicolored cloud dust that the sun had stirred up in the sky was settling by slow degrees.

"Here, Pheoby, take yo' ole plate. Ah ain't got a bit of use for a empty dish. Dat grub sho come in handy."

Pheoby laughed at her friend's rough joke. "Youse just as crazy as you ever was."

"Hand me dat wash-rag on dat chair by you, honey. Lemme scrub mah feet." She took the cloth and rubbed vigorously. Laughter came to her from the big road.

"Well, Ah see Mouth-Almighty is still sittin' in de same place. And Ah reckon they got *me* up in they mouth now."

"Yes indeed. You know if you pass some people and don't speak tuh suit 'em dey got tuh go way back in yo' life and see whut you ever done. They know mo' 'bout yuh than you do yo' self. An envious heart makes a treacherous ear. They done 'heard' 'bout you just what they hope done happened."

"If God don't think no mo' 'bout 'em then Ah do, they's a lost ball in de high grass."

"Ah hears what they say 'cause they just will collect round mah porch 'cause it's on de big road. Mah husband git so sick of 'em sometime he makes 'em all git for home."

"Sam is right too. They just wearin' out yo' sittin' chairs."

"Yeah, Sam say most of 'em goes to church so they'll be sure to rise in Judgment. Dat's de day dat every secret is

5

s'posed to be made known. They wants to be there and hear it *all*."

"Sam is *too* crazy! You can't stop laughin' when youse round him."

"Uuh hunh. He says he aims to be there hisself so he can find out who stole his corn-cob pipe."

"Pheoby, dat Sam of your'n just won't quit! Crazy thing!"

"Most of dese zigaboos is so het up over yo' business till they liable to hurry theyself to Judgment to find out about you if they don't soon know. You better make haste and tell 'em 'bout you and Tea Cake gittin' married, and if he taken all yo' money and went off wid some young gal, and where at he is now and where at is all yo' clothes dat you got to come back here in overhalls."

"Ah don't mean to bother wid tellin' 'em nothin', Pheoby. 'Tain't worth de trouble. You can tell 'em what Ah say if you wants to. Dat's just de same as me 'cause mah tongue is in mah friend's mouf."

"If you so desire Ah'll tell 'em what you tell me to tell 'em."

"To start off wid, people like dem wastes up too much time puttin' they mouf on things they don't know nothin' about. Now they got to look into me loving Tea Cake and see whether it was done right or not! They don't know if life is a mess of corn-meal dumplings, and if love is a bed-quilt!"

"So long as they get a name to gnaw on they don't care whose it is, and what about, 'specially if they can make it sound like evil."

"If they wants to see and know, why they don't come kiss and be kissed? Ah could then sit down and tell 'em things. Ah been a delegate to de big 'ssociation of life. Yessuh! De Grand Lodge, de big convention of livin' is just where Ah been dis year and a half y'all ain't seen me."

They sat there in the fresh young darkness close together. Pheoby eager to feel and do through Janie, but hating to show her zest for fear it might be thought mere curiosity. Janie full of that oldest human longing—self revelation. Pheoby held

6

her tongue for a long time, but she couldn't help moving her feet. So Janie spoke.

"They don't need to worry about me and my overhalls long as Ah still got nine hundred dollars in de bank. Tea Cake got me into wearing 'em—following behind him. Tea Cake ain't wasted up no money of mine, and he ain't left me for no young gal, neither. He give me every consolation in de world. He'd tell 'em so too, if he was here. If he wasn't gone."

Pheoby dilated all over with eagerness, "Tea Cake gone?"

"Yeah, Pheoby, Tea Cake is gone. And dat's de only reason you see me back here—cause Ah ain't got nothing to make me happy no more where Ah was at. Down in the Everglades there, down on the muck."

"It's hard for me to understand what you mean, de way you tell it. And then again Ah'm hard of understandin' at times."

"Naw, 'tain't nothin' lak you might think. So 'tain't no use in me telling you somethin' unless Ah give you de understandin' to go 'long wid it. Unless you see de fur, a mink skin ain't no different from a coon hide. Looka heah, Pheoby, is Sam waitin' on you for his supper?"

"It's all ready and waitin'. If he ain't got sense enough to eat it, dat's his hard luck."

"Well then, we can set right where we is and talk. Ah got the house all opened up to let dis breeze get a little catchin'.

"Pheoby, we been kissin'-friends for twenty years, so Ah depend on you for a good thought. And Ah'm talking to you from dat standpoint."

Time makes everything old so the kissing, young darkness became a monstropolous old thing while Janie talked.

7

CHAPTER 2

J anie saw her life like a great tree in leaf with the things
suffered, things enjoyed, things done and undone. Dawn
and doom was in the branches.

"Ah know exactly what Ah got to tell yuh, but it's hard to
know where to start at.

"Ah ain't never seen mah papa. And Ah didn't know 'im if
Ah did. Mah mama neither. She was gone from round dere
long before Ah wuz big enough tuh know. Mah grandma
raised me. Mah grandma and de white folks she worked wid.
She had a house out in de back-yard and dat's where Ah wuz
born. They was quality white folks up dere in West Florida.
Named Washburn. She had four gran'chillun on de place and
all of us played together and dat's how come Ah never called
mah Grandma nothin' but Nanny, 'cause dat's what everybody on de place called her. Nanny used to ketch us in our
devilment and lick every youngun on de place and Mis' Washburn did de same. Ah reckon dey never hit us ah lick amiss
'cause dem three boys and us two girls wuz pretty aggravatin',
Ah speck.

"Ah was wid dem white chillun so much till Ah didn't know
Ah wuzn't white till Ah was round six years old. Wouldn't
have found it out then, but a man come long takin' pictures

8

and without askin' anybody, Shelby, dat was de oldest boy, he told him to take us. Round a week later de man brought de picture for Mis' Washburn to see and pay him which she did, then give us all a good lickin'.

"So when we looked at de picture and everybody got pointed out there wasn't nobody left except a real dark little girl with long hair standing by Eleanor. Dat's where Ah wuz s'posed to be, but Ah couldn't recognize dat dark chile as me. So Ah ast, 'where is me? Ah don't see me.'

"Everybody laughed, even Mr. Washburn. Miss Nellie, de Mama of de chillun who come back home after her husband dead, she pointed to de dark one and said, 'Dat's you, Alphabet, don't you know yo' ownself?'

"Dey all useter call me Alphabet 'cause so many people had done named me different names. Ah looked at de picture a long time and seen it was mah dress and mah hair so Ah said:

"'Aw, aw! Ah'm colored!

"Den dey all laughed real hard. But before Ah seen de picture Ah thought Ah wuz just like de rest.

"Us lived dere havin' fun till de chillun at school got to teasin' me 'bout livin' in de white folks' back-yard. Dere wuz uh knotty head gal name Mayrella dat useter git mad every time she look at me. Mis' Washburn useter dress me up in all de clothes her gran'chillun didn't need no mo' which still wuz better'n whut de rest uh de colored chillun had. And then she useter put hair ribbon on mah head fuh me tuh wear. Dat useter rile Mayrella uh lot. So she would pick at me all de time and put some others up tuh do de same. They'd push me 'way from de ring plays and make out they couldn't play wid nobody dat lived on premises. Den they'd tell me not to be takin' on over mah looks 'cause they mama told 'em 'bout de hound dawgs huntin' mah papa all night long. 'Bout Mr. Washburn and de sheriff puttin' de bloodhounds on de trail tuh ketch mah papa for whut he done tuh mah mama. Dey didn't tell about how he wuz seen tryin' tuh git in touch wid mah mama later on so he could marry her. Naw, dey didn't talk dat part

9

of it atall. Dey made it sound real bad so as tuh crumple mah feathers. None of 'em didn't even remember whut his name wuz, but dey all knowed de bloodhound part by heart. Nanny didn't love tuh see me wid mah head hung down, so she figgered it would be mo' better fuh me if us had uh house. She got de land and everything and then Mis' Washburn helped out uh whole heap wid things."

Pheoby's hungry listening helped Janie to tell her story. So she went on thinking back to her young years and explaining them to her friend in soft, easy phrases while all around the house, the night time put on flesh and blackness.

She thought awhile and decided that her conscious life had commenced at Nanny's gate. On a late afternoon Nanny had called her to come inside the house because she had spied Janie letting Johnny Taylor kiss her over the gatepost.

It was a spring afternoon in West Florida. Janie had spent most of the day under a blossoming pear tree in the back-yard. She had been spending every minute that she could steal from her chores under that tree for the last three days. That was to say, ever since the first tiny bloom had opened. It had called her to come and gaze on a mystery. From barren brown stems to glistening leaf-buds; from the leaf-buds to snowy virginity of bloom. It stirred her tremendously. How? Why? It was like a flute song forgotten in another existence and remembered again. What? How? Why? This singing she heard that had nothing to do with her ears. The rose of the world was breathing out smell. It followed her through all her waking moments and caressed her in her sleep. It connected itself with other vaguely felt matters that had struck her outside observation and buried themselves in her flesh. Now they emerged and quested about her consciousness.

She was stretched on her back beneath the pear tree soaking in the alto chant of the visiting bees, the gold of the sun and the panting breath of the breeze when the inaudible voice of it all came to her. She saw a dust-bearing bee sink into the sanctum of a bloom; the thousand sister-calyxes arch to meet

10

the love embrace and the ecstatic shiver of the tree from root to tiniest branch creaming in every blossom and frothing with delight. So this was a marriage! She had been summoned to behold a revelation. Then Janie felt a pain remorseless sweet that left her limp and languid.

After a while she got up from where she was and went over the little garden field entire. She was seeking confirmation of the voice and vision, and everywhere she found and acknowledged answers. A personal answer for all other creations except herself. She felt an answer seeking her, but where? When? How? She found herself at the kitchen door and stumbled inside. In the air of the room were flies tumbling and singing, marrying and giving in marriage. When she reached the narrow hallway she was reminded that her grandmother was home with a sick headache. She was lying across the bed asleep so Janie tipped on out of the front door. Oh to be a pear tree—*any* tree in bloom! With kissing bees singing of the beginning of the world! She was sixteen. She had glossy leaves and bursting buds and she wanted to struggle with life but it seemed to elude her. Where were the singing bees for her? Nothing on the place nor in her grandma's house answered her. She searched as much of the world as she could from the top of the front steps and then went on down to the front gate and leaned over to gaze up and down the road. Looking, waiting, breathing short with impatience. Waiting for the world to be made.

Through pollinated air she saw a glorious being coming up the road. In her former blindness she had known him as shiftless Johnny Taylor, tall and lean. That was before the golden dust of pollen had beglamored his rags and her eyes.

In the last stages of Nanny's sleep, she dreamed of voices. Voices far-off but persistent, and gradually coming nearer. Janie's voice. Janie talking in whispery snatches with a male voice she couldn't quite place. That brought her wide awake. She bolted upright and peered out of the window and saw Johnny Taylor lacerating her Janie with a kiss.

11

"Janie!"

The old woman's voice was so lacking in command and reproof, so full of crumbling dissolution,—that Janie half believed that Nanny had not seen her. So she extended herself outside of her dream and went inside of the house. That was the end of her childhood.

Nanny's head and face looked like the standing roots of some old tree that had been torn away by storm. Foundation of ancient power that no longer mattered. The cooling palma christi leaves that Janie had bound about her grandma's head with a white rag had wilted down and become part and parcel of the woman. Her eyes didn't bore and pierce. They diffused and melted Janie, the room and the world into one comprehension.

"Janie, youse uh 'oman, now, so—"

"Naw, Nanny, naw Ah ain't no real 'oman yet."

The thought was too new and heavy for Janie. She fought it away.

Nanny closed her eyes and nodded a slow, weary affirmation many times before she gave it voice.

"Yeah, Janie, youse got yo' womanhood on yuh. So Ah mout ez well tell yuh whut Ah been savin' up for uh spell. Ah wants to see you married right away."

"Me, married? Naw, Nanny, no ma'am! Whut Ah know 'bout uh husband?"

"Whut Ah seen just now is plenty for me, honey, Ah don't want no trashy nigger, no breath-and-britches, lak Johnny Taylor usin' yo' body to wipe his foots on."

Nanny's words made Janie's kiss across the gatepost seem like a manure pile after a rain.

"Look at me, Janie. Don't set dere wid yo' head hung down. Look at yo' ole grandma!" Her voice began snagging on the prongs of her feelings. "Ah don't want to be talkin' to you lak dis. Fact is Ah done been on mah knees to mah Maker many's de time askin' *please*—for Him not to make de burden too heavy for me to bear."

12

"Nanny, Ah just—Ah didn't mean nothin' bad."

"Dat's what makes me skeered. You don't mean no harm. You don't even know where harm is at. Ah'm ole now. Ah can't be always guidin' yo' feet from harm and danger. Ah wants to see you married right away."

"Who Ah'm goin' tuh marry off-hand lak dat? Ah don't know nobody."

"De Lawd will provide. He know Ah done bore de burden in de heat uh de day. Somebody done spoke to me 'bout you long time ago. Ah ain't said nothin' 'cause dat wasn't de way Ah placed you. Ah wanted yuh to school out and pick from a higher bush and a sweeter berry. But dat ain't yo' idea, Ah see."

"Nanny, who—who dat been askin' you for me?"

"Brother Logan Killicks. He's a good man, too."

"Naw, Nanny, no ma'am! Is dat whut he been hangin' round here for? He look like some ole skullhead in de grave yard."

The older woman sat bolt upright and put her feet to the floor, and thrust back the leaves from her face.

"So you don't want to marry off decent like, do yuh? You just wants to hug and kiss and feel around with first one man and then another, huh? You wants to make me suck de same sorrow yo' mama did, eh? Mah ole head ain't gray enough. Mah back ain't bowed enough to suit yuh!"

The vision of Logan Killicks was desecrating the pear tree, but Janie didn't know how to tell Nanny that. She merely hunched over and pouted at the floor.

"Janie."

"Yes, ma'am."

"You answer me when Ah speak. Don't you set dere poutin' wid me after all Ah done went through for you!"

She slapped the girl's face violently, and forced her head back so that their eyes met in struggle. With her hand uplifted for the second blow she saw the huge tear that welled up from Janie's heart and stood in each eye. She saw the terrible agony

13

and the lips tightened down to hold back the cry and desisted. Instead she brushed back the heavy hair from Janie's face and stood there suffering and loving and weeping internally for both of them.

"Come to yo' Grandma, honey. Set in her lap lak yo' use tuh. Yo' Nanny wouldn't harm a hair uh yo' head. She don't want nobody else to do it neither if she kin help it. Honey, de white man is de ruler of everything as fur as Ah been able tuh find out. Maybe it's some place way off in de ocean where de black man is in power, but we don't know nothin' but what we see. So de white man throw down de load and tell de nigger man tuh pick it up. He pick it up because he have to, but he don't tote it. He hand it to his womenfolks. De nigger woman is de mule uh de world so fur as Ah can see. Ah been prayin' fuh it tuh be different wid you. Lawd, Lawd, Lawd!"

For a long time she sat rocking with the girl held tightly to her sunken breast. Janie's long legs dangled over one arm of the chair and the long braids of her hair swung low on the other side. Nanny half sung, half sobbed a running chant-prayer over the head of the weeping girl.

"Lawd have mercy! It was a long time on de way but Ah reckon it had to come. Oh Jesus! Do, Jesus! Ah done de best Ah could."

Finally, they both grew calm.

"Janie, how long you been 'lowin' Johnny Taylor to kiss you?"

"Only dis one time, Nanny. Ah don't love him at all. Whut made me do it is—oh, Ah don't know."

"Thank yuh, Massa Jesus."

"Ah ain't gointuh do it no mo', Nanny. Please don't make me marry Mr. Killicks."

" 'Tain't Logan Killicks Ah wants you to have, baby, it's protection. Ah ain't gittin' ole, honey. Ah'm *done* ole. One mornin' soon, now, de angel wid de sword is gointuh stop by here. De day and de hour is hid from me, but it won't be long. Ah ast de Lawd when you was uh infant in mah arms to let me stay here till you got grown. He done spared me to see de day. Mah daily prayer now is tuh let dese golden moments rolls on a few days longer till Ah see you safe in life."

"Lemme wait, Nanny, please, jus' a lil bit mo'."

"Don't think Ah don't feel wid you, Janie, 'cause Ah do. Ah couldn't love yuh no more if Ah had uh felt yo' birth pains mahself. Fact uh de matter, Ah loves yuh a whole heap more'n Ah do yo' mama, de one Ah did birth. But you got to take in consideration you ain't no everyday chile like most of 'em. You ain't got no papa, you might jus' as well say no mama, for de good she do yuh. You ain't got nobody but me. And mah head is ole and tilted towards de grave. Neither can you stand alone by yo'self. De thought uh you bein' kicked around from pillar tuh post is uh hurtin' thing. Every tear you drop squeezes a cup uh blood outa mah heart. Ah got tuh try and do for you befo' mah head is cold."

A sobbing sigh burst out of Janie. The old woman answered her with little soothing pats of the hand.

"You know, honey, us colored folks is branches without roots and that makes things come round in queer ways. You in particular. Ah was born back due in slavery so it wasn't for me to fulfill my dreams of whut a woman oughta be and to do. Dat's one of de hold-backs of slavery. But nothing can't stop you from wishin'. You can't beat nobody down so low till you can rob 'em of they will. Ah didn't want to be used for a work-ox and a brood-sow and Ah didn't want mah daughter used dat way neither. It sho wasn't mah will for things to happen lak they did. Ah even hated de way you was born. But, all de same Ah said thank God, Ah got another chance. Ah wanted to preach a great sermon about colored women sittin' on high, but they wasn't no pulpit for me. Freedom found me wid a baby daughter in mah arms, so Ah said Ah'd take a broom and a cook-pot and throw up a highway through de wilderness for her. She would expound what Ah felt. But somehow she got lost offa de highway and next thing Ah knowed here you was in de world. So whilst Ah was tendin' you of nights Ah said Ah'd save de text for you. Ah been waitin' a long time, Janie, but nothin' Ah been through ain't too much if you just take a stand on high ground lak Ah dreamed."

Old Nanny sat there rocking Janie like an infant and thinking back and back. Mind-pictures brought feelings, and feelings dragged out dramas from the hollows of her heart.

"Dat mornin' on de big plantation close to Savannah, a rider come in a gallop tellin' 'bout Sherman takin' Atlanta. Marse Robert's son had done been kilt at Chickamauga. So he grabbed his gun and straddled his best horse and went off wid de rest of de gray-headed men and young boys to drive de Yankees back into Tennessee.

"They was all cheerin' and cryin' and shoutin' for de men dat was ridin' off. Ah couldn't see nothin' cause yo' mama wasn't but a week old, and Ah was flat uh mah back. But pretty soon he let on he forgot somethin' and run into mah cabin and made me let down mah hair for de last time. He sorta wropped his hand in it, pulled mah big toe, lak he always done, and was gone after de rest lak lightnin'. Ah heard 'em give one last whoop for him. Then de big house and de quarters got sober and silent.

"It was de cool of de evenin' when Mistis come walkin' in mah door. She throwed de door wide open and stood dere lookin' at me outa her eyes and her face. Look lak she been livin' through uh hundred years in January without one day of spring. She come stood over me in de bed.

" 'Nanny, Ah come to see that baby uh yourn.'

"Ah tried not to feel de breeze off her face, but it got so cold in dere dat Ah was freezin' to death under the kivvers. So Ah couldn't move right away lak Ah aimed to. But Ah knowed Ah had to make haste and do it.

" 'You better git dat kivver offa dat youngun and dat quick!' she clashed at me. 'Look lak you don't know who is Mistis on dis plantation, Madam. But Ah aims to show you.'

"By dat time I had done managed tuh unkivver mah baby

16

enough for her to see de head and face.

" 'Nigger, whut's yo' baby doin' wid gray eyes and yaller hair? She begin tuh slap mah jaws ever which a'way. Ah never felt the fust ones 'cause Ah wuz too busy gittin' de kivver back over mah chile. But dem last lick burnt me lak fire. Ah had too many feelin's tuh tell which one tuh follow so Ah didn't cry and Ah didn't do nothin' else. But then she kept on astin me how come mah baby look white. She asted me dat maybe twenty-five or thirty times, lak she got tuh sayin' dat and couldn't help herself. So Ah told her, 'Ah don't know nothin' but what Ah'm told tuh do, 'cause Ah ain't nothin' but uh nigger and uh slave.'

"Instead of pacifyin' her lak Ah thought, look lak she got madder. But Ah reckon she was tired and wore out 'cause she didn't hit me no more. She went to de foot of de bed and wiped her hands on her handksher. 'Ah wouldn't dirty mah hands on yuh. But first thing in de mornin' de overseer will take you to de whippin' post and tie you down on yo' knees and cut de hide offa yo' yaller back. One hundred lashes wid a raw-hide on yo' bare back. Ah'll have you whipped till de blood run down to yo' heels! Ah mean to count de licks mahself. And if it kills you Ah'll stand de loss. Anyhow, as soon as dat brat is a month old Ah'm going to sell it offa dis place.'

"She flounced on off and let her wintertime wid me. Ah knowed mah body wasn't healed, but Ah couldn't consider dat. In de black dark Ah wrapped mah baby de best Ah knowed how and made it to de swamp by de river. Ah knowed de place was full uh moccasins and other bitin' snakes, but Ah was more skeered uh whut was behind me. Ah hide in dere day and night and suckled de baby every time she start to cry, for fear somebody might hear her and Ah'd git found. Ah ain't sayin' uh friend or two didn't feel mah care. And den de Good Lawd seen to it dat Ah wasn't taken. Ah don't see how come mah milk didn't kill mah chile, wid me so skeered and worried all de time. De noise uh de owls skeered me; de limbs of dem

17

cypress trees took to crawlin' and movin' round after dark, and two three times Ah heered panthers prowlin' round. But nothin' never hurt me 'cause de Lawd knowed how it was.

"Den, one night Ah heard de big guns boomin' lak thunder. It kept up all night long. And de next mornin' Ah could see uh big ship at a distance and a great stirrin' round. So Ah wrapped Leafy up in moss and fixed her good in a tree and picked mah way on down to de landin'. The men was all in blue, and Ah heard people say Sherman was comin' to meet de boats in Savannah, and all of us slaves was free. So Ah run got mah baby and got in quotation wid people and found a place Ah could stay.

"But it was a long time after dat befo' de Big Surrender at Richmond. Den de big bell ring in Atlanta and all de men in gray uniforms had to go to Moultrie, and bury their swords in de ground to show they was never to fight about slavery no mo'. So den we knowed we was free.

"Ah wouldn't marry nobody, though Ah could have uh heap uh times, cause Ah didn't want nobody mistreating mah baby. So Ah got with some good white people and come down here in West Florida to work and make de sun shine on both sides of de street for Leafy.

"Mah Madam help me wid her just lak she been doin' wid you. Ah put her in school when it got so it was a school to put her in. Ah was 'spectin' to make a school teacher outa her.

"But one day she didn't come home at de usual time and Ah waited and waited, but she never come all dat night. Ah took a lantern and went round askin' everybody but nobody ain't seen her. De next mornin' she come crawlin' in on her hands and knees. A sight to see. Dat school teacher had done hid her in de woods all night long, and he had done raped mah baby and run on off just before day.

"She was only seventeen, and somethin' lak dat to happen! Lawd a'mussy! Look lak Ah kin see it all over again. It was a long time before she was well, and by dat time we knowed you was on de way. And after you was born she took to drinkin'

18

likker and stayin' out nights. Couldn't git her to stay here and nowhere else. Lawd knows where she is right now. She ain't dead, 'cause Ah'd know it by mah feelings, but sometimes Ah wish she was at rest.

"And, Janie, maybe it wasn't much, but Ah done de best Ah kin by you. Ah raked and scraped and bought dis lil piece uh land so you wouldn't have to stay in de white folks' yard and tuck yo' head befo' other chillun at school. Dat was all right when you was little. But when you got big enough to understand things, Ah wanted you to look upon yo'self. Ah don't want yo' feathers always crumpled by folks throwin' up things in yo' face. And Ah can't die easy thinkin' maybe de menfolks white or black is makin' a spit cup outa you: Have some sympathy fuh me. Put me down easy, Janie, Ah'm a cracked plate."

CHAPTER 3

There are years that ask questions and years that answer. Janie had had no chance to know things, so she had to ask. Did marriage end the cosmic loneliness of the unmated? Did marriage compel love like the sun the day?

In the few days to live before she went to Logan Killicks and his often-mentioned sixty acres, Janie asked inside of herself and out. She was back and forth to the pear tree continuously wondering and thinking. Finally out of Nanny's talk and her own conjectures she made a sort of comfort for herself. Yes, she would love Logan after they were married. She could see no way for it to come about, but Nanny and the old folks had said it, so it must be so. Husbands and wives always loved each other, and that was what marriage meant. It was just so. Janie felt glad of the thought, for then it wouldn't seem so destructive and mouldy. She wouldn't be lonely anymore.

Janie and Logan got married in Nanny's parlor of a Saturday evening with three cakes and big platters of fried rabbit and chicken. Everything to eat in abundance. Nanny and Mrs. Washburn had seen to that. But nobody put anything on the seat of Logan's wagon to make it ride glorious on the way to his house. It was a lonesome place like a stump in the middle of the woods where nobody had ever been. The house was absent of flavor, too. But anyhow Janie went on inside to wait for love to begin. The new moon had been up and down three times before she got worried in mind. Then she went to see Nanny in Mrs. Washburn's kitchen on the day for beaten biscuits.

Nanny beamed all out with gladness and made her come up to the bread board so she could kiss her.

"Lawd a'mussy, honey, Ah sho is glad tuh see mah chile! G'wan inside and let Mis' Washburn know youse heah. Umph! Umph! Umph! How is dat husband uh yourn?"

Janie didn't go in where Mrs. Washburn was. She didn't say anything to match up with Nanny's gladness either. She just fell on a chair with her hips and sat there. Between the biscuits and her beaming pride Nanny didn't notice for a minute. But after a while she found the conversation getting lonesome so she looked up at Janie.

"Whut's de matter, sugar? You ain't none too spry dis mornin'."

"Oh, nothin' much, Ah reckon. Ah come to get a lil information from you."

The old woman looked amazed, then gave a big clatter of laughter. "Don't tell me you done got knocked up already, less see—dis Saturday it's two month and two weeks."

"No'm, Ah don't think so anyhow." Janie blushed a little.

"You ain't got nothin' to be shamed of, honey, youse uh married 'oman. You got yo' lawful husband same as Mis' Washburn or anybody else!"

"Ah'm all right dat way. Ah *know* 'tain't nothin' dere."

"You and Logan been fussin'? Lawd, Ah know dat grass-gut, liver-lipted nigger ain't done took and beat mah baby already! Ah'll take a stick and salivate 'im!"

"No'm, he ain't even talked 'bout hittin' me. He says he never mean to lay de weight uh his hand on me in malice. He chops all de wood he think Ah wants and den he totes it inside de kitchen for me. Keeps both water buckets full."

"Humph! don't 'spect all dat tuh keep up. He ain't kissin'

21

yo' mouf when he carry on over yuh lak dat. He's kissin' yo' foot and 'tain't in uh man tuh kiss foot long. Mouf kissin' is on uh equal and dat's natural but when dey got to bow down tuh love, dey soon straightens up."

"Yes'm."

"Well, if he do all dat whut you come in heah wid uh face long as mah arm for?"

" 'Cause you told me Ah mus gointer love him, and, and Ah don't. Maybe if somebody was to tell me how, Ah could do it."

"You come heah wid yo' mouf full uh foolishness on uh busy day. Heah you got uh prop tuh lean on all yo' bawn days, and big protection, and everybody got tuh tip dey hat tuh you and call you Mis' Killicks, and you come worryin' me 'bout love."

"But Nanny, Ah wants to want him sometimes. Ah don't want him to do all de wantin'."

"If you don't want him, you sho oughta. Heah you is wid de onliest organ in town, amongst colored folks, in yo' parlor. Got a house bought and paid for and sixty acres uh land right on de big road and . . . Lawd have mussy! Dat's de very prong all us black women gits hung on. Dis love! Dat's just whut's got us uh pullin' and uh haulin' and sweatin' and doin' from can't see in de mornin' till can't see at night. Dat's how come de ole folks say dat bein' uh fool don't kill nobody. It jus' makes you sweat. Ah betcha you wants some dressed up dude dat got to look at de sole of his shoe everytime he cross de street tuh see whether he got enough leather dere tuh make it across. You can buy and sell such as dem wid what you got. In fact you can buy 'em and give 'em away."

"Ah ain't studyin' 'bout none of 'em. At de same time Ah ain't takin' dat ole land tuh heart neither. Ah could throw ten acres of it over de fence every day and never look back to see where it fell. Ah feel de same way 'bout Mr. Killicks too. Some folks never was meant to be loved and he's one of 'em."

"How come?"

" 'Cause Ah hates de way his head is so long one way and so flat on de sides and dat pone uh fat back uh his neck."

"He never made his own head. You talk so silly."

"Ah don't keer who made it, Ah don't like de job. His belly is too big too, now, and his toe-nails look lak mule foots. And 'tain't nothin' in de way of him washin' his feet every evenin' before he comes tuh bed. 'Tain't nothin' tuh hinder him 'cause Ah places de water for him. Ah'd ruther be shot wid tacks than tuh turn over in de bed and stir up de air whilst he is in dere. He don't even never mention nothin' pretty."

She began to cry.

"Ah wants things sweet wid mah marriage lak when you sit under a pear tree and think. Ah . . ."

" 'Tain't no use in you cryin', Janie. Grandma done been long uh few roads herself. But folks is meant to cry 'bout somethin' or other. Better leave things de way dey is. Youse young yet. No tellin' whut mout happen befo' you die. Wait awhile, baby. Yo' mind will change."

Nanny sent Janie along with a stern mien, but she dwindled all the rest of the day as she worked. And when she gained the privacy of her own little shack she stayed on her knees so long she forgot she was there herself. There is a basin in the mind where words float around on thought and thought on sound and sight. Then there is a depth of thought untouched by words, and deeper still a gulf of formless feelings untouched by thought. Nanny entered this infinity of conscious pain again on her old knees. Towards morning she muttered, "Lawd, you know mah heart. Ah done de best Ah could do. De rest is left to you." She scuffled up from her knees and fell heavily across the bed. A month later she was dead.

So Janie waited a bloom time, and a green time and an orange time. But when the pollen again gilded the sun and sifted down on the world she began to stand around the gate and expect things. What things? She didn't know exactly. Her breath was gusty and short. She knew things that nobody had ever told her. For instance, the words of the trees and the wind. She often spoke to falling seeds and said, "Ah hope you fall on soft ground," because she had heard seeds saying that to each other as they passed. She knew the world was a stallion rolling in the blue pasture of ether. She knew that God tore down the old world every evening and built a new one by sun-up. It was wonderful to see it take form with the sun and emerge from the gray dust of its making. The familiar people and things had failed her so she hung over the gate and looked up the road towards way off. She knew now that marriage did not make love. Janie's first dream was dead, so she became a woman.

CHAPTER 4

Long before the year was up, Janie noticed that her husband had stopped talking in rhymes to her. He had ceased to wonder at her long black hair and finger it. Six months back he had told her, "If Ah kin haul de wood heah and chop it fuh yuh, look lak you oughta be able tuh tote it inside. Mah fust wife never bothered me 'bout choppin' no wood nohow. She'd grab dat ax and sling chips lak uh man. You done been spoilt rotten."

So Janie had told him, "Ah'm just as stiff as you is stout. If you can stand not to chop and tote wood Ah reckon you can stand not to git no dinner. 'Scuse mah freezolity, Mist' Killicks, but Ah don't mean to chop de first chip."

"Aw you know Ah'm gwine chop de wood fuh yuh. Even if you is stingy as you can be wid me. Yo' Grandma and me myself done spoilt yuh now, and Ah reckon Ah have tuh keep on wid it."

One morning soon he called her out of the kitchen to the barn. He had the mule all saddled at the gate.

"Looka heah, LilBit, help me out some. Cut up dese seed taters fuh me. Ah got tuh go step off a piece."

"Where you goin'?"

"Over tuh Lake City tuh see uh man about uh mule."

"Whut you need two mules fuh? Lessen you aims to swap off dis one."

"Naw, Ah needs two mules dis yeah. Taters is goin' tuh be taters in de fall. Bringin' big prices. Ah aims tuh run two plows, and dis man Ah'm talkin' 'bout is got uh mule all gentled up so even uh woman kin handle 'im."

Logan held his wad of tobacco real still in his jaw like a thermometer of his feelings while he studied Janie's face and waited for her to say something.

"So Ah thought Ah mout as well go see." He tagged on and swallowed to kill time but Janie said nothing except, "Ah'll cut de p'taters fuh yuh. When yuh comin' back?"

"Don't know exactly. Round dust dark Ah reckon. It's uh sorta long trip—specially if Ah hafter lead one on de way back."

When Janie had finished indoors she sat down in the barn with the potatoes. But springtime reached her in there so she moved everything to a place in the yard where she could see the road. The noon sun filtered through the leaves of the fine oak tree where she sat and made lacy patterns on the ground. She had been there a long time when she heard whistling coming down the road.

It was a cityfied, stylish dressed man with his hat set at an angle that didn't belong in these parts. His coat was over his arm, but he didn't need it to represent his clothes. The shirt with the silk sleeveholders was dazzling enough for the world. He whistled, mopped his face and walked like he knew where he was going. He was a seal-brown color but he acted like Mr. Washburn or somebody like that to Janie. Where would such a man be coming from and where was he going? He didn't look her way nor no other way except straight ahead, so Janie ran to the pump and jerked the handle hard while she pumped. It made a loud noise and also made her heavy hair fall down. So he stopped and looked hard, and then he asked her for a cool drink of water.

Janie pumped it off until she got a good look at the man.

He talked friendly while he drank.

Joe Starks was the name, yeah Joe Starks from in and through Georgy. Been workin' for white folks all his life. Saved up some money—round three hundred dollars, yes indeed, right here in his pocket. Kept hearin' 'bout them buildin' a new state down heah in Floridy and sort of wanted to come. But he was makin' money where he was. But when he heard all about 'em makin' a town all outa colored folks, he knowed dat was de place he wanted to be. He had always wanted to be a big voice, but de white folks had all de sayso where he come from and everywhere else, exceptin' dis place dat colored folks was buildin' theirselves. Dat was right too. De man dat built things oughta boss it. Let colored folks build things too if dey wants to crow over somethin'. He was glad he had his money all saved up. He meant to git dere whilst de town wuz yet a baby. He meant to buy in big. It had always been his wish and desire to be a big voice and he had to live nearly thirty years to find a chance. Where was Janie's papa and mama?

"Dey dead, Ah reckon. Ah wouldn't know 'bout 'em 'cause mah Grandma raised me. She dead too."

"She dead too! Well, who's lookin' after a lil girl-chile lak you?"

"Ah'm married."

"You married? You ain't hardly old enough to be weaned. Ah betcha you still craves sugar-tits, doncher?"

"Yeah, and Ah makes and sucks 'em when de notion strikes me. Drinks sweeten' water too."

"Ah loves dat mahself. Never specks to get too old to enjoy syrup sweeten' water when it's cools and nice."

"Us got plenty syrup in de barn. Ribbon-cane syrup. If you so desires—"

"Where yo' husband at, Mis' er-er."

"Mah name is Janie Mae Killicks since Ah got married. Useter be name Janie Mae Crawford. Mah husband is gone

27

tuh buy a mule fuh me tuh plow. He left me cuttin' up seed p'taters."

"You behind a plow! You ain't got no mo' business wid uh plow than uh hog is got wid uh holiday! You ain't got no business cuttin' up no seed p'taters neither. A pretty doll-baby lak you is made to sit on de front porch and rock and fan yo'self and eat p'taters dat other folks plant just special for you."

Janie laughed and drew two quarts of syrup from the barrel and Joe Starks pumped the water bucket full of cool water. They sat under the tree and talked. He was going on down to the new part of Florida, but no harm to stop and chat. He later decided he needed a rest anyway. It would do him good to rest a week or two.

Every day after that they managed to meet in the scrub oaks across the road and talk about when he would be a big ruler of things with her reaping the benefits. Janie pulled back a long time because he did not represent sun-up and pollen and blooming trees, but he spoke for far horizon. He spoke for change and chance. Still she hung back. The memory of Nanny was still powerful and strong.

"Janie, if you think Ah aims to tole you off and make a dog outa you, youse wrong. Ah wants to make a wife outa you."

"You mean dat, Joe?"

"De day you puts yo' hand in mine, Ah wouldn't let de sun go down on us single. Ah'm uh man wid principles. You ain't never knowed what it was to be treated lak a lady and Ah wants to be de one tuh show yuh. Call me Jody lak you do sometime."

"Jody," she smiled up at him, "but s'posin'—"

"Leave de s'posin' and everything else to me. Ah'll be down dis road uh little after sunup tomorrow mornin' to wait for you. You come go wid me. Den all de rest of yo' natural life you kin live lak you oughta. Kiss me and shake yo' head. When you do dat, yo' plentiful hair breaks lak day."

Janie debated the matter that night in bed.

28

"Logan, you 'sleep?"

"If Ah wuz, you'd be done woke me up callin' me."

"Ah wuz thinkin' real hard about us; about you and me."

"It's about time. Youse powerful independent around here sometime considerin'."

"Considerin' whut for instance?"

"Considerin' youse born in a carriage 'thout no top to it, and yo' mama and you bein' born and raised in de white folks back-yard."

"You didn't say all dat when you wuz begging Nanny for me to marry you."

"Ah thought you would 'preciate good treatment. Thought Ah'd take and make somethin' outa yuh. You think youse white folks by de way you act."

"S'posin' Ah wuz to run off and leave yuh sometime."

There! Janie had put words in his held-in fears. She might run off sure enough. The thought put a terrible ache in Logan's body, but he thought it best to put on scorn.

"Ah'm gettin' sleepy, Janie. Let's don't talk no mo'. 'Tain't too many mens would trust yuh, knowin' yo' folks lak dey do."

"Ah might take and find somebody dat did trust me and leave yuh."

"Shucks! 'Tain't no mo' fools lak me. A whole lot of mens will grin in yo' face, but dey ain't gwine tuh work and feed yuh. You won't git far and you won't be long, when dat big gut reach over and grab dat little one, you'll be too glad to come back here."

"You don't take nothin' to count but sow-belly and corn-bread."

"Ah'm sleepy. Ah don't aim to worry mah gut into a fiddle-string wid no s'posin'." He flopped over resentful in his agony and pretended sleep. He hoped that he had hurt her as she had hurt him.

Janie got up with him the next morning and had the break-fast halfway done when he bellowed from the barn.

"Janie!" Logan called harshly. "Come help me move dis

manure pile befo' de sun gits hot. You don't take a bit of interest in dis place. 'Tain't no use in foolin' round in dat kitchen all day long."

Janie walked to the door with the pan in her hand still stirring the cornmeal dough and looked towards the barn. The sun from ambush was threatening the world with red daggers, but the shadows were gray and solid-looking around the barn. Logan with his shovel looked like a black bear doing some clumsy dance on his hind legs.

"You don't need mah help out dere, Logan. Youse in yo' place and Ah'm in mine."

"You ain't got no particular place. It's wherever Ah need yuh. Git uh move on yuh, and dat quick."

"Mah mamma didn't tell me Ah wuz born in no hurry. So whut business Ah got rushin' now? Anyhow dat ain't whut youse mad about. Youse mad 'cause Ah don't fall down and wash-up dese sixty acres uh ground yuh got. You ain't done me no favor by marryin' me. And if dat's what you call yo'self doin', Ah don't thank yuh for it. Youse mad 'cause Ah'm tellin' yuh whut you already knowed."

Logan dropped his shovel and made two or three clumsy steps towards the house, then stopped abruptly.

"Don't you change too many words wid me dis mawnin', Janie, do Ah'll take and change ends wid yuh! Heah, Ah just as good as take you out de white folks' kitchen and set you down on yo' royal diasticutis and you take and low-rate me! Ah'll take holt uh dat ax and come in dere and kill yuh! You better dry up in dere! Ah'm too honest and hard-workin' for anybody in yo' family, dat's de reason you don't want me!" The last sentence was half a sob and half a cry. "Ah guess some low-lifed nigger is grinnin' in yo' face and lyin' tuh yuh. God damn yo' hide!"

Janie turned from the door without answering, and stood still in the middle of the floor without knowing it. She turned wrongside out just standing there and feeling. When the throbbing calmed a little she gave Logan's speech a hard thought and placed it beside other things she had seen and heard. When she had finished with that she dumped the dough on the skillet and smoothed it over with her hand. She wasn't even angry. Logan was accusing her of her mamma, her grand-mama and her feelings, and she couldn't do a thing about any of it. The sow-belly in the pan needed turning. She flipped it over and shoved it back. A little cold water in the coffee pot to settle it. Turned the hoe-cake with a plate and then made a little laugh. What was she losing so much time for? A feeling of sudden newness and change came over her. Janie hurried out of the front gate and turned south. Even if Joe was not there waiting for her, the change was bound to do her good.

The morning road air was like a new dress. That made her feel the apron tied around her waist. She untied it and flung it on a low bush beside the road and walked on, picking flowers and making a bouquet. After that she came to where Joe Starks was waiting for her with a hired rig. He was very solemn and helped her to the seat beside him. With him on it, it sat like some high, ruling chair. From now on until death she was going to have flower dust and springtime sprinkled over everything. A bee for her bloom. Her old thoughts were going to come in handy now, but new words would have to be made and said to fit them.

"Green Cove Springs," he told the driver. So they were married there before sundown, just like Joe had said. With new clothes of silk and wool.

They sat on the boarding house porch and saw the sun plunge into the same crack in the earth from which the night emerged.

CHAPTER 5

On the train the next day, Joe didn't make many speeches with rhymes to her, but he bought her the best things the butcher had, like apples and a glass lantern full of candies. Mostly he talked about plans for the town when he got there. They were bound to need somebody like him. Janie took a lot of looks at him and she was proud of what she saw. Kind of portly like rich white folks. Strange trains, and people and places didn't scare him neither. Where they got off the train at Maitland he found a buggy to carry them over to the colored town right away.

It was early in the afternoon when they got there, so Joe said they must walk over the place and look around. They locked arms and strolled from end to end of the town. Joe noted the scant dozen of shame-faced houses scattered in the sand and palmetto roots and said, "God, they call this a town? Why, 'tain't nothing but a raw place in de woods."

"It is a whole heap littler than Ah thought." Janie admitted her disappointment.

"Just like Ah thought," Joe said. "A whole heap uh talk and nobody doin' nothin'. I god, where's de Mayor?" he asked somebody. "Ah want tuh speak wid de Mayor."

Two men who were sitting on their shoulderblades under

a huge live oak tree almost sat upright at the tone of his voice. They stared at Joe's face, his clothes and his wife.

"Where y'all come from in sich uh big haste?" Lee Coker asked.

"Middle Georgy," Starks answered briskly. "Joe Starks is mah name, from in and through Georgy."

"You and yo' daughter goin' tuh join wid us in fellowship?" the other reclining figure asked. "Mighty glad tuh have yuh. Hicks is the name. Guv'nor Amos Hicks from Buford, South Carolina. Free, single, disengaged."

"I god, Ah ain't nowhere near old enough to have no grown daughter. This here is mah wife."

Hicks sank back and lost interest at once.

"Where is de Mayor?" Starks persisted. "Ah wants tuh talk wid *him.*"

"Youse uh mite too previous for dat," Coker told him. "Us ain't got none yit."

"Ain't got no Mayor! Well, who tells y'all what to do?"

"Nobody. Everybody's grown. And then agin, Ah reckon us just ain't thought about it. Ah know Ah ain't."

"Ah did think about it one day," Hicks said dreamily, "but then Ah forgot it and ain't thought about it since then."

"No wonder things ain't no better," Joe commented. "Ah'm buyin' in here, and buyin' in big. Soon's we find some place to sleep tonight us menfolks got to call people together and form a committee. Then we can get things movin' round here."

"Ah kin point yuh where yuh kin sleep," Hicks offered. "Man got his house done built and his wife ain't come yet."

Starks and Janie moved on off in the direction indicated with Hicks and Coker boring into their backs with looks.

"Dat man talks like a section foreman," Coker commented. "He's mighty compellment."

"Shucks!" said Hicks. "Mah britches is just as long as his. But dat wife uh hisn! Ah'm uh son of uh Combunction if Ah don't go tuh Georgy and git me one just like her."

"Whut wid?"

"Wid mah talk, man."

"It takes money tuh feed pretty women. Dey gits uh lavish uh talk."

"Not lak mine. Dey loves to hear me talk because dey can't understand it. Mah co-talkin' is too deep. Too much co to it."

"Umph!"

"You don't believe me, do yuh? You don't know de women Ah kin git to mah command."

"Umph!"

"You ain't never seen me when Ah'm out pleasurin' and givin' pleasure."

"Umph!"

"It's uh good thing he married her befo' she seen me. Ah kin be some trouble when Ah take uh notion."

"Umph!"

"Ah'm uh bitch's baby round lady people."

"Ah's much ruther see all dat than to hear 'bout it. Come on less go see whut he gointuh do 'bout dis town."

They got up and sauntered over to where Starks was living for the present. Already the town had found the strangers. Joe was on the porch talking to a small group of men. Janie could be seen through the bedroom window getting settled. Joe had rented the house for a month. The men were all around him, and he was talking to them by asking questions.

"Whut is de real name of de place?"

"Some say West Maitland and some say Eatonville. Dat's 'cause Cap'n Eaton give us some land along wid Mr. Laurence. But Cap'n Eaton give de first piece."

"How much did they give?"

"Oh 'bout fifty acres."

"How much is y'all got now?"

"Oh 'bout de same."

"Dat ain't near enough. Who owns de land joining on to whut yuh got?"

"Cap'n Eaton."

"Where *is* dis Cap'n Eaton?"

"Over dere in Maitland, 'ceptin' when he go viisitin' or somethin'."

"Lemme speak to mah wife a minute and Ah'm goin' see de man. You cannot have no town without some land to build it on. Y'all ain't got enough here to cuss a cat on without gittin' yo' mouf full of hair."

"He ain't got no mo' land tuh give away. Yuh needs plenty money if yuh wants any mo'."

"Ah specks to pay him."

The idea was funny to them and they wanted to laugh. They tried hard to hold it in, but enough incredulous laughter burst out of their eyes and leaked from the corners of their mouths to inform anyone of their thoughts. So Joe walked off abruptly. Most of them went along to show him the way and to be there when his bluff was called.

Hicks didn't go far. He turned back to the house as soon as he felt he wouldn't be missed from the crowd and mounted the porch.

"Evenin', Miz Starks."

"Good evenin'."

"You reckon you gointuh like round here?"

"Ah reckon so."

"Anything *Ah* kin do tuh help out, why you kin call on me."

"Much obliged."

There was a long dead pause. Janie was not jumping at her chance like she ought to. Look like she didn't hardly know he was there. She needed waking up.

"Folks must be mighty close-mouthed where you come from."

"Dat's right. But it must be different at yo' home."

He was a long time thinking but finally he saw and stumbled down the steps with a surly " 'Bye."

"Good bye."

That night Coker asked him about it.

"Ah saw yuh when yuh ducked back tuh Starks' house. Well, how didju make out?"

"Who, me? Ah ain't been near de place, man. Ah been down tuh de lake tryin' tuh ketch me uh fish."

"Umph!"

"Dat 'oman ain't so awfully pretty no how when yuh take de second look at her. Ah had to sorta pass by de house on de way back and seen her good. 'Tain't nothin' to her 'ceptin' dat long hair."

"Umph!"

"And anyhow, Ah done took uhlikin' tuh de man. Ah wouldn't harm him at all. She ain't half ez pretty ez uh gal Ah run off and left up in South Cal'lina."

"Hicks, Ah'd git mad and say you wuz lyin' if Ah didn't know yuh so good. You just talkin' to consolate yo'self by word of mouth. You got uh willin' mind, but youse too light behind. A whole heap uh men seen de same thing you seen but they got better sense than you. You oughta know you can't take no 'oman lak dat from no man lak him. A man dat ups and buys two hundred acres uh land at one whack and pays cash for it."

"Naw! He didn't buy it sho nuff?"

"He sho did. Come off wid de papers in his pocket. He done called a meetin' on his porch tomorrow. Ain't never seen no sich uh colored man befo' in all mah bawn days. He's gointuh put up uh store and git uh post office from de Goven'-ment."

That irritated Hicks and he didn't know why. He was the average mortal. It troubled him to get used to the world one way and then suddenly have it turn different. He wasn't ready to think of colored people in post offices yet. He laughed boisterously.

"Y'all let dat stray darky tell y'all any ole lie! Uh colored man sittin' up in uh post office!" He made an obscene sound.

"He's liable tuh do it too, Hicks. Ah hope so anyhow. Us colored folks is too envious of one 'nother. Dat's how come

36

us don't git no further than us do. Us talks about de white man keepin' us down! Shucks! He don't have tuh. Us keeps our own selves down."

"Now who said Ah didn't want de man tuh git us uh post office? He kin be de king uh Jerusalem fuh all Ah keer. Still and all, 'tain't no use in telling lies just 'cause uh heap uh folks don't know no better. Yo' common sense oughta tell yuh de white folks ain't goin' tuh 'low him tuh run no post office."

"Dat we don't know, Hicks. He say he kin and Ah b'lieve he know whut he's talkin' 'bout. Ah reckon if colored folks got they own town they kin have post offices and whatsoever they please, regardless. And then agin, Ah don't speck de white folks way off yonder give uh damn. Less us wait and see."

"Oh, Ah'm waitin' all right. Specks tuh keep on waitin' till hell freeze over."

"Aw, git reconciled! Dat woman don't want you. You got tuh learn dat all de women in de world ain't been brought up on no teppentine still, and no saw-mill camp. There's some women dat jus' ain't for you tuh broach. You can't git *her* wid no fish sandwich."

They argued a bit more then went on to the house where Joe was and found him in his shirt-sleeves, standing with his legs wide apart, asking questions and smoking a cigar.

"Where's de closest saw-mill?" He was asking Tony Taylor.

" 'Bout seben miles goin' t'wards Apopka," Tony told him.

"Thinkin' 'bout buildin' right away?"

"I god, yeah. But not de house Ah specks tuh live in. Dat kin wait till Ah make up mah mind where Ah wants it located. Ah figgers we all needs uh store in uh big hurry."

"Uh store?" Tony shouted in surprise.

"Yeah, uh store right heah in town wid everything in it you needs. 'Tain't uh bit uh use in everybody proagin' way over tuh Maitland tuh buy uh little meal and flour when they could git it right heah."

"Dat would be kinda nice, Brother Starks, since you mention it."

37

"I god, course it would! And then agin uh store is good in other ways. Ah got tuh have a place tuh be at when folks comes tuh buy land. And furthermo' everything is got tuh have uh center and uh heart tuh it, and uh town ain't no different from nowhere else. It would be natural fuh de store tuh be meetin' place fuh de town."

"Dat sho is de truth, now."

"Oh, we'll have dis town all fixed up tereckly. Don't miss bein' at de meetin' tuhmorrow."

Just about time for the committee meeting called to meet on his porch next day, the first wagon load of lumber drove up and Jody went to show them where to put it. Told Janie to hold the committee there until he got back, he didn't want to miss them, but he meant to count every foot of that lumber before it touched the ground. He could have saved his breath and Janie could have kept right on with what she was doing. In the first place everybody was late in coming; then the next thing as soon as they heard where Jody was, they kept right on up there where the new lumber was rattling off the wagon and being piled under the big live oak tree. So that's where the meeting was held with Tony Taylor acting as chairman and Jody doing all the talking. A day was named for roads and they all agreed to bring axes and things like that and chop out two roads running each way. That applied to everybody except Tony and Coker. They could carpenter, so Jody hired them to go to work on his store bright and soon the next morning. Jody himself would be busy driving around from town to town telling people about Eatonville and drumming up citizens to move there.

Janie was astonished to see the money Jody had spent for the land come back to him so fast. Ten new families bought lots and moved to town in six weeks. It all looked too big and rushing for her to keep track of. Before the store had a complete roof, Jody had canned goods piled on the floor and was selling so much he didn't have time to go off on his talking tours. She had her first taste of presiding over it the day it was

38

complete and finished. Jody told her to dress up and stand in the store all that evening. Everybody was coming sort of fixed up, and he didn't mean for nobody else's wife to rank with her. She must look on herself as the bell-cow, the other women were the gang. So she put on one of her bought dresses and went up the new-cut road all dressed in wine-colored red. Her silken ruffles rustled and muttered about her. The other women had on percale and calico with here and there a head-rag among the older ones.

Nobody was buying anything that night. They didn't come there for that. They had come to make a welcome. So Joe knocked in the head of a barrel of soda crackers and cut some cheese.

"Everybody come right forward and make merry. I god, it's mah treat." Jody gave one of his big heh heh laughs and stood back. Janie dipped up the lemonade like he told her. A big tin cup full for everybody. Tony Taylor felt so good when it was all gone that he felt to make a speech.

"Ladies and gent'men, we'se come tuhgether and gethered heah tuh welcome tuh our midst one who has seen fit tuh cast in his lot amongst us. He didn't just come hisself neither. He have seen fit tuh bring his, er, er, de light uh his home, dat is his wife amongst us also. She couldn't look no mo' better and no nobler if she wuz de queen uh England. It's uh pledger fuh her tuh be heah amongst us. Brother Starks, we welcomes you and all dat you have seen fit tuh bring amongst us—yo' belov-ed wife, yo' store, yo' land—"

A big-mouthed burst of laughter cut him short.

"Dat'll do, Tony," Lige Moss yelled out. "Mist' Starks is uh smart man, we'se all willin' tuh acknowledge tuh dat, but de day he comes waggin' down de road wid two hund'ed acres uf land over his shoulder, Ah wants tuh be dere tuh see it."

Another big blow-out of a laugh. Tony was a little peeved at having the one speech of his lifetime ruined like that.

"All y'all know whut wuz meant. Ah don't see how come—"

39

" 'Cause you jump up tuh make speeches and don't know how," Lige said.

"Ah wuz speakin' jus' all right befo' you stuck yo' bill in."

"Naw, you wuzn't, Tony. Youse way outa jurisdiction. You can't welcome uh man and his wife 'thout you make comparison about Isaac and Rebecca at de well, else it don't show de love between 'em if you don't."

Everybody agreed that that was right. It was sort of pitiful for Tony not to know he couldn't make a speech without saying that. Some tittered at his ignorance. So Tony said testily, "If all them dat's goin-tuh cut de monkey is done cut it and through wid, we'll thank Brother Starks fuh a respond."

So Joe Starks and his cigar took the center of the floor.

"Ah thanks you all for yo' kind welcome and for extendin' tuh me de right hand uh fellowship. Ah kin see dat dis town is full uh union and love. Ah means tuh put mah hands tuh de plow heah, and strain every nerve tuh make dis our town de metropolis uh de state. So maybe Ah better tell yuh in case you don't know dat if we expect tuh move on, us got tuh incorporate lak every other town. Us got tuh incorporate, and us got tuh have uh mayor, if things is tuh be done and done right. Ah welcome you all on behalf uh me and mah wife tuh dis store and tuh de other things tuh come. Amen."

Tony led the loud hand-clapping and was out in the center of the floor when it stopped.

"Brothers and sisters, since us can't never expect tuh better our choice, Ah move dat we make Brother Starks our Mayor until we kin see further."

"Second dat motion!!!" It was everybody talking at once, so it was no need of putting it to a vote.

"And now we'll listen tuh uh few words uh encouragement from Mrs. Mayor Starks."

The burst of applause was cut short by Joe taking the floor himself.

"Thank yuh fuh yo' compliments, but mah wife don't know nothin' 'bout no speech-makin'. Ah never married her for

40

nothin' lak dat. She's uh woman and her place is in de home."

Janie made her face laugh after a short pause, but it wasn't too easy. She had never thought of making a speech, and didn't know if she cared to make one at all. It must have been the way Joe spoke out without giving her a chance to say anything one way or another that took the bloom off of things. But anyway, she went down the road behind him that night feeling cold. He strode along invested with his new dignity, thought and planned out loud, unconscious of her thoughts.

"De mayor of uh town lak dis can't lay round home too much. De place needs buildin' up. Janie, Ah'll git hold uh somebody tuh help out in de store and you kin look after things whilst Ah drum up things otherwise."

"Oh Jody, Ah can't do nothin' wid no store lessen youse there. Ah could maybe come in and help you when things git rushed, but—"

"I god, Ah don't see how come yuh can't. 'Tain't nothin' atall tuh hinder yuh if yuh got uh thimble full uh sense. You got tuh. Ah got too much else on mah hands as Mayor. Dis town needs some light right now."

"Unh hunh, it *is* uh little dark right long heah."

" 'Course it is. 'Tain't no use in scufflin' over all dese stumps and roots in de dark. Ah'll call uh meetin' bout de dark and de roots right away. Ah'll sit on dis case first thing."

The very next day with money out of his own pocket he sent off to Sears, Roebuck and Company for the street lamp and told the town to meet the following Thursday night to vote on it. Nobody had ever thought of street lamps and some of them said it was a useless notion. They went so far as to vote against it, but the majority ruled.

But the whole town got vain over it after it came. That was because the Mayor didn't just take it out of the crate and stick it up on a post. He unwrapped it and had it wiped off carefully and put it up on a showcase for a week for everybody to see. Then he set a time for the lighting and sent word all around Orange County for one and all to come to the lamplighting.

He sent men out to the swamp to cut the finest and the straightest cypress post they could find, and kept on sending them back to hunt another one until they found one that pleased him. He had talked to the people already about the hospitality of the occasion.

"Y'all know we can't invite people to our town just dry long so. I god, naw. We got tuh feed 'em something, and 'tain't nothin' people laks better'n barbecue. Ah'll give one whole hawg mah ownself. Seem lak all de rest uh y'all put tuhgether oughta be able tuh scrape up two mo'. Tell yo' womenfolks tuh do 'round 'bout some pies and cakes and sweet p'tater pone."

That's the way it went, too. The women got together the sweets and the men looked after the meats. The day before the lighting, they dug a big hole in back of the store and filled it full of oak wood and burned it down to a glowing bed of coals. It took them the whole night to barbecue the three hogs. Hambo and Pearson had full charge while the others helped out with turning the meat now and then while Hambo swabbed it all over with the sauce. In between times they told stories, laughed and told more stories and sung songs. They cut all sorts of capers and whiffed the meat as it slowly came to perfection with the seasoning penetrating to the bone. The younger boys had to rig up the saw-horses with boards for the women to use as tables. Then it was after sun-up and everybody not needed went home to rest up for the feast.

By five o'clock the town was full of every kind of a vehicle and swarming with people. They wanted to see that lamp lit at dusk. Near the time, Joe assembled everybody in the street before the store and made a speech.

"Folkses, de sun is goin' down. De Sun-maker brings it up in de mornin', and de Sun-maker sends it tuh bed at night. Us poor weak humans can't do nothin' tuh hurry it up nor to slow it down. All we can do, if we want any light after de settin' or befo' de risin', is tuh make some light ourselves. So dat's

42

how come lamps was made. Dis evenin' we'se all assembled
heah tuh light uh lamp. Dis occasion is something for us all
tuh remember tuh our dyin' day. De first street lamp in uh
colored town. Lift yo' eyes and gaze on it. And when Ah touch
de match tuh dat lamp-wick let de light penetrate inside of
yuh, and let it shine, let it shine, let it shine. Brother Davis,
lead us in a word uh prayer. Ask uh blessin' on dis town in uh
most particular manner."

While Davis chanted a traditional prayer-poem with his
own variations, Joe mounted the box that had been placed for
the purpose and opened the brazen door of the lamp. As the
word Amen was said, he touched the lighted match to the
wick, and Mrs. Bogle's alto burst out in:

> We'll walk in de light, de beautiful light
> Come where the dew drops of mercy shine bright
> Shine all around us by day and by night
> Jesus, the light of the world.

They, all of them, all of the people took it up and sung it
over and over until it was wrung dry, and no further innova-
tions of tone and tempo were conceivable. Then they hushed
and ate barbecue.

When it was all over that night in bed Jody asked Janie,
"Well, honey, how yuh lak bein' Mrs. Mayor?"

"It's all right Ah reckon, but don't yuh think it keeps us in
uh kinda strain?"

"Strain? You mean de cookin' and waitin' on folks?"

"Naw, Jody, it jus' looks lak it keeps us in some way we ain't
natural wid one 'nother. You'se always off talkin' and fixin'
things, and Ah feels lak Ah'm jus' markin' time. Hope it soon
gits over."

"Over, Janie? I god, Ah ain't even started good. Ah told
you in de very first beginnin' dat Ah aimed tuh be uh big
voice. You oughta be glad, 'cause dat makes uh big woman
outa you."

A feeling of coldness and fear took hold of her. She felt far away from things and lonely.

Janie soon began to feel the impact of awe and envy against her sensibilities. The wife of the Mayor was not just another woman as she had supposed. She slept with authority and so she was part of it in the town mind. She couldn't get but so close to most of them in spirit. It was especially noticeable after Joe had forced through a town ditch to drain the street in front of the store. They had murmured hotly about slavery being over, but every man filled his assignment.

There was something about Joe Starks that cowed the town. It was not because of physical fear. He was no fist fighter. His bulk was not even imposing as men go. Neither was it because he was more literate than the rest. Something else made men give way before him. He had a bow-down command in his face, and every step he took made the thing more tangible.

Take for instance that new house of his. It had two stories with porches, with bannisters and such things. The rest of the town looked like servants' quarters surrounding the "big house." And different from everybody else in the town he put off moving in until it had been painted, in and out. And look at the way he painted it—a gloaty, sparkly white. The kind of promenading white that the houses of Bishop Whipple, W. B. Jackson and the Vanderpool's wore. It made the village feel funny talking to him—just like he was anybody else. Then there was the matter of the spittoons. No sooner was he all set as the Mayor—post master—landlord—storekeeper, than he bought a desk like Mr. Hill or Mr. Galloway over in Maitland with one of those swing-around chairs to it. What with him biting down on cigars and saving his breath on talk and swinging round in that chair, it weakened people. And then he spit in that gold-looking vase that anybody else would have been glad to put on their front-room table. Said it was a spittoon just like his used-to-be bossman used to have in his bank up there in Atlanta. Didn't have to get up and go to the door every time he had to spit. Didn't spit on his floor neither. Had that golded-up spitting pot right handy. But he went further than that. He bought a little lady-size spitting pot for Janie to spit in. Had it right in the parlor with little sprigs of flowers painted all around the sides. It took people by surprise because most of the women dipped snuff and of course had a spit-cup in the house. But how could they know up-to-date folks was spitting in flowery little things like that? It sort of made the rest of them feel that they had been taken advantage of. Like things had been kept from them. Maybe more things in the world besides spitting pots had been hid from them, when they wasn't told no better than to spit in tomato cans. It was bad enough for white people, but when one of your own color could be so different it put you on a wonder. It was like seeing your sister turn into a 'gator. A familiar strangeness. You keep seeing your sister in the 'gator and the 'gator in your sister, and you'd rather not. There was no doubt that the town respected him and even admired him in a way. But any man who walks in the way of power and property is bound to meet hate. So when speakers stood up when the occasion demanded and said "Our beloved Mayor," it was one of those statements that everybody says but nobody actually believes like "God is everywhere." It was just a handle to wind up the tongue with. As time went on and the benefits he had conferred upon the town receded in time they sat on his store porch while he was busy inside and discussed him. Like one day after he caught Henry Pitts with a wagon load of his ribbon cane and took the cane away from Pitts and made him leave town. Some of them thought Starks ought not to have done that. He had so much cane and everything else. But they didn't say that while Joe Starks was on the porch. When the mail came from Maitland and he went inside to sort it out everybody had their say.

Sim Jones started off as soon as he was sure that Starks couldn't hear him.

"It's uh sin and uh shame runnin' dat po' man way from

here lak dat. Colored folks oughtn't tuh be so hard on one 'nother."

"Ah don't see it dat way atall," Sam Watson said shortly. "Let colored folks learn to work for what dey git lak everybody else. Nobody ain't stopped Pitts from plantin' de cane he wanted tuh. Starks give him uh job, what mo' do he want?"

"Ah know dat too," Jones said, "but, Sam, Joe Starks is too exact wid folks. All he got he done made it offa de rest of us. He didn't have all dat when he come here."

"Yeah, but none uh all dis you see and you'se settin' on wasn't here neither, when he come. Give de devil his due."

"But now, Sam, you know dat all he do is big-belly round and tell other folks what tuh do. He loves obedience out of everybody under de sound of his voice."

"You kin feel a switch in his hand when he's talkin' to yuh," Oscar Scott complained. "Dat chastisin' feelin' he totes sorter gives yuh de protolapsis uh de cutinary linin'."

"He's uh whirlwind among breezes," Jeff Bruce threw in.

"Speakin' of winds, he's de wind and we'se de grass. We bend which ever way he blows," Sam Watson agreed, "but at dat us needs him. De town wouldn't be nothin' if it wasn't for him. He can't help bein' sorta bossy. Some folks needs thrones, and ruling-chairs and crowns tuh make they influence felt. He don't. He's got uh throne in de seat of his pants."

"Whut Ah don't lak 'bout de man is, he talks tuh unlettered folks wid books in his jaws," Hicks complained. "Showin' off his learnin'. To look at me you wouldn't think it, but Ah got uh brother pastorin' up round Ocala dat got good learnin'. If he wuz here, Joe Starks wouldn't make no fool outa him lak he do de rest uh y'all."

"Ah often wonder how dat lil wife uh hisn makes out wid him, 'cause he's uh man dat changes everything, but nothin' don't change him."

"You know many's de time Ah done thought about dat mahself. He gits on her ever now and then when she make little mistakes round de store."

"Whut make her keep her head tied up lak some ole 'oman round de store? Nobody couldn't *git* me tuh tie no rag on mah head if Ah had hair lak dat."

"Maybe he make her do it. Maybe he skeered some de rest of us mens might touch it round dat store. It sho is uh hidden mystery tuh me."

"She sho don't talk much. De way he rears and pitches in de store sometimes when she make uh mistake is sort of ungodly, but she don't seem to mind at all. Reckon dey understand one 'nother."

The town had a basketful of feelings good and bad about Joe's positions and possessions, but none had the temerity to challenge him. They bowed down to him rather, because he was all of these things, and then again he was all of these things because the town bowed down.

CHAPTER 6

E very morning the world flung itself over and exposed
the town to the sun. So Janie had another day. And every
day had a store in it, except Sundays. The store itself was
a pleasant place if only she didn't have to sell things. When the
people sat around on the porch and passed around the pictures
of their thoughts for the others to look at and see, it was nice.
The fact that the thought pictures were always crayon enlargements of life made it even nicer to listen to.

Take for instance the case of Matt Bonner's yellow mule.
They had him up for conversation every day the Lord sent.
Most especial if Matt was there himself to listen. Sam and Lige
and Walter were the ringleaders of the mule-talkers. The others threw in whatever they could chance upon, but it seemed
as if Sam and Lige and Walter could hear and see more about
that mule than the whole county put together. All they needed
was to see Matt's long spare shape coming down the street and
by the time he got to the porch they were ready for him.

"Hello, Matt."

"Evenin', Sam."

"Mighty glad you come 'long right now, Matt. Me and
some others wuz jus' about tuh come hunt yuh."

"Whut fuh, Sam?"

"Mighty serious matter, man. Serious!!"

"Yeah man," Lige would cut in, dolefully. "It needs yo' strict attention. You ought not tuh lose no time."

"Whut is it then? You oughta hurry up and tell me."

"Reckon we better not tell yuh heah at de store. It's too fur off tuh do any good. We better all walk on down by Lake Sabelia."

"Whut's wrong, man? Ah ain't after none uh y'alls foolishness now."

"Dat mule uh yourn, Matt. You better go see 'bout him. He's bad off."

"Where 'bouts? Did he wade in de lake and uh alligator ketch him?"

"Worser'n dat. De womenfolks got yo' mule. When Ah come round de lake 'bout noontime mah wife and some others had 'im flat on de ground usin' his sides fuh uh wash board."

The great clap of laughter that they have been holding in, bursts out. Sam never cracks a smile. "Yeah, Matt, dat mule so skinny till de women is usin' his rib bones fuh uh rub-board, and hangin' things out on his hock-bones tuh dry."

Matt realizes that they have tricked him again and the laughter makes him mad and when he gets mad he stammers.

"You'se uh stinkin' lie, Sam, and yo' feet ain't mates. Y-y-y-you!"

"Aw, man, 'tain't no use in you gittin' mad. Yuh know yuh don't feed de mule. How he gointuh git fat?"

"Ah-ah-ah d-d-does feed 'im! Ah g-g-gived 'im uh full cup uh cawn every feedin'."

"Lige knows all about dat cup uh cawn. He hid round yo' barn and watched yuh. 'Tain't no feed cup you measures dat cawn outa. It's uh tea cup."

"Ah does feed 'im. He's jus' too mean tuh git fat. He stay poor and rawbony jus' fuh spite. Skeered he'll hafta work some."

"Yeah, you feeds 'im. Feeds 'im offa 'come up' and seasons it wid raw-hide."

49

"Does feed de ornery varmint! Don't keer whut Ah do Ah can't git long wid 'im. He fights every inch in front uh de plow, and even lay back his ears tuh kick and bite when Ah go in de stall tuh feed 'im.''

"Git reconciled, Matt," Lige soothed. "Us all knows he's mean. Ah seen 'im when he took after one uh dem Roberts chillun in de street and woulda caught 'im and maybe trompled 'im tuh death if de wind hadn't of changed all of a sudden. Yuh see de youngun wuz tryin' tuh make it tuh de fence uh Starks' onion patch and de mule wuz dead in behind 'im and gainin' on 'im every jump, when all of a sudden de wind changed and blowed de mule way off his course, him bein' so poor and everything, and before de ornery varmint could tack, de youngun had done got over de fence." The porch laughed and Matt got mad again.

"Maybe de mule takes out after everybody," Sam said, " 'cause he thinks everybody he hear comin' is Matt Bonner comin' tuh work 'im on uh empty stomach.''

"Aw, naw, aw, naw. You stop dat right now," Walter objected. "Dat mule don't think Ah look lak no Matt Bonner. He ain't dat dumb. If Ah thought he didn't know no better Ah'd have mah picture took and give it tuh dat mule so's he could learn better. Ah ain't gointuh 'low 'im tuh hold nothin' lak dat against me."

Matt struggled to say something but his tongue failed him so he jumped down off the porch and walked away as mad as he could be. But that never halted the mule talk. There would be more stories about how poor the brute was; his age; his evil disposition and his latest caper. Everybody indulged in mule talk. He was next to the Mayor in prominence, and made better talking.

Janie loved the conversation and sometimes she thought up good stories on the mule, but Joe had forbidden her to indulge. He didn't want her talking after such trashy people. "You'se Mrs. Mayor Starks, Janie. I god, Ah can't see what uh woman uh yo' stability would want tuh be treasurin' all dat gum-grease from folks dat don't even own de house dey sleep in. 'Tain't no earthly use. They's jus' some puny humans playin' round de toes uh Time.''

Janie noted that while he didn't talk the mule himself, he sat and laughed at it. Laughed his big heh, heh laugh too. But then when Lige or Sam or Walter or some of the other big picture talkers were using a side of the world for a canvas, Joe would hustle her off inside the store to sell something. Look like he took pleasure in doing it. Why couldn't he go himself sometimes? She had come to hate the inside of that store anyway. That Post Office too. People always coming and asking for mail at the wrong time. Just when she was trying to count up something or write in an account book. Get her so hackled she'd make the wrong change for stamps. Then too, she couldn't read everybody's writing. Some folks wrote so funny and spelt things different from what she knew about. As a rule, Joe put up the mail himself, but sometimes when he was off she had to do it herself and it always ended up in a fuss.

The store itself kept her with a sick headache. The labor of getting things down off of a shelf or out of a barrel was nothing. And so long as people wanted only a can of tomatoes or a pound of rice it was all right. But supposing they went on and said a pound and a half of bacon and a half pound of lard? The whole thing changed from a little walking and stretching to a mathematical dilemma. Or maybe cheese was thirty-seven cents a pound and somebody came and asked for a dime's worth. She went through many silent rebellions over things like that. Such a waste of life and time. But Joe kept saying that she could do it if she wanted to and he wanted her to use her privileges. That was the rock she was battered against.

This business of the head-rag irked her endlessly. But Jody was set on it. Her hair was NOT going to show in the store. It didn't seem sensible at all. That was because Joe never told Janie how jealous he was. He never told her how often he had seen the other men figuratively wallowing in it as she went about things in the store. And one night he had caught Walter standing behind Janie and brushing the back of his hand back and forth across the loose end of her braid ever so lightly so as to enjoy the feel of it without Janie knowing what he was doing. Joe was at the back of the store and Walter didn't see him. He felt like rushing forth with the meat knife and chopping off the offending hand. That night he ordered Janie to tie up her hair around the store. That was all. She was there in the store for *him* to look at, not those others. But he never said things like that. It just wasn't in him. Take the matter of the yellow mule, for instance.

Late one afternoon Matt came from the west with a halter in his hand. "Been huntin' fuh mah mule. Anybody seen 'im?" he asked.

"Seen 'im soon dis mornin' over behind de schoolhouse," Lum said. " 'Bout ten o'clock or so. He musta been out all night tuh be way over dere dat early."

"He wuz," Matt answered. "Seen 'im last night but Ah couldn't ketch 'im. Ah'm 'bliged tuh git 'im in tuhnight 'cause Ah got some plowin' fuh tuhmorrow. Done promised tuh plow Thompson's grove."

"Reckon you'll ever git through de job wid dat mule-frame?" Lige asked.

"Aw dat mule is plenty strong. Jus' evil and don't want tuh be led."

"Dat's right. Dey tell me he brought you heah tuh dis town. Say you started tuh Miccanopy but de mule had better sense and brung yuh on heah."

"It's uh l-l-lie! Ah set out fuh dis town when Ah left West Floridy."

"You mean tuh tell me you rode dat mule all de way from West Floridy down heah?"

"Sho he did, Lige. But he didn't mean tuh. He wuz satisfied up dere, but de mule wuzn't. So one mornin' he got straddle uh de mule and he took and brought 'im on off. Mule had sense. Folks up dat way don't eat biscuit bread but once uh week."

There was always a little seriousness behind the teasing of Matt, so when he got huffed and walked on off nobody minded. He was known to buy side-meat by the slice. Carried home little bags of meal and flour in his hand. He didn't seem to mind too much so long as it didn't cost him anything.

About half an hour after he left they heard the braying of the mule at the edge of the woods. He was coming past the store very soon.

"Less ketch Matt's mule fuh 'im and have some fun."

"Now, Lum, you know dat mule ain't aimin' tuh let hisself be caught. Less watch *you* do it."

When the mule was in front of the store, Lum went out and tackled him. The brute jerked up his head, laid back his ears and rushed to the attack. Lum had to run for safety. Five or six more men left the porch and surrounded the fractious beast, goosing him in the sides and making him show his temper. But he had more spirit left than body. He was soon panting and heaving from the effort of spinning his old carcass about. Everybody was having fun at the mule-baiting. All but Janie.

She snatched her head away from the spectacle and began muttering to herself. "They oughta be shamed uh theyselves! Teasin' dat poor brute beast lak they is! Done been worked tuh death; done had his disposition ruint wid mistreatment, and now they got tuh finish devilin' 'im tuh death. Wisht Ah had mah way wid 'em all."

She walked away from the porch and found something to busy herself with in the back of the store so she did not hear Jody when he stopped laughing. She didn't know that he had heard her, but she did hear him yell out, "Lum, I god, dat's enough! Y'all done had yo' fun now. Stop yo' foolishness and go tell Matt Bonner Ah wants tuh have uh talk wid him right away."

Janie came back out front and sat down. She didn't say anything and neither did Joe. But after a while he looked down at his feet and said, "Janie, Ah reckon you better go fetch me dem old black gaiters. Dese tan shoes sets mah feet on fire. Plenty room in 'em, but they hurts regardless."

She got up without a word and went off for the shoes. A little war of defense for helpless things was going on inside her. People ought to have some regard for helpless things. She wanted to fight about it. "But Ah hates disagreement and confusion, so Ah better not talk. It makes it hard tuh git along." She didn't hurry back. She fumbled around long enough to get her face straight. When she got back, Joe was talking with Matt.

"Fifteen dollars? I god you'se as crazy as uh betsy bug! Five dollars."

"L-l-less we strack uh compermise, Brother Mayor. Less m-make it ten."

"Five dollars." Joe rolled his cigar in his mouth and rolled his eyes away indifferently.

"If dat mule is wuth somethin' tuh *you,* Brother Mayor, he's wuth mo' tuh me. More special when Ah got uh job uh work tuhmorrow."

"Five dollars."

"All right, Brother Mayor. If you wants tuh rob uh poor man lak me uh everything he got tuh make uh livin' wid, Ah'll take de five dollars. Dat mule been wid me twenty-three years. It's mighty hard."

Mayor Starks deliberately changed his shoes before he reached into his pocket for the money. By that time Matt was wringing and twisting like a hen on a hot brick. But as soon as his hand closed on the money his face broke into a grin.

"Beatyuh tradin' dat time, Starks! Dat mule is liable tuh be dead befo' de week is out. You won't git no work outa him."

"Didn't buy 'im fuh no work. I god, Ah bought dat varmint tuh let 'im rest. You didn't have gumption enough tuh do it."

A respectful silence fell on the place. Sam looked at Joe and said, "Dat's uh new idea 'bout varmints, Mayor Starks. But Ah laks it mah ownself. It's uh noble thing you done." Everybody agreed with that.

Janie stood still while they all made comments. When it was all done she stood in front of Joe and said, "Jody, dat wuz uh mighty fine thing fuh you tuh do. 'Tain't everybody would have thought of it, 'cause it ain't no everyday thought. Freein' dat mule makes uh mighty big man outa you. Something like George Washington and Lincoln. Abraham Lincoln, he had de whole United States tuh rule so he freed de Negroes. You got uh town so you freed uh mule. You have tuh have power tuh free things and dat makes you lak uh king uh something."

Hambo said, "Yo' wife is uh born orator, Starks. Us never knowed dat befo'. She put jus' de right words tuh our thoughts."

Joe bit down hard on his cigar and beamed all around, but he never said a word. The town talked it for three days and said that's just what they would have done if they had been rich men like Joe Starks. Anyhow a free mule in town was something new to talk about. Starks piled fodder under the big tree near the porch and the mule was usually around the store like the other citizens. Nearly everybody took the habit of fetching along a handful of fodder to throw on the pile. He almost got fat and they took a great pride in him. New lies sprung up about his free-mule doings. How he pushed open Lindsay's kitchen door and slept in the place one night and fought until they made coffee for his breakfast; how he stuck his head in the Pearsons' window while the family was at the table and Mrs. Pearson mistook him for Rev. Pearson and handed him a plate; he ran Mrs. Tully off of the croquet ground for having such an ugly shape; he ran and caught up with Becky Anderson on the way to Maitland so as to keep his head out of the sun under her umbrella; he got tired of listening to Redmond's long-winded prayer, and went inside the Baptist church and broke up the meeting. He did everything but let himself be bridled and visit Matt Bonner.

But way after a while he died. Lum found him under the big tree on his rawbony back with all four feet up in the air. That wasn't natural and it didn't look right, but Sam said it would have been more unnatural for him to have laid down on his side and died like any other beast. He had seen Death coming and had stood his ground and fought it like a natural man. He had fought it to the last breath. Naturally he didn't have time to straighten himself out. Death had to take him like it found him.

When the news got around, it was like the end of a war or something like that. Everybody that could knocked off from work to stand around and talk. But finally there was nothing to do but drag him out like all other dead brutes. Drag him out to the edge of the hammock which was far enough off to satisfy sanitary conditions in the town. The rest was up to the buzzards. Everybody was going to the dragging-out. The news had got Mayor Starks out of bed before time. His pair of gray horses was out under the tree and the men were fooling with the gear when Janie arrived at the store with Joe's breakfast.

"I god, Lum, you fasten up dis store good befo' you leave, you hear me?" He was eating fast and talking with one eye out of the door on the operations.

"Whut you tellin' 'im tuh fasten up for, Jody?" Janie asked, surprised.

" 'Cause it won't be nobody heah tuh look after de store. Ah'm goin' tuh de draggin'-out mahself."

" 'Tain't nothin' so important Ah got tuh do tuhday, Jody. How come Ah can't go long wid you tuh de draggin'-out?"

Joe was struck speechless for a minute. "Why, Janie! You wouldn't be seen at uh draggin'-out, wouldja? Wid any and everybody in uh passle pushin' and shovin' wid they no-manners selves? Naw, naw!"

"You would be dere wid me, wouldn't yuh?"

"Dat's right, but Ah'm uh man even if Ah is de Mayor. But de mayor's wife is somethin' different again. Anyhow they's liable tuh need me tuh say uh few words over de carcass, dis bein' uh special case. But *you* ain't goin' off in all dat mess uh commonness. Ah'm surprised at yuh fuh askin'."

He wiped his lips of ham gravy and put on his hat. "Shet

de door behind yuh, Janie. Lum is too busy wid de hawses."

After more shouting of advice and orders and useless comments, the town escorted the carcass off. No, the carcass moved off with the town, and left Janie standing in the doorway.

Out in the swamp they made great ceremony over the mule. They mocked everything human in death. Starks led off with a great eulogy on our departed citizen, our most distinguished citizen and the grief he left behind him, and the people loved the speech. It made him more solid than building the schoolhouse had done. He stood on the distended belly of the mule for a platform and made gestures. When he stepped down, they hoisted Sam up and he talked about the mule as a school teacher first. Then he set his hat like John Pearson and imitated his preaching. He spoke of the joys of mule-heaven to which the dear brother had departed this valley of sorrow; the mule-angels flying around; the miles of green corn and cool water, a pasture of pure bran with a river of molasses running through it; and most glorious of all, *No* Matt Bonner with plow lines and halters to come in and corrupt. Up there, mule-angels would have people to ride on and from his place beside the glittering throne, the dear departed brother would look down into hell and see the devil plowing Matt Bonner all day long in a hell-hot sun and laying the raw-hide to his back.

With that the sisters got mock-happy and shouted and had to be held up by the menfolks. Everybody enjoyed themselves to the highest and then finally the mule was left to the already impatient buzzards. They were holding a great flying-meet way up over the heads of the mourners and some of the nearby trees were already peopled with the stoop-shouldered forms.

As soon as the crowd was out of sight they closed in circles. The near ones got nearer and the far ones got near. A circle, a swoop and a hop with spread-out wings. Close in, close in till some of the more hungry or daring perched on the carcass. They wanted to begin, but the Parson wasn't there, so a messenger was sent to the ruler in a tree where he sat.

The flock had to wait the white-headed leader, but it was hard. They jostled each other and pecked at heads in hungry irritation. Some walked up and down the beast from head to tail, tail to head. The Parson sat motionless in a dead pine tree about two miles off. He had scented the matter as quickly as any of the rest, but decorum demanded that he sit oblivious until he was notified. Then he took off with ponderous flight and circled and lowered, circled and lowered until the others danced in joy and hunger at his approach.

He finally lit on the ground and walked around the body to see if it were really dead. Peered into its nose and mouth. Examined it well from end to end and leaped upon it and bowed, and the others danced a response. That being over, he balanced and asked:

"What killed this man?"

The chorus answered, "Bare, bare fat."

"What killed this man?"

"Bare, bare fat."

"What killed this man?"

"Bare, bare fat."

"Who'll stand his funeral?"

"We!!!!!"

"Well, all right now."

So he picked out the eyes in the ceremonial way and the feast went on. The yaller mule was gone from the town except for the porch talk, and for the children visiting his bleaching bones now and then in the spirit of adventure.

Joe returned to the store full of pleasure and good humor but he didn't want Janie to notice it because he saw that she was sullen and he resented that. She had no right to be, the way he thought things out. She wasn't even appreciative of his efforts and she had plenty cause to be. Here he was just pouring honor all over her; building a high chair for her to sit in and overlook the world and she here pouting over it!

58

Not that he wanted anybody else, but just too many women would be glad to be in her place. He ought to box her jaws! But he didn't feel like fighting today, so he made an attack upon her position backhand.

"Ah had tuh laugh at de people out dere in de woods dis mornin', Janie. You can't help but laugh at de capers they cuts. But all the same, Ah wish mah people would git mo' business in 'em and not spend so much time on foolishness."

"Everybody can't be lak you, Jody. Somebody is bound tuh want tuh laugh and play."

"Who don't love tuh laugh and play?"

"You make out like you don't, anyhow."

"I god, Ah don't make out no such uh lie! But it's uh time fuh all things. But it's awful tuh see so many people don't want nothin' but uh full belly and uh place tuh lay down and sleep afterwards. It makes me sad sometimes and then agin it makes me mad. They say things sometimes that tickles me nearly tuh death, but Ah won't laugh jus' tuh dis-incourage 'em." Janie took the easy way away from a fuss. She didn't change her mind but she agreed with her mouth. Her heart said, "Even so, but you don't have to cry about it."

But sometimes Sam Watson and Lige Moss forced a belly laugh out of Joe himself with their eternal arguments. It never ended because there was no end to reach. It was a contest in hyperbole and carried on for no other reason.

Maybe Sam would be sitting on the porch when Lige walked up. If nobody was there to speak of, nothing happened. But if the town was there like on Saturday night, Lige would come up with a very grave air. Couldn't even pass the time of day, for being so busy thinking. Then when he was asked what was the matter in order to start him off, he'd say, "Dis question done 'bout drove me crazy. And Sam, he know so much into things, Ah wants some information on de subject."

Walter Thomas was due to speak up and egg the matter on. "Yeah, Sam always got more information than he know what to do wid. He's bound to tell yuh whatever it is you wants tuh know."

Sam begins an elaborate show of avoiding the struggle. That draws everybody on the porch into it.

"How come you want me *tuh* tell yuh? You always claim God done met you round de corner and talked His inside business wid yuh. 'Tain't no use in you askin' *me* nothin'. Ah'm questionizin' *you.*"

"How you gointuh do dat, Sam, when Ah arrived dis conversation mahself? Ah'm askin' *you.*"

"Askin' me what? You ain't told me de subjick yit."

"Don't aim tuh tell yuh! Ah aims tuh keep yuh in de dark all de time. If you'se smart lak you let on you is, you kin find out."

"Yuh skeered to lemme know whut it is, 'cause yuh know Ah'll tear it tuh pieces. You got to have a subjick tuh talk from, do yuh can't talk. If uh man ain't got no bounds, he ain't got no place tuh stop."

By this time, they are the center of the world.

"Well all right then. Since you own up you ain't smart enough tuh find out whut Ah'm talkin' 'bout, Ah'll tell you. Whut is it dat keeps uh man from gettin' burnt on uh red-hot stove—caution or nature?"

"Shucks! Ah thought you had somethin' hard tuh ast me. Walter kin tell yuh dat."

"If de conversation is too deep for yuh, how come yuh don't tell me so, and hush up? Walter can't tell me nothin' uh de kind. Ah'm uh educated man, Ah keeps mah arrangements in mah hands, and if it kept me up all night long studyin' 'bout it, Walter ain't liable tuh be no help to me. Ah needs uh man lak you."

"And then agin, Lige, Ah'm gointuh tell yuh. Ah'm gointuh run dis conversation from uh gnat heel to uh lice. It's nature dat keeps uh man off of uh red-hot stove."

"Uuh huuh! Ah knowed you would going tuh crawl up in dat holler! But Ah aims tuh smoke yuh right out. 'Tain't no nature at all, it's caution, Sam."

" 'Tain't no sich uh thing! Nature tells yuh not tuh fool wid no red-hot stove, and you don't do it neither."

"Listen, Sam, if it was nature, nobody wouldn't have tuh look out for babies touchin' stoves, would they? 'Cause dey just naturally wouldn't touch it. But dey sho will. So it's caution."

"Naw it ain't, it's nature, cause nature makes caution. It's de strongest thing dat God ever made, now. Fact is it's de onliest thing God ever made. He made nature and nature made everything else."

"Naw nature didn't neither. A whole heap of things ain't even been made yit."

"Tell me somethin' you know of dat nature ain't made."

"She ain't made it so you kin ride uh butt-headed cow and hold on tuh de horns."

"Yeah, but dat ain't yo' point."

"Yeah it is too."

"Naw it ain't neither."

"Well what *is* mah point?"

"You ain't got none, so far."

"Yeah he is too," Walter cut in. "De red-hot stove is his point."

"He know mighty much, but he ain't proved it yit."

"Sam, Ah say it's caution, not nature dat keeps folks off uh red-hot stove."

"How is de son gointuh be before his paw? Nature is de first of everything. Ever since self was self, nature been keepin' folks off of red-hot stoves. Dat caution you talkin' 'bout ain't nothin' but uh humbug. He's uh inseck dat nothin' he got belongs to him. He got eyes, lak somethin' else; wings lak somethin' else—everything! Even his hum is de sound of somebody else."

"Man, whut you talkin' 'bout? Caution is de greatest thing in de world. If it wasn't for caution—"

"Show me somethin' dat caution ever made! Look whut

nature took and done. Nature got so high in uh black hen she got tuh lay uh white egg. Now you tell me, how come, whut got intuh man dat he got tuh have hair round his mouth? Nature!''

''Dat ain't—''

The porch was boiling now. Starks left the store to Hezekiah Potts, the delivery boy, and come took a seat in his high chair.

''Look at dat great big ole scoundrel-beast up dere at Hall's fillin' station—uh great big old scoundrel. He eats up all de folks outa de house and den eat de house.''

''Aw 'tain't no sich a varmint nowhere dat kin eat no house! Dat's uh lie. Ah wuz dere yiste'ddy and Ah ain't seen nothin' lak dat. Where is he?''

''Ah didn't see him but Ah reckon he is in de back-yard some place. But dey got his picture out front dere. They was nailin' it up when Ah come pass dere dis evenin'.''

''Well all right now, if he eats up houses how come he don't eat up de fillin' station?''

''Dat's 'cause dey got him tied up so he can't. Dey got uh great big picture tellin' how many gallons of dat Sinclair high-compression gas he drink at one time and how he's more'n uh million years old.''

'' 'Tain't *nothin'* no million years old!''

''De picture is right up dere where anybody kin see it. Dey can't make de picture till dey see de thing, kin dey?''

''How dey goin' to tell he's uh million years old? Nobody wasn't born dat fur back.''

''By de rings on his tail Ah reckon. Man, dese white folks got ways for tellin' anything dey wants tuh know.''

''Well, where he been at all dis time, then?''

''Dey caught him over dere in Egypt. Seem lak he used tuh hang round dere and eat up dem Pharaohs' tombstones. Dey got de picture of him doin' it. Nature is high in uh varmint lak dat. Nature and salt. Dat's whut makes up strong man lak Big John de Conquer. He was uh man wid salt in him. He could give uh flavor to *anything.*"

"Yeah, but he was uh man dat wuz more'n man. 'Tain't no mo' lak him. He wouldn't dig potatoes, and he wouldn't rake hay: He wouldn't take a whipping, and he wouldn't run away."

"Oh yeah, somebody else could if dey tried hard enough. Me mahself, Ah got salt in *me.* If Ah like man flesh, Ah could eat some man every day, some of 'em is so trashy they'd let me eat 'em."

"Lawd, Ah loves to talk about Big John. Less we tell lies on Ole John."

But here come Bootsie, and Teadi and Big 'oman down the street making out they are pretty by the way they walk. They have got that fresh, new taste about them like young mustard greens in the spring, and the young men on the porch are just bound to tell them about it and buy them some treats.

"Heah come mah order right now," Charlie Jones announces and scrambles off the porch to meet them. But he has plenty of competition. A pushing, shoving show of gallantry. They all beg the girls to just buy anything they can think of. Please let them pay for it. Joe is begged to wrap up all the candy in the store and order more. All the peanuts and soda water—everything!

"Gal, Ah'm crazy 'bout you," Charlie goes on to the entertainment of everybody. "Ah'll do anything in the world except work for you and give you mah money."

The girls and everybody else help laugh. They know it's not courtship. It's acting-out courtship and everybody is in the play. The three girls hold the center of the stage till Daisy Blunt comes walking down the street in the moonlight.

Daisy is walking a drum tune. You can almost hear it by looking at the way she walks. She is black and she knows that white clothes look good on her, so she wears them for dress up. She's got those big black eyes with plenty shiny white in them that makes them shine like brand new money and she knows what God gave women eyelashes for, too. Her hair is not what you might call straight. It's negro hair, but it's got a kind of white flavor. Like the piece of string out of a ham. It's not ham at all, but it's been around ham and got the flavor. It was spread down thick and heavy over her shoulders and looked just right under a big white hat.

"Lawd, Lawd, Lawd," that same Charlie Jones exclaims rushing over to Daisy. "It must be uh recess in heben if St. Peter is lettin' his angels out lak dis. You got three men already layin' at de point uh death 'bout yuh, and heah's uhnother fool dat's willin' tuh make time on yo' gang."

All the rest of the single men have crowded around Daisy by this time. She is parading and blushing at the same time.

"If you know anybody dat's 'bout tuh die 'bout me, yuh know more'n Ah do," Daisy bridled. "Wisht Ah knowed who it is."

"Now, Daisy, *you* know Jim, and Dave and Lum is 'bout tuh kill one 'nother 'bout you. Don't stand up here and tell dat big ole got-dat-wrong."

"Dey a mighty hush-mouf about it if dey is. Dey ain't never told me nothin'."

"Unhunh, you talked too fast. Heah, Jim and Dave is right upon de porch and Lum is inside de store."

A big burst of laughter at Daisy's discomfiture. The boys had to act out their rivalry too. Only this time, everybody knew they meant some of it. But all the same the porch enjoyed the play and helped out whenever extras were needed.

David said, "Jim don't love Daisy. He don't love yuh lak Ah do."

Jim bellowed indignantly, "Who don't love Daisy? Ah know you ain't talkin' 'bout me."

Dave: "Well all right, less prove dis thing right now. We'll prove right now who love dis gal de best. How much time is you willin' tuh make fuh Daisy?"

Jim: "Twenty yeahs!"

Dave: "See? Ah told yuh dat nigger didn't love yuh. Me,

64

Ah'll beg de Judge tuh hang me, and wouldn't take nothin' less than life.''

There was a big long laugh from the porch. Then Jim had to demand a test.

"Dave, how much would you be willin' tuh do for Daisy if she was to turn fool enough tuh marry yuh?''

"Me and Daisy done talked dat over, but if you just got tuh know, Ah'd buy Daisy uh passenger train and give it tuh her.''

"Humph! Is dat all? Ah'd buy her uh steamship and then Ah'd hire some mens tuh run it fur her.''

"Daisy, don't let Jim fool you wid his talk. He don't aim tuh do nothin' fuh yuh. Uh lil ole steamship! Daisy, Ah'll take uh job cleanin' out de Atlantic Ocean fuh you any time you say you so desire.'' There was a great laugh and then they hushed to listen.

"Daisy,'' Jim began, "you know mah heart and all de ranges uh mah mind. And you know if Ah wuz ridin' up in uh earoplane way up in de sky and Ah looked down and seen you walkin' and knowed you'd have tuh walk ten miles tuh git home, Ah'd step backward offa dat earoplane just to walk home wid you.''

There was one of those big blow-out laughs and Janie was wallowing in it. Then Jody ruined it all for her.

Mrs. Bogle came walking down the street towards the porch. Mrs. Bogle who was many times a grandmother, but had a blushing air of coquetry about her that cloaked her sunken cheeks. You saw a fluttering fan before her face and magnolia blooms and sleepy lakes under the moonlight when she walked. There was no obvious reason for it, it was just so. Her first husband had been a coachman but "studied jury" to win her. He had finally become a preacher to hold her till his death. Her second husband worked in Fohnes orange grove— but tried to preach when he caught her eye. He never got any further than a class leader, but that was something to offer her. It proved his love and pride. She was a wind on the ocean. She moved men, but the helm determined the port. Now, this night she mounted the steps and the men noticed her until she passed inside the door.

"I god, Janie," Starks said impatiently, "why don't you go on and see whut Mrs. Bogle want? Whut you waitin' on?"

Janie wanted to hear the rest of the play-acting and how it ended, but she got up sullenly and went inside. She came back to the porch with her bristles sticking out all over her and with dissatisfaction written all over her face. Joe saw it and lifted his own hackles a bit.

Jim Weston had secretly borrowed a dime and soon he was loudly beseeching Daisy to have a treat on him. Finally she consented to take a pickled pig foot on him. Janie was getting up a large order when they came in, so Lum waited on them. That is, he went back to the keg but came back without the pig foot.

"Mist' Starks, de pig feets is all gone!" he called out.

"Aw naw dey ain't, Lum. Ah bought uh whole new kag of 'em wid dat last order from Jacksonville. It come in yistiddy."

Joe came and helped Lum look but he couldn't find the new keg either, so he went to the nail over his desk that he used for a file to search for the order.

"Janie, where's dat last bill uh ladin'?"

"It's right dere on de nail, ain't it?"

"Naw it ain't neither. You ain't put it where Ah told yuh tuh. If you'd git yo' mind out de streets and keep it on yo' business maybe you could git somethin' straight sometimes."

"Aw, look around dere, Jody. Dat bill ain't apt tuh be gone off nowheres. If it ain't hangin' on de nail, it's on yo' desk. You bound tuh find it if you look."

"Wid you heah, Ah oughtn't tuh hafta do all dat lookin' and searchin'. Ah done told you time and time agin tuh stick all dem papers on dat nail! All you got tuh do is mind me. How come you can't do lak Ah tell yuh?"

"You sho loves to tell me whut to do, but Ah can't tell you nothin' Ah see!"

"Dat's 'cause you need tellin'," he rejoined hotly. "It would be pitiful if Ah didn't. Somebody got to think for women and chillun and chickens and cows. I god, they sho don't think none theirselves."

"Ah knows uh few things, and womenfolks thinks sometimes too!"

"Aw naw they don't. They just think they's thinkin'. When Ah see one thing Ah understands ten. You see ten things and don't understand one."

Times and scenes like that put Janie to thinking about the inside state of her marriage. Time came when she fought back with her tongue as best she could, but it didn't do her any good. It just made Joe do more. He wanted her submission and he'd keep on fighting until he felt he had it.

So gradually, she pressed her teeth together and learned to hush. The spirit of the marriage left the bedroom and took to living in the parlor. It was there to shake hands whenever company came to visit, but it never went back inside the bedroom again. So she put something in there to represent the spirit like a Virgin Mary image in a church. The bed was no longer a daisy-field for her and Joe to play in. It was a place where she went and laid down when she was sleepy and tired.

She wasn't petal-open anymore with him. She was twenty-four and seven years married when she knew. She found that out one day when he slapped her face in the kitchen. It happened over one of those dinners that chasten all women sometimes. They plan and they fix and they do, and then some kitchen-dwelling fiend slips a scorchy, soggy, tasteless mess into their pots and pans. Janie was a good cook, and Joe had looked forward to his dinner as a refuge from other things. So when the bread didn't rise, and the fish wasn't quite done at the bone, and the rice was scorched, he slapped Janie until she had a ringing sound in her ears and told her about her brains before he stalked on back to the store.

Janie stood where he left her for unmeasured time and thought. She stood there until something fell off the shelf inside her. Then she went inside there to see what it was. It was her image of Jody tumbled down and shattered. But looking at it she saw that it never was the flesh and blood figure of her dreams. Just something she had grabbed up to drape her dreams over. In a way she turned her back upon the image where it lay and looked further. She had no more blossomy openings dusting pollen over her man, neither any glistening young fruit where the petals used to be. She found that she had a host of thoughts she had never expressed to him, and numerous emotions she had never let Jody know about. Things packed up and put away in parts of her heart where he could never find them. She was saving up feelings for some man she had never seen. She had an inside and an outside now and suddenly she knew how not to mix them.

●She bathed and put on a fresh dress and head kerchief and went on to the store before Jody had time to send for her. That was a bow to the outside of things.

Jody was on the porch and the porch was full of Eatonville as usual at this time of the day. He was baiting Mrs. Tony Robbins as he always did when she came to the store. Janie could see Jody watching her out of the corner of his eye while he joked roughly with Mrs. Robbins. He wanted to be friendly with her again. His big, big laugh was as much for her as for the baiting. He was longing for peace but on his own terms.

"I god, Mrs. Robbins, whut make you come heah and worry me when you see Ah'm readin' mah newspaper?" Mayor Starks lowered the paper in pretended annoyance.

Mrs. Robbins struck her pity-pose and assumed the voice.

" 'Cause Ah'm hongry, Mist' Starks. 'Deed Ah is. Me and mah chillun is hongry. Tony don't fee-eed me!"

This was what the porch was waiting for. They burst into a laugh.

"Mrs. Robbins, how can you make out you'se hongry when Tony comes in here every Satitday and buys groceries lak a man? Three weeks' shame on yuh!"

"If he buy all dat you talkin' 'bout, Mist' Starks, God knows

68

whut he do wid it. He sho don't bring it home, and me and mah po' chillun is *so* hongry! Mist' Starks, please gimme uh lil piece uh meat fur me and mah chillun."

"Ah know you don't need it, but come on inside. You ain't goin' tuh lemme read till Ah give it to yuh."

Mrs. Tony's ecstasy was divine. "Thank you, Mist' Starks. You'se noble! You'se du most gentlemanfied man Ah ever did see. You'se uh king!"

The salt pork box was in the back of the store and during the walk Mrs. Tony was so eager she sometimes stepped on Joe's heels, sometimes she was a little before him. Something like a hungry cat when somebody approaches her pan with meat. Running a little, caressing a little and all the time making little urging-on cries.

"Yes, indeedy, Mist' Starks, you'se noble. You got sympathy for me and mah po' chillun. Tony don't give us nothin' tuh eat and we'se *so* hongry. Tony don't fee-eed me!"

This brought them to the meat box. Joe took up the big meat knife and selected a piece of side meat to cut. Mrs. Tony was all but dancing around him.

"Dat's right, Mist' Starks! Gimme uh lil piece 'bout dis wide." She indicated as wide as her wrist and hand. "Me and mah chillun is *so* hongry!"

Starks hardly looked at her measurements. He had seen them too often. He marked off a piece much smaller and sunk the blade in. Mrs. Tony all but fell to the floor in her agony.

"Lawd a'mussy! Mist' Starks, you ain't gointuh gimme dat lil tee-ninchy piece fuh me and all mah chillun, is yuh? Lawd, we'se *so* hongry!"

Starks cut right on and reached for a piece of wrapping paper. Mrs. Tony leaped away from the proffered cut of meat as if it were a rattlesnake.

"Ah wouldn't tetch it! Dat lil eyeful uh bacon for me and all mah chillun! Lawd, some folks is got everything and they's so gripin' and so mean!"

Starks made as if to throw the meat back in the box and close it. Mrs. Tony swooped like lightning and seized it, and started towards the door.

"Some folks ain't got no heart in dey bosom. They's willin' tuh see uh po' woman and her helpless chillun starve tuh death. God's gointuh put 'em under arrest, some uh dese days, wid dey stingy gripin' ways."

She stepped from the store porch and marched off in high dudgeon! Some laughed and some got mad.

"If dat wuz *mah* wife," said Walter Thomas, "Ah'd kill her cemetery dead."

"More special after Ah done bought her everything mah wages kin stand, lak Tony do," Coker said. "In de fust place Ah never would spend on *no* woman whut Tony spend on *her.*"

Starks came back and took his seat. He had to stop and add the meat to Tony's account.

"Well, Tony tells me tuh humor her along. He moved here from up de State hopin' tuh change her, but it ain't. He say he can't bear tuh leave her and he hate to kill her, so 'tain't nothin' tuh do but put up wid her."

"Dat's 'cause Tony love her too good," said Coker. "Ah could break her if she wuz mine. Ah'd break her or kill her. Makin' uh fool outa me in front of everybody."

"Tony won't never hit her. He says beatin' women is just like steppin' on baby chickens. He claims 'tain't no place on uh woman tuh hit," Joe Lindsay said with scornful disapproval, "but Ah'd kill uh baby just born dis mawnin' fuh uh thing lak dat. 'Tain't nothin' but low-down spitefulness 'ginst her husband make her do it."

"Dat's de God's truth," Jim Stone agreed. "Dat's de very reason."

Janie did what she had never done before, that is, thrust herself into the conversation.

"Sometimes God gits familiar wid us womenfolks too and talks His inside business. He told me how surprised He was 'bout y'all turning out so smart after Him makin' yuh different; and how surprised y'all is goin' tuh be if you ever find out you don't know half as much 'bout us as you think you do. It's so easy to make yo'self out God Almighty when you ain't got nothin' tuh strain against but women and chickens."

"You gettin' too moufy, Janie," Starks told her. "Go fetch me de checker-board *and* de checkers. Sam Watson, you'se mah fish."

CHAPTER 7

The years took all the fight out of Janie's face. For a while she thought it was gone from her soul. No matter what Jody did, she said nothing. She had learned how to talk some and leave some. She was a rut in the road. Plenty of life beneath the surface but it was kept beaten down by the wheels. Sometimes she stuck out into the future, imagining her life different from what it was. But mostly she lived between her hat and her heels, with her emotional disturbances like shade patterns in the woods—come and gone with the sun. She got nothing from Jody except what money could buy, and she was giving away what she didn't value.

Now and again she thought of a country road at sun-up and considered flight. To where? To what? Then too she considered thirty-five is twice seventeen and nothing was the same at all.

"Maybe he ain't nothin'," she cautioned herself, "but he is something in my mouth. He's got tuh be else Ah ain't got nothin' tuh live for. Ah'll lie and say he is. If Ah don't, life won't be nothin' but uh store and uh house."

She didn't read books so she didn't know that she was the world and the heavens boiled down to a drop. Man attempting to climb to painless heights from his dung hill.

Then one day she sat and watched the shadow of herself going about tending store and prostrating itself before Jody, while all the time she herself sat under a shady tree with the wind blowing through her hair and her clothes. Somebody near about making summertime out of lonesomeness.

This was the first time it happened, but after a while it got so common she ceased to be surprised. It was like a drug. In a way it was good because it reconciled her to things. She got so she received all things with the stolidness of the earth which soaks up urine and perfume with the same indifference.

One day she noticed that Joe didn't sit down. He just stood in front of a chair and fell in it. That made her look at him all over. Joe wasn't so young as he used to be. There was already something dead about him. He didn't rear back in his knees any longer. He squatted over his ankles when he walked. That stillness at the back of his neck. His prosperous-looking belly that used to thrust out so pugnaciously and intimidate folks, sagged like a load suspended from his loins. It didn't seem to be a part of him anymore. Eyes a little absent too.

Jody must have noticed it too. Maybe, he had seen it long before Janie did, and had been fearing for her to see. Because he began to talk about her age all the time, as if he didn't want her to stay young while he grew old. It was always "You oughta throw somethin' over yo' shoulders befo' you go outside. You ain't no young pullet no mo'. You'se uh ole hen now." One day he called her off the croquet grounds. "Dat's somethin' for de young folks, Janie, you out dere jumpin' round and won't be able tuh git out de bed tuhmorrer." If he thought to deceive her, he was wrong. For the first time she could see a man's head naked of its skull. Saw the cunning thoughts race in and out through the caves and promontories of his mind long before they darted out of the tunnel of his mouth. She saw he was hurting inside so she let it pass without talking. She just measured out a little time for him and set it aside to wait.

It got to be terrible in the store. The more his back ached

and his muscle dissolved into fat and the fat melted off his bones, the more fractious he became with Janie. Especially in the store. The more people in there the more ridicule he poured over her body to point attention away from his own. So one day Steve Mixon wanted some chewing tobacco and Janie cut it wrong. She hated that tobacco knife anyway. It worked very stiff. She fumbled with the thing and cut way away from the mark. Mixon didn't mind. He held it up for a joke to tease Janie a little.

"Looka heah, Brother Mayor, whut yo' wife done took and done." It was cut comical, so everybody laughed at it. "Uh woman and uh knife—no kind of uh knife, don't b'long tuhgether." There was some more good-natured laughter at the expense of women.

Jody didn't laugh. He hurried across from the post office side and took the plug of tobacco away from Mixon and cut it again. Cut it exactly on the mark and glared at Janie.

"I god amighty! A woman stay round uh store till she get old as Methusalem and still can't cut a little thing like a plug of tobacco! Don't stand dere rollin' yo' pop eyes at me wid yo' rump hangin' nearly to yo' knees!"

A big laugh started off in the store but people got to thinking and stopped. It was funny if you looked at it right quick, but it got pitiful if you thought about it awhile. It was like somebody snatched off part of a woman's clothes while she wasn't looking and the streets were crowded. Then too, Janie took the middle of the floor to talk right into Jody's face, and that was something that hadn't been done before.

"Stop mixin' up mah doings wid mah looks, Jody. When you git through tellin' me how tuh cut uh plug uh tobacco, then you kin tell me whether mah behind is on straight or not."

"Wha—whut's dat you say, Janie? You must be out yo' head."

"Naw, Ah ain't outa mah head neither."

"You must be. Talkin' any such language as dat."

"You de one started talkin' under people's clothes. Not me."

"Whut's de matter wid you, nohow? You ain't no young girl to be gettin' all insulted 'bout yo' looks. You ain't no young courtin' gal. You'se uh ole woman, nearly forty."

"Yeah, Ah'm nearly forty and you'se already fifty. How come you can't talk about dat sometimes instead of always pointin' at me?"

"T'ain't no use in gettin' all mad, Janie, 'cause Ah mention you ain't no young gal no mo'. Nobody in heah ain't lookin' for no wife outa yuh. Old as you is."

"Naw, Ah ain't no young gal no mo' but den Ah ain't no old woman neither. Ah reckon Ah looks mah age too. But Ah'm uh woman every inch of me, and Ah know it. Dat's uh whole lot more'n *you* kin say. You big-bellies round here and put out a lot of brag, but 'tain't nothin' to it but yo' big voice. Humph! Talkin' 'bout *me* lookin' old! When you pull down yo' britches, you look lak de change uh life."

"Great God from Zion!" Sam Watson gasped. "Y'all really playin' de dozens tuhnight."

"Wha—whut's dat you said?" Joe challenged, hoping his ears had fooled him.

"You heard her, you ain't blind," Walter taunted.

"Ah ruther be shot with tacks than tuh hear dat 'bout mahself," Lige Moss commiserated.

Then Joe Starks realized all the meanings and his vanity bled like a flood. Janie had robbed him of his illusion of irresistible maleness that all men cherish, which was terrible. The thing that Saul's daughter had done to David. But Janie had done worse, she had cast down his empty armor before men and they had laughed, would keep on laughing. When he paraded his possessions hereafter, they would not consider the two together. They'd look with envy at the things and pity the man that owned them. When he sat in judgment it would be the same. Good-for-nothing's like Dave and Lum and Jim wouldn't change place with him. For what can excuse a man in the eyes of other men for lack of strength? Raggedy-behind squirts of sixteen and seventeen would be giving him their merciless pity out of their eyes while their mouths said something humble. There was nothing to do in life anymore. Ambition was useless. And the cruel deceit of Janie! Making all that show of humbleness and scorning him all the time! Laughing at him, and now putting the town up to do the same. Joe Starks didn't know the words for all this, but he knew the feeling. So he struck Janie with all his might and drove her from the store.

CHAPTER 8

After that night Jody moved his things and slept in a room downstairs. He didn't really hate Janie, but he wanted her to think so. He had crawled off to lick his wounds. They didn't talk too much around the store either. Anybody that didn't know would have thought that things had blown over, it looked so quiet and peaceful around. But the stillness was the sleep of swords. So new thoughts had to be thought and new words said. She didn't want to live like that. Why must Joe be so mad with her for making him look small when he did it to her all the time? Had been doing it for years. Well, if she must eat out of a long-handled spoon, she must. Jody might get over his mad spell any time at all and begin to act like somebody towards her.

Then too she noticed how baggy Joe was getting all over. Like bags hanging from an ironing board. A little sack hung from the corners of his eyes and rested on his cheek-bones; a loose-filled bag of feathers hung from his ears and rested on his neck beneath his chin. A sack of flabby something hung from his loins and rested on his thighs when he sat down. But even these things were running down like candle grease as time moved on.

He made new alliances too. People he never bothered with

one way or another now seemed to have his ear. He had always been scornful of root-doctors and all their kind, but now she saw a faker from over around Altamonte Springs, hanging around the place almost daily. Always talking in low tones when she came near, or hushed altogether. She didn't know that he was driven by a desperate hope to appear the old-time body in her sight. She was sorry about the root-doctor because she feared that Joe was depending on the scoundrel to make him well when what he needed was a doctor, and a good one. She was worried about his not eating his meals, till she found out he was having old lady Davis to cook for him. She knew that she was a much better cook than the old woman, and cleaner about the kitchen. So she bought a beef-bone and made him some soup.

"Naw, thank you," he told her shortly. "Ah'm havin' uh hard enough time tuh try and git well as it is."

She was stunned at first and hurt afterwards. So she went straight to her bosom friend, Pheoby Watson, and told her about it.

"Ah'd ruther be dead than for Jody tuh think Ah'd hurt him," she sobbed to Pheoby. "It ain't always been too pleas-ant, 'cause you know how Joe worships de works of his own hands, but God in heben knows Ah wouldn't do one thing tuh hurt nobody. It's too underhand and mean."

"Janie, Ah thought maybe de thing would die down and you never would know nothin' 'bout it, but it's been singin' round here ever since de big fuss in de store dat Joe was 'fixed' and you wuz de one dat did it."

"Pheoby, for de longest time, Ah been feelin' dat somethin' set for still-bait, but dis is—is—oh Pheoby! Whut *kin* I do?"

"You can't do nothin' but make out you don't know it. It's too late fuh y'all tuh be splittin' up and gittin' divorce. Just g'wan back home and set down on yo' royal diasticutis and say nothin'. Nobody don't b'lieve it nohow."

"Tuh think Ah been wid Jody twenty yeahs and Ah just now got tuh bear de name uh poisonin' him! It's 'bout to kill me,

Pheoby. Sorrow dogged by sorrow is in mah heart."

"Dat's lie dat trashy nigger dat calls hisself uh two-headed doctor brought tuh 'im in order tuh git in wid Jody. He seen he wuz sick—everybody been knowin' dat for de last longest, and den Ah reckon he heard y'all wuz kind of at variance, so dat wuz his chance. Last summer dat multiplied cockroach wuz round heah tryin' tuh sell gophers!"

"Pheoby, Ah don't even b'lieve Jody b'lieve dat lie. He ain't never took no stock in de mess. He just make out he b'lieve it tuh hurt me. Ah'm stone dead from standin' still and tryin' tuh smile."

She cried often in the weeks that followed. Joe got too weak to look after things and took to his bed. But he relentlessly refused to admit her to his sick room. People came and went in the house. This one and that one came into her house with covered plates of broth and other sick-room dishes without taking the least notice of her as Joe's wife. People who never had known what it was to enter the gate of the Mayor's yard unless it were to do some menial job now paraded in and out as his confidants. They came to the store and ostentatiously looked over whatever she was doing and went back to report to him at the house. Said things like "Mr. Starks need *somebody* tuh sorta look out for 'im till he kin git on his feet again and look for hisself."

But Jody was never to get on his feet again. Janie had Sam Watson to bring her the news from the sick room, and when he told her how things were, she had him bring a doctor from Orlando without giving Joe a chance to refuse, and without saying she sent for him.

"Just a matter of time," the doctor told her. "When a man's kidneys stop working altogether, there is no way for him to live. He needed medical attention two years ago. Too late now."

So Janie began to think of Death. Death, that strange being with the huge square toes who lived way in the West. The great one who lived in the straight house like a platform without sides to it, and without a roof. What need has Death for a cover, and what winds can blow against him? He stands in his high house that overlooks the world. Stands watchful and motionless all day with his sword drawn back, waiting for the messenger to bid him come. Been standing there before there was a where or a when or a then. She was liable to find a feather from his wings lying in her yard any day now. She was sad and afraid too. Poor Jody! He ought not to have to wrassle in there by himself. She sent Sam in to suggest a visit, but Jody said No. These medical doctors wuz all right with the Godly sick, but they didn't know a thing about a case like his. He'd be all right just as soon as the two-headed man found what had been buried against him. He wasn't going to die at all. That was what he thought. But Sam told her different, so she knew. And then if he hadn't, the next morning she was bound to know, for people began to gather in the big yard under the palm and china-berry trees. People who would not have dared to foot the place before crept in and did not come to the house. Just squatted under the trees and waited. Rumor, that wingless bird, had shadowed over the town.

She got up that morning with the firm determination to go on in there and have a good talk with Jody. But she sat a long time with the walls creeping in on her. Four walls squeezing her breath out. Fear lest he depart while she sat trembling upstairs nerved her and she was inside the room before she caught her breath. She didn't make the cheerful, casual start that she had thought out. Something stood like an oxen's foot on her tongue, and then too, Jody, no Joe, gave her a ferocious look. A look with all the unthinkable coldness of outer space. She must talk to a man who was ten immensities away.

He was lying on his side facing the door like he was expecting somebody or something. A sort of changing look on his face. Weak-looking but sharp-pointed about the eyes. Through the thin counterpane she could see what was left of his belly huddled before him on the bed like some helpless thing seeking shelter.

The half-washed bedclothes hurt her pride for Jody. He had always been so clean.

"Whut you doin' in heah, Janie?"

"Come tuh see 'bout you and how you wuz makin' out."

He gave a deep-growling sound like a hog dying down in the swamp and trying to drive off disturbance. "Ah come in heah tuh git shet uh you but look lak 'tain't doin' me no good. G'wan out. Ah needs tuh rest."

"Naw, Jody, Ah come in heah tuh talk widja and Ah'm gointuh do it too. It's for both of our sakes Ah'm talkin'."

He gave another ground grumble and eased over on his back.

"Jody, maybe Ah ain't been sich uh good wife tuh you, but Jody—"

"Dat's 'cause you ain't got de right feelin' for nobody. You oughter have some sympathy 'bout yo'self. You ain't no hog."

"But, Jody, Ah meant tuh be awful nice."

"Much as Ah done fuh yuh. Holdin' me up tuh scorn. No sympathy!"

"Naw, Jody, it wasn't because Ah didn't have no sympathy. Ah had uh lavish uh dat. Ah just didn't never git no chance tuh use none of it. You wouldn't let me."

"Dat's right, blame everything on me. Ah wouldn't let you show no feelin'! When, Janie, dat's all Ah ever wanted or desired. Now you come blamin' me!"

" 'Tain't dat, Jody. Ah ain't here tuh blame nobody. Ah'm just tryin' tuh make you know what kinda person Ah is befo' it's too late."

"Too late?" he whispered.

His eyes buckled in a vacant-mouthed terror and she saw the awful surprise in his face and answered it.

"Yeah, Jody, don't keer whut dat multiplied cockroach told yuh tuh git yo' money, you got tuh die, and yuh can't live."

A deep sob came out of Jody's weak frame. It was like beating a bass drum in a hen-house. Then it rose high like pulling in a trombone.

"Janie! Janie! don't tell me Ah got tuh die, and Ah ain't used tuh thinkin' 'bout it."

" 'Tain't really no need of you dying, Jody, if you had of—de doctor—but it don't do no good bringin' dat up now. Dat's just whut Ah wants tuh say, Jody. You wouldn't listen. You done lived wid me for twenty years and you don't half know me atall. And you could have but you was so busy worshippin' de works of yo' own hands, and cuffin' folks around in their minds till you didn't see uh whole heap uh things yuh could have."

"Leave heah, Janie. Don't come heah—"

"Ah knowed you wasn't gointuh lissen tuh me. You changes everything but nothin' don't change you—not even death. But Ah ain't goin' outa here and Ah ain't gointuh hush. Naw, you gointuh listen tuh me one time befo' you die. Have yo' way all yo' life, trample and mash down and then die ruther than tuh let yo'self heah 'bout it. Listen, Jody, you ain't de Jody ah run off down de road wid. You'se whut's left after he died. Ah run off tuh keep house wid you in uh wonderful way. But you wasn't satisfied wid me de way Ah was. Naw! Mah own mind had tuh be squeezed and crowded out tuh make room for yours in me."

"Shut up! Ah wish thunder and lightnin' would kill yuh!"

"Ah know it. And now you got tuh die tuh find out dat you got tuh pacify somebody besides yo'self if you wants any love and any sympathy in dis world. You ain't tried tuh pacify *nobody* but yo'self. Too busy listening tuh yo' own big voice."

"All dis tearin' down talk!" Jody whispered with sweat globules forming all over his face and arms. "Git outa heah!"

"All dis bowin' down, all dis obedience under yo' voice—dat ain't whut Ah rushed off down de road tuh find out about you."

A sound of strife in Jody's throat, but his eyes stared unwillingly into a corner of the room so Janie knew the futile fight was not with her. The icy sword of the square-toed one had cut off his breath and left his hands in a pose of agonizing protest. Janie gave them peace on his breast, then she studied his dead face for a long time.

"Dis sittin' in de rulin' chair is been hard on Jody," she muttered out loud. She was full of pity for the first time in years. Jody had been hard on her and others, but life had mishandled him too. Poor Joe! Maybe if she had known some other way to try, she might have made his face different. But what that other way could be, she had no idea. She thought back and forth about what had happened in the making of a voice out of a man. Then thought about herself. Years ago, she had told her girl self to wait for her in the looking glass. It had been a long time since she had remembered. Perhaps she'd better look. She went over to the dresser and looked hard at her skin and features. The young girl was gone, but a handsome woman had taken her place. She tore off the kerchief from her head and let down her plentiful hair. The weight, the length, the glory was there. She took careful stock of herself, then combed her hair and tied it back up again. Then she starched and ironed her face, forming it into just what people wanted to see, and opened up the window and cried, "Come heah people! Jody is dead. Mah husband is gone from me."

CHAPTER 9

Joe's funeral was the finest thing Orange County had ever
seen with Negro eyes. The motor hearse, the Cadillac
and Buick carriages; Dr. Henderson there in his Lincoln;
the hosts from far and wide. Then again the gold and red and
purple, the gloat and glamor of the secret orders, each with
its insinuations of power and glory undreamed of by the unini-
tiated. People on farm houses and mules; babies riding astride
of brothers' and sisters' backs. The Elks band ranked at the
church door and playing "Safe in the Arms of Jesus" with such
a dominant drum rhythm that it could be stepped off smartly
by the long line as it filed inside. The Little Emperor of the
cross-roads was leaving Orange County as he had come—with
the out-stretched hand of power.

Janie starched and ironed her face and came set in the
funeral behind her veil. It was like a wall of stone and steel.
The funeral was going on outside. All things concerning death
and burial were said and done. Finish. End. Nevermore.
Darkness. Deep hole. Dissolution. Eternity. Weeping and
wailing outside. Inside the expensive black folds were resurrection and life. She did not reach outside for anything, nor
did the things of death reach inside to disturb her calm. She
sent her face to Joe's funeral, and herself went rollicking with

84

the springtime across the world. After a while the people finished their celebration and Janie went on home.

Before she slept that night she burnt up every one of her head rags and went about the house next morning with her hair in one thick braid swinging well below her waist. That was the only change people saw in her. She kept the store in the same way except of evenings she sat on the porch and listened and sent Hezekiah in to wait on late custom. She saw no reason to rush at changing things around. She would have the rest of her life to do as she pleased.

Most of the day she was at the store, but at night she was there in the big house and sometimes it creaked and cried all night under the weight of lonesomeness. Then she'd lie awake in bed asking lonesomeness some questions. She asked if she wanted to leave and go back where she had come from and try to find her mother. Maybe tend her grandmother's grave. Sort of look over the old stamping ground generally. Digging around inside of herself like that she found that she had no interest in that seldom-seen mother at all. She hated her grandmother and had hidden it from herself all these years under a cloak of pity. She had been getting ready for her great journey to the horizons in search of *people;* it was important to all the world that she should find them and they find her. But she had been whipped like a cur dog, and run off down a back road after *things.* It was all according to the way you see things. Some people could look at a mud-puddle and see an ocean with ships. But Nanny belonged to that other kind that loved to deal in scraps. Here Nanny had taken the biggest thing God ever made, the horizon—for no matter how far a person can go the horizon is still way beyond you—and pinched it in to such a little bit of a thing that she could tie it about her granddaughter's neck tight enough to choke her. She hated the old woman who had twisted her so in the name of love. Most humans didn't love one another nohow, and this mis-love was so strong that even common blood couldn't over-come it all the time. She had found a jewel down inside herself and she had wanted to walk where people could see her and gleam it around. But she had been set in the market-place to sell. Been set for still-bait. When God had made The Man, he made him out of stuff that sung all the time and glittered all over. Then after that some angels got jealous and chopped him into millions of pieces, but still he glittered and hummed. So they beat him down to nothing but sparks but each little spark had a shine and a song. So they covered each one over with mud. And the lonesomeness in the sparks make them hunt for one another, but the mud is deaf and dumb. Like all the other tumbling mud-balls, Janie had tried to show her shine.

Janie found out very soon that her widowhood and property was a great challenge in South Florida. Before Jody had been dead a month, she noticed how often men who had never been intimates of Joe, drove considerable distances to ask after her welfare and offer their services as advisor.

"Uh woman by herself is uh pitiful thing," she was told over and again. "Dey needs aid and assistance. God never meant 'em tuh try tuh stand by theirselves. You ain't been used tuh knockin' round and doin' fuh yo'self, Mis' Starks. You been well taken keer of, you needs uh man."

Janie laughed at all these well-wishers because she knew that they knew plenty of women alone; that she was not the first one they had ever seen. But most of the others were poor. Besides she liked being lonesome for a change. This freedom feeling was fine. These men didn't represent a thing she wanted to know about. She had already experienced them through Logan and Joe. She felt like slapping some of them for sitting around grinning at her like a pack of chessy cats, trying to make out they looked like love.

Ike Green sat on her case seriously one evening on the store porch when he was lucky enough to catch her alone.

"You wants be keerful 'bout who you marry, Mis' Starks. Dese strange men runnin' heah tryin' tuh take advantage of yo' condition."

"Marry!" Janie almost screamed. "Joe ain't had time tuh git cold yet. Ah ain't even give marryin' de first thought."

"But you will. You'se too young uh 'oman tuh stay single, and you'se too pretty for de mens tuh leave yuh alone. You'se bound tuh marry."

"Ah hope not. Ah mean, at dis present time it don't come befo' me. Joe ain't been dead two months. Ain't got settled down in his grave."

"Dat's whut you say now, but two months mo' and you'll sing another tune. Den you want tuh be keerful. Womenfolks is easy taken advantage of. You know what tuh let none uh dese stray niggers dat's settin' round heah git de inside track on yuh. They's jes lak uh pack uh hawgs, when dey see uh full trough. Whut yuh needs is uh man dat yuh done lived uh-round and know all about tuh sort of manage yo' things fuh yuh and ginerally do round."

Janie jumped upon her feet. "Lawd, Ike Green, you'se uh case! Dis subjick you bringin' up ain't fit tuh be talked about at all. Lemme go inside and help Hezekiah weigh up dat barrel uh sugar dat just come in." She rushed on inside the store and whispered to Hezekiah, "Ah'm gone tuh de house. Lemme know when dat ole pee-de-bed is gone and Ah'll be right back."

Six months of wearing black passed and not one suitor had ever gained the house porch. Janie talked and laughed in the store at times, but never seemed to want to go further. She was happy except for the store. She knew by her head that she was absolute owner, but it always seemed to her that she was still clerking for Joe and that soon he would come in and find something wrong that she had done. She almost apologized to the tenants the first time she collected the rents. Felt like a usurper. But she hid that feeling by sending Hezekiah who was the best imitation of Joe that his seventeen years could make. He had even taken to smoking, and smoking cigars, since Joe's death and tried to bite 'em tight in one side of his mouth like Joe. Every chance he got he was reared back in

Joe's swivel chair trying to thrust out his lean belly into a paunch. She'd laugh quietly at his no-harm posing and pretend she didn't see it. One day as she came in the back door of the store she heard him bawling at Tripp Crawford, "Naw indeed, we can't do nothin' uh de kind! I god, you ain't paid for dem last rations you done et up. I god, you won't git no mo' outa dis store than you got money tuh pay for. I god, dis ain't Gimme, Florida, dis is Eatonville." Another time she overheard him using Joe's favorite expression for pointing out the differences between himself and the careless-living, mouthy town. "Ah'm an educated man, Ah keep mah arrangements in mah hands." She laughed outright at that. His acting didn't hurt nobody and she wouldn't know what to do without him. He sensed that and came to treat her like baby-sister, as if to say "You poor little thing, give it to big brother. He'll fix it for you." His sense of ownership made him honest too, except for an occasional jaw-breaker, or a packet of sen-sen. The sen-sen was to let on to the other boys and the pullet-size girls that he had a liquor breath to cover. This business of managing stores and women store-owners was trying on a man's nerves. He needed a drink of liquor now and then to keep up.

When Janie emerged into her mourning white, she had hosts of admirers in and out of town. Everything open and frank. Men of property too among the crowd, but nobody seemed to get any further than the store. She was always too busy to take them to the house to entertain. They were all so respectful and stiff with her, that she might have been the Empress of Japan. They felt that it was not fitting to mention desire to the widow of Joseph Starks. You spoke of honor and respect. And all that they said and did was refracted by her inattention and shot off towards the rim-bones of nothing. She and Pheoby Watson visited back and forth and once in awhile sat around the lakes and fished. She was just basking in freedom for the most part without the need for thought. A Sanford undertaker was pressing his cause through Pheoby, and Janie was listening pleasantly but undisturbed. It might be nice to marry him, at that. No hurry. Such things take time to think about, or rather she pretended to Pheoby that that was what she was doing.

" 'Tain't dat Ah worries over Joe's death, Pheoby. Ah jus' loves dis freedom."

"Sh-sh-sh! Don't let nobody hear you say dat, Janie. Folks will say you ain't sorry he's gone."

"Let 'em say whut dey wants tuh, Pheoby. To my thinkin' mourning oughtn't tuh last no longer'n grief."

CHAPTER 10

One day Hezekiah asked off from work to go off with the ball team. Janie told him not to hurry back. She could close up the store herself this once. He cautioned her about the catches on the windows and doors and swaggered off to Winter Park.

Business was dull all day, because numbers of people had gone to the game. She decided to close early, because it was hardly worth the trouble of keeping open on an afternoon like this. She had set six o'clock as her limit.

At five-thirty a tall man came into the place. Janie was leaning on the counter making aimless pencil marks on a piece of wrapping paper. She knew she didn't know his name, but he looked familiar.

"Good evenin', Mis' Starks," he said with a sly grin as if they had a good joke together. She was in favor of the story that was making him laugh before she even heard it.

"Good evenin'," she answered pleasantly. "You got all de advantage 'cause Ah don't know yo' name."

"People wouldn't know me lak dey would *you.*"

"Ah guess standin' in uh store do make uh person git tuh be known in de vicinity. Look lak Ah seen you somewhere."

"Oh, Ah don't live no further than Orlandah. Ah'm easy

90

tuh see on Church Street most any day or night. You got any smokin' tobacco?"

She opened the glass case. "What kind?"

"Camels."

She handed over the cigarettes and took the money. He broke the pack and thrust one between his full, purple lips.

"You got a lil piece uh fire over dere, lady?"

They both laughed and she handed him two kitchen matches out of a box for that purpose. It was time for him to go but he didn't. He leaned on the counter with one elbow and cold-cocked her a look.

"Why ain't *you* at de ball game, too? Everybody else is dere."

"Well, Ah see somebody else besides me ain't dere. Ah just sold some cigarettes." They laughed again.

"Dat's 'cause Ah'm dumb. Ah got de thing all mixed up. Ah thought de game was gointuh be out at Hungerford. So Ah got uh ride tuh where dis road turns off from de Dixie Highway and walked over here and then Ah find out de game is in Winter Park."

That was funny to both of them too.

"So what you gointuh do now? All de cars in Eatonville is gone."

"How about playin' *you* some checkers? You looks hard tuh beat."

"Ah is, 'cause Ah can't play uh lick."

"You don't cherish de game, then?"

"Yes, Ah do, and then agin Ah don't know whether Ah do or not, 'cause nobody ain't never showed me how."

"Dis is de last day for *dat* excuse. You got uh board round heah?"

"Yes indeed. De men folks treasures de game round heah. Ah just ain't never learnt how."

He set it up and began to show her and she found herself glowing inside. Somebody wanted her to play. Somebody thought it natural for her to play. That was even nice. She looked him over and got little thrills from every one of his good points. Those full, lazy eyes with the lashes curling sharply away like drawn scimitars. The lean, over-padded shoulders and narrow waist. Even nice!

He was jumping her king! She screamed in protest against losing the king she had had such a hard time acquiring. Before she knew it she had grabbed his hand to stop him. He struggled gallantly to free himself. That is he struggled, but not hard enough to wrench a lady's fingers.

"Ah got uh right tuh take it. You left it right in mah way."

"Yeah, but Ah wuz lookin' off when you went and stuck yo' men right up next tuh mine. No fair!"

"You ain't supposed tuh look off, Mis' Starks. It's de biggest part uh de game tuh watch out! Leave go mah hand."

"No suh! Not mah king. You kin take another one, but not dat one."

They scrambled and upset the board and laughed at that.

"Anyhow it's time for uh Coca-Cola," he said. "Ah'll come teach yuh some mo' another time."

"It's all right tuh come teach me, but don't come tuh cheat me."

"Yuh can't beat uh woman. Dey jes won't stand fuh it. But Ah'll come teach yuh agin. You gointuh be uh good player too, after while."

"You reckon so? Jody useter tell me Ah never would learn. It wuz too heavy fuh mah brains."

"Folks is playin' it wid sense and folks is playin' it without. But you got good meat on yo' head. You'll learn. Have uh cool drink on me."

"Oh all right, thank yuh. Got plenty cold ones tuhday. Nobody ain't been heah tuh buy none. All gone off tuh de game."

"You oughta be at de next game. 'Tain't no use in *you* stayin' heah if everybody else is gone. You don't buy from yo'self, do yuh?"

"You crazy thing! 'Course Ah don't. But Ah'm worried 'bout you uh little."

"How come? 'Fraid Ah ain't gointuh pay fuh dese drinks?"

"Aw naw! How you gointuh git back home?"

"Wait round heah fuh a car. If none don't come, Ah got good shoe leather. 'Tain't but seben miles no how. Ah could walk dat in no time. Easy."

"If it wuz me, Ah'd wait on uh train. Seben miles is uh kinda long walk."

"It would be for you, 'cause you ain't used to it. But Ah'm seen women walk further'n dat. You could too, if yuh had it tuh do."

"Maybe so, but Ah'll ride de train long as Ah got railroad fare."

"Ah don't need no pocket-full uh money to ride de train lak uh woman. When Ah takes uh notion Ah rides anyhow—money or no money."

"Now ain't you somethin'! Mr. er—er—You never did tell me whut yo' name wuz."

"Ah sho didn't. Wuzn't expectin' fuh it to be needed. De name mah mama gimme is Vergible Woods. Dey calls me Tea Cake for short."

"Tea Cake! So you sweet as all dat?" She laughed and he gave her a little cut-eye look to get her meaning.

"Ah may be guilty. You better try me and see."

She did something halfway between a laugh and a frown and he set his hat on straight.

"B'lieve Ah done cut uh hawg, so Ah guess Ah better ketch air." He made an elaborate act of tipping to the door stealthily. Then looked back at her with an irresistible grin on his face. Janie burst out laughing in spite of herself. "You crazy thing!"

He turned and threw his hat at her feet. "If she don't throw it at me, Ah'll take a chance on comin' back," he announced, making gestures to indicate he was hidden behind a post. She picked up the hat and threw it after him with a laugh. "Even if she had uh brick she couldn't hurt yuh wid it," he said to an invisible companion. "De lady can't throw." He gestured to his companion, stepped out from behind the imaginary lamp post, set his coat and hat and strolled back to where Janie was as if he had just come in the store.

"Evenin', Mis' Starks. Could yuh lemme have uh pound uh knuckle puddin'* till Saturday? Ah'm sho tuh pay yuh then."

"You needs ten pounds, Mr. Tea Cake. Ah'll let yuh have all Ah got and you needn't bother 'bout payin' it back."

They joked and went on till the people began to come in. Then he took a seat and made talk and laughter with the rest until closing time. When everyone else had left he said, "Ah reckon Ah done over-layed mah leavin' time, but Ah figgured you needed somebody tuh help yuh shut up de place. Since nobody else ain't round heah, maybe Ah kin git de job."

"Thankyuh, Mr. Tea Cake. It is kinda strainin' fuh me."

"Who ever heard of uh teacake bein' called Mister! If you wanta be real hightoned and call me Mr. Woods, dat's de way you feel about it. If yuh wants tuh be uh lil friendly and call me Tea Cake, dat would be real nice." He was closing and bolting windows all the time he talked.

"All right, then. Thank yuh, Tea Cake. How's dat?"

"Jes lak uh lil girl wid her Easter dress on. Even nice!" He locked the door and shook it to be sure and handed her the key. "Come on now, Ah'll see yuh inside yo' door and git on down de Dixie."

Janie was halfway down the palm-lined walk before she had a thought for her safety. Maybe this strange man was up to something! But it was no place to show her fear there in the darkness between the house and the store. He had hold of her arm too. Then in a moment it was gone. Tea Cake wasn't strange. Seemed as if she had known him all her life. Look how she had been able to talk with him right off! He tipped his hat

---

*A beating with the fist.

94

at the door and was off with the briefest good night.

So she sat on the porch and watched the moon rise. Soon its amber fluid was drenching the earth, and quenching the thirst of the day.

CHAPTER 11

Janie wanted to ask Hezekiah about Tea Cake, but she was afraid he might misunderstand her and think she was interested. In the first place he looked too young for her. Must be around twenty-five and here *she* was around forty. Then again he didn't look like he had too much. Maybe he was hanging around to get in with her and strip her of all that she had. Just as well if she never saw him again. He was probably the kind of man who lived with various women but never married. Fact is, she decided to treat him so cold if he ever did foot the place that he'd be sure not to come hanging around there again.

He waited a week exactly to come back for Janie's snub. It was early in the afternoon and she and Hezekiah were alone. She heard somebody humming like they were feeling for pitch and looked towards the door. Tea Cake stood there mimicking the tuning of a guitar. He frowned and struggled with the pegs of his imaginary instrument watching her out of the corner of his eye with that secret joke playing over his face. Finally she smiled and he sung middle C, put his guitar under his arm and walked on back to where she was.

"Evenin', folks. Thought y'all might lak uh lil music this evenin' so Ah brought long mah box."

96

"Crazy thing!" Janie commented, beaming out with light.

He acknowledged the compliment with a smile and sat down on a box. "Anybody have uh Coca-Cola wid me?"

"Ah just had one," Janie temporized with her conscience.

"It'll hafter be done all over agin, Mis' Starks."

"How come?"

" 'Cause it wasn't done right dat time. 'Kiah bring us two bottles from de bottom uh de box."

"How you been makin' out since Ah seen yuh last, Tea Cake?"

"Can't kick. Could be worse. Made four days dis week and got de pay in mah pocket."

"We got a rich man round here, then. Buyin' passenger trains uh battleships this week?"

"Which one do *you* want? It all depends on you."

"Oh, if you'se treatin' me tuh it, Ah b'lieve Ah'll take de passenger train. If it blow up Ah'll still be on land."

"Choose de battleship if dat's whut you really want. Ah know where one is right now. Seen one round Key West de other day."

"How you gointuh git it?"

"Ah shucks, dem Admirals is always ole folks. Can't no ole man stop me from gittin' no ship for yuh if dat's whut you want. Ah'd git dat ship out from under him so slick till he'd be walkin' de water lak ole Peter befo' he knowed it."

They played away the evening again. Everybody was surprised at Janie playing checkers but they liked it. Three or four stood behind her and coached her moves and generally made merry with her in a restrained way. Finally everybody went home but Tea Cake.

"You kin close up, 'Kiah," Janie said. "Think Ah'll g'wan home."

Tea Cake fell in beside her and mounted the porch this time. So she offered him a seat and they made a lot of laughter out of nothing. Near eleven o'clock she remembered a piece of pound cake she had put away. Tea Cake went out to the

97

lemon tree at the corner of the kitchen and picked some lemons and squeezed them for her. So they had lemonade too.

"Moon's too pretty fuh anybody tuh be sleepin' it away," Tea Cake said after they had washed up the plates and glasses. "Less us go fishin'."

"Fishin'? Dis time uh night?"

"Unhhunh, fishin'. Ah know where de bream is beddin'. Seen 'em when Ah come round de lake dis evenin'. Where's yo' fishin' poles? Less go set on de lake."

It was so crazy digging worms by lamp light and setting out for Lake Sabelia after midnight that she felt like a child breaking rules. That's what made Janie like it. They caught two or three and got home just before day. Then she had to smuggle Tea Cake out by the back gate and that made it seem like some great secret she was keeping from the town.

"Mis' Janie," Hezekiah began sullenly next day, "you oughtn't 'low dat Tea Cake tuh be walkin' tuh de house wid yuh. Ah'll go wid yuh mahself after dis, if you'se skeered."

"What's de matter wid Tea Cake, 'Kiah? Is he uh thief uh somethin'?"

"Ah ain't never heard nobody say he stole nothin'."

"Is he bad 'bout totin' pistols and knives tuh hurt people wid?"

"Dey don't say he ever cut nobody or shot nobody neither."

"Well, is he—he—is he got uh wife or something lak dat? Not dat it's any uh mah business." She held her breath for the answer.

"No'm. And nobody wouldn't marry Tea Cake tuh starve tuh death lessen it's somebody jes lak him—ain't used to nothin'. 'Course he always keep hisself in changin' clothes. Dat long-legged Tea Cake ain't got doodly squat. He ain't got no business makin' hissef familiar wid nobody lak you. Ah said Ah wuz goin' to tell yuh so yuh could know."

"Oh dat's all right, Hezekiah. Thank yuh mighty much."

The next night when she mounted her steps Tea Cake was

there before her, sitting on the porch in the dark. He had a string of fresh-caught trout for a present.

"Ah'll clean 'em, you fry 'em and let's eat," he said with the assurance of not being refused. They went out into the kitchen and fixed up the hot fish and corn muffins and ate. Then Tea Cake went to the piano without so much as asking and began playing blues and singing, and throwing grins over his shoulder. The sounds lulled Janie to soft slumber and she woke up with Tea Cake combing her hair and scratching the dandruff from her scalp. It made her more comfortable and drowsy.

"Tea Cake, where you git uh comb from tuh be combin' mah hair wid?"

"Ah brought it wid me. Come prepared tuh lay mah hands on it tuhnight."

"Why, Tea Cake? Whut good do combin' mah hair do *you?* It's *mah* comfortable, not yourn."

"It's mine too. Ah ain't been sleepin' so good for more'n uh week cause Ah been wishin' so bad tuh git mah hands in yo' hair. It's so pretty. It feels jus' lak underneath uh dove's wing next to mah face."

"Umph! You'se mighty easy satisfied. Ah been had dis same hair next tuh mah face ever since Ah cried de fust time, and 'tain't never gimme me no thrill."

"Ah tell you lak you told me—you'se mighty hard tuh satisfy. Ah betcha dem lips don't satisfy yuh neither."

"Dat's right, Tea Cake. They's dere and Ah make use of 'em whenever it's necessary, but nothin' special tuh me."

"Umph! umph! umph! Ah betcha you don't never go tuh de lookin' glass and enjoy yo' eyes yo'self. You lets other folks git all de enjoyment out of 'em 'thout takin' in any of it yo'self."

"Naw, Ah never gazes at 'em in de lookin' glass. If anybody else gits any pleasure out of 'em Ah ain't been told about it."

"See dat? You'se got de world in uh jug and make out you don't know it. But Ah'm glad tuh be de one tuh tell yuh."

"Ah guess you done told plenty women all about it."

"Ah'm de Apostle Paul tuh de Gentiles. Ah tells 'em and then agin Ah shows 'em."

"Ah thought so." She yawned and made to get up from the sofa. "You done got me so sleepy wid yo' head-scratchin' Ah kin hardly make it tuh de bed." She stood up at once, collecting her hair. He sat still.

"Naw, you ain't sleepy, Mis' Janie. You jus' want me tuh go. You figger Ah'm uh rounder and uh pimp and you done wasted too much time talkin' wid me."

"Why, Tea Cake! Whut ever put dat notion in yo' head?"

"De way you looked at me when Ah said whut Ah did. Yo' face skeered me so bad till mah whiskers drawed up."

"Ah ain't got no business bein' mad at nothin' you do and say. You got it all wrong. Ah ain't mad atall."

"Ah know it and dat's what puts de shamery on me. You'se jus' disgusted wid me. Yo' face jus' left here and went off somewhere else. Naw, you ain't mad wid me. Ah be glad if you was, 'cause then Ah might do somethin' tuh please yuh. But lak it is—"

"Mah likes and dislikes ought not tuh make no difference wid you, Tea Cake. Dat's fuh yo' lady friend. Ah'm jus' uh sometime friend uh yourn."

Janie walked towards the stairway slowly, and Tea Cake sat where he was, as if he had frozen to his seat, in fear that once he got up, he'd never get back in it again. He swallowed hard and looked at her walk away.

"Ah didn't aim tuh let on tuh yuh 'bout it, leastways not right away, but Ah ruther be shot wid tacks than fuh you tuh act wid me lak you is right now. You got me in de go-long."

At the newel post Janie whirled around and for the space of a thought she was lit up like a transfiguration. Her next thought brought her crashing down. He's just saying anything for the time being, feeling he's got me so I'll b'lieve him. The next thought buried her under tons of cold futility. He's trading on being younger than me. Getting ready to laugh at me for an old fool. But oh, what wouldn't I give to be twelve years younger so I could b'lieve him!

"Aw, Tea Cake, you just say dat tuhnight because de fish and corn bread tasted sort of good. Tomorrow yo' mind would change."

"Naw, it wouldn't neither. Ah know better."

"Anyhow from what you told me when we wuz back dere in de kitchen Ah'm nearly twelve years older than you."

"Ah done thought all about dat and tried tuh struggle aginst it, but it don't do me no good. De thought uh mah youngness don't satisfy me lak yo' presence do."

"It makes uh whole heap uh difference wid most folks, Tea Cake."

"Things lak dat got uh whole lot tuh do wid convenience, but it ain't got nothin' tuh do wid love."

"Well, Ah love tuh find out whut you think after sun-up tomorrow. Dis is jus' yo' night thought."

"You got yo' ideas and Ah got mine. Ah got uh dollar dat says you'se wrong. But Ah reckon you don't bet money, neither."

"Ah never have done it so fur. But as de old folks always say, Ah'm born but Ah ain't dead. No tellin' whut Ah'm liable tuh do yet."

He got up suddenly and took his hat. "Good night, Mis' Janie. Look lak we done run our conversation from grass roots tuh pine trees. G'bye." He almost ran out of the door.

Janie hung over the newel post thinking so long that she all but went to sleep there. However, before she went to bed she took a good look at her mouth, eyes and hair.

All next day in the house and store she thought resisting thoughts about Tea Cake. She even ridiculed him in her mind and was a little ashamed of the association. But every hour or two the battle had to be fought all over again. She couldn't make him look just like any other man to her. He looked like the love thoughts of women. He could be a bee to a blossom—a pear tree blossom in the spring. He seemed to be crushing scent out of the world with his footsteps. Crushing aromatic herbs with every step he took. Spices hung about him. He was a glance from God.

So he didn't come that night and she laid in bed and pretended to think scornfully of him. "Bet he's hangin' round some jook or 'nother. Glad Ah treated him cold. Whut do Ah want wid some trashy nigger out de streets? Bet he's livin' wid some woman or 'nother and takin' me for uh fool. Glad Ah caught mahself in time." She tried to console herself that way.

The next morning she awoke hearing a knocking on the front door and found Tea Cake there.

"Hello, Mis' Janie, Ah hope Ah woke you up."

"You sho did, Tea Cake. Come in and rest yo' hat. Whut you doin' out so soon dis mornin'?"

"Thought Ah'd try tuh git heah soon enough tuh tell yuh mah daytime thoughts. Ah see yuh needs tuh know mah daytime feelings. Ah can't sense yuh intuh it at night."

"You crazy thing! Is dat whut you come here for at daybreak?"

"Sho is. You needs tellin' and showin', and dat's whut Ah'm doin'. Ah picked some strawberries too, Ah figgered you might like."

"Tea Cake, Ah 'clare Ah don't know whut tuh make outa you. You'se so crazy. You better lemme fix you some breakfast."

"Ain't got time. Ah got uh job uh work. Gottuh be back in Orlandah at eight o'clock. See yuh later, tell you straighter."

He bolted down the walk and was gone. But that night when she left the store, he was stretched out in the hammock on the porch with his hat over his face pretending to sleep. She called him. He pretended not to hear. He snored louder. She went to the hammock to shake him and he seized and pulled her in with him. After a little, she let him adjust her in his arms and laid there for a while.

"Tea Cake, Ah don't know 'bout you, but Ah'm hongry, come on let's eat some supper."

They went inside and their laughter rang out first from the

102

kitchen and all over the house.

Janie awoke next morning by feeling Tea Cake almost kissing her breath away. Holding her and caressing her as if he feared she might escape his grasp and fly away. Then he must dress hurriedly and get to his job on time. He wouldn't let her get him any breakfast at all. He wanted her to get her rest. He made her stay where she was. In her heart she wanted to get his breakfast for him. But she stayed in bed long after he was gone.

So much had been breathed out by the pores that Tea Cake still was there. She could feel him and almost see him bucking around the room in the upper air. After a long time of passive happiness, she got up and opened the window and let Tea Cake leap forth and mount to the sky on a wind. That was the beginning of things.

In the cool of the afternoon the fiend from hell specially sent to lovers arrived at Janie's ear. Doubt. All the fears that circumstance could provide and the heart feel, attacked her on every side. This was a new sensation for her, but no less excruciating. If only Tea Cake would make her certain! He did not return that night nor the next and so she plunged into the abyss and descended to the ninth darkness where light has never been.

But the fourth day after he came in the afternoon driving a battered car. Jumped out like a deer and made the gesture of tying it to a post on the store porch. Ready with his grin! She adored him and hated him at the same time. How could he make her suffer so and then come grinning like that with that darling way he had? He pinched her arm as he walked inside the door.

"Brought me somethin' tuh haul you off in," he told her with that secret chuckle. "Git yo' hat if you gointuh wear one. We got tuh go buy groceries."

"Ah sells groceries right here in dis store, Tea Cake, if you don't happen tuh know." She tried to look cold but she was smiling in spite of herself.

"Not de kind we want fuh de occasion. You sells groceries for ordinary people. We'se gointuh buy for *you*. De big Sunday School picnic is tomorrow—bet you done forget it—and we got tuh be dere wid uh swell basket and ourselves."

"Ah don't know 'bout dat, Tea Cake. Tell yuh whut you do. G'wan down tuh de house and wait for me. Be dere in uh minute."

As soon as she thought it looked right she slipped out of the back and joined Tea Cake. No need of fooling herself. Maybe he was just being polite.

"Tea Cake, you sure you want me tuh go tuh dis picnic wid yuh?"

"Me scramble 'round tuh git de money tuh take yuh—been workin' lak uh dawg for two whole weeks—and she come astin' me if Ah want her tuh go! Puttin' mahself tuh uh whole heap uh trouble tuh git dis car so you kin go over tuh Winter Park or Orlandah tuh buy de things you might need and dis woman set dere and ast me if Ah want her tuh go!"

"Don't git mad, Tea Cake, Ah just didn't want you doin' nothin' outa politeness. If dere's somebody else you'd ruther take, it's all right wid me."

"Naw, it ain't all right wid you. If it was you wouldn't be sayin' dat. Have de nerve tuh say whut you mean."

"Well, all right, Tea Cake, Ah wants tuh go wid you real bad, but,—oh, Tea Cake, don't make no false pretense wid me!"

"Janie, Ah hope God may kill me, if Ah'm lyin'. Nobody else on earth kin hold uh candle tuh you, baby. You got de keys to de kingdom."

CHAPTER 12

t was after the picnic that the town began to notice things and got mad. Tea Cake and Mrs. Mayor Starks! All the men that she could get, and fooling with somebody like Tea Cake! Another thing, Joe Starks hadn't been dead but nine months and here she goes sashaying off to a picnic in pink linen. Done quit attending church, like she used to. Gone off to Sanford in a car with Tea Cake and her all dressed in blue! It was a shame. Done took to high heel slippers and a ten dollar hat! Looking like some young girl, always in blue because Tea Cake told her to wear it. Poor Joe Starks. Bet he turns over in his grave every day. Tea Cake and Janie gone hunting. Tea Cake and Janie gone fishing. Tea Cake and Janie gone to Orlando to the movies. Tea Cake and Janie gone to a dance. Tea Cake making flower beds in Janie's yard and seeding the garden for her. Chopping down that tree she never did like by the dining room window. All those signs of possession. Tea Cake in a borrowed car teaching Janie to drive. Tea Cake and Janie playing checkers; playing coon-can; playing Florida flip on the store porch all afternoon as if nobody else was there. Day after day and week after week.

"Pheoby," Sam Watson said one night as he got in the bed, "Ah b'lieve yo' buddy is all tied up with dat Tea Cake shonough. Didn't b'lieve it at first."

"Aw she don't mean nothin' by it. Ah think she's sort of stuck on dat undertaker up at Sanford."

"It's somebody 'cause she looks might good dese days. New dresses and her hair combed a different way nearly every day. You got to have something to comb hair over. When you see uh woman doin' so much rakin' in her head, she's combin' at some man or 'nother."

" 'Course she kin do as she please, but dat's uh good chance she got up at Sanford. De man's wife died and he got uh lovely place tuh take her to—already furnished. Better'n her house Joe left her."

"You better sense her intuh things then 'cause Tea Cake can't do nothin' but help her spend whut she got. Ah reckon dat's whut he's after. Throwin' away whut Joe Starks worked hard tuh git tuhgether."

"Dat's de way it looks. Still and all, she's her own woman. She oughta know by now whut she wants tuh do."

"De men wuz talkin' 'bout it in de grove tuhday and givin' her and Tea Cake both de devil. Dey figger he's spendin' on her now in order tuh make her spend on him later."

"Umph! Umph! Umph!"

"Oh dey got it all figgered out. Maybe it ain't as bad as they say, but they talk it and make it sound real bad on her part."

"Dat's jealousy and malice. Some uh dem very mens wants tuh do whut dey claim deys skeered Tea Cake is doin'."

"De Pastor claim Tea Cake don't 'low her tuh come tuh church only once in awhile 'cause he want dat change tuh buy gas wid. Just draggin' de woman away from church. But any-how, she's yo' bosom friend, so you better go see 'bout her. Drop uh lil hint here and dere and if Tea Cake is tryin' tuh rob her she kin see and know. Ah laks de woman and Ah sho would hate tuh see her come up lak Mis' Tyler."

"Aw mah God, naw! Reckon Ah better step over dere tomorrow and have some chat wid Janie. She jus' ain't thinkin' whut she doin', dat's all."

The next morning Pheoby picked her way over to Janie's house like a hen to a neighbor's garden. Stopped and talked a little with everyone she met, turned aside momentarily to pause at a porch or two—going straight by walking crooked. So her firm intention looked like an accident and she didn't have to give her opinion to folks along the way.

Janie acted glad to see her and after a while Pheoby broached her with, "Janie, everybody's talkin' 'bout how dat Tea Cake is draggin' you round tuh places you ain't used tuh. Baseball games and huntin' and fishin'. He don't know you'se useter uh more high time crowd than dat. You always did class off."

"Jody classed me off. Ah didn't. Naw, Pheoby, Tea Cake ain't draggin' me off nowhere Ah don't want tuh go. Ah always did want tuh git round uh whole heap, but Jody wouldn't 'low me tuh. When Ah wasn't in de store he wanted me tuh jes sit wid folded hands and sit dere. And Ah'd sit dere wid de walls creepin' up on me and squeezin' all de life outa me. Pheoby, dese educated women got uh heap of things to sit down and consider. Somebody done tole 'em what to set down for. Nobody ain't told poor me, so sittin' still worries me. Ah wants tuh utilize mahself all over."

"But, Janie, Tea Cake, whilst he ain't no jail-bird, he ain't got uh dime tuh cry. Ain't you skeered he's jes after yo' money—him bein' younger than you?"

"He ain't never ast de first penny from me yet, and if he love property he ain't no different from all de rest of us. All dese ole men dat's settin' round me is after de same thing. They's three mo' widder women in town, how come dey don't break dey neck after dem? 'Cause dey ain't got nothin', dat's why."

"Folks seen you out in colors and dey thinks you ain't payin' de right amount uh respect tuh yo' dead husband."

"Ah ain't grievin' so why do Ah hafta mourn? Tea Cake love me in blue, so Ah wears it. Jody ain't never in his life picked out no color for me. De world picked out black and white for mournin', Joe didn't. So Ah wasn't wearin' it for him. Ah was wearin' it for de rest of y'all."

"But anyhow, watch yo'self, Janie, and don't be took advantage of. You know how dese young men is wid older women. Most of de time dey's after whut dey kin git, then dey's gone lak uh turkey through de corn."

"Tea Cake don't talk dat way. He's aimin' tuh make hisself permanent wid me. We done made up our mind tuh marry."

"Janie, you'se yo' own woman, and Ah hope you know whut you doin'. Ah sho hope you ain't lak uh possum—de older you gits, de less sense yuh got. Ah'd feel uh whole heap better 'bout yuh if you wuz marryin' dat man up dere in Sanford. He got somethin' tuh put long side uh whut you got and dat make it more better. He's endurable."

"Still and all Ah'd ruther be wid Tea Cake."

"Well, if yo' mind is already made up, 'tain't nothin' nobody kin do. But you'se takin' uh awful chance."

"No mo' than Ah took befo' and no mo' than anybody else takes when dey gits married. It always changes folks, and sometimes it brings out dirt and meanness dat even de person didn't know they had in 'em theyselves. You know dat. Maybe Tea Cake might turn out lak dat. Maybe not. Anyhow Ah'm ready and willin' tuh try 'im."

"Well, when you aim tuh step off?"

"Dat we don't know. De store is got tuh be sold and then we'se goin' off somewhere tuh git married."

"How come you sellin' out de store?"

" 'Cause Tea Cake ain't no Jody Starks, and if he tried tuh be, it would be uh complete flommuck. But de minute Ah marries 'im everybody is gointuh be makin' comparisons. So us is goin' off somewhere and start all over in Tea Cake's way. Dis ain't no business proposition, and no race after property and titles. Dis is uh love game. Ah done lived Grandma's way, now Ah means tuh live mine."

"What you mean by dat, Janie?"

"She was borned in slavery time when folks, dat is black folks, didn't sit down anytime dey felt lak it. So sittin' on porches lak de white madam looked lak uh mighty fine thing tuh her. Dat's whut she wanted for me—don't keer whut it cost. Git up on uh high chair and sit dere. She didn't have time tuh think whut tuh do after you got up on de stool uh do nothin'. De object wuz tuh git dere. So Ah got up on de high stool lak she told me, but Pheoby, Ah done nearly languished tuh death up dere. Ah felt like de world wuz cryin' extry and Ah ain't read de common news yet."

"Maybe so, Janie. Still and all Ah'd love tuh experience it for just one year. It look lak heben tuh me from where Ah'm at."

"Ah reckon so."

"But anyhow, Janie, you be keerful 'bout dis sellin' out and goin' off wid strange men. Look whut happened tuh Annie Tyler. Took whut little she had and went off tuh Tampa wid dat boy dey call Who Flung. It's somethin' tuh think about."

"It sho is. Still Ah ain't Mis' Tyler and Tea Cake ain't no Who Flung, and he ain't no stranger tuh me. We'se just as good as married already. But Ah ain't puttin' it in de street. Ah'm tellin' *you.*"

"Ah jus lak uh chicken. Chicken drink water, but he don't pee-pee."

"Oh, Ah know you don't talk. We ain't shame faced. We jus' ain't ready tuh make no big kerflommuck as yet."

"You doin' right not tuh talk it, but Janie, you'se takin' uh mighty big chance."

" 'Tain't so big uh chance as it seem lak, Pheoby. Ah'm older than Tea Cake, yes. But he done showed me where it's de thought dat makes de difference in ages. If people thinks de same they can make it all right. So in the beginnin' new thoughts had tuh be thought and new words said. After Ah got used tuh dat, we gits 'long jus' fine. He done taught me de maiden language all over. Wait till you see de new blue satin

Tea Cake done picked out for me tuh stand up wid him in. High heel slippers, necklace, earrings, *everything* he wants tuh see me in. Some of dese mornin's and it won't be long, you gointuh wake up callin' me and Ah'll be gone."

CHAPTER 13

Jacksonville. Tea Cake's letter had said Jacksonville. He had worked in the railroad shops up there before and his old boss had promised him a job come next pay day. No need for Janie to wait any longer. Wear the new blue dress because he meant to marry her right from the train. Hurry up and come because he was about to turn into pure sugar thinking about her. Come on, baby, papa Tea Cake never could be mad with you!

Janie's train left too early in the day for the town to witness much, but the few who saw her leave bore plenty witness. They had to give it to her, she sho looked good, but she had no business to do it. It was hard to love a woman that always made you feel so wishful.

The train beat on itself and danced on the shiny steel rails mile after mile. Every now and then the engineer would play on his whistle for the people in the towns he passed by. And the train shuffled on to Jacksonville, and to a whole lot of things she wanted to see and to know.

And there was Tea Cake in the big old station in a new blue suit and straw hat, hauling her off to a preacher's house first thing. Then right on to the room he had been sleeping in for two weeks all by himself waiting for her to come. And such another hugging and kissing and carrying on you never saw. It made her so glad she was scared of herself. They stayed at home and rested that night, but the next night they went to a show and after that they rode around on the trolley cars and sort of looked things over for themselves. Tea Cake was spending and doing out of his own pocket, so Janie never told him about the two hundred dollars she had pinned inside her shirt next to her skin. Pheoby had insisted that she bring it along and keep it secret just to be on the safe side. She had ten dollars over her fare in her pocket book. Let Tea Cake think that was all she had. Things might not turn out like she thought. Every minute since she had stepped off the train she had been laughing at Pheoby's advice. She meant to tell Tea Cake the joke some time when she was sure she wouldn't hurt his feelings. So it came around that she had been married a week and sent Pheoby a card with a picture on it.

That morning Tea Cake got up earlier than Janie did. She felt sleepy and told him to go get some fish to fry for breakfast. By the time he had gone and come back she would have finished her nap out. He told her he would and she turned over and went back to sleep. She woke up and Tea Cake still wasn't there and the clock said it was getting late, so she got up and washed her face and hands. Perhaps he was down in the kitchen fixing around to let her sleep. Janie went down and the landlady made her drink some coffee with her because she said her husband was dead and it was bad to be having your morning coffee by yourself.

"Yo' husband gone tuh work dis mornin', Mis' Woods? Ah seen him go out uh good while uh go. Me and you kin be comp'ny for one 'nother, can't us?"

"Oh yes, indeed, Mis' Samuels. You puts me in de mind uh mah friend back in Eatonville. Yeah, you'se nice and friendly jus' lak her."

Therefore Janie drank her coffee and sankled on back to her room without asking her landlady anything. Tea Cake must be hunting all over the city for that fish. She kept that thought in front of her in order not to think too much. When she heard the twelve o'clock whistle she decided to get up and dress. That was when she found out her two hundred dollars was gone. There was the little cloth purse with the safety pin on the chair beneath her clothes and the money just wasn't nowhere in the room. She knew from the beginning that the money wasn't any place she knew of if it wasn't in that little pocket book pinned to her pink silk vest. But the exercise of searching the room kept her busy and that was good for her to keep moving, even though she wasn't doing anything but turning around in her tracks.

But, don't care how firm your determination is, you can't keep turning round in one place like a horse grinding sugar cane. So Janie took to sitting over the room. Sit and look. The room inside looked like the mouth of an alligator—gaped wide open to swallow something down. Outside the window Jacksonville looked like it needed a fence around it to keep it from running out on ether's bosom. It was too big to be warm, let alone to need somebody like her. All day and night she worried time like a bone.

Way late in the morning the thought of Annie Tyler and Who Flung came to pay her a visit. Annie Tyler who at fifty-two had been left a widow with a good home and insurance money.

Mrs. Tyler with her dyed hair, newly straightened and her uncomfortable new false teeth, her leathery skin, blotchy with powder and her giggle. Her love affairs, affairs with boys in their late teens or early twenties for all of whom she spent her money on suits of clothes, shoes, watches and things like that and how they all left her as soon as their wants were satisfied. Then when her ready cash was gone, had come Who Flung to denounce his predecessor as a scoundrel and took up around the house himself. It was he who persuaded her to sell her house and come to Tampa with him. The town had seen her limp off. The undersized high-heel slippers were punishing her tired feet that looked like bunions all over. Her body

113

squeezed and crowded into a tight corset that shoved her middle up under her chin. But she had gone off laughing and sure. As sure as Janie had been.

Then two weeks later the porter and conductor of the north bound local had helped her off the train at Maitland. Hair all gray and black and bluish and reddish in streaks. All the capers that cheap dye could cut was showing in her hair. Those slippers bent and griped just like her work-worn feet. The corset gone and the shaking old woman hanging all over herself. Everything that you could see was hanging. Her chin hung from her ears and rippled down her neck like drapes. Her hanging bosom and stomach and buttocks and legs that draped down over her ankles. She groaned but never giggled.

She was broken and her pride was gone, so she told those who asked what had happened. Who Flung had taken her to a shabby room in a shabby house in a shabby street and promised to marry her next day. They stayed in the room two whole days then she woke up to find Who Flung and her money gone. She got up to stir around and see if she could find him, and found herself too worn out to do much. All she found out was that she was too old a vessel for new wine. The next day hunger had driven her out to shift. She had stood on the streets and smiled and smiled, and then smiled and begged and then just begged. After a week of world-bruising a young man from home had come along and seen her. She couldn't tell him how it was. She just told him she got off the train and somebody had stolen her purse. Naturally, he had believed her and taken her home with him to give her time to rest up a day or two, then he had bought her a ticket for home.

They put her to bed and sent for her married daughter from up around Ocala to come see about her. The daughter came as soon as she could and took Annie Tyler away to die in peace. She had waited all her life for something, and it had killed her when it found her.

The thing made itself into pictures and hung around Janie's bedside all night long. Anyhow, she wasn't going back to

Eatonville to be laughed at and pitied. She had ten dollars in her pocket and twelve hundred in the bank. But oh God, don't let Tea Cake be off somewhere hurt and Ah not know nothing about it. And God, please suh, don't let him love nobody else but me. Maybe Ah'm is uh fool, Lawd, lak dey say, but Lawd, Ah been so lonesome, and Ah been waitin', Jesus. Ah done waited uh long time.

Janie dozed off to sleep but she woke up in time to see the sun sending up spies ahead of him to mark out the road through the dark. He peeped up over the door sill of the world and made a little foolishness with red. But pretty soon, he laid all that aside and went about his business dressed all in white. But it was always going to be dark to Janie if Tea Cake didn't soon come back. She got out of the bed but a chair couldn't hold her. She dwindled down on the floor with her head in a rocking chair.

After a while there was somebody playing a guitar outside her door. Played right smart while. It sounded lovely too. But it was sad to hear it feeling blue like Janie was. Then whoever it was started to singing "Ring de bells of mercy. Call de sinner man home." Her heart all but smothered her.

"Tea Cake, is dat you?"

"You know so well it's me, Janie. How come you don't open de door?"

But he never waited. He walked on in with a guitar and a grin. Guitar hanging round his neck with a red silk cord and a grin hanging from his ears.

"Don't need tuh ast me where Ah been all dis time, 'cause it's mah all day job tuh tell yuh."

"Tea Cake, Ah—"

"Good Lawd, Janie, whut you doin' settin' on de floor?"

He took her head in his hands and eased himself into the chair. She still didn't say anything. He sat stroking her head and looking down into her face.

"Ah see whut it is. You doubted me 'bout de money. Thought Ah had done took it and gone. Ah don't blame yuh but it wasn't lak you think. De girl baby ain't born and her mama is dead, dat can git me tuh spend our money on her. Ah told yo' before dat you got de keys tuh de kingdom. You can depend on dat."

"Still and all you went off and left me all day and all night."

" 'Twasn't 'cause Ah wanted tuh stay off lak dat, and it sho Lawd, wuzn't no woman. If you didn't have de power tuh hold me and hold me tight, Ah wouldn't be callin' yuh Mis' Woods. Ah met plenty women before Ah knowed you tuh talk tuh. You'se de onliest woman in de world Ah ever even mentioned gitting married tuh. You bein' older don't make no difference. Don't never consider dat no mo'. If Ah ever gits tuh messin' round another woman it won't be on account of her age. It'll be because she got me in de same way you got me—so Ah can't help mahself."

He sat down on the floor beside her and kissed and playfully turned up the corner of her mouth until she smiled.

"Looka here, folks," he announced to an imaginary audience, "Sister Woods is 'bout tuh quit her husband!"

Janie laughed at that and let herself lean on him. Then she announced to the same audience, "Mis' Woods got herself uh new lil boy rooster, but he been off somewhere and won't tell her."

"First thing, though, us got tuh eat together, Janie. Then we can talk."

"One thing, Ah won't send you out after no fish."

He pinched her in the side and ignored what she said.

" 'Tain't no need of neither one of us workin' dis mornin'. Call Mis' Samuels and let her fix whatever you want."

"Tea Cake, if you don't hurry up and tell me, Ah'll take and beat yo' head flat as uh dime."

Tea Cake stuck out till he had some breakfast, then he talked and acted out the story.

He spied the money while he was tying his tie. He took it up and looked at it out of curiosity and put it in his pocket to count it while he was out to find some fish to fry. When he

116

found out how much it was, he was excited and felt like letting folks know who he was. Before he found the fish market he met a fellow he used to work with at the round house. One word brought on another one and pretty soon he made up his mind to spend some of it. He never had had his hand on so much money before in his life, so he made up his mind to see how it felt to be a millionaire. They went on out to Callahan round the railroad shops and he decided to give a big chicken and macaroni supper that night, free to all.

He bought up the stuff and they found somebody to pick the guitar so they could all dance some. So they sent the message all around for people to come. And come they did. A big table loaded down with fried chicken and biscuits and a wash-tub full of macaroni with plenty cheese in it. When the fellow began to pick the box the people begin to come from east, west, north and Australia. And he stood in the door and paid all the ugly women two dollars *not* to come in. One big meriny colored woman was so ugly till it was worth five dollars for her not to come in, so he gave it to her.

They had a big time till one man come in who thought he was bad. He tried to pull and haul over all the chickens and pick out the livers and gizzards to eat. Nobody else couldn't pacify him so they called Tea Cake to come see if he could stop him. So Tea Cake walked up and asked him, "Say, whut's de matter wid you, nohow?"

"Ah don't want nobody handin' me nothin'. Specially don't issue me out no rations. Ah always chooses mah rations." He kept right on plowing through the pile uh chicken. So Tea Cake got mad.

"You got mo' nerve than uh brass monkey. Tell me, what post office did *you* ever pee in? Ah craves tuh know."

"Whut you mean by dat now?" the fellow asked.

"Ah means dis—it takes jus' as much nerve tuh cut caper lak dat in uh United States Government Post Office as it do tuh comes pullin' and haulin' over any chicken Ah pay for. Hit de ground. Damned if Ah ain't gointuh try you dis night."

So they all went outside to see if Tea Cake could handle the boogerboo. Tea Cake knocked out two of his teeth, so that man went on off from there. Then two men tried to pick a fight with one another, so Tea Cake said they had to kiss and make up. They didn't want to do it. They'd rather go to jail, but everybody else liked the idea, so they made 'em do it. Afterwards, both of them spit and gagged and wiped their mouths with the back of their hands. One went outside and chewed a little grass like a sick dog, he said to keep it from killing him.

Then everybody began to holler at the music because the man couldn't play but three pieces. So Tea Cake took the guitar and played himself. He was glad of the chance because he hadn't had his hand on a box since he put his in the pawn shop to get some money to hire a car for Janie soon after he met her. He missed his music. So that put him in the notion he ought to have one. He bought the guitar on the spot and paid fifteen dollars cash. It was really worth sixty-five any day.

Just before day the party wore out. So Tea Cake hurried on back to his new wife. He had done found out how rich people feel and he had a fine guitar and twelve dollars left in his pocket and all he needed now was a great big old hug and kiss from Janie.

"You musta thought yo' wife was powerful ugly. Dem ugly women dat you paid two dollars not to come in, could git tuh de door. You never even 'lowed me tuh git dat close." She pouted.

"Janie, Ah would have give Jacksonville wid Tampa for a jump-back for you to be dere wid me. Ah started to come git yuh two three times."

"Well, how come yuh didn't come git me?"

"Janie, would you have come if Ah did?"

"Sho Ah would. Ah laks fun just as good as you do."

"Janie, Ah wanted tuh, mighty much, but Ah was skeered. Too skeered Ah might lose yuh."

"Why?"

"Dem wuzn't no high muckty mucks. Dem wuz railroad

hands and dey womenfolks. You ain't usetuh folks lak dat and Ah wuz skeered you might git all mad and quit me for takin' you 'mongst 'em. But Ah wanted yuh wid me jus' de same. Befo' us got married Ah made up mah mind not tuh let you see no commonness in me. When Ah git mad habits on, Ah'd go off and keep it out yo' sight. 'Tain't mah notion tuh drag *you* down wid me.''

"Looka heah, Tea Cake, if you ever go off from me and have a good time lak dat and then come back heah tellin' me how nice Ah is, Ah specks tuh kill yuh dead. You heah me?''

"So you aims tuh partake wid everything, hunh?''

"Yeah, Tea Cake, don't keer what it is.''

"Dat's all Ah wants tuh know. From now on you'se mah wife and mah woman and everything else in de world Ah needs.''

"Ah hope so.''

"And honey, don't you worry 'bout yo' lil ole two hundred dollars. It's big pay day dis comin' Saturday at de railroad yards. Ah'm gointuh take dis twelve dollars in mah pocket and win it all back and mo'.''

"How?''

"Honey, since you loose me and gïmme privilege tuh tell yuh all about mahself, Ah'll tell yuh. You done married one uh de best gamblers God ever made. Cards or dice either one. Ah can take uh shoe string and win uh tan-yard. Wish yuh could see me rollin'. But dis time it's gointuh be nothin' but tough men's talkin' all kinds uh talk so it ain't no place for you tuh be, but 'twon't be long befo' you see me.''

All the rest of the week Tea Cake was busy practising up on his dice. He would flip them on the bare floor, on the rug and on the bed. He'd squat and throw, sit in a chair and throw and stand and throw. It was very exciting to Janie who had never touched dice in her life. Then he'd take his deck of cards and shuffle and cut, shuffle and cut and deal out then examine each hand carefully, and do it again. So Saturday came. He went out and bought a new switch-blade knife and two decks of

119

star-back playing cards that morning and left Janie around noon.

"They'll start to paying off, pretty soon now. Ah wants tuh git in de game whilst de big money is in it. Ah ain't fuh no spuddin' tuhday. Ah'll come home wid de money or Ah'll come back on uh stretcher." He cut nine hairs out of the mole of her head for luck and went off happy.

Janie waited till midnight without worrying, but after that she began to be afraid. So she got up and sat around scared and miserable. Thinking and fearing all sorts of dangers. Wondering at herself as she had many times this week that she was not shocked at Tea Cake's gambling. It was part of him, so it was all right. She rather found herself angry at imaginary people who might try to criticize. Let the old hypocrites learn to mind their own business, and leave other folks alone. Tea Cake wasn't doing a bit more harm trying to win hisself a little money than they was always doing with their lying tongues. Tea Cake had more good nature under his toe-nails than they had in their so-called Christian hearts. She better not hear none of them old backbiters talking about *her* husband! Please, Jesus, don't let them nasty niggers hurt her boy. If they do, Master Jesus, grant her a good gun and a chance to shoot 'em. Tea Cake had a knife it was true, but that was only to protect hisself. God knows, Tea Cake wouldn't harm a fly.

Daylight was creeping around the cracks of the world when Janie heard a feeble rap on the door. She sprung to the door and flung it wide. Tea Cake was out there looking like he was asleep standing up. In some strange way it was frightening. Janie caught his arm to arouse him and he stumbled into the room and fell.

"Tea Cake! You chile! What's de matter, honey?"

"Dey cut me, dat's all. Don't cry. Git me out dis coat quick as yuh can."

He told her he wasn't cut but twice but she had to have him naked so she could look him all over and fix him up to a certain extent. He told her not to call a doctor unless he got much worse. It was mostly loss of blood anyhow.

"Ah won the money jus' lak ah told yuh. Round midnight Ah had yo' two hundred dollars and wuz ready tuh quit even though it wuz uh heap mo' money in de game. But dey wanted uh chance tuh win it back so Ah set back down tuh play some mo'. Ah knowed ole Double-Ugly wuz 'bout broke and wanted tuh fight 'bout it, so Ah set down tuh give 'im his chance tuh git back his money and then to give 'im uh quick trip tuh hell if he tried tuh pull dat razor Ah glimpsed in his pocket. Honey, no up-to-date man don't fool wid no razor. De man wid his switch-blade will be done cut yuh tuh death while you foolin' wid uh razor. But Double-Ugly brags he's too fast wid it tuh git hurt, but Ah knowed better.

"So round four o'clock Ah had done cleaned 'em out complete—all except two men dat got up and left while dey had money for groceries, and one man dat wuz lucky. Then Ah rose tuh bid 'em good bye agin. None of 'em didn't lak it, but dey all realized it wuz fair. Ah had done give 'em a fair chance. All but Double-Ugly. He claimed Ah switched de dice. Ah shoved de money down deep in mah pocket and picked up mah hat and coat wid mah left hand and kept mah right hand on mah knife. Ah didn't keer what he *said* long as he didn't try tuh *do* nothin'. Ah got mah hat on and one arm in mah coat as Ah got to de door. Right dere he jumped at me as Ah turned to see de doorstep outside and cut me twice in de back.

"Baby, Ah run mah other arm in mah coat-sleeve and grabbed dat nigger by his necktie befo' he could bat his eye and then Ah wuz all over 'im jus' lak gravy over rice. He lost his razor tryin' tuh git loose from me. He wuz hollerin' for me tuh turn him loose, but baby, Ah turnt him every way *but* loose. Ah left him on the doorstep and got here to yuh de quickest way Ah could. Ah know Ah ain't cut too deep 'cause he was too skeered tuh run up on me close enough. Sorta pull de flesh together with stickin' plaster. Ah'll be all right in uh day or so."

Janie was painting on iodine and crying.

"You ain't de one to be cryin', Janie. It's his ole lady oughta do dat. You done gimme luck. Look in mah left hand pants pocket and see whut yo' daddy brought yuh. When Ah tell yuh Ah'm gointuh bring it, Ah don't lie."

They counted it together—three hundred and twenty-two dollars. It was almost like Tea Cake had held up the Paymaster. He made her take the two hundred and put it back in the secret place. Then Janie told him about the other money she had in the bank.

"Put dat two hundred back wid de rest, Janie. Mah dice. Ah no need no assistance tuh help me feed mah woman. From now on, you gointuh eat whutever mah money can buy yuh and wear de same. When Ah ain't got nothin' you don't git nothin'."

"Dat's all right wid me."

He was getting drowsy, but he pinched her leg playfully because he was glad she took things the way he wanted her to. "Listen, mama, soon as Ah git over dis lil cuttin' scrape, we gointuh do somethin' crazy."

"Whut's dat?"

"We goin' on de muck."

"Whut's de muck, and where is it at?"

"Oh down in de Everglades round Clewiston and Belle Glade where dey raise all dat cane and string-beans and tomatuhs. Folks don't do nothin' down dere but make money and fun and foolishness. We must go dere."

He drifted off into sleep and Janie looked down on him and felt a self-crushing love. So her soul crawled out from its hiding place.

CHAPTER 14

To Janie's strange eyes, everything in the Everglades was big and new. Big Lake Okechobee, big beans, big cane, big weeds, big everything. Weeds that did well to grow waist high up the state were eight and often ten feet tall down there. Ground so rich that everything went wild. Volunteer cane just taking the place. Dirt roads so rich and black that a half mile of it would have fertilized a Kansas wheat field. Wild cane on either side of the road hiding the rest of the world. People wild too.

"Season don't open up till last of September, but we had tuh git heah ahead uh time tuh git us uh room," Tea Cake explained. "Two weeks from now, it'll be so many folks heah dey won't be lookin' fuh rooms, dey'll be jus' looking fuh somewhere tuh sleep. Now we got uh chance tuh git uh room at de hotel, where dey got uh bath tub. Yuh can't live on de muck 'thout yuh take uh bath every day. Do dat muck'll itch yuh lak ants. 'Tain't but one place round heah wid uh bath tub. 'Tain't nowhere near enough rooms."

"Whut we gointuh do round heah?"

"All day Ah'm pickin' beans. All night Ah'm pickin' mah box and rollin' dice. Between de beans and de dice Ah can't lose. Ah'm gone right now tuh pick me uh job uh work wid

123

de best man on de muck. Before de rest of 'em gits heah. You can always git jobs round heah in de season, but not wid de right folks.''

"When do de job open up, Tea Cake? Everybody round here look lak dey waitin' too."

"Dat's right. De big men haves uh certain time tuh open de season jus' lak in everything else. Mah boss-man didn't get sufficient seed. He's out huntin' up uh few mo' bushels. Den we'se gointuh plantin'."

"Bushels?"

"Yeah, bushels. Dis ain't no game fuh pennies. Po' man ain't got no business at de show."

The very next day he burst into the room in high excitement. "Boss done bought out another man and want me down on de lake. He got houses fuh de first ones dat git dere. Less go!"

They rattled nine miles in a borrowed car to the quarters that squatted so close that only the dyke separated them from great, sprawling Okechobee. Janie fussed around the shack making a home while Tea Cake planted beans. After hours they fished. Every now and then they'd run across a party of Indians in their long, narrow dug-outs calmly winning their living in the trackless ways of the 'Glades. Finally the beans were in. Nothing much to do but wait to pick them. Tea Cake picked his box a great deal for Janie, but he still didn't have enough to do. No need of gambling yet. The people who were pouring in were broke. They didn't come bringing money, they were coming to make some.

"Tell yuh whut, Janie, less buy us some shootin' tools and go huntin' round heah."

"Dat would be fine, Tea Cake, exceptin' you know Ah can't shoot. But Ah'd love tuh go wid *you.*"

"Oh, you needs tuh learn how. 'Tain't no need uh you not knowin' how tuh handle shootin' tools. Even if you didn't never find no game, it's always some trashy rascal dat needs uh good killin'," he laughed. "Less go intuh Palm Beach and spend some of our money."

Every day they were practising. Tea Cake made her shoot at little things just to give her good aim. Pistol and shot gun and rifle. It got so the others stood around and watched them. Some of the men would beg for a shot at the target themselves. It was the most exciting thing on the muck. Better than the jook and the pool-room unless some special band was playing for a dance. And the thing that got everybody was the way Janie caught on. She got to the place she could shoot a hawk out of a pine tree and not tear him up. Shoot his head off. She got to be a better shot than Tea Cake. They'd go out any late afternoon and come back loaded down with game. One night they got a boat and went out hunting alligators. Shining their phosphorescent eyes and shooting them in the dark. They could sell the hides and teeth in Palm Beach besides having fun together till work got pressing.

Day by day now, the hordes of workers poured in. Some came limping in with their shoes and sore feet from walking. It's hard trying to follow your shoe instead of your shoe following you. They came in wagons from way up in Georgia and they came in truck loads from east, west, north and south. Permanent transients with no attachments and tired looking men with their families and dogs in flivvers. All night, all day, hurrying in to pick beans. Skillets, beds, patched up spare inner tubes all hanging and dangling from the ancient cars on the outside and hopeful humanity, herded and hovered on the inside, chugging on to the muck. People ugly from ignorance and broken from being poor.

All night now the jooks clanged and clamored. Pianos living three lifetimes in one. Blues made and used right on the spot. Dancing, fighting, singing, crying, laughing, winning and losing love every hour. Work all day for money, fight all night for love. The rich black earth clinging to bodies and biting the skin like ants.

Finally no more sleeping places. Men made big fires and

125

fifty or sixty men slept around each fire. But they had to pay the man whose land they slept on. He ran the fire just like his boarding place—for pay. But nobody cared. They made good money, even to the children. So they spent good money. Next month and next year were other times. No need to mix them up with the present.

Tea Cake's house was a magnet, the unauthorized center of the "job." The way he would sit in the doorway and play his guitar made people stop and listen and maybe disappoint the jook for that night. He was always laughing and full of fun too. He kept everybody laughing in the bean field.

Janie stayed home and boiled big pots of blackeyed peas and rice. Sometimes baked big pans of navy beans with plenty of sugar and hunks of bacon laying on top. That was something Tea Cake loved so no matter if Janie had fixed beans two or three times during the week, they had baked beans again on Sunday. She always had some kind of dessert too, as Tea Cake said it give a man something to taper off on. Sometimes she'd straighten out the two-room house and take the rifle and have fried rabbit for supper when Tea Cake got home. She didn't leave him itching and scratching in his work clothes, either. The kettle of hot water was already waiting when he got in.

Then Tea Cake took to popping in at the kitchen door at odd hours. Between breakfast and dinner, sometimes. Then often around two o'clock he'd come home and tease and wrestle with her for a half hour and slip on back to work. So one day she asked him about it.

"Tea Cake, whut you doin' back in de quarters when everybody else is still workin'?"

"Come tuh see 'bout you. De boogerman liable tuh tote yuh off whilst Ah'm gone."

" 'Tain't no boogerman got me tuh study 'bout. Maybe you think Ah ain't treatin' yuh right and you watchin' me."

"Naw, naw, Janie. Ah *know* better'n dat. But since you got dat in yo' head, Ah'll have tuh tell yuh de real truth, so yuh can know. Janie, Ah gits lonesome out dere all day 'thout yuh.

After dis, you betta come git uh job uh work out dere lak de rest uh de women—so Ah won't be losin' time comin' home."

"Tea Cake, you'se uh mess! Can't do 'thout me dat lil time."

" 'Tain't no lil time. It's near 'bout all day."

So the very next morning Janie got ready to pick beans along with Tea Cake. There was a suppressed murmur when she picked up a basket and went to work. She was already getting to be a special case on the muck. It was generally assumed that she thought herself too good to work like the rest of the women and that Tea Cake "pomped her up tuh dat." But all day long the romping and playing they carried on behind the boss's back made her popular right away. It got the whole field to playing off and on. Then Tea Cake would help get supper afterwards.

"You don't think Ah'm tryin' tuh git outa takin' keer uh yuh, do yuh, Janie, 'cause Ah ast yuh tuh work long side uh me?" Tea Cake asked her at the end of her first week in the field.

"Ah naw, honey. Ah laks it. It's mo' nicer than settin' round dese quarters all day. Clerkin' in dat store wuz hard, but heah, we ain't got nothin' tuh do but do our work and come home and love."

The house was full of people every night. That is, all around the doorstep was full. Some were there to hear Tea Cake pick the box; some came to talk and tell stories, but most of them came to get into whatever game was going on or might go on. Sometimes Tea Cake lost heavily, for there were several good gamblers on the lake. Sometimes he won and made Janie proud of his skill. But outside of the two jooks, everything on that job went on around those two.

Sometimes Janie would think of the old days in the big white house and the store and laugh to herself. What if Eatonville could see her now in her blue denim overalls and heavy shoes? The crowd of people around her and a dice game on her floor! She was sorry for her friends back there and scornful of the others. The men held big arguments here like they used to do on the store porch. Only here, she could listen and laugh and even talk some herself if she wanted to. She got so she could tell big stories herself from listening to the rest. Because she loved to hear it, and the men loved to hear themselves, they would "woof" and "boogerboo" around the games to the limit. No matter how rough it was, people seldom got mad, because everything was done for a laugh. Everybody loved to hear Ed Dockery, Bootyny, and Sop-de-Bottom in a skin game. Ed Dockery was dealing one night and he looked over at Sop-de-Bottom's card and he could tell Sop thought he was going to win. He hollered, "Ah'll break up *dat* settin' uh eggs." Sop looked and said, "Root de peg." Bootyny asked, "What are you goin' tuh do? Do do!" Everybody was watching that next card fall. Ed got ready to turn. "Ah'm gointuh sweep out hell and burn up de broom." He slammed down another dollar. "Don't oversport yourself, Ed," Bootyny challenged. "You gittin' too yaller." Ed caught hold of the corner of the card. Sop dropped a dollar. "Ah'm gointuh shoot in de hearse, don't keer how sad de funeral be." Ed said, "You see how this man is teasin' hell?" Tea Cake nudged Sop not to bet. "You gointuh git caught in uh bullet storm if you don't watch out." Sop said, "Aw 'tain't nothin' tuh dat bear but his curly hair. Ah can look through muddy water and see dry land." Ed turned off the card and hollered, "Zachariah, Ah says come down out dat sycamore tree. You can't do no business." Nobody fell on that card. Everybody was scared of the next one. Ed looked around and saw Gabe standing behind his chair and hollered, "Move, from over me, Gabe! You too black. You draw heat! Sop, you wanta pick up dat bet whilst you got uh chance?" "Naw, man, Ah wish Ah had uh thousand-leg tuh put on it." "So yuh won't lissen, huh? Dumb niggers and free schools. Ah'm gointuh take and teach yuh. Ah'll main-line but Ah won't side-track." Ed flipped the next card and Sop fell and lost. Everybody hollered and laughed. Ed laughed and said, "Git off de muck! You ain't nothin'. Dat's all! Hot boilin' water won't help yuh none." Ed kept on laughing because he had been so scared before. "Sop, Bootyny, all y'all dat lemme win yo' money: Ah'm sending it straight off to Sears and Roebuck and buy me some clothes, and when Ah turn out Christmas day, it would take a doctor to tell me how near Ah is dressed tuh death."

CHAPTER 15

Janie learned what it felt like to be jealous. A little chunky girl took to picking a play out of Tea Cake in the fields and in the quarters. If he said anything at all, she'd take the opposite side and hit him or shove him and run away to make him chase her. Janie knew what she was up to—luring him away from the crowd. It kept up for two or three weeks with Nunkie getting bolder all the time. She'd hit Tea Cake playfully and the minute he so much as tapped her with his finger she'd fall against him or fall on the ground and have to be picked up. She'd be almost helpless. It took a good deal of handling to set her on her feet again. And another thing, Tea Cake didn't seem to be able to fend her off as promptly as Janie thought he ought to. She began to be snappish a little. A little seed of fear was growing into a tree. Maybe some day Tea Cake would weaken. Maybe he had already given secret encouragement and this was Nunkie's way of bragging about it. Other people began to notice too, and that put Janie more on a wonder.

One day they were working near where the beans ended and the sugar cane began. Janie had marched off a little from Tea Cake's side with another woman for a chat. When she

130

glanced around Tea Cake was gone. Nunkie too. She knew because she looked.

"Where's Tea Cake?" she asked Sop-de-Bottom.

He waved his hand towards the cane field and hurried away. Janie never thought at all. She just acted on feelings. She rushed into the cane and about the fifth row down she found Tea Cake and Nunkie struggling. She was on them before either knew.

"Whut's de matter heah?" Janie asked in a cold rage. They sprang apart.

"Nothin'," Tea Cake told her, standing shame-faced.

"Well, whut you doin' in heah? How come you ain't out dere wid de rest?"

"She grabbed mah workin' tickets outa mah shirt pocket and Ah run tuh git 'em back," Tea Cake explained, showing the tickets, considerably mauled about in the struggle.

Janie made a move to seize Nunkie but the girl fled. So she took out behind her over the humped-up cane rows. But Nunkie did not mean to be caught. So Janie went on home. The sight of the fields and the other happy people was too much for her that day. She walked slowly and thoughtfully to the quarters. It wasn't long before Tea Cake found her there and tried to talk. She cut him short with a blow and they fought from one room to the other, Janie trying to beat him, and Tea Cake kept holding her wrists and wherever he could to keep her from going too far.

"Ah b'lieve you been messin' round her!" she panted furiously.

"No sich uh thing!" Tea Cake retorted.

"Ah b'lieve yuh did."

"Don't keer how big uh lie get told, somebody kin b'lieve it!"

They fought on. "You done hurt mah heart, now you come wid uh lie tuh bruise mah ears! Turn go mah hands!" Janie seethed. But Tea Cake never let go. They wrestled on until they were doped with their own fumes and emanations; till their clothes had been torn away; till he hurled her to the floor and held her there melting her resistance with the heat of his body, doing things with their bodies to express the inexpressible; kissed her until she arched her body to meet him and they fell asleep in sweet exhaustion.

The next morning Janie asked like a woman, "You still love ole Nunkie?"

"Naw, never did, and you know it too. Ah didn't want her."

"Yeah, you did." She didn't say this because she believed it. She wanted to hear his denial. She had to crow over the fallen Nunkie.

"Whut would Ah do wid dat lil chunk of a woman wid you around? She ain't good for nothin' exceptin' tuh set up in uh corner by de kitchen stove and break wood over her head. You'se something tuh make uh man forgit tuh git old and forgit tuh die."

CHAPTER 16

The season closed and people went away like they had come—in droves. Tea Cake and Janie decided to stay since they wanted to make another season on the muck. There was nothing to do, after they had gathered several bushels of dried beans to save over and sell to the planters in the fall. So Janie began to look around and see people and things she hadn't noticed during the season.

For instance during the summer when she heard the subtle but compelling rhythms of the Bahaman drummers, she'd walk over and watch the dances. She did not laugh the "Saws" to scorn as she had heard the people doing in the season. She got to like it a lot and she and Tea Cake were on hand every night till the others teased them about it.

Janie came to know Mrs. Turner now. She had seen her several times during the season, but neither ever spoke. Now they got to be visiting friends.

Mrs. Turner was a milky sort of a woman that belonged to child-bed. Her shoulders rounded a little, and she must have been conscious of her pelvis because she kept it stuck out in front of her so she could always see it. Tea Cake made a lot of fun about Mrs. Turner's shape behind her back. He claimed that she had been shaped up by a cow kicking her from behind. She was an ironing board with things throwed at it. Then that same cow took and stepped in her mouth when she was a baby and left it wide and flat with her chin and nose almost meeting.

But Mrs. Turner's shape and features were entirely approved by Mrs. Turner. Her nose was slightly pointed and she was proud. Her thin lips were an ever delight to her eyes. Even her buttocks in bas-relief were a source of pride. To her way of thinking all these things set her aside from Negroes. That was why she sought out Janie to friend with. Janie's coffee-and-cream complexion and her luxurious hair made Mrs. Turner forgive her for wearing overalls like the other women who worked in the fields. She didn't forgive her for marrying a man as dark as Tea Cake, but she felt that she could remedy that. That was what her brother was born for. She seldom stayed long when she found Tea Cake at home, but when she happened to drop in and catch Janie alone, she'd spend hours chatting away. Her disfavorite subject was Negroes.

"Mis' Woods, Ah have often said to mah husband, Ah don't see how uh lady like Mis' Woods can stand all them common niggers round her place all de time."

"They don't worry me atall, Mis' Turner. Fact about de thing is, they tickles me wid they talk."

"You got mo' nerve than me. When somebody talked mah husband intuh comin' down heah tuh open up uh eatin' place Ah never dreamt so many different kins uh black folks could colleck in one place. Did Ah never woulda come. Ah ain't useter 'ssociatin' wid black folks. Mah son claims dey draws lightnin'." They laughed a little and after many of these talks Mrs. Turner said, "Yo' husband musta had plenty money when y'all got married."

"Whut make you think dat, Mis' Turner?"

"Tuh git hold of uh woman lak you. You got mo' nerve than me. Ah jus' couldn't see mahself married to no black man. It's too many black folks already. We oughta lighten up de race."

"Naw, mah husband didn't had nothin' but hisself. He's easy tuh love if you mess round 'im. Ah loves 'im."

"Why you, Mis' Woods! Ah don't b'lieve it. You'se jus' sorter hypnotized, dat's all."

"Naw, it's real. Ah couldn't stand it if he wuz tuh quit me. Don't know whut Ah'd do. He kin take most any lil thing and make summertime out of it when times is dull. Then we lives offa dat happiness he made till some mo' happiness come along."

"You'se different from me. Ah can't stand black niggers. Ah don't blame de white folks from hatin' 'em 'cause Ah can't stand 'em mahself. 'Nother thing, Ah hates tuh see folks lak me and you mixed up wid 'em. Us oughta class off."

"Us can't *do* it. We'se uh mingled people and all of us got black kinfolks as well as yaller kinfolks. How come you so against black?"

"And dey makes me tired. Always laughin'! Dey laughs too much and dey laughs too loud. Always singin' ol' nigger songs! Always cuttin' de monkey for white folks. If it wuzn't for so many black folks it wouldn't be no race problem. De white folks would take us in wid dem. De black ones is holdin' us back."

"You reckon? 'course Ah ain't never thought about it too much. But Ah don't figger dey even gointuh want us for comp'ny. We'se too poor."

" 'Tain't de poorness, it's de color and de features. Who want any lil ole black baby layin' up in de baby buggy lookin' lak uh fly in buttermilk? Who wants to be mixed up wid uh rusty black man, and uh black woman goin' down de street in all dem loud colors, and whoopin' and hollerin' and laughin' over nothin'? Ah don't know. Don't bring me no nigger doctor tuh hang over mah sick-bed. Ah done had six chillun— wuzn't lucky enough tuh raise but dat one—and ain't never had uh nigger tuh even feel mah pulse. White doctors always

135

gits mah money. Ah don't go in no nigger store tuh buy nothin' neither. Colored folks don't know nothin' 'bout no business. Deliver me!''

Mrs. Turner was almost screaming in fanatical earnestness by now. Janie was dumb and bewildered before and she clucked sympathetically and wished she knew what to say. It was so evident that Mrs. Turner took black folk as a personal affront to herself.

"Look at me! Ah ain't got no flat nose and liver lips. Ah'm uh featured woman. Ah got white folks' features in mah face. Still and all Ah got tuh be lumped in wid all de rest. It ain't fair. Even if dey don't take us in wid de whites, dey oughta make us uh class tuh ourselves."

"It don't worry me atall, but Ah reckon Ah ain't got no real head fur thinkin'."

"You oughta meet mah brother. He's real smart. Got dead straight hair. Dey made him uh delegate tuh de Sunday School Convention and he read uh paper on Booker T. Washington and tore him tuh pieces!"

"Booker T.? He wuz a great big man, wusn't he?"

" 'Sposed tuh be. All he ever done was cut de monkey for white folks. So dey pomped him up. But you know whut de ole folks say 'de higher de monkey climbs de mo' he show his behind' so dat's de way it wuz wid Booker T. Mah brother hit 'im every time dey give 'im chance tuh speak."

"Ah was raised on de notion dat he wuz uh great big man," was all that Janie knew to say.

"He didn't do nothin' but hold us back—talkin' 'bout work when de race ain't never done nothin' else. He wuz uh enemy tuh us, dat's whut. He wuz uh white folks' nigger."

According to all Janie had been taught this was sacrilege so she sat without speaking at all. But Mrs. Turner went on.

"Ah done sent fuh mah brother tuh come down and spend uh while wid us. He's sorter outa work now. Ah wants yuh tuh meet him mo' special. You and him would make up uh swell couple if you wuzn't already married. He's uh fine carpenter, when he kin git anything tuh do."

"Yeah, maybe so. But Ah *is* married now, so 'tain't no use in considerin'."

Mrs. Turner finally rose to go after being very firm about several other viewpoints of either herself, her son or her brother. She begged Janie to drop in on her anytime, but never once mentioning Tea Cake. Finally she was gone and Janie hurried to her kitchen to put on supper and found Tea Cake sitting in there with his head between his hands.

"Tea Cake! Ah didn't know you wuz home."

"Ah know yuh didn't. Ah been heah uh long time listenin' to dat heifer run me down tuh de dawgs uh try tuh tole you off from me."

"So dat whut she wuz up to? Ah didn't know."

" 'Course she is. She got some no-count brother she wants yuh tuh hook up wid and take keer of Ah reckon."

"Shucks! If dat's her notion she's barkin' up de wrong tree. Mah hands is full already."

"Thanky Ma'am. Ah hates dat woman lak poison. Keep her from round dis house. Her look lak uh white woman! Wid dat meriny skin and hair jus' as close tuh her head as ninety-nine is tuh uh hundred! Since she hate black folks so, she don't need our money in her ol' eatin' place. Ah'll pass de word along. We kin go tuh dat white man's place and git good treatment. Her and dat whittled-down husband uh hers! And dat son! He's jus' uh dirty trick her womb played on her. Ah'm telling her husband tuh keep her home. Ah don't want her round dis house."

One day Tea Cake met Turner and his son on the street. He was a vanishing-looking kind of a man as if there used to be parts about him that stuck out individually but now he hadn't a thing about him that wasn't dwindled and blurred. Just like he had been sand-papered down to a long oval mass. Tea Cake felt sorry for him without knowing why. So he didn't blurt out the insults he had intended. But he couldn't hold in everything. They talked about the prospects for the coming season for a moment, then Tea Cake said, "Yo' wife don't seem tuh have nothin' much tuh do, so she kin visit uh lot. Mine got too much tuh do tuh go visitin' and too much tuh spend time talkin' tuh folks dat visit her."

"Mah wife takes time fuh whatever she wants tuh do. Real strong headed dat way. Yes indeed." He laughed a high lungless laugh. "De chillun don't keep her in no mo' so she visits when she chooses."

"De chillun?" Tea Cake asked him in surprise. "You got any smaller than him?" He indicated the son who seemed around twenty or so. "Ah ain't seen yo' others."

"Ah reckon you ain't 'cause dey all passed on befo' dis one wuz born. We ain't had no luck atall wid our chillun. We lucky to raise him. He's de last stroke of exhausted nature."

He gave his powerless laugh again and Tea Cake and the boy joined in with him. Then Tea Cake walked on off and went home to Janie.

"Her husband can't do nothin' wid dat butt-headed woman. All you can do is treat her cold whenever she come round here."

Janie tried that, but short of telling Mrs. Turner bluntly, there was nothing she could do to discourage her completely. She felt honored by Janie's acquaintance and she quickly forgave and forgot snubs in order to keep it. Anyone who looked more white folkish than herself was better than she was in her criteria, therefore it was right that they should be cruel to her at times, just as she was cruel to those more negroid than herself in direct ratio to their negroness. Like the pecking-order in a chicken yard. Insensate cruelty to those you can whip, and groveling submission to those you can't. Once having set up her idols and built altars to them it was inevitable that she would worship there. It was inevitable that she should accept any inconsistency and cruelty from her deity as all good worshippers do from theirs. All gods who receive homage are cruel. All gods dispense suffering without reason. Otherwise they would not be worshipped. Through indiscriminate suffering men know fear and fear is the most divine emotion. It is the stones for altars and the beginning of wisdom. Half gods are worshipped in wine and flowers. Real gods require blood.

Mrs. Turner, like all other believers had built an altar to the unattainable—Caucasian characteristics for all. Her god would smite her, would hurl her from pinnacles and lose her in deserts, but she would not forsake his altars. Behind her crude words was a belief that somehow she and others through worship could attain her paradise—a heaven of straight-haired, thin-lipped, high-nose boned white seraphs. The physical impossibilities in no way injured faith. That was the mystery and mysteries are the chores of gods. Beyond her faith was a fanaticism to defend the altars of her god. It was distressing to emerge from her inner temple and find these black desecrators howling with laughter before the door. Oh, for an army, terrible with banners *and swords!*

So she didn't cling to Janie Woods the woman. She paid homage to Janie's Caucasian characteristics as such. And when she was with Janie she had a feeling of transmutation, as if she herself had become whiter and with straighter hair and she hated Tea Cake first for his defilement of divinity and next for his telling mockery of her. If she only knew something she could do about it! But she didn't. Once she was complaining about the carryings-on at the jook and Tea Cake snapped, "Aw, don't make God look so foolish—findin' fault wid everything He made."

So Mrs. Turner frowned most of the time. She had so much to disapprove of. It didn't affect Tea Cake and Janie too much. It just gave them something to talk about in the summertime when everything was dull on the muck. Otherwise they made little trips to Palm Beach, Fort Myers and Fort Lauderdale for their fun. Before they realized it the sun was cooler and the crowds came pouring onto the muck again.

CHAPTER 17

A great deal of the old crowd were back. But there were lots of new ones too. Some of these men made passes at Janie, and women who didn't know took out after Tea Cake. Didn't take them long to be put right, however. Still and all, jealousies arose now and then on both sides. When Mrs. Turner's brother came and she brought him over to be introduced, Tea Cake had a brainstorm. Before the week was over he had whipped Janie. Not because her behavior justified his jealousy, but it relieved that awful fear inside him. Being able to whip her reassured him in possession. No brutal beating at all. He just slapped her around a bit to show he was boss. Everybody talked about it next day in the fields. It aroused a sort of envy in both men and women. The way he petted and pampered her as if those two or three face slaps had nearly killed her made the women see visions and the helpless way she hung on him made men dream dreams.

"Tea Cake, you sho is a lucky man," Sop-de-Bottom told him. "Uh person can see every place you hit her. Ah bet she never raised her hand tuh hit yuh back, neither. Take some uh dese ol' rusty black women and dey would fight yuh all night long and next day nobody couldn't tell you ever hit 'em. Dat's de reason Ah done quit beatin' mah woman. You can't make no mark on 'em at all. Lawd! wouldn't Ah love tuh whip uh tender woman lak Janie! Ah bet she don't even holler. She jus' cries, eh Tea Cake?"

"Dat's right."

"See dat! Mah woman would spread her lungs all over Palm Beach County, let alone knock out mah jaw teeth. You don't know dat woman uh mine. She got ninety-nine rows uh jaw teeth and git her good and mad, she'll wade through solid rock up to her hip pockets."

"Mah Janie is uh high time woman and useter things. Ah didn't git her outa de middle uh de road. Ah got her outa uh big fine house. Right now she got money enough in de bank tuh buy up dese ziggaboos and give 'em away."

"Hush yo' mouf! And she down heah on de muck lak anybody else!"

"Janie is wherever *Ah* wants tuh be. Dat's de kind uh wife she is and Ah love her for it. Ah wouldn't be knockin' her around. Ah didn't wants whup her last night, but ol' Mis' Turner done sent for her brother tuh come tuh bait Janie in and take her way from me. Ah didn't whup Janie 'cause *she* done nothin'. Ah beat her tuh show dem Turners who is boss. Ah set in de kitchen one day and heard dat woman tell mah wife Ah'm too black fuh her. She don't see how Janie can stand me."

"Tell her husband on her."

"Shucks! Ah b'lieve he's skeered of her."

"Knock her teeth down her throat."

"Dat would look like she had some influence when she ain't. Ah jus' let her see dat Ah got control."

"So she live offa our money and don't lak black folks, huh? O.K. we'll have her gone from here befo' two weeks is up. Ah'm goin' right off tuh all de men and drop rocks aginst her."

"Ah ain't mad wid her for whut she done, 'cause she ain't done me nothin' yet. Ah'm mad at her for thinkin'. Her and her gang got tuh go."

"Us is wid yuh, Tea Cake. You know dat already. Dat

141

Turner woman is real smart, accordin' tuh her notions. Reckon she done heard 'bout dat money yo' wife got in de bank and she's bound tuh rope her in tuh her family one way or another.''

"Sop, Ah don't think it's half de money as it is de looks. She's color-struck. She ain't got de kind of uh mind you meet every day. She ain't a fact and neither do she make a good story when you tell about her.''

"Ah yeah, she's too smart tuh stay round heah. She figgers we'se jus' uh bunch uh dumb niggers so she think she'll grow horns. But dat's uh lie. She'll die butt-headed.''

Saturday afternoon when the work tickets were turned into cash everybody began to buy coon-dick and get drunk. By dusk dark Belle Glade was full of loud-talking, staggering men. Plenty women had gotten their knots charged too. The police chief in his speedy Ford was rushing from jook to jook and eating house trying to keep order, but making few arrests. Not enough jail-space for all the drunks so why bother with a few? All he could do to keep down fights and get the white men out of colored town by nine o'clock. Dick Sterrett and Coodemay seemed to be the worst off. Their likker told them to go from place to place pushing and shoving and loud-talking and they were doing it.

Way after a while they arrived at Mrs. Turner's eating house and found the place full to the limit. Tea Cake, Stew Beef, Sop-de-Bottom, Bootyny, Motor Boat and all the familiar crowd was there. Coodemay straightened up as if in surprise and asked, "Say, whut y'all doin' in heah?''

"Eatin','' Stew Beef told him. "Dey got beef stew, so you *know* Ah'd be heah.''

"We all laks tuh take uh rest from our women folks' cookin' once in uh while, so us all eatin' way from home tuhnight. Anyhow Mis' Turner got de best ole grub in town.''

Mrs. Turner back and forth in the dining room heard Sop when he said this and beamed.

"Ah speck you two last ones tuh come in is gointuh have

142

tuh wait for uh seat. Ah'm all full up now."

"Dat's all right," Sterrett objected. "You fry me some fish. Ah kin eat dat standin' up. Cuppa coffee on de side."

"Sling me up uh plate uh dat stew beef wid some coffee too, please ma'am. Sterrett is jus' ez drunk ez Ah is; and if he kin eat standin' up, Ah kin do de same." Coodemay leaned drunkenly against the wall and everybody laughed.

Pretty soon the girl that was waiting table for Mrs. Turner brought in the order and Sterrett took his fish and coffee in his hands and stood there. Coodemay wouldn't take his off the tray like he should have.

"Naw, you hold it fuh me, baby, and lemme eat," he told the waitress. He took the fork and started to eat off the tray.

"Nobody ain't got no time tuh hold yo' grub up in front uh yo' face," she told Coodemay. "Heah, take it yo'self."

"You'se right," Coodemay told her. "Gimme it heah. Sop kin gimme his chear."

"You'se uh lie," Sop retorted. "Ah ain't through and Ah ain't ready tuh git up."

Coodemay tried to shove Sop out of the chair and Sop resisted. That brought on a whole lot of shoving and scrambling and coffee got spilt on Sop. So he aimed at Coodemay with a saucer and hit Bootyny. Bootyny threw his thick coffee cup at Coodemay and just missed Stew Beef. So it got to be a big fight. Mrs. Turner came running in out of the kitchen. Then Tea Cake got up and caught hold of Coodemay by the collar.

"Looka heah, y'all, don't come in heah and raise no disturbance in de place. Mis' Turner is too nice uh woman fuh dat. In fact, she's more nicer than anybody else on de muck." Mrs. Turner beamed on Tea Cake.

"Ah knows dat. All of us knows it. But Ah don't give uh damn how nice she is, Ah got tuh have some place tuh set down and eat. Sop ain't gointuh bluff me, neither. Let 'im fight lak a man. Take yo' hands off me, Tea Cake."

"Naw, Ah won't neither. You comin' on outa de place."

"Who gointuh make me come out?"

"Me, dat's who. Ah'm in heah, ain't Ah? If you don't want tuh respect nice people lak Mrs. Turner, God knows you gointuh respect me! Come on outa heah, Coodemay."

"Turn him loose, Tea Cake!" Sterrett shouted. "Dat's *mah* buddy. Us come in heah together and he ain't goin' nowhere until Ah go mahself."

"Well, both of yuh is goin'!" Tea Cake shouted and fastened down on Coodemay. Dockery grabbed Sterrett and they wrassled all over the place. Some more joined in and dishes and tables began to crash.

Mrs. Turner saw with dismay that Tea Cake's taking them out was worse than letting them stay in. She ran out in the back somewhere and got her husband to put a stop to things. He came in, took a look and squinched down into a chair in an off corner and didn't open his mouth. So Mrs. Turner struggled into the mass and caught Tea Cake by the arm.

"Dat's all right, Tea Cake, Ah 'preciate yo' help, but leave 'em alone."

"Naw suh, Mis' Turner, Ah'm gointuh show 'em dey can't come runnin' over nice people and loud-talk no place whilst Ah'm around. Dey goin' outa heah!"

By that time everybody in and around the place was taking sides. Somehow or other Mrs. Turner fell down and nobody knew she was down there under all the fighting, and broken dishes and crippled up tables and broken-off chair legs and window panes and such things. It got so that the floor was knee-deep with something no matter where you put your foot down. But Tea Cake kept right on until Coodemay told him, "Ah'm wrong. Ah'm wrong! Y'all tried tuh tell me right and Ah wouldn't lissen. Ah ain't mad wid nobody. Just tuh show y'all Ah ain't mad, me and Sterrett gointuh buy everybody somethin' tuh drink. Ole man Vickers got some good coon-dick over round Pahokee. Come on everybody. Let's go git our knots charged." Everybody got in a good humor and left.

Mrs. Turner got up off the floor hollering for the police.

Look at her place! How come nobody didn't call the police? Then she found out that one of her hands was all stepped on and her fingers were bleeding pretty peart. Two or three people who were not there during the fracas poked their heads in at the door to sympathize but that made Mrs. Turner madder. She told them where to go in a hurry. Then she saw her husband sitting over there in the corner with his long bony legs all crossed up smoking his pipe.

"What kinda man is *you*, Turner? You see dese no count niggers come in heah and break up mah place! How kin you set and see yo' wife all trompled on? You ain't no kinda man at all. You seen dat Tea Cake shove me down! Yes you did! You ain't raised yo' hand tuh do nothin' about it."

Turner removed his pipe and answered: "Yeah, and you see how Ah did swell up too, didn't yuh? You tell Tea Cake he better be keerful Ah don't swell up again." At that Turner crossed his legs the other way and kept right on smoking his pipe.

Mrs. Turner hit at him the best she could with her hurt hand and then spoke her mind for half an hour.

"It's a good thing mah brother wuzn't round heah when it happened do he would uh kilt somebody. Mah son too. Dey got some manhood about 'em. We'se goin' back tuh Miami where folks is civilized."

Nobody told her right away that her son and brother were already on their way after pointed warnings outside the café. No time for fooling around. They were hurrying into Palm Beach. She'd find out about that later on.

Monday morning Coodemay and Sterrett stopped by and begged her pardon profusely and gave her five dollars apiece. Then Coodemay said, "Dey tell me Ah wuz drunk Sat'day night and clownin' down. Ah don't 'member uh thing 'bout it. But when Ah git tuh peepin' through mah likker, dey tell me Ah'm uh mess."

145

CHAPTER 18

Since Tea Cake and Janie had friended with the Bahaman workers in the 'Glades, they, the "Saws," had been gradually drawn into the American crowd. They quit hiding out to hold their dances when they found that their American friends didn't laugh at them as they feared. Many of the Americans learned to jump and liked it as much as the "Saws." So they began to hold dances night after night in the quarters, usually behind Tea Cake's house. Often now, Tea Cake and Janie stayed up so late at the fire dances that Tea Cake would not let her go with him to the field. He wanted her to get her rest.

So she was home by herself one afternoon when she saw a band of Seminoles passing by. The men walking in front and the laden, stolid women following them like burros. She had seen Indians several times in the 'Glades, in twos and threes, but this was a large party. They were headed towards the Palm Beach road and kept moving steadily. About an hour later another party appeared and went the same way. Then another just before sundown. This time she asked where they were all going and at last one of the men answered her.

"Going to high ground. Saw-grass bloom. Hurricane coming."

Everybody was talking about it that night. But nobody was worried. The fire dance kept up till nearly dawn. The next day, more Indians moved east, unhurried but steady. Still a blue sky and fair weather. Beans running fine and prices good, so the Indians could be, *must* be, wrong. You couldn't have a hurricane when you're making seven and eight dollars a day picking beans. Indians are dumb anyhow, always were. Another night of Stew Beef making dynamic subtleties with his drum and living, sculptural, grotesques in the dance. Next day, no Indians passed at all. It was hot and sultry and Janie left the field and went home.

Morning came without motion. The winds, to the tiniest, lisping baby breath had left the earth. Even before the sun gave light, dead day was creeping from bush to bush watching man.

Some rabbits scurried through the quarters going east. Some possums slunk by and their route was definite. One or two at a time, then more. By the time the people left the fields the procession was constant. Snakes, rattlesnakes began to cross the quarters. The men killed a few, but they could not be missed from the crawling horde. People stayed indoors until daylight. Several times during the night Janie heard the snort of big animals like deer. Once the muted voice of a panther. Going east and east. That night the palm and banana trees began that long distance talk with rain. Several people took fright and picked up and went in to Palm Beach anyway. A thousand buzzards held a flying meet and then went above the clouds and stayed.

One of the Bahaman boys stopped by Tea Cake's house in a car and hollered. Tea Cake came out throwin' laughter over his shoulder into the house.

"Hello Tea Cake."

"Hello 'Lias. You leavin', Ah see."

"Yeah man. You and Janie wanta go? Ah wouldn't give nobody else uh chawnce at uh seat till Ah found out if you all had anyway tuh go."

"Thank yuh ever so much, Lias. But we 'bout decided tuh stay."

"De crow gahn up, man."

"Dat ain't nothin'. You ain't seen de bossman go up, is yuh? Well all right now. Man, de money's too good on the muck. It's liable tuh fair off by tuhmorrer. Ah wouldn't leave if Ah wuz you."

"Mah uncle come for me. He say hurricane warning out in Palm Beach. Not so bad dere, but man, dis muck is too low and dat big lake is liable tuh bust."

"Ah naw, man. Some boys in dere now talkin' 'bout it. Some of 'em been in de 'Glades fuh years. 'Tain't nothin' but uh lil blow. You'll lose de whole day tuhmorrer tryin' tuh git back out heah."

"De Indians gahn east, man. It's dangerous."

"Dey don't always know. Indians don't know much uh nothin', tuh tell de truth. Else dey'd own dis country still. De white folks ain't gone nowhere. Dey oughta know if it's dangerous. You better stay heah, man. Big jumpin' dance tuhnight right heah, when it fair off."

Lias hesitated and started to climb out, but his uncle wouldn't let him. "Dis time tuhmorrer you gointuh wish you follow crow," he snorted and drove off. Lias waved back to them gaily.

"If Ah never see you no mo' on earth, Ah'll meet you in Africa."

Others hurried east like the Indians and rabbits and snakes and coons. But the majority sat around laughing and waiting for the sun to get friendly again.

Several men collected at Tea Cake's house and sat around stuffing courage into each other's ears. Janie baked a big pan of beans and something she called sweet biscuits and they all managed to be happy enough.

Most of the great flame-throwers were there and naturally, handling Big John de Conquer and his works. How he had done everything big on earth, then went up tuh heben without

148

dying atall. Went up there picking a guitar and got all de angels doing the ring-shout round and round de throne. Then everybody but God and Old Peter flew off on a flying race to Jericho and back and John de Conquer won the race; went on down to hell, beat the old devil and passed out ice water to everybody down there. Somebody tried to say that it was a mouth organ harp that John was playing, but the rest of them would not hear that. Don't care how good anybody could play a harp, God would rather to hear a guitar. That brought them back to Tea Cake. How come he couldn't hit that box a lick or two? Well, all right now, make us know it.

When it got good to everybody, Muck-Boy woke up and began to chant with the rhythm and everybody bore down on the last word of the line:

> Yo' mama don't wear no *Draws*
> Ah seen her when she took 'em *Off*
> She soaked 'em in alco*Hol*
> She sold 'em tuh de Santy *Claus*
> He told her 'twas aginst de *Law*
> To wear dem dirty *Draws*

Then Muck-Boy went crazy through the feet and danced himself and everybody else crazy. When he finished he sat back down on the floor and went to sleep again. Then they got to playing Florida flip and coon-can. Then it was dice. Not for money. This was a show-off game. Everybody posing his fancy shots. As always it broiled down to Tea Cake and Motor Boat. Tea Cake with his shy grin and Motor Boat with his face like a little black cherubim just from a church tower doing amazing things with anybody's dice. The others forgot the work and the weather watching them throw. It was art. A thousand dollars a throw in Madison Square Garden wouldn't have gotten any more breathless suspense. It would have just been more people holding in.

After a while somebody looked out and said, "It ain't gitting no fairer out dere. B'lieve Ah'll git on over tuh mah shack." Motor Boat and Tea Cake were still playing so everybody left them at it.

Sometime that night the winds came back. Everything in the world had a strong rattle, sharp and short like Stew Beef vibrating the drum head near the edge with his fingers. By morning Gabriel was playing the deep tones in the center of the drum. So when Janie looked out of her door she saw the drifting mists gathered in the west—that cloud field of the sky—to arm themselves with thunders and march forth against the world. Louder and higher and lower and wider the sound and motion spread, mounting, sinking, darking.

It woke up old Okechobee and the monster began to roll in his bed. Began to roll and complain like a peevish world on a grumble. The folks in the quarters and the people in the big houses further around the shore heard the big lake and wondered. The people felt uncomfortable but safe because there were the seawalls to chain the senseless monster in his bed. The folks let the people do the thinking. If the castles thought themselves secure, the cabins needn't worry. Their decision was already made as always. Chink up your cracks, shiver in your wet beds and wait on the mercy of the Lord. The bossman might have the thing stopped before morning anyway. It is so easy to be hopeful in the day time when you can see the things you wish on. But it was night, it stayed night. Night was striding across nothingness with the whole round world in his hands.

A big burst of thunder and lightning that trampled over the roof of the house. So Tea Cake and Motor stopped playing. Motor looked up in his angel-looking way and said, "Big Massa draw him chair upstairs."

"Ah'm glad y'all stop dat crap-shootin' even if it wasn't for money," Janie said. "Ole Massa is doin' *His* work now. Us oughta keep quiet."

They huddled closer and stared at the door. They just didn't use another part of their bodies, and they didn't look at anything but the door. The time was past for asking the white folks what to look for through that door. Six eyes were questioning *God.*

Through the screaming wind they heard things crashing and things hurtling and dashing with unbelievable velocity. A baby rabbit, terror ridden, squirmed through a hole in the floor and squatted off there in the shadows against the wall, seeming to know that nobody wanted its flesh at such a time. And the lake got madder and madder with only its dikes between them and him.

In a little wind-lull, Tea Cake touched Janie and said, "Ah reckon you wish now you had of stayed in yo' big house 'way from such as dis, don't yuh?"

"Naw."

"Naw?"

"Yeah, naw. People don't die till dey time come nohow, don't keer where you at. Ah'm wid mah husband in uh storm, dat's all."

"Thanky, Ma'am. But 'sposing you wuz tuh die, now. You wouldn't git mad at me for draggin' yuh heah?"

"Naw. We been tuhgether round two years. If you kin see de light at daybreak, you don't keer if you die at dusk. It's so many people never seen de light at all. Ah wuz fumblin' round and God opened de door."

He dropped to the floor and put his head in her lap. "Well then, Janie, you meant whut you didn't say, 'cause Ah never *knowed* you wuz so satisfied wid me lak dat. Ah kinda thought—"

The wind came back with triple fury, and put out the light for the last time. They sat in company with the others in other shanties, their eyes straining against crude walls and their souls asking if He meant to measure their puny might against His. They seemed to be staring at the dark, but their eyes were watching God.

As soon as Tea Cake went out pushing wind in front of him, he saw that the wind and water had given life to lots of things

151

that folks think of as dead and given death to so much that had been living things. Water everywhere. Stray fish swimming in the yard. Three inches more and the water would be in the house. Already in some. He decided to try to find a car to take them out of the 'Glades before worse things happened. He turned back to tell Janie about it so she could be ready to go.

"Git our insurance papers tuhgether, Janie. Ah'll tote mah box mahself and things lak dat."

"You got all de money out de dresser drawer, already?"

"Naw, git it quick and cut up piece off de table-cloth tuh wrap it up in. Us liable tuh git wet tuh our necks. Cut uh piece uh dat oilcloth quick fuh our papers. We got tuh go, if it ain't too late. De dish can't bear it out no longer."

He snatched the oilcloth off the table and took out his knife. Janie held it straight while he slashed off a strip.

"But Tea Cake, it's too awful out dere. Maybe it's better tuh stay heah in de wet than it is tuh try tuh—"

He stunned the argument with half a word. "Fix," he said and fought his way outside. He had seen more than Janie had.

Janie took a big needle and ran up a longish sack. Found some newspaper and wrapped up the paper money and papers and thrust them in and whipped over the open end with her needle. Before she could get it thoroughly hidden in the pocket of her overalls, Tea Cake burst in again.

" 'Tain't no cars, Janie."

"Ah thought not! Whut we gointuh do now?"

"We got tuh walk."

"In all dis weather, Tea Cake? Ah don't b'lieve Ah could make it out de quarters."

"Oh yeah you kin. Me and you and Motor Boat kin all lock arms and hold one 'nother down. Eh, Motor?"

"He's sleep on de bed in yonder," Janie said. Tea Cake called without moving.

"Motor Boat! You better git up from dere! Hell done broke loose in Georgy. Dis minute! How kin you sleep at uh time lak dis? Water knee deep in de yard."

They stepped out in water almost to their buttocks and managed to turn east. Tea Cake had to throw his box away, and Janie saw how it hurt him. Dodging flying missiles, floating dangers, avoiding stepping in holes and warmed on the wind now at their backs until they gained comparatively dry land. They had to fight to keep from being pushed the wrong way and to hold together. They saw other people like themselves struggling along. A house down, here and there, frightened cattle. But above all the drive of the wind and the water. And the lake. Under its multiplied roar could be heard a mighty sound of grinding rock and timber and a wail. They looked back. Saw people trying to run in raging waters and screaming when they found they couldn't. A huge barrier of the makings of the dike to which the cabins had been added was rolling and tumbling forward. Ten feet higher and as far as they could see the muttering wall advanced before the braced-up waters like a road crusher on a cosmic scale. The monstropolous beast had left his bed. The two hundred miles an hour wind had loosed his chains. He seized hold of his dikes and ran forward until he met the quarters; uprooted them like grass and rushed on after his supposed-to-be conquerors, rolling the dikes, rolling the houses, rolling the people in the houses along with other timbers. The sea was walking the earth with a heavy heel.

"De lake is comin'!" Tea Cake gasped.

"De lake!" In amazed horror from Motor Boat, "De lake!"

"It's comin' behind us!" Janie shuddered. "Us can't fly."

"But we still kin run," Tea Cake shouted and they ran. The gushing water ran faster. The great body was held back, but rivers spouted through fissures in the rolling wall and broke like day. The three fugitives ran past another line of shanties that topped a slight rise and gained a little. They cried out as best they could, "De lake is comin'!" and barred doors flew open and others joined them in flight crying the same as they went. "De lake is comin'!" and the pursuing waters growled

153

and shouted ahead, "Yes, Ah'm comin'!", and those who could fled on.

They made it to a tall house on a hump of ground and Janie said, "Less stop heah. Ah can't make it no further. Ah'm done give out."

"All of us is done give out," Tea Cake corrected. "We'se goin' inside out dis weather, kill or cure." He knocked with the handle of his knife, while they leaned their faces and shoulders against the wall. He knocked once more then he and Motor Boat went round to the back and forced a door. Nobody there.

"Dese people had mo' sense than Ah did," Tea Cake said as they dropped to the floor and lay there panting. "Us oughta went on wid 'Lias lak he ast me."

"You didn't know," Janie contended. "And when yuh don't know, yuh just don't know. De storms might not of come sho nuff."

They went to sleep promptly but Janie woke up first. She heard the sound of rushing water and sat up.

"Tea Cake! Motor Boat! De lake is comin'!"

The lake *was* coming on. Slower and wider, but coming. It had trampled on most of its supporting wall and lowered its front by spreading. But it came muttering and grumbling onward like a tired mammoth just the same.

"Dis is uh high tall house. Maybe it won't reach heah at all," Janie counseled. "And if it do, maybe it won't reach tuh de upstairs part."

"Janie, Lake Okechobee is forty miles wide and sixty miles long. Dat's uh whole heap uh water. If dis wind is shovin' dat whole lake disa way, dis house ain't nothin' tuh swaller. Us better go. Motor Boat!"

"Whut you want, man?"

"De lake is comin'!"

"Aw, naw it 'tain't."

"Yes, it is *so* comin'! Listen! You kin hear it way off."

"It kin jus' come on. Ah'll wait right here."

"Aw, get up, Motor Boat! Less make it tuh de Palm Beach road. Dat's on uh fill. We'se pretty safe dere."

"Ah'm safe here, man. Go ahead if yuh wants to. Ah'm sleepy."

"Whut you gointuh do if de lake reach heah?"

"Go upstairs."

"S'posing it come up dere?"

"Swim, man. Dat's all."

"Well, uh, Good bye, Motor Boat. Everything is pretty bad, yuh know. Us might git missed of one 'nother. You sho is a grand friend fuh uh man tuh have."

"Good bye, Tea Cake. Y'all oughta stay here and sleep, man. No use in goin' off and leavin' me lak dis."

"We don't wanta. Come on wid us. It might be night time when de water hem you up in heah. Dat's how come Ah won't stay. Come on, man."

"Tea Cake, Ah got tuh have mah sleep. Definitely."

"Good bye, then, Motor. Ah wish you all de luck. Goin' over tuh Nassau fuh dat visit widja when all dis is over."

"Definitely, Tea Cake. Mah mama's house is yours."

Tea Cake and Janie were some distance from the house before they struck serious water. Then they had to swim a distance, and Janie could not hold up more than a few strokes at a time, so Tea Cake bore her up till finally they hit a ridge that led on towards the fill. It seemed to him the wind was weakening a little so he kept looking for a place to rest and catch his breath. His wind was gone. Janie was tired and limping, but she had not had to do that hard swimming in the turbulent waters, so Tea Cake was much worse off. But they couldn't stop. Gaining the fill was something but it was no guarantee. The lake was coming. They had to reach the six-mile bridge. It was high and safe perhaps.

Everybody was walking the fill. Hurrying, dragging, falling, crying, calling out names hopefully and hopelessly. Wind and rain beating on old folks and beating on babies. Tea Cake stumbled once or twice in his weariness and Janie held him up.

So they reached the bridge at Six Mile Bend and thought to rest.

But it was crowded. White people had preempted that point of elevation and there was no more room. They could climb up one of its high sides and down the other, that was all. Miles further on, still no rest.

They passed a dead man in a sitting position on a hummock, entirely surrounded by wild animals and snakes. Common danger made common friends. Nothing sought a conquest over the other.

Another man clung to a cypress tree on a tiny island. A tin roof of a building hung from the branches by electric wires and the wind swung it back and forth like a mighty ax. The man dared not move a step to his right lest this crushing blade split him open. He dared not step left for a large rattlesnake was stretched full length with his head in the wind. There was a strip of water between the island and the fill, and the man clung to the tree and cried for help.

"De snake won't bite yuh," Tea Cake yelled to him. "He skeered tuh go intuh uh coil. Skeered he'll be blowed away. Step round dat side and swim off!"

Soon after that Tea Cake felt he couldn't walk anymore. Not right away. So he stretched long side of the road to rest. Janie spread herself between him and the wind and he closed his eyes and let the tiredness seep out of his limbs. On each side of the fill was a great expanse of water like lakes—water full of things living and dead. Things that didn't belong in water. As far as the eye could reach, water and wind playing upon it in fury. A large piece of tar-paper roofing sailed through the air and scudded along the fill until it hung against a tree. Janie saw it with joy. That was the very thing to cover Tea Cake with. She could lean against it and hold it down. The wind wasn't quite so bad as it was anyway. The very thing. Poor Tea Cake!

She crept on hands and knees to the piece of roofing and caught hold of it by either side. Immediately the wind lifted both of them and she saw herself sailing off the fill to the right, out and out over the lashing water. She screamed terribly and released the roofing which sailed away as she plunged downward into the water.

"Tea Cake!" He heard her and sprang up. Janie was trying to swim but fighting water too hard. He saw a cow swimming slowly towards the fill in an oblique line. A massive built dog was sitting on her shoulders and shivering and growling. The cow was approaching Janie. A few strokes would bring her there.

"Make it tuh de cow and grab hold of her tail! Don't use yo' feet. Jus' yo' hands is enough. Dat's right, come on!"

Janie achieved the tail of the cow and lifted her head up along the cow's rump, as far as she could above water. The cow sunk a little with the added load and thrashed a moment in terror. Thought she was being pulled down by a gator. Then she continued on. The dog stood up and growled like a lion, stiff-standing hackles, stiff muscles, teeth uncovered as he lashed up his fury for the charge. Tea Cake split the water like an otter, opening his knife as he dived. The dog raced down the back-bone of the cow to the attack and Janie screamed and slipped far back on the tail of the cow, just out of reach of the dog's angry jaws. He wanted to plunge in after her but dreaded the water, somehow. Tea Cake rose out of the water at the cow's rump and seized the dog by the neck. But he was a powerful dog and Tea Cake was over-tired. So he didn't kill the dog with one stroke as he had intended. But the dog couldn't free himself either. They fought and somehow he managed to bite Tea Cake high up on his cheek-bone once. Then Tea Cake finished him and sent him to the bottom to stay there. The cow relieved of a great weight was landing on the fill with Janie before Tea Cake stroked in and crawled weakly upon the fill again.

Janie began to fuss around his face where the dog had bitten him but he said it didn't amount to anything. "He'd uh raised hell though if he had uh grabbed me uh inch higher and bit me in mah eye. Yuh can't buy eyes in de store, yuh know." He flopped to the edge of the fill as if the storm wasn't going on at all. "Lemme rest awhile, then us got tuh make it on intuh town somehow."

It was next day by the sun and the clock when they reached Palm Beach. It was years later by their bodies. Winters and winters of hardship and suffering. The wheel kept turning round and round. Hope, hopelessness and despair. But the storm blew itself out as they approached the city of refuge.

Havoc was there with her mouth wide open. Back in the Everglades the wind had romped among lakes and trees. In the city it had raged among houses and men. Tea Cake and Janie stood on the edge of things and looked over the desolation.

"How kin Ah find uh doctor fuh yo' face in all dis mess?" Janie wailed.

"Ain't got de damn doctor tuh study 'bout. Us needs uh place tuh rest."

A great deal of their money and perseverance and they found a place to sleep. It was just that. No place to live at all. Just sleep. Tea Cake looked all around and sat heavily on the side of the bed.

"Well," he said humbly, "reckon you never 'spected tuh come tuh dis when you took up wid me, didja?"

"Once upon uh time, Ah never 'spected nothin', Tea Cake, but bein' dead from the standin' still and tryin' tuh laugh. But you come 'long and made somethin' outa me. So Ah'm thankful fuh anything we come through together."

"Thanky, Ma'am."

"You was twice noble tuh save me from dat dawg. Tea Cake, Ah don't speck you seen his eyes lak Ah did. He didn't aim tuh jus' bite me, Tea Cake. He aimed tuh kill me stone dead. Ah'm never tuh fuhgit dem eyes. He wuzn't nothin' all over but pure hate. Wonder where he come from?"

"Yeah, Ah did see 'im too. It wuz frightenin'. Ah didn't mean tuh take his hate neither. He had tuh die uh me one.

Mah switch blade said it wuz him."

"Po' me, he'd tore me tuh pieces, if it wuzn't fuh you, honey."

"You don't have tuh say, if it wuzn't fuh me, baby, cause Ah'm *heah,* and then Ah want yuh tuh know it's uh man heah."

CHAPTER 19

And then again Him-with-the-square-toes had gone back to his house. He stood once more and again in his high flat house without sides to it and without a roof with his soulless sword standing upright in his hand. His pale white horse had galloped over waters, and thundered over land. The time of dying was over. It was time to bury the dead.

"Janie, us been in dis dirty, slouchy place two days now, and dat's too much. Us got tuh git outa dis house and outa dis man's town. Ah never did lak round heah."

"Where we goin', Tea Cake? Dat we don't know."

"Maybe, we could go back up de state, if yuh want tuh go."

"Ah didn't say dat, but if dat is whut you—"

"Naw, Ah ain't said nothin' uh de kind. Ah wuz tryin' not tuh keep you outa yo' comfortable no longer'n you wanted tuh stay."

"If Ah'm in yo' way—"

"Will you lissen at dis woman? Me 'bout tuh bust mah britches tryin' tuh stay wid her and she heah—she oughta be shot wid tacks!"

"All right then, you name somethin' and we'll do it. We kin give it uh poor man's trial anyhow."

"Anyhow Ah done got rested up and de bed bugs is done got too bold round heah. Ah didn't notice when mah rest wuz broke. Ah'm goin' out and look around and see whut we kin do. Ah'll give *any*thing uh common trial."

"You better stay inside dis house and git some rest. 'Tain't nothin' tuh find out dere nohow."

"But Ah wants tuh look and see, Janie. Maybe it's some kinda work fuh me tuh help do."

"Whut dey want you tuh help do, you ain't gointuh like it. Dey's grabbin' all de menfolks dey kin git dey hands on and makin' 'em help bury de dead. Dey claims dey's after de unemployed, but dey ain't bein' too particular about whether you'se employed or not. You stay in dis house. De Red Cross is doin' all dat kin be done otherwise fuh de sick and de 'fflicted."

"Ah got money on me, Janie. Dey can't bother me. Anyhow Ah wants tuh go see how things is sho nuff. Ah wants tuh see if Ah kin hear anything 'bout de boys from de 'Glades. Maybe dey all come through all right. Maybe not."

Tea Cake went out and wandered around. Saw the hand of horror on everything. Houses without roofs, and roofs without houses. Steel and stone all crushed and crumbled like wood. The mother of malice had trifled with men.

While Tea Cake was standing and looking he saw two men coming towards him with rifles on their shoulders. Two white men, so he thought about what Janie had told him and flexed his knees to run. But in a moment he saw that wouldn't do him any good. They had already seen him and they were too close to miss him if they shot. Maybe they would pass on by. Maybe when they saw he had money they would realize he was not a tramp.

"Hello, there, Jim," the tallest one called out. "We been lookin' fuh you."

"Mah name ain't no Jim," Tea Cake said watchfully. "Whut you been lookin' fuh *me* fuh? Ah ain't done nothin'."

"Dat's whut we want yuh fuh—not doin' nothin'. Come on

less go bury some uh dese heah dead folks. Dey ain't gittin' buried fast enough."

Tea Cake hung back defensively. "Whut Ah got tuh do wid dat? Ah'm uh workin' man wid money in mah pocket. Jus' got blowed outa de 'Glades by de storm."

The short man made a quick move with his rifle. "Git on down de road dere, suh! Don't look out somebody'll be buryin'. *you!* G'wan in front uh me, suh!"

Tea Cake found that he was part of a small army that had been pressed into service to clear the wreckage in public places and bury the dead. Bodies had to be searched out, carried to certain gathering places and buried. Corpses were not just found in wrecked houses. They were under houses, tangled in shrubbery, floating in water, hanging in trees, drifting under wreckage.

Trucks lined with drag kept rolling in from the 'Glades and other outlying parts, each with its load of twenty-five bodies. Some bodies fully dressed, some naked and some in all degrees of dishevelment. Some bodies with calm faces and satisfied hands. Some dead with fighting faces and eyes flung wide open in wonder. Death had found them watching, trying to see beyond seeing.

Miserable, sullen men, black and white under guard had to keep on searching for bodies and digging graves. A huge ditch was dug across the white cemetery and a big ditch was opened across the black graveyard. Plenty quick-lime on hand to throw over the bodies as soon as they were received. They had already been unburied too long. The men were making every effort to get them covered up as quickly as possible. But the guards stopped them. They had received orders to be carried out.

"Hey, dere, y'all! Don't dump dem bodies in de hole lak dat! Examine every last one of 'em and find out if they's white or black."

"Us got tuh handle 'em slow lak dat? God have mussy! In de condition they's in got tuh examine 'em? Whut difference

162

do it make 'bout de color? Dey all needs buryin' in uh hurry.''

"Got orders from headquarters. They makin' coffins fuh all de white folks. 'Tain't nothin' but cheap pine, but dat's better'n nothin'. Don't dump no white folks in de hole jus' so.''

"Whut tuh do 'bout de colored folks? Got boxes fuh dem too?''

"Nope. They cain't find enough of 'em tuh go 'round. Jus' sprinkle plenty quick-lime over 'em and cover 'em up.''

"Shucks! Nobody can't tell nothin' 'bout some uh dese bodies, de shape dey's in. Can't tell whether dey's white or black.''

The guards had a long conference over that. After a while they came back and told the men, "Look at they hair, when you cain't tell no other way. And don't lemme ketch none uh y'all dumpin' white folks, and don't be wastin' no boxes on colored. They's too hard tuh git holt of right now.''

"They's mighty particular how dese dead folks goes tuh judgment,'' Tea Cake observed to the man working next to him. "Look lak dey think God don't know nothin' 'bout de Jim Crow law.''

Tea Cake had been working several hours when the thought of Janie worrying about him made him desperate. So when a truck drove up to be unloaded he bolted and ran. He was ordered to halt on pain of being shot at, but he kept right on and got away. He found Janie sad and crying just as he had thought. They calmed each other about his absence then Tea Cake brought up another matter.

"Janie, us got tuh git outa dis house and outa dis man's town. Ah don't mean tuh work lak dat no mo'.''

"Naw, naw, Tea Cake. Less stay right in heah until it's all over. If dey can't see yuh, dey can't bother yuh.''

"Aw naw. S'posin' dey come round searchin'? Less git outa heah tuhnight.''

"Where us goin', Tea Cake?''

"De quickest place is de 'Glades. Less make it on back down dere. Dis town is full uh trouble and compellment.''

"But, Tea Cake, de hurricane wuz down in de 'Glades too. It'll be dead folks tuh be buried down dere too."

"Yeah, Ah know, Janie, but it couldn't never be lak it 'tis heah. In de first place dey been bringin' bodies outa dere all day so it can't be but so many mo' tuh find. And then again it never wuz as many dere as it wuz heah. And then too, Janie, de white folks down dere knows us. It's bad bein' strange niggers wid white folks. Everybody is aginst yuh."

"Dat sho is de truth. De ones de white man know is nice colored folks. De ones he don't know is bad niggers." Janie said this and laughed and Tea Cake laughed with her.

"Janie, Ah done watched it time and time again; each and every white man think he know all de GOOD darkies already. He don't need tuh know no mo.' So far as he's concerned, all dem he don't know oughta be tried and sentenced tuh six months behind de United States privy house at hard smellin'."

"How come de United States privy house, Tea Cake?"

"Well, you know Old Uncle Sam always do have de biggest and de best uh everything. So de white man figger dat anything less than de Uncle Sam's consolidated water closet would be too easy. So Ah means tuh go where de white folks know me. Ah feels lak uh motherless chile round heah."

They got things together and stole out of the house and away. The next morning they were back on the muck. They worked hard all day fixing up a house to live in so that Tea Cake could go out looking for something to do the next day. He got out soon next morning more out of curiosity than eagerness to work. Stayed off all day. That night he came in beaming out with light.

"Who you reckon Ah seen, Janie? Bet you can't guess."

"Ah'll betcha uh fat man you seen Sop-de-Bottom."

"Yeah Ah seen him and Stew Beef and Dockery and 'Lias, and Coodemay and Bootyny. Guess who else!"

"Lawd knows. Is it Sterrett?"

"Naw, he got caught in the rush. 'Lias help bury him in Palm Beach. Guess who else?"

"Ah g'wan tell me, Tea Cake. Ah don't know. It can't be Motor Boat."

"Dat's jus' who it is. Ole Motor! De son of a gun laid up in dat house and slept and de lake come moved de house way off somewhere and Motor didn't know nothin' 'bout it till de storm wuz 'bout over."

"Naw!"

"Yeah man. Heah we nelly kill our fool selves runnin' way from danger and him lay up dere and sleep and float on off!"

"Well, you know dey say luck is uh fortune."

"Dat's right too. Look, Ah got uh job uh work. Help clearin' up things in general, and then dey goin' build dat dike sho nuff. Dat ground got to be cleared off too. Plenty work. Dey needs mo' men even."

So Tea Cake made three hearty weeks. He bought another rifle and a pistol and he and Janie bucked each other as to who was the best shot with Janie ranking him always with the rifle. She could knock the head off of a chicken-hawk sitting up a pine tree. Tea Cake was a little jealous, but proud of his pupil.

About the middle of the fourth week Tea Cake came home early one afternoon complaining of his head. Sick headache that made him lie down for a while. He woke up hungry. Janie had his supper ready but by the time he walked from the bedroom to the table, he said he didn't b'lieve he wanted a thing.

"Thought you tole me you wuz hongry!" Janie wailed.

"Ah thought so too," Tea Cake said very quietly and dropped his head in his hands.

"But Ah done baked yuh uh pan uh beans."

"Ah knows dey's good all right but Ah don't choose nothin' now, Ah thank yuh, Janie."

He went back to bed. Way in the midnight he woke Janie up in his nightmarish struggle with an enemy that was at his throat. Janie struck a light and quieted him.

"Whut's de matter, honey?" She soothed and soothed. "You got tuh tell me so Ah kin feel widja. Lemme bear de pain 'long widja, baby. Where hurt yuh, sugar?''

"Somethin' got after me in mah sleep, Janie." He all but cried, "Tried tuh choke me tuh death. Hadn't been fuh *you* Ah'd be dead."

"You sho wuz strainin' wid it. But you'se all right, honey. Ah'm heah."

He went on back to sleep, but there was no getting around it. He was sick in the morning. He tried to make it but Janie wouldn't hear of his going out at all.

"If Ah kin jus' make out de week," Tea Cake said.

"Folks wuz makin' weeks befo' you wuz born and they gointuh be makin' 'em after you'se gone. Lay back down, Tea Cake. Ah'm goin' git de doctor tuh come see 'bout yuh."

"Aw ain't dat bad, Janie. Looka heah! Ah kin walk all over de place."

"But you'se too sick tuh play wid. Plenty fever round heah since de storm."

"Gimme uh drink uh water befo' you leave, then."

Janie dipped up a glass of water and brought it to the bed. Tea Cake took it and filled his mouth then gagged horribly, disgorged that which was in his mouth and threw the glass upon the floor. Janie was frantic with alarm.

"Whut make you ack lak dat wid yo' drinkin' water, Tea Cake? You ast me tuh give it tuh yuh."

"Dat water is somethin' wrong wid it. It nelly choke me tuh death. Ah tole yuh somethin' jumped on me heah last night and choked me. You come makin' out ah wuz dreamin'."

"Maybe it wuz uh witch ridin' yuh, honey. Ah'll see can't Ah find some mustard seed whilst Ah's out. But Ah'm sho tuh fetch de doctor when Ah'm come."

Tea Cake didn't say anything against it and Janie herself hurried off. This sickness to her was worse than the storm. As soon as she was well out of sight, Tea Cake got up and dumped the water bucket and washed it clean. Then he struggled to the irrigation pump and filled it again. He was not accusing Janie of malice and design. He was accusing her of carelessness. She ought to realize that water buckets needed washing like every-thing else. He'd tell her about it good and proper when she got back. What was she thinking about nohow? He found himself very angry about it. He eased the bucket on the table and sat down to rest before taking a drink.

Finally he dipped up a drink. It was so good and cool! Come to think about it, he hadn't had a drink since yesterday. That was what he needed to give him an appetite for his beans. He found himself wanting it very much, so he threw back his head as he rushed the glass to his lips. But the demon was there before him, strangling, killing him quickly. It was a great relief to expel the water from his mouth. He sprawled on the bed again and lay there shivering until Janie and the doctor arrived. The white doctor who had been around so long that he was part of the muck. Who told the workmen stories with brawny sweaty words in them. He came into the house quickly, hat sitting on the left back corner of his head.

"Hi there, Tea Cake. What de hell's de matter with *you*?"

"Wisht Ah knowed, Doctah Simmons. But Ah sho is sick."

"Ah, naw Tea Cake. 'Tain't a thing wrong that a quart of coon-dick wouldn't cure. You haven't been gettin' yo' right likker lately, eh?" He slapped Tea Cake lustily across his back and Tea Cake tried to smile as he was expected to do. But it was hard. The doctor opened up his bag and went to work.

"You do look a little peaked, Tea Cake. You got a tempera-ture and yo' pulse is kinda off. What you been doin' here lately?"

"Nothin' 'cept workin' and gamin' uh little, doctah. But look lak water done turn't aginst me."

"Water? How do you mean?"

"Can't keep it on mah stomach, at all."

"What else?"

Janie came around the bed full of concern.

"Doctah, Tea Cake ain't tellin' yuh everything lak he oughta. We wuz caught in dat hurricane out heah, and Tea Cake over-strained hisself swimmin' such uh long time and

167

holdin' me up too, and walkin' all dem miles in de storm and then befo' he could git his rest he had tuh come git me out de water agin and fightin' wid dat big ole dawg and de dawg bitin' 'im in de face and everything. Ah been spectin' him tuh be sick befo' now.''

"Dawg bit 'im, did you say?''

"Aw twudn't nothin' much, doctah. It wuz all healed over in two three days,'' Tea Cake said impatiently. "Dat been over uh month ago, nohow. Dis is somethin' new, doctah. Ah figgers de water is yet bad. It's bound tuh be. Too many dead folks been in it fuh it tuh be good tuh drink fuh uh long time. Dat's de way Ah figgers it anyhow.''

"All right, Tea Cake. Ah'll send you some medicine and tell Janie how tuh take care of you. Anyhow, I want you in a bed by yo'self until you hear from me. Just you keep Janie out of yo' bed for awhile, hear? Come on out to the car with me, Janie. I want to send Tea Cake some pills to take right away.''

Outside he fumbled in his bag and gave Janie a tiny bottle with a few pellets inside.

"Give him one of these every hour to keep him quiet, Janie, and stay out of his way when he gets in one of his fits of gagging and choking.''

"How you know he's havin' 'em, doctah? Dat's jus' what Ah come out heah tuh tell yuh.''

"Janie, I'm pretty sure that was a mad dawg bit yo' husband. It's too late to get hold of de dawg's head. But de symptoms is all there. It's mighty bad dat it's gone on so long. Some shots right after it happened would have fixed him right up.''

"You mean he's liable tuh die, doctah?''

"Sho is. But de worst thing is he's liable tuh suffer somethin' awful befo' he goes.''

"Doctor, Ah loves him fit tuh kill. Tell me anything tuh do and Ah'll do it.''

" 'Bout de only thing you can do, Janie, is to put him in the County Hospital where they can tie him down and look after him.''

168

"But he don't like no hospital at all. He'd think Ah wuz tired uh doin' fuh 'im, when God knows Ah ain't. Ah can't stand de idea us tyin' Tea Cake lak he wuz uh mad dawg."

"It almost amounts to dat, Janie. He's got almost no chance to pull through and he's liable to bite somebody else, specially you, and then you'll be in the same fix he's in. It's mighty bad."

"Can't nothin' be done fuh his case, doctah? Us got plenty money in de bank in Orlandah, doctah. See can't yuh do somethin' special tuh save him. Anything it cost, doctah, Ah don't keer, but please, doctah."

"Do what I can. Ah'll phone into Palm Beach right away for the serum which he should have had three weeks ago. I'll do all I can to save him, Janie. But it looks too late. People in his condition can't swallow water, you know, and in other ways it's terrible."

Janie fooled around outside awhile to try and think it wasn't so. If she didn't see the sickness in his face she could imagine it wasn't really happening. Well, she thought, that big old dawg with the hatred in his eyes had killed her after all. She wished she had slipped off that cow-tail and drowned then and there and been done. But to kill her through Tea Cake was too much to bear. Tea Cake, the son of Evening Sun, had to die for loving her. She looked hard at the sky for a long time. Somewhere up there beyond blue ether's bosom sat He. Was He noticing what was going on around here? He must be because He knew everything. Did He *mean* to do this thing to Tea Cake and her? It wasn't anything she could fight. She could only ache and wait. Maybe it was some big tease and when He saw it had gone far enough He'd give her a sign. She looked hard for something up there to move for a sign. A star in the daytime, maybe, or the sun to shout, or even a mutter of thunder. Her arms went up in a desperate supplication for a minute. It wasn't exactly pleading, it was asking questions. The sky stayed hard looking and quiet so she went inside the house. God would do less than He had in His heart.

Tea Cake was lying with his eyes closed and Janie hoped he was asleep. He wasn't. A great fear had took hold of him. What was this thing that set his brains afire and grabbed at his throat with iron fingers? Where did it come from and why did it hang around him? He hoped it would stop before Janie noticed anything. He wanted to try to drink water again but he didn't want her to see him fail. As soon as she got out of the kitchen he meant to go to the bucket and drink right quick before anything had time to stop him. No need to worry Janie, until he couldn't help it. He heard her cleaning out the stove and saw her go out back to empty the ashes. He leaped at the bucket at once. But this time the sight of the water was enough. He was on the kitchen floor in great agony when she returned. She petted him, soothed him, and got him back to bed. She made up her mind to go see about that medicine from Palm Beach. Maybe she could find somebody to drive over there for it.

"Feel better now, Tea Cake, baby chile?"

"Uh huh, uh little."

"Well, b'lieve Ah'll rake up de front yard. De mens is got cane chewin's and peanut hulls all over de place. Don't want de doctah tuh come back heah and find it still de same."

"Don't take too long, Janie. Don't lak tuh be by mahself when Ah'm sick."

She ran down the road just as fast as she could. Halfway to town she met Sop-de-Bottom and Dockery coming towards her.

"Hello, Janie, how's Tea Cake?"

"Pretty bad off. Ah'm gointuh see 'bout medicine fuh 'im right now."

"Doctor told somebody he wuz sick so us come tuh see. Thought somethin' he never come tuh work."

"Y'all set wid 'im till Ah git back. He need de company right long in heah."

She fanned on down the road to town and found Dr. Simmons. Yes, he had had an answer. They didn't have any serum

170

but they had wired Miami to send it. She needn't worry. It would be there early the next morning if not before. People didn't fool around in a case like that. No, it wouldn't do for her to hire no car to go after it. Just go home and wait. That was all. When she reached home the visitors rose to go.

When they were alone Tea Cake wanted to put his head in Janie's lap and tell her how he felt and let her mama him in her sweet way. But something Sop had told him made his tongue lie cold and heavy like a dead lizard between his jaws. Mrs. Turner's brother was back on the muck and now he had this mysterious sickness. People didn't just take sick like this for nothing.

"Janie, whut is dat Turner woman's brother doin' back on de muck?"

"Ah don't know, Tea Cake. Didn't even knowed he wuz back."

"Accordin' tuh mah notion, you did. Whut you slip off from me just now for?"

"Tea Cake, Ah don't lak you astin' me no sich question. Dat shows how sick you is sho nuff. You'se jealous 'thout me givin' you cause."

"Well, whut didja slip off from de house 'thout tellin' me you wuz goin'. You ain't never done dat befo'."

"Dat wuz cause Ah wuz tryin' not tuh let yuh worry 'bout yo' condition. De doctah sent after some mo' medicine and Ah went tuh see if it come."

Tea Cake began to cry and Janie hovered him in her arms like a child. She sat on the side of the bed and sort of rocked him back to peace.

"Tea Cake, 'tain't no use in you bein' jealous uh me. In de first place Ah couldn't love nobody but yuh. And in de second place, Ah jus' uh ole woman dat nobody don't want but you."

"Naw, you ain't neither. You only sound ole when you tell folks when you wuz born, but wid de eye you'se young enough tuh suit most any man. Dat ain't no lie. Ah knows plenty mo' men would take yuh and work hard fuh de privilege. Ah done heard 'em talk."

"Maybe so, Tea Cake, Ah ain't never tried tuh find out. Ah jus' know dat God snatched me out de fire through you. And Ah loves yuh and feel glad."

"Thank yuh, ma'am, but don't say you'se ole. You'se uh lil girl baby all de time. God made it so you spent yo' ole age first wid somebody else, and saved up yo' young girl days to spend wid me."

"Ah feel dat uh way too, Tea Cake, and Ah thank yuh fuh sayin' it."

" 'Tain't no trouble tuh say whut's already so. You'se uh pretty woman outside uh bein' nice."

"Aw, Tea Cake."

"Yeah you is too. Everytime Ah see uh patch uh roses uh somethin' over sportin' they selves makin' out they pretty, Ah tell 'em 'Ah want yuh tuh see mah Janie sometime.' You must let de flowers see yuh sometimes, heah, Janie?"

"You keep dat up, Tea Cake, Ah'll b'lieve yuh after while," Janie said archly and fixed him back in bed. It was then she felt the pistol under the pillow. It gave her a quick ugly throb, but she didn't ask him about it since he didn't say. Never had Tea Cake slept with a pistol under his head before. "Neb' mind 'bout all dat cleanin' round de front yard," he told her as she straightened up from fixing the bed. "You stay where Ah kin see yuh."

"All right, Tea Cake, jus' as you say."

"And if Mis' Turner's lap-legged brother come prowlin' by heah you kin tell 'im Ah got him stopped wid four wheel brakes. 'Tain't no need of him standin' 'round watchin' de job."

"Ah won't be tellin' 'im nothin' 'cause Ah don't expect tuh see 'im."

Tea Cake had two bad attacks that night. Janie saw a changing look come in his face. Tea Cake was gone. Something else was looking out of his face. She made up her mind to be off after the doctor with the first glow of day. So she was up and dressed when Tea Cake awoke from the fitful sleep that had come to him just before day. He almost snarled when he saw her dressed to go.

"Where are you goin', Janie?"

"After de doctor, Tea Cake. You'se too sick tuh be heah in dis house 'thout de doctah. Maybe we oughta git yuh tuh de hospital."

"Ah ain't goin' tuh no hospital no where. Put dat in yo' pipe and smoke it. Guess you tired uh waitin' on me and doing fuh me. Dat ain't de way Ah been wid *you*. Ah never is been able tuh do enough fuh yuh."

"Tea Cake, you'se sick. You'se takin' everything in de way Ah don't mean it. Ah couldn't never be tired uh waitin' on you. Ah'm just skeered you'se too sick fuh me tuh handle. Ah wants yuh tuh git well, honey. Dat's all."

He gave her a look full of blank ferocity and gurgled in his throat. She saw him sitting up in bed and moving about so that he could watch her every move. And she was beginning to feel fear of this strange thing in Tea Cake's body. So when he went out to the outhouse she rushed to see if the pistol was loaded. It was a six shooter and three of the chambers were full. She started to unload it but she feared he might break it and find out she knew. That might urge his disordered mind to action. If that medicine would only come! She whirled the cylinder so that if he even did draw the gun on her it would snap three times before it would fire. She would at least have warning. She could either run or try to take it away before it was too late. Anyway Tea Cake wouldn't hurt *her*. He was jealous and wanted to scare her. She'd just be in the kitchen as usual and never let on. They'd laugh over it when he got well. She found the box of cartridges, however, and emptied it. Just as well to take the rifle fror. back of the head of the bed. She broke it and put the shell in her apron pocket and put it in a corner in the kitchen almost behind the stove where it was hard to see. She could outrun his knife if it came to that. Of course she was too fussy, but it did no harm to play safe. She ought not to let poor sick Tea Cake do something that would run him crazy when he found out what he had done.

She saw him coming from the outhouse with a queer loping gait, swinging his head from side to side and his jaws clenched in a funny way. This was too awful! Where was Dr. Simmons with that medicine? She was glad she was here to look after him. Folks would do such mean things to her Tea Cake if they saw him in such a fix. Treat Tea Cake like he was some mad dog when nobody in the world had more kindness about them. All he needed was for the doctor to come on with that medicine. He came back into the house without speaking, in fact, he did not seem to notice she was there and fell heavily into the bed and slept. Janie was standing by the stove washing up the dishes when he spoke to her in a queer cold voice.

"Janie, how come you can't sleep in de same bed wid me no mo'?"

"De doctah told you tuh sleep by yo'self, Tea Cake. Don't yuh remember him tellin' you dat yistiddy?"

"How come you ruther sleep on uh pallet than tuh sleep in de bed wid me?" Janie saw then that he had the gun in his hand that was hanging to his side. "Answer me when Ah speak."

"Tea Cake, Tea Cake, honey! Go lay down! Ah'll be too glad tuh be in dere wid yuh de minute de doctor say so. Go lay back down. He'll be heah wid some new medicine right away."

"Janie, Ah done went through everything tuh be good tuh you and it hurt me tuh mah heart tuh be ill treated lak Ah is."

The gun came up unsteadily but quickly and leveled at Janie's breast. She noted that even in his delirium he took good aim. Maybe he would point to scare her, that was all.

The pistol snapped once. Instinctively Janie's hand flew behind her on the rifle and brought it around. Most likely this would scare him off. If only the doctor would come! If anybody at all would come! She broke the rifle deftly and shoved in the shell as the second click told her that Tea Cake's suffer-

174

ing brain was urging him on to kill.

"Tea Cake, put down dat gun and go back tuh bed!" Janie yelled at him as the gun wavered weakly in his hand.

He steadied himself against the jamb of the door and Janie thought to run into him and grab his arm, but she saw the quick motion of taking aim and heard the click. Saw the ferocious look in his eyes and went mad with fear as she had done in the water that time. She threw up the barrel of the rifle in frenzied hope and fear. Hope that he'd see it and run, desperate fear for her life. But if Tea Cake could have counted costs he would not have been there with the pistol in his hands. No knowledge of fear nor rifles nor anything else was there. He paid no more attention to the pointing gun than if it were Janie's dog finger. She saw him stiffen himself all over as he leveled and took aim. The fiend in him must kill and Janie was the only thing living he saw.

The pistol and the rifle rang out almost together. The pistol just enough after the rifle to seem its echo. Tea Cake crumpled as his bullet buried itself in the joist over Janie's head. Janie saw the look on his face and leaped forward as he crashed forward in her arms. She was trying to hover him as he closed his teeth in the flesh of her forearm. They came down heavily like that. Janie struggled to a sitting position and pried the dead Tea Cake's teeth from her arm.

It was the meanest moment of eternity. A minute before she was just a scared human being fighting for its life. Now she was her sacrificing self with Tea Cake's head in her lap. She had wanted him to live so much and he was dead. No hour is ever eternity, but it has its right to weep. Janie held his head tightly to her breast and wept and thanked him wordlessly for giving her the chance for loving service. She had to hug him tight for soon he would be gone, and she had to tell him for the last time. Then the grief of outer darkness descended.

So that same day of Janie's great sorrow she was in jail. And when the doctor told the sheriff and the judge how it was, they all said she must be tried that same day. No need to punish her in jail by waiting. Three hours in jail and then they set the court for her case. The time was short and everything, but sufficient people were there. Plenty of white people came to look on this strangeness. And all the Negroes for miles around. Who was it didn't know about the love between Tea Cake and Janie?

The court set and Janie saw the judge who had put on a great robe to listen about her and Tea Cake. And twelve more white men had stopped whatever they were doing to listen and pass on what happened between Janie and Tea Cake Woods, and as to whether things were done right or not. That was funny too. Twelve strange men who didn't know a thing about people like Tea Cake and her were going to sit on the thing. Eight or ten white women had come to look at her too. They wore good clothes and had the pinky color that comes of good food. They were nobody's poor white folks. What need had *they* to leave their richness to come look on Janie in her overalls? But they didn't seem too mad, Janie thought. It would be nice if she could make *them* know how it was instead of those menfolks. Oh, and she hoped that undertaker was fixing Tea Cake up fine. They ought to let her go see about it. Yes, and there was Mr. Prescott that she knew right well and he was going to tell the twelve men to kill her for shooting Tea Cake. And a strange man from Palm Beach who was going to ask them not to kill her, and none of them knew.

Then she saw all of the colored people standing up in the back of the courtroom. Packed tight like a case of celery, only much darker than that. They were all against her, she could see. So many were there against her that a light slap from each one of them would have beat her to death. She felt them pelting her with dirty thoughts. They were there with their tongues cocked and loaded, the only real weapon left to weak folks. The only killing tool they are allowed to use in the presence of white folks.

So it was all ready after a while and they wanted people to talk so that they could know what was right to do about Janie

Woods, the relic of Tea Cake's Janie. The white part of the room got calmer the more serious it got, but a tongue storm struck the Negroes like wind among palm trees. They talked all of a sudden and all together like a choir and the top parts of their bodies moved on the rhythm of it. They sent word by the bailiff to Mr. Prescott they wanted to testify in the case. Tea Cake was a good boy. He had been good to that woman. No nigger woman ain't never been treated no better. Naw suh! He worked like a dog for her and nearly killed himself saving her in the storm, then soon as he got a little fever from the water, she had took up with another man. Sent for him to come there from way off. Hanging was too good. All they wanted was a chance to testify. The bailiff went up and the sheriff and the judge, and the police chief, and the lawyers all came together to listen for a few minutes, then they parted again and the sheriff took the stand and told how Janie had come to his house with the doctor and how he found things when he drove out to hers.

Then they called Dr. Simmons and he told about Tea Cake's sickness and how dangerous it was to Janie and the whole town, and how he was scared for her and thought to have Tea Cake locked up in the jail, but seeing Janie's care he neglected to do it. And how he found Janie all bit in the arm, sitting on the floor and petting Tea Cake's head when he got there. And the pistol right by his hand on the floor. Then he stepped down.

"Any further evidence to present, Mr. Prescott?" the judge asked.

"No, Your Honor. The State rests."

The palm tree dance began again among the Negroes in the back. They had come to talk. The State couldn't rest until it heard.

"Mistah Prescott, Ah got somethin' tuh say," Sop-de-Bottom spoke out anonymously from the anonymous herd.

The courtroom swung round on itself to look.

"If you know what's good for you, you better shut your

mouth up until somebody calls you," Mr. Prescott told him coldly.

"Yassuh, Mr. Prescott."

"We are handling this case. Another word out of *you,* out of any of you niggers back there, and I'll bind you over to the big court."

"Yassuh."

The white women made a little applause and Mr. Prescott glared at the back of the house and stepped down. Then the strange white man that was going to talk for her got up there. He whispered a little with the clerk and then called on Janie to take the stand and talk. After a few little questions he told her to tell just how it happened and to speak the truth, the whole truth and nothing but the truth. So help her God.

They all leaned over to listen while she talked. First thing she had to remember was she was not at home. She was in the courthouse fighting something and it wasn't death. It was worse than that. It was lying thoughts. She had to go way back to let them know how she and Tea Cake had been with one another so they could see she could never shoot Tea Cake out of malice.

She tried to make them see how terrible it was that things were fixed so that Tea Cake couldn't come back to himself until he had got rid of that mad dog that was in him and he couldn't get rid of the dog and live. He had to die to get rid of the dog. But she hadn't wanted to kill him. A man is up against a hard game when he must die to beat it. She made them see how she couldn't ever want to be rid of him. She didn't plead to anybody. She just sat there and told and when she was through she hushed. She had been through for some time before the judge and the lawyer and the rest seemed to know it. But she sat on in that trial chair until the lawyer told her she could come down.

"The defense rests," her lawyer said. Then he and Prescott whispered together and both of them talked to the judge in secret up high there where he sat. Then they both sat down.

"Gentlemen of the jury, it is for you to decide whether the defendant has committed a cold blooded murder or whether she is a poor broken creature, a devoted wife trapped by unfortunate circumstances who really in firing a rifle bullet into the heart of her late husband did a great act of mercy. If you find her a wanton killer you must bring in a verdict of first degree murder. If the evidence does not justify that then you must set her free. There is no middle course."

The jury filed out and the courtroom began to drone with talk, a few people got up and moved about. And Janie sat like a lump and waited. It was not death she feared. It was misunderstanding. If they made a verdict that she didn't want Tea Cake and wanted him dead, then that was a real sin and a shame. It was worse than murder. Then the jury was back again. Out five minutes by the courthouse clock.

"We find the death of Vergible Woods to be entirely accidental and justifiable, and that no blame should rest upon the defendant Janie Woods."

So she was free and the judge and everybody up there smiled with her and shook her hand. And the white women cried and stood around her like a protecting wall and the Negroes, with heads hung down, shuffled out and away. The sun was almost down and Janie had seen the sun rise on her troubled love and then she had shot Tea Cake and had been in jail and had been tried for her life and now she was free. Nothing to do with the little that was left of the day but to visit the kind white friends who had realized her feelings and thank them. So the sun went down.

She took a room at the boarding house for the night and heard the men talking around the front.

"Aw you know dem white mens wuzn't gointuh do nothin' tuh no woman dat look lak her."

"She didn't kill no white man, did she? Well, long as she don't shoot no white man she kin kill jus' as many niggers as she please."

"Yeah, de nigger women kin kill up all de mens dey wants

179

tuh, but you bet' not kill one uh dem. De white folks will sho hang yuh if yuh do."

"Well, you know whut dey say 'uh white man and uh nigger woman is de freest thing on earth.' Dey do as dey please."

Janie buried Tea Cake in Palm Beach. She knew he loved the 'Glades but it was too low for him to lie with water maybe washing over him with every heavy rain. Anyway, the 'Glades and its waters had killed him. She wanted him out of the way of storms, so she had a strong vault built in the cemetery at West Palm Beach. Janie had wired to Orlando for money to put him away. Tea Cake was the son of Evening Sun, and nothing was too good. The Undertaker did a handsome job and Tea Cake slept royally on his white silken couch among the roses she had bought. He looked almost ready to grin. Janie bought him a brand new guitar and put it in his hands. He would be thinking up new songs to play to her when she got there.

Sop and his friends had tried to hurt her but she knew it was because they loved Tea Cake and didn't understand. So she sent Sop word and to all the others through him. So the day of the funeral they came with shame and apology in their faces. They wanted her quick forgetfulness. So they filled up and overflowed the ten sedans that Janie had hired and added others to the line. Then the band played, and Tea Cake rode like a Pharaoh to his tomb. No expensive veils and robes for Janie this time. She went on in her overalls. She was too busy feeling grief to dress like grief.

CHAPTER 20

Because they really loved Janie just a little less than they had loved Tea Cake, and because they wanted to think well of themselves, they wanted their hostile attitude forgotten. So they blamed it all on Mrs. Turner's brother and ran him off the muck again. They'd show him about coming back there posing like he was good looking and putting himself where men's wives could look at him. Even if they didn't look it wasn't his fault, he had put himself in the way.

"Naw, Ah ain't mad wid Janie," Sop went around explaining. "Tea Cake had done gone crazy. You can't blame her for puhtectin' herself. She wuz crazy 'bout 'im. Look at de way she put him away. Ah ain't got anything in mah heart aginst her. And Ah never woulda thought uh thing, but de very first day dat lap-legged nigger come back heah makin' out he wuz lookin' fuh work, he come astin' me 'bout how wuz Mr. and Mrs. Woods makin' out. Dat goes tuh show yuh he wuz up tuh somethin'."

"So when Stew Beef and Bootyny and some of de rest of 'em got behind 'im he come runnin' tuh me tuh save 'im. Ah told 'im, don't come tuh *me* wid yo' hair blowin' back, 'cause, Ah'm gointuh send yuh, and Ah sho did. De bitches' baby!" That was enough, they eased their feelings by beating him and running him off. Anyway, their anger against Janie had lasted two whole days and that was too long to keep remembering anything. Too much of a strain.

They had begged Janie to stay on with them and she had stayed a few weeks to keep them from feeling bad. But the muck meant Tea Cake and Tea Cake wasn't there. So it was just a great expanse of black mud. She had given away everything in their little house except a package of garden seed that Tea Cake had bought to plant. The planting never got done because he had been waiting for the right time of the moon when his sickness overtook him. The seeds reminded Janie of Tea Cake more than anything else because he was always planting things. She had noticed them on the kitchen shelf when she came home from the funeral and had put them in her breast pocket. Now that she was home, she meant to plant them for remembrance.

Janie stirred her strong feet in the pan of water. The tiredness was gone so she dried them off on the towel.

"Now, dat's how everything wuz, Pheoby, jus' lak Ah told yuh. So Ah'm back home agin and Ah'm satisfied tuh be heah. Ah done been tuh de horizon and back and now Ah kin set heah in mah house and live by comparisons. Dis house ain't so absent of things lak it used tuh be befo' Tea Cake come along. It's full uh thoughts, 'specially dat bedroom.

"Ah know all dem sitters-and-talkers gointuh worry they guts into fiddle strings till dey find out whut we been talkin' 'bout. Dat's all right, Pheoby, tell 'em. Dey gointuh make 'miration 'cause mah love didn't work lak they love, if dey ever had any. Then you must tell 'em dat love ain't somethin' lak uh grindstone dat's de same thing everywhere and do de same thing tuh everything it touch. Love is lak de sea. It's uh movin' thing, but still and all, it takes its shape from de shore it meets, and it's different with every shore."

"Lawd!" Pheoby breathed out heavily, "Ah done growed ten feet higher from jus' listenin' tuh you, Janie. Ah ain't satisfied wid mahself no mo'. Ah means tuh make Sam take me fishin' wid him after this. Nobody better not criticize yuh in mah hearin'.''

"Now, Pheoby, don't feel too mean wid de rest of 'em 'cause dey's parched up from not knowin' things. Dem meatskins is *got* tuh rattle tuh make out they's alive. Let 'em consolate theyselves wid talk. 'Course, talkin' don't amount tuh uh hill uh beans when yuh can't do nothin' else. And listenin' tuh dat kind uh talk is jus' lak openin' yo' mouth and lettin' de moon shine down yo' throat. It's uh known fact, Pheoby, you got tuh *go* there tuh *know* there. Yo' papa and yo' mama and nobody else can't tell yuh and show yuh. Two things everybody's got tuh do fuh theyselves. They got tuh go tuh God, and they got tuh find out about livin' fuh theyselves.''

There was a finished silence after that so that for the first time they could hear the wind picking at the pine trees. It made Pheoby think of Sam waiting for her and getting fretful. It made Janie think about that room upstairs—her bedroom. Pheoby hugged Janie real hard and cut the darkness in flight.

Soon everything around downstairs was shut and fastened. Janie mounted the stairs with her lamp. The light in her hand was like a spark of sun-stuff washing her face in fire. Her shadow behind fell black and headlong down the stairs. Now, in her room, the place tasted fresh again. The wind through the open windows had broomed out all the fetid feeling of absence and nothingness. She closed in and sat down. Combing road-dust out of her hair. Thinking.

The day of the gun, and the bloody body, and the courthouse came and commenced to sing a sobbing sigh out of every corner in the room; out of each and every chair and thing. Commenced to sing, commenced to sob and sigh, singing and sobbing. Then Tea Cake came prancing around her where she was and the song of the sigh flew out of the window and lit in the top of the pine trees. Tea Cake, with the sun for a shawl. Of course he wasn't dead. He could never be dead until she herself had finished feeling and thinking. The kiss of

183

his memory made pictures of love and light against the wall. Here was peace. She pulled in her horizon like a great fish-net. Pulled it from around the waist of the world and draped it over her shoulder. So much of life in its meshes! She called in her soul to come and see.

AFTERWORD

❖

ZORA NEALE HURSTON: "A NEGRO WAY OF SAYING"

I.

The Reverend Harry Middleton Hyatt, an Episcopal priest whose five-volume classic collection, *Hoodoo, Conjuration, Witchcraft, and Rootwork,* more than amply returned an investment of forty years' research, once asked me during an interview in 1977 what had become of another eccentric collector whom he admired. "I met her in the field in the thirties. I think," he reflected for a few seconds, "that her first name was Zora." It was an innocent question, made reasonable by the body of confused and often contradictory rumors that make Zora Neale Hurston's own legend as richly curious and as dense as are the black myths she did so much to preserve in her classic anthropological works, *Mules and Men* and *Tell My Horse,* and in her fiction.

A graduate of Barnard, where she studied under Franz Boas, Zora Neale Hurston published seven books—four novels, two books of folklore, and an autobiography—and more than fifty shorter works between the middle of the Harlem

Renaissance and the end of the Korean War, when she was the dominant black woman writer in the United States. The dark obscurity into which her career then lapsed reflects her staunchly independent political stances rather than any deficiency of craft or vision. Virtually ignored after the early fifties, even by the Black Arts movement in the sixties, an otherwise noisy and intense spell of black image- and myth-making that rescued so many black writers from remaindered oblivion, Hurston embodied a more or less harmonious but nevertheless problematic unity of opposites. It is this complexity that refuses to lend itself to the glib categories of "radical" or "conservative," "black" or "Negro," "revolutionary" or "Uncle Tom"—categories of little use in literary criticism. It is this same complexity, embodied in her fiction, that, until Alice Walker published her important essay ("In Search of Zora Neale Hurston") in *Ms.* magazine in 1975, had made Hurston's place in black literary history an ambiguous one at best.

The rediscovery of Afro-American writers has usually turned on larger political criteria, of which the writer's work is supposedly a mere reflection. The deeply satisfying aspect of the rediscovery of Zora Neale Hurston is that black women generated it primarily to establish a maternal literary ancestry. Alice Walker's moving essay recounts her attempts to find Hurston's unmarked grave in the Garden of the Heavenly Rest, a segregated cemetery in Fort Pierce, Florida. Hurston became a metaphor for the black woman writer's search for tradition. The craft of Alice Walker, Gayl Jones, Gloria Naylor, and Toni Cade Bambara bears, in markedly different ways, strong affinities with Hurston's. Their attention to Hurston signifies a novel sophistication in black literature: they read Hurston not only for the spiritual kinship inherent in such relations but because she used black vernacular speech and rituals, in ways subtle and various, to chart the coming to consciousness of black women, so glaringly absent in other black fiction. This use of the vernacular became the fundamental framework for all but one of her novels and is particularly effective in her classic work *Their Eyes Were Watching God*, published in 1937, which is more closely related to Henry James's *The Portrait of a Lady* and Jean Toomer's *Cane* than to Langston Hughes's and Richard Wright's proletarian literature, so popular in the Depression.

The charting of Janie Crawford's fulfillment as an autonomous imagination, *Their Eyes* is a lyrical novel that correlates the need of her first two husbands for ownership of progressively larger physical space (and the gaudy accoutrements of upward mobility) with the suppression of self-awareness in their wife. Only with her third and last lover, a roustabout called Tea Cake whose unstructured frolics center around and about the Florida swamps, does Janie at last bloom, as does the large pear tree that stands beside her grandmother's tiny log cabin.

> She saw a dust bearing bee sink into the sanctum of a bloom; the thousand sister calyxes arch to meet the love embrace and the ecstatic shiver of the tree from root to tiniest branch creaming in every blossom and frothing with delight. So this was a marriage!

To plot Janie's journey from object to subject, the narrative of the novel shifts from third to a blend of first and third person (known as "free indirect discourse"), signifying this awareness of self in Janie. *Their Eyes* is a bold feminist novel, the first to be explicitly so in the Afro-American tradition. Yet in its concern with the project of finding a voice, with language as an instrument of injury and salvation, of selfhood and empowerment, it suggests many of the themes that inspirit Hurston's oeuvre as a whole.

II.

One of the most moving passages in American literature is Zora Neale Hurston's account of her last encounter with her dying mother, found in a chapter entitled "Wandering" in her autobiography, *Dust Tracks on a Road* (1942):

> As I crowded in, they lifted up the bed and turned it around so that Mama's eyes would face east. I thought that she looked to me as the head of the bed reversed. Her mouth was slightly open, but her breathing took up so much of her strength that she could not talk. But she looked at me, or so I felt, to speak for her. She depended on me for a voice.

We can begin to understand the rhetorical distance that separated Hurston from her contemporaries if we compare this passage with a similar scene published just three years later in *Black Boy* by Richard Wright, Hurston's dominant black male contemporary and rival: "Once, in the night, my mother called me to her bed and told me that she could not endure the pain, and she wanted to die. I held her hand and begged her to be quiet. That night I ceased to react to my mother; my feelings were frozen." If Hurston represents her final moments with her mother in terms of the search for voice, then Wright attributes to a similar experience a certain "somberness of spirit that I was never to lose," which "grew into a symbol in my mind, gathering to itself . . . the poverty, the ignorance, the helplessness. . . ." Few authors in the black tradition have less in common than Zora Neale Hurston and Richard Wright. And whereas Wright would reign through the forties as our predominant author, Hurston's fame reached its zenith in 1943 with a *Saturday Review* cover story honoring the success of *Dust Tracks*. Seven years later, she would be serving as a maid in Rivo Alto, Florida; ten years after that she would die in the County Welfare Home in Fort Pierce, Florida.

How could the recipient of two Guggenheims and the author of four novels, a dozen short stories, two musicals, two books on black mythology, dozens of essays, and a prizewinning autobiography virtually "disappear" from her readership for three full decades? There are no easy answers to this quandary, despite the concerted attempts of scholars to resolve it. It is clear, however, that the loving, diverse, and enthusiastic responses that Hurston's work engenders today were not shared by several of her influential black male contemporaries. The reasons for this are complex and stem largely from what we might think of as their "racial ideologies."

Part of Hurston's received heritage—and perhaps the paramount received notion that links the novel of manners in the Harlem Renaissance, the social realism of the thirties, and the cultural nationalism of the Black Arts movement—was the idea that racism had reduced black people to mere ciphers, to beings who only react to an omnipresent racial oppression, whose culture is "deprived" where different, and whose psyches are in the main "pathological." Albert Murray, the writer and social critic, calls this "the Social Science Fiction Monster." Socialists, separatists, and civil rights advocates alike have been devoured by this beast.

Hurston thought this idea degrading, its propagation a trap, and railed against it. It was, she said, upheld by "the sobbing school of Negrohood who hold that nature somehow has given them a dirty deal." Unlike Hughes and Wright, Hurston chose deliberately to ignore this "false picture that distorted. . . ." Freedom, she wrote in *Moses, Man of the Mountain,* "was something internal. . . . The man himself must make his own emancipation." And she declared her first novel a manifesto against the "arrogance" of whites assuming that "black lives are only defensive reactions to white actions." Her strategy was not calculated to please.

What we might think of as Hurston's mythic realism, lush and dense within a lyrical black idiom, seemed politically retrograde to the proponents of a social or critical realism. If Wright, Ellison, Brown, and Hurston were engaged in a battle over ideal fictional modes with which to represent the Negro, clearly Hurston lost the battle.

But not the war.

After Hurston and her choice of style for the black novel were silenced for nearly three decades, what we have witnessed since is clearly a marvelous instance of the return of the repressed. For Zora Neale Hurston has been "rediscovered" in a manner unprecedented in the black tradition: several black women writers, among whom are some of the most accomplished writers in America today, have openly turned to her works as sources of narrative strategies, to be repeated, imitated, and revised, in acts of textual bonding. Responding to Wright's critique, Hurston claimed that she had wanted at long last to write a black novel, and "not a treatise on sociology." It is this urge that resonates in Toni Morrison's *Song of Solomon* and *Beloved,* and in Walker's depiction of Hurston as our prime symbol of "racial health—a sense of black people as complete, complex, *undiminished* human beings, a sense that is lacking in so much black writing and literature." In a tradition in which male authors have ardently denied black literary paternity, this is a major development, one that heralds the refinement of our notion of tradition: Zora and her daughters are a tradition-within-the-tradition, a black woman's voice.

The resurgence of popular and academic readerships of Hurston's works signifies her multiple canonization in the black, the American, and the feminist traditions. Within the critical establishment, scholars of every stripe have found in Hurston texts for all seasons. More people have read Hurston's works since 1975 than did between that date and the publication of her first novel, in 1934.

III.

Rereading Hurston, I am always struck by the density of intimate experiences she cloaked in richly elaborated imagery. It is this concern for the figurative capacity of black language, for what a character in *Mules and Men* calls "a hidden meaning, jus' like de Bible . . . de inside meanin' of words," that unites Hurston's anthropological studies with her fiction. For the folklore Hurston collected so meticulously as Franz Boas's student at Barnard became metaphors, allegories, and performances in her novels, the traditional recurring canonical metaphors of black culture. Always more of a novelist than a social scientist, even Hurston's academic collections center on the quality of imagination that makes these lives whole and splendid. But it is in the novel that Hurston's use of the black idiom realizes its fullest effect. In *Jonah's Gourd Vine,* her first novel, for instance, the errant preacher, John, as described by Robert Hemenway "is a poet who graces his world with language but cannot find the words to secure his own personal grace." This concern for language and for the "natural" poets who "bring barbaric splendor of word and song into the very camp of the mockers" not only connects her two disciplines but also makes of "the suspended linguistic moment" a thing to behold indeed. Invariably, Hurston's writing depends for its strength on the text, not the context, as does John's climactic sermon, a *tour de force* of black image and metaphor. Image and metaphor define John's world; his failure to interpret himself leads finally to his self-destruction. As Robert Hemenway, Hurston's biographer, concludes, "Such passages eventually add up to a theory of language and behavior."

Using "the spy-glass of Anthropology," her work celebrates rather than moralizes; it shows rather than tells, such that "both behavior and art become self-evident as the tale texts and hoodoo rituals accrete during the reading." As author, she functions as "a midwife participating in the birth of a body of folklore, . . . the first wondering contacts with natural law." The myths she describes so accurately are in fact "alternative modes for perceiving reality," and never just condescending depictions of the quaint. Hurston sees "the Dozens," for example, that age-old black ritual of graceful insult, as, among other things, a verbal defense of the sanctity of the family, conjured through ingenious plays on words. Though attacked by Wright and virtually ignored by his literary heirs, Hurston's ideas about language and craft undergird many of the most successful contributions to Afro-American literature that followed.

IV.

We can understand Hurston's complex and contradictory legacy more fully if we examine *Dust Tracks on a Road,* her own controversial account of her life. Hurston did make significant parts of herself up, like a masquerader putting on a disguise for the ball, like a character in her fictions. In this way, Hurston *wrote* herself, and sought in her works to rewrite the "self" of "the race," in its several private and public guises, largely for ideological reasons. That which she chooses to reveal is the life of her imagination, as it sought to mold and interpret her environment. That which she silences or deletes, similarly, is all that her readership would draw upon to delimit or pigeonhole her life as a synecdoche of "the race problem," an exceptional part standing for the debased whole.

Hurston's achievement in *Dust Tracks* is twofold. First, she gives us a *writer's* life, rather than an account, as she says, of "the Negro problem." So many events in this text are figured in terms of Hurston's growing awareness and mastery of books and language, language and linguistic rituals as spoken and written both by masters of the Western tradition and by ordinary members of the black community. These two "speech communities," as it were, are Hurston's great sources of inspiration not only in her novels but also in her autobiography.

The representation of her sources of language seems to be her principal concern, as she constantly shifts back and forth between her "literate" narrator's voice and a highly idiomatic black voice found in wonderful passages of free indirect discourse. Hurston moves in and out of these distinct voices effortlessly, seamlessly, just as she does in *Their Eyes* to chart Janie's coming to consciousness. It is this usage of a *divided* voice, a double voice unreconciled, that strikes me as her great achievement, a verbal analogue of her double experiences as a woman in a male-dominated world and as a black person in a nonblack world, a woman writer's revision of W. E. B. Du Bois's metaphor of "double-consciousness" for the hyphenated African-American.

Her language, variegated by the twin voices that intertwine throughout the text, retains the power to unsettle.

There is something about poverty that smells like death.
Dead dreams dropping off the heart like leaves in a dry
season and rotting around the feet; impulses smothered too
long in the fetid air of underground caves. The soul lives
in a sickly air. People can be slave-ships in shoes.

Elsewhere she analyzes black "idioms" used by a culture "raised on simile and invective. They know how to call names," she concludes, then lists some, such as 'gator-mouthed, box-ankled, puzzle-gutted, shovel-footed: "Eyes looking like skint-ginny nuts, and mouth looking like a dish-pan full of broke-up crockery!"

Immediately following the passage about her mother's death, she writes:

The Master-Maker in His making had made Old Death.
Made him with big, soft feet and square toes. Made him

193

with a face that reflects the face of all things, but neither changes itself, nor is mirrored anywhere. Made the body of death out of infinite hunger. Made a weapon of his hand to satisfy his needs. This was the morning of the day of the beginning of things.

Language, in these passages, is not merely "adornment," as Hurston described a key black linguistic practice; rather, manner and meaning are perfectly in tune: she says the thing in the most meaningful manner. Nor is she being "cute," or pandering to a condescending white readership. She is "naming" emotions, as she says, in a language both deeply personal and culturally specific.

The second reason that *Dust Tracks* succeeds as literature arises from the first: Hurston's unresolved tension between her double voices signifies her full understanding of modernism. Hurston uses the two voices in her text to celebrate the psychological fragmentation both of modernity and of the black American. As Barbara Johnson has written, hers is a rhetoric of division, rather than a fiction of psychological or cultural unity. Zora Neale Hurston, the "real" Zora Neale Hurston that we long to locate in this text, dwells in the silence that separates these two voices: she is both, and neither; bilingual, and mute. This strategy helps to explain her attraction to so many contemporary critics and writers, who can turn to her works again and again only to be startled at her remarkable artistry.

But the life that Hurston could write was not the life she could live. In fact, Hurston's life, so much more readily than does the standard sociological rendering, reveals how economic limits determine our choices even more than does violence or love. Put simply, Hurston wrote well when she was comfortable, wrote poorly when she was not. Financial problems—book sales, grants and fellowships too few and too paltry, ignorant editors and a smothering patron—produced the sort of dependence that affects, if not determines, her style, a relation she explored somewhat ironically in "What White Publishers Won't Print." We cannot oversimplify the relation between Hurston's art and her life; nor can we reduce the complexity of her postwar politics, which, rooted in her distaste for the pathological image of blacks, were markedly conservative and Republican.

Nor can we sentimentalize her disastrous final decade, when she found herself working as a maid on the very day the *Saturday Evening Post* published her short story "Conscience of the Court" and often found herself without money, surviving after 1957 on unemployment benefits, substitute teaching, and welfare checks. "In her last days," Hemenway concludes dispassionately, "Zora lived a difficult life—alone, proud, ill, obsessed with a book she could not finish."

The excavation of her buried life helped a new generation read Hurston again. But ultimately we must find Hurston's legacy in her art, where she "ploughed up some literacy and laid by some alphabets." Her importance rests with the legacy of fiction and lore she constructed so cannily. As Hurston herself noted, "Roll your eyes in ecstasy and ape his every move, but until we have placed something upon his street corner that is our own, we are right back where we were when they filed our iron collar off." If, as a friend eulogized, "She didn't come to you empty," then she does not leave black literature empty. If her earlier obscurity and neglect today seem inconceivable, perhaps now, as she wrote of Moses, she has "crossed over."

HENRY LOUIS GATES, JR.

SELECTED BIBLIOGRAPHY

WORKS BY ZORA NEALE HURSTON

Jonah's Gourd Vine. Philadelphia: J. B. Lippincott, 1934.

Mules and Men. Philadelphia: J. B. Lippincott, 1935.

Their Eyes Were Watching God. Philadelphia: J. B. Lippincott, 1937.

Tell My Horse. Philadelphia: J. B. Lippincott, 1938.

Moses, Man of the Mountain. Philadelphia: J. B. Lippincott, 1939.

Dust Tracks on a Road. Philadelphia: J. B. Lippincott, 1942.

Seraph on the Suwanee. New York: Charles Scribner's Sons, 1948.

*I Love Myself When I Am Laughing . . . & Then Again When I Am
Looking Mean and Impressive: A Zora Neale Hurston Reader.* Edited
by Alice Walker. Old Westbury, N.Y.: The Feminist Press, 1979.

The Sanctified Church. Edited by Toni Cade Bambara. Berkeley: Turtle Island, 1981.

Spunk: The Selected Short Stories of Zora Neale Hurston. Berkeley: Turtle Island, 1985.

WORKS ABOUT ZORA NEALE HURSTON

Baker, Houston A., Jr. *Blues, Ideology, and Afro-American Literature: A Vernacular Theory,* pp. 15–63. Chicago: University of Chicago Press, 1984.

Bloom, Harold, ed. *Zora Neale Hurston.* New York: Chelsea House, 1986.

————, ed. *Zora Neale Hurston's "Their Eyes Were Watching God."* New York: Chelsea House, 1987.

Byrd, James W. "Zora Neale Hurston: A Novel Folklorist." *Tennessee Folklore Society Bulletin* 21 (1955): 37–41.

Cooke, Michael G. "Solitude: The Beginnings of Self-Realization in Zora Neale Hurston, Richard Wright, and Ralph Ellison." In Michael G. Cooke, *Afro-American Literature in the Twentieth Century,* pp. 71–110. New Haven: Yale University Press, 1984.

Dance, Daryl C. "Zora Neale Hurston." In *American Women Writers: Bibliographical Essays,* edited by Maurice Duke, et al. Westport, Conn.: Greenwood Press, 1983.

Gates, Henry Louis, Jr. "The Speakerly Text." In Henry Louis Gates, Jr., *The Signifying Monkey,* pp. 170–217. New York: Oxford University Press, 1988.

Giles, James R. "The Significance of Time in Zora Neale Hurston's *Their Eyes Were Watching God." Negro American Literature Forum* 6 (Summer 1972): 52–53, 60.

Hemenway, Robert E. *Zora Neale Hurston: A Literary Biography.* Chicago: University of Illinois Press, 1977.

Holloway, Karla. *The Character of the Word: The Texts of Zora Neale Hurston.* Westport, Conn.: Greenwood Press, 1987.

Holt, Elvin. "Zora Neale Hurston." In *Fifty Southern Writers After 1900,* edited by Joseph M. Flura and Robert Bain, pp. 259–69. Westport, Conn.: Greenwood Press, 1987.

Howard, Lillie Pearl. *Zora Neale Hurston.* Boston: Twayne, 1980.

————. "Zora Neale Hurston." In *Dictionary of Literary Biography,* vol. 51, edited by Trudier Harris, pp. 133–45. Detroit: Gale, 1987.

Jackson, Blyden. "Some Negroes in the Land of Goshen." *Tennessee Folklore Society Bulletin* 19 (4) (December 1953): 103–7.

Johnson, Barbara. "Metaphor, Metonymy, and Voice in *Their Eyes.*" In *Black Literature and Literary Theory,* edited by Henry Louis Gates, Jr., pp. 205–21. New York: Methuen, 1984.

———. "Thresholds of Difference: Structures of Address in Zora Neale Hurston." In *"Race," Writing and Difference,* edited by Henry Lewis Gates, Jr. Chicago: University of Chicago Press, 1986.

Jordan, June. "On Richard Wright and Zora Neale Hurston." *Black World* 23 (10) (August 1974): 4–8.

Kubitschek, Missy Dehn. " 'Tuh de Horizon and Back': The Female Quest in *Their Eyes.*" *Black American Literature Forum* 17 (3) (Fall 1983): 109–15.

Lionnet, Françoise. "Autoethnography: The Anarchic Style of *Dust Tracks on a Road.*" In Françoise Lionnet, *Autobiographical Voices: Race, Gender, Self-Portraiture,* pp. 97–130. Ithaca: Cornell University Press, 1989.

Lupton, Mary Jane. "Zora Neale Hurston and the Survival of the Female." *Southern Literary Journal* 15 (Fall 1982): 45–54.

Meese, Elizabeth. "Orality and Textuality in Zora Neale Hurston's *Their Eyes.*" In Elizabeth Meese, *Crossing the Double Cross: The Practice of Feminist Criticism,* pp. 39–55. Chapel Hill: University of North Carolina Press, 1986.

Newson, Adele S. *Zora Neale Hurston: A Reference Guide.* Boston: G. K. Hall, 1987.

Rayson, Ann. *"Dust Tracks on a Road:* Zora Neale Hurston and the Form of Black Autobiography." *Negro American Literature Forum* 7 (Summer 1973): 42–44.

Sheffey, Ruthe T., ed. *A Rainbow Round Her Shoulder: The Zora Neale Hurston Symposium Papers.* Baltimore: Morgan State University Press, 1982.

Smith, Barbara. "Sexual Politics and the Fiction of Zora Neale Hurston." *Radical Teacher* 8 (May 1978): 26–30.

Stepto, Robert B. *From Behind the Veil.* Urbana: University of Illinois Press, 1979.

Walker, Alice. "In Search of Zora Neale Hurston." *Ms.,* March 1975, pp. 74–79, 85–89.

Wall, Cheryl A. "Zora Neale Hurston: Changing Her Own Words." In *American Novelists Revisited: Essays in Feminist Criticism,* edited by Fritz Fleischmann, pp. 370–93. Boston: G. K. Hall, 1982.

Washington, Mary Helen. "Zora Neale Hurston: A Woman Half in Shadow." Introduction to *I Love Myself When I Am Laughing,* edited by Alice Walker. Old Westbury, N.Y.: Feminist Press, 1979.

———. " 'I Love the Way Janie Crawford Left Her Husbands': Zora Neale Hurston's Emergent Female Hero." In Mary Helen Washington, *Invented Lives: Narratives of Black Women, 1860–1960.* New York: Anchor Press, 1987.

Willis, Miriam. "Folklore and the Creative Artist: Lydia Cabrera and Zora Neale Hurston." *CLA Journal* 27 (September 1983): 81–90.

Wolff, Maria Tai. "Listening and Living: Reading and Experience in *Their Eyes.*" *BALF* 16 (1) (Spring 1982): 29–33.

CHRONOLOGY

January 7, 1891	Born in Eatonville, Florida, the fifth of eight children, to John Hurston, a carpenter and Baptist preacher, and Lucy Potts Hurston, a former schoolteacher.
September 1917– June 1918	Attends Morgan Academy in Baltimore, completing the high school requirements.
Summer 1918	Works as a waitress in a nightclub and a manicurist in a black-owned barbershop that serves only whites.
1918–19	Attends Howard Prep School, Washington, D.C.
1919–24	Attends Howard University; receives an associate degree in 1920.
1921	Publishes her first story, "John Redding Goes to Sea," in the *Stylus,* the campus literary society's magazine.
December 1924	Publishes "Drenched in Light," a short story, in *Opportunity.*
1925	Submits a story, "Spunk," and a play, *Color Struck,* to *Opportunity*'s literary contest. Both

win second-place awards; publishes "Spunk" in the June number.

1925–27	Attends Barnard College, studying anthropology with Franz Boas.
1926	Begins field work for Boas in Harlem.
January 1926	Publishes "John Redding Goes to Sea" in *Opportunity*.
Summer 1926	Organizes *Fire!* with Langston Hughes and Wallace Thurman; they publish only one issue, in November 1926. The issue includes Hurston's "Sweat."
August 1926	Publishes "Muttsy" in *Opportunity*.
September 1926	Publishes "Possum or Pig" in the *Forum*.
September–November 1926	Publishes "The Eatonville Anthology" in the *Messenger*.
1927	Publishes *The First One,* a play, in Charles S. Johnson's *Ebony and Topaz*.
February 1927	Goes to Florida to collect folklore.
May 19, 1927	Marries Herbert Sheen.
September 1927	First visits Mrs. Rufus Osgood Mason, seeking patronage.
October 1927	Publishes an account of the black settlement at St. Augustine, Florida, in the *Journal of Negro History;* also in this issue: "Cudjo's Own Story of the Last African Slaver."
December 1927	Signs a contract with Mason, enabling her to return to the South to collect folklore.
1928	Satirized as "Sweetie Mae Carr" in Wallace Thurman's novel about the Harlem Renaissance *Infants of the Spring;* receives a bachelor of arts degree from Barnard.
January 1928	Relations with Sheen break off.

May 1928	Publishes "How It Feels to Be Colored Me" in the *World Tomorrow*.
1930–32	Organizes the field notes that become *Mules and Men*.
May–June 1930	Works on the play *Mule Bone* with Langston Hughes.
1931	Publishes "Hoodoo in America" in the *Journal of American Folklore*.
February 1931	Breaks with Langston Hughes over the authorship of *Mule Bone*.
July 7, 1931	Divorces Sheen.
September 1931	Writes for a theatrical revue called *Fast and Furious*.
January 1932	Writes and stages a theatrical revue called *The Great Day,* first performed on January 10 on Broadway at the John Golden Theatre; works with the creative literature department of Rollins College, Winter Park, Florida, to produce a concert program of Negro music.
1933	Writes "The Fiery Chariot."
January 1933	Stages *From Sun to Sun* (a version of *Great Day*) at Rollins College.
August 1933	Publishes "The Gilded Six-Bits" in *Story*.
1934	Publishes six essays in Nancy Cunard's anthology, *Negro*.
January 1934	Goes to Bethune-Cookman College to establish a school of dramatic arts "based on pure Negro expression."
May 1934	Publishes *Jonah's Gourd Vine,* originally titled *Big Nigger;* it is a Book-of-the-Month Club selection.

September 1934	Publishes "The Fire and the Cloud" in the *Challenge*.
November 1934	*Singing Steel* (a version of *Great Day*) performed in Chicago.
January 1935	Makes an abortive attempt to study for a Ph.D in anthropology at Columbia University on a fellowship from the Rosenwald Foundation. In fact, she seldom attends classes.
August 1935	Joins the WPA Federal Theatre Project as a "dramatic coach."
October 1935	*Mules and Men* published.
March 1936	Awarded a Guggenheim Fellowship to study West Indian Obeah practices.
April–September 1936	In Jamaica.
September–March 1937	In Haiti; writes *Their Eyes Were Watching God* in seven weeks.
May 1937	Returns to Haiti on a renewed Guggenheim.
September 1937	Returns to the United States; *Their Eyes Were Watching God* published, September 18.
February–March 1938	Writes *Tell My Horse;* it is published the same year.
April 1938	Joins the Federal Writers Project in Florida to work on *The Florida Negro*.
1939	Publishes "Now Take Noses" in *Cordially Yours*.
June 1939	Receives an honorary Doctor of Letters degree from Morgan State College.
June 27, 1939	Marries Albert Price III in Florida.

Summer 1939	Hired as a drama instructor by North Carolina College for Negroes at Durham; meets Paul Green, professor of drama, at the University of North Carolina.
November 1939	*Moses, Man of the Mountain* published.
February 1940	Files for divorce from Price, though the two are reconciled briefly.
Summer 1940	Makes a folklore-collecting trip to South Carolina.
Spring–July 1941	Writes *Dust Tracks on a Road.*
July 1941	Publishes "Cock Robin, Beale Street" in the *Southern Literary Messenger.*
October 1941–January 1942	Works as a story consultant at Paramount Pictures.
July 1942	Publishes "Story in Harlem Slang" in the *American Mercury.*
September 5, 1942	Publishes a profile of Lawrence Silas in the *Saturday Evening Post.*
November 1942	*Dust Tracks on a Road* published.
February 1943	Awarded the Anisfield-Wolf Book Award in Race Relations for *Dust Tracks;* on the cover of the *Saturday Review.*
March 1943	Receives Howard University's Distinguished Alumni Award.
May 1943	Publishes "The 'Pet Negro' Syndrome" in the *American Mercury.*
November 1943	Divorce from Price granted.
June 1944	Publishes "My Most Humiliating Jim Crow Experience" in the *Negro Digest.*
1945	Writes *Mrs. Doctor;* it is rejected by Lippincott.

March 1945	Publishes "The Rise of the Begging Joints" in the *American Mercury.*
December 1945	Publishes "Crazy for This Democracy" in the *Negro Digest.*
1947	Publishes a review of Robert Tallant's *Voodoo in New Orleans* in the *Journal of American Folklore.*
May 1947	Goes to British Honduras to research black communities in Central America; writes *Seraph on the Suwanee;* stays in Honduras until March 1948.
September 1948	Falsely accused of molesting a ten-year-old boy and arrested; case finally dismissed in March 1949.
October 1948	*Seraph on the Suwanee* published.
March 1950	Publishes "Conscience of the Court" in the *Saturday Evening Post,* while working as a maid in Rivo Island, Florida.
April 1950	Publishes "What White Publishers Won't Print" in the *Saturday Evening Post.*
November 1950	Publishes "I Saw Negro Votes Peddled" in the *American Legion* magazine.
Winter 1950–51	Moves to Belle Glade, Florida.
June 1951	Publishes "Why the Negro Won't Buy Communism" in the *American Legion* magazine.
December 8, 1951	Publishes "A Negro Voter Sizes Up Taft" in the *Saturday Evening Post.*
1952	Hired by the *Pittsburgh Courier* to cover the Ruby McCollum case.
May 1956	Receives an award for "education and human relations" at Bethune-Cookman College.

June 1956	Works as a librarian at Patrick Air Force Base in Florida; fired in 1957.
1957–59	Writes a column on "Hoodoo and Black Magic" for the *Fort Pierce Chronicle.*
1958	Works as a substitute teacher at Lincoln Park Academy, Fort Pierce.
Early 1959	Suffers a stroke.
October 1959	Forced to enter the St. Lucie County Welfare Home.
January 28, 1960	Dies in the St. Lucie County Welfare Home of "hypertensive heart disease"; buried in an unmarked grave in the Garden of Heavenly Rest, Fort Pierce.
August 1973	Alice Walker discovers and marks Hurston's grave.
March 1975	Walker publishes "In Search of Zora Neale Hurston," in *Ms.,* launching a Hurston revival.